Danielle Steel has been ~~~~~~~~~~~~~~~~~~~~~~~~~~~~st popular authors, with over 530 million copies of her novels sold. Her many international bestsellers include *Loving, Star, Fine Things, The Ring, Summer's End, Season of Passion* and other highly acclaimed novels.

Visit the Danielle Steel website at www.daniellesteel.com

By Danielle Steel

★ published outside the UK under the title PASSION'S PROMISE

DANIELLE STEEL
OMNIBUS

Kaleidoscope

Family Album

sphere

SPHERE

This omnibus edition first published in Great Britain in 2011 by Sphere

Copyright © Danielle Steel 2011

Previously published separately:
Kaleidoscope first published in Great Britain in 1987 by Michael Joseph Ltd
Published by Sphere Books Ltd 1988
Reissued by Sphere in 2009
Copyright © Danielle Steel 1987
Family Album first published in Great Britain in 1985 by Michael Joseph Ltd
Published by Sphere Books Ltd 1985
Reissued by Sphere in 2009
Copyright © Benitreto Productions 1985

The moral right of the author has been asserted.

*All characters and events in this publication, other than those
clearly in the public domain, are fictitious and any resemblance
to real persons, living or dead, is purely coincidental.*

All rights reserved.
No part of this publication may be reproduced, stored in a
retrieval system, or transmitted, in any form or by any means, without
the prior permission in writing of the publisher, nor be otherwise circulated
in any form of binding or cover other than that in which it is published
and without a similar condition including this condition being
imposed on the subsequent purchaser.

A CIP catalogue record for this book
is available from the British Library.

ISBN 978-0-7515-4780-1

Printed and bound in Great Britain by
Clays Ltd, St Ives plc

Sphere
An imprint of
Little, Brown Book Group
100 Victoria Embankment
London EC4Y 0DY

An Hachette UK Company
www.hachette.co.uk

www.littlebrown.co.uk

KALEIDOSCOPE

To three very special little sisters:
Samantha, Victoria, and Vanessa,
precious little ladies,

and their very big sister, Beatrix,
who is so lovely,

and their three big brothers,
Trevor, Todd, and Nicky,
who are very special too.

May each of you be blessed
with good lives, and good fortune,
good hearts, and good people to love you
and who you love well.
May you always be safe, and strong,
and happy . . . and together!

And may each turn of the kaleidoscope
bring you joy!
The first turn, which was our turn
brought you to us, one by one,
special gifts, greatly loved, precious people.
And may your own turns bring you love,
and flowers . . . never demons . . .
Hold fast to each other, beloved ones,
bring each other strength, and laughter
and good times and love . . . just as once
we brought them to you.

With my love, for you and your Daddy,
and with ours, for each other,
and you.
With all my heart.

                                    d.s.

kaleidoscope

the first,
   shimmering moment
      of life,
like a diamond
      in the sea,
   glittering
      in the noonday
         sun,
brightly lit
   and glowing
         flame,
a brand new name,
   a shining light,
then gentle twist
   and darkest night
         comes
            for the first
               time,
   then happy rhymes
      and gentle songs,
         hearts that belong
until one stands
      alone,
   from brightest
            dawn
   to deepest dusk,
from morning sun
to twilight dreams,
   fantastic schemes,

and lives
    that sometimes
        go awry,
such shining
        hopes,
such sudden turns,
    from bright
        to dark
from grim
    to grand
    from joy
        to sorrow,
always waiting
    for tomorrow
and a twist
    of fate,
a ray of hope . . .
    with the faintest
        sleight of hand,
the alteration
    of all life's
        schemes
    and all its scope . . .
all with one tiny turn
    of life's kaleidoscope.

Part I

SOLANGE

Chapter 1

The rains were torrential north-east of Naples on the twenty-fourth of December 1943, and Sam Walker huddled in his foxhole with his rain-gear pulled tightly around him. He was twenty-one years old and had never been in Europe before the war. It was a hell of a way to see the world, and he had seen more than he'd ever wanted. He had been overseas since November of '42, fighting in North Africa, and taking part in Operation Torch until May of '43. He had thought Africa was bad with the deadly heat and desert winds and the sandstorms that left you half blind with red eyes that burned for days and tears constantly pouring down your cheeks, but this was worse. His hands were so numb he could hardly hold the cigarette butt his buddy had given him as a Christmas gift, let alone light it.

The wind from the mountains went right through your bones, it was the worst winter Italy had ever seen, or so they said, and he suddenly longed for the torrid heat of the desert. He had reached Sicily in July, with the 45th Infantry, attached to Clark's Fifth Army, and after Sicily they had been in the battle of Naples in October. And the battle of Termoli after that, but for two months now they had crawled over rocks and through ditches towards Rome, hiding in barns when they found them, stealing what food they could, fighting the Germans

3

every inch of the way, and bleeding over every step they covered.

'Shit . . .' His last match was drenched, and by then so was the butt that had been his only Christmas present. He was twenty-one years old, and when the Japanese struck Pearl Harbor he had been at Harvard. Harvard – the thought of it would have made him laugh if he hadn't been so bone-tired.

Harvard . . . With its perfect life and its pristine Quad and its bright young faces so sure they would one day run the world. If they only knew . . . It was difficult to believe now that he had ever been a part of all that. He had worked so damn hard to get there. He was a 'townie' from Somerville, and all his life he had dreamed of going to Harvard. His sister had laughed at him; all she had wanted was to marry one of the boys in her high school senior class – any of them would do – and she had certainly slept with enough of them to audition for the part. She was three years older than Sam and she had already been married and divorced by the time Sam finally got into Harvard, after working at every odd job he could for a year after finishing high school. Their parents had died when he was fifteen, in a car accident on a trip to Cape Cod, and he had wound up living with Eileen and her eighteen-year-old 'husband'. Sam had walked out four months before Eileen's erstwhile spouse, and they had hardly seen each other after that. He had gone to see her once, to say goodbye, three days after he'd been drafted. She'd been working in a bar, had dyed her hair blond, and he had hardly recognized her in the dim light when he'd first seen her. She'd looked embarrassed at first, and there was the same cunning light in her eyes he had remembered and always hated. Eileen looked out for number one, and her little brother had never meant much to her.

4

'Well, good luck . . .' She'd stood awkwardly staring at him in a dark corner of the bar, as he wondered if he should kiss her goodbye, but she'd seemed anxious to get back to work, and didn't seem to have anything more to say to him. 'Let me know where you are . . .'

'Yeah . . , sure . . . take care of yourself . . .' He had felt twelve years old again, saying goodbye to her, and he remembered all of the things he had never liked about his sister. It was hard to remember anything he had liked. They had always seemed like two people from different worlds, different lives, almost different planets. She had tortured him as a child, by telling him he was adopted, and he had believed her until their mother had whipped her one day and told Sam in her pathetic boozy way that Eileen was lying. Eileen always lied, she lied about everything, and whenever possible she had blamed Sam for whatever she'd done, and most of the time their father believed her. Sam had felt foreign to all of them, the big, burly father who had worked on a fishing boat all his life, the mother who drank too much, and the sister who partied all night. He had lain in his bed at times, imagining what it would be like to be part of a 'real' family, the kind with hot meals on the table, and clean sheets on the bed . . . a family from Beacon Hill perhaps . . . who summered on Cape Cod . . . a family with little children and dogs, and parents who laughed a lot. He couldn't remember ever seeing his parents laugh or smile or hold hands, and sometimes he wondered if they ever had. Secretly, he hated them for the tawdry lives they led, and the life they had condemned him to. He wanted so much more than that. And they hated him in return for his good grades, his bright mind, his starring roles in his high school plays, and the things he said to them, about other lives, other worlds, other people. He had once confided in his father that he wanted to go to Harvard one day, and his father had stared at him as though he were a stranger. And he was, to all of them. When he finally went to Harvard, it was a dream come true, and the scholarship he had won had been the gift of a lifetime . . . the gift of a lifetime . . . and then that magical first day, after working so hard for so long, and then suddenly three months later it was over.

The rain beat on his frozen hands and he heard a voice next to him for the first time, as he glanced over his shoulder.

'Need a light?'

He nodded, startled out of his memories, and looked up to see a tall blond man with blue eyes and rivers of rain pouring down his thin cheeks. They all looked like they were crying.

'Yeah . . . thanks . . .' Sam smiled, and for a moment his eyes danced as they had years before. He had been full of mischief once, aeons before. He had dreamt of being the life and soul of the drama club at Harvard. 'Nice Christmas, huh?'

The other man smiled. He looked older than Sam, but even Sam looked older than his years now. After North Africa and the Italian Campaign, they all felt like old men, and some of them looked it. 'Arthur Patterson.' He introduced himself formally and Sam laughed out loud as a gust of wind swept them both against the side of the foxhole.

'Charming place, Italy, isn't it? I've always wanted to come here. A truly marvellous vacation.' He looked around him as though seeing beautiful girls in bathing suits and beaches with endless lovely bodies, as Patterson grinned and chuckled in spite of himself.

'Been here long?'

'Oh, about a thousand years. I was in North Africa last

Christmas. Terrific place. We were invited by Rommel.'
He gratefully took the light from the tall blond man, lit
the butt and got two good drags before burning his fingers.
He'd have offered it to his new friend but there wasn't
time before the rain put out the mere half inch that
remained, and he looked apologetically at his benefactor.
'I'm Sam Walker, by the way.'

'Where you from?'

He wanted to say Harvard, just for old times' sake, but
that would have sounded crazy. 'Boston.'

'New York.' As though it mattered now. Nothing
mattered now, they were all names of places that didn't
exist. All that existed were Palermo, Sicily, and Salerno,
and Naples, and Rome, their ultimate goal, if they ever
got there.

The tall blond man looked around him, squinting in the
wind and rain. 'I was a lawyer before all this.'

Sam would have been impressed, but like the places
they were from, the people they had been no longer
mattered. 'I wanted to be an actor.' It was something he
had told hardly anyone, certainly not his parents before
they died, or his sister after that, and only a few friends,
but even they had laughed at him. And his teachers had
told him that he needed to study something more
worthwhile. But none of them understood just what acting
meant to him, what happened when he stepped on stage.
It was like magic reaching from his soul, transforming
him into the character he was playing. Gone were the
parents he had hated, the sister he had loathed and all his
own fears and insecurities with them. But no one seemed
to understand that. Not even at Harvard. Harvard men
weren't actors, they were doctors and lawyers and busi-
nessmen, heads of corporations and foundations, and
ambassadors . . . He laughed softly to himself again. He

7

sure as hell was an ambassador now, with a gun in his hand, and his bayonet fixed all the time so that he could run it through the guts of his enemies as he had time and time again in the past year. He wondered how many men Patterson had killed, and how he felt about it now, but it was a question you didn't ask anyone, you just lived with your own thoughts and the memories of the twisted faces and staring eyes as you pulled your bayonet out again and wiped it on the ground. He looked up at Arthur Patterson with the eyes of an old man and wondered briefly if either of them would be alive to see another Christmas.

'What made you want to be an actor?'

'Hmm?' He was startled by the serious look in the other man's eyes, as they both sank to a sitting position on a rock planted in the mud near their feet as the water in the foxhole swirled around them. 'Oh, that . . . Christ, I don't know . . . it seemed like an interesting thing to do.' But it was more than that, much more than that, it was the only time he felt whole, that he felt powerful and sure of himself. But he couldn't tell this guy that. It was ridiculous to talk about dreams sitting in a foxhole on Christmas Eve.

'I was in the glee club at Princeton.' It was an absurd exchange, and suddenly Sam Walker gave a crack of laughter.

'Do you realise how crazy we are? Talking about glee clubs and drama clubs and Princeton, sitting in this goddam foxhole? Do you realise we probably won't even be alive by next week, and I'm telling you I wanted to be an actor . . .' He suddenly wanted to cry through his own laughter. It was all so goddam awful, but it was real, it was so real they could taste it and feel it and smell it. He had smelled nothing but death for a year, and he was sick of it. They all were, while the generals planned their attack on

Rome. Who gave a damn about Rome anyway? Or Naples or Palermo? What were they fighting for? Freedom in Boston and New York and San Francisco? They already were free, and at home people were driving to work, and dancing at the USO and going to the movies. What the hell did they know about all this? Nothing. Absolutely goddam nothing. Sam looked up at the tall blond man and shook his head, his eyes full of wisdom and sadness, the sudden laughter gone. He wanted to go home . . . to anyone . . . even his sister, who had not written to him once since he'd left Boston. He'd written to her twice and then decided it wasn't worth the trouble. The thought of her always made him angry. She had embarrassed him for all of his teenage years, and several before that, just as his mother had . . . and his stolid, taciturn father. He hated all of them, and now he was here, alone, with a stranger who had been in the glee club at Princeton, but he already liked him.

'Where'd you go to school? Patterson seemed desperate to hold on to the past, to remember old times, as though thinking about it would take them back there, but Sam knew better than that. The present was right here, in the filth and frozen rain of the foxhole.

Sam looked at him with a lopsided grin, wishing he had another cigarette, a real one, not just half an inch of someone else's. 'Harvard.' At Harvard he had had real cigarettes, any time he wanted – Lucky Strikes. The thought of them almost made him weep with longing.

Patterson looked impressed. 'And you wanted to be an actor?'

Sam shrugged. 'I guess . . . I was majoring in English lit. I probably would have ended up teaching somewhere, and running the school plays for snotty freshmen.'

'That's not a bad life. I went to St Paul's, we had a hell

9

of a drama club there.' Sam stared at him, wondering if he was for real . . . Princeton, St Paul's . . . what were they all doing here? What were any of them doing here? . . . especially the boys who had died here.

'You married?' Sam was curious about him now, like a Christmas angel who had been visited on him, he appeared different in every possible way, and yet they seemed to have some things in common.

Arthur shook his head. 'I was too busy starting my career. I worked for a law firm in New York. I'd been there for eight months when I signed up.' He was twenty-seven and his eyes were serious and sad where Sam's were full of mischief. Sam's hair was as black as Arthur's was fair, and he had a medium build with powerful shoulders, long legs for his size, and a kind of energy about him which Arthur seemed to lack. Everything about Arthur Patterson was more restrained, more tentative, quieter, but then Sam was also younger.

'I have a sister in Boston – if she hasn't got herself killed by some guy in a bar by now.' It seemed important to share information about themselves, as though they might not have another chance, and they each wanted someone to know them. They wanted to be known before they died, to make friends, to be remembered. 'We never got along. I went to see her before I left, but she hasn't written since I've been gone. You? Sisters? Brothers?'

Arthur smiled for the first time in a while. 'I'm an only child, of only children. My father died when I was away at school, and my mother never remarried. This is pretty hard on her. I can tell in her letters.'

'I'll bet.' Sam nodded, trying to think of what Arthur's mother would be like, trying to envisage her: a tall, spare woman with white hair that had once been blond, probably from New England. 'My parents died in a car accident when I was fifteen.' He didn't tell Arthur that it was no loss, that he had hated them, and they had never understood him. It would have been too maudlin now, and it was no longer important. 'Have you heard anything about where we go from here?' It was time to think about the war again, there was no point dwelling too much in the past. It would get them nowhere. Reality was here, north-east of Naples. 'I heard something about Cassino yesterday, that's over the mountains. It ought to be fun getting there.' Then they could worry about snow instead of rain. Sam wondered what other tortures they had in store for them at the hands of the generals who owned their lives now.

'The sergeant said something about Anzio last night, on the coast.'

'Great.' Sam smiled wickedly. 'Maybe we can go swimming.'

Arthur Patterson smiled, he liked this outspoken boy from Boston. One sensed that beneath the bitterness born of war there was a light heart and a bright mind, and at least it was someone he could talk to. The war had been hard on Arthur in a lot of ways. Spoiled as a boy, over-protected as a young man, particularly after his father died, and brought up by a doting mother in a highly civilized world, war had come as a brutal shock to him. He had never been uncomfortable in his life, or endangered, or frightened, and he had been all of those endlessly since arriving in Europe. He admired Sam for surviving it as well as he had.

Sam pulled out the K-rations he had been saving as his Christmas treat, and opened them with a wry face. He had already given away the candy to some local children. 'Care for a little Christmas turkey? The dressing's a little rich, but the chestnuts are marvellous.' He offered the pathetic tin with a flourish and Arthur laughed. He liked Sam a lot. He liked everything about him, and instinctively sensed that he had the kind of courage he himself didn't have. He just wanted to survive and get home again to a warm bed, and clean sheets, and women with blonde hair and good legs who had gone to Wellesley or Vassar.

'Thanks, I've already eaten.'

'Mmm . . .' Sam murmured convincingly, as though eating pheasant under glass, 'fabulous cuisine, isn't it? I never realised the food was this good in Italy.'

'What's that, Walker?' The sergeant had just crawled past them, and stopped to stare at them both. He had no problems with Sam, but he kept an eye on him, the boy had too much fire for his own good, and had already risked his life foolishly more than once. Patterson was another story, no guts, and too goddam much education. 'You got a problem?'

'No, Sergeant. I was just saying how great the food is here. Care for a hot biscuit?' He held out the half-empty tin as the sergeant growled.

'Cut it out, Walker. No one invited you over here for a party.'

'Damn . . . I must have misread the invitation.' Undaunted by the sergeant's stripes or the scowl, he laughed and finished his rations as the sergeant crawled past them in the driving rain, and then glanced over his shoulder.

'We're moving on tomorrow, gentlemen, if you can take time out from your busy social schedules.'

'We'll do our best, Sergeant . . . our very best . . .' With a grin in spite of himself, he moved on, and Arthur Patterson shuddered. The sergeant admired Sam's ability to laugh, and make the other men laugh too. It was something they all needed desperately, particularly now. And he knew they were in for tougher times ahead. Maybe even Walker wouldn't be laughing.

'That guy's been riding my ass since I got here,' Arthur complained to Sam.

'It's part of his charm,' Sam muttered as he felt in his pockets for another butt, in case he'd forgotten one, and then like the gift of the Magi, Arthur pulled out an almost whole cigarette. 'My God, man, where did you get that?' His eyes grew wide with desire as Arthur lit it and handed it to him. 'I haven't seen that much tobacco since the one I took off a dead German last week.' Arthur shuddered at the thought, but he imagined Sam was capable of it. It was partially the callousness of youth, and partially the fact that Sam Walker had courage. Even sitting quietly in the foxhole, cracking bad jokes, and talking about Harvard, one sensed that.

They slept huddled side by side that night and the rain abated the next morning. The following night they slept in a barn they'd taken over in a minor skirmish, and two days later they headed for the Volturno River. It was a brutal march that cost them more than a dozen men, but by then Sam and Arthur were fast friends. It was Sam who literally dragged Arthur and finally half carried him when he swore he could no longer walk, and it was Sam who saved him from a sniper who would have killed them all.

When the invasions at Nettuno and Anzio failed, the brunt of breaking through the German line at Cassino fell to Sam and Arthur's division. And this time Arthur was wounded. He took a bullet in the arm, and at first Sam thought he was dead when he turned to him as the shot whizzed past him. Arthur lay with blood all over his chest, and his eyes glazed, as Sam ripped his shirt open, and then discovered that he had been hit in the arm. He carried him behind the lines to the medics and stayed with him until he was sure he was all right, and then he went back and fought until the last retreat, but it was a depressing ordeal for all of them.

The next four months were a nightmare. In total, 59,000 men died at Anzio. And Sam and Arthur felt as though they had crawled through every inch of mud and snow in Italy as the rains continued, and they made their way north to Rome. Arthur was restored to duty rapidly, and Sam was thrilled to have him near at hand again. In the weeks before Arthur was shot, they had developed a bond which neither of them spoke of, but both felt deeply. They both knew it was a friendship that would stand the test of time, they were living through hell together and it was something neither of them would ever forget. It meant a lot more than anything in their past, and for the moment even anything in their future.

'Come on, Patterson, get off your dead ass.' They had been resting in a valley south of Rome, in the steady march to defeat Mussolini. 'The sergeant says we move out in half an hour.' Patterson groaned, without moving. 'Lazy fart, you didn't even have to fight in Cassino.' In the weeks after Arthur had been hit, they had struggled for Cassino, and fought until the entire town was reduced to rubble. The smoke had been so thick that it had actually taken several hours to see that the huge monastery had been totally destroyed and had virtually disappeared from the shelling. There had been no major battles since then, but constant skirmishes with the Italians and the Germans. But since 14th May, their efforts had been stepped up, as they joined the Eighth Army to cross the Garigliano and Rapido rivers, and by the following week all of the men were exhausted. Arthur looked as though he could have slept for a week, if only Sam would let him. 'Up, man, up!' Sam nudged him with his boot. 'Or are you waiting for an invitation from the Germans?'

Arthur squinted up at him through one eye, wishing he could doze for another moment. The wound still bothered him from time to time, and he tired more easily than Sam, but he had before the wound too. Sam was tireless, but Arthur told himself that he was also younger. 'You better watch it, Walker . . . you're beginning to sound just like the sergeant.'

'You gentlemen have a problem?' He always seemed to appear at the least opportune moments, and to have a sixth sense about when his men were talking about him, and in less than flattering terms. As usual, he had materialized behind Sam, and Arthur scrambled quickly to his feet with a guilty look. The man had an uncanny knack for finding him at his least prepossessing. 'Resting again, Patterson?' Shit. There was no pleasing the man. They had been marching for weeks, but like Sam, the sergeant never seemed to get tired. 'The war's almost over, if you can just stay awake long enough to watch us win it.' Sam grinned, and the crusty sergeant stared at him, but there was an *entente* between the two men, a mutual respect which totally eluded Arthur. He thought he was a sonofabitch to his very core, but he knew that secretly Sam liked him.

'You planning to get your beauty sleep too, Walker, or can we get you two on your feet long enough to join us in Rome?'

'We'll try, Sergeant . . . we'll try.' Sam smiled sweetly, as the sergeant roared over his head to the others.

'Move 'em outtttt!!!! . . .' He hurried on ahead to roust them and ten minutes later they were heading north again, and it felt to Arthur as though they never stopped until 4th June, when, exhausted beyond words, he found himself literally staggering through the Piazza Venezia in Rome, being pelted with flowers, and kissed by shrieking Italians. Everywhere around them was noise and laughter and singing and the shouts of his own men, and Sam with a week-old beard shouting in delight at him and everyone in sight.

'We made it! We made it! *We made it!*' There were tears of joy in Sam's eyes, matched by those in the eyes of the women who kissed him, fat ones, thin ones, old ones, young ones, women in black and in rags and in aprons and cardboard shoes, women who might have, at another time, been beautiful but no longer were after the ravages of war, except to Sam they all looked beautiful. One of them put a huge yellow flower into the mouth of his gun and Sam held her in his arms so long and hard that Arthur grew embarrassed watching.

They dined that night in one of the little trattorias that had been thrown open for them, along with a hundred other soldiers and Italian women. It was a festival of excitement and food and song, and for a few hours it seemed like ample reward for the agonies they'd been through. The mud and the filth and the rain and the snows were almost forgotten. But not for long. They had three weeks of revelry in Rome and then the sergeant gave them the word that they were moving out. Some of the men were staying in Rome, but Sam and Arthur were not among them. Instead, they would be joining Bradley's First Army near Coutances in France, and for a while, they told themselves it couldn't be a very difficult assignment. It was early summer, and in Italy and France the countryside was beautiful, the air was warm, and the women welcomed them, along with a few German snipers.

The sergeant saved Sam's hide this time, and in return two days later Sam kept the entire platoon from being caught in an ambush. But on the whole, it was an easy move with the German army in full retreat by mid-August. They were to press through France, join General LeClerc's French division and march on Paris. As the word filtered through the ranks, Sam quietly celebrated with Arthur.

'Paris, Arthur . . . sonofabitch! I've always wanted to go there!' It was as though he'd been invited to stay at the Ritz and go to the Opera and the *Folies-Bergère*.

'Don't get your hopes up, Walker. You may not have noticed, but there's a war on. We may not live long enough to see Paris.'

'That's what I love about you, Arthur. You're always so optimistic and cheerful.' But nothing could dampen Sam's spirits. All he could think of was the Paris he had read about and dreamed about for years. In his mind, nothing had changed, and it would all be there, waiting for him, and for Arthur. He could talk of nothing else as they marched through towns and villages filled with excitement and the end of four years of bitter occupation. Sam was obsessed by the dream of a lifetime, and even the thrill of Rome was forgotten now as they fought their way to Chartres in the next two days, and the Germans were retreating methodically toward Paris, as though leading them to their goal, and what Arthur was sure would be total destruction.

'You're crazy. Has anyone told you that, Walker? Crazy. Totally insane. You act as though you're going on a vacation.' Arthur stared at him in total disbelief as Sam rattled on between killing Germans. He even forgot to raid their pockets for cigarettes, he was so excited.

In the early hours of 25th August Sam's dream came true. And in an eerie hush, with eyes watching them from every window, they marched into Paris. It was totally unlike their victorious march on Rome. Here, the people were frightened, cautious, slow to come out of their houses and hiding places, and then little by little, they emerged, and suddenly there were shouts and embraces and tears, not unlike Rome, but it all took a little longer.

By two-thirty that afternoon, General von Choltitz had surrendered and Paris had been officially liberated by the Allies, and when they marched down the Champs-Elysées in the victory parade four days later on 29th August Sam unashamedly cried as he marched with his comrades. The thought of how far they had come and how much they had accomplished, and that they had freed the Paris of his dreams left him breathless. And the shouts from the people who lined the streets only made him cry more, as the troops marched from the Arc de Triomphe to Notre Dame for a service of thanksgiving. Sam realized he had never been as grateful for anything in his life as he was for having survived the war this far, and having come to this remarkable city to bring freedom to its people.

After the services at Notre Dame, Arthur and Sam were deeply moved as they left the Cathedral and they walked slowly down the rue d'Arcole. They were free for the rest of the afternoon, and for a moment Sam couldn't even think of what he wanted to do, he just wanted to walk and drink it all in and smile at the people. They stopped for a cup of coffee at a tiny bistro on a corner, and were given a small steaming cup of the chicory everyone drank, and a plate of tiny biscuits by the owner's wife as she kissed them on both cheeks. When it came time to leave she wouldn't let them pay, no matter how much they insisted. Arthur spoke a little French, and Sam could only gesture his thanks and kiss the woman again. They knew only too well how short of food everyone was, and the gift of biscuits was like bars of gold, offered to a stranger.

Sam was speechless with awe as they left the bistro.

Maybe the war hadn't been so bad after all. Maybe it was all worth it. He was twenty-two years old, and he felt as though he had conquered the world, or at least the only part that mattered. Arthur smiled down at him as they walked. For some reason, Rome had moved him more. Perhaps because he had also spent time there before the war, and Rome had always been a special place for him, the way Paris seemed to be for Sam, even though he had never been there.

'I don't ever want to go home, you know that, Patterson? Sounds nuts, doesn't it?' As he said it, he noticed a young woman walking ahead of them, and he was distracted when Arthur answered. She had flaming red hair pulled back in a knot at the nape of her neck, and a navy-blue crepe dress that was so old it was shiny, but which showed all the rich curves of her figure. There was a proud tilt to her head, as though she had nothing to thank anyone for – she had survived the Germans, and she owed nothing to anyone now, not even the Americans or the Allies who had freed Paris. Everything she felt was spoken by the way she carried herself, and Sam stared at her shapely legs and the sway of her hips as they followed her down the street, all conversation with Arthur halted.

'. . . Don't you think?' Arthur asked him.

'What?' Sam couldn't concentrate on what he was saying. All he could see was the red hair and the slim shoulders, and the proud way she moved. She stopped at the corner, and then crossed the bridge over the Seine and turned down the Quai de Montebello as Sam unconsciously followed her.

'Where are you going?'

'I don't know yet.' His voice was intense, his blue eyes serious, as though if he lost her from sight for a moment, something terrible would happen.

'What are you doing?'

'Hmm? . . . ' He looked at Arthur for the merest instant and then quickened his pace, as though terrified to lose the girl. And then suddenly, Arthur saw her too. He looked at her just in time to see her face turned toward them, as though she suddenly sensed them behind her. She had a face like a cameo, with creamy white skin, delicate features and huge green eyes that bore right into them, one by one, and her gaze seemed to stop on Sam, as though warning him to keep his distance.

He was paralysed by his lack of French and the crushing look she gave him, but when she began to walk again, he followed her with even greater determination. 'Have you ever seen a face like that?' he asked Arthur without glancing at him. 'She's the most beautiful woman I've ever seen.' There was an aura about her that easily captivated the attention, and a strength one could sense even at a distance. This was not a girl throwing flowers at the Allied troops, or ready to throw her arms around the nearest soldier. This was a woman who had survived the war, and was ready to thank no one for it.

'She's a pretty girl,' Arthur agreed, sensing the inadequacy of his own words, but feeling somewhat embarrassed, too, by Sam's dogged pursuit of her every step. 'I don't think she's too pleased at having us follow her, though.' That was clearly an understatement.

'Say something to her.' Sam was totally mesmerized by her as the distance between them narrowed.

'Are you crazy? That wasn't exactly a friendly look she threw us a minute ago.' And they both watched her disappear into a shop, while they stood helplessly outside on the pavement.

'Now what?' Arthur looked embarrassed to be pursuing this woman on a Paris street. Liberation or no, it seemed an awkward thing to be doing, and he didn't like it.

'We'll wait for her. Let's invite her out for a cup of coffee.' He suddenly wished he had saved the plate of tiny biscuits. She was awfully thin; she probably hadn't seen anything like that in years, and she deserved them. All he'd done was crawl his way across North Africa and Italy on his belly, and march through France on his knees. Hell, what was that in comparison to surviving occupation by the Germans, particularly as a woman. Suddenly, he wanted to save her from everything that had ever happened to her, and anything that could happen now with thousands of Allied troops running crazed all over Paris.

She emerged from the shop carrying two eggs in a basket and a loaf of bread, and she glanced at them with obvious annoyance when she saw them waiting outside for her. Her eyes blazed as she said something directly to Sam which he didn't understand and he quickly turned to Arthur for a translation.

'What did she say?' It was obviously not anything endearing, but even that didn't seem to matter now. At least she had spoken to them, and there was a faint blush on Arthur's cheeks as he glanced at Sam in annoyance. This was most unlike him. He had behaved himself on the whole in Rome and every place else they went, with the exception of a few pinches and hugs and kisses, but this was something new, and Arthur was not at all sure he liked it.

'She said that if we take one step near her, she's going to go to our commanding officer and have us arrested. And frankly, Walker, I think she means it.'

'Tell her you're a general.' Sam grinned, seeming to regain some of his aplomb and good humour, as his desperation left him. 'Christ . . . tell her I'm in love with her.'

'Shall I offer her a candy bar and silk stockings too, while I'm at it? For heaven's sake, Sam, come to your senses and leave the girl alone.' She stopped in another shop just then, and it was obvious that Sam had no intention of leaving. 'Come on . . .' Arthur tried to induce him to leave, but to no avail, she came out of the shop as they were still arguing about it, and this time she walked right up to both of them, and stood so close to them that Sam thought he was going to faint from the sheer impact of being so near to her body. Her skin was so creamy-looking that he wanted to reach out and touch her arm, as she blazed at them in her very limited English.

'Go out! Go back! Go away!' she said, but despite the odd choice of words, they both got the message. She looked as though she were going to slap them, particularly Arthur, as though she expected him to be the sensible one and do something about Sam. '*C'est compris?*'

'No . . .' Sam immediately launched into frantic conversation with her. 'No *compris* . . . I don't speak French . . . I'm American . . . My name is Sam Walker, and this is Arthur Patterson. We just wanted to say hello and . . .' He gave her his most winning smile, and something in her eyes was angry and hurt beyond anything Sam could have understood, anything he had ever felt or experienced, and he felt desperately sorry for her.

'*Non!*' She waved her arms at them. '*Merde! Voilà! C'est compris?*'

'*Merde?*' Sam looked blank and turned to Arthur for translation. 'What's "*merde*"?'

'It means shit.'

'Very nice.' Sam smiled as though she had invited them

to tea. 'Would you like to join us for a cup of coffee . . . *café*?' He was still smiling at her as he spoke to Arthur, 'Christ, Patterson, how do I invite her for a cup of coffee? Say something will you, please?'

'*Je m'excuse* . . .' he said apologetically, trying to remember his schoolboy French, most of which seemed to have escaped him in the face of this incredible-looking French woman. Sam was right. She was the most beautiful girl he'd ever seen. '*Je regrette . . . mon ami est très excité . . . voulez-vous un café?*' he said lamely at the end, suddenly not wanting to let go of her either. Her response was one of immediate outrage.

'*Quel sacré culot . . . bande de salopards . . . allez-vous faire . . .*' And then, with tears in her eyes, she suddenly shook her head and hurried past them, going back the way she had come, with her head down now, but her shoulders still as proud as ever, walking faster in shoes they could see were well worn and too big for her, like the dark blue dress that looked as though it might have been her mother's.

'What did she say, Arthur?' Sam was already hurrying after her, and had to scurry through a crowd of soldiers who seemed to have sprung up from nowhere.

'I think she was about to tell us to go to hell, I didn't quite catch the rest. I think it was argot.'

'What's that? A dialect?' Sam looked instantly worried, French was complicated enough without worrying about dialects, but he was more concerned about losing her in the press of people on the street.

'It's Paris slang.' She had darted into a short street, the rue des Grands-Degrés, stopped suddenly in a doorway, and then disappeared, loudly banging the door behind her, as Sam stopped and sighed with a victorious grin. 'What are you looking so pleased about?' Arthur asked.

'We know where she lives now.' The rest would be easy.

'How do you know she's not visiting someone?' Arthur was fascinated by the intensity of his passion. He had never felt anything like it himself, but he had also never seen anyone like her. She was truly lovely.

'She'll come out sooner or later. She has to.'

'And you plan to stand here and wait for her all day? Walker, you *are* crazy!' Arthur shook his head in dismay. He didn't intend to spend all his time in Paris loitering outside some girl's doorway ... a girl who obviously didn't want to speak to him, when there were a thousand others who would have been thrilled to show them all sorts of gratitude and passion. 'I am *not* going to stand here all day for chrissake ... if you think ...'

Sam looked nonplussed. 'So go. I'll meet you later. Back at the café where we had coffee.'

'And you're just going to wait here?'

'You got it.' He lit a cigarette, and lounged happily against the wall of what he assumed was her building. He was thinking of going inside, but that could wait. Presumably, she'd come out again ... eventually ... and he had every intention of waiting.

Arthur stood on the pavement fuming and trying to convince him to do something more constructive with his time, but to no avail. Sam had no intention of leaving. And in total irritation, Arthur gave up, and decided to hang around with him, partially because he didn't want to leave Sam and partially because he found her intriguing too. It was less than an hour before she emerged, carrying some books in a string bag. Her hair was combed loose now, and she looked even more beautiful than she had an hour before. She saw them immediately as she stepped out of her house, started to back inside for a moment, and then decided against it. With her head held high, she

24

walked past them, and Sam ever so gently touched her arm to catch her attention. At first she looked as though she were going to brush past, and then she stopped, the green eyes blazing, and looked at him. The look she gave him spoke volumes, but she also looked as though she understood there was no point in trying to say anything because he wouldn't understand, and what's more he didn't want to.

'Would you like to go have something to eat with us, mademoiselle?' He made the gesture of eating and his eyes never left hers. There was something very compelling about the way he looked at her, as though he wanted her to understand that he wasn't going to hurt her or take advantage of her. He just wanted to look at her ... to see her ... and maybe even to reach out and touch her. '*Oui?*' He looked boyishly hopeful and she shook her head.

'*Non.* Okay?' Her French accent on the single word sounded endearing and he smiled as Arthur watched the exchange, unable to speak up in his limited French. Something about the girl left him speechless. 'No ...' She repeated the gesture Sam had made to indicate eating and shook her head.

'Why?' He struggled to find the word in French. '*Pourquoi?*' He suddenly glanced at her hand in panic. Maybe she was married. Maybe her husband was going to kill him. But there was no ring there. She seemed awfully young, but maybe she was a widow.

'*Parce que,*' she spoke slowly, wondering if he would understand, but almost certain he wouldn't, '*je ne veux pas.*' Arthur spoke up then in a whisper.

'She says she doesn't want to.'

'Why?' Sam looked hurt. 'We're nice guys. Only lunch – food ...' He made the eating gesture again, '... *café* ... okay? ... five minutes?' He held up five fingers on one hand. 'Okay?' He held out both hands, palms up, in a gesture of helplessness and peace, and she looked suddenly weary as she shook her head. She looked as though she had had years of this, years of soldiers harassing her, of strangers in her homeland.

'No German . . . no American . . . no . . . no *café* . . . no . . .' She did the now familiar eating gesture again.

Sam folded his hands in supplication and for a minute he looked as though he might burst into tears. But at least she was still standing there, listening to him. He pointed to himself and then to Arthur. 'North Africa . . . Italy . . . now France . . .' He pretended to shoot, he pantomimed Arthur's wounded arm, and looked at her imploringly, 'One *café* . . . five minutes . . . please . . .'

She seemed almost sorry this time when she shook her head and then started to turn away. '*Non . . . je regrette . . .*' And then she walked away quickly as they stared after her. Even Sam didn't follow her this time. There was no point. But when Arthur started to walk away, Sam wouldn't follow.

'Come on, man, she's gone, and she doesn't want to see us.'

'I don't care.' He sounded like a disappointed schoolboy. 'Maybe she'll change her mind when she comes back.'

'The only thing that'll be different is that maybe this time she'll have her father and seven brothers come and knock our teeth out. She told us no, and she meant it, now let's not waste all day standing here. There are a million other women in Paris, dying to show their gratitude to the liberating heroes.'

'I don't give a damn.' Sam wasn't moving. 'This girl's different.'

'You're damn right she is.' Arthur was finally getting angry. Very angry. 'She told us to take a hike. And personally, I intend to follow her advice, no matter how good her legs are. Are you coming, or not?'

Sam hesitated for a moment and then followed him, but with obvious regret. And wherever they went that day, all he could think of was the beautiful girl with red hair on the rue d'Arcole with the green eyes that blazed fire and sadness. There was something about her that haunted him, and after dinner that night, he left Arthur at the table with three girls, and quietly slipped away to walk slowly down her street, just to be near her. It was a crazy thing to do, and even he knew it, but he couldn't help himself. He wanted to see her one more time, even if only from a distance. It wasn't just her looks, there was something more about her. Something he couldn't define or understand, but he wanted to know her . . . or at least see her. He had to.

He stopped at a little café across the street, and ordered a cup of the bitter coffee that everyone drank black and without sugar, and sat staring at her doorway, and then watched in amazement as he saw her walking down the street with her string bag still full of books, and walk slowly up the steps to her house and stop there for a moment, looking for a key in her purse and glancing over her shoulder, as though to be sure no one was following her. Sam leapt to his feet, dropped a handful of coins on the table, and ran across the street, and she glanced up, startled. She looked as though she were going to bolt, but then held her ground with defiance. In occupied Paris, she had faced more ominous men than Sam, and she looked as though she were ready to face one more. But her eyes were more tired than angry this time when she faced him.

'*Bonjour*, mademoiselle.' He looked more sheepish now than he had before, and she shook her head, like a mother scolding a schoolboy.

'*Pourquoi vous me poursuivez?*'

He had no idea what she had said, and this time he didn't have Arthur to rely on, but she spoke more English than he had originally thought. She repeated her question to him in her gentle husky voice. 'Why you do that?'

'I want to talk to you.' He spoke softly, as though caressing the graceful arms that shivered slightly in the cool night air. She had no sweater, only the ugly old blue dress.

She waved vaguely toward the people in the streets, as though offering them up instead. 'Many girls in Paris . . . happy talking Americans.' Her eyes grew hard then. 'Happy talking Germans, happy talking Americans . . .' He understood her.

'And you only speak to Frenchmen?'

She smiled and shrugged. 'French people talk Germans too . . . Americans . . .' She wanted to tell him how France had betrayed itself, how ugly it had been, but there was no way to say all that with the little English she knew, and after all he was a stranger.

'What is your name? Mine is Sam.'

She hesitated for a long time, thinking he didn't need to know it, and then shrugged, as though talking to herself. 'Solange Bertrand.' But she did not hold out her hand in introduction. 'You go?' She looked at him hopefully and he gestured toward the café across the street.

'One cup of coffee, then I go? Please?'

For an instant, he thought she would get angry again, and then, her shoulders drooping for the first time, she seemed to hesitate.

'*Je suis très fatiguée.*' She pointed to the books. He knew she couldn't be going to school at the moment. Everything was disrupted.

'Do you go to school usually?'

28

'Teaching . . . little boy at home . . . very sick . . . *tuber-culose.*'

He nodded. Everything about her seemed noble. 'Aren't you hungry?' She didn't seem to understand and he made the eating gesture again, and this time she laughed, showing beautiful teeth and a smile that made his heart do cartwheels.

'*D'accord . . . d'accord . . .*' She held up one hand, fingers splayed. '*Cinq minutes . . .* five minute!'

'You'll have to drink fast and their coffee is pretty hot . . .' He felt as though he were flying as he took the string bag from her and led her across the street to the café. The owner greeted her as though he knew her, and seemed interested by the fact that she was there with an American soldier. She called him Julien and they chatted for a moment before she ordered a cup of tea, but she refused to order anything to eat until Sam ordered for her. He ordered some cheese and bread, and in spite of herself, she devoured it. He noticed then for the first time, how thin she was when he looked at her closely. The proud shoulders were mostly bones, and she had long graceful fingers. She sipped the hot tea carefully and seemed grateful for the steaming liquid.

'Why you do this?' she asked him after she had sipped the tea. She shook her head slowly. '*Je ne comprends pas.*'

He was unable to explain even to her why he felt so compelled to speak to her, but the moment he had laid eyes on her, he knew he had to.

'I'm not sure.' He looked pensive, and she seemed not to understand. He threw up his hands to show her he didn't know himself. And then he tried to explain it, touching his heart, and then his eyes. 'I felt something different the first time I saw you.'

She seemed to disapprove and glanced at the other girls

in the café, with American soldiers, but he was quick to shake his head. 'No, no . . . not like that . . . more . . .' He indicated 'bigger' with his hands, and she looked sadly at him as though she knew better.

'*Ça n'existe pas* . . . it do not exist.'

'What doesn't?'

She touched her heart and indicated 'bigger', as he had.

'Have you lost someone in the war? . . .' He hated to ask, 'Your husband?'

Slowly she shook her head, and then not knowing why, she told him. 'My father . . . my brother . . . the Germans kill them . . . my mother die of *tuberculose* . . . My father, my brother, *dans la Résistance*.'

'And you?'

'*J'ai soigné ma mère* . . . I . . . take sick my mother . . .'

'You took care of your mother?' She nodded.

'*J'ai eu peur* . . .' She waved her hand in annoyance at herself, and then indicated fright, '*de la Résistance* . . . because my mother she need me very much . . . My brother was sixteen . . .' Her eyes filled with tears then, and without thinking he reached out and touched Solange's hand, and miraculously she let him, for an instant at least, before drawing it away to take another sip of tea, which gave her the breather she needed from the emotions of the moment.

'Do you have other family?' She looked blank. 'More brothers? Sisters? Aunts and uncles?'

She shook her head, her eyes serious. She had been alone for two years now. Alone against the Germans. Tutoring to make enough money to survive. She had often thought of the Resistance after her mother died, but she was too frightened, and her brother had died such a pointless death. He hadn't died for glory, he had died, betrayed by one of their French neighbours. Everyone seemed to be collaborating, and a traitor. Except for a handful of loyal Frenchmen, and they were being hunted down and slaughtered. Everything had changed. And Solange along with it. The laughing, ebullient girl she had once been, had become a smouldering, angry, distant woman. And yet this boy had somehow reached out and touched her and she knew it. Worse yet, she liked it. It made her feel human again.

'How old are you, Solange?'

'*Dix-neuf . . .*' She thought about it for a minute, trying to find the right numbers in English. 'Ninety,' she said quietly and then he laughed at her, and shook his head.

'No, I don't think so. Nineteen?' Suddenly, she realized what she had said, and she laughed too, looking suddenly young again and more beautiful than ever. 'You look terrific for ninety.'

'*Et vous?*' She asked the same question of him.

'Twenty-two.' It was suddenly like boy-and-girl exchanges anywhere except that they had both seen so much of life. She in Paris, and he with his bayonet, killing Germans.

'*Vous étiez étudiant? . . .* student?'

He nodded. 'At a place called Harvard, in Boston.' He was still proud of it, even now, oddly enough with her it still seemed to matter, and he was doubly proud when he saw a light of recognition in her eyes.

''Arvard?'

'You've heard of it?'

'*Bien sûr . . .* of course! . . . like la Sorbonne, no?'

'Probably.' He was pleased that she knew it, and they exchanged a smile. The tea and bread and cheese were long gone, but she didn't seem so anxious to leave now. 'Could I see you tomorrow, Solange? To go for a walk maybe? Or lunch? . . . dinner?' He realized how hungry

31

she was now, how little food she probably had, and he felt it his duty to feed her.

She started to shake her head and indicated the books in the string bag.

'After? . . . or before? . . . please . . . I don't know how long I will be here.' There was already talk of their leaving Paris and moving on to Germany, and he couldn't bear the thought of leaving her. Not now . . . not yet . . . and maybe not ever. It was his first taste of puppy love, and he was totally in her thrall as he gazed into the green eyes that seemed so much gentler now, and so full of wisdom.

She sighed. He was so persistent. And in spite of herself, she liked him. During the entire Occupation, she had not made friends with a single German, and certainly no soldier, and she didn't see why the Liberation should be any different, and yet . . . and yet, this boy was different. And she knew it.

'*D'accord*,' she said reluctantly.

'Don't look so excited,' he teased and she looked confused as he smiled, and took her hand again. 'Thank you.'

They stood up slowly then and he walked her to her door across the street. She gave him a formal little handshake and thanked him for dinner, and then with a resolute sound, the heavy door closed behind her. As Sam made his way slowly through the streets of Paris, he felt as though his whole life had changed in only a few hours. He wasn't sure how, but he knew that this woman . . . this girl . . . this extraordinary creature . . . had come into his life for a reason.

Chapter 2

'Where were you last night?' Arthur yawned as they had breakfast together in the dining room of the hotel where they were quartered. It was the Hôtel Idéal on the rue Saint-Sebastien, and troops were being billeted in similar quarters all over Paris. Arthur himself had had a particularly pleasant evening, which ended with too much wine, but not too many women.

'I had dinner with Solange,' Sam said casually as he finished his coffee, trying to make it sound like any ordinary date, which they both knew it wasn't.

'Who's that? Someone you picked up after you left me?'

'Nope.' Sam looked him right in the eye, with the famous grin full of mischief. 'You remember her . . . we met her yesterday on the rue d'Arcole . . . red hair, green eyes . . . nice legs . . . great walk . . .'

'Are you serious?' He looked stunned, and then he laughed, it was obvious that Sam was teasing. 'For a minute, I believed you. Seriously, where were you?'

'I told you. With Solange.' And this time he looked as though he meant it.

'Walker, do you mean it? *That girl*? Where in hell did you find her?'

'Outside her house. I went back, just in case, and she was coming home. She tutors a kid with tuberculosis.'

'How the hell do you know? As I recall, she only spoke French to us, argot at that.' Arthur looked stunned.

'She speaks a little English. Not a lot, but enough. Other than the fact she told me she was ninety years old, we got along great.' He smiled a proprietary smile at Arthur. It was clear that Solange was already his woman, and looking at him, Arthur felt a pang of regret for not having persisted. There was something about Sam, and people like him. Invariably in life, they won all the prizes.

'How old is she?' He was curious now. Like Sam, he wanted to know everything about her.

'Nineteen.'

'And her father didn't come after you with a butcher's knife?'

Sam shook his head quietly. 'Her father and brother were killed by the Germans. Her mother died of tuberculosis. She's alone.'

Arthur look impressed. They really had had a conversation. 'Are you seeing her again?'

Sam nodded, and then smiled knowingly at his friend. 'Yes, I am, and she doesn't know it yet, Patterson, but after the war, we're going to get married.'

Arthur's jaw almost dropped as he stared at his friend, but this time he didn't even bother to tell him he was crazy, because he suddenly sensed that Sam meant it.

Sam and Solange met again for dinner that night, and this time, she told him what it was like living in Paris with the Germans. In a subtler way, it was worse than what he'd been through, and she had been defenceless. She'd had to live by her wits, avoiding being arrested or tortured or merely raped by the Germans who felt they owned Paris and all the women in it. And after her father had died, she had had to support her mother. They had had hardly any food, and she had given almost everything to

34

her mother. They had lost their apartment eventually, and her mother had died in her arms in a rented room – the room she still lived in now. It was filled with ugly memories and sad ghosts, but she had nowhere else to go now. And after what she'd seen during the war, there was no one left that she trusted. Her brother's betrayal had been the final blow to any feeling she had once had for France or her fellow Frenchmen.

'I'd like you to come to America one day,' he said as though testing the waters, watching her eat. He kept ordering food, and was gratified that she ate it.

She shrugged in answer to his invitation, as though it were an impossible dream, not even worth thinking about. 'Very far . . .' She gestured and then explained in French, '*C'est très loin.*' In every possible way, was what she was thinking.

'Not so far.'

'And you? 'Arvard again after the war?'

'Maybe.' If it even mattered anymore. It was hard to imagine going back to school again. Maybe he would try acting after all. He and Arthur had talked about it a lot, at night, in the foxhole. It made sense there. But it was hard to know what would make sense once they got home. Things would be very different. 'I want to be an actor.' He tried it out on her, to see what she would say, and she looked intrigued by it.

'An actor?' And then she nodded, as though it made sense to her and he wanted to kiss her. He smiled at her and she wasn't quite sure why, and then he ordered a bowl of fruit for her, which was the first she'd had in months, or even dreamt of. His generosity embarrassed her, yet in another way it seemed very natural, as though they were old friends. It was difficult to imagine that this was only their second dinner together.

Their friendship seemed to flourish as they took walks along the Seine, and stopped in little bistros and cafés to talk and eat and finally hold hands. Sam had hardly seen Arthur in days, and when they met over breakfast, Sam didn't like what he had to say. Patton crossed the Meuse two days after their victory parade down the Champs-Elysées, and the day after was at Metz on the Moselle on the way to Belgium. It was unlikely that they would be allowed to languish in Paris for much longer. And on 3rd September Brussels was liberated by the British, and the following day Antwerp as well.

'They're going to have our asses back out there any day, Sam, mark my words,' Patterson said gloomily over coffee, and Sam knew he was right, but he was desperate to stay with Solange now. And on the day Brussels had fallen to the British, he had gone to her room, and he had gently pulled away the old blue dress that had been her mother's and made love to her for the first time. And to his amazement, and delight, he had discovered that she was a virgin. She had lain in his arms afterwards with tears of happiness washing her cheeks as he kissed her. And Sam had fallen more desperately in love with her than ever.

'I love you so much Sam.' Her voice was husky and gentle as she carefully pronounced the words.

'So do I, Solange . . . so do I . . .' He couldn't bear the thought of leaving her, and he knew she hated the thought too. She seemed so much more dependent on him now, more trusting and open. But two weeks later, he got his orders. They were moving on to the German Front, there was a war to fight after all, and at least the end was in sight now. Everyone was certain that with the rest of Europe liberated, Germany would fall quickly . . . maybe even by Christmas, he promised her late one night, as he sculpted her exquisite body with hungry fingers. She had flesh of a

36

satin he had never touched before, and hair that fell past her shoulders and over her breasts like benign fire as he kissed her.

'I love you, Solange ... oh God, how I love you.' He had never known anyone like her. Surely not in Boston, or anywhere since then. 'Will you marry me when the war is over?' Her eyes were full of tears when he asked her, and she didn't answer. He forced her to look at him, and the tears spilled slowly down her cheeks as though she knew something he didn't. 'What's the matter, sweetheart?'

She could hardly force herself to say the words, and it was even harder for her in English. 'Many things change in war, Sam ...' He loved the way she said his name, he loved the way she breathed and spoke and smelled. He loved everything about her with a passion that seemed to sweep him right into the heavens. He had never before felt any of the emotions she brought him. 'You go to 'Arvard again ... après ... and ...' she shrugged helplessly, 'you will forget Paris.' What she really meant was that he would forget her, and he stared at her in amazement.

'Do you really think I could forget this? Do you really think this is some kind of soldier's sport? Dammit, I *love* you!' For the first time, she saw him angry, and he made love to her this time with a vengeance. 'I love you. Do you understand that? *This* is what's important! And when the war is over, I'm taking you home with me. Will you come?'

She nodded slowly, still unable to believe that he would really want her when the war was over ... if he even lived through it. She could not bear the thought of that. She had lost everyone in the war, and perhaps now she would lose him too. It was enough to make her fearful of loving him, and yet, like him, she was unable to stop it. It was a passion greater than both of them.

37

Sam felt as though his soul was being torn from hers. On the day he left Paris she had come to say goodbye, and she and Sam were both speechless with tears when he finally left her. Arthur had never seen him like that as the troops marched out of the Porte Saint-Cloud. Sam had to force himself not to look back again, or he might have deserted. He couldn't bear seeing her standing there as he marched away. She was sobbing the last time he saw her.

When they reached the Ardennes, Sam fought with an even greater vengeance than he had before. It was as though the harder he fought the quicker he could get back to Solange and take her home with him. But by the end of September, the dream was beginning to fade, not the dream of Solange, but the dream of seeing the war end by Christmas. The Germans were not as weakened as everyone had thought, and they fought ruthlessly. It was only at the end of October that Aachen fell, restoring some hope to Sam and Arthur and their comrades. In Arnhem, they weren't as lucky, and by then winter had set in, and the bitter winds and freezing cold began to remind Sam and Arthur of the previous winter they had spent in the Italian trenches.

From November to December they fought in the bitter cold and snows and felt as though they were getting nowhere. Hitler had added new Panzer brigades, and the tanks just seemed to keep on coming forever.

'Christ, do you believe this shit?' Sam looked exhausted as he and Arthur sat in the dark one night, their hands frozen, their feet numb, their faces tingling in the cold, and it was the first time Arthur had seen him so discouraged. All he talked about was spending Christmas with Solange, and it was long since obvious to all of them now that that was not going to happen.

On 16th December, the Battle of the Bulge began and

for a solid week, the Germans pounded the Allies. It wasn't until the skies cleared on the 23rd, that the Allies were able to begin pushing them back, and even then victory for the Allies was uncertain. It was even more disheartening to learn that on 17th December, ninety prisoners of war had been killed by the Germans at Mamedy, in a singularly heartless gesture that violated all of the ethics of war, if any such thing still existed.

And on Christmas Eve, Arthur and Sam sat side by side in a snow-filled trench, trying to keep warm and sharing their rations.

'I don't know, Patterson ... I think the turkey was better last year. Think we should look for a new chef?' But despite the words so typical of Sam, his eyes were glazed with exhaustion and he wore a week's beard on his thin cheeks. He seemed to have aged ten years since he had left Paris, perhaps because he had so much at stake now.

Their sergeant had been killed crossing the Ardennes, and suddenly Sam found himself missing him ... Solange ... even his sister in Boston, from whom he had still heard nothing.

'I wonder what she's doing in Paris?' Sam said the words almost to himself, thinking of Solange, and if Arthur hadn't been so bitter cold to the bone, he would have smiled at him.

'Thinking about you probably. Lucky bastard.' He still remembered how beautiful she was, and wished he had been as persistent as Sam in speaking to her. He spoke French after all, but ... that was silly. She was Sam's girl now.

'Care for some chocolate cake?' Sam held out a piece of rock-hard biscuit he'd been carrying around in his jacket for a week and Arthur declined with a wry face. 'Waiting for the soufflé? I don't blame you.'

'Cut it out, you're making me hungry.' But in truth, they were too cold to eat, too cold, and too tired, and too frightened.

The Germans didn't begin to fall back until two days afterwards, and the Battle of the Bulge was finally over. In March, they took the Bridge at Remagen near Bonn, and in April they met the Ninth Army at Lippstadt and then went on to take 325,000 German prisoners near the Ruhr, and it finally looked as though the end was approaching. And on 25th April at Torgau, they joined forces with the Russians. Roosevelt had died two weeks before, and the news had saddened everyone, but the men on the front were intent on winning and getting home. The Battle of Berlin had begun, and on 2nd May, Berlin was silent at last. On 7th May, Germany surrendered, and Arthur and Sam stood looking at each other, with tears running down their faces. Was it over? Could it be? From North Africa to Italy to France, and now Germany, it felt as though they had crossed half the world, and they had. They had freed it.

'My God, Sam . . .' Arthur whispered to him as they heard the news . . . 'It's over . . . I don't believe it.' They embraced like the brothers they had become, and Sam had an odd feeling of nostalgia that that moment would never come again, and then a moment later he was grateful that it wouldn't. He threw his helmet in the air, and gave a tremendous whoop, but it wasn't Arthur he was thinking of now. It was Solange . . . he was going *home*! And just as he had promised her eight months before, he was going to take her with him.

Chapter 3

The Army had given him three days leave before shipping him back to the States in May 1945, and Sam had headed straight for Paris, where he had found Solange just as he had left her. There was such relief on her face when she saw him that it was easy to read what her feelings were, and the three days flew by faster than either of them could have dreamed.

And she cried copiously this time when he left her at the station to return to Berlin, and from there back to the States for his discharge. He had thought of marrying her before he left Paris, but there was too much red tape, and it would be easier to marry her in the States. He had promised to send for her by the end of the summer. But he had to make some money first. He had already decided not to go back to Harvard, and he wanted to try his luck as an actor. But he was willing to do anything to make the money he needed to pay Solange's passage. He was going to have her come to the States on a tourist visa, and marry her the minute she arrived. He could hardly stand the thought of the months ahead without her.

In New York Arthur had talked him into moving in with him until Sam found an apartment, and all Sam could think of was getting settled.

'Don't cry, sweetheart. I promise . . . no later than September.' That gave him four months to get everything

41

organized and have enough money to support her. He was twenty-three years old, he had survived the war, and he had the world by the tail now.

'I love you, Sam!' she shouted as the train pulled away, and she waved for as long as he could see her.

'Cute girl you got, Private,' an admiring sergeant said as they settled down on the train, and Sam only nodded. He wasn't anxious to discuss Solange with anyone, and he wasn't particularly keen on the other soldiers' constantly admiring glances. She was a beautiful young woman, but she was more than that. She was his now.

The train pulled into the Berlin Station at midnight, and Sam made his way back to his quarters to look for Arthur. Arthur had been keeping himself busy with the German girls, and he seemed to have a decided preference for tall blondes. He was in seventh heaven in Germany, and Sam teased him about it constantly, but when he came in that night, Arthur wasn't there, and Sam went to bed, his head filled with thoughts of his bride to be, and the life they would share in New York. And before he knew it, it was eight o'clock the next morning. He left Germany two days after that with Arthur scheduled to come home two weeks later.

Sam was flown to Fort Dix, New Jersey, to muster out, and he took the train to New York from there, and as he stepped off the train in Penn Station, he felt as though he had landed on the moon. After three years in Europe, fighting in the filth and the mud and the rain and the snow, it seemed incredible to be home and see people going about their normal lives. He could hardly adjust to any of it, not even the little hotel where he stayed on the West Side, and he was desperately lonely for Arthur and Solange as he pounded the pavement, going to agents and acting schools, and looking for jobs

42

that would help him keep body and soul together in the meantime.

The army had given him one hundred and fifty-four dollars when he was discharged and his funds were dwindling rapidly. It was a huge relief when Arthur came home two weeks later and Sam could move in with him and his mother. He hadn't wanted to impose on her before that. But it was a joy to be with him again, not just because of the money he was saving but because at last he had someone to talk to. They talked for hours in the bedroom they shared, like two kids. Although Arthur's mother often complained that she could hear them, and she wore a disapproving look whenever she spoke to Sam, which was not often. It was as though the war had somehow been Sam's fault, and their laughter and re-membered tales only helped to prove that they'd been having a good time, and had stayed away just to cause her anguish. She seemed to view Sam as a constant, unhappy reminder of a difficult time and it was a relief when Arthur found a place of his own, and let Sam stay with him there. By then, Sam had a job as a waiter at P. J. Clarke's on Third Avenue, and had enrolled in an acting school on West Thirty-ninth, but he hadn't been offered any parts. He was beginning to wonder if it was all a hopeless dream, when someone finally auditioned him for an off-Broadway show. He didn't get the part, but he felt a little closer than he had before, and he knew where he had gone wrong. He discussed it at length with his acting coach, and when he auditioned a second time in late July, this time he got a walk-on part in another off-Broadway show, and he wrote about it to Solange as a major victory. But it was far more exciting to both of them when in September, he finally sent her enough money to come over. It was just enough for her fare, and a few extra dollars to buy some clothes, and he had explained at length to her that they would be living on his waiter's salary and tips, and the going would be rough for a long time. But there was no doubt in his mind that he wanted her with him.

She arrived on 26th September, tourist class, on the *De Grasse*, which was still the only ship sailing out of Le Havre since the war had ended. And Sam stood staring at the decks with a pair of binoculars Arthur had given him. He searched every face he could see, and for a moment he panicked, fearing she hadn't made the journey . . . and then . . . on a lower deck, he saw a white dress, and a small white hat, and beneath it the red hair he loved so much and the face he had longed for. He waved frantically, but there were too many people on the dock and he knew she hadn't seen him.

It took hours for Solange to clear customs as he waited impatiently. It was a brilliantly sunny day, and it was warm on the docks, with a gentle breeze. It was a perfect day for her to come home to him. Then suddenly she was free and flew into his arms, her hat askew and tears pouring down her cheeks as he kissed her and held her in his powerful arms as he cried too. It was the moment he had wanted so desperately, and he laughed with relief and joy and kissed her.

'Oh God, Solange, how I love you.' It was a passion almost beyond reason or measure. He couldn't bear to tear himself away from her, he missed most of his acting classes after she first arrived, and he could hardly stand going to work every night at five o'clock. He had found a tiny studio apartment for them in the East Forties, under the elevated train, and every night, no matter how cold it was, she would walk him to work. And at two-thirty, when he came home, he would bring her food, and she was always waiting up for him. They would eat after they had made love, sometimes at four o'clock in the morning. And then finally at Christmas, she insisted that he had to get serious about his career, and start thinking seriously about his acting. It still seemed like a remote dream to him, and she was far more real, but he knew she was right. Sometimes she would go to acting classes with him, and she was struck by how talented he was, as was everyone in the class. But his teacher was merciless, and demanded more and more from him. In the mornings, he would read plays, and scan the papers for auditions.

They saw Arthur from time to time too, but less than Sam would have liked. It was difficult because Sam worked at night, and Arthur now had a steady girlfriend. A girl who had graduated from Vassar before the war, with a nasal voice, and smooth blond hair which she wore in a page-boy. She did not seem particularly amused by Sam, and always seemed to find an opportunity to mention that Sam was a 'waiter'. What's more, she made it obvious to everyone that she hated Solange, much to Arthur's embarrassment. And when they were alone, she always referred to Sam and Solange as 'the gypsies'. Her name was Marjorie and she was not touched by Arthur's tales of the war, or by the fact that Solange had survived the occupation of France and lost her entire family. She had spent the war doing volunteer work for the Red Cross and the Junior League, which she felt sure was far more noble. And it was obvious that at twenty-eight, she was terrified of never getting married. There were a lot of girls like her after the war, girls who would have got married years before, if all the best men hadn't been overseas, as they claimed. And she was working hard on Arthur to change her status. But Arthur had problems of his own. His mother hadn't been well, he told Sam, and it worried her to think of him getting married to Marjorie.

He was back at his old law firm, and doing well, but he was afraid to upset his mother who thought he should find someone a little younger ... or different ... or never. Sam had seen her for what she was when he stayed with them, and he felt sorry for Arthur and the pressures he let everyone put him under. His mother wanted to keep a grip on him and live vicariously through him. And she saw all the women in his life, and even his male friends as competition. She wanted her son to herself, and she tried to make him feel guilty for every moment he didn't spend with her.

'*Il manque de courage*,' Solange had said bluntly about Arthur after she came to the States, waving her hands as they chatted one night, over one of their three am dinners. 'He has ... no ... guts ...' She looked victorious over finding the right word. 'No heart ... no ... courage.'

'He has a lot of heart, Solange. He's just not as forceful as he could be.' And his mother had a hold on him like a vice, but Sam didn't say that.

'*Voilà*.' She agreed. 'No courage. He should marry Marjorie if he wants to or say *au revoir*, or perhaps,' she said mischievously, 'he should beat her.' Sam had laughed at the thought but he couldn't disagree with her. 'And he should say to his mother ... *merde*!' Sam laughed even harder at that one. They got on famously, in bed and out. They shared most of the same views, she had a heart of gold, and she was fiercely devoted to him, and she was even very fond of Arthur, which meant a lot to Sam. He had been the best man at their wedding at City Hall three days after she arrived on the *De Grasse*, and he had taken care of all of Solange's papers. She called him her '*grand frère*', her big brother, and looked at him lovingly with her huge green eyes, and he always looked as though he would gladly die for her.

But in the end, Marjorie got her way, and in the spring of 1946, they had a small wedding in Philadelphia, where she came from. In Sam's eyes, Arthur had traded one difficult woman for another, but he didn't say so. Arthur's mother was too ill to go, she said her heart was simply not strong enough to allow her to travel, and she had stayed home on the advice of her doctor. Solange and Sam hadn't gone either, but in their case it was because they were not invited. Arthur had explained endlessly that it was a tiny wedding, only family, only Marjorie's very closest friends, too far . . . too complicated . . . sure they wouldn't have liked . . . he had agonized over it every time he saw Sam, but Solange saw the announcement in the papers. It was a wedding for five hundred guests in St Peter's Episcopal Church in Philadelphia, with a reception at the Philadelphia Club. Arthur had seen the notice too and prayed that the Walkers hadn't seen it.

'That was not nice of him, Sam.' Solange was hurt, and disappointed for Sam, but Sam seemed surprisingly understanding.

'It's Marjorie's fault, not his.'

'*Quand même* . . .' Still . . . it only confirmed what she had previously said. Arthur had no guts, and Sam suspected that Marjorie was going to seriously hamper their friendship.

Time did not prove him wrong, and he and Arthur met for lunch, sometimes with Solange, but their meetings did not include Arthur's wife, who had announced, now that she had his ring firmly on her left hand, that she wanted to go to law school, and did not intend to have any children until much later. Arthur was still reeling from the blow. He had hoped to have children as soon as possible, and she had nurtured that hope during their entire courtship.

But Sam and Solange had enough to fill their own lives,

without worrying about Arthur and his bride. Solange was totally involved in Sam, night and day, and encouraging him constantly now to get serious about his acting. By the autumn of 1947, she knew every play on Broadway, had wormed her way into rehearsals whenever possible, and read every trade paper and notice available, while Sam went to acting school every day and went to all the auditions she directed him to. It was a joint effort which bore fruit, sooner than they expected.

His big break came just after Christmas. He got a leading role in an off-Broadway play, and got extraordinarily good reviews which won him the respect of the critics. The play closed in four and a half months, but the experience had been invaluable. And that summer he did summer stock at Stockbridge, Massachusetts, and while they were there, he decided to look up his sister. It was embarrassing to realize that in the three years since he'd been home from the war, he had never tried to find her, and Solange scolded him for his lack of family devotion. Until she met Eileen and Jack Jones, and then she understood a little better why he had preferred to ignore her. He tracked her down from the old neighbourhood and found her married to an ex-Marine, who greeted them with a constant flood of lewd jokes. Eileen said very little and she was probably more than a little drunk as they sat in her living room on an ugly street, in an ugly suburb of Boston. Her hair was still bleached blond, with dark roots, and her dress was so tight she might as well have worn nothing, which would obviously have pleased her husband. It was difficult to believe that she and Sam were even remotely related and it was a relief when Sam and Solange finally left their home, and Sam took a deep breath of fresh air and looked at his wife with a rueful grin mixed with disappointment.

'Well, darling, that's my sister.'

'I don't understand . . . what happened to her?' It still amazed Solange, who had grown more beautiful as she grew older, and dressed beautifully in spite of their limited funds. She looked like an actress herself, or a very successful model.

'She was always like that,' Sam explained. 'We never got along.' He sighed. 'To be honest with you, I never liked her.'

'It's too bad.' It was a relief to get away from them. And they both knew she was no loss in their lives. But the loss of more frequent contact with Arthur was one they both regretted. He came up to see Sam in summer stock once that summer, and was greatly impressed by his performance. And of course he made all the appropriate apologies for Marjorie, who felt terrible not to be able to join them, but she had supposedly gone to visit her parents at their summer home near Philadelphia. She was entering Columbia Law School in the autumn, and was anxious to get a holiday before beginning the school year. And of course Solange and Sam didn't question him any further.

But in September, Arthur and Marjorie became a great deal less important. Sam got an offer for his first big part and Solange was so excited she went out and bought a magnum of champagne which they drank in total abandon together. It was for the leading role in *Wilderness*, and promised to be one of the most important plays on Broadway. It was a fabulous part for Sam, and both of them were hysterical with excitement. Arthur handled the contracts, Sam told P. J. Clarke's he wouldn't be coming back that autumn, and they went into rehearsal almost immediately. The play was handsomely backed, and produced by one of Broadway's most successful producers. Sam Walker's career was launched, and he was going to be in good company that winter. Rex Harrison was going to be appearing in *Anne of the Thousand Days* at the Schubert, with Joyce Redman. Henry Fonda and David Wayne were already in *Mister Roberts* at the Alvin, and Anne Jackson was opening on 6th October in Tennessee Williams's *Summer and Smoke* at the Music Box Theater. This was going to be a year they would always remember.

Arthur took them both to lunch at '21' to celebrate. He explained that Marjorie was already busy with law school and couldn't join them, and Solange had an announcement of her own. She had already told Sam the night before, and he was flying high. Suddenly, they had everything they wanted. He and Solange were going to have a baby. It was due in April, and by then Sam would have settled into the play. Everything was just perfect, and Arthur looked at them wistfully over lunch. He was only thirty-two years old, but lately he seemed much older. He had wanted children too, but by the time Marjorie finished law school she'd be thirty-three years old and anxious to start on her career. Realistically, he knew he would never have a child now, and for some reason it made Solange and Sam's baby seem even more important.

'I envy you both.' Not only the baby, but everything they had, the love that was so obvious, the excitement over Sam's career. Everything seemed to be beginning for them. Sam was twenty-six years old, and Solange was twenty-three. It seemed light-years from the day they had first seen her, after the liberation of Paris. She was so elegant and sleek, she was even more beautiful now, and she seemed so constantly full of life and excitement.

And the excitement didn't dim that autumn, as Sam rehearsed the play night and day, and honed it to perfection. He came home exhausted at night, but never too exhausted to make love to Solange, or tell her about the cast, or the changes in the play. His leading lady was Barbara George, a major star of Broadway, and she was teaching him a great deal, all of which he told Solange with fire in his eyes and the laughter that made her love him.

They opened on 9th December, the day after Rex Harrison in Anderson's play, and Sam's reviews were even better than those he'd had before. It was difficult to believe ... more than that ... incredible ... He had made it!

Chapter 4

The baby was born while they were still riding high on his enormous success on Broadway. Solange timed it perfectly, she went into labour after the curtain call on Saturday night, and the baby was born at ten o'clock the next morning at Doctors Hospital on East End Avenue. It was a natural birth, and they had a little girl, she nestled in her mother's arms, with her father's dark hair and her mother's green eyes the first time that Sam saw her. He was overwhelmed by how pretty she was, and how beautiful Solange looked, tired but proud, as though she knew an important secret now, and had worked hard to learn it.

Arthur was their first visitor the next day, and his eyes grew damp as he looked through the window at the baby. They had named her Hilary, and Solange loved the name even though it was difficult for her to say it. She had never mastered the American 'H', and she called her 'Ilary', and whispered to her in French when they brought the baby to her for her to nurse. They had asked Arthur to be her godfather, and he was deeply touched, but instead of Marjorie, Sam had asked his leading lady, Barbara George, to be the baby's godmother.

The christening was at St Patrick's Cathedral with full pomp and circumstance. The baby wore a beautiful lace gown that her godmother had bought her at Bergdorf Goodman. And Solange was wearing a new mink coat and a diamond ring that Sam had bought her for having the baby. Their circumstances had greatly improved since his role in *Wilderness*, and they moved to a larger apartment on Lexington Avenue, which wasn't luxurious, but it was a great deal nicer than the one they'd had under the Third Avenue elevated train. The baby had come home to her new room, overlooking a little back garden, and Sam and Solange had a cosy room of their own, and a spacious living-room to entertain their friends. There seemed to be a constant flow of people in their apartment now, new friends, actors mostly, and people in Sam's play. Solange didn't mind having them around, on the contrary, she liked it.

The play ran for a full year, and closed after the Christmas of 1949. Sam had many offers within a month, and when he finally chose one he liked he barely had time to catch his breath with Solange and Hilary before he went to rehearsals. Hilary was nine months old by then, and crawling everywhere. She turned up at his feet in his bathroom, when he was shaving, and under the breakfast table in the morning as he drank his coffee, with a constant chorus of 'Da Da Da's' which delighted him. He wanted to have another child soon, hopefully a boy, but Solange wanted to wait. She was content with little Hilary and wanted to give her her full attention. She was a devoted mother, and she seemed even more loving with Sam now since the baby had been born. It was as though it had increased her supply of love for him tenfold.

And motherhood certainly hadn't harmed her looks. She was an incredibly beautiful girl, even more so now, and the press had begun to talk about her increasingly as Sam Walker's fabulous-looking wife. She had been interviewed more than once, but she always directed the attention back to Sam, and talked about what an important actor he was. And the critics agreed with her more than ever after the opening of his new play. It ran for two years, and when it finally closed, Sam decided to take some time off, and Solange almost immediately got pregnant. And nine months later, another daughter, redheaded this time, like her mother, was born on the opening night of Sam's new play. Solange had to rush to the hospital with Arthur just after the curtain went up. She felt terrible not to see Sam's opening night, but she barely made it to the hospital, squeezing Arthur's hand, while he begged the driver to go faster. Alexandra was born ten minutes after they arrived, on a stretcher just outside the delivery room. The baby gave a lusty cry, and Solange lay back with a soft moan, spent with the effort. Arthur came to see her as soon as she was put in a room, and teased her about their going back in time for the final curtain with the baby. Solange loved the idea and wished she could actually do it. Instead, she made him promise to bring Sam back with him afterwards, and Arthur left promising to see her the next day.

Sam didn't get to the hospital till the next morning. He explained that he'd been tied up with endless cast parties, and he pretended not to see the hurt look in her eyes. She had waited for him all night and he hadn't even called her. He brought her a spectacular emerald bracelet, but still, she had silent questions about where he had been, and she was desperately hurt that he hadn't come to see her. He was so much less attentive these days, because the play was a demanding one, he said, and she knew this part was the most difficult of all, but still . . . to her, their baby was more important. But all he could talk about was his leading lady. He seemed obsessed with her. And it was Arthur who took Solange and Alexandra home from the hospital while Sam was at rehearsal. He seemed to be out constantly and she didn't say anything to Sam when he came home late at night, but she always noticed. She particularly noticed the heady scent of another woman's perfume, and although she didn't say it to him, she knew that lately their marriage was different. She felt a void in her own life as a result, an emptiness that was a constant pain, and only Arthur seemed to understand it. He was the only one she could talk to. He had his own problems as well. He still wanted children, and Marjorie wouldn't hear of it. And for his own part, Arthur thought Sam was a damn fool, but he never said so. He only did his best to bolster Solange's spirits during their frequent lunches. It wasn't fair to hurt a woman who was so much in love with her husband. And he often found himself wishing that he had won over Sam, years before, but it was too late now. Solange was married to Sam, and she adored him.

'And you, Arthur, what about you, are you happy? No, of course not,' she answered for him and he didn't disagree. How could one be happy, with a woman like Marjorie? She was a selfish, ambitious iceberg. 'You should force her to have babies if you want them.' She looked serious and he laughed. It was impossible to force Marjorie to do anything she didn't want to do. Impossible for him anyway. He wasn't that kind of person.

'You can't force a woman to have a baby.' He smiled ruefully. 'You'd only have an unhappy mother and eventually an unhappy child. Not like yours.' They were perfect little cherubs, her children Hilary and Alexandra, and he adored them. Hilary was still as dark as Sam, while Alexandra had bright red hair and big green eyes. He smiled at Solange then, and saw the sadness in her face. She knew what Sam was up to, just as everyone else in New York did, she had heard the rumours, and there were constant items about him in the papers.

'He's a damn fool. He's thirty-one years old and he's got the world by the tail . . . and a wife most men would give their right arm for.'

'What would I do with a right arm?' She smiled at him philosophically, looking very Gallic. 'I want his heart, not his arm . . . or all that expensive jewellery. I always know when something is wrong — he comes home with boxes full of diamonds.'

'I know.' Arthur frowned. He still advised Sam on his business affairs, and for some time now had been urging Sam to save money. But Sam was still playing, and enjoying the initial impact of his success. He was buying and buying and buying: toys for the girls, furs and jewels for his wife, clothes for himself, and expensive presents for the women he got involved with. There had been several Arthur knew about, and he disapproved of them all, and he always hoped that Solange knew nothing about them. But he sensed that this time was different. This was the first time he'd had the feeling she was really unhappy.

'I don't know what to do, Arthur. I don't know if I should make a scene, tell him I know what's going on, or sit back quietly and wait for it to be over. Because it will be over soon. It always is with Sam . . . and then he comes home to me.' She smiled a smile that would have brought Arthur to his knees, if he'd been standing, and if it had been meant for him, but it wasn't.

'You're a very sensible woman, Solange. Most Americans aren't. Most women in this country go crazy if they think their husband is having an affair. They hire detectives, sue for divorce, take him for everything he's worth . . .' She was amazing.

But she only smiled at him again, that wise little smile that said she was a thousand years old, even if she only looked twenty. 'I don't want "things", Arthur. I only want my husband.' It was obvious that she adored him. And Arthur envied his friend, though not for the first time. He had always wondered what would have happened if he had pursued Solange, if he had spoken to her that day on the rue d'Arcole. What if . . . it was something he would foolishly ask himself for a lifetime. And it didn't matter now. Sam was the lucky one. Luckier than he knew. The bastard.

'I suppose he'll quiet down again.' Solange sighed and finished her wine. 'With each leading lady now we have a little problem, and then eventually he gets tired of them. It's hard for him, he becomes so involved in the play . . . the theatre is a hard life for him. It's so extremely demanding.' She looked as though she genuinely believed what she said, but Arthur shook his head.

'It's not that demanding. He's spoiled. Spoiled by success, by the women he meets . . . and by you, Solange. You treat him like a god, for heaven's sake.'

'He is – to me. He means everything to me.' Her huge eyes reached out to Arthur and her words cut him to the quick.

'Then sit tight. He'll come home again. He's just playing, Solange. As long as you understand that, perhaps it isn't so important.'

She nodded. It was good advice. And she was always prepared to sit it out. She would rather have died than lose him.

The affair went on for six months finally, and then ended brutally, with the attempted suicide of his leading lady. After which she left the play, for reasons of 'ill health', and Sam's life returned to normal. It was callous of him in some ways, but Solange was relieved to see it. For now, the threat was over. It was 1954 by then, and he stayed with the play for another year and as usual returned to his wife and children. It was the longest run he had ever had in any play, and they were both sad when it was over. He took her and the girls to Europe after that for a summer in Saint-Tropez. It was something he had always talked about. He had been there during the war, though only for a day, and he had always wanted to go back there.

They sent Arthur a postcard from Saint-Tropez and another from Cannes, and then they went on a little pilgrimage to Paris, and Solange showed the children where she had lived as a child. It was emotional for her going back. It was ten years since she had left, and there were painful memories for her there, but happy ones too. Hilary was only six years old, but Solange hoped she would enjoy the trip, and Alexandra was still only a baby. They had brought along a nurse to help them with the children. It was a far cry from the way Solange had left France, with her steamship ticket in her pocket and barely enough money to eat. She had left owning three dresses and two pairs of shoes, and the hat on her head, and an old worn-out coat that had been her mother's. And now here she was with trunks of clothes. They had arrived travelling first class on the *Liberté*, and they stayed at the Ritz in Paris. Sam took her to Givenchy and Chanel and Dior to buy her clothes, and to Cartier where he insisted on buying her a new diamond bracelet.

'But I don't need it, Sam!' she protested laughingly as he forced it on her arm. He was as loving as he had always been, and he had been spoiling her as though she were a new mistress. He had acquired some expensive habits in recent years, and sometimes it frightened Solange. Like Arthur, she wanted him to start saving money for their children.

'Every girl needs a diamond bracelet, Solange.'

'But I have three!' She pulled her arm away with a grin

58

and shook her head. '*Non, chéri! Je ne veux pas!* I want you to save our money.' He looked momentarily annoyed as he glanced at her.

'You sound just like Arthur.'

'Well, he's right. We have to start thinking of the children.'

'Fine.' He pointed to another bracelet in the case, indicating for the salesgirl to take it out. 'We'll take two of them.'

'*Ah non*, Sam! *Quand même voyons!*' Since returning to Paris, she had slipped back into French again, and it pleased her to hear Hilary speaking to people easily. She spoke only French with the two girls, and Hilary was completely bilingual. Alexandra didn't speak yet at all, but when she would, she would speak French too. In some ways, Solange had not totally renounced her homeland. And it felt good to be back again. There were places and memories that still warmed her heart and as they walked into the Place Vendôme at night, with the lights and the statue of Napoleon, she felt her heart soar in a way that it hadn't since she'd left Paris.

They had dinner at Maxim's that night, and at La Tour d'Argent the following day, and the day they left Paris, Sam gave her both diamond bracelets, and a new ring. Solange tried to discourage him, but she knew it was hopeless, and as they sailed back to the States, she thought about what a lovely trip it had been. It had felt good to go back, and good to go home again as they returned. New York was home now. She had lived there for ten years and it meant a great deal to her. They had an apartment on Sutton Place now, with a spectacular view of the river, and lovely rooms for the girls. It was a split-level flat which allowed them to entertain lavishly, and Marilyn Monroe had an apartment nearby. She was a good friend of Sam's, and always spent time with him when she was in New York, but Solange knew they had never had an affair. And she liked Marilyn very much, she was an amusing girl, and she kept telling Solange she should be in movies, which only made Solange laugh.

'One star in the family is enough!' she always said, with her still noticeable French accent.

Sam was offered a part in a new play that autumn but he turned it down. He didn't think it was challenging enough for him. And he surprised everyone by agreeing to make a movie. They went to Hollywood for the film, and Solange found it a completely amazing place, filled with remarkable people who couldn't tell the difference between fantasy and real life. They lived in a 'bungalow' at the Beverly Hills Hotel, with another smaller one for the children and the nurse, and for a year it was a totally unreal existence. Solange thought the movie was very good, but Sam was not pleased and he was relieved to get back to New York and start rehearsals for a new play in January of 1956. He became totally involved in his craft again, and within two months he was also involved with his leading lady. And this time, Solange was seriously annoyed. She had lunch with Arthur regularly, and more often than she liked, she found herself crying on his shoulder. Arthur's marriage was in form only. Marjorie was always occupied elsewhere, and his mother had died while they were in California the year before. He seemed terribly alone suddenly, just as alone as Solange felt, despite Sam's denials and constant gifts, and he was always especially nice to his daughters when he felt guilty.

'Why? Why do you do this to me?' She waved the gossip column at him one morning at breakfast.

'You're imagining things again, Solange. You do this every time I start work on a new play.'

'Ah . . .' She threw the paper in the sink, 'It's because you sleep with your leading lady *every* time you start work on a new play. Do you have to work on the leading lady too? Couldn't one of the other actors do that? Your understudy perhaps. Couldn't that be one of his duties?'

Sam laughed at her and pulled her close to him, pulling her down on his lap and nuzzling the mane of resplendent red hair that was more beautiful than ever. 'I love you, crazy one.'

'Don't call me crazy. I only know you too well, Mr Walker. You cannot fool me. Not at all!' She wagged a finger at him, but somehow she always forgave him. He drank too much, and when he did was sometimes hostile and threatening when he came home. It was impossible for her to stay angry at him. She loved him too much. Too much for her own good, Arthur said, and maybe he was right. But it was the only thing about Sam she would have changed. His other women. The rest she loved just as it was. That spring she got pregnant again, and the baby was born just after Christmas when Sam was in California. It was another little girl and they named her Megan. Once again Arthur took her to the hospital and it took Solange two days to track Sam down in California. She had heard the rumours again, and she knew what he was doing in Hollywood. And this time she was fed up and she told him so when he came back to New York, when the baby was three weeks old. She even threatened to divorce him, which was totally unlike her.

'You humiliate me to the entire world . . . you make a fool out of me, and you expect me to sit here and take it. I want a divorce, Sam.'

'You're out of your mind. You're imagining things. Who've you been talking to again? Arthur?' But he looked worried.

'Arthur has nothing to do with this. And all you have to do is read the newspapers. It's in every column from here to LA, Sam. Every year, every month, every movie, every play, it's a new showgirl, a new leading lady, a new woman. You've done it for too long. You've done nothing but play, and you're so impressed with yourself that you think you owe it to yourself. Then fine, okay, but I owe myself something too. I owe myself a husband who loves me and is willing to be faithful too.'

'And you?' He tried to turn the tables on her, even though he knew how desperately devoted she had been. 'What about all your goddam lunches with Arthur?'

'I have no one else to talk to, Sam. At least he won't call the papers and tell them what I say.' They both knew that everyone else would. She wasn't wrong. She was Sam Walker's wife after all. And he was a star now. 'At least I can cry on his shoulder.'

'While he cries in your soup. You're the most pathetic pair I've ever heard of. And remember what I told you, Solange. I will not give you a divorce. Period. Amen. So don't ask me again.'

'I don't have to ask you.' It was the first time she had openly threatened him.

'Oh no?' There was a thin trace of fear in his voice, carefully masked, but she knew it.

'All I have to do is have you followed. I could have divorced you fifty times by now.'

He had slammed out of the house without saying another word, and he had left for California again the next day. It had delayed rehearsals of his play by a month, but they always forgave Sam Walker.

When he returned things were just as stormy with Solange. She knew whom he had taken to the West Coast and she was finally fed up with him. One night he came back to find her waiting for him, and when she confronted him, their fighting was so loud that it woke Hilary. Alexandra's room was further down the hall, and Megan was only eleven months old then. But Hilary was eight years old. And she remembered everything. The ambulances and the police . . . the sirens . . . and her mother being taken out in a sheet . . . she remembered what they had said . . . and her father crying as they led him away. He hadn't even seen her standing near the door, watching. And then she remembered the nurse calling Uncle Arthur.

He had come almost at once, his face grey. He couldn't believe what they had told him. There had to be some mistake . . . had to be . . . it wasn't possible. He knew they had been having problems for a while, but Sam adored her, just as she loved him. It was a love that had often gone well beyond reason, a love that forgave him everything, a love that had led him to follow her doggedly down the rue d'Arcole right from the beginning. It was a love that touched everyone who came near them . . . a love that . . . he just couldn't understand it as he sat in their apartment as the dawn came and the doorman brought the paper upstairs and knocked discreetly on their front door. But it was all there, as Arthur held out a trembling hand and took the paper. It was all there . . . the end of a dream . . . the end of a life . . . Sam had killed her.

Part II

ARTHUR

Chapter 5

The door to the holding cell slammed hard behind Arthur as he waited to see him. Sam was being held at the 17th Precinct on East Fifty-first Street and it was after noon before they let Arthur in to see him. They had interrogated him until then, for hours and hours, although they had no need to. He had admitted everything. He had sobbed. He had stared glassy-eyed . . . he had remembered every minute of those first hours in Paris. He didn't understand why he had done it . . . he knew he'd been drunk . . . she had frightened him by saying she was leaving. But still . . . he couldn't understand why he'd done it except that he didn't want to lose her and she had said . . . she had said . . . With a look of despair he stared up at Arthur when they led him in. And Sam seemed almost not to see him.

'Sam . . .' Arthur's voice was hoarse. He had been crying all morning. And he reached out to touch Sam's arm, as though to bring him back from the edge of the abyss. Sam looked as though he wanted to die himself. He stood in the centre of the room after they left him there and just stared at Arthur.

'I killed her, Arthur . . . I killed her.' He seemed almost not to see him . . . only her face when he strangled her . . . the red hair he loved so much . . . why? . . . why had he done it? . . . why had she said all those terrible things to him? He looked blindly at his friend as the tears began to roll down his cheeks again.

'Sit down, Sam ... come on.' He gently helped him into one of the room's two straight-backed chairs, facing each other over a narrow, battered table. 'We have to talk.' Sam seemed barely coherent, but they had to talk. 'Do you want to talk about what happened?'

Sam only stared at him. It was all much too simple. 'I killed her.'

'I know that, Sam. But what happened before that? Did she provoke you?' He had to find him a good defence attorney, and before he did, he had to know what they were up against. Now Sam was not just his best friend, he was indirectly a client. 'Did she strike you?'

Sam shook his head, his eyes distant and vague. 'She said a lot of terrible things ... she was very angry.'

Arthur suspected why, but he asked anyway. 'Why was she angry?'

Sam stared at the floor, remembering Solange's fury. He had never seen her like that. He knew he had pushed her too far this time. And he was desperate not to lose her. But he had anyway ... the only woman he loved ... He looked up at Arthur in despair. 'She knew I was having an affair again ... it didn't mean anything ... it never did ...'

'Except to Solange, Sam.' His voice was quiet, and he had to remind himself that it was Sam he was defending, not Solange now.

Sam looked at him strangely in answer, and he was silent for a long time.

'Did she threaten to divorce you?'

He nodded, and then he had to clear the air. He had to ask him. He had to know. It was, in a sense, why he had killed her. Except that he was also drunk and had lost control and the things she said were so terrible, and he was terrified that she meant it and he would lose her. 'She said you and she were having an affair. Is that true?' His eyes pierced his friend's, and Arthur looked back at him with sorrow.

'What do you think?'

'I've never thought about it before. I know you were close to her . . . you two used to go to lunch a lot . . .'

'But did she ever hide it?' Like all good lawyers, he knew the answer before he asked the question.

'No . . . she always told me . . . at least I think so . . .'

'Don't you think she was just trying to get back at you by saying that, for all the pain you'd caused her, and how else could she?'

Now, in the clear light of day, he knew that. But the night before, in the heat of passion, Sam had believed her . . . he had gone crazy . . . and he had actually killed her. The thought of it made the panic rise in his throat like a hand reaching up from his guts to strangle him, and he knew he deserved it. He deserved to die for what he had done to Solange. He began to cry again and Arthur held his shoulders.

'What's going to happen to the girls now?' He suddenly looked up at Arthur with fresh panic.

Arthur had been thinking about it all morning. 'I'm sure you have enough money to take care of them while all this is pending.' And there was the nurse, and a maid in the apartment. They lived extremely well at the apartment on Sutton Place.

Sam looked bleak as he stared at his friend. 'How much is all this going to cost me?' It had cost Solange her life, and now . . . Arthur had to fight his own feelings again and again. How could he have done this to her? And yet, Sam was his friend, more than that, he was almost his brother. They had survived the war side by side, Sam had carried him across the mountains, and to the medics when he was wounded near Cassino. They had liberated Paris and Rome . . . Paris . . . and the rue d'Arcole where they had first seen her. It was all so tightly interwoven, and now it wasn't just a matter of Sam and Solange, there were their daughters to think of. Hilary, Alexandra, and Megan. But Arthur tried to force his thoughts back to answer Sam's question. He wanted to know how much his defence would cost him.

'It depends on who you hire to defend you. I want to think of who to recommend. But you should have the best. This is going to be a very big trial, and there will be a lot of sympathy for Solange. You've had a lot of press with your lady friends in recent years, Sam, and that is not going to help you.'

But Sam was shaking his head with determination. 'I don't want someone else. I want you to defend me.' He looked up at Arthur and Arthur almost visibly shuddered.

'I can't do that.' His voice was a croak in the room full of echoes.

'Why not?'

'Because I'm your friend. And I'm not a criminal attorney.'

'I don't care. You're the best there is. I don't want anyone else. I want you.' His eyes filled with tears, it was all so horrible, it was beyond belief, but it was happening, it *was* real. He had made it real. He had made reality from a nightmare.

Arthur's face was suddenly covered by a thin film of perspiration. This was bad enough, but to defend him on top of it. He just couldn't. 'I don't think I can do it, Sam. I don't have the experience in this field. It would be a tremendous disadvantage to you. You can't do this . . .'

. . . to either of us . . . Oh God, please. He wanted to cry. But Sam was adamant as he looked up at him with pleading eyes.

'You have to. For me, for the girls . . . for Solange . . . please . . .' For Solange? Christ, he had killed her. But the worst of it was that Arthur knew Solange would have wanted him to do anything Sam wanted. He knew better than anyone how desperately she had loved him.

'We'll both have to think it over, but I am convinced it would be a terrible mistake. You need the *best*, Sam, not a tax attorney you drafted into this out of some misguided allegiance. I *can't* do it! I just *can't*!' It was the most emotional Sam had ever heard him, but he still wanted Arthur to defend him. 'But more importantly right now, is there anyone you want me to call for the girls?'

Sam thought about it and shook his head. There was no one they were close to, except Arthur, and the thousands of acquaintances they had had in the theatre. But Solange had had no close friends. She had been totally involved in Sam's life, his children and his career. She never had time for anyone else, nor any particular interest.

'Any family I should call?' He knew he should know that after the years they spent in Europe together, but suddenly he couldn't remember. He knew Sam's parents were dead, but he couldn't remember if there was anyone else, some remote relative he should call, but Sam only shook his head.

'No one who would be important to the girls. There's my sister in Boston, but for God's sake, don't call her.'

'Why not?'

'I haven't seen her in years, not since before Hilary was even born. She's a real tramp. Just forget her.'

But Arthur couldn't afford to forget anyone now. Maybe an aunt was just what the girls would be needing.

'What's her name? Just in case. You never know in a situation like this . . .'

'Eileen. Eileen Jones. She's married to an ex-Marine named Jack. And they live in Charlestown. But believe me, you'd hate them.' Sam stood up, and walked across the holding cell to stare out the barred window.

'I'm not planning to invite them down for the weekend, for chrissake, but right now a relative or two might come in handy.' He had three daughters, two of them practically babies, and he had no one in the world to take care of them except a nurse and a maid . . . and Arthur . . .

And then Sam turned to face Arthur again. 'Can I see them?' His eyes filled with tears at the thought . . . his little angels . . . his babies . . . how could he have done this to them? He had robbed them of their mother, a mother who would have assured them of a happy childhood and a perfect life, a mother who never failed them in any way, who was always there for them, who gave them every kiss, every hug, every bath, played every game, read every story, and whispered with them when she put them to bed at night, with giggles and tickles and cuddles, and now . . . the very thought made him shudder. He wondered if he could even take care of them himself when he got out. But there was no point thinking about it. He would have to.

But Arthur was looking at him now. 'Do you really want to see them here?'

'I guess not.' Sam's voice was the merest whisper. 'I just thought . . . I wanted to try and explain . . . to Hilary at least . . .'

'You can do that later. Right now, we have to get you out of this.'

'Do you think you can?' It was the first time Sam had asked him that, and Arthur didn't like the prospect.

'I think someone else would have a better chance of doing it for you than I would.'

'I don't care. I already told you, Arthur. I only want you to defend me.'

'I think it's going to be a tough fight . . . for anyone . . . to be honest with you, Sam.' He hated to say the words, but he owed him the truth after all. 'You'll have to plead insanity . . . crime of passion . . . you've admitted everything. It's all pretty cut-and-dried, and in the past few years you've got yourself a hell of a reputation.' It was true, they both knew that, and Arthur had always wanted to tell him what a damn fool he was, but for a different reason. He had hated him for hurting Solange, and so needlessly, but on the other hand, they were friends, and Sam's success had come so fast and hard that Arthur suspected it was difficult for him to deal with. He was only thirty-five now, and he had become a big star when he was only in his twenties. It was a lot to digest and a lot to live up to, and he had paid a price for it . . . but so had she . . . more than Sam ever knew. There was a lot about Solange he hadn't noticed, he was so wrapped up in himself and his career that in recent years he had become self-centred, and spoiled. Even his daughters seemed to know that. Alexandra had even said to Arthur recently, 'We have to make a big fuss about Daddy when he's home, or he gets very angry. Our Daddy needs a lot of attention.' It was true and Solange had explained that to them, teaching them how to stay out of his way when he was tired, or having them bring him little treats, like the chocolates he loved, or a plate of fresh fruit, and something cool to drink, or sing a little song she had taught them just for him. The entire household had been trained to revolve around Daddy.

And now they had lost both Solange and Sam. Arthur

thought about it all the way back to the office that afternoon, after he left Sam. And on his own, he decided to call their godparents and see if he could arouse any interest. With Sam in jail, and Solange gone, they had no one now except Arthur. But the godparents they had chosen had been chosen for their important names and pretty faces, well-known actors most of them, and none of them had any real interest in the children. They were much more interested in talking about the news with Arthur, why had Sam done it, had he gone crazy, had Solange done something to provoke him, what was going to happen now, when was the trial? . . . but absolutely nothing about the children, which left him right back where he started, as the only person they had to depend on, in Sam's absence. He was going to hang on to their aunt's name, just in case, but in the meantime, he was going to follow Sam's instructions and not call her.

The next thing he did was to check into Sam's bank accounts, so he could handle his affairs. And he was horrified at what he found there. The balance was infinitely less than he had expected. Sam spent everything he made, mainly on his lifestyle and his girlfriends. In fact, he had already borrowed ahead against future salary in his next play, and aside from the small amount of cash in his checking account, he was in debt up to his eyeballs. There was barely enough to pay the maid's and nurse's salaries over the next few months, until the trial was over. It was a hell of a spot to put the children in, and Arthur remembered Solange saying as much to him years before. She had always wanted Sam to think of the girls, and save some money. But instead he bought her diamond bracelets and fur coats, and God only knew what he spent on his other women. He was known to be a generous man, and he had never skimped on anything, once he could afford to. But now it left him with ten thousand dollars in the bank and ten times that in debts. It was amazing how little one knew about one's friends, and Arthur wished he had talked to him more sternly years before. He had never realized that Sam was irresponsible to this extent, and now it represented disaster for his children.

Arthur had tried to talk to Marjorie about it, bemoaning the children's fate, and hoping to stir her sympathy for them. But he was disappointed to find she only had harsh words for them, making comments about their undoubtedly being gypsies like their parents. She seemed to have no compassion whatsoever for them.

But in the next few days he barely saw his wife. He had his hands full with Sam and the girls, the press constantly badgering all of them, even the children, and he had to make the funeral arrangements for Solange. There was no one else to do it.

The funeral was set for three days after Sam had gone to jail. She lay in state for two days, and on the third day, they held the service. And it was amazing to Arthur how many people came, mostly out of respect for Sam, but there were a great many people who had known and liked her. 'She was a lovely girl . . .' he heard countless people say, '. . . absolutely beautiful . . . didn't know how lucky he was . . . should have been an actress too . . . always wanted her to model for me . . . wonderful with her kids . . . hell of a girl . . . lucky man to have a wife like that . . . she was French to her very soul . . . incredible girl . . . don't understand why he did it . . . she was crazy about him . . .' It went on and on, and Arthur sat in the front row, with the girls and their nurse, trying not to cry as they closed the lid of the coffin. Hilary sat very stiff next to him, and once she walked right up to it and stared down at Solange, and then she kissed her, and returned to her seat with a wooden look of grief, as though she were numb from the immensity of her pain, but she wouldn't let Arthur touch her. In fact, she wouldn't let anyone close to her. She only held tightly to Alexandra's hand, answering all her questions about why Mommy was sleeping in the box covered with white roses. Arthur had paid for all the flowers himself, he hadn't wanted to deplete their funds any further, even for their mother's funeral service.

Alexandra thought Solange looked just like Snow White after she had eaten the apple, and she kept asking Hilary when she was going to wake up . . . and if Daddy was going to come and kiss her.

'No, she's going to go on sleeping like that, Axie.' Her voice was very quiet as the organist played the Ave Maria in church.

'Why?'

'Because she is.' She shushed her. 'Now be quiet.' She tightened her grip on her sister's hand, and her face went dead white as she watched her mother's coffin roll slowly past her. She stood silently, and then suddenly reached out and pulled two white roses from the heavy blanket of flowers that covered the casket, and handed one of them to Alexandra. Alexandra started to cry, and whispered that she wanted Mommy to wake up, and she couldn't breathe like that with the box closed. It was as though she knew her mother was dead, but none of them could face it. Even little Megan had begun to cry, as though she understood too, and the nurse had to take her outside where she could wail in the winter sunshine. It seemed incongruous to bury her on such a pretty day, but perhaps not . . . everything about Solange had always been filled with light and flowers and sunshine, from her flaming red hair to the brilliant green eyes to the lithe body that was always in motion.

Arthur took the children back to the apartment in the limousine, and then went to the cemetery himself to see that everything was attended to. And then he went to see Sam at Rikers Island. He brought him one white rose from the casket, like the one Hilary had given Axie.

Arthur looked very tall and thin and pale, as he entered the holding cell in his dark suit with his Homburg in his hand. He looked like the messenger of Death, and in a way he was. Sam looked up at him and trembled.

'I thought you'd want this.' He held out the white rose, and with a trembling hand, Sam took it.

'How are the girls?'

'They're doing very well. Hilary is keeping them all intact. It's as though she's taken on Solange's role, as their mother.'

Sam dropped into a chair and put his head in his hands, still clutching the rose Arthur had brought him, but it had the smell of death, and sadness, and funerals. There was no joy left in his love for her, or his life; he felt as though everything were over. And in an important way it was. He lay in his cell day and night, and thought only of Solange. Even his daughters seemed remote now. He wondered how much they would hate him in later years, when they discovered, and fully understood, that he had murdered their mother. It would make any kind of relationship with them impossible. Everything was impossible now. And life was no longer worth living. He had already said as much to Arthur, who told him he had to think of the girls now. He owed them everything. But what did he have to give? His debts? His guilt? His bad habits? His overwhelming remorse for killing the one woman he loved . . . he was certain they would never understand.

'I've been thinking about the girls, Sam.' Arthur cleared his throat, praying that Sam wouldn't fight him. 'I'd like to sell all of Solange's jewellery so that they have a little money to fall back on, and you're going to need quite a lot for attorney's fees, particularly if I can convince you to get another attorney. In my case, all we have to do is satisfy the firm for my time. I don't want anything out of it personally or directly.' The last thing he wanted was to make money for defending Sam. But he still didn't want to do it at all. Sam had killed the only woman he had ever loved and admired, in fact almost worshipped, and no matter how close they were, or how great the bond, it was going to be almost impossible for Arthur to defend him. He had tried to explain that to him, but Sam didn't want to hear it.

'What do you think about selling the jewellery?' He looked down at Sam, who turned to him with a deathly pale face covered with beard stubble.

'Fine. If it'll help the girls, get rid of it. Do you want the keys to the safe deposit box at the bank?'

'I've already found them. Solange kept everything in remarkably good order.'

Sam only nodded, unable to answer him. It was hardly surprising that she had. She was a very remarkable woman. But they both knew that. And it didn't matter now . . . she was gone . . . in the box Arthur had watched them lower into the ground only hours before. The thought of it was still with him, and like the aura of sorrow around him, Sam could feel it.

'I'll take care of it this week.' He wanted as much money as possible on hand, for the girls, and Sam's defence fund.

The trial had been set for the following June, which was still months away, and Arthur wanted to be sure that there was no problem for the girls. And they were going to need money too for extensive psychiatric evaluations of

Sam. Arthur was going to plead temporary insanity, which was the only possible defence, given the circumstances and his confession.

It was an endless period of time. The nurse they had was not particularly pleasant to them. Solange had never selected her nurses with great care because she was around all the time anyway, and it was she who took care of the girls whenever possible, so the charm and skill of the nurse was never very important. Christmas itself was a ghastly day. With both parents gone, the children already seemed like little orphans.

Arthur took Alexandra and Hilary out to lunch on Christmas Day, but it was more depressing than joyful. And Alexandra saw it. Her eyes moved seriously back and forth between the two of them and then she looked up at Hilary with sorrow and confusion.

'Why are you mad at Uncle Arthur?'

'I'm not.' Hilary kept her eyes on her plate and then glared briefly at her little sister.

'Yes, you are. You took your hand away when he tried to hold it.'

'Eat your turkey, Axie.'

Hilary seemed oblivious to the Christmas songs played by the violins in the Palm Court at the Plaza. She was lost in her own thoughts, and Arthur was sorry Marjorie hadn't come with him. She was having lunch at the Colony Club instead with another woman lawyer. And he had begged her to come, but she had flatly refused.

'I'm not interested in those children, and you shouldn't be taking them out either. You're not their family, they just have to adjust to the reality of their situation.'

'At eight and five years of age? It's Christmas, for God's sake. The least we can do is . . .'

'I don't want to hear it. If you want to play Noble

Saviour, don't drag me into it.' And with that, she'd left the room so he had come alone, with Hilary and Alexandra.

In fact Marjorie's adamant stance *vis-à-vis* the girls was only an extension of her dislike for the Walkers generally, and more specifically her disapproval of his frequent lunches with Solange. It wasn't that she was jealous. It was more that she disapproved of her fawning French ways, and the fact that Sam was an actor, no matter how successful.

Sam had no contact whatsoever with the girls that Christmas. He was not allowed to call them, and wouldn't have anyway, he was too depressed to think of anyone, except Solange and why he had killed her. He couldn't even bear thinking of the children.

Arthur had tried bringing photographs of them to Sam, but he was totally withdrawn these days, talking only of Solange and the past, and chronicling his sins and mistakes and transgressions endlessly. He was like an old man, whose entire life was behind him. And Arthur was having a hard time getting him interested in the case. He seemed to have no excitement about his defence, and often said that he deserved to be punished, which was hardly encouraging for Arthur.

The rest of the winter slid by agonizingly. Hilary seemed to be running the household more than adequately, and the younger children were doing well, although Hilary had a constant look of pain and anguish around her eyes, which frightened Arthur. But she wanted no comfort from him, in fact, since her mother's death she hadn't come near him. He reminded her that he was her godfather and that he loved her very much, but she stood politely listening, and never responded. She was an odd, distant girl, unusually quiet now that Solange was gone, and she spoke of her father as though she no longer knew him, as though he had died years before her mother. It was obvious that she was deeply affected by what had happened, and it was difficult to remind oneself that she was only eight years old. She seemed so marked by tragedy and it was painful to realize how much it had aged her.

Arthur tried to have dinner with them as often as he could, and he was growing worried about paying for the help, their schools, their food, and the apartment. Little Megan had been sick several times, and there were doctor's bills, and new shoes. Most of the money from Solange's jewellery had gone to defend Sam, and what was left was barely enough to make a difference. And their meagre funds were dwindling. And there were times when he wondered if Hilary knew it. She was forcing everyone into economies, and had even learned to mend her own clothes, much to Arthur's amazement. Megan had already begun to regard Hilary as her mother.

By the spring, Sam had lost thirty pounds, and all the psychiatric evaluations had been completed. The doctors who saw him all said that he was suffering from a deep depression. They were also willing to say that he had acted, in killing Solange, under the passion of the moment, and had perhaps been insane while he did it, although they all found him sane, normal and intelligent. His only problem was his very understandable depression. Arthur almost felt as though he couldn't reach him, and Sam did nothing to help prepare his own defence. He seemed uninterested in all of Arthur's efforts, and Arthur worked all night on his defence for months, looking up similar cases in the past, searching for improper technicalities, and desperately seeking new angles.

But the trial itself was a nightmare. The prosecutor was swift and sure, and he had found every tramp, whore, and starlet whom Sam had ever slept with. There was a parade of women dragged through, testifying to the fact that he drank too much, was sometimes violent when he was drunk, and had no morals whatsoever. And the portrait of Solange painted by the prosecution was one Arthur could hardly disagree with. They described a woman of intelligence and wit and charm and almost saintly devotion to her husband, anxious to do anything possible for him, to help further his career, and keep him happy, while taking extraordinarily good care of their three daughters. She was said to have kept a lovely home, kept aloof from all the Broadway and Hollywood mischief most stars' wives seemed to get into, and it was bluntly said that despite extensive research on the subject, the prosecution had been unable to find anyone who was able to say they thought Solange had ever cheated on her husband. She was thought to have been entirely faithful to him, in fact everyone spoken to said that Solange Walker had adored her husband. The prosecution also pointed out that he had absolutely no reason whatsoever to kill her. There was no '*crime passionnel*', there was no justification she had given him for becoming crazed, or temporarily insane, he had simply wantonly, carelessly, wickedly killed her. They even tried to ask for a charge of murder in the first degree, suggesting that it was premeditated, and that he wanted to be free of her to pursue all his other floozies. While Arthur, on the other hand, tried to manoeuvre a manslaughter charge, indicating that it had all been an unfortunate accident. But in the end, after less than a day's deliberation, and more than three weeks of trial, the jury convicted him of murder. Arthur felt as though a stone wall had fallen on his head, and Sam was led from the courtroom looking glassy-eyed and vague. It was obvious that he was in shock, and his depression had worsened considerably during the

82

trial. It had been difficult to get any real feeling from him when he was on the stand, or to believe that he had actually loved his wife. But he was so far gone in his own guilt and depression that he could no longer depict any semblance of real emotion, and Arthur had feared that would hurt him terribly with the jury.

Arthur asked to see his client in the holding cell immediately after the verdict, but Sam had refused to see him, and a request from Arthur to see him in his cell had been denied. Arthur left in total despair and frustration, feeling that he had failed Sam terribly. But he had warned him, and begged him to get a criminal attorney. Arthur flailed himself all the way back to his apartment for having allowed Sam to force him into defending him. He had two stiff drinks, thought about going to see the girls, and then decided that he couldn't face it. Marjorie had left a message that she wouldn't be home for dinner. As he sat at his desk in the dark he decided it was just as well. She had never been fond of Sam anyway, and what Arthur really needed was the warm touch and unconditional love of Solange. It was what they all needed and what Sam had robbed them of. For a long moment, Arthur found himself wondering if the jury had been right, and as he shuddered at his own thoughts, the phone rang. It was the sergeant at the jail, and he said he had news for him about his client. Maybe Sam was ready to see him after all, Arthur thought as he squinted at his watch in the summer twilight. It was eight-fifteen, and he was exhausted and more than a little drunk, but for Sam, he'd go there.

'Your client committed suicide in his cell an hour ago, Mr Patterson. We just found him.'

Arthur felt his heart stop, and the bile rise. He was going to throw up, or faint, or maybe just die. 'What?' It was barely a whisper. The sergeant repeated the same words as Arthur sank into a chair with a shudder, his entire body trembling. 'My God, why didn't you watch him?' He'd been depressed for months, they should have thought of that. In fact, one of the psychiatrists had warned them. But no one had really thought . . . and now they were both gone. It was almost more than Arthur could bear . . . his only friend . . . and the only woman he had ever truly loved . . . and now he had the girls to think about. What in God's name was he going to do about them? He was going to have to discuss it seriously with Marjorie when she got home. They had no one else now. Sam and Solange were both gone, and their daughters were now truly orphans.

Chapter 6

'Are you out of your mind, Arthur?' Marjorie was staring at him in complete disbelief. She looked as though he had just taken all his clothes off in public. He had been waiting up for her when she got home. And she barely reacted when he told her about Sam's suicide. What stunned her was Arthur's suggestion that they take in Hilary, Alexandra, and Megan. It was the only possible solution he could think of. They had no money and no family, and with a bigger apartment and a live-in maid, he and Marjorie could manage easily – if she would let him do it. 'Are you crazy? What in God's name would we do with three small children? We've never even wanted children of our own, why would we turn our lives upside down for the children of strangers?'

He gulped, trying to clear his head, and wishing he had waited till morning. He had had too much to drink by the time she came home, and he was afraid that his arguments wouldn't be convincing. 'Sam Walker was my best friend. He saved my life during the war . . . those children are not strangers to us, Marjorie, even if you'd like to think so.'

'But do you have any idea of the responsibility involved in having *one* child, let alone *three*?'

'Hilary is like a mother to them. She'd make everything easy for you, Marjorie. Truly.' He felt as though he were sixteen again, begging his mother for a car, and not winning the battle either. 'And I've always wanted children. You were the one who decided you couldn't handle kids *and* a career . . .' He tried to look at her reproachfully but she seemed not to care. She had no guilt, only righteous indignation.

'I will *not* take on three children. We don't have any space, the time, the lifestyle. You're as busy as I am. And besides, raising three girls would cost a fortune. No! Just forget it, Arthur. Put them in an institution.' And the tragedy, as Arthur listened to her get ready for bed, was that she meant it.

He tried again, the next morning over breakfast, but to no avail. Her mind was made up, and he didn't have the strength, or the ingenuity, to change it.

'I don't want children of my own, why would I want someone else's? And *theirs*! My God, Arthur, I always knew you were blind but I never thought you were stupid. The man was a murderer, not to mention everything else, can you imagine what traits those children will inherit? And their mother . . .' Arthur looked ominous as she got started again, but she was too involved in her own speech to notice. 'She always looked like a French whore to me. God only knows what she did over there during the war before she caught Sam Walker.'

'That's enough, Marjorie. You don't know what you're talking about. I was there when Sam met her.'

'In a bordello?' she asked viciously and he suddenly wanted to slap her. But there was no point. She had won. He was not going to be able to take in Sam's children.

'I won't discuss brothels with you, Marjorie, and I can tell you for certain that Solange Walker was never in one. I'm just sorry you're not willing to be more compassionate about this, Marjorie. It disappoints me greatly.' But she didn't give a damn. She left for work without saying another word to Arthur.

As far as she was concerned, it was his problem. And it was. Their parents were his closest friends. He was Hilary's godfather. Those children weren't strangers to him, no matter what Marjorie wished. They were flesh and blood, and he loved them.

And Sam and Solange had loved them too. It was desperately important to Arthur that they not lose a sense of that, or feel that they were being abandoned. The idea of putting them up for adoption sounded barbaric to him, but he just didn't know what else to do with them. And things got even more complicated the following week when both the maid and the nurse announced that they were leaving. They had stayed long enough in terrible conditions. They wanted a real home with parents for the children, and a couple at home, not a murdered wife and husband who'd been in jail. They both seemed outraged by the scandal that had been foisted on *them* and had remarkably little compassion for the children. And for Arthur, it meant finding new people to care for them, which seemed even more complicated now. Finally, by the week's end, he took out the name Sam had given him, of his sister. Eileen Jones. He wondered if he would even find her in Boston. But he thought that if he did, perhaps he could induce her to take care of them for a while. Then he could let the apartment on Sutton Place go, and it would save them a great deal of money. They were almost out of funds anyway. But having them stay with their aunt would give Arthur some time to make other arrangements, or convince Marjorie that they had to take them. Either way, he needed time, and having them stay with Sam's sister would give him the breather he needed. More than anything he wanted to convince Marjorie that what he wanted was right, and not crazy, as she kept insisting. It required some adjustments, to be sure, but they were three little human beings, and well worth adjusting for, even if she didn't think so. But then what? And if they didn't take them in, who on earth would? That was what worried Arthur.

But first he had to find their aunt, and see if she would take them, even if only for the summer. She couldn't be as bad as Sam said. She was his sister after all, and blood was thicker than water. He had his secretary call Boston information, and they finally turned up a Jack and Eileen Jones in Charlestown, a suburb which boasted a naval yard, and which his secretary told him was right on the water. It sounded perfect for a little summer holiday, and Arthur called her up without preamble. She sounded stunned to hear from Arthur, and she said she had read about the trial, and her brother's subsequent suicide in the papers. She didn't sound particularly emotional about his death, and she asked Arthur bluntly if Sam had left any money.

'Not a great deal, I'm afraid, which is why I'm calling.' He decided to get right to the point and see if she would help him. He had nowhere else to turn now. 'As you may know, Sam and Solange had three little girls, Hilary, Alexandra and Megan, and for the moment, there is literally no one to take them. I want to speak to you about the possibility of . . . to see if you might be interested in giving them a home, temporarily or permanently, whichever suits you.'

There was a stunned silence at the other end. And then her sharp voice that had none of the polish of her brother's. 'Holy shit. Are you kidding, mister? Three kids? I don't even have kids of my own. Why would I want Sam's three brats?'

'Because they need you. If you just kept them for the summer, it would give me time to find another suitable home for them. But for the moment, they have nowhere to go.' He tried to appeal to her sympathies, but another thought had occurred to Eileen Jones.

'Will you pay me to take them in?'

Arthur paused, but only for a second. 'I can certainly give you enough money to pay for their needs while they're with you.'

'That isn't what I meant, but I'll take that too.'

'I see.' Arthur could see why Sam wasn't fond of her, but there was no one else for him to turn to. 'Would three hundred dollars do as a fee for you, Mrs Jones? A hundred for each child?'

'For how long?' She sounded suspicious of him. Suspicious and greedy.

'Until I find a home for them . . . a few weeks, a month, perhaps the summer.'

'No more than that. I'm not runnin' an orphanage up here, you know. And my husband won't like it.' But she knew he'd like the three hundred dollars, and she was hoping they could squeeze some more out of Arthur.

'Do you have room for them, Mrs Jones?'

'I got a spare room. Two of them can sleep in one bed, and we'll figure something out for the other one.'

'That would be Megan. She'll need a crib. She's just over a year old.' He wanted to ask if she knew how to take care of a baby. He wanted to ask a lot of things, but he didn't dare. He had no choice. He just had to trust that she'd do the best she could, for Sam's sake. And the children were so adorable, he was sure she'd fall in love with them the minute she saw them.

But it was something less than love at first sight when Arthur drove the three girls to Charlestown. He had explained to Hilary the day before that they were going to stay with Aunt Eileen for the summer. He told the maid to pack all their things, and explained quietly that she and the nurse would be free to leave after the girls left in the morning. He suggested that Hilary and Alexandra take their favourite toys. And he did not tell anyone that he would be closing the apartment and selling everything as soon as the children had left it. They would be better off with whatever meagre amount he could eke from the sale of the furniture, and not having their funds depleted by paying rent for an apartment on Sutton Place. Sam's debts were still astronomical, and there just was no money coming in from anywhere for them. He was glad to be getting rid of the apartment and the two servants.

Hilary had eyed him suspiciously when he told them about the trip to Boston. Much of her affection for him seemed to have cooled since her mother's death, but it was difficult to tell if that was just her way of expressing pain, or due to some other reason.

'Why are you sending us away?'

'Because it'll be nicer for you there than it is here. Your aunt lives near the water in Boston. It'll be cooler, if nothing else, and you can't just sit here in New York all summer, Hilary.'

'But we're coming back, right?'

'Of course you are.' He felt a wave of guilt and terror wash over him. What if she could see that he was lying?

'Then why did you tell Millie to pack all our things?'

'Because I thought you might need them. Now, don't be unreasonable, Hilary. It'll be nice for all of you to get to know your father's sister.'

Hilary was standing very quietly in the centre of the room, in a yellow organdie dress with white piqué trim, her shining black hair – like Sam's – perfectly combed into two smooth braids, her big green eyes as wise as Solange's had been, her little white anklets immaculate, and her patent leather Mary Janes shined to perfection And she studied him, as though she knew he were hiding something from her. In a way, she frightened him, she was so knowing and so cool, and so fiercely protective of her sisters. She had taken the news of her father's suicide stoically. She had barely cried, and she had comforted Alexandra, and explained that Daddy had gone to heaven to be with Mommy. It all seemed terribly hard for Alexandra to understand, she was only five after all, but Hilary made everything easier for her, as she did for all of them. It was as though Solange had left her there to care for all of them in her absence.

'Why didn't we ever meet Aunt Eileen before? Didn't my Daddy like her?' She was perceptive just as Solange had been, and she didn't take any nonsense. The way her eyes flashed over him reminded him so much of her mother.

'I don't think they were close, Hilary, but that doesn't mean she's not a nice person.'

Hilary nodded, she was willing to suspend judgment. Temporarily. But it was easy to see what she thought when they arrived in Charlestown.

The house was a small frame house on a dark street, with shutters that had fallen off in the bitter winds of the previous winters. The paint was peeling everywhere, the yard was overgrown with weeds, and two of the front steps were broken. It was a less than auspicious welcome, as Hilary walked up the steps, holding Alexandra's hand, and Arthur carried the baby. The nurse had come with them, for the trip, but she was returning to New York with Arthur.

He rang the doorbell ineffectively, and finally realized

that it, too, was broken. And then he knocked hard on the window. He could feel Hilary's eyes on him and her silent question, asking him why they had come here. He didn't dare look at her now, he couldn't have borne to see Solange's eyes looking up at him, filled with silent reproach and unspent fury.

'Yeah?' The door opened finally, and a woman with blond stringy hair yanked the door open wearing a frayed dirty bathrobe. 'What do *you* want?' She stared at the crew on the front steps with obvious annoyance, a cigarette hanging out of the corner of her mouth, her eyes squinting shut to defend themselves from the smoke wafting up, and then she realized who they were. She smiled uncomfortably, and for a fraction of an instant, she looked like Sam, but barely. One had to be looking for the resemblance.

'Mrs Jones?' Arthur's heart was sinking slowly to his feet, and he felt no better as they walked into the living room. There was a broken couch, three battered chairs with the stuffing pouring out, a coffee table that had seen better days, and a small Formica dinner set, with a television blaring in the distance. Inside, the house looked even worse than it did outside. Eileen Jones apparently did not spend a great deal of time keeping house for her husband.

It was a Saturday afternoon and there was a baseball game blaring on the radio, at the same time as Gabby Hayes came on the TV. The noise was deafening, and the children looked stunned by it. Everyone stood awkwardly in the middle of the living room, looking at each other.

'Want a beer?' She looked at Arthur, ignoring the children. And it was difficult to believe that this was Sam Walker's sister. He had been so impeccably groomed, such a handsome man, he had had such presence and power and magnetism about him. One had felt instantly drawn to Sam, and together with Solange they had made a dazzling couple. But this woman was a parody of all that was cheap and beaten and ugly. She looked well beyond her thirty-nine years, and the ravages of booze had taken their toll on her early. She might have been attractive once, but anything pleasant in her looks was long gone. She only looked hard and bitter and ugly. Her dyed hair was thin, dirty and unkempt, cut just below her ears, and hanging limp and greasy. She had Sam's brilliant blue eyes, but there was a dullness to them, with terrible bags beneath them from excessive drinking. Her skin was sallow, and her waist was thickened by beer, while her legs looked like two little toothpicks. She was totally foreign to everything the girls had ever seen, and Arthur realized that Hilary was staring at her in shock and horror.

'This is Hilary.' He tried to encourage her forward to shake the woman's hand, but she wouldn't budge. 'And Alexandra,' who sniffed the stale beer that seemed to permeate the air, and made a face as she looked up at Hilary's obvious disapproval, 'and Megan.' He indicated the baby, who glanced at the battered blonde with wide eyes. She was the only one who didn't seem worried by her summer home or her hostess. The other two looked terrified, and Hilary had to fight back tears when she saw the room they were to be given to sleep in. Eileen Jones walked them back to it without ceremony, waved in the direction of the sagging, narrow bed that stood unmade in one corner. The room itself was a narrow cell without windows, barely big enough for the bed it held, with a crib folded against one wall that looked as though she had fished it out of someone else's garbage, which is precisely where Eileen had found it, shortly after Arthur had called her.

'We'll get the sheets on the bed later.' She smiled artificially at her oldest niece. 'Maybe you can help me.' And then, with no particular interest she glanced at Arthur. 'Got her mother's eyes though.'

Arthur looked puzzled. 'You knew Solange?' Solange had never mentioned this woman to him.

'I met her once. Sam was doing a play up here or something.'

And then suddenly Arthur remembered. Solange had hated her. But so had Sam. They had come by when he was doing summer stock in Stockbridge after the war. It seemed light years ago, but so did everything now. Arthur looked around him with a lump in his throat, hating to leave the girls there. And for a moment he hated his wife for condemning the children to this. How could she do this? But she didn't know, he reminded himself, as he fought back his own guilt and resentment. He had to force himself not to think about it and remind himself that this arrangement was only for the summer. And then ... that was the real problem. And then what? Marjorie was intransigent. And he had already put out feelers everywhere, for people who would help, people who might want to take them in, people who had large families of their own, or people with no children of their own, but who might be willing to have them. He had spoken to all of his partners at the law firm.

Hilary was still standing awkwardly in the doorway of what was to be their room, staring with dismay at their new quarters. There was no closet, no chest for their things, there wasn't even a chair or a lamp or a table. There was a bare bulb hanging from the ceiling, which dangled near the doorway.

'You got the money?' Eileen turned to him, and feeling awkward handing it over to her in front of the girls, he reached into his jacket for an envelope.

'That includes a reasonable amount for their expenses.'

Being far less genteel than Arthur, she opened the envelope and thumbed through it. He had given her a thousand dollars, including the fee, and if she played her cards right, and fed them nothing but macaroni and cheese for the next two months, she'd have plenty of money left over. She smiled happily at the girls, took a swig of her beer, and saluted Arthur as she tossed her cigarette into the sink with perfect aim. She did it often. 'That's just fine, Mr Patterson. We have any problems, I'll call you.'

'I thought I might come up to see them in a few weeks, if you and your husband don't mind, to see how they're doing.' Hilary stared at him unbelievingly. He was actually going to leave them in this place, with the filth and the beer bottles and the unmade bed ... and that awful woman. And if she had been withdrawn before, she was icy now, as he left them. 'I'll call you in a few days, Hilary, and don't be afraid to call if you need me.' All she could do was nod. She couldn't believe he was doing this to them, after everything else he'd done. For a moment, she wanted to kill him. And instead she turned to look down at Alexandra, who was crying softly.

'Don't be silly, Axie. This is going to be fun. Remember, Uncle Arthur said we could go to the ocean.'

'Yeah?' Eileen laughed raucously as they heard the car drive away. 'Where you going to do that? In the shipyard?' She laughed again. A thousand bucks was a hell of a nice price for a few months of inconvenience, and with luck they wouldn't be too bad. The baby looked like kind of a pain in the ass, and the five-year-old looked like a whiner, but the oldest one seemed to have it all in control. With luck, she'd take care of everything. Maybe she'd even cook and clean house. Eileen fell onto the couch in front of the TV with a fresh beer, and lit a cigarette. Maybe she and Jack would go out for dinner.

'Excuse me.' Hilary stood awkwardly next to the television, holding the baby. 'Where are the sheets for our bed?'

'On the back porch, I think. If you can find 'em.' She never spoke another word to them, as Hilary quietly got them organized. She found torn sheets, but at least they were clean, and she put them on the bed, but there were no pillows and no blanket. And she put a makeshift sheet in the baby's crib, propping it between her bed and the wall, for fear it would topple over if she didn't. As she had suspected, it was broken.

She washed Alexandra's face then and took her to the bathroom, changed Megan's nappy, and gave all three of them a drink of water, as they sat quietly in their new room, looking around them.

'It's so ugly here,' Axie whispered, afraid that the lady with the cigarette and the beer would hear her. 'Is she really Daddy's sister?'

Hilary nodded. It was difficult to believe, and not pleasant to think about, but she was their aunt and they were stuck with her for the summer. There was no place for them to put their toys, and the dresses the nurse had packed for them had to remain in their suitcases. It was five o'clock before Eileen saw them again, and as she had suspected, Hilary had everything in control.

'Excuse me.' She stood in front of her with her shining dark hair and big green eyes, like a miniature spokesman. 'Could you give my sisters something to eat? They're both hungry.' Eileen hadn't even thought of that. There was nothing in the house. She opened the fridge and there was nothing there except beer and some rotting lemons and stale bread. Eileen and Jack never ate at home if they could help it. All they did was drink there.

'Sure, kid. Which one are you?'

'Hilary.' There was something very distant in her eyes, as though the last nine months had left her broken. She was only nine years old and she had already had more pain and grief than most people have in a lifetime.

'Can you go to the store for me, and get yourself something to eat? A couple of cans of tuna ought to do it.'

'Tuna?' Hilary looked as though she'd never heard the word. She was used to hot meals prepared by the maid on Sutton Place, and her mother before that. Thick soups, and rich stews, and steaks cooked medium rare, and chocolate cakes with vanilla ice cream. 'Tuna fish?'

'Yeah. Here's some money.' She handed her a few dollars, as though she expected her to create an entire dinner with two dollars. Even Hilary knew that was impossible. Her nurse gave her more than that just when she went to get ice cream. 'The store's on the corner, you can't miss it. And buy me another beer too, will ya?' She was always afraid of running out, even when she had plenty.

Hilary took her sisters with her, only because she was afraid of what would happen if she didn't. And the store looked as seamy as everything else around them. Most of the houses were either crumbling brick, or wood with faded, peeling paint on them. And everything in the neighbourhood looked as though it was battered and beaten and broken. Hilary bought two cans of tuna fish, a jar of baby food, a loaf of bread, some mayonnaise, butter, half a dozen eggs, a container of milk and a can of beer for their hostess. Hilary figured she could make a halfway decent dinner out of all of it, and she could use the rest of the eggs and the bread to make breakfast the next morning. But as she came in the front door struggling to carry the package and Megan and still hold Axie's hand, Eileen asked her two questions.

'Where's my beer?'

'I have it in the bag.'

'Then get it,' she barked at Hilary, and Axie started to whimper. She hated people who shouted at her, or her sisters. Their mother never had, and even their nurse didn't shout at them, even though they didn't like her much and she said ugly things about their parents.

Hilary handed Eileen the beer as quickly as she could, and Eileen glared at her and asked the second question. 'Where's the change?'

Hilary handed her three cents, and Eileen threw it back at her, hitting the baby near the eye with one of the pennies. 'What'd you do, buy yourself a T-bone? This isn't Park Avenue, you know. Where the hell's the rest of the money?' She seemed to have forgotten the thousand dollars Arthur had given her for just this purpose.

'I had to buy them dinner,' Hilary explained. 'And there was nothing for breakfast tomorrow morning.'

'When I want you to buy breakfast, I'll tell you. You got that? And next time, don't spend so goddam much money.'

Hilary was stunned at what she was hearing, and her hands shook as she made them dinner. With expert ease, she had food in front of them in less than ten minutes. A soft-boiled egg and toast and baby food for Megan, and tuna fish sandwiches with mayonnaise for herself and Axie, and big glasses of milk for all three of them, which they drank gratefully. They were hungry and exhausted after the drive from New York and the emotional shock of Eileen and Charlestown.

Hilary did not offer her aunt anything to eat, and Eileen showed no interest in what they were doing. Hilary had them eat in their own room. The simultaneous blare of the radio and television made it impossible to talk and Eileen frightened all of them, even the baby. But just as Hilary was putting their dishes in the sink and starting to wash them, Eileen's husband came home, and Hilary was even more frightened when she saw him. He was a huge, burly man with enormous arms and powerful shoulders, and he was wearing work pants and an undershirt. The cloud of booze that surrounded him reached her all the way to the kitchen. He started to yell at Eileen almost the instant he walked in the door, but before he could hit her, she waved the envelope at him and showed him what he thought was all the money. Five hundred dollars. He broke into a big foolish grin, never suspecting that his wife had hidden an equal amount in a pile of old stockings where she kept her own money.

'Wooo . . . baby! Look at that! Ain't it purty?' Hilary watched him, long before he had seen her. 'What's that for?'

'Them.' She pointed vaguely to the back of the house and Jack suddenly spotted Hilary in the kitchen.

'Who's that?' He looked blank, and Hilary noticed that he had an incredibly stupid face, and eyes that reminded her of a pig. She hated him on sight, he was even worse than Eileen, and he looked meaner.

'Remember my brother's kids I told you about?'

'The one who snuffed his old lady?'

'Yeah. Him. Well, they came today.'

'How long we gotta keep 'em?' He looked less than pleased as he glanced over Hilary like a piece of meat. He did not seem to think of their arrival as good news, in spite of the windfall.

'A few weeks, till that lawyer finds them some place to live.'

So that was it. Hilary heard the news with a shiver. Arthur hadn't explained it to them before they left, and she suddenly wondered what would happen to their apartment.

But Eileen was smiling at her husband, as Hilary watched them. She was impervious to the children in the back room, as was he. It was as though they didn't exist, and to the Joneses they didn't. 'Hey, baby, let's go dancing tonight.' They both looked too drunk to Hilary, but Jack Jones seemed to like the idea, as Hilary watched them. He had an oily-looking face and thinning hair, and thick hands that looked like roast beef.

'Can we leave the kids?'

'Sure, why not? The older one does everything.'

'Everything?' He leered at his wife and moved closer, as Hilary sensed with a shiver that what he was suggesting was improper, but Eileen only laughed at him and pulled him closer.

'Come on, you horny old sailor ... she's only nine years old for chrissake ...' Eileen was laughing at him as he pressed his mouth down hard on hers, and slipped a fat hand into her bathrobe.

'And how old were you the first time?'

'Thirteen,' she said primly, but they both knew she was lying, and then with a raucous laugh she went to get herself another beer, and saw that Hilary was watching. 'What the hell are you doing here, spying on us, you little brat?'

'I was just ... cleaning up after dinner ... I'm sorry ... I ...'

'Go to your room!' she shouted, slamming the refrigerator door with a vengeance. 'Goddam kids.' She knew they were going to be a real nuisance before she got rid of them again, but as long as Jack didn't mind too much, they were good for the money.

The Joneses went out at eight o'clock that night. Megan and Alexandra were already asleep in their narrow airless room, but Hilary was lying in the dark, thinking of their mother. She would never have let something like this happen to them. Never. She would have read Eileen the riot act, taken her children home, and somewhere, somehow, she would have made a home for them, and that was just what Hilary had to do. And she knew it. She had to find a way, and a place to go ... and enough money to do it. She wasn't going to let anything happen to her little sisters. She would do anything to protect them. And in the meantime she just had to keep them away from Jack and Eileen, keep them amused, outside in the weed-choked yard, or in their room. She'd make their meals, give them their baths, take care of their clothes. She lay in bed and planned everything until she fell asleep, and she didn't wake up again until morning, when Megan woke her up at six-fifteen with a dirty nappy. She was a good-natured child with her mother's red hair, which hung in loose coppery curls, and she had her father's big blue eyes, just as Hilary herself had her father's dark hair and her mother's green eyes. But it was Alexandra who really looked like their mother, and it tore at Hilary's heart sometimes to see her looking so much like Solange, and she sounded just like her whenever she giggled.

She made the girls' breakfast before Jack and Eileen woke up, and she took them outside to play, after dressing them in matching blue gingham dresses. She wore a red dress herself with a little apron. Her mother had bought it for her before she died, and she still loved it best of all. And it comforted her to wear it now, and think of her mother.

It was noon before Eileen Jones appeared in the doorway to glare at them. She looked as though she were sick, and had they been older, they would have known she was desperately hung over.

'Can't you brats shut up? You make enough noise for a whole neighbourhood. Christ!' The screen door slammed and she went back inside, and they didn't see her again until after lunch. She stayed inside all day and watched television and drank beer, and Jack seemed to go somewhere else to do his drinking. The only change during the week was that Jack left earlier and wore work clothes. He rarely spoke to them, except once in a while, he'd make a crack at Hilary, and tell her she'd be nice-looking one day, and she never knew what to say to him. Eileen didn't speak to them at all. And it seemed aeons before they heard from Arthur. He called exactly one week after he had left them and inquired how everything was. Hilary spoke mechanically and told him they were fine, but it was obvious to anyone that they weren't. Axie had started having nightmares and Megan was waking up at night. The room was breathlessly hot and the food inadequate. Hilary did everything she could to compensate for all of it, but there was only so much she could do. She was a nine-year-old child after all, and she was slowly drowning in deep waters.

But she told none of that to Arthur.

'We're fine.' But she sounded tired and unenthusiastic.

'I'll call you again in a few days.' But he didn't. He had his hands full at the office, with a difficult case, and he was still trying to finish sorting out Sam's affairs, and find someone to take the girls, but by August, it was plainly obvious that that wasn't going to happen. And he had given up trying to convince his wife. She had finally told him it was her or the children. The die was cast. Arthur was not going to take them.

Chapter 7

By the end of the summer two of Arthur's colleagues came to him quietly, quite unexpectedly, and offered to solve his problem.

The first to do so was one of the oldest partners in the firm. George Gorham was nearing retirement age, but only the year before, he had married an extremely attractive young socialite in her early twenties. Margaret Millington had been one of the prettiest débutantes of the year when she came out, and after that she had impressed everyone by doing extremely well at Vassar. But then she had left the usual expected mould, and instead of marrying one of the young men her parents expected her to, she had become involved with George Gorham. A widower, he was forty years older than she, and perfect for her in every way. Except that he was unable to have children. He had been honest with her and she insisted that it didn't matter. But he was afraid it might some day, and he didn't want to lose her. And little Alexandra would fill the only void between them. He had discussed with Margaret adopting all of the Walker children and keeping the family intact, and although it seemed a noble deed, it seemed a little excessive to them. He didn't feel young enough to take on a child of Megan's age, and a child as old as Hilary when she was adopted could present problems. But a five-year-old sounded ideal to them, and Margaret was ecstatic.

And on the same day that George approached Arthur about adopting Alexandra, David Abrams had privately come to see Arthur. He was only thirty-four, and he and his wife Rebecca were both attorneys, although Rebecca worked for another firm with more liberal leanings. They had been married since their senior year in college and had been attempting to have a baby since their last year in law school, with no success. And they had finally been told that the situation was hopeless. Rebecca was unable to have children. It had been a tremendous blow to both of them, particularly as they had hoped to have several children, but now they found they would be grateful for one, which was really all they could afford at the moment. Like the Gorhams, they had briefly thought of adopting all three, but they felt unable to take on that large a burden. What they wanted was to adopt Megan, the baby.

Which left only Hilary. And Arthur with an enormous decision. Should he break up the family? Did he have a right to do that? But then again, Sam had murdered Solange, and in so doing, had destroyed all of their lives. Maybe all Arthur could do was save each one separately. The Gorhams were wonderful people, and both of them were enormously wealthy. There was no doubt in Arthur's mind that Alexandra would have everything she needed, and from what George had said, it was obvious that they would love her deeply. What's more, they would be near by, and Arthur could keep an eye on things, not that he needed to with George and Margaret Gorham.

And although Rebecca and David Abrams were less comfortably circumstanced than George, they were certainly two hard-working young people, with promising careers ahead of them, with families from New York, so it was unlikely they would stray far, and once again Arthur could play guardian angel to Megan.

But it was Hilary who worried him most. What would happen to her now? It was a great shame that neither the Gorhams nor the Abramses were willing to take on a second child, but when he inquired again, both of them were definite when they said they wouldn't. He mentioned it to Marjorie once again, but her answer was an adamant 'no'. And he sensed that their relationship might be in jeopardy if he persisted. He had promised her weeks before not to bring the subject up again. But that left Hilary with nowhere to go, except where she was, with the Joneses in Boston, if they would even keep her. There was going to be about ten thousand dollars in Sam's estate after everything was sold, and Arthur thought about the possibility of offering that to the Joneses for the care and feeding of Hilary for as long as it lasted. It was better than nothing, but not much, and he was unhappy with the solution as he made the final arrangements for the others. The papers were drawn up, and both couples were wildly excited. Rebecca planned to take a month off from work, and Margaret and George planned a trip to Europe in the autumn with their new daughter. George had already ravaged F A O Schwarz and Alexandra's new room looked like a toy store, whereas Rebecca had bought enough sweaters and snowsuits and underwear for quintuplets. They were two very lucky little girls and their arrivals were anticipated with breathless excitement But it was Hilary who continued to worry Arthur.

In mid-August, he had a brief conversation with Eileen Jones, and explained the situation to her. And she bluntly said that for ten thousand dollars, she'd keep her indefinitely, but she didn't see why she had to adopt her. She could just live with them. And cook and clean, although she didn't fill in those details for Arthur. It was like having a live-in maid, she was already having her do everything, and Hilary was so deathly afraid of her that she did whatever she told her. She had struck Alexandra once hard, across the face, for some minor infraction she never explained, and she had hit the baby more than once, whenever she touched the television or the radio, or ventured out of their room at all, which it was difficult not to. It was a tiny room for the three of them, particularly a baby who was not quite two and didn't understand that she was being confined to her quarters.

But in any case, Eileen agreed to keep Hilary, as long as she got the ten thousand dollars in cash. She was becoming a very profitable little venture for Eileen. And this time she would tell Jack about two thousand dollars and keep eight for herself, giving him a long song and dance that she was doing it for the memory of her brother.

'I thought you didn't like him.'

'He was still my brother . . . and it's still his kid. Besides she's a pretty good kid, and a good worker.'

'Kids are a pain in the ass.' Jack knew at firsthand. His last wife had had three of them, and they had driven him crazy. 'But if you want to take care of her, she's your problem, not mine. Just so she don't bug me.'

'If she does, just whack her.'

'Yeah.' That seemed to mollify him, and he agreed to let Eileen keep her. And that night she locked herself in the bathroom, checked that her other money was still there, and figured that with the eight she got to keep from the cheque for Hilary, she'd have close to ten thousand dollars hidden among her suspender belt and nylons. It gave her a good feeling, in case she ever decided to walk out on her husband. And maybe she'd take the kid with her, and maybe she wouldn't. Depends if she was any use to her or not, otherwise let Jack worry about feeding her, or let the lawyer take her back. She didn't owe the kid anything. But the kid owed her. After all, she had agreed to keep her, hadn't she? She owed her a lot, from Eileen's point of view. And Eileen owed her nothing.

Arthur came up looking sombre with a nurse he had hired for the day, and he was startled to see Hilary looking so thin and the others so pale after their months in Boston. They looked like little waifs and he found himself hoping that they were all healthy. And he asked Hilary to come outside with him so they could talk for a while. He wanted to know how she really was, but when she went outside, she told him nothing. It was as though she had put an even greater distance between them, and he didn't even suspect how much she hated him for leaving them in this hellhole. She had spent two months trying to eke out enough sustenance for her sisters, barely able to feed them, let alone herself, on the meagre allotment Eileen gave her. She had washed, scrubbed, cooked, and baby-sat, and constantly protected them from the threatened beatings of their aunt and uncle. And at night she sang them to sleep and held them when they cried for their mother. And Arthur knew none of that as he watched Hilary's face and wondered why she was so distant.

And now, he had to tell her the news no one had prepared her for. Her sisters were leaving, and she wasn't. They would never be together again, except on visits, if their new parents would allow it, and Arthur already knew that the Abramses wouldn't. They didn't want Megan to know anything about her past life, her parents, or even her sisters. She was disappearing into a new life. Forever.

'Hilary . . .' he began awkwardly, sitting on the back steps of the Joneses house, off the laundry porch, with the weeds scratching their legs, and the flies buzzing around them. 'I . . . I thought . . . I have . . . some things to tell you.' He wished he could tell her anything but what he had to. He knew how attached she was to them, but it wasn't his fault it had come to this, he kept reminding himself. He had done his best . . . if only Marjorie had been willing to take them . . .

'Is something wrong, Uncle Arthur?' Maybe he was going to tell her now they weren't going back to their apartment, but Eileen had already told them it was gone, and she had adjusted. As long as they were together, that was all that mattered, even here. She turned her big green eyes up to him, and he felt as though Solange had reached out and touched him, but it only made him feel worse now.

'I . . . your sisters are going away for a little while.' There was no other way to tell her, except directly.

'Megan and Axie?' She looked startled and confused as she turned the familiar emerald gaze on him again.

'Why? Why are they going anywhere?'

'Because.' Oh God . . . please don't make me do this to her. There was a sob of anguish lodged in his chest. But he had to tell her. 'Because, Hilary, there's no way to keep you together anymore. Your aunt doesn't feel she can, and no one else felt they could either. Megan and Alexandra are going to two very nice families in New York, to live with them. And you're going to stay here with your aunt in Boston.' It would have been easier to run a knife through her heart, and when he saw the tears spill from her eyes he envied Sam the easy fate he had chosen, and hated him for it all at once. 'Hilary, please . . . darling, I tried, I really did . . .' He reached out to her, but she escaped him, darting through the weeds toward the front of the house again, as though they might already be gone, and shouting back at him.

'No! No! I won't let you!' She ran inside, and offering no explanation she rushed into their ugly room and pulled both girls close to her. She had left them playing on her bed, and Axie baby-sitting for Megan. She held them close to her, with tears streaming down her cheeks, feeling desperate and helpless, and knowing that there was no way to fight him. She had nowhere to go, and no money to take them with, and no one to help her, and she was only nine years old. But they couldn't do this to her . . . they couldn't . . . they were all she had . . . her mother and father had betrayed her . . . and Uncle Arthur . . . and her aunt and uncle hated her and she hated them . . . all she had in the world were Megan and Axie.

'What's the matter, Hillie?' Alexandra was staring up at her with her big blue eyes, and Megan cried when Hilary held her too tight, so she simply let her go and clung to Axie.

'I love you . . . that's all . . . I just love you . . . with all my heart. Will you always remember that, Axie?'

'Yes.' The little voice was sober, as though she knew something important was happening. They had been through a lot together, the three of them, and they had an unusual bond to each other, as though they sensed each other's moods and possible danger. 'Is something bad going to happen again, Hillie? Like Mommy and Daddy? Are you going away in a box too?'

She started to cry and Hilary was quick to shake her head. 'No, no. Don't be afraid, Axie. Uncle Arthur wants to take you and Megan on a little trip back to New York to visit friends of his.' She knew she had to make it easy for them, no matter how painful it was for her. But she could tolerate anything for them. But for Megan it would be the easiest of all. She would cry when they took her away from her sisters, but she would never remember . . . never . . . and Hilary would never forget them. She would carry them with her for the rest of her life, and one day she would find them. She swore it to herself as she held Alexandra, and a moment later, Arthur and the nurse he had hired appeared in the doorway.

'We should go soon, Hilary.'

She nodded, blinded by tears, and suddenly Alexandra began to wail. 'I don't want to leave Hillie.' She clung to her hand, and wiping away her own tears, Hilary kissed her gently.

'You have to go to help take care of Megan, otherwise she'll be scared. Okay? Will you take care of her for me?'

Alexandra nodded through her tears. No matter what they told her, she knew something terrible was going to happen, and as Hilary packed her things, she was sure of it. Eileen was staying out of their way. She was so excited about the fresh green bills Arthur had given her that all she could do was sit in the locked bathroom and count them. She was going to hide most of it from Jack, but she wanted to look at it all together first.

So Hilary was alone as she helped put Alexandra and Megan in the car. The girls sat in the back with the nurse, Megan holding her arms out to Hilary as she cried, and Alexandra sobbing uncontrollably as Arthur got behind the wheel with a last look at Hilary.

'I'll come back to see you soon.' She said nothing to him. He had betrayed her. And the cries from the back seat almost overwhelmed her as she fought to keep control, and stepped back, waving at them, shouting at the car, for as long as they could hear her.

'I love you, Axie . . . I love you, Megan . . . I love you . . .' Her voice broke into a sob as she stood in the street, waving at the retreating car until it turned a corner and was gone, taking her whole life with it. And as the car disappeared, she sank to her knees sobbing their names, wishing that someone would kill her. She wasn't aware of anything until she felt someone shaking her, and a hard hand cracked her across the face. She looked up, blinded by her tears, to see Eileen standing over her, clutching her battered purse under her arm with a look of victory.

She spoke harshly to the child, as she always did. 'What the hell are you doing?' And then she realized that they must have gone. 'Crying won't do anything. Go inside and clean up, you little fool. People are going to think we been treating you bad.' She dragged her to her feet and shoved her into the house as Hilary sobbed uncontrollably, and another hard slap across her face did nothing to help it. She staggered inside to her room, and threw herself across the bed, which still smelled of the two children who had just left it. She could smell the powder she had used only moments ago on Megan when she changed her and the shampoo on Axie's bright red curls. The agony was more than Hilary could bear.

She lay there and sobbed for hours, until at last she fell asleep, exhausted, drained, battered by the realities of her existence. And she fell into a deep fitful sleep where she was running . . . running . . . running after a car . . . trying to find them . . . looking everywhere . . . and all she could hear in the distance was Eileen's drunken laughter.

Part III

HILARY

Chapter 8

That year, after tearing flesh from flesh, Arthur called Hilary several times, but she refused to come to the phone and talk to him, and eventually his own guilt made him call her less and less often. He knew that the other girls were all right. The Gorhams were ecstatic over Alexandra, she was a delightful little girl, and the Abramses were in love with 'their' baby. But he had no grip on Hilary now, no idea how she was, since Eileen did not keep him informed, and Hilary wouldn't speak to him on the phone.

He went to Boston to see her once, just before Thanksgiving. But Hilary sat in the living room as though numb. She had nothing to say to him, and he left with a feeling of guilt and quiet desperation. He felt as though he had destroyed the child, and yet what choice did he have, and Eileen was her aunt after all. He told himself a thousand stories to calm his conscience as he drove home again, and it was Christmas when he called again, but this time no one answered, and after that he was busy with his own life. George Gorham had died suddenly, and quite unexpectedly David Abrams had decided to move to California, which meant that a great deal more work fell to Arthur. There were, of course, several other partners in the firm, but Arthur was among the senior men there and a great many decisions fell to him, particularly about

George's estate which was very involved. He saw Margaret at the funeral of course, but she had decided not to bring Alexandra.

It was spring before Arthur saw Hilary again, and he found her even more withdrawn, with a bleak look of despair that was frightening. The house was immaculate, which was at least some relief to him, at least Eileen was making more of an effort. He had no idea that she used Hilary as a full-time maid now. At the age of ten, it fell to her to do everything, including pull the weeds outside, wash and iron her aunt's and uncle's clothes, clean, cook, and do laundry. It was remarkable that she got decent grades in school, but somehow she always did, in spite of everything. She had no friends, and no desire to make any. What did she have in common with them? The other kids in school had normal homes, they had mothers and fathers and sisters. She had an aunt and uncle who hated her and drank too much, and a thousand chores to do before finishing her homework and going to bed around midnight. And lately, Eileen wasn't feeling well. She talked about her health all the time, she was losing weight, even with all the beer she drank, and she had been to several doctors. She had overheard Jack saying something about Florida. He had friends who worked in a naval shipyard there and they thought they could get him a civilian job. He thought maybe the warm weather would be good for Eileen, and they could move down before next winter.

But Hilary never mentioned this to Arthur. It didn't matter to him. And she didn't care about him any more, or about anything. The only thing she cared about was finding Axie and Megan again, and she knew that one day she would. All she had to do was wait until she turned eighteen, and then she would find them. She dreamt about it at night, and she could still feel Axie's soft red curls on her cheek on the bed next to her and Megan's soft baby breath when she held her . . . and one day . . . one day . . . she would find them.

They moved to Jacksonville, Florida, that October, and by then Eileen was very sick. She could hardly eat or walk, and by Christmas she was bedridden, and Hilary instinctively knew that she was dying. Jack seemed to take no interest in her, and he was out constantly, drinking and carousing, and sometimes she saw him around the neighbourhood, coming out of someone's house, and kissing another woman. And it was her job to take care of Eileen, to do everything that had to be done for a dying woman. She didn't want to go to a hospital, and Jack said they couldn't afford it. So Hilary did everything, from the time she got home from school, until the next morning. Sometimes she didn't sleep at all. She just lay on the floor next to Eileen's bed, and tended her as she was needed. Jack didn't sleep in her room any more anyway. He slept on a big sleeping porch at the back of the house, and came and went as it suited him, without even seeing his wife for days sometimes. And Eileen cried and asked Hilary where he was at night, and Hilary would lie to her and say he was sleeping.

But even Eileen's illness didn't bring out any kindness in her, no gentleness, no gratitude for the impossible tasks Hilary was performing. She expected it of her, and even as weak as she was, if she thought Hilary could do more, she would threaten to beat her. It was an empty threat now, but Hilary still hated her, she had from the first day she saw her.

Eileen lived for another year and a half after they reached Florida, and when Hilary was twelve, she finally died, staring at Hilary as though she wanted to say something to her, but Hilary was sure it wouldn't have been anything kindly.

And life was simpler in some ways after that, and more complicated in others. She didn't have to provide nursing care any more. But she had to steer clear of Jack, and the women he dragged in with him. He had told her bluntly the day after Eileen died that he was willing to let her stay under his roof as long as she didn't cause any trouble. He had also told her to clear out her aunt's things, keep what she wanted, and throw out the rest. He didn't seem to want any reminders of her. She had taken her time doing it, feeling somehow that Eileen was going to come back and punish her for going through her things, but she finally got through the last of it. She gave the clothes away to a church bazaar, and threw all the cheap make-up out. She was about to throw out all her underwear when she noticed a little cloth pouch in one of the drawers and went through it just to be sure it was nothing important. There was over ten thousand dollars there, mostly in small bills, and a few fifties, as though she'd gathered it over the years, hiding it from everyone, and probably from Jack as well. Hilary sat staring at the pouch for a long time, and then silently she slipped it into a pocket, and that night she hid it among her own things. It was just what she needed to escape one day, and find Megan and Alexandra.

For the next year, Jack scarcely took any notice of her. He was too busy chasing all the neighbourhood women. By then, he had lost several jobs, but he always seemed able to find another one. He didn't care what he did, as long as he had a roof over his head, a woman in his bed at night, and a six-pack of beer in the fridge. But when Hilary turned thirteen, he suddenly became more demanding. He seemed to be complaining all the time, and asked her to do things for him. He didn't think she was keeping the house clean enough, and when he came home for dinner, which was rare, he complained that her cooking was lousy. There was suddenly no pleasing him, and he acted as though it mattered to him, whereas before he had taken no notice of her at all. Now he even criticized the way she dressed and said her clothes were too baggy and her skirts were too long. It was 1962 and mini-skirts were in, and he told her she should dress more like the girls she saw in magazines or on TV.

'Don't you want the boys to look at you? he asked boozily one afternoon. He had just come home from a softball game with some friends, most of whom were ex-Marines like him, but he was forty-five years old and three decades of drinking had taken their toll on him. He was overweight, and had a beer belly that hung way out over his blue jeans. 'Don't you like boys, Hilary?'

He kept hounding her and she was tired of it. She never had time to notice boys. She was too busy going to school and cleaning house for him. She was going into ninth grade in the autumn, a year early. And now she had ten thousand dollars hidden in her underwear drawer. She had everything she needed.

'Not particularly,' she finally answered him. 'I don't have time for boys.'

'Oh yeah? What about men? You got time for men, little Hillie?'

She didn't bother to answer him. Instead, she went to the kitchen to cook dinner, thinking about how southern he had become after only a few years. He spoke with a drawl, and a southern accent that sounded like he was born in Florida. You'd never have known he was from Boston. And thinking of it made her think back to her brief time there with them . . . she still remembered it as the place she had lost Megan and Axie. She had never heard from Arthur Patterson again, not since they'd moved to Florida, not that she cared anyway. She hated him. And it never occurred to her that the reason he hadn't called was because Jack and Eileen hadn't left an address when they moved. They had disappeared without a trace, and Arthur had no idea how to find them. He had his hands full with his own life anyway by then. Around the time the Joneses had moved to Florida, Marjorie had left him.

'What's for dinner?' Jack appeared in the kitchen with a beer-can in his hand and a cigarette. He seemed to be eyeing her with greater interest these days, and she didn't like it. It made her uncomfortable, and made her feel as though he was taking her clothes off with his eyes.

'Hamburgers.'

'That's nice.' But he was staring at her firm young breasts as he said it. She had long, shapely legs and a tiny waist, and the thick black hair she had inherited from Sam hung in a black sheet to her waist. She was a beautiful girl, and it was becoming difficult to hide it. She looked years older than she was, and her eyes held the pain of a lifetime.

Jack patted her on the behind, and brushed past her without needing to, and for the first time he stood by her side the entire time while she was making dinner for him. He made her so uncomfortable that she was unable to eat once the hamburgers were ready. She pushed the food around on her plate, and left the kitchen as quickly as she could, after washing the dishes. She heard him go out then, a little while after that, and she was asleep in her bed in her room off the kitchen long before he came home around midnight. There was a pouring tropical rain, and there had been lightning and thunder, and he staggered into the house, extremely drunk, but with the intention of doing something . . . if he could just remember what it was . . . dammit . . . it had slipped his mind . . . he was still cursing when he passed her room, and then suddenly he remembered, and gave a laugh as he stood outside her door for a long moment.

He didn't bother to knock, instead he just turned the knob and walked into her room, his wet shoes squeezing water onto the linoleum floor and his breathing heavy, from years of cigarettes, but she didn't hear him. The sheet of black hair was fanned out across her face, and one arm was tossed over her head, as she slept on top of the covers in a childish cotton nightgown.

'Purrrrtyyyy . . .' He purred to himself and coughed, which almost woke her. She stirred and turned over, revealing a graceful hip and one long leg as she slept only inches away from him. And slowly he began unbuttoning his shirt until it dropped on the floor and lay there in a wet heap. He unzipped his trousers and slipped them off with his shoes, and he stood next to her in his shorts and socks, and a moment later, they lay with the rest of his clothes next to her bed. And only the vast amount of liquor he had drunk kept him from getting a bigger erection. He came to life slowly, watching her, aching with desire, and the secret lust he had hidden for years, but now she was old enough . . . hell, he could have years of her, his very own piece right at home . . . before she grew up and moved out, and maybe after this she'd never want to. He groaned as he lay down on the bed beside her, and the cloud of boozy fumes he exhaled along with the stench of unwashed perspiration woke her.

'Hmm . . .' She opened one eye, not sure where she was and then gave a gasp and leapt out of bed. But he was quicker than that and had taken a firm grasp of her nightgown. It tore right off her tall frame as he held it, and she stood naked and trembling before him, as he lay in her bed and watched her.

'My, my . . . ain't that a purty sight, little Hillie?' She tried to cover her nakedness and she wanted to cry, or run, but she wasn't sure what to do. She just stood there, terrified. She knew that if she tried to run away, he'd catch her. 'Come on back to bed, it's not time to get up yet. First Uncle Jack's got a few things to show you.' She could see him long and hard and ominous where she'd been lying, and she was old enough to know what he intended to do to her, and she would die before she'd let him.

'Don't touch me!' she ran through the open doorway to the kitchen, and he followed her in the dark, stumbling and naked and slipping on the wet patches he had left on the floor moments earlier.

'Come on, ya little tramp . . . you know what you want. And I'm going to give it to you.' As he said it, he lunged for her arm, and tried to drag her back to her bedroom. But she fought like a cat, and scratched his face and his arm, trying to kick him as he dragged her.

'Let go of me!' She pulled herself free and almost made it to the back door before he caught her again, but for an instant, she had time to reach out for something she suddenly remembered on the draining board. She hid it carefully from him, and seeming to become docile finally, she let him lead her back to her bedroom. It was a daring thing to do, but she would rather kill him than let him rape her.

'That's a good girl . . . now you want ole Uncle Jack, don't ya, little Hillie . . .' She said nothing in answer and he didn't seem to notice as he pushed her roughly back onto her bed and prepared to mount her, but with a sudden flash of silver he felt something cold and sharp and ugly pointing at his belly.

'If you touch me, I'll cut your balls off . . . and I mean

it . . .' Everything about her tone of voice said she did, and he believed her. He backed off just a fraction of an inch, and she followed him with the knife point. 'Get out of my room.'

'Fine, fine . . . Christ . . .' he muttered as he backed out of the room and almost fell over the threshold. 'Put that thing away for chrissake, will you, dammit?'

'Not till you're out of here.' She was following him with the knife still pointed at his testicles, which seemed to worry him greatly.

'Little bitch . . . that what they teach you in school these days? In my day, the girls were a hell of a lot nicer.' She didn't answer him and he backed away, and then suddenly he had slapped the knife out of her hand and slapped her so hard across the face that she fell against the opposite wall and she wasn't sure which hurt her most, her nose bleeding profusely all over her face, or the back of her head which felt as though he had crushed it. 'There you little bitch, how does that feel?'

She grunted and struggled to her feet, still hell-bent on protecting her virtue, but he wasn't interested in it anymore, he just wanted to punish her for humiliating him. He knew he could always get the rest of her later. Hell, there was nowhere for her to go. She was his now. He practically owned her.

'Now, you gonna behave yourself for Uncle Jack next time?' He backhanded her again, his eyes glinting evilly, and this time she fell against a chair and it caught against her ribs, cutting deep into one breast, and she could feel herself bleeding there too. Her ears were ringing, and her lip was split, she thought her jaw might be broken, and she had a huge gash on one breast before it was all over and she crawled away from him. He had passed out on the couch by then, still naked, totally drunk, and pleased with his night's work. She couldn't resist him next time. He was sure of it. He had taught her a good lesson. So good, that she dragged herself, naked in the pouring rain, until she passed out cold on their neighbour's doorstep. She lay there for hours, unconscious in the rain, bleeding from her various wounds, until Mrs Archer found her there the next day when she opened her front door to get her paper.

'Oh my God! . . . oh my *God*!' she screamed, backing into the house, and running to find her husband. 'My God . . . Bert, there's a dead woman on our doorstep and she's naked!' He ran to the door and found her there, half in and half out of the door, still bleeding and still unconscious.

'Christ . . . it's that kid from next door, the one whose aunt died . . . the one you never see . . . we've got to call the police.' But Mollie was already dialling. The police came almost immediately, and the ambulance was there even before that. They took her to Brewster Hospital and half an hour later she came around, and saw the Archers staring at her in the emergency room. Mrs Archer started to cry, she reminded her so much of her daughter. And it was obvious she had been beaten and raped and deposited on their doorstep. But the examination showed later on that she hadn't been raped at all, just beaten to within an inch of her life. She had stitches in various places, and the gash on her breast was bad, but the worst was the concussion he'd given her when he threw her against the wall the first time. She threw up almost as soon as she awoke and she lost consciousness several times, but the doctors assured Mrs Archer she'd be all right, and they left her there several hours later. She was unwilling to talk about who had beaten her up, but the police weren't through with their investigation.

'Who do you think would do such a thing to her?' Mrs Archer asked her husband on the way home, but it was days before the truth came to light, and Hilary didn't tell them. Jack gave it away himself the third time the police went to see him, and they brought charges against him, which Hilary begged them to drop.

'He'll kill me if you do that.' She was terrified now. He would kill her now for sure, or worse.

But the police changed everything. 'Hilary, you don't have to go back, you know. You could go to a foster home.'

'What's that?' Her eyes were wide with fear, but what could be worse than the hell she'd been living?

'It's a temporary home, even a long-term one sometimes where kids can live who don't have anywhere else to go.'

'You mean like an institution?'

The officer shook his head. 'No, like real folks who take kids like you into their homes. What do you think?'

'I think I'd like to do that.' In order to set it up, she had to be processed through the Florida courts as a homeless minor. And it turned out to be much easier than anyone had thought when she explained that she was an orphan and had never been adopted by her aunt and uncle. She went back to see him only once, and Mollie Archer came with her and stood uneasily in the doorway. Hilary had wanted to get her things and she was afraid of confronting Jack. It was the first time she'd seen him since the night he beat her, and she was terrified of what he'd do to her for setting the police on him. But he only stared at her in venomous fury and dared to say very little with Mrs Archer standing by her.

She packed her few belongings in the only suitcase she owned, and tucked the little cloth pouch carefully into the lining. She knew she had to take good care of it now, it was the only friend she had in the world . . . her escape money to find her sisters . . . her ten thousand dollars. If

Jack had known it existed and that she had it, he would surely have killed her for it.

Jack slammed the door behind her and locked it loudly, and she walked quietly across the backyard to Mrs Archer's house and waited for the juvenile authorities to pick her up again. They had a foster home for her and the people were coming for her in the morning. It was all so effortless, and for a moment, she allowed herself to think that it was going to be easy now. Smooth sailing, and then back to New York in a few years, to find Megan and Axie, and one day, they'd be living with her and she'd take care of them again. She'd be able to do that, with the windfall she'd found hidden among Eileen's nylons. It was the only nice thing her aunt had ever done for her, and even that she hadn't meant to do. But it didn't matter now. The money was in Hilary's suitcase and she intended to guard it with her life. To her, it was an absolute fortune.

The social worker came for her, as promised, in the morning, and after a brief appearance in court took her to a family in a battered-looking house in a poor suburb of Jacksonville. The woman opened the door wearing a warm smile and an apron, there were five other kids inside varying from about ten to fourteen from what Hilary could see, and the place instantly reminded her of the house Eileen and Jack had lived in in Boston. It had the same fetid smell, worn-out furniture, and battered look. But with half a dozen kids living there, it was hardly surprising.

The woman's name was Louise and she showed Hilary to her room, a room she was to share with three other girls, all of them living on narrow army cots Louise had bought from army surplus. There was a black girl sitting on one of them, she was tall and thin, with big black eyes and she glanced over at Hilary with curiosity as she walked into the room and put down her things as the social worker introduced them.

'Hilary, this is Maida. She's been here for nine months.' The social worker smiled and disappeared, back to Louise and the mob of children in the kitchen. The house looked busy and full but wasn't welcoming somehow, and it gave Hilary the feeling that she had just been dropped off at a work camp.

'Hilary . . . what kinda name is dat?' Maida stared at her with hostility now that the social worker was gone and looked her over from the collar of her ugly dress to the cheap shoes Eileen had bought her. It was not a pretty outfit, and it was a far cry from the organdies and velvets of her childhood, forgotten luxuries by now. And with her serious green eyes, she looked at the black girl and wondered what life would be like here. 'Where you from girl?'

'New York . . . Boston . . . I've been here for two years.'

The black girl nodded, she was reed thin and Hilary could see she bit her nails to the quick. She was tall and angry and nervous. 'Yeah? So why you come here? You ma and pa in jail?' Hers were. Her mother was a prostitute and her father was a pimp and a pusher.

'My parents are dead.' Hilary's voice was dead too as she said it, and her eyes were guarded as she stood just inside the doorway.

'You got brothers and sisters?' She didn't see what difference it made and she was about to say yes, and then decided against it and merely shook her head. Maida seemed satisfied with her answer. 'You gonna work hard for Louise, sweetheart. She a bitch to work for.' It was not entirely welcome information, but somehow Hilary had suspected as she walked in the door that this was not going to be as easy as they'd told her.

'What do you have to do?'

'Clean the house, take care of her kids, the yard, the vegetable garden out back . . . laundry . . . anything she tells you to do. Kinda like slavery, except you get to sleep in the main house and she lets you eat here.' There was an evil smile in Maida's eyes and Hilary wasn't sure whether to laugh or not. 'But it still beats juvie.'

'What's that?' She was a neophyte to all this, to foster homes and juvenile halls and parents who had gone to jail, even though her own father had died there. It was difficult to absorb the changes he had wrought in her life with one night of unbridled fury. Hilary often thought late at night, when she allowed herself to think about it, that he might as well have killed her along with her mother. It would have been a great deal simpler, instead of this slow death he had condemned her to, far from home and those she loved, abandoned among strangers.

'Where you been, girl?' Maida looked annoyed. 'You know, juvie . . . juvenile hall . . .' She made a big deal of mouthing it, as Hilary nodded. 'That's jail for kids. If they don't find you a foster home, you go there, and they lock you up and treat you like shit. I'd rather work my ass off for Louise until my Ma gets out again. She'll be out soon and I can go home then.' This time she'd been caught in a drug bust with her 'husband'. 'What 'bout you? How long you think you gonna be here? You got relatives to go to?' She figured Hilary's parents had just died and maybe this was only a temporary arrangement. There was something different about Hilary, the way she spoke, the way she moved, the silent way she stared at everything, as though she didn't really belong here. But she shook her head in answer to

Maida's question, just as the social worker walked back into the doorway.

'You girls getting acquainted?' The woman smiled, as though totally unaware of the jungle she worked in. To her, these were all nice kids, and she was finding them lovely homes, and everyone was happy.

Both girls looked at her as though she were crazy, but Maida was the first to speak. 'Yeah. That's what we doin' ... gettin' acquainted. Right, Hilary?' Hilary nodded, wondering what she was supposed to say and relieved when the social worker took her back to the kitchen. There was something about Maida that scared her.

'Maida's done very well here,' the social worker confided as they walked down a dreary hall to the kitchen.

The children had gone back outside, and Louise was waiting for them, but all signs of any food they'd been eating was gone, and Hilary felt her stomach growl as she wondered if they'd give her something to eat, or if she'd have to wait until dinner.

'Ready to get to work?' Louise asked, and Hilary nodded, having got the answer to her question. The social worker seemed to disappear, and Louise directed her outside to a shovel and some rakes. She was told to dig a trench, and promised that some of the boys would help her, but they never showed. The boys were smoking cigarettes behind the barn, and Hilary was left to wield the shovel by herself, grunting and perspiring. She had worked hard in the last four years, but never at manual labour. She had cleaned Eileen and Jack's house, done their laundry, cooked their meals, and nursed Eileen until she died, but this was harder than anything she'd done before, and there were tears of exhaustion in her eyes when Louise finally called them in out of the torrid heat and told them to come to dinner.

She found Maida there, looking victorious as she stood by the stove. To her had fallen the ladylike task of cooking dinner, if one could call it that. It was a few pieces of meat and gristle floating in a sea of watery grease, which Louise cheerfully called stew as she ladled out small portions to each of them and sat down to say grace. And despite the pangs of hunger that she felt, and the dizziness from being in the hot sun all day, Hilary was unable to make herself eat it.

'Come on, eat up, you gotta keep up your strength.' Louise grinned horribly at her, it was all like some awful fairy-tale, about a witch who was going to eat the children. Hilary remembered tales like that from her childhood, but they never seemed quite as real as this, and the witch always died and the children went back to being princesses and princes.

'I'm sorry . . . I'm not very hungry . . .' Hilary apologized weakly as the boys laughed at her.

'You sick?' Louise looked annoyed. 'They didn't tell me you was sick . . .' She looked as though she were about to send her back to some unknown fate and Hilary remembered Maida's unpleasant description of 'juvie'. Jail for kids. That was all she needed. But she had nowhere else to go now. She couldn't go back to Jack. She knew what he'd do to her this time. So it was Louise or juvie.

'No, no, I'm not sick . . . it's just the sun . . . it was hot outside . . .'

'Aww . . .' The other kids were quick to make fun of her and Maida gave her a vicious pinch as she helped wash the dishes. It was an odd arrangement, Hilary realized again. They weren't like friends or family, Louise didn't pretend to mother them, they were just like a hired work force she'd brought in to do her work, and that was how they treated her as well. It all seemed very temporary and very distant. Louise's husband seemed to come and go. He had lost one leg in the war and the other was severely crippled. He was unable to work as a result, and Louise took these kids in to do his share of the work, and her own, and for the money it brought her. The State paid her for each child she took in, and she didn't get rich on it, but it gave her decent money. The maximum she could take in was seven, and they knew there would be another one coming soon, because with Hilary there were only six. There was a pale, blonde, fifteen-year-old girl named Georgine, as well as Maida, and three rowdy boys in their early teens. Two of them had been leering at Hilary since dinner. None of them were handsome kids, and few of them even looked healthy. It would have been hard to on the diet they were given. Louise cut all the corners she could, but Hilary was used to that from living with Eileen and Jack, although Louise seemed to have perfected the art even further.

At seven-thirty she shouted at the kids to get ready for bed. They had been sitting in their rooms, talking, complaining, exchanging stories about parents in jail, and their own experiences in juvie. It was all totally foreign to Hilary, who sat on her bed in frightened silence. The boys had their own room next door, and Georgine and Maida talked as though Hilary wasn't there. They shoved their way past her in their nightgowns eventually, and slammed the door in her face when they went to the bathroom.

I can take it, she told herself . . . it's better than Jack . . . this isn't so awful . . . She remembered the money hidden in her suitcase and prayed no one would find it. She only had to live through five more years of this . . . five years of foster homes or juvie . . . or Jack . . . she felt tears sting her eyes as she finally closed the door to the bathroom, and she sat down and sobbed silently into the torn scratchy towel Louise had given her that morning. It was impossible to believe that this was what her life had come to. And within minutes, the boys were pounding on the door, and she had to give up the bathroom, as a trail of cockroaches ran across the bathtub.

'What you doin' in there, Mama? Want a hand?' one of the black boys asked, and the others laughed at his delightful sense of humour. Hilary only brushed past them and went back to her own room, just in time for Maida to turn the light out. And a moment later, Hilary was stunned when Louise appeared in the doorway, with a ring of keys in one hand. She looked as though she were going to lock them in, but Hilary knew that was impossible, or so she thought. She could hear raucous laughter from the boys' room.

'Lock-up time,' Maida supplied the information and with that Louise slammed the door, and they could hear the key turn in the lock. The other two girls looked as though it was perfectly normal, and Hilary stared at them in the dim light from outside their windows.

'Why did she do that?'

'So we don't meet up with the boys. She likes everything nice and clean and wholesome.' And then suddenly Maida laughed as though it were a very funny joke and so did Georgine. They seemed to laugh endlessly as Hilary watched them.

'What if we have to go to the bathroom?'

'You piss in your bed,' Georgine supplied.

'But *you* clean it up tomorrow mornin',' Maida added, and then they snickered again.

'What if there's a fire?' Hilary was terrified, but Maida only laughed again.

'Then you fry, baby. Like a little potato chip with your lily-white skin turnin' all brown like mine.' In truth they could have broken the window and escaped, but Hilary didn't think of that as she felt rising waves of panic. She lay down in her bed and pulled up the sheets, trying not to think of all the terrible things that could happen. No one had ever locked her in a room before, and the experience was frightening beyond anything she'd ever thought of.

She lay silently, staring at the ceiling, her breathing shallow and quick. She felt as though someone were smothering her with a pillow, and she could hear the other two girls whispering, and then she heard sheets rustling and a series of giggles. She turned just to see what was going on and was in no way prepared for what she saw when she did so. Maida was naked in Georgine's bed, and Georgine had thrown her tattered nightgown to the floor, and they were caressing each other's bodies in the moonlight, kissing and fondling each other, as Maida moaned and rolled her eyes. Hilary wanted to turn away, but she was so horrified she didn't move and the older girl saw her and snapped at her.

'What's the matter honey, you never seen two girls making it before?' Hilary shook her head silently, and as Maida nestled her head down between Georgine's legs she laughed hoarsely and then pushed her away with another crack of laughter. 'Wait a minute.' She turned to Hilary, 'Want to try it?' Hilary shook her head again, terrified, and there was no escape from them. The door was locked, and she had to lie there listening, even if she didn't watch them. 'You might like it.'

'No . . . no . . .' In effect this was what had brought her here . . . except that it had been Jack and not two girls, and she couldn't even imagine what they would do to her, but they forgot her quickly as they went on with their nightly pleasure. They moaned and writhed and Maida screamed once, so loudly that Hilary was afraid Louise would come and beat them all, but there were no sounds in the silence except Maida's and Georgine's, the sound of hard breathing and panting and moaning, and then finally, as Hilary cried softly in her bed, they lay spent and fell asleep in each others's arms, and Hilary lay awake until morning.

The next day they worked hard again. Hilary went back to digging in the garden, and was told to scrub down the inside of the shed. The boys hassled her as they had before, and she was told to cook lunch this time. She tried to make something decent for all of them, but it was impossible with the meagre supplies Louise left out. They had thin slices of Spam and leftover frozen chips. It was barely enough to stay alive on, working in the hot summer sun, and that night she had to listen to Maida and Georgine go through their moaning and panting. This time she turned her back, pulled the covers over her head and tried to pretend she couldn't hear them. But it was two days later when Georgine slipped into her bed, and began gently stroking her back beneath her nightgown. It was the first gentle touch she had known since her mother died, but this was different, Hilary knew, and it was not welcome.

'Don't, please . . .' Hilary pulled away from her, half falling out of bed, but the girl took a strong grip on her, running an arm like steel around her waist and holding her close as she lay behind her. Hilary could feel the older girl's breasts on her back, and then her free hand stroking her nipples.

'Come on, honey, doesn't that feel nice . . . yeah . . . ain't that fine . . . Maida and I are tired of just having fun with each other, we want to share it with you too . . . you could be our friend now.' And with that the hand that had stroked Hilary's firm young breasts drifted down towards her thighs so tightly clenched in terror.

'Oh please . . . please . . . don't!' She was whimpering

and crying, in some ways this was worse than Jack. And she had no escape, no butcher's knife, nowhere to run. She couldn't escape these girls, locked into a room with them, and Georgine had a grip on her that Hilary could not pry away from, and as she held her down, her legs wrapped around Hilary's like steel snakes, Maida came stealthily from the other bed and began to stroke her, as Georgine forced her legs as far apart as Hilary's struggles would let her.

'Like this . . . you see . . .' Maida showed her things she didn't want to know, and reached into places Hilary had never touched herself as she began to scream in terror. But Georgine put one hand firmly on her mouth and let Maida do the stroking. They seemed to fondle her endlessly and softly only at first, then harder and rougher, as she sobbed and sobbed in their arms, and finally they tired of her, but when Georgine climbed out of her bed, Hilary was bleeding profusely. 'Shit, you got your period?' She looked annoyed as she saw the mess in the bed and on her legs. You could see it even in the moonlight. But Maida knew better, she had done everything she liked to do. She grinned at Georgine and down at the stricken girl.

'Nah . . . she was a virgin.'

Georgine grinned evilly. She'd come around, she knew. They always did. After the first time. And if she didn't, they'd rough her up a little, and she'd be scared not to.

The next day, Hilary washed her sheets as soon as Louise unlocked the door and apologized when she screamed at her for making a mess. The boys even laughed at her when they saw her scrubbing. It was as though all the pain and humiliation in the world was heaped on her head, as though someone somewhere wanted to destroy her. She wondered where her sisters were, and prayed that nothing like this happened to them. But she knew it wouldn't.

They were going to the homes of friends of Arthur Patterson's, and people like that didn't know about things like this ... they didn't know of the tortures people like Eileen and Jack and Louise and Maida and Georgine could conjure, and as she washed her sheets, and dug the ditch Louise wanted deeper, Hilary prayed that her own torture would be enough, that Axie and Megan would be safe from lives like this. She promised God that He could do anything He wanted to her, as long as He kept them safe ... please God ... please ... she muttered in the broiling sun as Georgine came up behind her.

'Hi baby, you talkin' to yourself?'

'I ... no ...' She turned away rapidly so Georgine couldn't see her blushing crimson.

'That was nice last night ... you're gonna like it better next time.'

But Hilary wheeled on her, and although she didn't know it, she looked just like her mother. 'No! I'm not! Don't ever touch me again, you hear me?' She clutched the shovel ominously, and Georgine laughed as she walked away. She knew Hilary would have no weapons in her room that night, and of course she didn't. They did the same thing to her again, and the next day Hilary looked glazed. There was no escaping them, and when the social worker came back in a week she looked at Hilary and asked her if she was working too hard. Hilary hesitated and then shook her head. Georgine told her that if she complained she'd wind up in juvie, and everyone did it there, sometimes they even used lead pipes and soda bottles ... 'not like me and Maida'. And Hilary believed them. Anything was possible now. Any anguish. Any torture. She only nodded and told the social worker everything was fine, and went on living her silent nightmare.

It went on for seven months, until Georgine turned

sixteen and was released as an emancipated minor, and Maida's mother was paroled from jail, and Maida went back to her, which left Hilary the only girl with three boys, while they waited for two new girls to replace the others. But for several days, Hilary was alone with the boys next door, and Louise figured one girl and three boys was not a dangerous combination, so she didn't bother locking Hilary's door, which left her no protection. The boys came stealthily one night, and Hilary lay wide awake, terrified, as she saw them enter her room and silently close the door behind them. She fought them like a cat, but she lost to their strength and they did exactly what they'd come for, and the next morning, Hilary called the social worker and asked to be transferred to juvenile hall. She offered no explanation, and Louise seemed not to care when they took her two days later. Hilary had stolen a knife and fork from the dinner table and the second time she had been well prepared for her midnight callers. One boy almost lost a hand, and they had retreated in terror. But she was still glad when she left Louise's care, and she said nothing to the social worker of what had happened.

At juvenile hall, they put her in solitary, because all she did was mope and wouldn't answer anyone's questions. It took them two weeks to decide she wasn't sick. She was rail thin, and weak from refusing to get up, but they thought that once she was put in with the other kids she might cheer up again. Her 'illness' was labelled 'teenage psychosis'.

She was assigned work in the laundry room, and put in a dorm with fifteen girls, and at night she heard the same moans and screams that she had learned from Maida. But this time no one bothered her, no one talked to her, no one touched her. And a month later they put her in another foster home with three other girls. The woman in charge was pleasant this time, not warm put polite, religious in a serious, joyless way, and talked frequently of a God who would punish them if they did not embrace Him. They tried hard to break through her shell, and they knew she was a bright girl but eventually her icy silences discouraged them. She was able to reach out to no one. And after two months, they sent her back to juvenile hall and 'exchanged' her for another girl, a friendly eleven-year-old who chatted and smiled and did all the things Hilary wouldn't.

Hilary went back to juvenile hall for good this time, and made no friends there. She went to school, did her work, and read everything she could lay her hands on. She had figured one thing out. She was going to get out, and get an education, and the harder she worked, the more she knew it would be her only salvation. She poured herself into her school work, and graduated at seventeen with honours, and the day afterwards her caseworker called her into her office.

'Congratulations, Hilary, we heard how well you did.' But no one had been there. No one had ever been there for Hilary, not in nine years, and now she knew there was never going to be. That was her destiny, and she accepted that. Except if she could find Megan and Alexandra ... but even that hope was dim now. She still had the ten thousand dollars, hidden in the lining of her suitcase, but her hope of finding them now was slim ... unless she went to Arthur ... but would they even remember her? Alexandra would be twelve, and Megan only nine ... to them, she would be a stranger. All she had left really was herself. She knew that now, as she looked at the caseworker without any trace of emotion.

'Thank you.'

'You have a choice to make now.'

'I do?' Surely nothing pleasant. Hilary had learned that

much, and she was always ready to defend herself against the miseries someone else wanted to inflict upon her. She had learned a lot since her first foster home, and her first days in juvie.

'Normally, our wards remain here until they reach eighteen, as you know, but in a case such as yours, when you graduate from high school before that date, you have the option of leaving as an emancipated minor.'

'Which means what?' Hilary gazed at her suspiciously from behind walls of steel. Her brilliant green eyes were her only peep-holes.

'It means you're free Hilary, if you want to be. Or you can stay here until you decide what you want to do after you leave here. Have you given it any thought?' Only four years' worth.

'Some.'

'And?' Talking to her was like pulling teeth but a lot of them were like that, too. too bruised by life to trust anyone. It was a tragedy, but there was no way to change that. 'Want to tell me your plans?'

'Do I have to in order to get out?' Like the parole she'd heard so much about. Everyone she knew in juvie had parents in jail, waiting to get out on parole. This was no different. But the caseworker shook her head.

'No, you don't, Hilary. But I'd like to help if I can.'

'I'll be all right.'

'Where do you want to go?'

'New York probably. It's where I'm from. It's what I know.' Although she had been gone from there for more than half her life, it still seemed like home to her. And, of course, there were her sisters . . .

'It's a big city. Do you have friends there?'

She shook her head. If she did, would she have spent four years in the Jacksonville juvenile hall? It was a stupid

139

question. And at least she still had her ten thousand dollars. That was going to be her salvation. She didn't need friends. All she needed was a job and a place to stay. But one thing was for sure, she wasn't staying here. 'I guess I'll be going pretty soon. How soon can I go?' Her eyes lit up for the first time at the prospect of leaving.

'We can have your release papers in order by next week. Soon enough for you?' The caseworker smiled with regret. They had failed dismally with her. It happened that way sometimes, it was rotten luck when it did, but it was hard to say who would survive the system and who wouldn't. She stood up and held out a hand which Hilary shook cautiously. She trusted nothing and no one. 'We'll let you know as soon as you can go.'

'Thank you.' She left the room quietly and went to the single room she lived in. She no longer had to sleep in a dorm or share with anyone. She had long-term seniority, and in a few days she'd be leaving. She lay on her bed with a smile and stared up at the ceiling. It was all over, the agony, the pain, the humiliation, the horror of her life for the last nine years. She was going to be on her own now. She lay there smiling as she hadn't in years. And a week later, to the day, she was on a bus, no regrets, no sorrow, no friends to leave behind. Her eyes were cold and hard and green, dreaming of a world she did not know yet. And the past was a nightmare left behind her.

Chapter 9

The bus stopped in Savannah, Raleigh, Richmond, Washington, and Baltimore, and took two days to reach New York, as Hilary sat staring soundlessly out of the window. Other passengers had said a word or two when they stopped for lunch, or when they stretched at night, two sailors had even tried to pick her up, but she dealt with them in no uncertain terms, and after that, no one came near her. She was a solitary figure as she stepped down from the bus in New York, and in her heart she felt a terrifying trembling. She was home . . . after nine years . . . she had left here as a little girl, a week after her father committed suicide, to go to stay with her aunt in Boston. And it had taken all these years to come home, but she had done it.

The juvenile authorities of Florida had given her two hundred and eighty-seven dollars to start her life, and she had the ten thousand from Eileen. The first thing she did was go to a bank on Forty-second Street. The second thing she did was go to a hotel room. She took a room in a small, seedy hotel in the Thirties on the East Side, but her room was simple and spare and no one bothered her when she went in or out. She ate at a coffee shop on the corner, and read the want ads for jobs. She had taken a typing class in high school, but she had no other skills and she had no delusions about what lay ahead. She had to start at the bottom. But she had other plans as well. She wasn't going to stop there. The spectres of the women she'd seen in the past nine years had left their mark. She was never going to be like them. She was going to work and go to college at night, and do everything she had to. And one day she was going to be important, she promised herself. One day she was going to be *someone*.

On her second day in New York, she went to Alexander's Department store on Lexington Avenue and spent five hundred dollars on clothes. It seemed like a terrifying portion of her fortune, but she knew she would have to look right if she was going to get a job. She selected dark colours, simple styles, a few skirts and blouses, and patent leather pumps and a matching bag. She looked like a pretty young girl as she tried her things on in her room downtown, and no one would have suspected the horrors she had endured since her parents died.

She went on her first job interview and was told she was too young, and then three more which required shorthand skills she didn't have, and finally a job in an accountant's office where she was interviewed by a bald, obese man, perspiring profusely with a damp handkerchief clutched in one hand.

'You type?' He leered at her, as she sat watching him. She had dealt with worse than that and he didn't frighten her. And she also needed the job. She couldn't go on living forever on her dwindling funds. She had to find work pretty soon, and she would even have been willing to work for him, if he would behave himself. 'Shorthand too?' She shook her head and he didn't seem to care. 'How old are you?'

'Nineteen,' she lied. She had learned that much in the first interview. No one wanted to hire a seventeen-year-old girl. So she lied to them.

'Have you been to secretarial school?' She shook her head again and he shrugged, and then stood up, with a small stack of papers in one hand, and moved around the desk, as though to show them to her, but when he reached her side, he caressed her breast instead, and she was on her feet with lightning speed, the back of her hand across his face before she had thought of it, and they both gasped simultaneously as he stared at her.

'If you touch me again, I'll scream so loud I'll have the police up here,' she warned, her green eyes flashing at him, her whole body tense, her hands trembling as she looked at him. 'How dare you do that?' Why did they all do things like that to her? . . . her Uncle Jack . . . and the girls at the foster home . . . and the boys at Louise's place . . . it kept happening to her. She didn't understand that it was because she was beautiful. She thought of it as some kind of punishment, something she must have done as a child that she was being tortured for now. It didn't seem fair that it happened to her all the time, and she backed slowly toward the door, never taking her eyes off his face.

'Look, I'm sorry . . . no big deal . . . Miss . . . what's your name? . . . come on . . .' He waddled towards her hurriedly and she slammed the door in his face and ran down the stairs as fast as she could go. She walked all the way back to her hotel after that, feeling dirty and depressed, and wondering if she'd ever find a job.

But she finally did, at an employment agency, as a receptionist. They liked the way she looked, suspected she was younger than she said, but she was intelligent, neat and clean, typed halfway decently and could answer the phone, and that was enough for them. They offered her ninety-five dollars a week and it seemed like a windfall to her. She took the job and went flying back to her hotel to get ready for work the next day. She had her first job!

And it would be a quick climb up from there. She didn't know what she wanted to do yet, but she already knew where she wanted to go to school. She'd been reading all the newspaper ads, and she made some calls. She had already applied, and she was waiting to hear from them, and then she'd really be on her way.

Now there was only one thing left to do, and she decided to tackle it that afternoon. After that, she didn't know when she'd have the time, and she didn't want to call him. She wanted to see him personally. Only once. She'd get the information from him and then all she had to do was call . . . the thought of it made her tremble as she changed her clothes again. She wore a simple navy-blue dress, dark stockings, and her patent leather shoes. The dress was short, as was the style, but it was respectable. And she tied her hair in a simple knot that made her look older than she was. She washed her face, dried it on one of the hotel's little rough towels, and went downstairs again. And this time she didn't take a bus. She didn't want to waste time. She took a cab instead, and stood outside looking up when she arrived at Forty-eighth and Park Avenue. It was a glass building trimmed with chrome, and it seemed to stretch all the way to the sky as she looked up at it.

The lift shuddered as it rose to the thirty-eighth floor, and she held her breath wondering if it would get stuck. She had never been anywhere like this before, not that she remembered anyway . . . there were other things she did remember though . . . a trip with her parents to France on the *Liberté* . . . the apartment on Sutton Place . . . tea at the Plaza with Solange, with little cakes and hot chocolate with tons of whipped cream . . . and she remembered the night her mother died and the things she and Sam had said . . .

The lift doors opened easily and she found herself in a

reception area with thick green carpeting, and a young girl at a desk. She wore a pink linen suit and had short blond hair, and she had the pert look all receptionists were supposed to have. It reminded Hilary of the job she was starting the next day. But she knew she would never look like that. Her looks weren't 'cute', her hair wasn't blond, and she didn't look as though she'd bounce out of her seat if someone asked her to. Instead, Hilary looked quiet and serious as she approached, and looked straight into the girl's eyes.

'I'm here to see Mr Patterson.'

'Is he expecting you?' she beamed, and Hilary did not smile in reply. She shook her head honestly, and spoke in a restrained voice. Inwardly, she was intimidated by the surroundings, but outwardly nothing showed. She looked perfectly at ease and totally in control.

'No, he's not. But I'd like to see him now.'

'Your name?' Little Miss Smile went into high beam.

'Hilary Walker.' And then she added, as though it would make a difference, 'He's my godfather.'

'Oh. Of course,' the little blonde said, and then hit a series of buttons and picked up a phone, speaking inaudibly into it. That was another part of the job, speaking into phones so no one else could hear . . . Mr So and So is here to see you, sir . . . oh, you're out? . . . tell him what? . . . It was an art Hilary would have to perfect at the employment agency. And then the girl astonished Hilary. She looked up at her with her perfect smile and waved to a door on her right. 'You may go right in. Mr Patterson's secretary will meet you to show you to his office.' She looked impressed. It wasn't easy to get in to see Arthur Patterson, but the girl was his goddaughter after all.

Hilary stepped inside and looked down a long carpeted corridor. The firm occupied the entire floor and she could see all the way down the hall to a corner office a block away from her. It was an impressive hallway lined with leather-bound legal books, and populated by secretaries at their desks outside the attorneys' offices. She had never been there before, even as a child, and they had moved since then anyway.

'Miss Walker?' An elderly woman with short grey hair and a kindly smile stepped up to her and pointed into the distance down the hall.

'Yes.'

'Mr Patterson is waiting for you.' As though it had been planned, as though he had known she would come, as though he had been waiting for nine years. But what could he possibly know, sitting here? What could he know of lives like Eileen and Jack's, of caring for her as she died, or fighting him off with a butcher's knife, of nearly starving in their home for all those years, and the foster home in Jacksonville, and Maida and Georgine ... and juvenile hall ... and even the sweaty little man who had 'interviewed' her only days ago. What did he know of any of it? And all she knew was that he had killed her mother, as surely as if he had done it with his own hands, and her father, too, eventually. And now here he sat, and she only wanted one thing from him, and then she would leave and never see him again. She never wanted to lay eyes on him again after today.

The secretary stopped at the doorway and knocked. A discreet brass and leather sign on the door said *Arthur Patterson* and then she heard his voice. It was still familiar to her. She could still remember him lying to her eight years before ... I'm just going to take them away for a little while, Hilary ... I'll come back for you. He never did, and she didn't care, she hated him anyway. She could remember kneeling in the street after he drove off, calling her sisters' names and she had to fight back tears again, but it was almost over now . . . almost. It was almost exactly eight years since she had last seen them.

'You may come in.' The secretary smiled and stepped aside as she opened the door, and Hilary walked in quietly. She didn't see the desk at first, and then she saw it, a simple slab of glass and chrome, in front of a window offering a full view of New York, and there he sat, incongruous in the modern décor. He was fifty years old and he looked at least ten years older than that, tall, thin, balding, with sad eyes and a pale face. But he was even paler than usual now as he stood up and looked at her. It was as though he had seen a ghost, as she stood in front of him. She was beautiful and tall, with Sam's shiny black hair, but there the resemblance to him stopped . . . she had Solange's eyes . . . and the same way of moving her head . . . and she stood in front of him just as proudly now as Solange had once walked on the rue d'Arcole in Paris twenty-two years before. It was like seeing a ghost . . . if you changed the black hair to red . . . it was Solange again . . . but with angry, bitter eyes, with something fierce in her face that Solange had never had, something that said if you come near me I will kill you before I let you lay a hand on me, and Arthur instantly feared what might have happened to her, what could possibly have made her look like that? And yet she was safe and sound, obviously, and standing in front of him in his office, fully grown and very beautiful. It was a miracle, and he walked slowly towards her, holding out a hand, with dreams of recapturing the past. It was a way of having Sam and Solange back, of sharing once more in their magic. Hilary was going to bring it all back to him. But as he approached, he could sense the wall built around the girl, and she began to back away when he got close to her, and instinctively he stopped approaching.

'Hilary, are you all right?' It was a little late to ask, and she hated the weakness she saw in his eyes. She never understood till then how totally without courage he was. He had no balls, she realized now, that was why he had abandoned her, after betraying them . . . no guts . . . it was something Solange had accused him of a lifetime ago, although Hilary didn't know it.

'I'm fine.' She wasted no time with him. She had not come for a warm reunion with a family friend, she had come to ask him the only thing she cared about, the only thing she had cared about for eight years. 'I want to know where my sisters are.' Her eyes were icy hard and neither of them moved as she watched his face, not sure of what she saw, terror or grief, and she waited with bated breath for what he would say next.

But whereas he was pale before, he looked ghostly now. He realized that he could not fob her off, that she wanted nothing to do with him. She only wanted them, and he could not give them to her, no matter how much he would have wanted to do so. 'Hilary . . . why don't we sit down . . .' He waved toward a chair and she shook her head, her eyes riveted to his.

'I'm not interested in sitting down with you. You killed my parents, you destroyed my family. I have nothing to say to you. But I want to know where Alexandra and Megan are. That's all I want. When you tell me that, I'll go.' She waited patiently, the same proud tilt of her head that had made Solange so unique . . . so extraordinary . . . he stared at her, seeing someone else, but there was no escaping Hilary. She was a force to be reckoned with, and he understood that fully now. He also sensed that she knew more than he had thought so long ago, but he didn't question her now. He told her the truth, his eyes filled with regret, and damp with tears for what had been and

148

was no more. A family had died at his hands. She was right. And he had never got over it. He had started no family of his own, and Marjorie had left him years before. The woman he loved was gone, her children cast to the winds. And he held himself responsible for what had happened to all of them, even Sam. But there was no way to explain that to this girl, or to excuse himself, least of all to her. God only knew what she had been through in the past eight years.

'I don't know where they are, Hilary. I don't even know where you've been. When I went to Boston to see you seven years ago, you were all gone . . . the Joneses had left no forwarding address with anyone. I was unable to find you . . .' His voice trailed off, filled with regret, because his own guilt had been so great, he had been secretly relieved not to have to face her again, and he suspected now she knew that about him. She had all-seeing eyes, and she looked as though she had an unforgiving heart. There was nothing warm about this girl, nothing gentle, or kind. She was entirely made of granite and barbed wire, shafts of steel and broken glass. There were ugly things inside this girl, he could see it in her eyes, and for an instant he was afraid of her as though, given the opportunity, she might harm him. And under the circumstances, he wasn't sure that he blamed her.

'You couldn't have tried very hard to find me.' Her voice sounded hard. She wasn't interested in his explanations or apologies. 'We went to Florida.'

'And then?' He needed to know what had happened to her, why she looked like that. He had to know . . . and to . . . he felt a sob catch his throat and prayed he wouldn't cry in front of her. 'What happened to you?' He wished she would sit down . . . that they could talk . . . that she would listen to him . . . he could talk to her now. He could explain about Marjorie, who was now a Superior Court judge. He could tell her why he couldn't take them to live with him . . . why nobody wanted all three of them . . . why he had done what he did. 'Are Jack and Eileen still . . . were they good to you?'

She laughed bitterly, sounding very old, and her eyes looked very green. She was thinking of Jack and that night . . . and the pathetic wraith Eileen had become before she died. 'Eileen died, and I've been a ward of the Jacksonville juvenile courts for the last four years. I've been in foster homes, and juvenile hall, and now I'm free, Mr Patterson. I don't owe anyone anything, and most of all not you. All I want now are my sisters.' Her heart was pounding as she realized he had lost them.

'Why didn't you call me when she died?' He sounded horrified. 'Surely you didn't have to go to foster homes . . . juvenile hall . . .' Those were places he never thought about, couldn't bear to think of now. 'Hilary, I'm so sorry . . .'

But her eyes flashed green fire again, and she waved a hand at him. 'Don't give me that shit. You never gave a damn about us, and you don't now. It's easy for you to sound pious and tell me how sorry you are. To tell you the truth, I don't give a damn. It doesn't change anything that happened to me. All I want from you are the addresses of where my sisters live, and don't tell me you don't know. You have to know. You took them there.' It had never occurred to her that he would lose track of them as he had of her. That was impossible. He *had* to know, and she searched his eyes now, but what she saw there was frightening. She saw remorse and guilt, and a man who was actually frightened of her.

He sat down in a chair and shook his head in despair, and then he looked up at her with sad, empty eyes.

'Alexandra went to one of my partners here in the firm. He had a lovely young wife, from a good family. And she was much younger than he. They didn't have children, and they were desperate to adopt Alexandra when I told them about her. And they did ... they worshipped her.' He looked at Hilary as though hoping to mollify her somewhat but it was no use, her eyes were like green ice, and her hands trembled as she silently sat down in a chair and listened to what he had to say. 'They took her to Europe, they went everywhere with her ... but six months later, George died of a heart attack. Margaret was in shock and she took Alexandra away with her. The last I heard was that they were in the south of France ... we sent papers on the estate to her in Paris years ago ... and I don't know anything after that. I think she stayed over there, but I'm really not sure. We've had no reason to stay in touch with her, and ...' his voice trailed away, as two tears rolled down his cheeks.

'So you don't know where Alexandra is.' Hilary sounded numb. 'And the woman's name?'

'Gorham. Margaret Gorham. But she could have re-married by now ... any number of things could have happened. She could be back in the States somewhere. I don't think she's back in New York, I think I'd have heard of it if she were.' He looked lamely at her.

'And Megan?'

'She was adopted by David and Rebecca Abrams, right after I ... after she ...' He could barely control himself, and Hilary was trembling from head to foot. '... after I brought her back to New York. He was not a partner of the firm, he merely worked for us, and several months later they left. She was an attorney too, and they had had an offer from a law firm in Los Angeles that wanted both of them. They were anxious to start a new life anyway, and they made a point of telling me that they did not want to stay in touch. They wanted to give Megan a new life, far away from all that had happened to her. I haven't heard from the n since they left. If he's a member of the California bar, I could possibly locate him, if he's still there . . . I don't know . . .'

'You sonofabitch.' She glared at him with hatred on her face. 'You let us all drift away. You set us adrift, as though getting rid of us would rid you of your own guilt, but it didn't, did it?' She had read him perfectly. 'It destroyed your life too, and you deserve that. You deserve everything that's happened to you. May you rot in hell, Arthur Patterson. You'll live with this for the rest of your life. You killed two people, and destroyed three more lives. That's five people on your soul. Can you live with that?' She walked to where he sat and looked down on him with contempt far beyond her years. 'Can you sleep at night? I don't think you can . . . and God only knows what happened to the other two. God only knows what lives you've condemned them to. I know what mine was like. But it's not over yet. I won't let you spoil my life. I'm going to make something of myself . . . and maybe one day I'll find my sisters . . . maybe . . . But in the meantime,' – she walked slowly to the door, with tears pouring slowly down her face, she had expected so much from him, and her disappointment was so great now – 'I never want to see you again, Arthur Patterson. Never. You won't soothe your conscience with me. We won't be "friends" again, dear Godfather.' She stood and looked at him for a long, long time, before her final words, and she spoke them in a whisper that haunted him for the rest of his life. 'I will never forgive what you did to us . . . never . . . and I will hate you for the rest of my life. Remember that . . . remember what you did and how much I hate you.' And then, like the ghost of Christmas past, she closed his office door, and slipped away, and he did not have the courage to follow her. He sat slumped in his chair, like an old man, remembering Solange, and crying for what he had done to her. Hilary was right, he would not be absolved of what he had done to them all. He couldn't forgive himself, and like Hilary, he wondered now where the other two girls were.

But there were no answers to that. Hilary went from the office on Park Avenue to the Public Library and did the only thing she knew how to do. She opened the Manhattan phone book and found no George or Margaret Gorham there. She found only five in all, and when she called, none of them knew anything about Margaret or Alexandra, and it was obvious they had never heard of them. And a listing of the attorneys of the California bar was equally discouraging. There was no David Abrams listed there, which meant he had left California long before, and God only knew where he had gone. She didn't have the resources to do more than that, she couldn't hunt them down. She couldn't do anything. She had counted on Arthur to know, and he knew nothing at all. Her sisters were gone. Forever this time. And the dream that had kept her alive slipped quietly from her heart, like a rock falling to her feet. She walked slowly back to her hotel, tears streaming down her cheeks. It was as though they had died finally, as she remembered the white roses at her mother's funeral. They no longer existed in her life, hadn't for years . . . and seeing him again reminded her of that terrible day when they'd been taken from her . . . Axie, I love you! . . . she could still remember screaming the words as the car drove away, and falling to her knees in the dirt. It seemed as though she had never got up since. But she would now . . . she had to . . . she would make it alone, as she had for all these years ... but she would always remember them. Always.

She felt them slip away from her as she walked into her hotel, like people she had loved, who had finally died. She was alone, as she always had been.

Part IV

ALEXANDRA

Chapter 10

The house on the avenue Foch stood protected by a tall, impeccably trimmed hedge that shielded everything behind it from the pedestrians' view. There were gardens groomed to perfection, and a solid brick *hôtel particulier* built in the eighteenth century, with handsomely carved doors, brass knockers and knobs, beautiful shutters painted dark green, with silk and damask curtains hung at the windows.

It was a house closed off from a far more public world shielded from all publicity, a house in which perfection reigned, filled with Fabergé objects and crystal chandeliers and impeccable antiquities. It was the house of the Baron and Baroness Henri de Morigny, one of France's oldest families. His was a house of great nobility and dwindling wealth, until he married the lovely daughter of old Comte de Borne fourteen years before. The house on the avenue Foch had been a wedding present from the Count, and as a gift to Henri, Alexandra had restored his family seat for him, a handsome château in Dordogne, and a hunting box in Sologne as well. And since then they had bought a summer house in Saint-Jean–Cap-Ferrat, where they went every year with their children. It was a life of considerable luxury, and endless grace. It was the only life Alexandra de Morigny had ever known, and she played the perfect wife at all times for her husband. She ran his house, planned his dinners, entertained his friends, followed his instructions, and brought up their two daughters, Axelle and Marie-Louise, to perfection. The girls were the greatest joy in her life, and she sat at her desk with a quiet smile, thinking of them that afternoon. They would be home from school very soon, and she would walk the dogs with them in the Bois. It was a good chance to talk, to find out what was going on, who they liked, and they 'hated', who might be having trouble at school, and then they would come home for the girls to do their *devoirs*, have their bath, dine and play and go to bed. Alexandra always stayed with them until her own dinner with Henri. They were six and twelve, as different as night and day, and they were the joy and laughter in her life. Marie-Louise was serious and a great deal like Henri, but Axelle was just as she had been as a child, a little bit shy, totally trusting, and enormously affectionate. It was wonderful just being with her, stroking her pale red curls and looking into those huge blue eyes. Alexandra's heart sang just thinking of it. And she sat smiling as she stared into space, and didn't hear his step on the highly polished parquet floor as he entered the room and watched her. He was almost in front of her before she awoke from her reverie, and she looked up to see the tall, handsome man she had married. He was fifty-nine years old, and powerfuly built, with strong lines in his face, and hard eyes that bore into her, as they always did, as though he were about to ask a very important question. It was a face that was not often amused, but he was a man she could trust and depend on. And she respected him. She had fallen in love with him at nineteen, and they had been engaged for two years. Her father had wanted to be sure that she was not making a mistake or acting on an impulse. Henri was twenty-five years older than she after all, but she had been absolutely certain. She wanted someone just like her father, the old Comte de Borne. He had been sixty when she was born, or he would have been. He had adopted her when she was six years old, and he worshipped her. He had never had children of his own, and he had just lost his wife of forty years when he married her mother. He had gone to the South of France, to grieve, and instead he had met Margaret Gorham, doing precisely the same thing after the death of her husband. She was twenty-seven years old and it was a whirlwind romance – within six months they were married, and Pierre de Borne adopted Alexandra. And only he and Margaret shared the secret that she'd been adopted once before when she came to Margaret and George Gorham at the age of five in New York. It was not something anyone needed to know, and it was no longer important. She was Alexandra de Borne, and she was as dear to the Count's heart as though she had been his natural daughter. Perhaps more so. She grew up cosseted and spoiled and adored as few children are, and in return she worshipped the man she knew as her father. It was to Pierre that she turned with every woe, or wish, or dream, sharing all her secrets with him, confessing her misdeeds, of which there were few, while Margaret looked on, content in every way, filled with love for her husband and child, and full of mischief of her own. Margaret was, in effect, the child of the family, pulling pranks on both of them, hiding unexpectedly, wearing ridiculous costumes to make them laugh. She was an oversized child who loved to laugh, and enjoy every moment. And Alexandra was oddly enough like Pierre, affectionate, shy, and filled with admiration for Margaret's wild schemes and irresistible laughter.

Alexandra was protected and greatly loved and it surprised everyone when she fell in love at nineteen and said she wanted to get married. And Pierre de Borne was not pleased at the prospect of his daughter marrying Henri de Morigny, mostly because he was so much older. He also thought him far too serious, and a difficult man in the bargain. Morigny had never married before, and the old Count knew that he'd been waiting for just the right girl, with an important family, an equally important fortune, and if at all possible, a title. And Alexandra certainly had all of that to offer him. But what did he offer her, her father asked her. Was he warm enough, would he be kind to her? Pierre talked constantly of it to Margaret, and she was just as concerned as he was. But Alexandra was positive she wanted Henri and never wavered. She was married at twenty-one at the church on their country estate in Rambouillet. Seven hundred people were there, from all of Europe's finest families. And they spent their honeymoon in Tahiti, drinking exotic punches and making love on the private beach of the house Henri had rented for her. And when they returned to Paris, Alexandra loved him with even greater passion than she had before, and all she wanted was to have his babies. It took them over a year to conceive, in spite of all of Henri's most romantic efforts.

Her father lived just long enough to hold his first grandchild, two years after Alexandra's marriage. And then he died peacefully in his sleep at the age of eighty-three. Margaret was bereft and Alexandra was stunned, she couldn't imagine a life without him, couldn't imagine not having his hand to hold, his wise eyes to look into. It made her suddenly extremely dependent on Henri, whom she adored, and also a little bit frightened of him. He became suddenly all-important to her and she was obsessed by her fears of losing him too, and knew she couldn't have stood it. Alexandra had always had an irrational fear of losing the people she loved and who loved her. And it worried Margaret considerably because she thought Henri took advantage of it to control her. And in some ways he treated Alexandra like a child, someone to be scolded, and spoken to in firm tones and told what to do, as though she didn't know herself. In Margaret's eyes, he was more a father than a husband, and Alexandra did everything to please him, no matter how trivial or foolish. He had aspirations towards politics and it made him maniacal about appearances. Everything had to be perfect, constantly circumspect, Alexandra had to be impeccable at all times, the children had to be ten times more polite than any others. Margaret found it exhausting just having tea with them, and it worried her at times that Alexandra seemed to think it was all normal. Anything was all right, as long as it pleased her husband.

'That's just the way he is, Maman. He doesn't mean any harm. He's a serious man and he wants everything to be perfect.' Alexandra's own father had never been as demanding of his daughter, or his wife, and he had had a marvellous sense of humour. Margaret found Henri a dead bore, in comparison to her late husband, but she never said it in so many words. All she wanted was Alexandra's happiness, it was all Pierre had ever wanted for her too. And he left her most of his fortune when he died, leaving Margaret more than enough to amuse herself with for another forty years. She was only forty-five when he died, and in many ways she seemed far younger, mostly because she enjoyed herself so much, and she was still very attractive. She was three years younger than Alexandra's husband.

Margaret de Borne always had a good time, something amusing to say, something outrageous and entertaining to do. She was pursued by every eligible man in Europe, and she had no desire whatever to remarry. She had been happy with George years before, and she had had everything she wanted with Pierre. There was no point trying to top that, she knew she never could and didn't want to try it. But Alexandra was another story, and Margaret worried about her more than Alexandra suspected.

Henri expected so much from her. So much so that Pierre and Margaret had decided not to tell him of Alexandra's background, which she herself didn't remember. She only remembered 'Papa' as she called Pierre, although Margaret knew she had some vague other memories as well, but they were long buried. She no longer seemed to have any recollection whatsoever of George Gorham. They had told her simply that buried deep in her memory was the fact that she'd been adopted by Pierre after her father died, a man she no longer remembered, and it never occurred to her, nor did they tell her, that she had in fact been born of other parents entirely, and Margaret was not her mother at all, that she had been adopted once before, after her own parents' tragic death. Pierre had been adamant with Margaret before he died. He did not want Alexandra's husband to know anything about either of her adoptions. But he had said nothing about it to Alexandra, not wanting to stir the memories or her conscience. She was such a decent girl, she might have felt obliged to tell her husband. It was much easier if she didn't remember. Her father knew Henri well enough to know what a maniac he was about his blood-line.

And Margaret did not disagree with her husband about their son-in-law, so for Alexandra's sake, she also remained silent. And remarkably, after so many years, no one even remembered that Alexandra was adopted.

And Margaret rejoiced when Marie-Louise was born, and then mourned when Alexandra lost a baby boy a year later. And then came Axelle after an excruciating pregnancy and endless labour. And after that, her doctor urged her not to try again. He told her she couldn't have any more children without jeopardizing her life. And she was content with the two little girls they had. Only Henri was bitterly disappointed, and resentful for a long time that she had not produced a son for him. And for years after Axelle was born, he told her so whenever he was angry. And always made her feel vaguely guilty towards her husband, as though she had somehow shortchanged him, and owed him something more because of her failure.

The loss of a son was a cross Henri had to bear and having Margaret de Borne as a mother-in-law was yet another. She drove him mad with her long, American legs, her endless stride, which he declared unfeminine, her booming laugh – too loud – her ghastly accent in French, which, to him, was like fingernails on a blackboard. He hated her pranks, detested her sense of humour, and cringed almost visibly whenever she arrived, bringing water pistols in the form of lipsticks for the girls, dime store toys they adored, or at the other extreme, boxes and boxes of clothes from New York, including matching navy-blue coats with little mink muffs, which he told Alexandra were extremely vulgar. He detested everything she brought and everything she said, and was grateful Alexandra was nothing like her. He could never imagine why the old Count had married a woman like her. And he thanked God every day that Alexandra was so much more restrained than her mother. Alexandra was intelligent and kind and discreet, and still very shy, and obedient, which was one of the qualities he liked most about her.

He looked down at her as she sat at her desk, and smiled at her in a quiet, distant way. He was not a man to show his emotions, but although he expected a great deal from

Alexandra, and showed no romance, he nonetheless had deep feelings for her. He knew that without her his life would not be the same, not only financially but in subtler ways that were even more important. She ran a beautiful home for him, she had elegance and style, and her impeccable breeding showed in countless ways. Alexandra de Borne de Morigny was every inch a lady.

'You look as though you're dreaming, Alexandra.' He spoke to her quietly, with only slight reproach. He never raised his voice to her or anyone, he had no need to. People ran to obey his orders from just a single glance, as did Alexandra. He was distinguished and powerful, with dark eyes and grey hair. He had been extremely handsome and virile and athletic in his youth, and he had aged admirably. He still had a powerful frame and handsome face, and he did not look fifty-nine years old, any more than Alexandra looked thirty-four with her big innocent green eyes, and the silky strawberry-blonde hair that she usually wore up in elegant French twists and chignons.

'Have you organized everything for the dinner next week?' He handed her a checklist of things for her to go over again. She had a secretary to assist her with such things, but she preferred doing most of it herself. That way she could assure him of the perfection he expected.

'Everything's done.' She smiled up at him with respectful eyes filled with admiration, and he looked serious, as he always did, and a little distant.

'Please be sure of it.' He eyed her with a warning like that you would give a child, and she smiled at him. Sometimes he frightened her, but not very often. She knew how good-hearted he was, beneath the constant demands for perfection.

'We're dining at the Elysée tomorrow night,' he informed her.

'That's nice. Any particular reason?' She smiled at him, unimpressed. They dined there often.

'They're announcing the new Minister of Defence.' It did not sound fascinating to her, but dinners at the Elysée never were. But Henri thought they were extremely important. He was still toying with the idea of a political career when he retired from his bank, which was still a few years in the future.

'I'm having lunch at my mother's tomorrow. But I'll be home in plenty of time to get ready for the evening.' She looked away, glancing at the papers on her desk, not wanting to see the disapproval in her eyes. She hated that, always had. She had always hoped he'd come to love her mother, but she had given up in recent years, and it was an open secret that Henri disapproved of Margaret.

Almost as revenge, his voice seemed to grow cold when he spoke again. 'I'll be out for dinner tonight.' He offered no reason or excuse, and she would not have asked for one in any case. 'I suppose you'll want to dine with the children.'

She nodded, meeting his eyes again, wondering where he was going. She knew he'd had one mistress only a few years before, and hoped it was not something he was starting fresh now. It was something she accepted about him. It was hardly unusual, in France. 'I'll tell the cook.' She loved eating with the girls, as long as it didn't mean something ominous between them, and this time she wasn't quite certain. 'A business dinner, darling?' She tried to keep her voice light as she watched him.

He scowled at her disapprovingly. The question was out of place and he nodded, as his daughters bounded into the room, not expecting him to be there. There were shrieks of delight, and Marie-Louise's long, coltish legs in her short navy-blue skirt, her eyes shy and admiring as she saw Henri, and then a warm hug for her mother as he watched them. He never showed Alexandra affection in front of them. But Axelle was the image of her, she looked like a miniature as she sat happily on her mother's lap, playing with the things on the desk, and almost overturning a bottle of ink as Henri cringed in anticipation of disaster.

'Axelle!' he said sternly as she gazed up at him, unconcerned, unafraid, and with endless mischief in her eyes. At times he feared she would turn out to be like her maternal grandmother, and he was strict with her because of it. 'Be careful what you do in your mother's study.'

'I am, Papa.' She smiled up at him with her angelic blue eyes. Her mouth formed a natural pout, her cheeks were still round, and she still had the baby fat of a little girl, unlike Marie-Louise, who was long and tall and elegant, and already looked more like her father. 'They sent me out of the room today in school,' Axelle announced proudly to everyone in the room, and Alexandra laughed. She was only sorry her father wasn't alive to see them both, she knew he would have been totally in love with Axelle, and of course very proud of Marie-Louise too. They were both lovely girls, and Alexandra was very proud of them.

'That's nothing to brag about, mademoiselle. What did you do?' Henri questioned, watching them with hidden pride of his own. He loved them both, although he never said it and still regretted not having a son to bear his name. He often thought it was a shame Alexandra hadn't been able to give him that, and he thought of it as her only important failure. And she felt that.

'Can I have some gum?' Axelle whispered audibly and Alexandra blushed. It was a treat she sometimes gave the girls when Henri wasn't around, because it was forbidden to them by their father. But Axelle always gave her away. Marie-Louise preferred liquorice and chocolates, but Axelle loved to blow enormous bubbles with great wads of pink goo.

'Certainly not.' Henri frowned at all three of them, reminded Alexandra of the list he had left on her desk, and went into his own study next door, firmly closing the door behind him, and then opening it just a crack, watched with a grin, as his wife handed out sweets and bubble-gum to the girls. He loved watching Axelle with the sticky stuff all over her face, but he felt it was not appropriate for him to admit it. He silently closed the door, and went to his desk with a sigh, as the girls enjoyed their time with their mother.

'Papa's home early.' Marie-Louise observed quietly as she sank gracefully into a Louis-XV *fauteuil* near her mother's desk, munching a piece of liquorice. She had large, dark soulful eyes and a natural elegance about her. She was going to be a beautiful girl in a few years, and already was in many ways. But Axelle was the more striking of the two, and her hair had her mother's natural red colour, although Alexandra used a rinse to dim the red and had worn it blond for years, because Henri preferred it. He thought red hair 'inappropriate', even though in her case it was natural. But she wore it blond, to please her husband.

'He's going out tonight,' Alexandra said matter-of-factly, handing Axelle another piece of bubble-gum, and Marie-Louise a chocolate.

'You too?' Axelle's eyes instantly filled with tears, although she was quick to take the gum from her mother's hand, and Alexandra laughed and shook her head in answer.

'No, I'm not. He's going to a business dinner, and I'm dining with you tonight.'

'Hurray!' Axelle exulted with a mouthful of gum, and Marie-Louise smiled. She loved it when her mother ate with them, particularly when their father was out. They always laughed a lot, and she told them stories about when she was a little girl, and the wonderful tricks Grandma helped her play on her father.

'Does your nanny know you're home?' she asked the girls, but she could see from Axelle's dirty hands and face that they had come to her without the governess's knowledge. The nurse always sent them in immaculately dressed and spotlessly groomed, and she preferred them like this, a little more natural, and totally relaxed in her presence.

'I think we forgot to tell Nanny we were home,' Marie-Louise confessed as Axelle blew an expert balloon with the pink gum, and the three of them laughed together.

'You'd better not let her see that.' Alexandra smiled and set Axelle back on her feet. 'You'd better tell her you're home.' The chauffeur usually brought them home from school in the Citroën, although Alexandra liked to pick them up whenever she could make it. 'I have some things to do now.' She wanted to go over Henri's list, to make sure she didn't forget anything for his dinner party the following week. She already knew who the guests would be. She had invited everyone three weeks before, on their formal *cartons*, and reminders had been sent out, formally engraved and edged in gold, letting their guests know that the Baron and Baroness de Morigny were expecting them at 14 avenue Foch, for a dinner in black tie, at eight o'clock. She already knew what she was going to wear, the flowers had been ordered, the menu set. Everything was in order, she saw, as the girls left the room, and she read carefully down the list. And she knew Henri would produce their best wines for the occasion. Probably a Château Margaux '61, or a Lafite-Rothschild '45. There would be Cristalle champagne, and Château d'Yquem afterwards, and eventually *poire* and a host of other liqueurs as the men smoked their cigars, and the ladies withdrew to another drawing-room reserved for their use while the gentlemen enjoyed their cigars and brandy and allegedly ribald stories. It was a custom few people still used, but Henri liked the old customs, and Alexandra always did things the way Henri liked them. It would never have occurred to her to suggest something different to him. She had always done things his way. Always. And to perfection.

She sat quietly in her study, after the girls left, thinking of her husband and wondering where he was going that night, and then thinking of her daughters. She heard their voices in the garden outside, and knew they were playing with the nurse. They would soon be out of school, and they would be going to Cap Ferrat as they always did for the summer. It was good for the children there, and Henri would join them in a few weeks, after settling things at his office in Paris. They would undoubtedly join friends on their yacht, and perhaps go to Italy or Greece for a few days, leaving the children alone with the nurse and the other servants. It was a golden life, the only one Alexandra had ever known, and yet sometimes, once in a great while, Alexandra allowed herself to wonder what life would have been like if she'd married a different man, someone easier, or perhaps younger. And then feeling guilty for the thought, she would force it from her mind, and realise how fortunate she was to be married to her husband.

When she saw Henri again that night, just before he went out, he looked handsome and impeccable in a beautifully tailored dark blue suit, with a perfectly starched white shirt and dark blue tie, his sapphire cufflinks glinting discreetly at his wrists, and his eyes were bright and alive. He always seemed full of energy, full of some secret reserve and strength that belied his almost sixty years, and made him seem much younger.

'You look very handsome, as usual,' she smiled at him. She had changed into a pink satin dressing-gown with matching mules, and her hair was piled on her head with a cascade of curls loosely falling from it. She looked beautiful, but it was obvious from the look in her eyes that she was totally unaware of it.

'Thank you, my dear. I won't be back late.' His words were banal, but the look in his eyes was gentle and loving. He knew she would wait up for him as she always did, in her own room, with the light on, and if he wished, he could come to see her. In most instances, he would knock softly on the door, and come in for a visit before he went to bed, in his own bedroom next door to hers. He preferred separate bedrooms. He had insisted on them since they were married. She had cried about it for weeks at first, and tried to change his mind on the subject for the first several months, if not years. But Henri was firm with her. He needed his own space, his own privacy, and assured her she would need hers in time as well. And he meant it. It was just a habit he had, like so many others. Eventually, she had grown used to it. They had connecting doors which gave easy access to the rooms, and the door between them didn't keep him from appearing in her room in his dressing-gown, late at night, with a frequency that always pleased her. And he still felt desire when he looked at her, as he did now. But there were other women who appealed to him too. He always tried to be discreet, although he suspected that occasionally she knew, by instinct if nothing else. Women had an uncanny knack for things like that. He had discovered that in his youth, and he had a great respect for it.

'Have a good time.' She kissed him lightly on the cheek, and went down to the smaller dining-room to have dinner with the girls. She heard his car pull away moments afterwards, and turned to help Axelle cut her meat, trying not to think of where he was going.

'Why does Daddy go out alone?' Axelle asked casually with a mouth full of food, and Marie-Louise frowned disapprovingly.

'That's rude to ask,' she chided, but Alexandra smiled.

'It's all right. Sometimes he has business dinners where he prefers to go alone.'

'Are they very dull?' She was interested in everything.

'Sometimes.' Alexandra laughed. 'I'd rather be here with both of you.'

'I'm glad.' Axelle grinned, and announced a loose tooth, as Marie-Louise winced in disgust at her younger sister. She was past all that, and Axelle's offer to wiggle it for them revolted her still further.

'Stop that! You make me sick!' She made a face and Alexandra smiled at them. She was never happier than when she was with her daughters. She spent a little while in Marie-Louise's room that night and discovered she had a new best friend at school, and then read stories to Axelle, and kissed them both, and said their prayers with them before retiring to her own room. It was odd. Sometimes Marie-Louise reminded her of someone else, but she was never sure whom. Henri perhaps . . . maybe that was it . . . and then she forced the thought from her mind, as she slipped off her dressing-gown, took a hot bath, and eventually climbed into bed with a new book.

It was after midnight when Henri finally came home, and she heard him in his room, before he finally came in to say good-night to her. 'Still up?' She nodded with a smile. She liked waiting up for him, sometimes he was more relaxed at night and more likely to open up to her, about his ideas, or plans, or problems.

'Did you have a nice evening?'

'It was all right.' His eyes seemed to search hers, and then he said something unusual for him, something that relieved her mind more than he could ever have imagined. Perhaps he didn't have a new mistress after all, she thought with immense relief. 'I should have taken you along. I was bored without you.' It was unlike him to pay her a compliment like that, and she smiled and patted her bed for him to sit down, and when he did she leaned over and kissed him.

'Thank you, Henri. I missed you too . . .' Her voice was gentle and her smile was the private one that always stirred him. 'I had a nice time with the girls tonight. Marie-Louise is serious and so grown up now, and Axelle is still . . . well, she's still a baby.' She laughed and he smiled. He was proud of them too, even if he didn't show it.

'They're good little girls.' He leaned over and kissed her neck. 'Just like their Maman . . . you're a good girl too, my darling.' They were tender words she loved to hear and they warmed her.

'Am I?' She smiled mischievously at him. 'What a shame . . .' She laughed then, and he lay next to her, touching her breast with one hand, and kissing her with the full measure of his desire. He hadn't intended to make love to her that night, but she looked so lovely, lying in her bed, with the pink and grey sheets, and her pink satin nightgown. And it was so hard for him to tell her how much he cared sometimes. It was easier to show her here, in the dim light of her boudoir. He loved their hours in bed, their nights side by side until he tiptoed quietly to his own room in the morning. He was deeply attached to her, and to the girls, but it was always difficult for him to show that. And he expected so much of her . . . of himself . . . he wanted her to be everything he had always dreamed of in a way, and in some ways that was why he had married her. He could never have married someone less than Alexandra. But the daughter of the Comte de Borne was of a breeding worthy of him, her upbringing suited her perfectly to become his wife, and in the past fourteen years she had proved him right. He was proud of who she was and all he had taught her. She was perfect in every way, and he could never have settled for anything less than Alexandra. He wanted her on a pedestal . . . except for these rare times . . . in his arms . . . in her bed . . . then he could allow her to be someone else, for a few moments at least. And with a contented sigh, and a last look at her afterwards, smiling happily at him, he turned over and fell asleep, totally sated.

Chapter 11

The chauffeur drove the Citroën over the Pont Alexandre III to the Left Bank, and moments later, passing the Invalides, was on the rue de Varenne. It always felt like going home to her. As beautiful as the *hôtel particulier* on the avenue Foch was, as handsomely decorated, after all these years her parents' house on the rue de Varenne still felt like home to Alexandra.

Her heart always seemed to give a happy little leap as she saw the house, and the caretaker opened the gates so they could drive into the court, and then there was still that moment of sadness, that tiny jolt, as she realized that her father would never be there again. After all these years, she still felt his absence sorely. But the prospect of seeing her mother was a comfort and a joy, and it was a homecoming each time she saw her.

Their old butler was standing smiling beside the front door, holding it open wide in welcome. And beyond, Alexandra could see the priceless artefacts her parents had collected. Beautifully inlaid pieces of furniture, Louis-XV chests covered with rich pink marbles and dripping with handsome bronzes. Urns they had bought at auction in London. And Renoirs and Degases and Turners and Van Goghs, and the Cassatts her mother was so fond of. It was a house filled with beautiful things, all of which would one day be hers, which was a prospect she didn't even like to think of, but the only one that consoled Henri for the exasperation of being related to Margaret.

'Darling, are you here?' the familiar voice called from upstairs, from the sitting-room overlooking the garden that she was so fond of. And Alexandra hurried up the marble staircase, feeling like a child again, with a happy smile, anxious to see her mother. She found her sitting on a couch, doing needlepoint with her glasses on the very end of her nose, and a glass of wine on the table next to her, and her Labrador retriever stretched out in front of the fire. Axelle and Marie-Louise loved the dog, who was old and good-natured, but Henri always cringed as she slobbered and licked and kissed and left her hair all over everyone who touched her. 'Darling!' Margaret dropped her needlepoint and stood to her full six foot, a pretty woman with blond hair and green eyes not unlike Alexandra's, in a bright pink Chanel suit with a navy-blue blouse and matching shoes, and ruby earrings the size of doorknobs. 'My God, who died?' She backed off suddenly after kissing Alexandra.

She looked at her daughter with a frown, and Alexandra grinned at her. Her mother always wore bright, striking clothes from wonderful designers – Chanel and Givenchy and Dior and de Ribes – and almost always in brilliant colours. They suited her too, but Henri preferred her in black and navy-blue and beige, and in the country in grey flannel. She had come to her mother's home in a new black dress from Dior, with a matching jacket. 'Now stop that. This is new, and Henri loves it.' Unlike her exchanges with her husband and her children, Alexandra always spoke to her mother in English, and although she spoke it well, she had a noticeable French accent.

'It looks awful. You should burn it.' Margaret de Borne sat down on her couch again, indicated to the butler to pour Alexandra a glass of wine, and went back to her needlepoint as she smiled happily at her daughter. She always loved her visits, and their private exchanges. She enjoyed going out with her too, but this was always a little more special. They both went out more than they needed to, so they didn't need each other as an excuse to go to the latest fashionable places. Instead, they preferred to eat a simple lunch of salad and cheese and fruit on trays in Margaret's sitting-room overlooking her garden. She glanced at her daughter again and shook her head in obvious dismay. 'I wish you'd stop doing your hair that colour. sweetheart. You look like one of those fading blondes from California. If I had hair your colour, I would flaunt it. I'd make it even more red!' She shook her glasses at her for emphasis before setting them down to sip her wine. She had always loved the red of Alexandra's hair before she began to rinse it blond. It seemed such a waste of one of nature's great gifts. Her own hair had to be helped considerably now twice a month at Alexandre's.

'You know Henri hates it red. It's too loud. He thinks it looks more ladylike this way.'

'Henri . . . the poor man is so afraid to be a little out of the ordinary. I'm surprised he doesn't make you wear a black wig and cover the whole thing. Seriously, darling, God gave you red hair, and you ought to enjoy it.'

'I don't mind it like this.' She smiled easily and sipped her wine. She was used to her mother's complaints about her husband. His were far worse about Margaret. And Alexandra had lived with it for fourteen years. She was only sorry they had never come to like each other, but she had given up long since. It was obvious they were never going to fall in love with each other.

'You're too good-natured. How do you like these, by the way?' She smiled happily, pointing at the new ruby earrings she was wearing. She could afford to indulge herself, partially thanks to Pierre's generosity when he died, and partially thanks to her own handsome fortune. 'I just got them.'

'I thought so.' Alexandra laughed. Her mother was always buying beautiful clothes and fabulous baubles. It was good for her, she looked well in what she bought and it made her happy, despite what Henri said about a woman spending 'that kind of money'. 'They're very pretty, and they suit you to perfection.'

'Van Cleef.' Margaret looked pleased with herself. 'And a terrific bargain.'

But at that, Alexandra laughed heartily as she set down her wineglass. 'I can just imagine.'

'No, really! They were under a hundred thousand.'

'Dollars or francs?'

'Are you kidding? Dollars of course.' Margaret grinned without a trace of guilt as Alexandra laughed at her.

'I thought so.' Alexandra smiled. It was not exactly the kind of bargain Henri would have approved of. And after thirty years in France, her mother still spoke more English than French, and calculated everything in dollars. 'What else have you been up to?'

'The usual. I had lunch with Mimi de Saint Bré yesterday.' She was another American woman who had married a titled Frenchman, and like Margaret, she had a good mind and a wild sense of humour. 'We're going to New York together next week.'

'What for?'

'Just to get our hair done and do some shopping. I haven't been in months and thought it might be fun before the summer. After that, I'm meeting friends in Rome, and I thought I might go to San Remo for a few weeks. I haven't made up my mind yet.'

'Why don't you stay with us for a few weeks afterwards?' Alexandra looked delighted at the prospect, but her mother looked cautious.

'I don't want to make your husband nervous.'

'Just don't bring the girls whoopee cushions and those hand buzzers and everything will be fine.' They both laughed at the memory. Henri had almost fainted when he sat down in the living-room with guests, and landed on one of the whoopee cushions Margaret and the children had planted.

'Do you remember how awful that was?' Margaret could hardly stop laughing at the memory, and there were tears in Alexandra's eyes when she stopped laughing. It had been awful for Henri, but in truth it was desperately funny, and they had all been banished to their rooms afterwards, including Margaret, who had taught Marie-Louise how to make apple-pie beds, which had complicated matters even further. There was no doubt in anyone's mind that she was not Henri's favourite house-guest. 'Actually, I thought I'd see what I could find for them in New York . . . nothing quite so outrageous of course . . .' But her eyes twinkled wickedly at the prospect. She used to buy silly jokes like that for her late husband, and he had always loved them. For him, being married to Margaret was like having another child. Alexandra had always been a bit more serious than that, even as a little girl, and especially after she got married.

'I'll tell Henri you're coming.'

Margaret grinned. 'Wait until you really want to annoy him.'

'Mother!' Alexandra laughed. Her mother had very few illusions. 'You make him sound so awful and he isn't!' She always defended her husband, and to Henri, she defended her mother. She was loyal to both.

'He is not awful, darling.' Margaret grinned. 'Just stuffy.'

The afternoon seemed to fly by, as it always did when they were together, and at four-thirty Alexandra looked at her watch and stretched regretfully. She was so comfortable in the cosy room, looking out at the garden, and in her mother's company. They always had such a good time together. Margaret was still her closest friend, and always had been.

'I should go . . . much as I hate to . . .' Alexandra stood up with obvious regret as Margaret watched her.

'Why? Are you giving a party tonight?'

'No, that's next week. Tonight we're dining at the Elysée, and Henri will get nervous if I don't come home early and start getting ready.'

'You ought to do something wonderful to surprise him, like wear a skintight dress covered with rhinestones, and tease your hair straight up. It would do them good at the Elysée.' She chuckled at the thought and Alexandra smiled. Her mother probably would have done something just like that, and Henri would have called his attorneys in the morning. With him, that was always the implication. Step out of line and . . . Alexandra never tested his mettle in that direction. She loved him too much to risk everything for pranks like her mother's. And besides, she wasn't like that.

'You're a lot braver than I am, Maman.'

'That's only because I'm not married to your husband. I can do exactly what I want now. And before, your father always let me get away with anything I wanted. I was very lucky.' She smiled gently at her daughter.

'Papa was lucky too. And he knew it,' Alexandra reminded her and the two women embraced and walked slowly downstairs, as the butler waited to let her out with his usual warm smile. He had been with them since she was a little girl, and he called her 'Madame Alexandra' as he helped her into her car and closed the door firmly. She waved at her mother as the driver took her home in the Citroën, and she felt the same sadness she always did when she left her mother. Life had been so simple on the rue de Varenne, living with her parents ... before ... but that wasn't fair either. She loved Henri, and of course, the children. They were the life-force of her existence. But seeing her mother always made her long for a life that was simpler, and a time when she didn't have quite so much to live up to.

She was still thinking of it as she slipped out of her dress and ran her bath, and took out a serious, well-covered black evening gown for their dinner that night at the Elysée Palace.

The girls came in to say hello to her while she was in the tub, and she heard Henri go into his study while she was getting dressed, but he didn't come in to speak to her and she didn't see him until they met in the front hall, ready to go out for the evening. Her dress had long sleeves and a high neck, and a long slender skirt with beautiful gold embroidery on it. It was exquisitely made and from an old collection of Saint-Laurent. She wore it with a short sable jacket and a pair of outstanding diamond earrings given to her by her father.

'You look lovely tonight.' His eyes were admiring, his voice restrained, and his manner impeccably formal.

'Thank you.' She turned to him with her blond good looks, her hair swept into a smooth French twist, exactly as it had been worn years before by Grace Kelly. It was a good look for Alexandra, and one that Henri approved of. 'Did you have a good day?' Her eyes looked lonely, and she suddenly wished he would kiss her, but he didn't.

'Very pleasant, thank you,' he answered. There were times when they were like two strangers, and the intimacies of the night before seemed all but forgotten in the formality of the moment. He helped her into the car, and the driver pulled away, with both of them lost in thought in separate worlds in the back seat, and two little girls in nightgowns watching from the upstairs window.

Chapter 12

The day after Hilary saw Arthur Patterson, when he had told her he didn't know how to find her sisters, Hilary felt as though the world had come to an end. She was seventeen years old and she felt as though her life was over. For years she had lived only to find Megan and Axie. And now there was no hope. They were gone forever.

She began her first job the next day with an aching void in her chest, but her face was calm, her eyes cool, and no one would have known the agony of despair she was feeling. The only thing that kept her going was her determination to survive in spite of everything, and her hatred for Arthur.

She felt like a machine as she moved through the days and nights, but she performed her job well. She improved her typing, studied shorthand from a book, and went to college at night, just as she had promised herself she would years before. She did everything she had said she would, but through it all there was not so much a sense of accomplishment but of heartless determination. She was going to succeed at all costs, but even she didn't know why she wanted to make it. There was no one to prove anything to. No one who cared. No one to love or who loved her.

She only kept the job for a year, and then she got a better one. She heard about it before anyone else, at the employment agency where she worked, and she went to the interview before anyone else even knew about it. It was as a receptionist at CBA-News. It was a fabulous job that paid almost twice what her current job did, and she had to be quick, smart, and good, and she was all three. The woman who interviewed her was very impressed with her. She got the job, and managed to stay on in school. And she got steady raises from then on. She eventually became a secretary, and then a production assistant, and within five years a producer. She was incredibly bright, and by then she had graduated from college. She was twenty-three years old and she was well on her way to a real career. She was respected by her superiors, and feared by some of her employees, most in fact, and she seemed to have few friends at work. She kept aloof and worked hard, staying late most of the time, and turning in projects deserving the praise she won. She was a remarkable girl, and when she became one of the main producers of the evening news at twenty-five, Adam Kane, the man in charge of network news, invited her out to celebrate. She hesitated and then decided it would be politically unwise to refuse him. She accepted gracefully and found herself dining at the Brussels with him, drinking champagne and talking shop, discussing how important the network was and where she hoped to go eventually. He was surprised to hear that she had long-range goals, particularly since they were more ambitious than his own plans for the future.

'Hey, hold on there . . . what is this? – staff meeting for Women's Lib?' He was an attractive man with brown hair and gentle brown eyes, and a philosophical way of looking at life. 'Why such big plans?' She was the first woman he'd ever known who had admitted her ambitions to him, and he admitted to her that he found it frightening. He and his wife had just got divorced because she didn't think she wanted to be a 'wife anymore', and it had shaken him to the core. They had two little boys and a house in Darien, and now suddenly he was living alone on the West Side, and women were talking to him about 'goals within corporate management'. He laughed softly as he looked at her. She was so beautiful and so young and so intense and yet there was something missing. 'What's happened to women who want to have babies and live in the suburbs? Is that totally out of fashion?'

She smiled at him, aware that she might have over-stated her case, but she so seldom went out with men. She forgot that one had to be quiet about things, and this one was nice. She liked working for him. 'I guess that's out for some of us.' She didn't apologize for it. She knew where she wanted to go, and nothing would stop her until she got there. She was still running from the demons of the past sixteen years and knew she probably would forever. She accepted that now, though she didn't explain it to him. She never told anyone anything. She lived alone, and she went to work, and other than that, she had no interest in anything. He sensed that now, and it frightened him, for her. He knew how much more there was to life. He was thirty-eight years old and he had married at twenty-three. And now he was discovering endless new horizons.

'Don't you want a husband and kids one day?'

She shook her head. He looked as though she could be honest with him. 'That's not very important to me.' More than that, she didn't want anyone she could lose . . . least of all two little girls . . . two little children someone could take away from her . . . She knew she would never let that happen to her. She wanted to be alone, and she was, and it only hurt occasionally, like now, as she looked at this man

184

and wondered what it woud be like to be close to him. Or was it only the champagne, she wondered.

'My children are the best thing in my life, Hilary. Don't cheat yourself of that.' She couldn't tell him that in a way, she had already had kids. She never told anyone that, and knew she never would. Ever.

'Why does everyone think you have to have kids to be complete?'

'These days they don't. Most women think like you, but they're wrong. Hilary, the women who don't have children now are going to panic in ten or fifteen years, mark my words, we're going to see a whole generation of women fighting their own biology before it's too late. But now they're all cool, they figure they've got years ahead of them. But it's a mistake to rule it out. You've never been married?' He looked into her eyes and he liked what he saw there, courage and honesty and integrity and intelligence. But he saw fear too. She was running from something and he couldn't figure out what it was that had hurt her. Maybe, maybe she'd had a bad experience with someone . . . not unlike his with Barb. He still couldn't believe she had left him and taken his children.

Hilary shook her head in answer to his question. 'No, I've never been married.' And then she laughed. 'I'm only twenty-five. What's the big rush?'

'These days none at all. I was just curious. I was twenty-three when I got married. My wife was twenty-one. It was real important to us. But that was fifteen years ago, things have changed a hell of a lot since then. This is 1974. We got married in '59.' And then he smiled at her over the last of their champagne. 'What were you doing then? You were probably just a kid.'

Her eyes clouded over then, thinking back. 1959 . . . she'd been in Boston then, with Eileen and Jack . . . or were they in Jacksonville by then? ... the thought of it almost made her feel ill. Axie and Megan were already gone. 'Oh, nothing much. I was living with an aunt in Boston around then.' She tried to make it sound ordinary, almost fun.

'Where were your folks?'

'They died when I was eight ... and nine ...'

'Separately?' She nodded, anxious to change the subject back to work again. She didn't want to talk to him about this. Not to him or anyone. 'How terrible. In accidents?' She nodded non-committally and finished her champagne at one gulp. 'Were you an only child?'

She looked him in the eye then with something cold and hard he didn't understand and nodded at him. 'Yes, I was.'

'It doesn't sound like much fun.' He felt sorry for her and she hated that too. She didn't want pity from him or from anyone. She tried to smile at him to lighten the mood, but he was looking so intensely at her, it made her nervous.

'Maybe that's why I love my work so much. It's home to me.' That seemed pathetic to him, but he didn't say so.

'Where'd you go to school?'

'NYU.' But she didn't tell him she'd gone at night, while she was working.

He nodded. 'Barb and I went to UC Berkeley.'

'That must have been fun.' She smiled and he reached out to her, not anxious to talk about his ex-wife anymore, but only about her.

'I'm glad we went out to dinner tonight. I've been wanting to talk to you for a long time. You do a hell of a job at the network.'

'I should.' She grinned, 'I've been around CBA for long enough. Years.' Six years of pushing and shoving her way up, until she was a producer. She had a right to be proud of herself and she was. It was a long, long way from the Jacksonville juvenile home, or the foster homes she'd been in, or even her life with Jack and Eileen in Boston.

'Do you think you'll stay?' he asked, and she stared at him.

'At CBA? Why would I go anywhere?'

'Because in this business people move around a lot.' He certainly had, and he wasn't unusual in their field.

She shook her head at him, with a look of determination in her eyes that startled him. 'I'm not going anywhere, my friend. I've got my eye on an office wayyyy upstairs.' And he sensed that she meant it more than she had meant anything else she'd said that night.

'Why?' That kind of ambition puzzled him. He was successful, and he liked his job, but he had never aspired to great heights, and he couldn't imagine wanting that, particularly not if you were a beautiful young girl.

'Because it's important to me.' She was being honest with him. 'It means security. And accomplishment. And it's something tangible I can take home with me at night.'

But he knew better than that. 'Until they fire you and hire someone else. Don't hang everything on your job, Hilary. You'll end up alone one day, and disappointed.'

'That doesn't frighten me.' She'd been alone all her life. She was used to it. In fact, she liked it that way, no one could hurt her or let her down, or betray her that way.

She was an odd girl, he thought, and he had never known anyone as independent as she was. He took her home that night, and hoped she would invite him upstairs but she only shook his hand with a warm smile and thanked him for the evening. And he went home so horny for her that as soon as he got upstairs, he called her. He didn't even care if he woke her up, and he doubted that she was asleep yet.

Her voice was husky when she picked up the phone, and he closed his eyes, listening to her. He was a nice guy, and he hated living alone. And she was so damn beautiful . . . he knew his boys would love her too . . . 'Hello?'

'Hi, Hilary . . . I just wanted to tell you what a nice time I had tonight.'

She laughed softly at him, and he liked the sound of that too. 'So did I. But don't you try to distract me at work, Mr Kane. I'm not planning to lose my job over anyone. Not even you.'

'I got that. Want to have lunch sometime this week?'

'Sure. If I'm not too swamped.'

'Tomorrow sound okay?'

She laughed again, a delicious mixture of hot smoke and icy cool. 'Why don't you relax, Adam. I told you, I'm not going anywhere.'

'Good. Then let's take advantage of it. I'll pick you up in your office at twelve-fifteen. Okay?' He sounded like a little kid, and she was smiling in the dark, lying in bed, and much as she hated to admit it, even to herself, he did something to her no other man had till then. And she trusted him. Maybe it was all right . . . just for a lunch or two . . . what harm could that do? She hadn't allowed herself anything more since coming to New York, and oddly enough she had never wanted anyone. Other people had boyfriends, and affairs, and broken hearts. And all Hilary wanted were promotions and raises and work. That was her lover, and so far it had treated her very well. 'Twelve-fifteen?' he repeated in the face of silence from her.

'Fine.' Her voice flowed over the single word, and he felt as though he were floating when he hung up.

There was a single rose on her desk the next day, and they had lunch at the Veau d'Or and she didn't get back to her office till three o'clock.

'This is terrible, Adam. I never do things like this.' She threw the long black hair over her shoulder, and rolled up the sleeves of her shirt. It was a beautiful warm day and she didn't even feel like going back to work. 'You're a miserable influence. I just got a promotion and now you're going to get me canned.'

'Good, then will you marry me? We can move to New Jersey and have ten kids.'

'How depressing.' She looked at him with her icy green eyes, and he felt something he never had before. She became a challenge. There was a wall around her he would have done anything to climb, but he still wasn't sure how far she'd let him go. They were still circling each other carefully, but he had so much to say to her and she was such intelligent company. And he appealed to her in a way no one had before. It was a dangerous combination, and at times it frightened her, particularly when he distracted her from her work, but after all he was her boss.

He invited her to dinner on Saturday, but she declined, and she turned down his next two invitations to lunch, but he looked so unhappy about it when he stopped to talk to her that she finally relented and agreed to go out with him the following Friday night. They went to P. J. Clarke's, for a hamburger, and then a walk up Third Avenue to her new apartment on Fifty-ninth Street.

'Why do you keep such a distance between us?' He looked sincerely unhappy about it. He was crazy about her, and he was dying for her to let him get closer.

'I'm not sure it's such a good idea. It could make things awfully complicated at work. You're my boss. Adam.'

She smiled up at him, and, as attracted to him as she was, she was afraid of repercussions at the office.

And then he smiled at her regretfully. 'Not for much longer, I'm afraid, if that makes any difference to you. I'm being transferred to sales in two weeks. I just heard about it today.'

'How do you feel about that?' She was concerned for him. It was kind of a sidestep, and in his shoes she'd have been crushed, but he didn't look too disturbed as he shrugged and smiled at her.

'No big deal. I might like it better than where I am . . . except for you, of course. Will you see me more often then?' It would certainly make things easier for her, but she still wasn't sure if she should get involved with him. Life was so much easier living as a celibate.

Celibacy had become a way of life to her, and giving it up meant risking a part of herself. 'Hilary?' He was looking down at her as they walked, and he gently took her hand. He seemed very young as he smiled at her, and in some ways he still was. 'I want to be with you . . . you mean a lot to me . . .'

'Adam, you don't even know who I am . . . I could be anyone . . . *La femme aux yeux verts* . . .' The words slipped out and she laughed.

'What does that mean?'

'It's French.' She had revived her French in college, and was surprised to find it was still there, dormant but not dead, a final gift from her mother. 'It means the woman with green eyes.'

'How come you speak French?' He wanted to know everything about her, and there was so little she wanted to tell him.

'I spoke it a long time ago . . . when I was a little girl. And I picked it up again in college.'

'Did your parents speak French?' She could have told him then, could have begun to open up, could have said something about Solange, but she decided it was safer not to.

'No, I just learned it at school, I guess.' He nodded, satisfied with the answer she'd given him, and when they reached her apartment, after a moment's hesitation, she invited him upstairs. They listened to Roberta Flack on her stereo, and talked for hours over a bottle of wine, and he stood up regretfully around one o'clock and looked down at her with a wistful smile.

'I'd like to spend the night with you, Hilary, but I get the feeling you're not ready for that ... are you?' She shook her head, not sure she would ever be. People had tried to get close to her but she was not even remotely tempted. 'Are you involved with anyone?' He had meant to ask before but he had put it off. She shook her head in answer, looking at him strangely.

'No, I'm not ... I haven't been in ... a long time ...'

'For any particular reason?'

'A lot of them. Most of them too complicated to explain.' He sat on her couch and looked at her quietly.

'Why don't you try me?'

She shrugged again. She didn't want to tell him what she'd been through. That was nobody's business. She led a different life now, in another place, another world. She didn't want to drag those things with her, and yet she did, in spite of all her efforts to deny them. 'I'm sorry, Adam ... I can't ...'

'Why not?' He reached out and took her hands in his. 'Don't you trust me?'

'It's not that.' She felt her eyes fill with tears and she hated herself for it. 'I don't want to talk about it ... really ...' She stood up and walked away, her proud shoulders straightened against the world and all it had done to her. And without knowing it, she looked exactly like her mother.

'Hilary . . .' He walked up to her from behind and put his arms around her. 'Why don't you let yourself go? I know how strong you are, I've seen it at work, but this is different . . . this is us . . . this isn't a war zone.'

Her voice was tired as she spoke to him with her head bowed. 'Life is a war zone, Adam.'

'It doesn't have to be.' He was so gentle, and so innocent. She envied him his simple life. The most difficult thing that had ever happened to him was his wife's deciding she wanted to be free and no longer married. But he knew nothing of the agonies Hilary had endured. He couldn't even begin to understand them. 'Life can be so sweet . . . if you let it . . .'

'It's not as easy as that.' She sighed and looked at him. 'I don't think you understand the kind of life I've led, and I don't think I could explain it.'

'Then why not go from here? Isn't that possible, and leave the past behind you?'

'Maybe.' She wasn't sure it could be done, but she was willing to try it. He reached out and kissed her gently at first, and then suddenly with more passion. He had wanted her for weeks, months, since the first time he'd seen her, and now he couldn't hold back. He peeled her clothes from her and dropped his own, and carried her to her bed, where he began making love to her. But she lay distant and cold, and secretly frightened. Some of the things he did to her were the same things that Maida and Georgine had done . . . and some of the things reminded her of the boys who raped her the day after Maida and Georgine left. It was too much to overcome, even with a good man like Adam. And it didn't take him long to realize that she didn't want to go on. He pulled away, still throbbing with desire for her and unable to understand what had happened.

'What's wrong? . . .' His voice was hoarse, his eyes bleary with unspent passion. 'I want you so much.'

'I'm sorry . . .' She whispered the words, and turned over on her side, staring at the far wall, wondering if she would ever be normal. Perhaps she would never overcome the past. She was twenty-five years old, and she was beginning to suspect that. There were too many people left that she hated . . . Arthur Patterson . . . Jack Jones . . . the boys who had raped her . . . Maida and Georgine . . . Eileen . . . the people at juvenile hall . . . and in the far distance, even her father. It was too big a burden to carry around and still allow her to function as a woman. 'It's not you,' she tried to explain. 'I just can't.'

'Why? You have to tell me.' He was trying to sit calmly at the edge of the bed, trying to reach out and understand her. And she sat up quietly and turned around. Maybe it was better to shock him than to hurt him.

'I was raped a long time ago . . .' She didn't want to say more, and hoped that would be enough, but of course it wasn't.

'How? . . . by whom?'

'It's a long story.' And which one should she tell him? Maida and Georgine, who were the first, or the boys who had come later? Or Jack who had done his best to precede them all and then had beaten her to within an inch of her life when he didn't get what he wanted. They were all possible candidates for the role, but she couldn't even imagine Adam able to withstand any truth she might tell him.

'When was it?'

'When I was thirteen . . .' That much was true at least.

They had all happened before her fourteenth birthday. She took a gulp of air. 'And there hasn't been anyone since then. I guess I should have told you.'

'Christ.' He looked deeply shaken by what she'd said. 'It certainly would have helped. How was I supposed to know something like that?'

'I didn't think it would matter.'

'Oh really? You were raped twelve years ago, haven't had relations with anyone since, and you actually thought it wouldn't make a difference? How can you do that to yourself, and to me, for chrissake? What about counselling? Have you had a lot of that since then?' He assumed she had, of course, everyone he knew was in therapy. He'd gone right back to his own shrink as soon as his wife left him.

'No.' She spoke very calmly, and got up to put on a bathrobe. She had a long, languid body and beautiful graceful legs that made him ache with wanting her again, but he tried to force himself not to think about it.

'What do you mean "no"? You got help after the rape, no? Yes? Right?'

She smiled at him. Hardly. 'No. Wrong. I guess I didn't need it.'

'Are you crazy?'

'All right, let's say it wasn't available to me at the time.'

'Where were you? The North Pole? Where is there in the modern world that therapy isn't available?' Oh God, he understood nothing of what her life had been like. Therapy? Where? In Louise's home, or at juvie?

'I told you, Adam.' She was getting annoyed, but he was getting frantic. 'I don't want to discuss it. It's too complicated.'

'Too complicated or too painful?' She averted her eyes, so he couldn't see the pain he had already inflicted.

'Why don't we just forget it?'

'What, the relationship? Why? You're not a quitter, Hilary.' Now he was sincerely angry. She would have done anything for her job, but not for him, or the relationship they might have, if she was willing.

'Why don't we just forget the problem, Adam. It'll go away by itself eventually.'

'Really? How long's it been now? Twelve years, you said, and I wouldn't exactly say you're cured. How long would you like to wait for it to "go away"? Thirty years maybe? Or how about fifty? You ought to feel a lot better by then, and Christ you'd only be sixty-three, you could have a great sex life, Hilary, *be serious!*' He took her by the hand and pulled her down on the bed beside him, but he wanted too much from her, and Hilary already knew she couldn't give it to him. He wanted everything, heart and soul, commitment and marriage and children. She could sense that in him, he wanted everything his wife had taken back and more. And she knew for a certainty that she didn't have it in her. She had nothing left to give him. All she could do was take, or maybe extend herself for a little while, if no one asked too much, but the rest was gone. All her love had been given too long ago, and all her energies were reserved for where she was going at the network. 'I want you to go into therapy.' He sat staring at her, as though announcing he wanted her to have brain surgery, and she had no intention of obliging him. God only knew what they'd find there.

'I can't.'

'That's bullshit. Why not?'

'I don't have the time.'

'You're twenty-five years old and you have a problem.'

'It's not one I can't live with.'

'You're not living, you're existing.' But slowly, she was

195

getting angry too. He had no right to make judgments on how she was living, just because she didn't want to make love with him.

'Maybe it'll get better.' But she didn't sound as though she really cared and that disturbed him.

'By itself?' She nodded. 'I doubt it.'

'Give it time, Adam. This is only the first time.'

He sat silently for a long time, watching her. He saw more than she wanted. 'There's a lot you're not telling me, isn't there?'

She smiled, sphinxlike. 'It's not that important, Adam.'

'I don't believe you. I think you live your whole life behind a walled fortress.'

'I used to . . . a long time ago . . .'

'Why?'

'Because there used to be a lot of people out to hurt me.'

'And now?'

'I don't let them.'

He looked sorry for her, and leaned down to kiss her with a gentle hand on her shoulder, as they sat on the edge of her unmade bed, where their passion had been so unsuccessful. 'I won't hurt you, Hil . . . I swear . . .' There were tears in his eyes, and she wished she could feel something for him, but she couldn't. She couldn't feel anything for anyone, and she knew that now, except perhaps if he awoke some unborn passion in her, but she couldn't imagine that either. 'I love you . . .'

She had no answer to those words, and only looked at him sadly. And then he smiled at her and kissed her again. He understood, and that touched her. 'It's okay . . . you don't have to say anything . . . just let me love you . . .' He lay her back against the pillows, and gently sculpted her body with one finger, drawing it close to her centre, and then, moving it away, drifting around her breasts and all the way down her belly, and then up again, touching her with his tongue and his heart and his fingers, but with nothing else, and after hours of it, she was writhing and begging him for something more, but he wouldn't do it. Instead, he let her feel him, and touched her gently with his throbbing organ. He ran it over her like a satin hand, and she bent down and began to kiss it, and touch him gently until he was writhing as she was, and then first with his lips, and then with his fingers he touched her, and felt her grow frightened and rigid.

'It's all right, Hil . . . it's all right . . . I won't hurt you . . . I . . . please, baby . . . please let me . . . please . . . Oh God, you're so beautiful . . .' He crooned to her like a mother with a baby and slowly he entered her and soothed her until he came, but he knew that she had not joined him. But at least it was a little better. 'I'm sorry, Hil . . .' He wanted more for her, he wanted everything that he felt, but it was too much to ask for.

'Don't be. It was lovely.' She lay quietly beside him, and eventually he slept and she watched him, wondering if she would ever feel for him what he wanted, if she could ever feel it for anyone, or if her body was too filled with hatred.

He left the next morning before she dressed for work, and asked her to lunch later that morning, but she said that she was too busy. He wanted to see her that night, but she had a meeting. And in desperation he asked her to join him on Sunday with his boys. They were spending the weekend with him. She looked strangely hesitant over that, as though she were about to say no, but he looked so hurt that she accepted.

'They're great kids, you'll love them.'

'I'm sure I will.' She smiled. But she was filled with

trepidation. She had avoided children for years, and she was not anxious to get to know his, or grow too attached to them. She had had her fill of children long since. The only two she had ever loved had been taken from her.

They arranged a meeting place in Central Park, and on Sunday morning she wore jeans, and a T-shirt, and went out to meet him. He had promised to bring the baseballs and the picnic and the children. And as she spotted them beneath a tree, the littlest one on his lap, and the six-year-old sitting beside him, she felt something stir in her heart that was so long gone she almost couldn't bear it. She stopped in her tracks and wanted to run, but she couldn't do that to him. But as she approached it only grew worse. What she saw in his eyes was the kind of love she had had for Megan and Axie.

She never made it to lunch. She watched them throw baseballs for half an hour, and then she pleaded a terrible headache. She ran from the park in tears, and went all the way back to her apartment without stopping for a light or a car or a person.

She lay in bed all day and sobbed, and then forced herself to realize again that Megan and Alexandra were gone from her life forever. She had to make herself remember that. There was no point hanging on to them. No one knew where they were anyway and it would have been close to impossible to find them. There was no point torturing herself now. And they were no longer children, they were women. Aiexandra would have been twenty-two by then, and Megan would be eighteen. But there was no point thinking about them anymore. They were no longer lost children, and she was never going to see them again. But she didn't want to see any other children either. She couldn't bear it.

And when the phone began ringing that evening, she

quietly took it off the hook and left it there. The next day she acted as though nothing had happened. She was pleasant and businesslike and friendly, and distant and Adam never knew what had hit him. As planned, he was transferred on to sales the following week, and he never went out with Hilary again. She saw to it that they never even ran into each other. And she never took his calls. It was as though none of it had ever happened. And what she didn't know was that he felt sorry for her. But he finally realized that he couldn't help her.

For the next several years Hilary concentrated even harder on her career. She had risen to a higher production position by then and was twenty-seven years old, and she had carefully kept away from all liaisons since her brush with Adam. She was too busy working her way up to want anything else in her life, and all of the men she met seemed to be divorced and have children. Until she met William Brock, CBA's newest anchor. Tall, blond, and handsome, he had been a major football star and had been recently hired by the network. Twice divorced, he had no children, and no desire to have them. He dated his way around the station with gusto, until he got to Hilary, and her ice-like green eyes fascinated him. He treated her with caution and respect, and sent her everything from flowers to a fur coat.

'That was cute, Bill.' She dropped it on his desk, box and all, on her way to her office one morning.

'Not your size, darling?'

'Not my style, Mr Brock. In every possible way.' She was not given to romances at the office, or anywhere else for that matter, and becoming a notch on Bill Brock's belt was the last thing she wanted. He invited her to Honolulu for a week, Jamaica for a weekend, skiing in Vermont, dinner at the Côte Basque, and anything else he could think of. But he didn't stand a chance, until one stormy night, when she couldn't get a cab home and he gave her a lift in his Ferrari. He started heading downtown from the network, and Hilary tapped him on the shoulder. 'Nice try, Bill. I live on Fifty-ninth Street.'

'I live on Fifth Avenue and Eleventh.'

'Congratulations, now take me home, or do I have to get out and walk?' She wasn't kidding and he skidded to a stop, but before she could say anything further, he kissed her.

'Your place or mine, Madam Producer, or shall we do something really crazy and go to the Plaza?' She laughed at his outrageous spirit, and demanded that he take her home, but she was no longer surprised when he stopped on the way, to take her to dinner. They stopped for a hamburger at one of his favourite hangouts, and she was surprised at how intelligent he was, beneath the playboy veneer, and the overdeveloped male body. 'And you, pretty lady? What makes you tick behind those green eyes that look like emeralds?'

'Ambition.' He was the first person she had been that honest with, but for some reason she thought he'd understand that.

'I've had a taste of that myself. It's addictive once you get started.'

'I know it.' But it was all she had to keep her going . . . getting to the top so that nothing could ever get to her again. She wouldn't feel safe till she got there. But that she didn't explain to him. 'There's nothing like it, is there? Were you sorry to give up football, Bill?'

'Sort of. It's a great game, but I got tired of having my knees kicked around and my nose broken. You can't take that kind of abuse forever.' He smiled at her in just the way that melted most women's hearts, paid the bill, and escorted her back to his Ferrari. He dropped her off at her place without a fight, and she was almost sorry as she let herself into her apartment. Somehow, she had expected a little more than that, an attempt at least, something. She was already undressed and in her nightgown, half an hour later, when the bell rang.

'Who is it?' she asked on the intercom.

'Bill. I forgot to ask you something about the show tomorrow.' She frowned and then grinned. He sounded sincere but it was probably a ploy. She decided to keep it that way, and let him stand in the snow while he talked to her.

'What is it?'

'What?'

'I said what is it?'

'I can't hear you!' He started to buzz frantically and she tried to outshout him on the intercom and then finally gave up, and buzzed him in. If it was a ruse, she would put him in his place, and quickly. She was waiting in the doorway when he came up, red-faced, smiling, and covered with the snow that was still falling. 'Something's wrong with your intercom.' He was out of breath and devastatingly handsome.

'Oh, really? Nice of you to come by. Ever heard of the telephone, Mr Brock?'

'No, ma'am, I haven't.' Without further ado, he swept her off her feet, picked her up like a rag doll, walked into her apartment and kicked the door closed behind him. She was laughing at him as he did it. It was such an incongruous scene, and there was something boyish and wonderful about him, but not so wonderful that she wanted to get involved with him, no matter how handsome he was, or how attractive. 'Where's your bedroom, Miss Walker?' He was all innocence as she laughed at him. He was like a schoolboy playing a prank on her. But he was also extremely sexy.

'In there. Why?'

'You'll see in a minute.' He deposited her on the bed, walked into the bathroom as she stared at him, and emerged five seconds later, stark naked. She was so stunned that she stood staring at him. He was the most outrageous man she had ever known, but also the most appealing. And without further ado, he began making love to her, and despite her initial resistance, his expertise melted whatever reserve she had, and she was soon moaning for him and within a very short time, he obliged her. He lay breathless in her arms, and then rolled over and smiled as she stared at him in amazement. It had aroused feelings in her she had never known existed, and before she could say anything, he began making love to her again, and she thought she would go mad as he made love to her again and again and again until morning. It was an experience she had never had before and was sure she would never have again, but it convinced her that not everything inside her was entirely dead, and maybe one day the right man might come along and find it. But in the meantime, Bill Brock had done something to her she would never forget. And when he left the next morning, she stared out the window at him wistfully as he drove off in his red Ferrari.

She knew then she would remember him for the rest of her life, but she didn't expect anything more from him. He was not looking for a relationship, or a girlfriend, or a mistress or a wife, or even a friendship. Life to him was one constant stream of pretty girls, and making love was something he did like eating and sleeping and drinking. He didn't really care who he did it with, or how often, or if he ever did it again with the same one. He just wanted to be able to do it, when and where and with whom he wanted.

When he sent Hilary a huge bouquet of roses the next day, and a diamond bracelet from Harry Winston, she gave the bracelet back, with a smile, and he didn't seem surprised. But he also didn't ask her out again. He had other fish to fry, and she was just one of a universe full of pretty women. She was disappointed but not surprised. The only surprise she got was when she went to the doctor two months later. She had had the flu for weeks, and instead of better, she was getting worse. And she was totally exhausted. All she wanted to do was sleep, the thought of food made her sick, she couldn't even stand the smell of coffee when she went into the office in the morning. So finally, after six weeks of it, she called her doctor and made an appointment. He suggested a series of blood tests, a thorough examination, and after the blood tests, he was thinking of putting her on antibiotics.

'It could be some kind of stomach virus, Miss Walker. Have you been anywhere exotic recently?'

She shook her head, depressed to be feeling so poorly. She felt two hundred years old and all she wanted to do was put her head down and sleep all day long. It was depressing to feel that lousy. But two days later she knew why. The test results came back, and the doctor did not suggest antibiotics. She was pregnant. He had done a routine pregnancy test, and a VDRL too, checking her for syphilis. When she heard the news she felt she would rather have had the latter than the former. She put the phone down in shock, staring around her office. She knew exactly whose it was. He was the only man she had slept with in two years, and she hadn't used any precautions and neither had he. It had never occurred to her, she didn't have any to use. He was only the second man she'd ever slept with in her adult life, since the tragedies of her youth. And now she was pregnant.

There was only one solution to the problem. And she called the doctor back within the hour and made the appointment. She left her office at lunchtime in a state of shock, and went home to think about the predicament she was in. Should she tell him? Should she not? Would he laugh? Would he figure it was exclusively her problem? And what about the abortion? Was it wrong? Was it a sin? A part of her wanted to be rid of it instantly, and another part of her remembered Axie as a baby, and little Megan again ... that sweet smell of powder and the silky hair nestled in her arms at night. She remembered the little noises she made before she went to sleep at night, and suddenly Hilary thought she couldn't do it. She had already lost two children she loved, how could she kill this one? Perhaps this was God's way of making it up to her, of making it all right again, of giving her back one of the babies she had lost, of filling the empty years ahead of her with more than just work ... and the baby would be so beautiful with a father like Bill Brock, and he need never know ... it could be all hers ... all hers ... and suddenly with every ounce of her being, she wanted to protect it.

She suddenly understood why her skirts had been getting tight, even though she'd been losing weight. Her waist had been growing, and she felt a tiny bulge in her stomach. The doctor had told her, when she talked to him, that she was eight weeks pregnant. Eight weeks ... two months ... and inside her there was a tiny baby. She couldn't let herself kill it. Yet she had to, what kind of career could she have with a baby around her neck, who would help her? ... but that smell ... and the sweet cry ... she still remembered the first time she'd seen Axie ... but what if someone took this baby from her too, as they had Megan and Axie, what if Bill Brock found out and wanted his child. For the rest of the week, Hilary was torn by mounting panic. She had no one to talk to, nowhere to turn. She was left only with her own guilt and confusion and panic. She wanted desperately to keep the baby, but couldn't imagine how she could, but more importantly, she was terrified that one day she would lose it, that somehow, someone would take it from her, and she never wanted to love anyone that much again. It was that fear that was the deciding factor. It was too much to ask of her, the rest she could handle, but not the terrible fear of loss, she knew too well the agony it would cause her. She could never risk that again, with children of her own, or anyone else's. She would sacrifice this child in the memory of Megan and Axie. There would never be children in her life and heart again. And as she walked into the doctor's office that Friday afternoon, she thought she was going to faint as she went through the doorway.

She gave the nurse her name, and signed a form with trembling hands, and then they let her sit in the waiting room for an hour. She had taken the afternoon off from work, and she had lain awake the night before. Some part of her was shrieking at her to save the life of this baby. But the voice of the past was too important to her. It out-shouted all else and reminded her of the terrible pain of losing Megan and Alexandra. She kept thinking of the day they'd driven away, and the unbearable agony of it . . . but the agony of tearing this child from within her was no smaller.

As the nurse led her down a corridor and into a small room she felt her knees grow weak. She was instructed to take off her clothes, put on a gown and paper slippers and report to the nurse across the hall.

'Thank you,' Hilary whispered almost inaudibly,

wishing somebody would stop her before it was too late. But there was no one to do it.

The nurse across the hall looked at her as though she had committed a federal offence, and handed her a clipboard with more forms to sign. Just glancing at them made Hilary feel ill, and she sank onto a narrow wooden bench.

'You all right?' the woman asked uninterestedly.

'I'm a little dizzy.'

She nodded, unconcerned, and told her to lie on the table.

'The doctor will be here in a few minutes.' But an hour and a half later, Hilary was still waiting. She had begun to shake from head to foot well over an hour before, and she had finally thrown up out of sheer nervousness. She hadn't had anything to eat since that morning. The nurse with the clipboard finally came back, looked at her, smelt the air, and Hilary blushed.

'I'm sorry, I . . . I don't feel well.'

'It'll probably happen again afterwards,' she said matter-of-factly. 'He'll be right in. We had a little problem down the hall.' And all Hilary could think about was the baby still alive inside her, the longer they took, the longer it would live, and soon they would have to kill it. She felt desperation choke her, but there was no way out, she couldn't allow herself to love this baby, couldn't go through it ever again. A part of her tried to tell her this was different, but the rest of her knew that it wasn't. She had loved Megan and Alexandra like her own . . . and she had lost them. And one day someone would take this baby from her too. She couldn't let that happen. She had to stop it now . . . before it destroyed her.

'Ready, young lady?' The doctor blew into the room like a hurricane, in surgical garb, with a green hat to cover his hair, and a small mask hanging around his neck. She could almost sense the blood dripping from him from his last abortion.

'I . . . yes . . .' Her voice was a barely audible croak and she felt as though she was going to throw up again or start crying. 'Are you going to give me something to put me to sleep?' They had told her nothing about it.

'You don't need any of that. It'll be all over in a few minutes.' How few? How long would it take? What were they going to do to her baby?

She lay flat on the table, and the nurse forced her feet into the stirrups, they were wider than usual, and the nurse secured them with straps so that Hilary couldn't move, and she felt a sudden wave of panic.

'Why are you doing that?'

'So you don't hurt yourself.' She was about to tie down Hilary's hands too but she begged her not to.

'I promise I won't touch anything . . . I swear . . . please . . .' It was like some medieval torture, and the nurse turned to the doctor and he nodded as he put on a fresh mask.

'Just relax. It won't take long, and then you'll be rid of this.' . . . rid of this . . . she tried to be comforted by the words, but she wasn't. She told herself she was doing the right thing, but everything inside her shrieked that she was killing a baby. They had only taken Megan and Axie away, no one had killed them. It was wrong, it was a sin, it was terrible . . . she wanted . . . she felt the local anaesthetic jab into her sharply, and she wanted to cry and wanted to ask the nurse to hold her hand, but the nurse looked uninterested as she assisted the doctor. And suddenly Hilary heard a terrible machine, it sounded like it was going to eat the walls. It was the vacuum.

'What's that?' She leapt to half-sitting position, unable

to move her legs, and she still felt a sharp pain where they had put the needle in her cervix.

'Just what it sounds like. It's a vacuum. Now lie back. We'll be ready in a minute. Count to ten.' She felt an incredible pain as something sharp and metallic shoved its way inside her. No torture ever concocted by Maida and Georgine had equalled this ... not even the boys with their hard bodies pressed into hers ... this was awful, it was beyond bearing, it was ... she let out a scream, and the metal piece inside her felt as though it was tearing her apart. It was forcing her uterus to open, dilating it so that they could take out the baby. 'You're further along than we thought, Miss Walker, we're going to have to open a little wider.' The local seemed to have done nothing for her and the pain was excruciating as her legs trembled violently and the doctor gave a grunt of satisfaction. 'That's it.' He said something to the nurse as Hilary threw up all over herself, but the nurse was too busy assisting the doctor to notice or help her. And then suddenly Hilary knew this was the wrong thing ... she couldn't do it ... she had to keep the baby, and she raised her head again, trying not to vomit so she could tell him.

'No, please ... don't ... please ... Stop!' But he only spoke soothingly to her. It was much too late to stop now. They had to finish what they had started.

'It's almost over, Hilary. Just a little bit longer.'

'No ... please I can't stand it ... I don't want to ... the baby ...' She was feeling faint again, and her whole body was wracked by convulsive shaking.

'There will be lots of babies in your life ... you're a young girl, and one day it'll be the right one.' He gave another ominous grunt, which she knew now meant he was going to inflict more pain on her, and suddenly he inserted the vacuum. She felt as though every ounce of her body was being sucked out by that machine and she threw up again as it went on endlessly, and then finally there was silence.

'Now just a little scraping,' he explained, and she saw the room reel as she felt him scrape what was left out of her, but the baby was long gone ... she had lost the others, and now she had killed this one. It was all she could think of as she lay there, wanting to die like her baby. She was a murderer now, just like her father. Her father had killed his wife, and now she had killed her own baby.

'That's all now.' She heard the voice she had come to hate, and they took out all their tools, and left her lying there, still trembling and strapped to the table. She could feel something wet and warm pouring out of her, and she knew she was bleeding profusely, but she didn't care anymore what they did to her. She didn't care if she died. In fact, she hoped so. 'Just rest for a little while, Hilary.' He stared into her face, patted her shoulder, and left the room with a resounding bang, as she lay strapped to the table and sobbed in a pool of her own vomit.

They came back for her in an hour, handed her a damp cloth and a sheet of instructions. She was to call them if the bleeding seemed too heavy, and otherwise she was to stay in bed for twenty-four hours and she'd be fine. That was it. It was all over. She staggered outside once she was dressed, still trembling violently, and hailed a cab, and gave him her address. And she was shocked to realize it was six o'clock. She had been in the doctor's office for almost six hours.

'What'sa matta, lady, you sick?' She looked terrible, even to him, even in the darkness. Her eyes were suddenly dark-ringed, her face was green, and she was shaking so hard she could hardly talk. And she only nodded in answer.

'Yeah . . . I got . . . the flu . . .' Her teeth were chattering and he nodded.

'Everybody's got it.' He grinned at her then, she was probably a pretty girl when she wasn't sick. 'Just don't kiss me.' She tried to smile at him, but she couldn't. She felt as though she would never smile again, at anyone. How could she? How could she ever look herself in the eye again? She had killed a baby.

She crawled into her bed when she got home, without even getting undressed, and she slept until four o'clock on Saturday morning. The cramps she felt woke her up, but when checked, nothing seemed to be out of order. She had survived it. She had done it. And she knew she would never forget it.

On Monday, she went to work looking pale and wan, but she went, and she did her work, and she went home again, with a stack of papers. She was going to bury herself in her work, and she was going to do anything to numb herself, and she did. She worked like a machine for the next six months and for another year after that. She became the wunderkind of CBA Network. She became the kind of woman people admired and everyone feared, the kind of person no one wanted to like.

'Terrifying, isn't she?' one of the new secretaries said the day Hilary turned thirty. 'She lives and breathes nothing but this network, and God help you if you cross her. At least that's what people say. Personally, she scares me.' The other girl agreed and they went to the powder room to discuss the two new men in the newsroom. But Hilary was immune there too. She seemed to have no interest in anyone, except her work, her career, and the network.

When she was thirty-two years old, she became a vice-president, and two years after that, she got another promotion. At thirty-six, she was the most senior woman in management, and at thirty-eight she was the number three person at the network, and there was no doubt in anyone's mind that one day she would run it. And probably sooner rather than later. *The New York Times* ran a big piece about her shortly afterwards discussing her policies and her plans, and *The Wall Street Journal* did another piece on her shortly afterwards. Hilary Walker had made it.

Chapter 13

The air on Park Avenue seemed to crush him as he left his doctor's office two hours later. He wasn't surprised. He had expected it, and yet . . . Arthur Patterson had secretly hoped for something different. But the pain had been so great. The pills had barely helped him for the last month, and yet he had tried to tell himself it was something else. He stopped to catch his breath as he reached the corner. It was four-thirty, and he was totally exhausted as the pain ripped through his chest again, and he coughed pathetically. A passerby stopped to look, wondering if he should help, but Arthur caught his breath and got back into the car, barely speaking to the driver.

He was still thinking of his doctor's words and dire prediction. He had no right to ask for more, reasonably. He was almost seventy-two years old, and he had led a full life . . . more or less . . . he had been married once . . . Marjorie had died three years before, and he'd gone to her funeral, surprised to discover that she had remarried only a few years before, a retired congressman. He had wondered as he stood there, in the dim light of St James, if she had been satisfied with her life . . . if she had ever been truly happy.

And now he was going to die too. It was odd that it didn't frighten him more. He was only sorry. He had so little to leave the world, a law practice that had slowed down years before, although he still went to the office every day, or whenever he was well enough. He wondered if his partners would miss him when he was gone. There was certainly no one else who would notice his absence, except possibly his secretary, who would just be reassigned to one of the other lawyers.

The doorman gave him a hand as he got out of the cab, and he took the lift upstairs, making idle conversation as he always did, with the liftman on duty. They discussed the early heat, and the baseball scores, and he let himself into his apartment with a sigh of exhaustion. It was so odd to think about it now. Soon it would all be gone . . . and then as he walked into the living-room, he began to cry. For no reason he could think of, Solange had come to mind . . . Solange with her fiery red hair and her emerald eyes . . . he had loved her so much so long ago. He wondered if he would see her now, when he died, if there was an afterlife . . . a heaven and a hell, as he'd been taught as a boy . . . He closed his eyes as he sank heavily into a chair . . . Solange . . . he spoke her name in a whisper as the tears rolled down his cheeks, and as he opened his eyes again, he had a sudden feeling of desperation. He had let her down so desperately, and Sam . . . the daughters they had loved so much had been cast to the winds and totally disappeared. He had let them disappear. It had all been his fault. He could have taken them in, if only he'd had the courage. But it was too late now. Much too late. Solange had died more than thirty years before . . . and Sam . . . and yet, he knew without a doubt, what he had to do now. He had to do one last thing. He had to find them.

He sat in the same chair until the room grew dark, thinking back over the years, all the way to the trenches near Cassino, to his wound and the time Sam had saved him . . . and the liberation of Paris and the first time he'd seen her. There was no going back. No changing what had happened. And perhaps it would make no difference now. But he knew that before he died, he had to find them, to explain to them . . . to bring them together again, for one last time, and with the crushing agony of memory, he remembered that day in Charlestown when he had gone to get Megan and Alexandra, and Hilary had begged him so piteously not to take them.

He lay awake in his bed for most of the night, thinking of the little girls, wondering how he would find them, or if they could be found in time. There was only one thing he could leave them. The rest was all stocks and bonds. But perhaps the house in Connecticut would mean something to them. He had bought it years before, as a summer place, but seldom ever used it. It was a large, rambling old Victorian house, and he liked going there, but he had kept it more as a home for his sunset years. And now the sunset was coming. There would be no time for retirement, for quiet gardening, for long walks down to the seashore. For him, it was all over. The doctor said it was too late to operate. The X-rays told their own tale. The cancer had spread too far, and he was too ill now to withstand any dramatic treatment. It was difficult to estimate how much time he had. Three months, perhaps six, or less if the disease spread very quickly.

He got up at midnight to take a sleeping pill, but it was daylight before he fell asleep, sleeping fitfully and dreaming of Hilary's sobs as he drove a car away from her, clutching something to him, he wasn't sure what, and then suddenly Hilary's face became her mother's, and it was Solange crying in his arms, asking him why he had killed her.

Chapter 14

Arthur Patterson left his office at noon the next day, exhausted from his sleepless night, but determined to go back. He had conferred with one of his partners at eleven o'clock, and got the name of a man who was thought to be the best in the business. He did not explain why he needed him, and the partner did not ask any questions.

Arthur had placed the call himself, and was surprised that John Chapman was willing to see him that day, when he explained that it was urgent. But Chapman knew who he was, and it was rare that the senior partner of an important law firm called him himself, and with such obvious desperation. He said he would see him shortly after noon, although he had only an hour at his disposal. And Arthur thanked him profusely, and hurried out of his office, patting his pocket to make sure he had his pills. He couldn't afford to be without them.

'Will you be back after lunch, Mr Patterson?' his secretary inquired as he hurried past her, coughing as was now his habit.

'I don't think so,' he said barely audibly, and she shook her head as he stepped into the lift. He looked terrible and he was too old to be coming to work every day now. She wished someone would force him to retire.

It was a short cab ride from Arthur's office to Chapman's,

and he was impressed when he saw the well appointed offices Chapman kept on Fifty-seventh, off Fifth. It was a smaller building than those that housed Brokaw, Miller and Patterson, but it was respectable and well kept, and Chapman had most of a floor, with a discreet sign on the door that said only JOHN CHAPMAN. A receptionist took his name, and several other people appeared to be waiting for Chapman's associates. Most of the people in the waiting room looked like attorneys.

'Mr Chapman will see you now,' the young woman said, and ushered him inside. Chapman had an office high above Fifty-seventh street with thick carpeting and English antiques, and like his own office, it was filled with law books. It was comforting to be in surroundings that looked so familiar. He had been afraid at first that the place he was being sent to would be sleazy, and it was a relief to find that it wasn't.

The door opened to reveal a handsome blond man in a tweed jacket and grey slacks, with lively grey eyes, and the look of someone who had gone to Princeton or Harvard. In fact, he had gone to both. He had done his undergraduate work at Princeton, and had gone to law school at Harvard.

'Mr Patterson?' He came easily around the desk, and shook Arthur's hand, startled at first by how frail it seemed in his grip. He had played football in college, and even as tall as he was, Arthur was dwarfed by the young attorney who was thirty years his junior. 'Please sit down.' He indicated a chair with a warm smile, and sat down in the chair next to Arthur.

'I'm very grateful to you . . .' Arthur coughed, trying to catch his breath, '. . . for seeing me on such short notice. It's a matter of both urgency and importance, and I'm afraid I . . . don't have much time.' He meant it just the way it sounded as he coughed again, but John Chapman assumed he was referring to a deadline associated with a court case.

'I was impressed that you were handling the matter yourself, sir.'

'Thank you.'

He knew who Arthur was, and it was most unusual for the senior partner of the firm to contact an investigation service himself, no matter how illustrious the outfit was, and John Chapman's was one of the best-known in the country. It operated more like a law firm than just an investigative bureau, and his own legal background made him extremely helpful. He grabbed a pad and pen as Arthur coughed again, and prepared to jot down some notes about what Arthur wanted.

'Would you like to explain to me, Mr Patterson, so I can have an idea how we may be of service?' He was quiet and professional and had the precise diction of the upper classes, and yet he seemed oddly unassuming, easy-going almost, and Patterson found himself curious about him. Why hadn't he gone into his father's firm? His father was the head of the most important law firm in Boston, and two of his brothers were prominent attorneys in New York. And yet he had chosen this rather unorthodox career instead. It was intriguing, but Arthur didn't have the time to think about it now. He had to save his strength to tell him what he wanted.

'It's a personal . . . matter.' He wheezed, and then took a sip of water Chapman had quietly poured him while he waited. 'Of the utmost confidentiality and importance. You are not to discuss this with anyone.' Arthur flashed his eyes at him, but the effort was wasted on Chapman.

'I don't discuss my cases with anyone, Mr Patterson. Period.'

'I'd also like you to do this yourself, if it's possible. One of my associates tells me you're the best in the business. I want to hire that talent, and no one else's.'

Chapman pursed his lips, waiting to hear the rest, making no commitment to Arthur. 'That depends on what's involved. I try to stay involved in all of our cases, to as great an extent as I'm able.'

'I want you to do this yourself. And we don't have much time.' He coughed and took another sip of water. 'I'm dying.'

Chapman watched him carefully, curious now. The old man was shaking with anticipation, and clutching a file he had taken out of a briefcase. Perhaps it was an old unsolved case he was determined to tie up before he died. It was odd the things people did when they were dying.

'The doctor thinks I might have three months, maybe six, maybe less. I think three months is more like it. I want to find three young women.' Chapman looked surprised. It was an odd request from an old man, unless they were his daughters. 'They were the daughters of close friends of mine, my closest friends. Their parents died thirty years ago, and two of them were adopted shortly after, the third one was left with her aunt and uncle. They were respectively one, five, and nine years old when I lost track of them, and I have no idea where they are now. I know who adopted the two younger girls, and I know the oldest one wound up in Jacksonville, Florida, and then came to New York twenty-one years ago, but that's all I know. I've included all the information I have in this file, including clippings about their parents. Their father was a very well-known Broadway actor.'

'Did the parents die simultaneously in an accident?' It was only curiosity on his part. Thus far, it was an intriguing story.

'No.' Arthur took a painful breath and continued. 'He killed their mother, no one ever really knew why, except that they had an argument and he seems to have gone crazy. I defended him in 1958.' Arthur's face went a little greyer as Chapman watched him, surprised that he had taken a criminal case. There had to be more to the story than he was telling. 'He was convicted and committed suicide in his cell the night of his conviction. I tried to place the girls in a home together.' He seemed close to breaking down as John Chapman watched him, sorry for him, it was obviously painful for him to remember, and worse still to discuss it with this stranger. Any attorney would have felt responsible . . . but not responsible enough to go looking for the children thirty years later. Or was it that he felt guilty? 'But no one wanted to take all three. I had to place them in separate homes, and leave the older girl with the aunt and uncle.' He didn't tell him that he had considered taking them himself, but didn't do it because his then wife wouldn't let him. 'There was also a recent clipping about a young woman at C B A,' he went on, 'by the same name as the oldest girl. I think there's a possibility it might be her, but it could be just a coincidence. I included the clipping and you ought to check it out.' Chapman nodded. And Arthur remembered finding the article in *The Times* only weeks before, and praying it was the right Hilary Walker. His hand had trembled as he held the column he'd clipped out and stared at the picture. She didn't look like anyone he knew, but that didn't necessarily mean anything. Newspaper photos often didn't. 'That's it, Chapman. I want to find those three young women.' Young to him perhaps, but certainly grown-up, Chapman thought to himself. He did a quick calculation and realized they were thirty-eight, thirty-four, and thirty years old. It wasn't going to be easy to find them. And

Arthur confirmed that. 'The adoptive parents of the two younger girls moved away years ago, and I have no idea where they went . . . I just hope you can find them.'

'So do I.' Chapman took the file in his hands, and looked sombre as he questioned Arthur. 'And when I do?'

'First, I want you to locate them, and then come back to me and tell me that you've found them. Then I want you to explain to them who they are, who I am, that I am an old family friend, and that I want to reunite them with their sisters. I'd like to do it in my home in Connecticut, if that's possible. I'm afraid I can't travel anymore . . . they'll have to come here.'

'And if they refuse?' It was possible. Anything was possible. He had seen everything in the seventeen years he'd been in the business.

'You can't let them.'

'They may not even remember having sisters, two of them anyway, and it may be a tremendous shock and disruption to them.' He wondered if there was a sizeable inheritance being attached to it, but he didn't want to press Arthur on the subject.

'I owe it to them to bring them together again. It was my fault that they were separated . . . that I was never able to find a home for all of them. I want to know that they're all right, that they don't need anything . . . I owe that much to their parents.'

John was tempted to tell him that it was a little late, but he didn't want to be disrespectful. At thirty-eight and thirty-four and thirty, it couldn't matter very much to them any more why they had been taken from their sisters, if they even remembered having any in the first place. But it was not his place to question the wisdom of Arthur Patterson's final wishes. Arthur was sitting watching him with quiet desperation.

'Will you do it?' It was a barely audible whisper.

'I'll try.'

'Will you do it yourself?'

'Most of it, if that's possible. I want to read the file first, before I make a definite commitment. I may have operatives already in the field in areas we're interested in who could do the job better and more quickly than I could.' Arthur nodded, that much made sense to him. 'I'll get to the file as quickly as possible, and I'll call you with an appraisal of the situation.'

Arthur was painfully honest with him. 'There's not much there, Chapman. Not much more than I told you.'

'That's all right. Something may jump out at me.' He discreetly looked at the clock he could see over Arthur's left shoulder. It was almost one-fifteen, and he hated to keep Sasha waiting. 'I'll call you in the next day or two.' He stood up and Arthur followed suit unsteadily.

'I'm deeply grateful to you, Chapman.'

'That's all right, Mr Patterson. I hope you won't be disappointed.' Arthur nodded thoughtfully, barely able to consider that. Chapman *had* to find them. 'I should warn you as well, this could be an expensive project.' Arthur looked up at him then with a wintery smile.

'I've got nothing else to spend it on now, do I?'

Chapman smiled at him. It was a difficult question to answer, and he walked him quietly to the outer office, shook his hand, thanked him for coming, and then hurried back to his office to lock the slim file in the safe, and head out of the door at a dead run. Sasha was going to kill him.

Chapter 15

John Chapman flew out of his office building on Fifty-seventh Street, and raced the two long blocks west, glancing at his watch, and catching his reflection in shop windows. Tiffany . . . I. Miller . . . Henri Bendel . . . it seemed to take hours to get there and he knew how she hated him to be late, but he couldn't hurry Arthur Patterson out of his office after all. The man was ancient and he was dying, and Chapman was intrigued by the case. But he also knew Sasha wouldn't understand that.

She was twenty-eight years old, sinew from head to foot, and every ounce of her was disciplined to perfection. She wore her blond hair pulled back so tight that it looked as though it were painted on her head, her green eyes had a Slavic tilt, and she wore her lips in a constant pout, which had seduced him from the first time he'd seen her. They had met at a friend's house, a ballet buff, who raved about how talented she was, and how extraordinary she'd been as a little girl. And now she was even more so as a big one. The daughter of Russian émigrés, she had studied for years at the Ballet Russe de Monte Carlo, and then gone on to Juilliard as a young girl, where she'd been a star already in her early teens. At twenty she had been invited to join the American Ballet Theatre. And at twenty-eight, she was not a prima, but she was a fine dancer with a solid career to be proud of. She indulged in the jealousies of her troupe, and it irked her not to be one of the prima ballerinas, but in truth she was too small to be more than one of the corps of dancers. She had the consolation of being very good, and she told John that every chance she got, when she wasn't complaining about her feet or the fact that he was late coming to meet her. But even though she wasn't easy to get along with, for months John Chapman had found her enchanting . . . her discipline, her intense routine, her talent coupled with her tiny face, her feet that seemed to move on butterfly wings when she danced, the huge green eyes . . . there was something very special about her.

'You're half an hour late.' She glared at him halfway through a cup of borscht, when he breathlessly reached her table at the Russian Tea Room. The atmosphere was precisely as it had been for the past fifty years, and they both loved blinis and caviar. Besides, it was close to where she rehearsed, and they met there half a dozen times a week, for lunch or after rehearsals, or even after performances, late at night, for a quick bite before they went home to his apartment. She lived with four other dancers, and it was impossible to talk, let alone make love, in the West Side walkup that was always filthy and draughty. But her green eyes were looking up at him in reproach as he apologized and sat down. 'I was thinking of leaving.' She looked like an angry child and he realized, as he always did, how much he loved her.

'I'm glad you didn't.' He gently touched her hand, and smiled at the familiar waiter. He was an old Russian who chatted with Sasha in her maternal tongue. She had been born in Paris, but still spoke Russian with her parents.

'I was hungry.' Her eyes bore into his mercilessly. 'That's the only reason why I waited.'

'I'm sorry. I had an important case. The head of a major

223

law firm needed some help, I couldn't shove him out of the door.' He smiled placatingly at her, wondering how long it would take him to get back in her good graces. Usually not long – her anger was hard and quick to burst into flame, but generally it abated fairly quickly. 'I'm sorry, darling.' He touched her hand again, and she looked only slightly mollified by his contrition.

'I had a very difficult morning.' She looked petulant, and more beautiful than ever.

'Something wrong?' He knew how she worried about her feet and her legs and her arms . . . it was not easy being a dancer. A pulled muscle, a torn ligament, and her life would be changed forever.

'They were trying to introduce a new choreographer, and he's impossible. He makes Balanchine look lazy by comparison. This man is mad. You cannot dance the way he asks you.'

'*You* can.' Chapman smiled proudly at her. He thought her a remarkable dancer. And this time, she smiled at him. He was almost forgiven.

'I'm trying. But I think he's trying to kill us.' She sighed and finished her borscht. She didn't want to eat too much before rehearsal that afternoon, but she was still hungry. He had just ordered blinis, and she was tempted but that was too heavy for her when she was dancing. 'Maybe I'll have a salad.' She told the waiter in Russian and he nodded and disappeared as she told John about her woes of the morning. She asked him nothing about his case. She never did. All she ever thought of was dancing.

'Are you rehearsing tonight?' he asked with eyes full of understanding. He was a kind man, and he didn't mind their life revolving around her work. He was used to that. His ex-wife had been a writer, and he had sat patiently for seven years while she churned out mysteries that had eventually become major bestsellers. He had respected her as a woman and a friend, but it hadn't been much of a marriage. Everything had come second to her work, even her husband. She had been a difficult woman. The whole world had to come to a shrieking halt when she started a book, and she expected John to protect her from any possible interruption. And he had done a fair job of it, until the loneliness of his life with her overwhelmed him. Her only friends were her characters, every plot she wrote became real to her, and she wouldn't even speak to him while she was working. She worked from eight in the morning until midnight, every day, and then went to bed, mute with exhaustion. In the morning, she'd start again, but she didn't talk to him over coffee because she was already thinking about the book. It had been lonely being married to Eloise. She wrote under the name of Eloise Wharton. And when she wasn't working on a book, she was either in a major depression because she wasn't working, or she was on tour in thirty cities in forty-five days, pushing her latest epic. He figured out before he asked her for a divorce that they spoke to each other on the average something like thirty hours a year, which was something less than what he needed for a happy marriage. They loved each other, but she loved her work more. And he wasn't even sure how much she understood when he left her. She had been deep in a book, and there had been only the vaguest of answers as he said goodbye and closed the front door behind him. It was a relief, oddly enough, and he discovered that it was less lonely being alone than being with her. He could play the stereo, sing when he liked, have friends over who made as much noise as they wanted. He went out with other women. Life was fine. And the only thing he regretted was that they had never had any children. He and Eloise had been divorced for five years, and he was only now starting to think about getting remarried. In fact, he had been thinking about it a great deal lately.

Sasha had nodded in answer to his question about rehearsal. 'We are rehearsing until eleven.' She still spoke English like someone who had learned it as a foreigner, and yet she had no clearly discernible accent.

'Can I pick you up?' His eyes filled with hope, and he told himself that he was not repeating the same pattern. He was not leading his life entirely around Sasha's dancing. Besides, she was so much more alive than Eloise had been. She was so vital, and exciting. Eloise lived in a dark room, with a single light burning over her head, haunted by imaginary people. And she hadn't changed in the last five years. She had only become more successful. She was one of the most successful mystery writers in the country. The new Agatha Christie, *The New York Times* had hailed her, and *Publishers Weekly* agreed. She was forty-one years old, and she lived in a world of fantasy. Not like Sasha . . . not at all . . .

'Thank you. I'll be at the stage door at eleven-ten.' And he knew she meant it. She had the precision of a surgeon. 'Don't be late.' She frowned and wagged a graceful finger.

He smiled at her, and touched her knee under the table. 'I won't. I'm not working tonight.' All he wanted to do was read the file Arthur Patterson had left him, and that couldn't take him more than an hour, possibly even less. In fact, that was what he was afraid of, that there wasn't anything in it of any real substance. 'I'll just look over the files on this new case.'

'Don't get too interested.' She frowned at him. He had done that before, and been an hour late after a performance. She wouldn't tolerate that from him, or anyone in fact. She didn't have to. As she pointed out to him regularly, she was a *real* artist.

'Do you want me to take you back?' He looked hopeful, like a schoolboy anxious to please her. It was something about him that had pleased every woman he'd been involved with, even Sasha, although she didn't admit it to him. She never told him how much she loved him, or how much she liked his company. It was beneath her to say those things, and he didn't need to know them.

'I'm meeting some of the others in five minutes, John. On the corner. I'll see you tonight?' She stood up, tiny and exquisitely erect, her back like a beautifully sculpted slab of marble, and one eyebrow raised over the olive-green eyes. 'On time, yes?'

'You're a tyrant.' He stood to kiss her and watched her go, as he sipped his tea, and then paid the bill. Something about her always left him feeling unnerved and excited. As though he wanted more, as though he couldn't get enough, as though she would never let him possess her. It was as though she danced away from his grasp each time he reached out for her, but in some ways he liked it. He liked chasing her. He liked everything about her. She was so much more alive than Eloise, and the endless numbers of women attorneys and ad. execs he had taken out in the five years since he'd divorced her. Sasha was entirely different.

He walked back to the office, more slowly this time, thinking of Sasha at first, and then of Arthur Patterson and the three women he wanted him to find. It was an odd story and he couldn't help wondering if there was more to it than Arthur was telling. There was a piece missing to the puzzle somehow, maybe even several of them. Why did he want to bring them back? What did it matter if they met now? They were grown women, having led separate lives, what could they possibly have in common? And why did Arthur Patterson feel so guilty? What had he done? Or what hadn't he done? And who were these women's parents? John's mind whirled over the questions as he walked along. He was good at what he did because he had an uncanny knack for seeing the pieces that were missing and then finding them, like the proverbial needle in the haystack. He had found more than a few, and had been crucial in several major cases. His most astounding work had been in the field of criminal law, and he was respected by attorneys and courts all over the country. Arthur Patterson had come to the right place. But John Chapman wondered if he could find the missing women.

He took the file home with him that night and pored over the little that was there. It was pathetic how little there was, though. Arthur had been right. There wasn't much there to help him. Only what he had said in the office. There were all the clippings of the trial, which John read first, intrigued by the unspoken elements of the story. Why had Sam Walker really killed his wife? Was it premeditated, as some thought, or a crime of passion? What had the woman done to him, and who was she? In a way, he didn't need to know those things, and yet the questions intrigued him. He read reviews of several of Walker's plays, and remembered seeing him once as a little boy. All he remembered was that it was an impressive performance and he was very handsome. But more than that he didn't remember.

There was a brief note in Arthur's trembling hand, explaining that he and Sam Walker had been buddies in the army. There was a list of the places they had been, and a description of their first meeting with Solange, which was surprisingly lyrical for a man his age, and one who had written nothing but legal documents and briefs all his

228

life. And John wondered if therein lay some of the answers. Perhaps Arthur had been in love with her. Or perhaps it didn't matter. The facts were still the same. Sam had killed Solange for whatever reason, leaving their three children orphans.

The eldest had gone to relatives at a Charlestown, Mass., address, an Eileen and Jack Jones, and Arthur knew she had gone to Jacksonville from there, because she had told him so when she'd come to his office in 1966, seeking her sisters' addresses. Arthur had mentioned in a footnote that she had been less than cordial. He said too that she mentioned having been in juvenile hall in Jacksonville, and John wondered if she had fallen foul of the law as a young girl. If so, she might have done so again, and he might be able to find a rap sheet on her. That would make her easier to find anyway, especially if she was sitting in prison somewhere. But at least he could tell Patterson he'd found her.

The second one had gone to one of Arthur's partners, who had then died, and the widow was God knows where, remarried to God knew who. That one was a healthy project. He'd have to start with the Gorham files at the firm, and pray they'd had to contact her for something in recent years, maybe a trust or some other lingering detail of the estate Arthur knew nothing of since he was not one of Gorham's trustees . . . and then there was the baby.

The youngest child had also virtually disappeared, but not without warning. Arthur had told him that David Abrams felt strongly about Patterson's not maintaining contact with the child, that they wanted her to have a new life, totally divorced from her past, and wanted to ensure that she did so. John even found himself wondering if that had been part of their reason for moving to California, to start a new life, where no one even knew that the child was adopted.

And after that, there was nothing. There was one clipping at the back of the file, the one Arthur had mentioned, but despite the similarity of name, like Arthur, John thought it was a long shot. It was the article from *The New York Times*, about a Hilary Walker's promotion at CBA Network, and it was highly unlikely that she was the same girl. Even Arthur didn't recognize her, and it was too sweet and easy to find her within easy reach, and successful. John had been in the business of finding people for long enough that he knew a false hope when he saw one. He'd look into it of course, but he was sure she would turn out to be a different Hilary Walker.

And that was it. There was nothing else. He sat back in his chair, and thought about all three. How to find them, where to start. The wheels were already turning. And then with a sudden start, he glanced at his watch.

'Sonofabitch . . .' He muttered to himself. It was just after ten-thirty. He grabbed his jacket off the back of a chair, and hurried down the three flights of his brownstone. He had the top floor of a lovely house on East Sixty-ninth Street. And he was lucky enough to find a cab almost at once, but with post-theatre traffic, he barely made it to the stage door in time to meet Sasha.

She came out at precisely eleven-ten, as he knew she would, looking tired, wearing jeans and sneakers and carrying her dance bag.

'How was it?' There was always the tension of someone having performed major surgery, not unlike Eloise's struggles with difficult denouements in the plot. But somehow this seemed more exciting.

'It was awful.'

He knew better than to believe her, and put a protective arm around her as he took her dance-bag. 'You expect too much of yourself, little one.' She was so tiny, it always made him feel protective of her, and in any case, he was that kind of person.

'No, it was terrible. My feet were killing me. It's going to rain tonight. I can always tell.' John had learned that dancers' feet were a constant source of agony, and a constant topic of conversation.

'I'll massage them when we get home,' he promised as they climbed into a cab and headed back to East Sixty-ninth Street.

The apartment was peaceful and quiet when they arrived. There were only two other tenants in the building, one a doctor who never seemed to be there. He was younger than John, and when he wasn't on call, delivering babies at New York Hospital, he seemed to be staying with assorted women. And the other was a woman who worked for IBM and travelled eight to ten months of the year. So most of the time he was alone in the building. He had a view of the little garden outside, and the larger gardens of the town houses on Sixty-eighth Street. 'Do you want a drink?' he inquired, poking his head out of his well-ordered kitchen.

'Just some tea, thanks.' She sat down on the couch with a sigh and stretched her arms and her back and her legs. She never cooked anything in his small kitchen. It never dawned on her to do things like that for him or herself. John always did them for her.

He emerged a few minutes later, bringing her tea in a glass, the way she liked it. It was a Russian tradition he had come to like, and he had bought special glass mugs just for that purpose. He had been equally expert at preparing Eloise's snacks while she was working. But in return, she had cooked him some wonderful dinners between books. She loved to bake, and had a real flair for

French cuisine. Unlike Sasha, who thought being expected to make toast was an affront to her as an artist.

'Are you coming to the performance tomorrow?' she asked as she slowly pulled the pins from her hair, and it began to cascade in long blond sheets past her shoulders.

John looked at her with regret. He hated to remind her. He knew that whenever he did it would create a scene between them. It annoyed her when he went anywhere. She expected him to be always near. And the next afternoon he was flying to Boston.

'I'm going up to the Cape for the weekend, Sash. I said something about it a few weeks ago, but you may have forgotten. It's my mother's birthday. I tried to get out of it, but I really couldn't. It's her seventieth, and it's important.' Both of his brothers were going to be there, and their wives, and their children. It always made him feel inadequate somehow, going there without an entourage to show for his years of marriage and assorted romances. Everything they had was tangible and obvious: wives who had nice sapphires or diamonds as engagement rings and anniversary presents, kids who had skinned knees and missing teeth, and in the case of his oldest nephew, even a high school diploma. It was going to be a long weekend. But he knew it would be fun too. He was fond of his two brothers, one older, one younger. His sisters-in-law were a bit difficult, but the kids were great. And there was no way he could bring Sasha. Even at his age, his parents would have frowned on his bringing a woman with him for a family occasion. 'I'll be home Sunday.'

'Don't bother.' She straightened her back and dropped both feet to the floor gracefully. 'I have rehearsal Sunday afternoon. And I'm not interested in crumbs left over from your parents' table.' She looked so outraged that he could only laugh at her choice of words. Sometimes her English was outlandish.

'Is that what I am, Sash? A crumb?' It was more than obvious that she thought so.

'I don't understand what is so sacred about your family. You've met my parents, my aunt, my grandmother. Are your parents so much better than mine? They would disapprove because I'm a dancer?' She sounded terribly Russian and looked extremely dramatic as she paced around the room, her hair flying and her hands shoved into the back pockets of her blue jeans, her tiny little body tense with emotion.

'They're very private, that's all.' And very Bostonian. A writer had been difficult enough. A ballerina would drive his mother totally crazy. She had a healthy respect for the arts, but preferably on a stage, not in her son's bedroom. 'They don't understand relationships like ours.'

'Neither do I. Are we together or are we not?' She stood in front of him looking like an enchanting elf, but an elf who was extremely angry. She felt shut out by the family he never introduced her to, and without his ever saying so, she was aware of their disapproval.

'Of course we're together. But as far as they're concerned, you don't acknowledge those things until you're married, or at least engaged.' And she was the one who resisted that. She saw no need for a permanent statement.

'They think we're immoral?'

'Maybe. They prefer not to think about it. They don't want to have to confront this kind of thing, so they don't. And as their son, I have to respect that. They're pretty old, Sash. My mother is going to be seventy on Saturday, my father is seventy-nine. It's a little late to force them into acknowledging modern arrangements.'

'That's ridiculous.' She stormed across the room again,

and then stood glaring at him from the kitchen doorway. 'And if you were any kind of man at all, you would take me anyway, and force them to acknowledge my existence.'

'I'd rather invite them to see you dance the next time they're here. That would be a better introduction. Don't you think so?'

Sasha thought it over as she crossed the room again, only slightly mollified, and then she sat down on the couch and began to put on her sneakers. He knew it was a bad omen. She was always storming out at two in the morning and going back to her apartment.

'What are you doing?'

'I'm going home. Where I belong.' She looked at him malevolently and he sighed. He hated scenes, and she doted on them. They seemed to be part of her art form.

'Don't be silly.' He stretched out a hand and touched her shoulder. It felt like rock beneath his fingers. 'We each have things in our lives we have to do on our own. You have your work and your ballet friends and your rehearsals. I have my own work, and a few other obligations.'

'I don't want to hear it. The truth is, Mr Chapman,' she stood up and glared at him, swinging her dance-bag over her shoulder, 'that you're a snob, and you're afraid your parents won't think I'm good enough. And do you know what? I don't care. You can have your *Mayflower* and your Plymouth Rock and your Boston. I don't need to be in the social register, I will be in *Who's Who* one day. And if that's not good enough,' – she made a gesture that said it all, and stalked to the door. And for once he didn't stop her. He knew that by Sunday she'd cool off, and he couldn't appease her by not going.

'I'm sorry you feel that way, Sash.' She slammed the

door in answer, and he sat down with a sigh. Sometimes she was so unbelievably childish. And so self-centred. He didn't let himself think about it often, but she hadn't once asked him about his new case. The only time she noticed his life was when, for whatever reason, it enraged her.

He turned off the lights in the living-room, and went to bed without putting their glasses in the sink. The cleaning lady could do it in the morning. And as he lay in bed, he thought about her accusations ... that he was a snob ... and that his parents wouldn't approve of her. In some ways, she was right. His parents would not have been enchanted by Sasha Riva. They would have thought her too limited, and extremely difficult, inadequately educated and ill-informed, and yes, it would matter to them that she wasn't 'social'. It wasn't something that mattered to him a great deal, but he knew that to them, it was important. Eloise had been something else. She and his mother had never really got along, and she thought his sisters-in-law unspeakably boring. But she was from an excellent family, and had graduated from Yale *summa cum laude*. You couldn't fault Eloise's breeding, or her education. And she was intelligent and amazingly witty, none of which had made her a good wife. Far from it. Not that Sasha showed much greater promise. He thought about calling Sasha after she got home, but he was too tired to hunt her down, wake her room-mates up, and beg her forgiveness because he was going to Cape Cod to see his mother. Instead he burrowed into the pillow and fell asleep, and didn't wake up until the alarm rang the next morning.

He showered and shaved, made himself coffee and left for work, and he noticed when he read the newspaper on the subway that Eloise had a new bestseller. Good for her. It was all she had in life, and he knew how happy it made

235

her. He envied her sometimes. He would have liked to be as fulfilled, as obsessed, as totally enthralled with what he did that it didn't matter what else happened in his life. He loved his work, but he wanted so much more than that. And so far, he hadn't found it. It was one of the reasons why he was excited about the Patterson case. There was something about it that excited him and he hadn't been this excited about his work in aeons. The first thing he wanted to do was find the oldest one, Hilary. There was something about her that haunted him. And God only knew what had happened to her after Arthur had abandoned her in Charlestown. He knew from her visit to Arthur's office in later years that she had wound up in Jacksonville, Florida. Somehow, but how or when or why, neither of them knew, and maybe it wasn't important. And what had happened to her afterwards was a mystery too. She had never contacted Arthur again. She had simply disappeared. And then there was the clipping from *The New York Times* Arthur had given him of the woman named Hilary Walker at CBA Network. But was that even the same woman? He doubted it. It seemed extremely unlikely.

Chapter 16

John got to the office before nine o'clock. He had a lot to do before leaving early for the weekend, there was something he wanted to do before he left. He wanted to try calling the Hilary Walker in Arthur's clipping. It probably wasn't the woman he wanted but it was worth a shot. It was a lead, and he couldn't afford to ignore it. She might just be at CBA, right under their noses, working near the top at a major network.

He glanced at his watch. It was nine-fifteen, and he picked up the phone himself. He called information, and then dialled the number.

'Hilary Walker, please.' His mouth felt a little dry, and he was surprised. He didn't know why he was getting to care about the Patterson case so much, except that something happened to him when he wondered what had become of the child in Charlestown.

A secretary answered, and he asked for her again.

'May I tell her who's calling?' a voice asked.

'John Chapman of Chapman Associates, she doesn't know me, and it's a matter of some urgency, if you'd be good enough to tell her that.'

'Just a moment please.' The girl at the other end gave away nothing. She had called Hilary on the intercom, and she couldn't figure out who the hell John Chapman was or why he was calling. She had a major production meeting to run at ten o'clock and she didn't have time to waste with crank callers.

'Ask him if I can call him back later,' she told the secretary and then countermanded her own orders. 'Oh never mind, I'll talk to him myself.' She pushed the button with the flashing light, and her cool, deep voice came on the line. 'Yes? This is Hilary Walker.' And for an odd moment, John was reminded of his mother's deep voice. She was the only other woman he knew with a voice as deep as that, but he got down to business with her quickly. Whether she was the right Hilary Walker or not, this one was a very busy woman.

'Thank you for taking my call, I appreciate it, and I'm going to be direct with you, in the interest of saving time. My name is John Chapman, I'm the head of Chapman Associates, I'm looking for a woman named Hilary Walker. Her father was Sam, her mother Solange, and she lived with a couple named Jack and Eileen Jones in Boston. Are you that woman?' It was fortunate that he could not see her face at the other end. She was chalk-white and shaking from head to foot as one hand clutched her desk, but her voice betrayed nothing.

'No, I'm not. What is this about?' Her first instinct had been to deny it, but she had to know why he was looking for her. Was it for the others? Not that it mattered any-more. They were long gone, and probably didn't even remember her. She had given all that up years before. All she had now was the network. And much more likely, it was Arthur. The bastard.

'This is part of an investigation for a client. He was hoping to find this Miss Walker. And he saw the articles about you in *The Times* and *The Wall Street Journal*, and hoped that you might be the right one. It was a long shot, and I'm sorry to have disturbed you.' He could hear in her voice that she wasn't the right one, and he had to admit he was disappointed.

'I'm awfully sorry not to be able to help you, Mr Chapman.' Her voice was smooth and cool, but she was definitely not moved by his inquiry. It would have been much too simple if she had been the right one.

'Thank you for your time, Miss Walker.'

'Not at all.' And with that, she hung up, and he quietly hung up the phone. He had struck out. And he couldn't see the woman who sat pale and shaken at her desk across town. It was like getting a phone call from a ghost. She was sure it was Arthur looking for her, the old sonofabitch, well he'd never find her. She had no reason to reach out to him, to soothe his conscience for him. He had never done anything for her or her sisters. To hell with him. And John Chapman. And all of them. She didn't need them.

She walked into the meeting at ten o'clock and tore heads off for the rest of the day. But she was still shaken when she left the meeting and so was everyone else. She had fired three producers, and threatened everyone else in the meeting. She was merciless, but then again she was known for it. She was only slightly worse after the call from John Chapman.

Chapter 17

In his office, John Chapman sat staring into space in disappointment. The woman in the article was not the Hilary Walker they wanted . . . *he* wanted . . . He sighed deeply and put the clipping back in the file with a notation. Later, he would have to call and tell Arthur. But two of his associates were anxious to speak to him in the meantime.

Three of their biggest cases were coming to court, and they had got the goods in all three. It was very rewarding. And at noon, John looked at his watch and made a decision. He had handled pretty much everything he wanted to, the rest could wait until Monday. His parents weren't expecting him till dinnertime, and if he caught the two o'clock commuter flight out of La Guardia, he'd be in Boston at three, and he could stop in Charlestown on his way to his folks. He'd still be there in plenty of time, and he wanted to see if he could turn up anything on Hilary Walker. He had what he needed to go straight to Jacksonville on her, but he still liked to be thorough in his investigations. And a trip to Charlestown might turn something up on one of the others. It was worth a look in any case, and he was going in that direction.

He told his secretary where he'd be in case she needed him, and took a cab back to his apartment. It took him ten minutes to pack a bag. He knew exactly what he needed for a weekend in the farmhouse. And by one o'clock he was already on his way to La Guardia. He bought a seat on the commuter flight, arrived at three-ten, and rented a car at the airport. And from there it was a thirty-minute drive to Charlestown.

He checked the information in the file again and made sure he had the correct address, and cringed inwardly as he began driving down the streets of Charlestown. It was one of those areas that had been ugly forty years before, and had not improved with age. There were other sections that had been lucky in recent years, and were being restored by loving hands, but these houses were not among them. And if they had been ugly when Hilary lived there, they were worse now. They were truly awful. Filthy, broken down, with paint peeling everywhere, and many of the houses boarded up and crumbling. There were signs here and there, on houses that had been condemned by the city, and John could almost feel the rats waiting to sneak out at nightfall. It was an awful place, and the house where he stopped was one of the worst among them. He stood for a moment, looking at it from the pavement, the weeds were shoulder-high in the yard, and the smell of rubbish was heavy in the air, and the front door was almost falling off its hinges.

With trepidation, he walked up the front steps, trying to avoid the two broken ones so as not to fall through, and he knocked on the door resoundingly. The doorbell was hanging by a thread and clearly broken. And although he heard noises within, no one came to the door for a long time, and then finally a toothless old woman answered. She stared at him, confused, and then asked him what he wanted.

'I was looking for Eileen and Jack Jones. They lived here a long time ago. Did you know them?' He spoke loudly, in case she was deaf. But she did not seem so much deaf as stupid.

'Never heard of 'em. Why don't you ask Charlie across the street. He been living here since the war. Maybe he knew 'em.'

'Thank you.' A glance into the house told John that it was depressing beyond belief, and he only hoped that it had been more pleasant when Hilary and her sisters lived there. Though it was hard to imagine it ever having been much better. The street had become a slum, but it didn't look as though it had ever been pretty. 'Thank you very much.' He smiled pleasantly, and she slammed the door in his face, not because she was annoyed, but only because she didn't know there was any other way to do it.

He looked up and down the street, and thought of talking to some of the other residents. But he went first to the house she had pointed to. He wondered if anyone would be home at four o'clock on a Friday afternoon, but the old man she had called 'Charlie' was rocking on his front porch, smoking a pipe, and talking to an old mangy dog who lay beside him.

'Hi there.' He looked friendly, and smiled at John as he came up the steps.

'Hello. Are you Charlie?' John smiled pleasantly. He had been good at this, in the days when he actually did the legwork. Now he just determined it from his desk on Fifty-seventh Street, but there was a certain thrill to doing this part of it again. He had tried to explain to Sasha once how much he loved it. But she couldn't understand it. To her, there was only dancing ... and Lincoln Center ... and rehearsals. Nothing else mattered. Sometimes he even found himself wondering if he did.

'Yes, I'm Charlie.' The old man answered. 'Who wants to know?'

John stuck out a hand. 'My name is John Chapman. I'm looking for some people who lived here years ago. In that house.' He pointed. 'Eileen and Jack Jones. Do you remember them by any chance, sir?' He was always polite, friendly, at ease, the kind of guy everyone wanted to talk to.

'Sure, I do. Got Jack a job once. Didn't keep it long of course. Drank like a sonofabitch, and she did too. I heard it finally killed her.' John nodded as though it were something he already knew. That was part of the art form. 'I used to work in the navy yard. Damn good work too, durin' the war. I was 4-F 'cause I had rheumatic fever as a boy. Spent the whole war right here, close to home, with my wife and my kids. Sounds kinda unpatriotic now, but I was lucky.'

'You had children then, did you?' John looked at him with interest.

'They're all growed now.' He rocked back and forth and a sad look came into his eyes as he gnawed on his pipe. 'And my wife's gone. Died fourteen years ago this summer. She was a good woman.' John nodded again, letting the old man ramble on. 'My boys come to see me from time to time, when they can. Daughter lives in Chicago. Went to see her last year, Christmas, colder'n a witch's teat. Got six kids too. Her husband's a preacher.' It was an interesting history and John patted the dog as he listened.

'Do you remember three little girls who came to live with the Joneses about thirty years ago . . . right about this time of year . . . it was the summer of '58, to be precise. Three little girls. One about nine years old, one five, and the littlest one was a baby. She must've been about a year old.'

'Naw . . . can't say as I do . . . they never had any kids,

Jack and Eileen. Just as well. They weren't real nice people. Used to have some knock-down drag-out fights those two. Nearly called the cops on 'em one night. I figured he'd kill her.' It sounded like a charming home in which to leave three children.

'They were her brother's children. They were just here for the summer, but one of them stayed on afterwards . . .' He let his voice trail off, hoping to jog Charlie's memory, and suddenly the old man looked up at him with a frown, and pointed the pipe into John's face with a burst of recognition.

'Now that you say all that, I do remember . . . some terrible thing . . . he had killed his wife, and the little girls were orphans. I only seen 'em once or twice, but I remember, Ruth, that's my wife, tellin' me how cute they were and how terrible Eileen was to 'em, that it was a crime to leave those children with her. Half starved 'em, Ruth said, she took 'em some dinner once or twice, but she was sure Jack and Eileen ate it and never gave it to the children. I never knew what happened to 'em though. They left pretty soon after that. Eileen took sick, and they went somewhere. Arizona, I think . . . California . . . someplace warm seems like . . . but she died anyway. Drank herself to death if you ask me. Don't know what happened to them little girls though. I guess Jack musta kep 'em.'

'Only one of them. The rest of them left that summer. They just kept the oldest one.'

'I guess Ruth musta known that. I forget.' He leaned back in his chair, as though remembering more than Jack and Eileen, it was all so long ago, and his wife had been alive then . . . it was bittersweet to remember back that far . . . he seemed to forget John as he rocked back and forth in his rocking chair, and he had given John what he'd come for. He hadn't learned anything he desperately needed to know, but it was a little piece of the puzzle. It explained some of Arthur's guilt. He must have known how terrible they were, and yet he had left them there . . . and left Hilary to them . . . in effect abandoned her to them. He could only begin to imagine what her life had been like in the house across the street, with the kind of people Charlie had described to him. The thought of it made John shudder.

'Do you think anyone else along here would remember them?' John asked, but Charlie shook his head, still lost in his reverie, and then he looked up at John and answered.

'No one lived here that long, 'cept me. The others all been here ten, fifteen years . . . most of 'em less. They stay a year or two, then move away.' It was easy to see why. 'My eldest boy wants me to come live with him, but I like it here . . . I lived here with his ma . . . I'll die here one day.' He said it philosophically. It was all right with him. 'I ain't goin'.'

'Thanks for your time. You've been a big help to me.' He smiled down at Charlie who looked up at him with open curiosity for the first time.

'Why you want to find Eileen and Jack? Somebody leave 'em some money?' It hardly seemed likely, even to him, but it was an intriguing idea, but John was as quick to shake his head.

'No. Actually, I'm looking for the three girls. A friend of their parents wants to find them.'

'That's a hell of a long time ago to lose someone and then go looking for 'em.' John knew only too well how true that was.

'I know. That's why you've been such a help. You put the picture together with little tiny pieces of what people remember and now and then you get lucky, like I did

245

with you. Thank you, Charlie.' He shook the old man's hand, and Charlie waved his pipe at him.

'They pay you good for a job like that? Seems like a lot of wild-goose chasin' to me.'

'Sometimes it is.' He left the previous question unanswered and waved as he stepped off the porch and walked back to his car. It was depressing just driving down the street, and it was as though he felt Hilary's eyes on him, as though he were Arthur leaving her there, and he couldn't help wondering how Arthur could have done it.

The drive to his parents' house after that took less than an hour, and his older brother was already there when he arrived, drinking a gin and tonic on the terrace with his father.

'Hi, Dad. You look great.' The old man looked more like sixty than nearly eighty. There was no tremor in his voice, he still had his hair, and he had the same long, lanky legs as John as he strode across the terrace to put an arm around his shoulders.

'Well, how's my black-sheep son?' They always teased him, but they were proud of him too. He was successful, attractive, led an interesting life. The only thing his parents regretted for him was that he had divorced Eloise, they had always hoped the two would stay together and have children. 'Keeping yourself out of trouble?'

'Not if I can help it. Hello, Charles.' He shook hands with his brother and the two men smiled. There was always a certain distance between them, and yet John was fond of him. He was a partner in an important law firm in New York and he had done well. He was forty-six years old, he was powerful in the field of international law, he had an attractive wife who was president of the Junior League, and he had three very nice children. By the standards of John's family, Charles was the major achiever. But John always felt there was something missing from Charles's life, excitement perhaps, or maybe just plain old romance.

And with that, Lesley, his wife, walked out of the house with her mother-in-law, who gave a whoop of delight when she saw John talking to his brother and father.

'The prodigal son has arrived,' she intoned in her husky voice, hugging him close to her. She was still a handsome woman at seventy, and even in her plain yellow linen dress, there was an innate elegance about her. She wore her hair in an elegant knot, a string of pearls around her neck that her husband had given on her wedding day, and the rings that had been in her family for five generations. 'Don't you look well, darling! What have you been up to?'

'A little work on the way up. I just started a new investigation.' She looked pleased. She enjoyed her sons. They were all handsome and different and intelligent, and she loved them all, but secretly she had always loved John just a little bit more than the others.

'I hear you've got involved with the ballet,' Lesley said coolly, eyeing John carefully over her Bloody Mary. There was something mean-spirited about the girl which always irked John, but he was amazed that no one else even seemed to notice. She was one of those women who had everything and should have enjoyed it – two lovely daughters, a charming son, a handsome, successful husband – and yet she seemed to begrudge everyone everything they had, particularly John. She always felt that somehow he had done better than Charles, and it annoyed her. 'I had no idea you were interested in the dance, John.'

'You never know, do you?' He smiled non-committally, amazed that she had heard about Sasha, and then he chuckled to himself inwardly, thinking that maybe she had been meeting a lover at the Russian Tea Room.

Moments later, Philip arrived, looking very tanned after his European holiday. He and his family lived in Connecticut, and he played tennis constantly. He had a son and a daughter and a wife with blond hair and blue eyes and freckles. She looked exactly like what she was, the childhood sweetheart he had married at college. He was thirty-eight years old, and so was she, and she won all the tennis tournaments in Greenwich. They were truly the perfect family, except for John who had never quite fitted into the mould, and never done what was expected.

And bringing Sasha up here would have complicated things even further. Eloise had been difficult enough. When she wanted to be sociable, she was great, and when she didn't, she would bring a typewriter, and insist on working till lunchtime, which drove Lesley nuts, and made mother worry that she wasn't having a good time. Eloise was definitely not easy. But Sasha would have really been a shock to them with her leotards and her skintight blue jeans and her fits of petulance and her scenes of defiance. The very thought of her made him grin to himself as he looked at the ocean.

'What's so funny, big brother?' Philip clapped him on the back, and John asked him all about Europe. The hardest thing of all was that they were all such nice people, and he loved them, but they bored him to death, and by Sunday afternoon it was a relief to be driving to the airport. He felt guilty for thinking it, but they all led such normal, suburban lives. By the end of a weekend, he always felt like a misfit. At least his mother had had a nice time. Each of her sons had given her something special that was important to her. John had bought her a beautiful antique diamond brooch with a matching bracelet, and it was just the kind of thing he knew his mother loved. Charles had given her stock, which John thought was an odd gift, but she seemed to be pleased with it, and Philip had given her something she had said she wanted for years, but never bought herself. A grand piano was being delivered to the house in Boston on Monday. It was just like him to do something like that, and John thought it was a terrific gift and wished he'd thought of it himself. But she seemed happy with the brooch and bracelet.

He returned the rented car at the airport, and flew back on the commuter with a mob of people returning from the weekend, and by eight o'clock he was back in his apartment making himself a sandwich for dinner, and going through Arthur Patterson's file again. He didn't know anything more than he did before, except the kind of home Hilary had been left in. And he knew exactly what he was going to do the next morning.

But Sasha was far from thrilled when he told her when she came to his apartment later that evening. 'What? You're going away *again*?' She was furious. 'What is it this time?'

John tried to pacify her as best he could, they had been on their way to bed when he mentioned it to her, which was a mistake, he recognized now, but he was still hoping to make love to her that night. It had been days, and with Sasha you had to hit it right, when she wasn't too tired, when her muscles weren't too delicate, when she didn't have a big performance the next day. It was a real feat getting her to bed at all, and he wasn't about to blow it for Arthur's investigation.

'I told you, baby, I have a big case, and I'm handling this one myself.'

'I thought you were the boss. The choreographer, as it were.' He smiled at the comparison and nodded.

'I am. But this is an exception. I agreed to do the legwork myself, if I could. It's a very important case to my client.'

'What's it about?' She looked at him suspiciously, as she stretched out again on his bed, with all her clothes on.

'I'm looking for three girls . . . three women actually. He lost track of them thirty years ago, and he has to find them quickly. He's dying.' He couldn't tell her more than that, even that was something of a violation of Arthur's confidence, but he wanted to spark Sasha's interest and her allegiance.

'Are they his daughters?' He shook his head as he un-buttoned his shirt. 'Ex-wives?' He shook his head again. 'Girlfriends?' He smiled and shook his head again. 'Then what are they?'

'They're sisters.'

'And they're in Florida?' She thought it all sounded very boring.

'One of them was a long time ago. I have to start way back. I thought I had her here in New York, but I didn't. So now we go back to the beginning.'

'How long will you be gone?'

'A few days. I should be back by Friday. We can do something nice this weekend.'

'No, we can't. I have rehearsals.' There was no denying, her schedule was not easy.

'All right, then we'll work around it.' He was used to that.

'You're sure you're not just going to Florida on holiday?'

'Hardly. I can think of a lot of places I'd much rather go, with you, my lovely.' He slid across the bed, took her by surprise and kissed her, and this time she laughed. She let him undress her, and wound her sinewy legs around his

250

body in a way that drove him mad as they began to make love, and then suddenly she pulled away, and he was afraid he had hurt her. He looked at her through his veil of desire and whispered in a hoarse voice, 'Are you all right?'

She nodded, but she looked worried. 'Do you know what I could do to myself in positions like this?' But she seemed to forget about it as his ardour increased and along with it, her own passion. But she was always thinking about herself, her dancing, her muscles, her feet, her body.

'I love you, Sash,' he whispered as they lay in each other's arms afterwards, but she was oddly silent. Her eyes were open and she was looking at the far wall and she seemed upset as he watched her. 'What's the matter, sweetheart?'

'That sonofabitch screamed at me all afternoon today, as though I were doing something wrong . . . and I know I wasn't . . .' She was obsessed with her dancing, and for a moment it depressed him. He had been there before, only the last time it had been her goddam characters and her books, and the plot she couldn't get a grip on. Women like them were exhausting. He wanted Sasha to be different, yet he wanted her to care about him, and in the moments when he was honest with himself, he was not sure that she did. He wasn't even sure she was capable of it. She was totally engrossed in herself. And when he got up to get something to drink from the kitchen, she didn't even seem to notice his absence. He sat on the couch for a long time, in the dark, listening to the noises from the street, and wondered if he would ever find a woman who cared about him, a woman who cared about his work, his life, his friends, his needs, and enjoyed being with him.

'What are you doing in here?' She was standing in the doorway, silhouetted gracefully in the moonlight, her voice a whisper in the darkened room, and she couldn't see the sadness in his eyes as he watched her.

'Thinking.'

'What about?' She came to sit beside him and for a moment it almost seemed as though she cared and then she looked down at her feet and groaned. 'God, I should go back to the doctor.'

'Why?'

'They hurt all the time now.'

'Have you ever thought about giving up dancing, Sash?'

She stared at him as though he were crazy. 'Are you mad? I would rather die. If they told me I couldn't dance anymore, I would kill myself.' And she sounded as though she meant it.

'What about children? Don't you want kids?' He should have asked her all those things long before, but it had been hard to distract her from her dancing.

'Maybe later.' She sounded vague. Eloise used to say the same kind of thing to him. Until she was thirty-six, and decided it would interfere too much with her career, and had her tubes tied while he was away on business. And she was probably right. She was happier alone.

'Sometimes if you put it off, "later" never happens.'

'Then it was never meant to be. I don't need children to be fulfilled.' She said it proudly.

'What do you need, Sash? Do you need a husband?' Or did she only need the ballet? That was the real question.

'I've never thought I was old enough to worry about being married.' She said it honestly, looking up at him in the moonlight. But he was forty-two years old, and he was thinking of all those things, he had been for a long time now. He didn't want to be alone forever. He wanted

252

someone to love him, and whom he could love, not just between books and ballets and rehearsals.

'You're twenty-eight. You should start to think about your future.'

'I think about it every day, with that old maniac screaming at me.'

'I don't mean your professional future, I mean your real life.'

'That *is* my real life, John.' But that was precisely what he was afraid of.

'And where do I fit into all that?' It was a night for soul-searching, and he wasn't sure if he should have started it. But it couldn't be helped. Sooner or later they'd have to talk about something other than her feet and her rehearsals.

'That's up to you. I can't offer you more than this for the moment. If it's enough, wonderful. And if it's not . . .' She shrugged. At least she was honest. And he wondered if he could change her mind, if he could induce her to marry him . . . to want a child . . . but it was crazy to do that again. He seemed to have this incredible penchant for challenges and lost causes. 'You ought to try climbing Everest sometime,' his younger brother had told him once, 'it might relieve some of the tension.' He had met Sasha twice and thought John was crazy. 'Do you want me to stay tonight?' she was asking him now. She was perfectly willing to go. She didn't mind the chaos of her apartment on the West Side with the eight million room-mates and fourteen million dance-bags.

'I'd like you to stay.' In truth, he wanted a great deal more from her. More even than she had to give, and he was only beginning to understand that.

'Then I'll go to bed now.' She got up matter-of-factly and went back to his bedroom. 'I have an early rehearsal tomorrow.' And he had to fly to Jacksonville. And more than that, he wanted to make love to her again, but she said she was too tired and her muscles were sore when he got back into bed with her and tried it.

Chapter 18

The flight to Jacksonville was brief and gave Chapman time to read some of his papers. He signed half a dozen things he had to read, but his mind always drifted back to Hilary . . . and the life she must have led with Eileen and Jack Jones, according to the description of the old man in Charlestown.

In Jacksonville, he went directly to the juvenile hall, asked for the senior administrator, and explained his investigation. It was unusual in cases like that to lay files open to anyone, but so many years had passed, and the girl would be thirty-eight years old. There could be no harm in looking back into the past now. And John assured them of his total discretion.

The signature of the judge assigned to the juvenile court had to be obtained, and John was told to come back the following morning. In the meantime, he checked into a motel downtown, and wandered the streets aimlessly. He spent some time going through the phone book and found five Jack Joneses, and then on a whim, he decided to call them. Three of them were black, and the fourth one didn't answer. But the fifth said his father had grown up in Boston and he thought he'd been married to a woman named Eileen who died before his dad married his mother. He said he was eighteen years old, and his dad had died of cirrhosis ten years before, but he'd be happy to tell him anything he could. John asked if he knew where his father used to live, say twenty-five years before, if maybe his mother knew, but the answer to that was simple.

'He's always lived in the same house. We still live here.' Chapman's interest rose sharply and he asked if he could come out and see it.

'Sure.' He gave him the address, and John was not surprised to discover that it had much the same feeling as their neighbourhood in Charlestown, the same seedy, depressing kind of area, near a naval yard, only this one was mostly black, and there were young boys on motorcycles cruising the area, which made Chapman nervous.

It was not a nice place to be, and like the Charlestown place, it looked as though it never had been.

Jack Jones Jr. was waiting for him, with a motorcycle parked in his own front yard, and he looked as though Chapman's visit made him feel important. He rattled on briefly about his dad, showed him some pictures, and invited him inside to meet his mother. Inside the house there was a terrible stench, of stale urine, old booze, and the filth of a lifetime. The house was beyond grim, and the woman Jack Jr. introduced as his mother was pathetic. She was probably only in her late forties, but already toothless, and she looked thirty years older, and it was impossible for John to determine if her infirmities were due to abuse or an illness. She smiled vaguely at him, and stared into space beyond him, while Jack Jr. made excuses for her, but she remembered nothing about a niece of Jack's previous wife. In fact, several times she seemed not to know who her own son was. Eventually, John gave up, and was on his way out, when Jack Jr. suggested he might want to talk to the neighbours. They had lived there for years, and even knew Jack Sr. when he was married to his

256

late wife. John thanked him and knocked on the door, and an elderly woman came to the screen door with caution.

'Yeah?'

'May I speak to you for a moment, ma'am?' It had been years since he had done this himself, and he suddenly remembered how difficult it was to win people's trust. He suddenly recalled how many doors had slammed in his face in the old days.

'You a cop?' It was a familiar question.

'No, I'm not. I'm looking for a woman named Hilary Walker. She lived here a long time ago, when she was a little girl. Would you have any idea where she might be today?'

The woman shook her head and seemed to be looking John over. 'What you want with her?'

'A friend of her parents wants to find her.'

'They shouldda looked for her twenty-five years ago. Poor kid . . .' She shook her head, remembering, and John knew he'd struck pay dirt. She was still talking to him through the screen door, but slowly it swung open, and she stood there in a house dress and slippers, staring at John, but not inviting him in. 'That so-called uncle of hers beat her to within an inch of her life. She crawled out of that place in the pouring rain and damn near died on my doorstep. My husband and I, we took her to the hospital, and she almost didn't make it. They said he'd tried to rape her.'

'Did anyone bring charges against him?' Chapman stared at her, horrified. The story was getting worse. Hilary's fate had truly been a nightmare.

But she only shook her head. 'She was too scared . . . little Hilary.' She shook her head. 'I'd forgotten her all this time.'

'What happened after that?'

'She went to a couple of foster homes, and eventually I think she just stayed in juvie. We went to see her twice, I think it was, but it was like . . . well, there was somethin' missin' outta that girl, not that you could blame her. She didn't warm up to no one.' It was easy to understand that, in the face of what he was hearing.

'Thank you. Thank you very much.' So that was the reason for juvenile hall, not that she had broken the law herself. Or maybe she'd done that too eventually. Sometimes that was the way it happened.

But in her case, it hadn't. They handed the files to him the first thing the next morning. The judge had signed the order without a problem. But the file on Hilary Walker was far from exciting. She had been a model student, had given no problems to the State, had been in two foster homes, whose addresses were given, and had then spent three years in juvenile hall without event. She had been given two hundred and eighty-seven dollars upon completion of her last year of high school, and five days later, she had left, never to be heard from again. It was a slim file, and told him precious little about the girl, except that her caseworkers' reports said that she was withdrawn, had no known friends, but posed no disciplinary problem either. The caseworkers who had known her then were all long since gone, and he imagined that both foster homes had disappeared too, but just to be sure, he went to the addresses listed in her file. The first woman was, amazingly, still alive and at the same address, and she thought she remembered her although she wasn't sure.

'She was the one who was so high and mighty. Didn't stay long neither. Can't remember how she worked. She started pining, and they sent her back to the hall. That's all I remember 'bout her now.' But it was enough, the woman's harsh words about other girls, the home itself told its own tale. And the second foster home had been torn down for a development years before. No wonder the woman at CBA knew nothing about her. The girl who had been here had gone God knows where to finish her life in the same kind of misery and squalor it had started, or been condemned to at the age of eight, when her father killed her mother, and then committed suicide and their best friend had abandoned her, after taking her sisters from her. In some ways, John felt as though Arthur had led her to slaughter. And it was easy to understand why she had come to Arthur's office twenty-one years before to vent her hatred. The question was, where had she gone from there? The trail was as cold as death, and he had no idea where to go from here. Where did one begin looking for a girl who had known so much pain and misery at such early age? He had run her rap sheet through various states and the FBI, and nothing had turned up, but that didn't mean anything. She could have changed her name, got married several times. She could have died in the past twenty-one years. She could have done a number of things. But if she was still in New York, John promised himself he would find her.

He left Jacksonville without regret, and with a sense of relief to be escaping the humidity and the squalor he had seen there. He could only imagine how Hilary felt on her way to New York to find her sisters, only to find that Arthur had not kept track of them, any more than he had of her. What a bitter disappointment it must have been for her.

He got home on Thursday night, and left a message on Sasha's answering machine. He knew it was the night of her big performance, but it was ten o'clock when he finally got home, and he was exhausted.

And the next day at the office, he reported to Arthur Patterson what he'd found, and there was a long, sad silence at the other end. John Chapman couldn't see the silent tears rolling down Arthur's cheeks as he listened.

'After she visited you, the trail's cold. I have no idea where she went from there, but I'm working on it.' He had already given one of his assistants a list of things he wanted: he wanted him to check out schools, hospitals, employment agencies, youth hostels, hotels, all the way back to 1966. It was no small task, but somewhere something would turn up, and they could go on from there. Meanwhile, he was going to start looking for Alexandra. 'I'll need to come down to your office on Monday. I want to go through the files on George Gorham's estate. I want to see if they contacted his widow recently.' Arthur nodded his head, and brushed away the tears he had shed for Hilary. John Chapman was certainly thorough.

It was a terrible thought to realize what had been Hilary's fate . . . but how could he have known . . . if only . . . he began coughing terribly as he thought of it, and eventually had to hang up the phone. And John went back to work. There was a mountain of files waiting for him on his desk, after being in Florida all week, and he stayed in the office until seven-thirty, and then stopped for a hamburger at the Auto Pub on the way home. It was nine o'clock when he got home, and the phone was ringing. It was Sasha.

'Where've you been all night long?' She sounded suspicious and angry.

'At my office. And I stopped and had something to eat on the way home. And how are you, Miss Riva?' There had been no preamble, no inquiry as to how he was, and she hadn't called him in Florida all week, even though he'd left his number on her machine, but he knew she'd been busy with rehearsals.

'I'm all right. I thought I'd done something to one of my tendons yesterday, but thank God, I hadn't.' Nothing had changed in his absence.

'I'm glad. Want to come over for a drink?' He half wanted to see her and half didn't. The week in Florida had been incredibly depressing and he needed cheering up, but on the other hand he didn't want to listen to the familiar litany about her ligaments and her tendons.

'I'm exhausted. I'm already at the apartment. But I'm free this weekend. We could do something tomorrow.'

'Why don't we go somewhere? How about the Hamptons or Fire Island?' The summer had already set in, and it was hot everywhere. It was going to be a beautiful weekend.

'Dominic Montaigne is having a birthday party on Sunday. I promised him I'd be there, and I can't let him down. I'm really sorry.' Ballet, ballerinas, dancers, rehearsals, performances. It was endless.

'That's all right. We could go for the day. I'd love to get out of town and lie on a beach somewhere.'

'So would I.' But he knew she would lie down for exactly half an hour and then she would start prancing around and flexing muscles, so nothing got stiff while she was relaxing. And there were times when it was extremely unnerving.

'I'll pick you up at nine o'clock. Okay?' She agreed, and he hung up, feeling suddenly sad, and indescribably lonely. She was never there for him when he needed her, and instead he found himself thinking about a girl he didn't know, who had been bounced between foster homes and juvenile hall more than twenty years before. It was crazy to be thinking about her now. He felt like Eloise with her imaginary characters. It made about as much sense, but she had become so real to him in the last week. Much more than he wanted.

The next day he and Sasha went to the beach. In the end they just went to Montauk, on Long Island, and it was relaxing and nice. He jogged along the beach while she exercised, and they stopped for a lobster dinner on the way home. It was eleven-thirty that night before they got back to his apartment, and fell into bed like two kids. She was in a good mood, and they made love without Sasha complaining once that his passion was going to do her great bodily harm or permanent damage. And wrapped around each other, they slept until ten o'clock the next morning, when she bounded out of bed, looked at her watch, and gave a shriek that woke him.

'What's wrong? . . . where are you? . . .' He squinted in the sunlight streaming across his room, and saw her rushing into the bathroom, and heard her turn on the shower. He threw back the sheets, and lumbered slowly in to see what she was up to. 'What are you doing in there?' The bathroom was full of steam, she had her hair tied in a knot on top of her head, and her face was turned full into the shower.

'What does it look like?'

'What are you doing up so early?'

'I promised Dominic I'd be there by eleven-thirty.'

'Oh for chrissake. What's the hurry?'

'I'm making lunch for everyone,' she announced as she turned off the shower and started to dry herself off.

'That's interesting. You never cook here.' He was annoyed. They had had such a nice day the day before, and now she was in such a hurry to leave him. He had wanted to make love to her again before she left, but she was all business.

262

'This is different,' she explained, looking as though what she said made sense. 'These are dancers.'

'Do they eat differently than everyone else?'

'Don't be silly.' He wasn't silly. He was just tired of the endless aggravation. 'I'll call you tonight when I get home.'

'Don't bother.' He walked out of the bathroom, picked up a cigarette on his dresser, and lit it. He rarely smoked, but when she upset him particularly it seemed to ease the tension, or added to it, he was never quite sure which, but it did something.

'John,' she smiled angelically at him as she brushed her hair with his hairbrush, 'don't be childish. I'd take you along, but they're all dancers. No one brings outsiders to these events. You know,' she smiled and for the first time he saw something vengeful in her eyes – 'kind of like when you visit your family in Boston.' So that was it. Or part of it anyway. Well, to hell with her games, and her dancers. 'Will I see you tomorrow night?' She hesitated doelike in the bedroom.

'Possibly, I have a lot of work to do on Monday.'

She walked over to him with her firm, lithe body straining against his and kissed him hard on the lips which visibly aroused him. He was standing naked in his bedroom doorway. 'I love you.' She had a way of taunting him that he half loved and half hated, and before he could say anything to her, she was gone, and he wanted to scream in frustration.

For lack of anything better to do, he called his younger brother, and spent the day in Greenwich with them, playing doubles with Pattie and Philip and their son, and swimming in the pool with their daughter. It was a relaxed, easy day, and he was always embarrassed to admit to himself, as he did on the drive home, how intensely they bored him. But they were decent people, and they were family after all, and it had been a pleasant escape from New York and the reminders of Sasha.

The phone was ringing when he got home, but he didn't answer it. He didn't want to hear about Dominic and Pascal and Pierre and André and Josef and Ivan or any of the others. He was sick to death of them all, and even a little bit of Sasha. And the next morning, he went to Arthur's law firm and went through the files of George Gorham's estate himself after Arthur gave him carte blanche, and he found exactly what he had wanted. Arthur could have found it himself, years before, if he had looked. The last contact they had had with Margaret Millington Gorham was in 1962, at which time she was already the Comtesse de Borne and living on the rue de Varenne in Paris. There had been no contact since then, but she couldn't be too hard to find. And a search of the Paris telephone directory that afternoon showed her still living at the same address, listed as Borne, P. de, and the address was the same one. Now if she was only still alive and could tell him where Alexandra was, he'd be in business.

Chapter 19

'Not again!' Sasha looked outraged, but he was unmoved this time. Business was business. 'What did you do, get a job with the airlines?' She was incensed. This was his third trip in as many weeks.

'I won't be gone long.' Things were a little cooler between them than they had been.

'Where to this time?'

He smiled. Jacksonville it wasn't. 'Paris. At least my working conditions are pleasant.' She didn't answer him at first and then she shrugged. For all she knew he was lying and flying all over with assorted girlfriends. He had certainly never done all this travelling before. It seemed odd that he was suddenly doing 'the legwork' himself, as he'd told her. 'I should be back by Friday. Monday at the latest.'

'Have you forgotten? I go out on tour next week for three weeks. I won't see you till I get back. Unless you want to fly in to see me one night.' But he knew what that was like, a whole troupe of dancers completely hysterical and on edge, and Sasha barely coherent enough to acknowledge his existence.

'That'll be all right, I'm going to be busy too.' But they wouldn't see each other for a month. A year ago that would have worried him. Now he thought it might be a relief, for him at least. Her obsession with her work was beginning to oppress him.

They slept side by side that night, without making love, and he dropped her off at her apartment the next morning on his way to the airport.

'I'll see you when you get back.' He kissed her on the mouth, and she smiled up at him, looking very innocent and pure.

'Have a good trip. I'll miss you.' Unusually kind words for her, ordinarily she would have been predicting the weather from the pain in her feet. And her sudden gentleness made him sorry to see her go. The problem with her was that she really had no idea how totally egocentric she was. To her, it seemed perfectly normal.

He waved at her from the cab, and promised to call from Paris as they rounded the corner, and a moment later, he sat lost in thought, wondering what he was going to find in Paris. Surely not a life like Hilary's if Margaret Gorham had married a French count. At least he hoped not.

At Arthur's request, he flew first class, and his flight landed in Paris at midnight, local time. He went directly to the Hotel Bristol after clearing customs, and was in bed by two o'clock, but he was too tired to sleep, and it was five in the morning before he fell asleep, and he was horrified to discover that it was eleven o'clock when he woke up again later. He instantly jumped out of bed, ordered coffee and croissants, and dialled Margaret's number, before taking his shower.

He asked for the Comtesse de Borne when the phone was answered by a male voice, speaking French, and stumbled in his limited French when the butler asked him, '*De la part de qui, monsieur?*' He gave him his name but was unable to translate the words *but she doesn't know me*. But whatever was said at her end, she was on the phone with him a moment later.

'Monsieur Chapote?' she said in French with a heavy American accent, sounding puzzled.

'Sorry.' He smiled. He liked her voice. 'John Chapman, from New York.'

'Good God. André can never get American names. Do I know you?' She was blunt and direct, and there was something in her voice that suggested quick laughter.

'No, ma'am. I'm here on a business matter I'd like to discuss with you at your earliest convenience.' He had no intention of telling her over the phone though.

'Oh.' She sounded a little startled. 'All my business matters are handled in New York.' She told him the name of the firm. 'Except my husband's, of course. Is this about an investment?'

'No.' He didn't want to frighten her, but he had to tell her something. 'Actually, it's a little more personal than that. It's about an investigation I'm conducting for a ~~rtner of your late husband's.'

'Pierre? But he didn't have any partners.' It was a very confusing conversation.

'I'm sorry. I meant Mr Gorham.'

'Oh poor George . . . but that was so long ago. He died in 1959 . . . that was almost thirty years ago, Mr . . . er . . . Chapman.'

'I understand that, and this goes back an awfully long time.'

'Was there anything wrong?' She sounded worried.

'Not at all. We were just hoping you could help us find someone. It would be a great help to us if you could. But I'd rather not go into the entire matter over the phone. If you could spare me a few moments, I would like very much to see you . . .'

'All right.' But she sounded uncertain. She wished she could ask Pierre, or someone, if they thought she should see this man. What if he were a charlatan, or a criminal of some kind . . . not that he sounded like it. 'Perhaps tomorrow, Mr Chapman? And the name of your firm in New York?'

He smiled. She was right to check him out. 'Chapman Associates on Fifty-seventh Street. My name is John Chapman. What time would you like to meet?'

'Eleven o'clock?' She wanted to get this meeting out of the way. He was beginning to make her nervous. But when she checked him out with her attorneys in New York, they knew the firm, and her attorney was even personally acquainted with John Chapman, and he assured her that he was entirely above-board. He just couldn't imagine what Chapman was doing, speaking to Margaret de Borne in Paris.

He arrived punctually the next morning, and the elderly butler let him in with a subdued bow, and then led him upstairs to wait in the countess's formal study. It was a room filled with beautiful Louis-XV furniture, and a tiny Russian chandelier with what looked like a million crystals that caught the sunlight shining into the room and cast it into a myriad of rainbows against the walls. It was the prettiest thing John had ever seen, and he didn't even hear her come in, as he stared at the beautiful lights, and the lovely garden in the distance.

'Mr Chapman?' She was tall and elegant, with a firm handshake and a strong voice, and the look in her eyes was warm and friendly. She was wearing a yellow Chanel suit, and their classic shoes, and a beautiful pair of yellow diamond earrings that had been a gift from her late husband. She smiled warmly at John and waved at one of the room's larger chairs. Most of them were extremely small and not very inviting, which always made her smile. She laughed as they both sat down. 'I'm afraid none of these pieces were designed for people of our proportions. I don't use this room very often. It was designed as a "lady's study" and I've never quite got the hang of it. My six-year-old granddaughter is the only person I know who looks comfortable here. My apologies.'

'Not at all, Countess. It's lovely.' It seemed odd to be calling her that, particularly with her easy smile and happy laughter, but he thought she might have expected the formality, and he wanted her as his ally. 'I'm afraid I'm here on a rather sensitive matter. I've been hired by Arthur Patterson.' He waited for the name to have an effect on her, but she didn't look as though she knew it. 'He was a partner of Mr Gorham's many years ago, and he was instrumental in bringing Alexandra Walker to you for adoption.' He watched her eyes, and she suddenly looked as though she were going to faint. Her face went pale as she watched him. She waited for him to go on without saying a word. But it was obvious that she now remembered Arthur.

'He is very ill now, and for whatever reasons – all of them personal I assume – he is anxious to find all three Walker girls. Their parents were close friends of his, and he feels an obligation to know that they're all right, before he . . .' As he groped for the right word, she interrupted.

'Isn't it a little late, Mr Chapman? They're certainly no longer children.'

'I agree. But he seems to have let it go until the eleventh hour, and now he wants the reassurance that they've had a good life.'

'At whose expense?'

'I beg your pardon?'

She looked angry. And she stood up and began to pace the room, walking through the shower of rainbows. 'At whose expense does he want that reassurance? Surely those

269

young women no longer care about Arthur Patterson, if they even knew him. And if they did, they won't remember him now. They were all very young children.' Chapman's heart sank at the look in her eyes. It was obvious that she was prepared to do anything to keep him from her daughter.'What on God's earth does it matter? They're all grown up. They don't know him. They don't even know each other.'

John Chapman sighed. In a way she was right. But he was working for Arthur. 'That is part of the reason for my investigation.' He spoke in a gentle voice, anxious to calm her down and show her that she could trust him. 'Mr Patterson wants to bring the sisters back together.'

'Oh, my God.' She sat down hard again, in one of the uncomfortable small Louis-XV chairs. And then, with intransigence, 'I won't allow it. What need is there to torture them? My daughter is thirty-four years old, God only knows how old the others are. Why would they want to discover two unknown sisters? It can only be an embarrassment to them, not to mention painful. Do you know what the circumstances of their parents' deaths were, Mr Chapman?' He nodded, and she went on, 'So do I. But my daughter does not, and there is no need for her to know it. George and I loved her very much, like our own, and the Count took her in as his own daughter. She has grown up as our child, with every advantage that could be given her, she has a happy life with a husband and children of her own. She does not need this heartache.' Not to mention how she would keep it from her husband. The very thought terrified Margaret. Not only was she adopted, but her real father had *murdered* her mother.

'I understand that, but maybe she would like to meet her sisters . . . it's possible . . . maybe she has a right to make that choice herself. Does she know she's adopted? Margaret hesitated thoughtfully.

'Yes. And no. We told her . . . a long time ago . . . but I'm not sure she remembers. It's no longer of any importance. To anyone, Mr Chapman. I will not tell her about your visit.'

'That's not fair to her.' He spoke in a quiet voice. 'And if you force me to, I'll find her. I would prefer it if you spoke to her, and explained the reason for my visit. I think that would be a lot easier for her.'

Margaret de Borne's eyes filled with tears of anger. 'That's blackmail. You're forcing me to tell her something that will make her very unhappy.'

'If she doesn't wish to see them, she doesn't have to. She has a right to refuse to see them herself. No one can force her. But she has the right to choose. Maybe she'd like to see them.'

'Why? Why after thirty years? What kind of people are they now? What does she have in common with them? Nothing.' It was certainly true in the case of Hilary, but he didn't yet know about Megan. While Hilary was being kicked around and raped by her uncle and living in nightmarish foster homes, her sister was riding ponies in Paris. It seemed an unfair turn of fate. At least one of them had been blessed, from all appearances, but it only made him ache more for Hilary. Life had not been kind to her for a single moment.

'Countess . . . please . . . help me make it easy for her. She has a right to know. And I have an obligation to tell her.'

'Tell her what?'

'That she has two sisters somewhere in the world, and perhaps they want to see her.'

'Have you found them yet?'

He shook his head. 'No, but I think we will.' He was being optimistic, but he didn't want to share his fears with her.

'Why don't you come back when you've found them.'

'I can't afford to waste a moment. I've already told you, Mr Patterson is dying.'

'It's a shame he didn't die before he decided to ruin everyone's life.' She sounded bitter and very angry. For years, she had shielded Alexandra from the truth, and now this stranger, this man, was coming to hurt her. It made her want to kill him, and John felt sorry for her. She was a nice woman, and it was unfortunate that this was so upsetting for her.

'I'm sorry. Truly, I am.'

She looked at him long and hard. 'Perhaps you are. Can't you just tell him you couldn't find her?' John shook his head and she sighed.

'I'll have to think about this. It will come as a great shock to her, particularly if I have to tell her about her parents.' But at least, John thought to himself, she was old enough to withstand it. She wasn't a young girl, or a child. Maybe it was just as well he had waited. 'I'll be seeing her tomorrow for lunch. I'll speak to her about it then, if I find an appropriate moment.'

He nodded. He couldn't ask for much more. 'I'm at the Bristol. I would like to speak to her myself, after you've told her.'

'She may not wish to see you, Mr Chapman. In fact, I hope she doesn't.' Margaret de Borne stood to her full height and did not hold out her hand, as she rang for the butler. 'Thank you for your visit. Good day, Mr Chapman.'

'Thank you, Countess.'

He was escorted downstairs by André, who wore a

stern look of disapproval. It was obvious to him by the way the Countess had said goodbye that John Chapman was *persona non grata*, and he treated him accordingly as he closed the door resoundingly behind him.

Chapter 20

Alexandra found her mother, as usual, in the small flowery sitting-room she preferred, but she was not doing needle-point when she arrived, and most uncharacteristically, her mother was wearing a navy-blue dress and very little jewellery.

'You look very serious today, Maman. Did you have a meeting at the bank this morning?' Alexandra kissed her warmly, and Margaret smiled up at her, but the smile looked distracted and halfhearted. She had barely slept the night before, after Chapman's visit that morning.

'No, no, I'm fine,' Margaret said distractedly, and looked around the room, as though hoping for an escape. And Alexandra frowned, watching her.

'Is something wrong?' She hadn't seen her that nervous since her father died, and wondered if something had happened to upset her.

'No, just some unpleasant business meetings yesterday.' She smiled nervously. 'Nothing to worry about, darling. Ah, here's lunch.' She looked enormously relieved, and dived into her salad, giving Alexandra the latest gossip she had heard at her hairdresser's, and it was a relief to Alexandra to hear her mother laughing. But it was obvious that she was troubled about something, and as the meal drew to a close, she fell strangely silent.

'Maman.' She eyed her mother seriously. 'What's bothering you? I can tell, something's wrong. Now what is it?' She hoped it wasn't her health. She was remarkably youthful, but nonetheless ... And then suddenly she worried that that was why she had just gone to New York the week before. Perhaps it was to see a doctor, and not go shopping. She had brought back marvellous things for the girls, and a beautiful new Galanos for Alexandra.

But Margaret only looked at her mournfully, wishing she had never heard of John Chapman. She took a deep breath, and waited while André poured their coffee, and then discreetly left the room. Not that it mattered, he was terribly deaf, and spoke no English. But nonetheless, Margaret waited.

'I had a rather unpleasant visit yesterday. Sort of a ghost from the past.' She looked at her daughter, and her eyes filled with tears, and Alexandra was shocked. She had never seen her mother look so worried.

'What kind of a ghost?'

'Ohhh ...' Margaret dragged her feet, unable to find her footing. And she looked at her daughter and dabbed at her eyes. 'I don't know where to begin. It's such a long and confusing story.' She blew her nose discreetly in a lace handkerchief she'd had tucked in her sleeve, and held out a hand to Alexandra. Alexandra moved closer to her, and held her mother's hand tightly in her own. It was obvious that whatever the news from this man had been, it had been ghastly. Margaret was looking up at her and fighting back tears as Alexandra gently stroked her hand to reassure her. 'Do you remember a long time ago, a very long time ago, before I married Pierre?'

'Not really, Maman.' It was all a distant blur now. She supposed if she tried very hard, she might remember something. 'Why? What is it that I'm supposed to remember?'

'Do you remember that I was married to someone

275

before your father? I mean before Pierre . . .' It was going to be just as difficult as she expected, and Alexandra narrowed her eyes thoughtfully, and then nodded.

'Yes . . . sort of . . . I suppose that was my real father . . . but to be honest I don't remember him. All I remember is Papa.'

Margaret nodded. That's what she had always thought. 'Well, I was married before, and that was obvious because I think you might remember that Pierre adopted you right after we got married.'

Alexandra smiled at the dim memory. She had almost forgotten, until her mother jogged her memory. But now she vaguely remembered. They had gone to a lawyer's office, and the *mairie*, and then they had all gone to lunch at Maxim's to celebrate. It had been the happiest day of her life . . . and it was odd that in a way she had forgotten. 'You know, it's funny. I think I'd almost forgotten I was adopted.' And then she blushed. 'I suppose I should have told Henri, but I never really thought it was important. And Papa said . . .' They both knew what Pierre had told her. And she had instinctively sensed that Henri would be very angry if he knew she were adopted. So she had never told him or allowed herself to remember.

'Your father thought of you that way. You were like his own flesh and blood . . . and more . . .' she added softly. And then she went on with her painful story. 'But you were adopted,' she paused as though trying to gain courage – 'not only by Pierre . . . but by my previous late husband. We adopted you when you were five years old, your parents were both dead, and a partner of George's firm came and spoke to us about you . . . and we fell in love with you the first time we saw you.' The tears were pouring copiously down her cheeks and dripping on their clasped hands, as Alexandra stared at her. What was she saying? What did she mean? Margaret was not her mother? Suddenly, her arms went around Margaret, and she held her tight, as though afraid to lose her.

'I don't remember that part at all, I thought . . . I always thought . . . that you were my mother . . .' How could she have forgotten? . . . How was it possible? . . . Not that it really changed anything. But who had her parents been, and who was really her mother?

Margaret sniffed and blew her nose again. This was even harder than she had expected. 'You were nearly four when your parents died . . . your mother anyway . . . and your father died a few months later. You were left with an aunt, I believe, on your father's side, but she didn't feel able to keep all . . . to keep you . . .' She stumbled and went on. 'So a friend of the family was looking for someone to adopt you. And you made us the happiest people in the world, and six months later George died, and we came to France, and you remember the rest after that.' She was glossing over some of it, but Alexandra was still trying to digest the fact that Margaret wasn't her mother.

'How did my parents die?' There was a long silence as their eyes met and held, and Alexandra felt a chill go up her spine. She knew deep in her heart that something terrible had happened. Margaret closed her eyes and then opened them, speaking in a gentle voice.

'There was a terrible argument no one ever understood . . . he was a famous actor on Broadway, and they said she was very beautiful . . .'

'That's not what I asked you, Maman . . .' The tears were pouring down Alexandra's cheeks as she waited. She knew, she already knew, that was the awful part, but now she needed to hear it from Margaret.

'Your father killed her.'

Alexandra spoke in a haunted whisper, looking beyond her mother at the garden. 'And my father committed suicide. They told me he had killed himself . . .' Her hand flew to her lips and a sob escaped her, as Margaret took her in her arms and let her cry. 'And I forgot . . . I forgot all of it . . . how could I forget that? . . . and my mother had red hair . . . and . . . she spoke French, didn't she? Oh my God . . . but that's all I remember.' And then she looked up at Margaret again, the pain of the memories etched on her face ravaged by the tears born of what she suddenly remembered. 'Was she French?'

Margaret spoke with obvious pain as she answered. It was terrible beyond words, and she hated John Chapman and Arthur Patterson for visiting this on them unnecessarily, so many years later. 'I think she was French . . . probably . . .' And she probably had red hair, because Alexandra did, when she wasn't rinsing it blond to please her husband. And little Axelle looked so exactly as Alexandra had at the same age. It was like seeing her again as she had the first time each time Margaret saw her.

'Why did my father kill himself? Because he killed her?' She wanted to know. It was awful, but suddenly she needed the answers to questions that were so long forgotten.

'He killed himself because he was convicted of killing her. It was a terrible, shocking story. And it left you and . . . it left you an orphan.' But she couldn't keep avoiding the rest of the story. That was the worst of it. She had to tell her. She took Alexandra's hand in her own again, and gently stroked the graceful fingers that looked nothing like her own. In fact, physically, they were very different, but Alexandra had never given it much thought. And suddenly she understood it . . . but all she could remember was the red hair, and nothing else . . . there was no face to go with it. She felt her heart was being torn from her chest, as though pain and memories long buried were rising to haunt her. 'You had . . . you had two sisters as well.' Her words struck through Alexandra like a knife, and she could feel them echo in her head like ricocheting bullets . . . two sisters . . . two sisters . . . two sisters . . . Axie, I love you . . . I love you . . . My God, how could she have forgotten? She remembered the touch, the smell . . . black, black hair, and big sad eyes . . . Hillie . . . Hillie . . . and a baby. Without thinking Alexandra pulled away from her mother and walked across the room to stare out at the garden. 'We couldn't take all three of you . . . we didn't feel . . .' Alexandra wasn't listening to the voice, the apologies, she kept hearing the same words . . . 'always remember how much I love you . . . I love you, Axie . . .' and a little girl sobbing uncontrollably. Who was that little girl? Was it her sister?

'What were their names?' She had to know now. She had to, but Margaret shook her head. She knew very little about the others.

'I don't know. I only know that one was older than you . . .'

Alexandra finished the sentence for her as though in a trance, '. . . and the other one was a baby.' She stared at Margaret as though in great pain. 'I remember them, Maman . . . I remember something now. How could I have forgotten?'

'Maybe it was all too painful for you then. Maybe it was easier to forget. You didn't do anything wrong. You had a right to a new life. We loved you very much, and we did everything we could to make you happy.' She looked so bereft, suddenly it was as though with one fell swoop she had lost her only daughter, and Alexandra went to her and put her arms around the woman she had known as her mother for thirty years.

'You *are* my mother, Maman. You always will be. None of this will ever change that.'

'Do you mean that?' She needed to hear it, and cried unashamedly as Alexandra reassured her. 'It's so awful that these people have come back to haunt you now, they have no right to do so.'

'Why have they come back?' Alexandra looked at her with eyes full of questions.

'Arthur Patterson, the man who arranged your adoption was a friend of your family . . . of your parents . . . and he wants to know now that you and your . . .' She almost choked on the word, '. . . sisters . . . are all right. And if possible he wants to bring you together.' Alexandra looked shocked.

'Do they know where the others are?'

'Not yet. But they're looking. And they found you, so I suppose they'll find the others.'

Alexandra nodded. It was a lot to absorb at once. Suddenly, in one afternoon, she had acquired two sisters, and a father who had killed a mother with red hair who was probably French, and the mother she'd loved all her life was no longer her mother, not to mention two adopted fathers she'd discovered instead of one. It was a bit much to swallow at one sitting, and she smiled weakly at Margaret and took a big swig of wine, with an apologetic look.

'I think I need it.'

'So do I.' And with that, Margaret stood up, and rang for André, and when he appeared she told him to bring her a double bourbon. 'American habits die hard, particularly in moments of crisis.' And then she turned to Alexandra, over her drink, as she slowly swirled the ice cubes with one finger.

'Do you want to see them, Alex?'

Alexandra looked up at her thoughtfully. 'I don't know. What if we all hate each other and are terribly different? Thirty years is a long time.'

'That's what I told Chapman. In truth, it's ridiculous. What can you possibly have in common?'

Alexandra agreed, and yet there was an undeniable attraction to meeting the others. But there was another problem she had to deal with first, a more pressing one. Her husband. 'What do you suppose Henri would say to all this, Maman?' She eyed her mother cautiously, but they both knew what Henri would say. He would be outraged. 'Do you really suppose it will make a difference to him?' Margaret could see that she desperately wanted reassurance. But she couldn't give it to her. The scandal would surely be too much for Alex's husband.

'It shouldn't, if he loves you. But I think it would be a shock to him. That's inevitable. And frankly, I still don't see why you should tell him. Your father and I talked about it when you married him, and we decided it wasn't important. We love you, you are our daughter in every possible way and what happened thirty years ago is no one's business. Perhaps not even your husband's.'

'But that's so dishonest, Maman. I owe it to him to tell him. Don't I?' Her eyes were still full of questions.

'Why? Why upset him needlessly?' Margaret tried to sound calm, but the whole thing was turning into a nightmare.

'Because the fact that I'm the daughter of the Comte de Borne is very important to him, Maman. He believes in all that lineage, and you know it. He's barely able to tolerate the fact that you're American, for heaven's sake, and only the fact that he knows what a fancy family you're from makes him willing to overlook it. How about telling him

281

instead that my father was an actor, and killed my mother, origin unknown. I am the daugher of an unknown murderer and suicide, American to boot, with two unidentified sisters.' She grinned in spite of herself. It was a difficult situation. 'Frankly, I think he'd drop dead from a heart attack. And if he survived, he'd divorce me. And take my daughters if he could get away with it. But if I don't tell him, I'm being dishonest.'

'Don't be foolish, Alex. This isn't the Dark Ages. He couldn't be that unreasonable. And besides, I still don't think you should tell him.'

'You don't know my husband. If I tell him, he might leave me and the girls, but the rest of it's not so far-fetched. Particularly with his political aspirations. My God, mother, he'd die . . . And if he found out some other way . . . if I didn't tell him . . . if someone else found out.' Alexandra visibly shuddered as she paced the room, and Margaret couldn't disagree with her.

'I told you. Don't tell him.'

'And if he finds out? If there's a scandal? At least before I didn't know most of it myself. But now that I do, how can I not tell him? That's deceitful.' It was before, too, but now she was hiding a veritable mountain of information.

'Oh don't be so bloody innocent, for heaven's sake.' She took a huge sip of bourbon and looked at her daughter. 'You can't always be the perfect wife. You have to think of yourself from time to time, not that you do it very often. And it would be stupid to make a confession to Henri. What purpose would it serve except to cause you a great many problems?' And she could hardly disagree with her mother. There was so much at risk. She could lose everything. Her husband. Her marriage. Her children.

'But what if I decide I want to see the others? How do I explain that? How do I slip away to America to meet my sisters? I can't exactly say I'm coming here to lunch and then disappear for five days, can I?'

'Are you so sure you want to go?' Margaret was disappointed to hear it, but Alexandra shook her head.

'I'm not at all sure . . . but if I wanted to, I don't know what I'd tell my husband.' Margaret's solution would have been not to go at all then, but she knew it wasn't fair to say that. She had her own reasons for not wanting Alexandra to go, it was foolish but she was afraid that in some way she would lose her, to the spectre of a mother long dead, and two sisters who would help prove that blood was thicker than water. It was childish, but she wanted Alexandra to turn her back on them. But she was wise enough not to say it.

'I don't think you should say anything to him, Alexandra. Nothing at all. You would be wisest if you kept your own counsel.' She scribbled something on a piece of paper then, and handed her John Chapman's name, and the name of his hotel and phone number. 'Mr Chapman wants you to call him, so he can explain it all to you. If you want to, you can call him at the Bristol.'

'Why is he here?'

Margaret hesitated, but only for an instant. 'To see you.'

'That's why he came to Paris?' Margaret nodded in answer. 'Then I'll call him. I owe him that at least.' And as she slipped the paper with his name into her bag, she saw the time. It was after five o'clock, and she was horrified. She had to get home to Henri and the children. It had been an amazing afternoon, full of unexpected admissions. And Margaret walked her to the door, and hugged her long and hard before she left, as Alexandra looked into her eyes with tears rolling down her cheeks again. 'Maman, please know how much I love you.'

'You'll always be my little girl.' The tears began sliding down her cheeks again, and the two women held each other for a long time before Alexandra left her. It had been a shocking afternoon and she could hardly think straight on the drive home. She kept hearing a voice from the distant past . . . Axie . . . always remember how much I love you . . .

Chapter 21

Alexandra was still in shock when she got home. It was difficult to absorb everything her mother had told her. She felt as though she were moving in a dream, and she kept trying to remember things that had been gone for years . . . the woman with red hair . . . and the little girl she had called Hillie.

'You're late.' Henri was waiting in her study as she walked into the room, feeling as though she had lead weights on her shoulders.

'I'm sorry, I . . .' She jumped when she saw him, startled from her reverie. But to Henri, it made her look guilty. 'My mother had some papers I had to discuss with her . . . I didn't think it would take . . . Henri, I'm sorry.' There were tears in her eyes when she turned to him, and he was looking at her as though he didn't believe her.

'Where were you?'

'I told you . . .' Her hands trembled as she hung up the jacket to her suit. He made her feel as though she had somehow betrayed him. 'I was at my mother's.' She tried to make her voice sound calm, but she sounded nervous, even to her own ears.

'Until now? It's six o'clock.' His voice was filled with disapproval, but suddenly she turned on him, her nerves frayed beyond control. She needed time to think, to absorb what she'd been told . . . she needed time to remember.

'Look, I'm sorry I'm late. I told you, I was at my mother's.'

He backed down quietly, but he still looked angry. 'See that it doesn't happen again. I don't know why she keeps you this late. She knows you have important obligations.'

Alexandra clenched her teeth so as not to answer him. Her mother had kept her late so that she could tell her she had been adopted twice . . . and her natural father had murdered her mother . . . that she had two sisters she'd entirely forgotten about . . . little things like that. Nothing important.

She dressed hastily in a black silk dress, and sheer black stockings. She slipped into black satin pumps, washed her face, changed her make-up, re-did her hair and put her lipstick and compact in a black satin handbag. And within twenty minutes she was downstairs again, joining Henri in the front hall as they left for the evening. She barely had time to say good-night to the girls, and when she did, she almost cried. As she looked at them, she was reminded of the sisters she had all but forgotten.

'Be good to each other, you two,' she whispered as she kissed Marie-Louise good-night. 'You don't know how lucky you are to have each other.' And a life such as theirs, filled with people who loved them, safe from harm. She herself had been lucky to be adopted by Margaret and Pierre. But now suddenly, as she looked at Henri, she felt as though she had a guilty secret.

'Why doesn't your mother take her problems to her attorney or her banker?' Henri asked in a voice filled with annoyance as they drove to the restaurant where they were meeting some new acquaintances of Henri.

Alexandra looked vague as she glanced out the window. 'She thought I could help her. That's all.' He laughed, as though it were a ridiculous suggestion.

'She could at least come to me. I could be of assistance.'
But she knew perfectly well that Margaret would never
go to her husband. They barely tolerated each other.

They arrived at Taillevent, and Alexandra looked
around the familiar décor distractedly as Henri led her to
their guests and made the necessary introductions. The
room was filled with *tout Paris*, men in dark suits, and
beautiful, elegantly dressed women. The room was as
magnificent as it always was, with the rich panelling,
magnificent chandeliers, and goblets filled with fresh
flowers. It was a place where only the most elite were
able to get in, and even they had to wait months for a
reservation.

It was Henri's favourite restaurant, and he enjoyed going
there with her and their friends, and even business associates like tonight. The people he was dining with were
potential backers for his political career, and Alexandra
could sense that the evening was extremely important.
But no matter how hard she tried, she found herself unable
to concentrate, and by the end of the evening she was near
tears, as Henri glared at her, and she fought desperately to
stay afloat in the conversation.

'Excuse me?' she said for a least the tenth time that
evening. She had totally missed what the woman said . . .
had it been something about the south of France? . . . or was
it something about her children? 'I'm terribly sorry . . .'
Alexandra's eyes filled with tears and she dabbed at her
eyes with her napkin, as though she were coughing. She
felt as though the evening was never going to end, and
Henri was furious with her when they left.

'How could you do that to me?' he railed on the ride
home. 'Your attitude was an open insult!'

'Henri, I'm sorry . . . I wasn't feeling well . . . I couldn't
concentrate . . . I . . .' But all she could think of was John

287

Chapman at the Bristol, and how desperately she wanted to call him.

'If you weren't well, you shouldn't have come tonight. You did more harm than good.' He was livid.

'I'm sorry . . . I tried . . . truly I did . . .' There were tears sliding down her cheeks. She hated to let him down, but there was so much on her mind now.

'You have no excuse!' he raged. But she did. And she couldn't tell him. 'I won't tolerate your behaving like that.' And then, the final blow, 'You're always impossible after you've seen your mother.' As though she were a naughty child, and he had a right to scold her.

'My mother has nothing to do with it, Henri.' Alexandra spoke in a quiet voice as she blew her nose, and he glared at her as they stopped at a light on the way home. He didn't even care if their driver heard him.

'Then where were you tonight until six o'clock?' That again. Alexandra only shook her head, and stared out the window, and then looked back at him again.

'I told you. I was at my mother's.'

'Was anyone else there?' He had never been suspicious of her before, and it hurt her deeply.

'Of course not. My God, what do you suspect me of?' She wanted to tell him that she didn't engage in the same sports as he, but she didn't want to open a Pandora's box that would cause even greater problems. She reached out and touched his hand then, but he showed no inclination to soften. 'Henri, please . . .'

'You disgraced me tonight.'

'I'm sorry. I had a terrible headache.'

He never said another word to her, but when they reached the house on the avenue Foch, he courteously opened the door to her, and then went to his own rooms, and firmly closed the door behind him.

Chapter 22

As soon as Henri had left for the office the next morning, Alexandra looked up the number of the Bristol and dialled it. She asked for John Chapman, feeling her hand tremble on the phone, and her voice cracked as she identified herself to him. It was like high espionage, and she was extremely nervous. If Henri had any idea what she was doing, or what she had learned, he would very probably divorce her.

'You've spoken to your mother?' Chapman had a calm, smooth voice, and she found him easy to talk to.

'Yesterday ... I ... I had forgotten everything.' Even that she was adopted. She had allowed herself to deny it to herself for all these years ... not to mention the fact that she'd been adopted once before ... and Hillie ... and the woman with red hair ... But Chapman didn't seem to condemn her.

'Maybe it was easier for you not to remember. There was no reason to.' He paused for a moment, and then spoke to her gently. 'Could we meet some time today? ... er ... uh ... I'm terribly sorry, I don't know your married name. All I know is your mother's name.' He sounded very polite and well bred and well educated. She had been nervous that he might be one of those seedy investigators one saw in B-movies.

'De Morigny. Alexandra de Morigny.' She didn't bother with the title. It seemed very unimportant.

'Thank you. I was hoping we could meet. Perhaps later this morning. I'd like to show you the files I have. Perhaps you have something to add to them ... or in any case, you have a right to know as much as we do.'

'Thank you very much. I could meet you at your hotel ...' She glanced at the clock on her desk, and made a rapid calculation. She had to bathe and dress, and leave instructions for the staff. Henri was having guests for dinner. 'At eleven. Would that be all right?'

'Perfect.' And with luck, he could catch a flight to New York that night. He had a lot of work to do, and he didn't want to cool his heels in Paris forever. 'I'll meet you in the lobby. I'm six feet two, I have blond hair parted on the side, and I'll be wearing a tweed jacket, a blue shirt and grey trousers.' He sounded more like a college student than a private eye, and she smiled as she imagined the outfit. He sounded like one of her American cousins. And then she realized that he didn't know what she looked like.

'I have blond hair too. I'm one metre sixty ...' And then she laughed. 'I'm sorry. I always forget what that is in English. Five foot five, I think. And I'll be wearing a grey suit.' She had a grey silk suit in mind, one that Henri liked, not that it mattered. And when she dressed, she wore it with a pink silk blouse, and a pink Hermès scarf and the Bvlgari coins on her ears that she wore when she didn't want to wear anything flashy. She looked respectable and chic, as she walked slowly into the Bristol, feeling her heart pound as her heels clicked on the marble floor and she glanced around the lobby. She was about to go to the desk and have him paged, but she saw him instantly, sitting quietly in a chair, holding a copy of the Paris *Herald Tribune*, and he stood up and smiled at her, walking towards her on long legs, and with a smile that left her a little breathless. He had perfect teeth, and gentle eyes, and she liked him instantly. He looked as though he would have made a good friend, and she shook hands with him solemnly, trying not to look at the briefcase he carried in his other hand. She knew that within it lay the secrets of her past, and that of her sisters.

'I'm sorry I'm late.' She spoke barely above a whisper, and he sensed easily that she was frightened. 'I drove myself, and I had a terrible time finding a parking place. I finally just gave the car to the doorman.' He nodded, and they sat down in a corner, in two large red velvet chairs that seemed perfectly suited to the occasion.

'Would you like a drink? Or a cup of tea? But she was too nervous to eat or drink, and she shook her head as he pulled the file out of his briefcase. It was much thicker than it had been when Arthur Patterson first gave it to John. There was what he knew of Hilary's life in it now. And soon there would be Alexandra's.

'Thank you, I'm fine.' Her eyes looked deep into his. 'Are you close to finding the others?'

'We hope so. The last trace we have of Hilary was when she went to see Arthur Patterson about twenty years ago, to find you and your younger sister, and she was furious to discover that he hadn't kept track of any of you. I suppose she tried to find you herself, and obviously couldn't. In any case, she held him responsible for the break-up of your family, and I imagine she hates him. And that is not difficult to understand, from what we know of her early life.

'I don't know what's happened to Megan yet, but certainly compared to you, Hilary got the worst deal possible.' He told her what he knew and Alexandra's eyes filled with tears as she listened, thinking of what a terrible fate a life like that would be for anyone. She tried to imagine it happening to her own two little girls, and the very thought made her ill. No wonder Hilary was bitter. She had every right to be. Abandoned, beaten, forgotten. 'I gather that when she went to New York, she went to see Patterson, and after that we've lost her. But I have a very intense investigation going on this week, and I imagine there will be more recent information on Hilary when I get back. We already thought we'd found her once, but it was a mistake.' He was referring to the woman at CBA. But wherever she was, he would find her. 'But next time it won't be.'

'My God, what an awful life.' Alexandra discreetly wiped the tears away and he offered her the file for her own inspection. She could hardly bear what she read, and looked up at him finally with anguish on her face. 'How could she survive it?' Alexandra felt a wave of guilt wash over her as she thought of her own life in comparison to her sister's. 'Why did this happen?'

'I don't know that. The turns of fate are not always kind, Mrs de Morigny.'

'I know.' She spoke softly, but she had never seen it quite so clearly. It was like one of the kaleidoscopes she gave to her children, you turned it just a fraction, and all of the same pieces fell into a totally different pattern. One moment they were flowers, and the next moment they were demons breathing fire. It seemed so wrong to her that Hilary should have been left to the demons. With effort, she turned her thoughts back to John Chapman. 'What can I do to help you find them?'

'Nothing at the moment, unless you remember anything specific that might help us. But your knowledge would have ended a long time ago, I don't think it's of much use now. I'll call you as soon as I've found the others, and Mr Patterson would like you to come to his home in Connecticut to meet them. It's the one thing he wants to do before he dies.' It seemed a noble wish, but less so if you thought of the pain he had caused them.

'What's he like? It's odd, but I don't remember him at all.' Nor did she remember her father. She had glanced at the clippings of Sam in John Chapman's file, and had been struck by how handsome he was, and how successful. There were only two photographs of her mother, one of a smiling young woman with cascading shafts of bright red hair, and in a funny way, she looked a little bit like Alexandra's youngest daughter. And the other photograph showed the three little girls, Alexandra and Hilary, in matching white dresses and shiny black shoes, and the baby in a long ruffled gown in her mother's arms, taken after Megan was born, on the last Easter their mother was alive. It was taken outside their house on Sutton Place, but it didn't look familiar to Alexandra.

Chapman tried to answer her question. 'Mr Patterson is very old, and very sick. I don't think he'll live much longer. He's very anxious to get the three of you together before he dies. It means a great deal to him.'

'And if he dies before you find them?' Alexandra asked bluntly.

'He's made provisions to continue the investigation and bring you together. But he would like to be around to see it.' She nodded. He had thought of everything. It was only a shame he hadn't thought of it thirty years sooner. It would have made a big difference to Hilary. And she said as much to John Chapman. 'If he was so close to my parents, why didn't he take us, and keep us together?'

John Chapman shook his head. 'I don't know. He said something about his wife not feeling able to cope with it. I think he regrets it now. Sometimes we make terrible mistakes, but we only see it in hindsight.' He dared to ask her then what Arthur wanted to know. 'Are you happy,

Alexandra? Forgive me for asking . . .' But it meant a great deal to Arthur. And she smiled at John.

'I have always been very happy. I have been blessed with wonderful parents whom I have loved deeply. Pierre de Borne was a remarkable man, and I'm only grateful he lived as long as he did. He was the joy of my life,' she blushed, 'and I of his.' And then she smiled more broadly. 'And you met my mother yesterday. She's wonderful, isn't she? She's my closest friend and greatest ally. This has been very hard for her.' Alexandra's face sobered as she thought of her mother's tears the day before. 'It was terribly hard for her to remind me of the past. I don't suppose it will be easy for anyone to dredge all this up, particularly given the way it all happened.' She sighed and looked hard at him. 'Does anyone really know why he killed her?'

'Not really.' He shook his head. 'Some sort of an argument, I believe. I think he was drunk. Temporary insanity, as the defence said. Mr Patterson maintains to this day that Sam, your father, adored her.

'It's difficult to understand people giving way to that kind of violence and emotions.'

She nodded, but she was thinking about Hilary and they still hadn't found out about Megan. 'I hope Megan's all right. I hope they both are.' It was as though she knew them now, as though they had already come back to her, like her own children. 'I have two little girls of my own, Axelle and Marie-Louise. It's odd,' she mused thoughtfully, 'I think Marie-Louise looks rather like Hilary.' It was odd too that Alexandra had returned to her mother's native country.

And then Chapman asked her a difficult question. 'Have you told your husband about all this?'

Slowly, she shook her head. 'I'm afraid Henri won't

understand it. I think he'll be very upset that my parents didn't tell him when we got married. And until you find the others, there's no point confronting him. It will only make him unhappy.' It was a story she had been telling herself since the night before, and she was almost convinced now.

'And when we find the others?'

'Then I'll have to tell him something.' She smiled uncomfortably. 'I don't normally go off to America at the drop of a hat, Mr Chapman.'

'You did not deceive him, you didn't know all this.' He was trying to soothe her, but she knew better.

'My parents did though. He will be very angry. He believes me to be the daugher of the Comte de Borne. The bloodline means a great deal to Henri. He can trace his family back nine hundred years. I don't really think that a murderer and a French war-bride were exactly what he had in mind for the grandparents of his children.' Perhaps it was just as well they had never had a son. Then he would never forgive her. And perhaps he wouldn't as it was. Chapman felt sorry for her as he watched her face. He sensed that her husband was not an easy person.

'I think he'll adjust. You've obviously been married for a long time. And he loves you. That counts for a lot.'

'Not to everyone, Mr Chapman.' She smiled wistfully. And how could he be so sure that Henri loved her? She wasn't sure of it herself sometimes. He owned her, like a fine piece of Louis-XV furniture, or a very good painting. And if the painting turned out to be a fraud? Would he still love it enough to keep it? She knew some would, but she wasn't at all sure Henri was among them. He was obsessed with quality and veracity and perfection. And she knew now that her pedigree was badly flawed. It was not difficult to imagine Henri's reaction.

Chapman was looking at her gently as they sat quietly in a corner of his hotel, and he realized that he liked her. She was gentle and shy, and she had kind eyes, the kind of eyes he had always wanted to find in a woman. She was so graceful, and so gentle. He hoped that Arthur's investigation was not going to cause her pain. She had done nothing to deserve it.

'May I invite you to lunch, Alexandra? And will you forgive me for being so informal?' He smiled his boyish smile at her and she laughed.

'You know all the secrets of my life. I hardly expect you to call me by my husband's title.'

'Oh dear . . . is he titled too then?'

'Of course.' She laughed again, and when she did she looked so much younger. 'The Baron Henri Edouard Antoine Xavier Saint-Brumier de Morigny. Lovely name, isn't it?' She was almost giggling. It had been a very tense morning, and she needed the relief. They both did.

'Does it all fit on his driver's licence?'

She laughed at the thought. And then sobered. 'And you, Mr Chapman, what do you think of all this? You're an intelligent man. It must all seem rather shocking.'

'Nothing shocks me anymore. I think it's a shame so many lives were destroyed by one act of madness. And in some ways, I think it's a shame to disturb the embers. But it's not for me to make those judgments, and perhaps it will bring some comfort to some of you to be reunited. Are you curious about the others?' She nodded. She had to admit she was.

'I remember Hilary a little bit . . . just flashes and little bits, ever since speaking to my mother yesterday.' And then she sighed. 'It was a tremendous shock for her.'

'And for you too.' There was compassion in his eyes

and he wanted to reach out and touch her hand, but he didn't. 'I'm sorry to cause you so much trouble.'

'You haven't yet.' But he would, when he found the others.

'Can I induce you to have lunch with me, in spite of all that?' He liked her, and funnily enough, he wanted to get to know her. He told himself it was so he could report back to his client, but he knew it was more than that. The pieces of the mystery were beginning to fall into place, and she was a lovely woman, and he liked her.

She hesitated for only a fraction of an instant, calculating what harm it could do, and decided it could do none. 'I'd love it.'

'Any suggestions? I haven't been here recently, and I'm afraid I'm not very much up-to-date on the in places.'

'The best places, Mr Chapman, are the old ones.' She stood up and smiled, and he put everything back in his briefcase and locked it. For an odd moment, she wanted to ask him for the picture of her as a little girl with her sisters, but she imagined that he needed it to show to the others, when he found them. And now suddenly she understood why there were no photographs of her as a baby. She thought of it as they crossed the lobby and he insisted that she call him John, and he noticed an odd look in her eyes then.

'I just realized something I'd never really understood before. My parents have no photographs of me as a baby. And I just accepted it, as though it were normal.'

'You had no reason to doubt them. Where are we going for lunch?'

'I thought we'd have lunch at the Ritz, with all the little old ladies.' She grinned and he laughed as she took his arm and they began walking.

'It sounds delightful.'

'They make me look terribly young and attractive.'

'You are, or haven't you noticed that lately?'

'I try not to look. I only see the wrinkles.' But it was only idle talk, she didn't even look thirty, and she had exquisite skin and silky hair, which reminded him that she looked different than he had expected.

'You know, it's funny. I thought you'd have red hair.'

She smiled guiltily, and looked very feminine, and he was struck again by how pretty she was, in a subtle way. It was almost as though she were trying to hide it, with her ladylike hair-do and subdued clothes. He wondered what she would look like if she really let herself go wild. Probably a great deal like her mother.

'I do have red hair.' The smile dimmed and then faded. 'My husband doesn't like it, so I rinse it blond. Axelle, my younger daughter, has red hair too. But I haven't been a redhead in years. Henri thinks it vulgar.' She said it in a matter-of-fact way and John silently decided that Henri was clearly an idiot.

Their lunch at the Ritz was relaxed and easy and pleasant. They talked about Boston and New York, and Cape Cod and Saint-Jean-Cap-Ferrat, where they each spent their summers. They talked about sailing, and summers as a child, and how he had started his career instead of going into law, as was expected. They were like comfortable old friends, and they were both sorry when she finally left him at his hotel, and she got back into the car she had left with the doorman.

'Call me as soon as you know something, John.'

'I promise.' He touched her hand on the wheel, and then leant in to kiss her cheek. 'Take care of yourself. And I hope next time I see you, you have flaming red hair!' They both laughed, and she waved and drove into the flow of traffic, feeling as though she had made a new friend. He was handsome and charming and bright, and she wondered why he wasn't married. He had said only that he was divorced and had a penchant for difficult women and had let it go at that. But she liked him so much, she couldn't imagine why someone hadn't snatched him up the moment he'd got divorced from his first wife.

But her mind drifted quickly back to the reason he had come to Paris to see her. It was all more than a little bit amazing. And she was stunned to realize as she walked in the door that it was already four o'clock. And she was giving a dinner party that evening. She hastily checked on the flowers and the wines, saw the chef, and glanced around to make sure that everything was in order. And then she went to see her daughters, playing in the garden with a friend. They were excited that school was almost over, and they'd be leaving for Cap Ferrat soon.

At six-thirty, she went to dress, and she heard Henri in his study, but she didn't want to disturb him. Instead she ran her bath and laid out her dress, a white silk floor-length gown. She usually wore it with long diamond earrings that had belonged to Henri's late mother. And she was just taking them out of her jewellery box when the door opened and he strode into the room with a look of fury.

'Hello darling,' she stood up to greet him, but the smile froze on her face when she saw him. 'Is something wrong? I checked everything for tonight and it looked fine to me . . .' But it was obvious that something terrible had happened in the meantime.

'What exactly do you think you're doing, making a fool of me, all over Paris?'

'My God, Henri, what are you talking about?'

'I mean that you were seen today, lunching with a man at the Ritz, thinking you were hiding.'

Her face went very white, but she stood extremely still as she explained it. 'If I thought I were hiding, I would hardly go to the Ritz. It was a business lunch. He's here from New York, on some business matters for my mother.'

'I heard that yesterday, Alexandra. And you won't get away with it twice. But it certainly explains your behaviour last night. You couldn't think straight. Well, I'm not going to tolerate an outrage of this kind. You will leave for Cap Ferrat in the morning.' She was being banished, like a naughty child, and tears filled her eyes at the injustice of what he was thinking.

'Henri, I have never cheated on you. You must believe that.' She didn't dare approach him, and they stood at opposite ends of the room, she in bleak despair, and he in outrage.

'I believed that until now. But you cannot expect me to believe it in this instance.'

'It's true.'

'That's nonsense. And I have every intention of telling your mother what I think of her providing a smokescreen for you. I do not wish to see her at Cap Ferrat this summer.'

'Henri, that's not fair. She wants to see the children . . .'

'She should have thought of that before she began covering for you with your lovers.'

'I don't have any lovers!' Alexandra screamed. 'And my mother has nothing to do with this . . .'

'Aha . . . I thought this was a business matter for her.' He advanced to her slowly, victory in his eyes, and Alexandra sank into a chair, beaten and desperately unhappy.

'It is . . .'

'What kind of business matter is it?' He roughly tilted her chin up so she had to face him, but he knew she wasn't entirely telling him the truth, and she could do nothing about it. To tell him the whole truth would have been far worse. She knew that.

'I can't explain it right now. It's all confidential business matters of my parents.' She looked pale and shaken, and he stalked out of the room again, and then turned to look at her from the doorway.

'I never would have expected this of you, Alexandra. See to it that it never happens again, or you will be going back to your mother's house, *without your daughters*. Have your things packed for the Riviera by noon tomorrow.' And with that he slammed the doors to her boudoir, and she sat and sobbed in despair. She had had such a pleasant time with John, and it was all so harmless, and now Henri thought she was cheating on him. And then suddenly, she realized she had to call him. She went hastily to the phone on her desk, and called the Bristol. Fortunately, he was there, and she was able to tell him that they were leaving for Cap Ferrat several weeks early, in case he needed to reach her. She gave him the number and thanked him for lunch again, never letting on for a moment how much pain it had just caused her.

'I hope I'll be in touch with you again soon.'

'So do I.' But she was ashamed for thinking it for several reasons. He was so kind and so understanding. But he had his own life to lead, and so did she. She had enough trouble without indulging in fantasies about him.

'I'll call as soon as I hear something.'

'Thank you, John. Have a good trip back.'

'I will. I'm leaving in the morning.' He had hoped to get on a flight that night, but he had returned to the hotel so late after lunch that he was no longer in the mood to pack and run, and he decided that a last night in Paris wouldn't do any harm. He was feeling relaxed and pleased after his lunch with Alexandra, and when he'd called Sasha from the hotel she was in one of her impossible moods. He was suddenly in no hurry to get back. He was looking forward to dinner at a bistro nearby, and a pleasant stroll through the streets of Paris.

He said goodbye to Alexandra and she hung up and walked slowly into her bathroom, unable to believe that Henri so easily thought the worst of her, and wondering what the summer would be like now. But she got a taste of it that night. He spoke to her in tones of ice, and until the next morning when she and the girls left, he treated her like a pariah.

'You will do no entertaining until I arrive, is that clear? You are to stay *in* the villa, and I will call you.' He treated her like a convict who had attempted to escape and her own fury was building slowly as they said goodbye the next morning.

'May I go to the beach, or should I stay in my room wearing a ball and chain?'

'I'm sorry you feel our marriage such a burden, Alexandra. I never realized it caused you such anguish.' He had an answer to everything and for the first time she hated him as they drove away. The chauffeur and two maids were accompanying them on the trip, and they were putting the Citroën and the Peugeot station wagon on the overnight train to the Riviera.

'Why was Papa in such a bad mood?' Axelle inquired as they drove through the traffic to the station. 'Was he mad at you?'

'Just a little bit.' She smoothed the coppery curls as Hilary had done for her so long ago, and she smiled now at the distant memory of her sister. She was excited now at the prospect of seeing them again. She just hoped that Chapman would find them soon, and that she would be able to get away to see them. But Axelle didn't give her the time to ponder it as they drove through Paris.

'Papa didn't look a "little bit" mad to me. He looked *very* mad. Did you do something terrible, Maman?' Alexandra smiled and took Axelle's hand in her own. It was going to be nice to get to the Riviera, and perhaps nice too to have a few weeks' breather from her husband.

'I only did something a little bit foolish.'

'Like when you bought the hat he hated with all feathers and the veil?' Axelle had loved it, and Henri had made Alexandra send it back the same day.

'Something like that.'

'Did you buy another hat?'

'Hmm . . . yes . . . uh . . . sort of . . .'

'Was it pretty?'

'Oh yes,' Alexandra smiled at her younger child, 'very.'

Axelle smiled up at her with obvious pleasure as they reached the station.

Chapter 23

The material they had dug up on Hilary in John's absence was excellent and he was immensely pleased. They had found her enrolment in night school, her job at the employment agency, and from there they had followed her to CBA. It was perfect. They had everything they needed, and as Chapman looked through the file, he realized that they had been right the first time. It *was* the right Hilary Walker he'd spoken to when he called her at CBA, and it was equally obvious she didn't want to be found. So be it, he would wait until he found Megan, and then confront her himself. For the moment, he would let her think she had lost him.

But as he thought of her, he felt that same odd tug in his heart he felt every time he read her file. He wanted to tell her that everything was all right, that people still cared about her, that she could stop running. It was terrible to think about her angry and alone, and then he realized that there might be a lot more to her current life than he knew. He ordered his assistant to begin a fullscale investigation of Hilary Walker at CBA Network. She could be married, divorced, have six children of her own. The broken little girl he had been following from Boston to Jacksonville to New York might well be leading a happy life now. And for the most part, he hoped so. And yet, he knew that he would not feel at peace about her until he met her. It was crazy, but he was obsessed by the women in his case, their lives, and their good and bad fortunes. So much so that he called his ex-wife, and asked her to lunch, and tried to press her into explaining to him again how she felt about her characters when she was writing.

'Do you ever fall in love with them, Ellie?' He looked at her in confusion, as they sat next to the fountain at the Four Seasons. It was where all the city's publishing notables ate lunch and he knew it was her favourite place, even though he still preferred the sensual, artsy chaos of the Russian Tea Room. But Eloise was a different girl. She was tall and cool and controlled, she had masterminded a successful career and done it brilliantly, and she seemed better suited to the cool marble and discreet fountains of the Four Seasons.

'Fall in love with them? What do you mean? Are you thinking of writing a book?' She looked amused and he shook his head.

'No, I'm just working on this crazy investigation. It goes back about thirty years, and the people are so damn real to me, I can't think straight anymore. I dream about them at night . . . I think about them in the daytime . . . little girls who are practically middle-aged women now tear at my heart and I want to help them.'

'It sounds more like food poisoning than love,' she grinned, and then she reached out and patted his hand sympathetically. She still liked him. They had lunch with each other a couple of times a year, and he had even introduced her to Sasha, but Eloise had told him bluntly on the phone the next day that she thought he could do a lot better. 'You got it bad, kid. Sounds like you ought to write a book about it.'

'No one would believe the story. And besides, I can't.

That's not my bag. You know that. It's just that it's driving me crazy. How can people on paper become real?'

'Somehow they do.'

'Do they finally go away?'

'Yes, when you resolve it,' she said reassuringly, eating her salad. 'When I finish a book, the characters finally disappear. For good. But before that, it's like being haunted.'

'That's it!' He waved his fork at her. 'That's it exactly!' He was being haunted by Hilary, and when he wasn't being tormented by Hilary, he was thinking of Alexandra. He had called her as soon as he was sure that it was Hilary at the network, and she had been jubilant. Now she was waiting for news of Megan, and John had been putting pressure on all his operatives to speed it up, because Patterson seemed to be fading. 'What do I do to get rid of this thing?'

'Finish it. Wind up the case, do whatever you have to do, and then it'll go away. That's how it works for me. Is it a tough case?' Unlike Sasha, she was always interested, but then she was always looking for new stories.

'Very. But we're two-thirds there. I just have to find one more piece of the puzzle and we've got it. It's kind of an exotic tale, I'll tell you about it when the case is closed.'

'I could use a good story. I'm starting a new one next week. I rented a place on Long Island for the summer.' It was amazing. The woman worked like a fiend, but it was obvious that she loved it. And then she grinned at her ex-husband. Their relationship was more like brother and sister now that they were no longer married. 'How's your ballerina?' She said it without venom. She wished him well. She hadn't been crazy about the girl when she met her, but she knew he was.

But he shrugged as he answered. 'So-so. People involved

306

in ballet seem to live in their own world. She doesn't have a great grasp on reality, mine anyway.'

'Worse than writers?' Eloise smiled.

'Much worse. At least you didn't complain about your feet night and day, and worry about every muscle in your body. Just breathing is a threat to them, they might do something to themselves that could keep them from dancing.'

'Sounds exhausting.' She finished her salad, took a sip of wine, and smiled at him. He was one of the nicest people she knew, and sometimes she was sorry they hadn't stayed married. She wondered if she should have tried harder but she was also smart enough to know it wasn't in her. And it wouldn't have been right for them. She needed to be alone with her work, and she had always felt he should be married and have children. 'Somehow I don't see her as the final answer for you.'

'Neither do I. But it's taken me a while to see that. There aren't a hell of a lot of people out there who intrigue me. Most of them aren't too bright, or they're not nice, or they really don't give a damn about anyone but themselves.' Without meaning to, he realized he had just described Sasha. She had been wearing thin on him ever since he'd got back from Paris. 'What about you? Prince Charming heading toward you on the horizon?'

She shrugged with an easy smile, and waved at a publisher she knew. 'I don't have time for much of that stuff. Nothing much has changed as far as that goes. It's hard to have a career and a real life.'

'But it *can* be done,' he always pointed out to her, 'if you want to.'

'Maybe I don't.' She was always honest with him. 'Maybe I don't want more than I've got. My typewriter and my old nightgowns.'

307

'El, that's terrible. It's a hell of a waste.'

'No, it's not. I never really wanted all that other stuff. I would have hated having kids.'

'Why?' It seemed so wrong to him. People were meant to have children. He had wanted one for the p twenty years. It just hadn't worked out for him to have one.

'They're too demanding. Too distracting. I'd have to give too much of myself. That's why I was such a lousy wife to you. I wanted to save it all for my books. I guess that's crazy, but it makes me happy.' And he knew it did. They were both better off the way things were now. And then suddenly he laughed.

'You were always too damn honest. I was just going to tell you I met a great woman in this case.' Eloise raised an eyebrow with interest. 'She just happens to be married to a French baron, and not exactly available.'

'She sounds a lot better than your ballerina.'

'She is. But she's totally wrapped up in her proper life. It's a damn shame too . . . she's lovely.'

'You'll find the right one, one of these days. Just stay away from the artsy ones. They make lousy wives. Take it from me. I know!' She smiled ruefully, and leaned over to kiss his cheek as they left the table.

'Don't be so hard on yourself. We were both young.'

'And you were terrific.' She stopped to say hello to her editor-in-chief, and they walked out into the sunshine together. Then John wished her luck on her new book, hailed a cab for her, and walked back to his office on East Fifty-seventh.

And there was a windfall for him when he got back to the office. One of his assistants had found the Abramses in San Francisco.

'Are you serious?' He was jubilant. They had tried everything and turned up nothing. But they had finally given up looking for David, and in doing so had found Rebecca. It turned out that they had left Los Angeles in the early sixties and gone to the deep South to march with Martin Luther King and participate in sit-ins and voter registration campaigns. They had provided free legal service to blacks in Georgia, Louisiana, and Mississippi, and had eventually set up a fullscale legal aid office in Biloxi. And eventually from there they had gone to Atlanta. It was only in 1981 they had finally gone back to California, but David had retired after extensive surgery, and Rebecca had joined an exclusively female practice in San Francisco, to defend women involved in feminist causes. For all their lives, they had been the classic liberals.

John's assistant had explained nothing to them. John had left strict orders that once Megan was located he would make contact. He had his secretary make an appointment with Rebecca Abrams, and he was set to fly out the following afternoon, which was perfect. Sasha was still on tour, and there was something he had wanted to do for days. It was something he hadn't done himself in years, but he knew now that he had to do it. It was part of what he had tried to explain to Eloise at lunch . . . part of being haunted.

He left the office just before four o'clock and took a cab to the network. He flashed a security badge and a police pass downstairs, both of which had been hard-earned and almost impossible to come by, and the network security were satisfied and instantly let him into the inner sanctum.

He took the lift upstairs, and waited inconspicuously in the reception area. He picked up a phone there and dialled her extension, and her secretary told him she was in a meeting.

'In her office, or upstairs?' He sounded like someone

who knew and the secretary was quick to give him the information.

'She's here. She's with Mr Baker.'

'Any idea what time she'll be through?'

'She said she's leaving at five-thirty.'

'Thanks.' Chapman hung up the house phone and the secretary had no idea who had phoned, but she assumed that it was someone who knew Hilary, obviously someone higher up at the network.

She came out at exactly five-fifteen, and John recognized her at once, even without the receptionist's good-night as she sped past. 'Good-night, Miss Walker.' Hilary turned to glance at her sharply and then nodded, she didn't seem to notice anyone else in the waiting area, or John as he followed her to the lifts and stepped into one beside her. He almost felt weak at the sight of her, he could see every strand of the shining black hair twisted into a knot, the graceful hands, the long neck, he could even smell the crisp scent of her perfume. She walked with a sure step, a long stride, and when he bumped into her once, she looked up at him with green eyes that pierced straight to his soul, eyes that said don't touch me, don't ever come near me. She got on a bus on Madison Avenue, instead of fighting for a cab, and she got out at Seventy-ninth Street. She walked two blocks further north, and then he realized she was going to a doctor's appointment. He waited patiently outside, and then followed her again when she took a cab and went to Elaine's where she met another woman. He sat in a booth close to theirs, and was intrigued by what might be said. The other woman was a well-known anchor from the network, and she looked upset. She started to cry once, and Hilary looked unmoved. She watched her, unhappy, but not sympathetic. And then finally John remembered as the two women shook hands outside the restaurant, that the woman who was the anchor had been fired when he was in Paris. It had created an enormous stir, and she was either pleading with Hilary for her job, or telling her side of the story. Her firing had supposedly come from higher up, but maybe she thought if she could gain Hilary's ear, she might get back in. But it was obvious from the unhappy look on Hilary's face as she walked slowly downtown alone, that she couldn't help her. She stopped to glance in shop windows once or twice, and walked with a purposeful stride, yet a feminine sway to her hips, which kept him riveted as he watched her. She turned on Seventy-second Street finally and walked all the way to the river, to an old brownstone set near a tiny park. It was a pretty place, yet everything he sensed about her told him she was lonely. She had a solitary air, and a kind of hardness and determination about her that suggested walls she had built long before and never taken down since. As he had when he read her file, he felt intensely sorry for her, and he felt sad as he walked the few blocks back to his own apartment. She lived so nearby, yet she seemed to exist in a universe of her own, a universe filled with work and little else, and yet it was not fair for him to make that judgment. Maybe she was happy after all, maybe she had a boyfriend she was deeply in love with, but everything about her present and her past suggested a solitary person with no one to love and no one who loved her. And when he walked into his apartment and turned on the light, he had an overwhelming urge to call her, to hold out a hand, to become her friend, to tell her that Alexandra still cared . . . all was not lost . . . yet . . . or maybe she wouldn't care. As he had explained to Eloise at lunch, he felt as though he were being haunted.

He tried to get some sleep, but he tossed and turned, and finally, for lack of something better to do, he turned on the light and called Sasha in Denver. She was in her room, she had just got in from the concert hall and her feet were killing her.

'I'm glad nothing's changed.' He laughed as he lay on his back, thinking of her. He wondered if he'd been too hard on her when he talked about her at lunch. She still excited him in some ways, and that night he missed her. 'Want to meet me in San Francisco?'

'When?' she sounded non-committal.

'I'm going tomorrow. I should be through in a couple of days. When do you finish in Denver?'

'Tomorrow. We go to Los Angeles. San Francisco cancelled.'

'I'll meet you in L A.'

'I don't think you should.' There was a long silence, and he frowned.

'What's up?'

'It might upset some of the other dancers,' she said vaguely and he sat up slowly in bed. He was no fool, and he had played this game before. But it was not a game he liked playing.

'Would it upset anyone in particular, Sasha?'

'Oh I don't know. It's too late to talk about it tonight.' And as she said it, he heard a male voice in the background.

'Is that Dominic, or Pierre, or Petrov?'

'It's Ivan,' she said petulantly. 'He pulled a hamstring tonight, and he was very upset.'

'Tell him I'm sorry. But tell him after you explain to me what the hell's going on. Sash, I'm too old for this kind of bullshit.'

'You don't understand the pressures of being a dancer,' she whined into the phone, and he sank back against his pillows.

'Well, I've tried for chrissake. What is it that I don't understand exactly?'

'Dancers need other dancers.'

'Ah ... now we get to the root of the problem. You mean like Ivan?'

'No, no ... well ... yes ... but it's not what you think.'

'How the hell do you know what I think, Sasha? You're so busy worrying about yourself and your feet and your ass and your tendons you wouldn't notice what anyone thought if they wrote it out in neon.'

'That's not fair!' She was suddenly crying, and for the first time in months he found he didn't care. Suddenly, in the space of one phone call, it was over. He had had it.

'It may not be fair, baby,' he spoke in his deep, gentle voice, 'but it happens to be true. I think maybe you and I had better take our bows, and step back gracefully while the curtain comes down. If I read the programme correctly, the fourth act just ended.'

'Why don't we talk when I get back?'

'About what? Your feet? ... or about how dancers need other dancers? I'm not a dancer, Sash. I'm a man. I have a very demanding job, I have a full life I want to share with a woman I love and who loves me. I even want to have children. Can you see yourself doing that?'

'No.' At least she was honest. The thought of it horrified her. She had no intention of giving up dancing for a year at any point in her life, and then fighting to get back all her muscles. 'Why is that so important?'

'Because it just is, and I'm forty-two years old. I can't waste my time with games like this anymore. I gave to the artistic community once. I made my contribution. Now I want something different.'

'That's what I mean ... you don't understand the

313

pressures of being a dancer. John, babies aren't important.'

'They are to me, little one. And so are a lot of other things you don't have room for. You don't need me. You don't need anyone. Be honest with yourself.' There was a long empty silence as she listened, and suddenly he wanted to get off the phone. There was nothing left to say. They had said it all, and run out of words a long time since. They just hadn't noticed. 'Goodbye, Sash . . . take it easy. I'll see you when you get back. Maybe we'll have lunch or a drink.' He knew she'd want the things she'd left in his apartment, but the truth was that he wasn't even anxious to see her.

'Are you really telling me it's over?' She sounded shocked and he could hear the male voice in the background again. He wondered if they were sharing a room, not that it really mattered.

'I guess I am.'

'Is that why you called me?'

'No. I guess it just happened. It was time.'

'Is there someone else?' He smiled at the question.

'Not really.' In a funny way there were three of them, the three women he was searching for day and night who filled his thoughts and his heart now, but not in the way Sasha had meant it.

'No one important . . . take it easy, Sash.' And with that, he quietly hung up and turned out the light. And he smiled to himself as he went back to sleep. He felt free for the first time in months, and he was glad he had called her. It was finally over.

Chapter 24

The flight to San Francisco was easy and he arrived at two in the afternoon, local time, which gave him plenty of time to get to Rebecca's office at four o'clock. When he got there, it was an old Victorian in a run-down neighbourhood. But he was surprised when he stepped inside, to find the house well maintained, pleasantly decorated, and filled with plants, and Rebecca Abrams herself was an attractive woman. She was in her early sixties and wore her grey hair in a single braid down her back. She wore clean blue jeans and a starched white shirt, red espadrilles and a red flower in her hair, and she looked like a very attractive, very intelligent, well-preserved elderly hippie. She smiled warmly at John, and ushered him into her office. She had no idea what he wanted, and didn't look perturbed when he left his suitcase in her outer office.

'You don't look like most of our clients, Mr Chapman.' She smiled warmly at him and pointed to a sunny little kitchen off her office. 'Would you like some coffee or tea? We have about a dozen different kinds of herb tea.' She smiled at him again and he shook his head. He hated to upset her, but he suspected that he was going to.

'I'm here on a personal matter, Mrs Abrams. I've been looking for you and your husband for quite some time, and I had a little trouble finding you. My last address for you was in New York, in 1957.'

Rebecca Abrams smiled again, and sat back peacefully in her chair. She had been doing yoga for years, and it showed in her tranquil manner. 'We've moved around quite a bit over the years. We spent a lot of time in the south, and then we came back here when my husband got ill. He had a quadruple bypass six and a half years ago, and we both decided that it was time for him to take it easy and enjoy life. So now I'm practising solo, or rather with a group of women I enjoy very much. But it's a different kind of practice than I had with David, although some of the concepts aren't so different. We deal with a lot of cases that involve discrimination and civil rights. We've been doing this for many years.'

'And your husband?'

'He teaches twice a week, at Boalt. He gardens. He's busy doing a thousand things he enjoys.'

'And your daughter?' Chapman held his breath.

'She's fine. She's still in Kentucky. How do you know our family, Mr Chapman?' She frowned slightly but the smile still didn't leave her eyes.

'I don't. I'm afraid I come to you rather indirectly. I'm an attorney too, and I run a firm called Chapman Associates in New York. Unlike you, I've never been terribly in love with the law, and I got hooked on investigations years ago, so that's what I do. And my client, in this case, is Arthur Patterson. I don't know if the name rings a bell, but he was instrumental in bringing Megan to you in 1958. I'm sure that now you remember.'

She nodded, the smile had faded now in earnest. 'Is something wrong? Why would Mr Patterson wish to contact us now?' She looked frightened, as though he could still take her away from them. That was what she had always been afraid of.

'Simply put, Mrs Abrams, he's dying. And he wants to

know that the girls are all right, that they're happy and well, and not in any kind of need. And he hopes to bring them together once before he dies, so that they have the benefit of knowing their sisters.'

'Now?' She looked horrified. 'After thirty years? Why would they possibly want to meet their sisters?' She looked as though she were about to throw him out of her office.

'He felt it might mean something to them, and I can appreciate your feelings. Thirty years is a long time to wait before having any contact.'

She shook her head as though in disbelief. 'We told him at the time of the adopting that we wanted no continued contact with him or the other girls. That was the main reason why we left New York and went to L A. I don't think it would be fair to Megan to drag her past out now.'

'Maybe she should make that choice. You mentioned that she is still in Kentucky.'

'She's finishing her residency there, in Appalachia. She's a doctor. She's specialized in obstetrics.' Rebecca said it with deep pride, but she looked at John with open hostility.

'May I contact her there?' To him it was a formality, but to her it was an offence and she half rose in her seat as she answered.

'No, you may not, Mr Chapman.' She sat back down again and glared at him in outrage. 'I can't believe you'd come to us after all these years and expect us to expose Megan to that pain and confusion. Are you aware of the cause of her parents' death?'

'I am. Is Megan?'

'Of course not. In fact, I will tell you very bluntly, Mr Chapman, this whole thing is totally out of the question. My daughter doesn't know she's adopted.' She looked him straight in the eye and he felt his heart stop. How could they not tell her? As liberal as they were, and as free-thinking, they had never told her she was adopted. It certainly complicated the matter for them.

'Do you have other children, Mrs Abrams?'

'No we don't. And my husband and I felt she had no need to know. She is our only child, and she came to us when she was a baby. There was absolutely no reason to tell her as she got older.'

'Would you be willing to tell her now?' He looked deep into her eyes and was frightened of what he saw there. Rebecca Abrams was not going to make this any easier for him. But at least he knew where Megan was now. If he had to, he would find her in Kentucky. It seemed a cruel thing to do, but she had a right to know about her sisters.

Rebecca hesitated for a long time. 'I don't know, Mr Chapman. Honestly, I don't think so. I'm going to have to discuss this with my husband, and with his doctor first. He's not well, and I don't want to upset him.'

'I understand. Will you get back to me in a day or two? I'm staying at the Mark Hopkins.'

'I'll get back to you when I can.' She stood up to indicate that the interview was over, and she might as well have been wearing a navy-blue pin-stripe suit. She looked as formidable as if she'd been wearing one. 'Will you be going back to New York in the meantime?'

'I'd rather wait for the answer here, in case your husband would like to see me.'

'I'll let you know.' She shook his hand, but the look in her eyes was not warm as she led him to the door and closed it behind him. And when she went back to her desk after he was gone, she put her head down on her arms and cried. It was thirty years later, but they were still going to try to take away her baby. They were going to awake a

318

curiosity she had never had, and bonds she never knew, and introduce her to blood relatives she had never longed for. It wasn't fair after all they had done for her, and given how much they loved her.

She went to see David's doctor that afternoon, and he felt that David was strong enough to hear the news. But it took her two days to get up the courage to tell him, and when she did she sobbed in his arms, and poured out all her fears and he stroked the long grey hair and held her close and told her how much he loved her.

'No one's going to take Meg away from us, sweetheart. How could they?' He was touched by her reaction. When Megan had been a little girl, she had worried about the same things. She had wanted Megan to be theirs, and no one else's.

'All of a sudden, she'll want to know everything about her biological parents.'

'So we'll tell her.'

'But what if she feels different about us after that?'

'You know better than that, Becky. Why should she? She loves us too. In all the important senses of the word, we're her parents. She knows what that means as well as we do. But that doesn't mean she won't want to see her sisters. If someone told me tomorrow I had two sisters I'd never known, I'd want to see them too, but it wouldn't make me love you any less, or Megan.' But Rebecca was still frightened and they talked about it long into the night. Rebecca wanted to keep their pact of silence, and David felt that they owed it to Megan to tell her. It took them another full day to resolve it. And when they finally called, John felt relief sweep over him, he had been going crazy in his hotel room. But he didn't want to leave until he knew where things stood; and he didn't want to press them.

She invited him to come to their house in Tiburon that night, and the three of them talked for a long time about the difficulties of telling Megan after so many years that she was adopted, and it was obvious that Rebecca was still fearful, but David was both adamant and supportive. He told John that his only request was that they wanted to tell Megan themselves, and in person. She was due home in two weeks for a brief vacation, and they would tell her then. They would call him as soon as she knew, and he was welcome to speak to her after that and set up the meeting that Arthur Patterson wanted so badly. And John had no recourse but to accept. They had all the cards in their hands and he wanted to do the right thing for them, and for Megan.

He went home that weekend, and called Arthur Patterson at home. It was obvious that he was not doing well, and John knew he had given up going to the office. He explained that he had found the Abramses, and that they wanted to tell Megan themselves. It meant waiting two weeks, but Chapman felt there was no choice. It was the only decent thing to do, and Arthur reluctantly agreed, and hoped he would live long enough to complete his mission.

'What's left to do now?' he asked John.

'Wait to hear from them. Then I'll set up the meeting with Megan and the others. Alexandra is ready to come when I call her, and I still have to deal with Hilary. But I don't want to do that until the last minute.' He instinctively sensed that the later he did it, the more likely she might be to come to the meeting. 'That gives us another two weeks to cool our heels. I'll let you know if I hear anything sooner.'

'Thank you, John.' And then, unexpectedly. 'You've done a fine job. I'm amazed that you've found them.'

'So am I.' John smiled at his end. He had never really thought he would, and he had . . . and in a few weeks they would be back together, and his job would be over. Part of him felt bereft at the thought, and another part felt relieved and he thought of what Eloise had said when they had lunch. He would be free when it was over.

Chapter 25

The call came from the Abramses in two and a half weeks, as promised, and John could tell from the strain in David's voice that telling Megan hadn't been easy for them.

'She took it very well.' His voice broke, 'We were very proud of her ... we always have been ...' and then he went on, sounding stronger. 'She said she'd call you herself when she gets back to Kentucky, if you'd like to talk to her.'

'Would it be possible for me to talk to her now?' John asked carefully and David had conferred with someone at the other end and then handed the phone to someone, whose voice John recognized within moments. Without the French accent, she sounded just like Alexandra, she had the same intonations, the same voice, the same laughter.

'Mr Chapman?'

'Yes.'

'This is all something of a surprise.' She sounded matter-of-fact, and young, but very pleasant.

'I'm sorry about that. I truly am.'

'It couldn't be helped, I understand you wanted to speak to me.'

'I did. I was hoping to meet you in Kentucky briefly before I set up the meeting. When do you suppose you could come to Connecticut to meet with the others?'

'I won't know that till I get back. My schedule won't be set until the day I return. But I could call you then, if you like.'

'I'd appreciate it very much.' And she did. She called punctually the day she arrived, and John wondered if that meant she was anxious to meet the others or if she was just that kind of person.

She told him that she would be free to see him, in Kentucky, that Sunday afternoon, between one and five. And she would be able to come to Connecticut for two days three weeks later, but no sooner.

Chapman frowned as he listened to her, wondering if Arthur would live that long, and he shared his concerns with her.

'I can try and trade with one of the other docs, but it won't change things by more than a few days. We're terribly understaffed, and you'll see what we're up against when you come down here.'

'You could make it in three weeks though?'

'I could. Unless there were a major emergency, but I can never predict that.'

'I understand.' She was businesslike and very firm for a young woman of thirty, and while she had the same voice, she seemed very different from the others. She was intent on a single purpose, and she had been brought up with values and traditions much different from those of Hilary or Alexandra. She was hell-bent on helping unfortunates and fighting the war on poverty. It was something Alexandra had certainly never thought of, and Hilary had been far too busy surviving to concern herself with the more esoteric problems of the masses. It was intriguing how different they were. And John remembered something Alexandra had said to him in Paris.

The kaleidoscope had taken yet another turn and

produced a totally different image . . . this time the demons had been turned into snow-covered mountains.

He agreed to come to Kentucky the following Saturday afternoon, and would meet her at the hospital during her free time. He thanked her for spending it with him, and he confirmed the meeting with her sisters. They set it for September first, and he called Arthur as soon as he hung up. And the following morning he called Alexandra on the Riviera. They had a terrible connection but eventually the line cleared and she could hear him.

'Already?' She sounded excited. 'You've found them both?' It was amazing. 'Where was Megan?'

He smiled at her gentle voice. She already spoke of her like a sister she had never lost, who had merely been gone on a long vacation. 'She's a doctor in Kentucky.'

'Oh my God. And Hilary's all right?'

'Yes. I've seen her.'

'Has she agreed to come on the first?' She held her breath waiting for the answer, and her hopes were dashed as soon as John told her he hadn't called her.

'I don't want to give her too much time to think about it. I'll give her a call in a week or so.'

'What if she goes away?' Alexandra was worried.

'Don't worry. I'll find her.' They both laughed and a moment later they hung up, and Alexandra hurriedly called her mother. She was staying at Cap d'Antibes, at the Hôtel du Cap where she always stayed. And Henri had finally relented on her exile.

'Maman?'

'Yes, darling, is something wrong?' Alexandra sounded breathless, and suddenly very young, like one of her own daughters.

'He's found them both.'

'Both what?' She had just got up and was drinking her

coffee and reading the *Herald Tribune*. She couldn't imagine what Alexandra might have lost that someone else might have found. 'What on earth are you talking about?'

'My sisters! Chapman found them both!' She sounded ecstatic and Margaret's blood suddenly ran cold. She had somehow hoped that he wouldn't find them.

'How nice.' She tried to force herself to sound happy. 'Are they well?'

'One of them is a doctor, the younger one, and the other one, Hilary, works for a television network in New York.'

'They sound like quite an illustrious group. And you're a baroness. They ought to make a film about you.' But she was not amused, and Alexandra knew it.

'Don't worry, Maman. It's not going to change anything. Please know that.'

Margaret wished she could be sure of that. Her fears were not so different from those of Rebecca Abrams. 'When are you meeting them?'

'On the first of September. I just got the call. I'm going to Connecticut.'

'What are you going to tell Henri?'

'I haven't figured that out yet. I thought maybe I'd tell him I was going with you . . . or perhaps on business for you.'

'He won't believe that.'

'No. But I can hardly tell him the truth. I'll think of something.' They talked for a moment longer and then hung up, and five minutes later Margaret called her back, and her first words stunned Alexandra.

'I'm going with you.'

'What? . . . Maman . . . you can't . . .'

'Why not?' She had made up her mind, and thought it an excellent idea, aside from providing Alexandra with the alibi that she needed. Besides, that way she could keep an eye on things, and stay close to Alexandra. She was desperately afraid of that meeting.

'It's such a lot of trouble for you. You weren't even going back to Paris until the end of September. You told me you were going to Rome for a few weeks.'

'So? I can go to Rome in October. Or on the way back from New York. All I wanted to do was visit Marisa' — one of her oldest friends — 'and buy some decent shoes. But I'd much rather go to New York with you,' and then, almost shyly, '. . . if you'll have me.'

'Oh Mother . . .' Tears sprang to her eyes as she thought of it. She sensed how frightened Margaret was, but she didn't need to be. No one, no blood relative, no husband, no friend, could ever replace her. 'Of course I'd love you to come. It just seems like such an imposition.'

'Don't be ridiculous. I'd be a nervous wreck if I stayed here.' And then she had a totally crazy idea, but she liked it. 'Shall we take Axelle and Marie-Louise?' Alexandra's face lit up at the thought. She didn't like just leaving them at the end of the summer, even for only a few days. And Henri couldn't possibly object to a family trip like that.

'That's a wonderful idea. The three of you can stay in New York while I go to Connecticut, and then we can all have a little fun before we go back to Paris. The girls don't start school until the eleventh.'

'Marvellous, I'll call the Pierre and make the reservations today. You call the airlines. What day will we arrive?'

'Friday is the first . . . maybe we should fly on Thursday, the thirty-first of August.'

'Perfect. I'll make reservations for ten days. We can always change them if you want to come back sooner.'

'Maman . . .' There was a lump in her throat the size of

326

a fist as she thought of the only mother she had ever known. 'I love you.'

'Everything's going to be fine, darling. Just fine.' And for the first time since John Chapman had appeared at the rue de Varenne, she really thought so.

Alexandra didn't say anything to Henri for another week. And then she mentioned it casually to him one afternoon as they lay on the terrace.

'My mother wants me to go to New York with her, at the end of the summer.' She said it easily but he looked up at her angrily. He was still angry at her for her supposed transgression before they'd left Paris. They had never discussed it again, but she knew he hadn't forgiven her.

'What's that all about now?'

'Nothing. She has some business to take care of in New York. Some investments of her family's that need looking into, and she asked me to come along and bring the girls.'

'That's ridiculous. Why would you go to New York in August?' He was suspicious of both of them, and the plot they were obviously cooking up against him.

'It's actually not till the very end of August. And it might be fun for the girls to do something a little different.'

'Nonsense. You can go to New York some other time, this winter without the children.' But the harshness of his words sent a chill down her spine. He didn't know it, but nothing was going to stop her from going, or from taking her children with her.

'No, Henri. I'm going now. With my mother. *And* the children.'

He bolted to a sitting position and stared at her angrily. 'Aren't you getting rather independent suddenly, Alexandra? May I remind you that I make the decisions here, for you, as well as the children.' He had never put it quite so bluntly, but it was true, or had been until then. But slowly, things had begun to change, since John Chapman had come to Paris.

'I don't think this is worth getting excited about, Henri. It's an invitation from my mother, for myself and the girls.'

'And if I forbid you to go?' His face was red with unspent fury, and her shocking behaviour.

'I will have to go anyway. My mother has asked me to come with her.'

'Your mother is not an invalid. I'll call her myself and tell her you're not going.' But this time Alexandra stood up and faced him. She spoke in a quiet voice, but there was no mistaking the steel beneath the velvet.

'I do not wish to disobey you, but I must go to New York with my mother.'

'Why? Tell me that. Give me one valid reason.'

'It's too complicated to explain. It's all family business.'

'Alexandra, you're lying to me.' He was right, but she had no choice, the truth was too frightening to share with him.

'Please don't say that. I won't be gone long. Just a few days.'

'Why, dammit, why?' He pounded his fist on the glass table and she jumped.

'Henri, please, you're being unreasonable.' And she was frightened that he could force her to tell him. 'My mother wants to visit her family, and she wants me to come along. There's nothing wrong with that.'

'What's wrong with it is that I didn't say you could go, and I see no reason for you to do so.'

'Perhaps because I want to.'

'You don't make those kinds of decisions for yourself. You are not a single woman.'

'Nor am I a slave. You can't decide everything for me, for heaven's sake. This is the twentieth century, not the Dark Ages.'

'And you are not some sort of modern Women's Libber to do as you please. Or if that's what you wish, Alexandra, you may not do it under my roof. Please keep that in mind before you start making your own travel arrangements.'

'This is ridiculous. You act as though I've committed a crime.'

'Not at all. But it is I who decide what you'll do when. That's how it's been for fourteen years, and I see no reason to change it.'

'And if I do?' she asked ominously. For the first time in her life the way he treated her truly rankled. She knew he was a kind and decent man, but he ran her life in such a way that she was no longer happy with it. And what's more, he knew it.

'You'll have trouble with me if you try out this independence. I'm warning you now.'

'And I'm telling you, as politely as I can, that I'm going to New York with my mother on the thirty-first of August.'

'That remains to be seen. And if I let you go, you are not taking my daughters. Is that clear?' It was all a power play and she suddenly hated him for it. All he needed was a whip to complete the image he was making.

'Are they prisoners here too then?'

'Is that how you see yourself?'

'Lately, yes. Ever since you sent me down here as a punishment for a sin I didn't commit. You've treated me like a criminal all summer.'

'Perhaps it's your own guilt that makes you feel that way, my dear.'

'Not at all. And I refuse to feel guilty about a trip with my mother, or to bow and scrape and beg, I don't need to do that. I'm a grown woman, and I can certainly do something like that, if I choose to.'

'Ah, the young baroness spreads her wings. Are you telling me that you don't need my support because of the size of your own income?'

'I would never say such a thing, Henri.' She was shocked at how bitter he seemed to be. But he was furious that she wouldn't bend to his wishes.

'You don't need to, my dear. In any case, I've decided. You're not going.'

She looked at him and shook her head in despair. He didn't understand that he was choosing the wrong issue on which to take his stand. Nothing could have kept her from going. Not even her husband.

Chapter 26

When John Chapman arrived in Kentucky, it was like landing on another planet. He had to change planes twice, and a jeep met him and took him over three hours of bumpy roads into the mountains, until he was deposited at a 'motel' with a single room and an outdoor toilet. He sat huddled in his room that night, listening to the owls outside and sounds he had never heard before, and he wondered what Megan would be like when he met her the next day.

He slept fitfully, and woke early. He walked to the town's only restaurant and ate fried eggs and grits, and had a cup of truly awful coffee. And the jeep came for him again after lunchtime, with a toothless driver, who was only sixteen years old, and drove him to the hospital, high up in the mountains, under tall pine trees and surrounded by shacks where assorted families lived, most of them with a dozen children running around barefoot in what could only be called rags, followed by packs of mangy dogs hoping to find some crumbs, or leftover food the children might have forgotten. It seemed difficult to believe that this godforsaken outpost could be huddled in such beautiful country, and only hours away from places like New York, or Washington or Atlanta. The poverty John saw was staggering. Young boys who looked like bent-over old men from poor working conditions, bad health, and acute malnutrition; young women with no teeth and thin hair. Children with swollen bellies from lack of food. John wondered how she could stand working there, and walked into the hospital, not sure of what he'd find there.

He was directed to a clinic around the back, and he went there, only to find twenty or thirty women, sitting patiently on benches, surrounded by screaming kids, and obviously pregnant again with what in some cases was their eighth or ninth child even though they were only twenty. It was an amazing sight, and when he looked toward the desk, he saw a head of bright red hair, braided and in pigtails, on a pretty girl in jeans and hiking boots, and as she walked toward him, he knew without a doubt, it was Megan. She looked incredibly like Alexandra.

'Hello, Doctor.' She smiled at the greeting and led him to a small room nearby, where they could talk privately. He showed her the file he had shown Alexandra, and told her about Alexandra as well, and explained that the meeting was set for September first, as she had suggested. 'Can you still make it?' He looked worried and she reassured him with a warm smile. She had some of the mannerisms of Rebecca, but actually she looked a great deal like Alexandra.

'I can. If I can get away from them.' She waved toward the army of women waiting on the benches.

'It's an awesome sight.'

'I know.' She nodded seriously. 'That's why I came here. They need help desperately. Medical care, and food, and education. It's incredible to think that this exists right in our own country.' He nodded, unable to disagree with her, and impressed that she was doing something about it.

She looked over the file again, thoughtfully, and then asked him some questions about her parents. She wanted to know the same thing Alexandra had asked him. Why had Sam killed Solange? And then, what had happened to the others? She was saddened by what she read of Hilary, and smiled after he finished talking about Alexandra.

'Her life sounds a far cry from mine, doesn't it? A French baroness. That's a long way from Kentucky, Mr Chapman.' She said it with a drawl and he laughed with her, but she still wanted to meet both her sisters. No matter how different they were. 'You know, my mother is very frightened about the meeting.'

'I sensed that when we met. Your father was trying to reassure her.'

'I think it's very threatening to any adoptive parent to have their adopted child seek out their birth family. I saw that during my residency, before I came here. But she has nothing to worry about.' She smiled up at him with ease. She knew exactly who she was, where she was going, and why she wanted to go there, not unlike the people who had formed her. David and Rebecca had lived by their beliefs too, and they were exactly the kind of parents she needed. Decent, intelligent, filled with integrity and love for the people and causes they believed in. And Megan knew it too. She had told her mother that before coming back here. 'She'll be all right. I promised to call her after it was all over. I think they'll probably visit me after that, if I know my parents.' They both laughed, and John watched her eyes. They were filled with light and life and excitement. She was a girl who loved what she was doing and felt fulfilled, and it was exciting just being near her. She was so different from girls like Sasha, who were so totally wrapped up in themselves. This girl thought of no one but the needy people around her. And halfway through the afternoon, she had to leave him to do an emergency Caesarean section. She was back in two hours and apologized for the delay.

'This is supposed to be my free afternoon. But it's always like this, that's why I don't get too far.' And then she invited him to dinner at her place. She lived in a simple shack, with simple furniture and beautiful quilts she had bought from some of her patients. She cooked up a plain pot of stew and they relaxed and talked about her youth and her parents and the people she had met. She seemed to love her parents deeply and she was grateful for all they had done for her, yet at the same time it seemed to intrigue her to think that she had once belonged to entirely different people.

She smiled once over her glass of wine, and looked very young and girlish. 'In a funny way, it's kind of exciting.' He laughed and patted her hand. In a way she seemed the least distressed, the most secure, the happiest of the three women. She was doing exactly what she wanted.

And afterwards she drove him back to where he was staying in the jeep her father had given her when she'd moved to the mountains. John wanted to sit in the moonlight and talk to her for hours, but she had to get back. She went back on duty at four-thirty the next morning.

'Will I see you in Connecticut on the first?' She asked him cautiously, as he looked down at her in the moonlight.

'I'll be there.' He smiled. 'For a while anyway. I promised Mr Patterson I'd be there to greet all of you and help get things started.'

'See you then.' She waved as she drove off and John stood looking after her for a long time, as he heard the owls hooting in the tree, and felt the mountain air soft on his cheeks, and for a moment he wished he could stay with her for ever.

Chapter 27

Alexandra had already done all her packing, and all she had left to do was organize the girls when Henri confronted her in the hallway, and grabbed her by the arm.

'I thought you understood me. I told you, you are not going to New York.'

'Henri, I have to.' She didn't want to fight with him about it. It was something she had to do, and it wasn't fair to try to stop her now. He followed her back into their bedroom where he stood glaring at her in silent fury as her suitcases lay open on the bed.

'Why are you being so obstinate about this?' He knew instinctively it had to be a man. There was no other conceivable reason.

'Because it's very important to me.'

'You've told me nothing that explains that. Why does a trip to New York with your mother mean so much to you now? Would you care to explain that?'

Her eyes filled with tears as she looked at him across the bed. He had been so unkind to her all summer, and it was so unfair of him to be difficult now. 'I really can't explain it. It has to do with something that happened a long time ago.'

'Something that involved a man?' He looked at her accusingly, and as she watched him in the harsh sunlight of the Riviera, he suddenly looked very old, and she wondered if perhaps he was frightened . . . frightened that she was involved with a younger man. It made her feel sorry for him and for a moment she let her guard down, as she shook her head.

'No, it has nothing whatsoever to do with a man. It has to do with my parents.' That was true, but she did not mean the Comte and Comtesse de Borne.

'What about them? Alexandra, I expect you to tell me what's going on.' And then suddenly, as though she could fight him no longer, she sat down in a chair, and began to cry. But he did not approach her. He offered her no comfort. From all that he knew, she still owed him an explanation, and perhaps much more.

'I didn't want to explain this to you . . . it . . . it's difficult to explain. I've only known it myself since June.' She looked up at him with deeply troubled eyes, and he suddenly realized that something was very wrong, that the transgressions he had punished her for for two months were perhaps not what he had thought them. A shiver of guilt sliced through him, but only briefly, as he waited, standing near the window, as she went on. 'My mother . . . my parents . . . there was something they should have told you . . . I should have told you, except that I had almost forgotten, and I told myself it wasn't important. But I suppose now that it was . . .' There was an inner shudder of horror as he waited and she caught her breath and continued. 'Henri, I was adopted.' He stared at her in utter amazement.

'You were? Why didn't someone tell me? Your father never said anything.' He looked horrified, but she bravely went on. She was going to tell him all of it, no matter what it cost.

'I was also adopted before that. By Margaret and her previous husband as well.' She waited for the full impact

336

to hit him, and as it did, he sat down slowly on the bed and went pale as he stared at Alexandra.

'Are you serious? You were not the biological child of Margaret and Pierre de Borne?' It was as though someone had just told him the Renoir for which he had paid five million dollars was a fraud. His lovely wife with the impeccable breeding was not a countess by birth, but an unknown. She nodded. She knew how deeply it had shocked her when Margaret told her, and she knew how much more Henri would be stunned. 'And before that? Margaret is not even your mother?' His voice was a whisper and Alexandra nodded, ready to tell him all.

'No, she's not.'

He gave a bitter crack of laughter. 'And to think how often I've worried that you or the children were too much like her. Then who are your parents? Do you even know?' She could be anyone ... a girl from the streets ... from the gutter ... of unknown parents and breeding. The thought of it almost made him ill. For ten centuries his family had married and bred with the utmost caution, and he had married a complete stranger of unknown background.

'I have known for two months. And I've wanted to spare you. That has been the secret I've been keeping from you. Nothing else.' But he was not appeased, he looked at her angrily, and strode across the room with fury, as he glanced at her over his shoulder.

'I'd have much preferred if it was a man.'

'I'm sorry to disappoint you.' She spoke with great sadness. He was letting her down. She had inwardly prayed that he would accept her ... that it wouldn't matter to him. But she had known better than that. These things meant too much to her husband for him to be magnanimous about a surprise of this kind. And she

337

had known it. She had only wished it might be different, but it wasn't.

'And your parents? Who are they? The real ones . . .'

She took a deep, brave breath and told him. 'My mother was a Frenchwoman, I know only that her name was Solange Bertrand, a "commoner" as you would put it. My father met her when he liberated Paris with the Allied forces. I know nothing more. My father was an actor, a well-known one, much respected, named Sam Walker. They were said to be very much in love, and they had three daughters, of which I am the second one. And then . . .' She almost choked on her words as she told him, but in an odd way it was a relief to say the words, '. . . as a result of some madness, he killed her. And when he was convicted of the crime, he committed suicide in his cell, leaving me and my sisters penniless and orphaned. We were left with an aunt for a few months, and then a friend of the family, an attorney, found homes for us, and got us adopted, two of us anyway. I was very fortunate in that I was given to Margaret and her first husband, a lawyer named George Gorham. I was five years old at the time. They say I was four when my father killed my mother, which is why I don't recall it. And I don't remember anything about the man named George Gorham. Apparently, six months later, he died, and my mother . . . Margaret, that is . . . came to France to recover, and she met my father . . . Pierre . . . and you know most of the rest. He adopted me as soon as he married my mother, which you did not know, and I suppose I had forgotten, and we lived happily ever after, and then you came along, Henri.' She tried to smile, but her face froze as she watched him.

'What a tidy little story.' Henri looked at her with unleashed fury. 'How dare you perpetrate that hoax on me for all these years? And even if you had forgotten, as you say, your mother certainly hadn't. And your "father", as you call him ... *bande de salopards*! ... I could sue you for divorce on the basis of fraud ... and damages in the bargain!'

'Do you call your daughters "damages", Henri? I had no idea ... truly ...' The tears coursed slowly down her cheeks and onto her yellow silk blouse as she watched him, but she saw no mercy there.

'I call the entire charade disgraceful! And this trip to New York? What is that all about? To put flowers on your parents' grave?'

'The lawyer who placed us for adoption was my parents' closest friend, and he is dying. He has spent months trying to locate my sisters, and he wishes to bring us together. He feels he owes it to us for whatever pain he caused us in taking us away from each other. I was very fortunate, but at least one of us was not.'

'And what is she? A prostitute in the streets of New York? My God, it's unbelievable! In one hour I have inherited a war bride, a murderer, a suicide, and God knows what else in the bargain, and you expect me to wave my handkerchief and shed tears of joy that you are being reunited with your sisters, whom even you cannot care about after all this time. And your mother? What part has she played in this? Is she responsible for getting you back in touch with the attorney? Did she think you needed a little excitement in your life? I know how dull she thinks me, but I assure you this is not my idea of excitement.'

'Nor is it hers.' Alexandra looked at him proudly. She had told him who she was, and if he chose to reject her, it was his loss, his sin, his lack of compassion. She had done everything possible to protect him and he had demanded an answer to his questions. Now he had it. And it remained

339

to be seen what he would do about it. 'My mother was heartbroken to have to tell me. She never wanted any of this to come out. But *I* want to see my sisters. *I* want to see who they are. And no, my sister is not a prostitute. She runs a major television network, and she has had a tragic life. My younger sister is a doctor, working in Appalachia. And I don't even know if I'll like them, or if they'll like me. But I want to see them, Henri. I want to know who they are, and who I am, other than just your wife.'

'That's no longer enough for you, is it? You had to bring this on our heads. Can you begin to imagine what this would do to my career if it got out? What would happen to my bank? To my political connections? My relatives? Can you imagine what your own children would think if they knew their grandfather murdered their grandmother. My God . . .' He sat down again, boggled at the thought. 'I can't even begin to imagine it.'

'Neither can I.' Alexandra said in a small voice. 'But I don't see why it should get out. No one is going to publicize this meeting. The children don't even know why I'm going. They just think that Grandma invited us, and we're going to New York. I'm going to spend one weekend in Connecticut, "with friends", while the girls and my mother stay in New York.'

'I don't understand why you want them with you. It makes no sense.' But it did to her . . . and to Margaret.

'Maybe I need them for emotional support.' And then she took a big step, one she hadn't imagined a moment earlier. 'You're welcome to come along. It's a little frightening going back thirty years to see people you don't know, but must have once loved.'

'I can't even begin to imagine. And no, I will not join you. In fact, Alexandra . . .' He stood up and looked at her sadly. As far as he could see, their lives had been shattered, in his eyes, beyond repair. 'I implore you not to go. I don't have any idea what, if anything, can be salvaged from our marriage, but it serves no purpose to go and see these people. They're beneath you. You must not go back there . . .' And then, in a whisper, 'Please don't.'

But this time, she could not oblige him. After fourteen years of devoted obedience to Henri de Morigny, she could not do more. She had to go to New York, for her own sake, and maybe even for that of her children. But she had to go, and face these women, reach out and touch them, maybe even love them, or not, and put to bed some old ghosts she hadn't even known existed. 'I'm sorry, Henri . . . I have to . . . I hope you can understand that. It's terribly important to me. And none of this has to hurt our marriage. I'm doing something I need to do . . . for me . . . not to hurt you.' She went to him then and gently tried to put her arms around him, but he wouldn't let her. He treated her like a stranger, which in his mind, she was now.

'I don't even know who you are any more.'

'Does my family tree make so much difference?' But she knew the answer to that, before she asked the question, and he shook his head sadly, and walked out of the room, as she blew her nose resolutely, and walked down the hall to pack for her daughters. No matter what happened to her marriage, there was no question in her mind. She had to go to New York. She *had* to. She was going.

Chapter 28

It was only three days before the scheduled meeting, when John Chapman went back to the network, flashed all his passes, and went upstairs to her office. He smiled at her secretary, and looked as though he belonged there, as he asked if Hilary was in her office.

'She's leaving in a few minutes . . .' She was about to ask him who he was, but he slipped past her and she shrugged. She couldn't keep track of everyone who went in to see Miss Walker. They were legion, and he looked all right. In fact, he looked a lot better than that. She smiled to herself, wondering if this was someone Hilary was involved with. No one ever knew anything about Hilary's private life. And as the door closed silently behind him, he stood in Hilary's office, and she looked up, startled.

'Yes?' She thought it was a delivery of some kind, a script, or urgent instructions. She was used to new faces popping in and out of her office, but not this one. And he stood staring at her quietly, as though he knew her well. It was an odd feeling as he approached her, and she was suddenly frightened as she reached for the phone to call for help. But as he smiled at her, she felt foolish. He looked intelligent and coherent and handsome, but she still couldn't figure out who in hell he was or what he was doing there as he spoke to her in a deep, gentle voice.

'Miss Walker?' But he didn't need to ask the question. He knew exactly who she was, possibly even better than she herself did. 'I'm sorry to barge in on you like this. I have to speak to you for a moment.' She stood up behind her desk, as though to take control of the situation as he approached her. The green eyes were as cold as ice, and her voice was curt.

'I'm on my way out. You'll have to see me tomorrow. What department are you from?'

It was a tough question and he wasn't sure what to answer. He didn't want her to call security and have him thrown out. Instead, he said something totally outrageous. 'I'm here because of Megan and Alexandra . . .' He waited to see the effect, and like a deep knife wound, or a gunshot, at first there was no bleeding. Her eyes were still steady green ice. '. . . They want to see you.'

'Who are you?' This time her hand was shaking as she reached for the phone, and he beat her to it, and held it in its cradle.

'Please . . . just give me five minutes. I won't hurt you. It's a long story, but I'll make it as quick as I can.' And suddenly she knew that he was the man who had called her, and he knew that she remembered.

'I don't want to see them.'

'They want to see you. Both of them. Alexandra is coming all the way from France . . . Megan from Kentucky . . .' He was stalling and she was showing signs of pain in her eyes . . . incredible sorrow . . .

'That old sonofabitch sent you, didn't he? Why now?' She stood to her full height and watched him, abandoning her grip on the phone.

'He's dying.'

'Good.'

'Maybe he wants to repent of his sins. He wants to

bring the three of you together, this weekend, at his house in Connecticut. He has spent months finding you . . .'

'Bullshit.' She cut him off. 'I know better. I went to him twenty years ago, and he had no idea and no interest where anyone was. Who found us? You did?' He nodded, not sure if she would hate him or not. He was just stirring up more pain for her. And she had long since put the past to rest. She had given up on finding her sisters after the last time she saw Arthur. After ten years, the dream had died. And now after more than twenty years, she didn't want to revive it. She didn't need them anymore. She had cut everything out of her life that might remind her of them. There were no men, no children, no love life of any kind. There was work, soothing work, and lots of it, and the people she trampled on the way up. She didn't have to feel guilty or sorry. She was heading in one direction. And she was all by herself. 'It's too late, whoever you are.'

'Chapman, John Chapman.'

'Well, tell him I'm not interested. He's twenty years too late . . . make that thirty.' She looked unspeakably bitter as she sat down. In some ways, he noticed, she looked younger than she was, and in others she looked older. She had eyes that were older and sadder than time.

'And what do I tell your sisters?'

'Tell them . . . Tell them . . .' Her voice faltered and she looked up at him sadly. 'Tell them I loved them then but . . . it's too late for me now.' He shook his head and sat down across the desk from her, praying that he could touch something still living in her heart, if anything had survived the endless pain she'd endured in her childhood.

'It's not too late, Hilary . . . it can't be . . . you were everything to them then . . .' Arthur had said so. He had once described to John how she cared for the other two

344

girls, and just talking about it had made him cry. 'You can't turn your back on them now.'

She looked into his eyes, wondering who this man was, how he had found her, and how he knew so much. 'They don't need me anymore, Chapman. They're grown up now. What are they? Secretaries? Housewives?' It was the best fate she could hope for them, as John Chapman smiled.

'One's a baroness in France, with two children, and the other's a doctor in Kentucky. They're both interesting women. I think you'd like them.' But that was beside the point, even though she was curious about them.

'Who's the doctor?' It was difficult to imagine either of those little girls as a doctor.

'Megan. She's terrific. And so is Alexandra. She's warm and compassionate and kind.'

'She was, even as a baby.' Her voice was a whisper, and then dropping her face into her hands, she shook her head. 'The thought of finding them kept me alive through ten years of hell. I stole ten thousand dollars from my aunt, and I was going to come to New York to find them.' She laughed into her hands, and Chapman could see that there were tears on her desk. 'And then he told me he hadn't kept track of them . . . he had no idea where they were . . . I couldn't find them either.' She looked up at John with empty, broken eyes. 'What's the point now, except to cause each other pain with the memories of what happened?'

'You're the only one who has those, Hilary. The others have nothing. Alexandra remembers you, and Megan knows nothing at all. All you have now is each other. What happened to your parents is no longer important. Just the three of you . . . you can't turn your back on that now.'

'That old bastard destroyed us. Why should I let him soothe his conscience by getting us back together now? My life won't change if I don't see them. That's all over. They're gone. Just ... like my parents ... like the past.'

'Your parents are gone forever ... but your sisters aren't. They're real and alive, and they want to know you. Even if you go and you hate them, at least you can tell yourself you tried.' But she shook her head slowly and stood up again, her eyes shooting emerald fire at him.

'I won't do it. Tell Patterson how much I hate him ... no ... you couldn't even imagine how much I hate him.'

'Why? I know he didn't keep the three of you together, but was there more?' He had wanted to ask her that since he first read her file.

'It doesn't matter any more. He knows what he did to us. Let him live with it. For me ... it's over ... I have my life ... my work ... I don't need more than that.'

'It's a hell of an empty life, Hilary. I know, because that's all I have. Who do you talk to at night in the silence? Who holds your hand when you're sick or tired or scared? I have an ex-wife and my parents and two brothers. Who do you have? Can you afford to turn your back on those two women?'

'Get out of my office.' She walked to the door and pulled it open. She had heard enough, and she couldn't take any more. But he took a piece of paper out of his pocket. On it were the instructions of how to get to Arthur's place in Connecticut on the first of September, the phone number, the address, and he looked into her eyes as he laid it on her desk and then walked to the door.

'I've lived your life, Hilary Walker, for months now. I've cried for you. I've been to Charlestown, to Jacksonville, I've talked to the neighbour who found you near death on her doorstep, I've been to your foster homes. I know how badly he hurt you . . . I know what a rotten deal you got,' and there were tears in his eyes as he looked down at her and spoke, 'but please God, please don't do this . . . don't turn your back on them now. They need you, and you need them . . . Hilary . . . please . . . go to the meeting. I'll be there to help you. I'll do anything I can.' She was looking up at him in amazement, wondering how he had known all that. 'Just be there . . . please . . .' And with that he squeezed her arm gently, and left her office, as she stood there, staring after him, all the old pain in the past revived in her, along with a new confusion. She didn't want to go and see them . . . she didn't want to remember Axie's bright red curls and Megan's little cries in the night. They were gone now. Gone forever. And she couldn't go back any more. Not even for John Chapman.

Chapter 29

'You're really going?' Henri stood looking at her across their bedroom. In Cap Ferrat they shared one bedroom, or they had, until Alexandra had confessed everything to him. He had moved into the guest room that night. And the gesture needed no explanation.

'I am.' She looked serious and firm. The girls were dressed and ready. Their bags were downstairs, and Margaret was meeting them at the airport in Nice. They had managed to book a direct flight to New York without going back to Paris.

'You won't reconsider?'

She shook her head slowly. 'I'm sorry, darling. I can't.' She walked toward him in the hope that he would let her touch him, but when she reached his side, he took a step back from her, and it cut her to the quick when he did it.

'Please don't,' he said quietly. 'Have a good trip then.'

'I'll be back no later than the tenth.' He nodded. 'And I'll be at the Pierre in New York, if you need me. I'll call you.'

'That won't be necessary. I'll be very busy.' He turned away and walked out on to the terrace, and with a last look at his back, she left and went downstairs. She didn't see him watching her as they drove away, or the tears in his eyes as he stared out at the sea and thought about her. He knew he loved her a great deal and now he felt as though he had lost her. It was incredible to him . . . all that had happened . . . he just didn't understand it. How they could have let it happen . . . in a way, he realized, she was as much the victim of circumstance as he. But to him it was so much more important, and now she was off on this wild-goose chase to meet two unknown sisters. He only wished he could have stopped her, but it was obvious that he couldn't.

Margaret had insisted they take first class on the flight, and the girls were enchanted as they ordered Shirley Temples, and blew at each other through the little red straws.

'Girls, please!' Alexandra admonished, still thinking of her husband, and Margaret told her to let them have some fun. And then as the two little girls walked down the aisles to see if they could find any children to play with, Margaret asked her how Henri had taken the news. Alexandra had told her only briefly several days before that she had told him the entire truth before leaving.

'He didn't say so in so many words,' Alexandra said solemnly to her mother, 'but I think it's over. I'm sure I'll come home to find he's contacted his attorneys.'

'But you didn't have to tell him, either. You could have just told him I was dragging you to New York.'

'He knew it was something else, Maman. I had to tell him something, so I told him the truth.' And despite the price to pay, she didn't regret it. At least she had a clear conscience.

'I think that was a great mistake.' And she didn't tell Alexandra, but she suspected that her daughter's suspicions were right. Henri would almost surely ask for a divorce. Not even ask for it, demand it, and Alexandra would never put up a fight. Margaret just prayed he left her the

349

children. None of it was pleasant to think about, and it distracted her when Axelle and Marie-Louise came back to announce that in spite of the fact that every seat was sold, and packed, there was 'no one' on the flight.

'In other words, there are no children?' Margaret inquired with a grin and they laughed. 'Then you'll just have to put up with us.' She played Old Maid and Fish and War and taught them Gin Rummy, and they watched the movie, as Alexandra sat lost in her own thoughts. She had a great deal to think about ... her parents ... her sisters ... and her husband, if she still had one when she went back to France. But she was still sure she had made the right decision, and the next morning, after a good night's sleep at the Pierre, she called the concierge and made an appointment. She went only a few blocks away to Bergdorf's, and she was very pleased with the results. When she met her mother and the girls for lunch, they were stunned. She had had the blond rinse stripped off her hair, and she was once more a redhead.

'Maman, you look just like me!' Axelle squealed in delight and Margaret laughed as Marie-Louise clapped her hands.

'What on earth brought that on?' Margaret inquired over the girls' heads.

'I've wanted to do it for a long time. Maybe it's that I am who I am now, for better or worse. But I'm not hiding any more.' And it felt good to her, as Margaret watched her.

'I love you,' Margaret whispered as she touched her daughter's hand.

They had lunch at '21', and stopped at Schwarz's for a 'little gift' from Grandma. As usual, she spoiled both the girls. And as planned, at four o'clock, Alexandra's limousine was waiting. She had explained to the girls that she was spending the weekend with some old friends in Connecticut, and they were staying in the city with their grandmother.

'I'll call you tonight,' she promised as she got into the car with one small suitcase, wearing a very chic black linen dress from Chanel.

'We're going to the movies with Grandma!' Axelle shouted.

She held her mother tight, hugged the girls, and then blew kisses to all three of them, and her eyes held her mother's for a long moment as they drove away. She was sure she could see tears on her mother's cheeks while she was waving, and tears stung Alexandra's eyes as well. It was frightening to be going back into the past, and ahead into the future, all at the same time. But it was also very exciting.

Chapter 30

The drive to Stonington on the Connecticut shore took slightly less than two hours, and Alexandra sat in the back seat, thinking of the people she had left behind her. Margaret, and the love she had lavished on her for thirty years, Axelle and Marie-Louise, so infinitely precious to her, perhaps even more so now . . . and Henri, so angry at her seeming betrayal of him. She had thought of calling him that morning, before she left, but she couldn't think of what to say. In fact, there seemed to be nothing left to say at all. She knew how he felt about her trip to the States. He had forbidden her to go, and for the first time in their married life, she had disobeyed him. And suddenly, as she drove along in the back of the hired limousine, she felt oddly free, and different than she had in a long time . . . almost the way she used to feel when she was a little girl, running with her father in the fields near their country house, with the wind in her hair, totally sure of herself, and completely happy. She felt as though he were with her now, as she took the journey back into the past that she felt so compelled to take. And without thinking, she ran a hand through her hair and smiled to herself. She was Alexandra de Borne again . . . Alexandra Walker, she whispered in the silent car. And for the first time in fourteen years, she was once more a redhead.

There was an electronic gate when they arrived, and

they were buzzed in by an unknown voice, but other than that bit of security the property looked simple and unimpressive. There was a long winding drive up a hill, and after a sharp turn, there was a pretty Victorian house with a wide porch and widow's walk. It looked like someone's grandmother's house, or that of a great-aunt. There was a lot of wicker furniture on the porch, and an old barn behind the house. It looked cosy and inviting, and Alexandra stepped out of the limousine carefully, looking around, thinking how pretty it was, and how much her children would like it. And then she saw a familiar face watching her from the porch, and she smiled as he hurried towards her.

'Hello! . . . how was your trip?' It was John Chapman, in khaki slacks and an open blue shirt. He looked totally at ease and his eyes were warm and friendly as he shook her hand and then took her suitcase from the chauffeur.

'It was fine, thank you very much. What a nice place this is.'

'It is, isn't it? I've been poking around all afternoon. There are some wonderful old things in the barn, I guess Mr Patterson has owned this place for years. Come on in, you'll love the house.' And he walked her slowly towards it, silently admiring the shining red hair that was so different from the quiet blonde she'd been before. And then finally he decided to go ahead and say it. 'Your hair looks wonderful, if it isn't rude to say it.'

But she only laughed and shook her head. She was pleased that he liked it. 'I decided to go back to my natural colour in honour of this trip. It's going to be hard enough for us to recognize each other without complicating things any further.' She smiled and their eyes met, and she finally got up the courage to ask him what she most wanted to know. 'Have the others arrived yet?'

He knit his brows and glanced at her, trying to look

unconcerned, but he was still worried about Hilary. She had given no indication that she would come, and he was desperately afraid that she wouldn't. 'Not yet. Megan said she'd get here around six o'clock. And Hilary ...' His voice drifted off and Alexandra looked at him long and hard and then nodded. She understood, and it saddened her. But it wasn't really surprising.

'She hasn't agreed to come, has she?'

'Not in so many words. But I told her how badly you wanted her to. I thought it was fair to say that.' She nodded in answer and silently prayed that her sister would have the courage to face them. She knew that the past was deeply painful for her, more so than for the others, and she might just decide not to do it. But Alexandra hoped that she would. Deep within, a small forgotten child desperately needed to see her. 'We'll keep our fingers crossed,' Chapman added as they walked into the front hall. There was a small sitting-room on the right, and a large parlour on the left, with a cosy fireplace, and well-kept Victorian furniture. She wondered where Arthur Patterson was, their benefactor who had brought them back together, and she asked John as much in a whisper.

'He's upstairs, resting.' He had brought two nurses with him, and when John saw him that morning, he realized that it was a miracle the man was still alive at all. It was as though he had hung on, just for this, and couldn't possibly hang on much longer. He had aged twenty years in the past four months, and it was obvious that he was in great pain all the time now. But he was coherent and alert, and anxious to see the three women he'd finally brought back together.

'Are you sure they'll come?' he'd pressed John, and Chapman had assured him, praying that Hilary wouldn't let them down. But as much as she hated Patterson, maybe it wouldn't be such a bad thing after all if she didn't come. Chapman wasn't sure how well the old man would weather that kind of confrontation. And after lunch, his nurses had put him to bed, and urged John to let him rest until dinner. He was determined to come downstairs that night and dine with his guests. And the plan was for John to leave after dinner. By then the women would have settled in, he would have introduced them all to each other and the rest was up to them ... and to Arthur.

Alexandra was peeking around the living-room, and from there, wandered into the dining-room with the long English table.

'It looks as though he spent a lot of time here,' Alexandra observed, 'the place looks well loved.' He smiled at her choice of words, and said he wasn't sure how much time Arthur had spent in Connecticut, and he didn't add that Arthur had told him he wanted to die there.

'Would you like to go upstairs?'

'Thank you.' She smiled up at him, wondering how old he was. He seemed so boyish in some ways, and yet so mature. He was serious and yet fun ... a world away from Henri, and yet he looked childish to her compared to her husband. She was so accustomed to Henri's forceful ways, his habits of command, his way of striding into a room and taking charge, with his stern face and his powerful shoulders, and it was odd how suddenly she missed it. He made other men seem weak, and too young, and as though somehow, no matter how nice they were, they lacked something. And she couldn't help wondering if things would ever be the same again, if he'd even take her back when she returned to France ... maybe she'd be forced to live with her mother again, or find her own house. For the time being, everything was uncertain.

John showed her to a sunny room at the corner of the

house; it was still hot from the afternoon sun, and the bedspread was sparkling white with lace trim, with a cosy rocking chair next to it, and the same Victorian furniture that seemed to fill the house. There was a love-seat and a porcelain washstand, and someone had put flowers in the room, and for some reason the room made her feel young again, as though she were a young girl coming home. And there were tears in her eyes when she turned to John and thanked him.

'It's so odd being here,' she tried to explain but she couldn't find the words, 'it's like being very young and very old . . . visiting the past . . . it's all very confusing.'

'I understand.' He left her to freshen up, and she came downstairs in a little while in a beige linen suit, her make-up fresh, her beige shoes with the familiar black toe of Chanel, and her red hair bringing it all to life. She looked elegant and in control, and she turned as she heard a stir of voices on the stairs behind her. It was Arthur coming downstairs with the assistance of the two nurses. He was bent over and frail, and he groaned with every step, but suddenly as he saw her, he stopped, and gave a startled sound, and then tears began to roll down his cheeks, as Alexandra walked halfway up the stairs to meet him.

'Hello, Mr Patterson,' she said, quietly, and as he trembled she bent down and kissed his cheek. 'Thank you for bringing me here.' But he was trembling so violently, he couldn't speak. He only took her hand and squeezed it hard, with the last of his strength, and then allowed her to assist him downstairs with the help of one nurse, and when they had settled him in a comfortable chair in the large sitting-room, he stared up at her and spoke at last in a voice hoarse from his illness.

'My God, you look so much like her. Are you Alexandra

or Megan?' He still remembered little Hilary's jet-black hair, exactly like her father's.

'I am Alexandra, sir.' She looked serious and deeply touched and he began to cry again as she spoke.

'You even have the same accent. Through all those years, she always had that lilt of French . . .' He shook his head, stunned by the resemblance between Alexandra and her mother. And it was an odd feeling for Alexandra, to be so like someone she had never known, and yet who was her mother.

'Were you very fond of her?' It was something to talk about as they waited for the others. John had appeared again and he offered her a glass of wine, which she declined. She wanted to concentrate on Arthur Patterson and wait for her sisters. She was growing more tense and excited with each passing moment.

But he nodded his head now, thinking of Alexandra's questions. 'Yes, I was very fond of her . . . she was such a lovely girl . . . so beautiful, so proud . . . so strong . . . with so much life in her . . .' With a faded smile, he told Alexandra of the first time he and Sam had seen her in Paris. 'I thought she was going to call the MPs on us, and she would have . . . except that your father was so damn handsome and charming.' He smiled, thinking back to Sam. What good friends they had been, and what good times they had had in the war years. 'He was a wonderful actor too.' He told her about some of his plays, as she listened quietly, and then suddenly there was the sound of a car outside, and John disappeared, and a moment later they heard voices.

Arthur seemed to be listening too, and unconsciously, he reached out and took Alexandra's hand and held it firmly in his own, just as the front door opened. And from where he was sitting, he could see her as she entered. She looked around, just as Alexandra had done, and then saw them watching her, and like a shy child, she walked into the room, looking suddenly like a younger double of Alexandra.

Alexandra rose slowly to her feet and instinctively walked to her with outstretched arms. It was like finding a piece of the past and looking in the mirror all at the same time. The only difference was that Alexandra's eyes were green and Megan's were blue. But otherwise, it was obvious that they were sisters. 'Megan?' she asked in a cautious voice, but it was obvious who she was. The younger girl nodded, and they went into each other's arms, with tears in their eyes, even though they had both promised themselves that they were going to control their emotions. And as Alexandra held her close, she felt for a moment as though she remembered.

'You look so much like me!' Megan laughed through her tears and hugged her again, and then pulled away to observe her with a wry smile. 'Except you don't dress as well.' She was still wearing the jeans and hiking boots and T-shirt she had worn at the hospital until she'd left that afternoon. But it was what she usually wore in any case, just like Rebecca. 'My God, you're beautiful.' She laughed, and shyly stepped back as Alexandra took her hand, and then took it upon herself to introduce her to Arthur.

'How do you do, Mr Patterson,' Megan greeted him politely, almost like a young girl, and he stared at her with satisfaction. She was almost as pretty as Solange, but not quite, and she didn't have Alexandra's sophistication, but she had something of her own that stood out, a kind of purity and intelligence that were clearly etched on her face. She looked like a lovely young woman.

'So you're the doctor, are you?'

'Yes, sir. Just about. I'm finishing my residency right now. I'll be all through by Christmas.'

He nodded again, looking from one woman to the other. There was no bitterness there, no anger, they had led good lives and it showed. He had chosen well for them . . . but not for poor Hilary. After Chapman's warning, he was afraid of what she would say to him if she came, but nonetheless he wanted to see her.

They waited until almost eight o'clock, alternately silent and then speaking all at once, nervous and uncomfortable and strange, with Arthur telling them stories of the past, and Megan and Alexandra trying to share their lives with him and each other. Alexandra had brought photographs of the girls, and Henri, and her parents. Megan had done the same, bringing photographs of Rebecca and David, the house in Tiburon, and the hospital where she worked in Kentucky. It was as though they wanted to bring each other up to date as quickly as possible. They had thirty years to account for. And it was obvious how different their lives were. The hospital in Kentucky stood out next to the photographs of the girls in front of the villa in Cap Ferrat. And Henri looked every inch the seigneur in front of his château in the Dordogne, as the photographs of Margaret and Rebecca stood side by side for a moment, the one in jeans with a flower in her hair, the other in an evening dress going to a ball in Monte Carlo the year before. And Megan mentioned it with a shy smile as they walked in to dinner with Arthur walking slowly behind them with John's assistance.

'It's funny how different our lives have been, isn't it? And yet we're still sisters . . . we still look alike . . . we still come from the same parents, and probably have similar likes and dislikes and habits we've inherited without even knowing it. And yet look at us, you grew up in all that pomp and circumstance in France, and I spent half my childhood living with friends, while my parents went to jail for causes they believed in.' And yet she didn't sound unhappy. She sounded proud of them, and she was. It was all amazing to think about, and it silenced both of them as they took their seats on either side of Arthur. John's place was next to Megan, and there was an empty chair next to Alexandra, and it was becoming obvious now that Hilary was not going to join them. Alexandra felt her heart sink, and made idle chit-chat for a while, as Arthur seemed to doze, and then suddenly there was the sound of a car outside. John left the table quietly. There were angry voices outside, and then suddenly the front door flew open, as the two women watched, mesmerized, and Arthur woke up, as though he sensed that someone else was coming to see him.

'Did something happen?' he asked Alexandra, confused for an instant as he woke up and she patted his hand, never taking her eyes from the door, and then she saw her. Tall and thin and lanky as their father had been, with a long stride, and jet-black hair, and green eyes that she suddenly turned on them. She was wearing a wrinkled navy linen business suit. She had had every intention of not coming, and then suddenly after work she had decided to rent a car and come up and tell Arthur once and for all what she thought of him. And then maybe she would be free of him for the rest of her life. She didn't even care if she saw the others. They were strangers to her now. It was Arthur who interested her as she strode into the room and stood facing him, but it was impossible to ignore the two women with red hair who flanked him, and her eyes were drawn first to Megan, and then to Alexandra, as John stood carefully just behind her. He could sense the tension in the room, the anguish of the woman who stood so close to

360

him. He wanted to put his arms around her but she looked as though she might explode, and then suddenly she stopped, as her eyes met Alexandra's, and Alexandra came slowly to her feet and crossed the room like a sleepwalker and the words escaped her without rhyme or reason.

'H . . . Hillie . . .' She could see the face of a little girl with long black hair, and yet here was this woman . . . with the same black hair . . . the same green eyes . . . without knowing why, she started to cry, and without wanting to, Hilary's arms went around her.

'Axie . . . little Axie . . .' It was the first time she'd held her since the day they'd torn her from her, and left her alone with Eileen and Jack in Charlestown, crying for the sisters she had so dearly loved, and she could barely stand the pain now of remembering it, as she held the tall, perfumed, beautifully coiffed woman from Paris . . . except all she saw there was the face of the child she had once loved, and she whispered the same words over and over again as she cried . . . 'I love you, Axie . . .' They held each other like that for a long time, as Megan watched silently, and then suddenly Arthur began to cough, and John hurried to give him a glass of water. The housekeeper who was serving them dinner brought the pills the nurse had given her, and Megan checked the dose and gave them to John, as Hilary slowly turned towards them. 'You must be Megan.' She smiled through her tears, and held Alexandra's hand as they pulled apart from the embrace. 'You've changed quite a bit since the last time I saw you.' The three women laughed, but Hilary's eyes clouded as she saw the old man, and she held tight to Alexandra's hand as she spoke to him. 'I said I wouldn't come, and I meant it, Arthur.' He nodded, meeting her eyes with fear and pain, and he saw everything there that he had dreaded seeing. She hated him, and one could see it there like black poison. But he also knew he deserved it. He knew better than anyone. 'I never wanted to see you again.'

'I'm glad you did come, Hillie,' Alexandra said in her gentle voice. 'I wanted so much to see you . . . both,' she added, smiling at Megan, but Hilary wasn't smiling now, and she dropped her sister's hand as she advanced on Arthur.

'Why did you do this to us? Bring us here after all these years, to taunt us with what we didn't have, what we missed, who we might have been if we'd stayed together?'

He choked on his own words, and clutched the table with both hands as he faced her. 'I felt I owed it to you to make up to you for what I'd done.' He could barely breathe as he spoke to her, but it didn't worry her.

'And do you think you can make it up?' She laughed bitterly and they all ached for her, but John was frightened of what she would do now. She had waited thirty years for this, and he had always sensed the full measure of her hatred for Arthur. 'Do you really think you can wipe out thirty years of loneliness and pain with one dinner?'

'Your sisters have been luckier than you, Hilary.' He spoke honestly. 'And they don't hate me as much as you do.'

'They don't know as much as I do . . . do they, Arthur . . . *do they*?' she shouted into the silent room, the words echoing off the walls as he trembled.

'That's all in the past. Hilary.' It was a conversation between only the two of them. Only they knew of what they were speaking, as the others wondered.

'Is it? How about you? Have you been able to live with yourself for all these years, after killing my parents?' Her green eyes blazed and Alexandra advanced to gently touch her arm, but Hilary shook her off.

'Hillie, don't . . . it doesn't matter now . . .'

'Doesn't it?' She wheeled on her sister. 'How do you know that? How could you possibly know, living the good life in France, while I sat on my ass in juvenile hall, after getting raped, trying to figure out how to find you. And that sonofabitch didn't even know where you were, he didn't know where any of us were. He didn't even care enough to keep track of us after he ripped you out of my arms that day, crying and sobbing . . . you don't remember that now, but I do. I've remembered it . . . I've remembered both of you . . .' She looked from Alexandra to Megan. '. . . every day of my life and I've cried for you because I never found you. And now you tell me it doesn't matter? That I shouldn't hate him for killing our parents? How can you say that?' The tears were pouring down her cheeks unashamedly.

'But he didn't kill them.' Alexandra spoke for herself and Megan. 'His only failing was in not keeping us together, or keeping track of us over the years, but perhaps he couldn't help it.' She looked benevolently at the old man, and Megan silently nodded, unable to understand why Hilary hated him so much. He had failed them, but he had not betrayed them the way Hilary said. But she was shaking her head and laughing at them through the tears.

'You don't know anything. You were babies. I was standing there the night Mama died . . . the night Daddy killed her . . . I was listening . . . I heard what they said . . .' She began to sob and John stood nearby, ready to help her if she collapsed or needed him. He was near her, as he had been for months, although she didn't know it. 'I heard her screams . . .' Hilary went on, 'when he hit her and hit her and hit her, and then strangled her into silence until she died . . .' She was gulping down the sobs and she stood right in front of Arthur now. 'And do you know why he did that?' Her eyes never left Arthur's face, she had waited a lifetime for this. 'He did it because she was having an affair with *him*, and she told Father so . . .' She was listening to the voices of the past as she spoke, and she almost looked as though she were in another world, remembering back to the night her father had killed her mother. 'He had been cheating on her, she said, with lots of different women for years . . . all his leading ladies, she said . . . and he said it wasn't true . . . he said she was crazy . . . and she said she had proof . . . she knew who he'd just taken to California . . . who he'd been with the night before . . . and she said it didn't make any difference to her any more . . . that she had someone of her own, and that if he wasn't careful, she'd leave him and take us with her. And he said he'd kill her if she did, and she laughed . . . she kept laughing at him . . . and he said she could never take away his baby girls . . . and she laughed . . . and then she told him who it was . . .' She was crying so hard she could hardly speak, but she went on, as Arthur shook more and more violently in his seat and she stood inches from him, shouting down at him and crying. 'She told him, didn't she, Arthur . . . didn't she?' Hilary shouted. And then she looked at her sisters, and told them what she had always known, and they hadn't. 'She was having an affair with Arthur, Daddy's best friend . . . and he said he would kill her for it, and she only laughed, and when he told her she couldn't take us away, she told him that only two of us were his . . .' There was a stunned silence in the room, and Arthur sat back in his chair as though he'd been struck by lightning. And Hilary's voice was quiet when she spoke this time. She had done what she had come for. 'She told him that Megan was Arthur's child,' she said in a dull voice, staring down at him with contempt. 'And then Daddy killed her.' She sank into the chair next to him, crying softly, as Alexandra put an arm around her shoulders and the old man whimpered softly in his chair.

'I never knew . . . she never told me . . .' He looked at Megan pathetically. 'You must believe me . . . I never knew . . . I always thought you were his, like the others . . .' He was crying openly, and Megan looked even more shocked than she had at the rest of the recital. And Arthur seemed to be making his excuses to the room in general. 'If I had known . . .' But Hilary only looked at him and shook her head.

'What would you have done differently? Kept her with you, and left the rest of us to rot? You wouldn't have done anything. You didn't stand by my mother, or your own child, you betrayed your best friend, and what you did killed them both. You have their blood on your hands . . . and ours, without you, our lives would have been very different. How could you live with yourself all these years, knowing what you'd done? How could you defend him after betraying him?'

'He begged me to, Hilary . . . I didn't want to. I begged him to let me find another attorney. But he didn't want me to. And in truth, he didn't want to live after your mother died.' His voice dropped down to a whisper. 'Neither did I. It ended both our lives . . . I loved her deeply from the first moment I saw her.' The tears rolled down his cheeks as Megan stared at him. He was no longer just a family friend. This was her father.

And Hilary stared at him emptily, as though seeing him for the first time. He was an old, dying man, and there was no undoing what he had done. For him, it was all over, no matter whose blood was on his hands. The blood was long since dry . . . the people all but forgotten. She stood up then, and looked down at him. 'I came here to tell you how much I hated you. And do you know something strange, Arthur, after all these years, I'm not really sure it still matters.' She felt Alexandra's hand on her shoulder and turned to look into her eyes. She was exhausted from the emotions of the evening and turned to look at both the girls. 'I loved you both a great deal a long time ago ... but maybe that's too far in the past too ...' She felt drained, spent, she had nothing left to give or take, but Alexandra wouldn't let her go, and Megan was watching her too. She was the one to speak first.

'It's a long time ago for all of us, but we still came. I didn't remember any of you. And I didn't know Mr Patterson was my father. We came to honour the past, but also to go on from here. We all have other parents now, other lives, other people we care about. We haven't lived in a void for thirty years, none of us, not even you with your anger and your hatred.' It was a quiet reproach but it was powerful and it struck home. 'You can't just come here and drop a bomb like this in our laps, and then go. You owe it to us to repair the wounds, just as we owe it to you to do the same. And that's why we all came here.' There were tears slowly running down her cheeks, as she looked at Hilary, and John Chapman silently wanted to cheer her. It would ruin everything if Hilary left now. It would destroy her life once and for all. She had to stay, in spite of Arthur, and face them.

Hilary looked at Alexandra, as though seeking confirmation and she nodded and spoke in her quiet voice. 'Please stay Hillie ... I've waited so long for this.' They had all taken such risks, paid such a high price. She had defied Henri, possibly at great expense, all for the pleasure of seeing her sisters. 'It took a lot of courage to come here. For all of us. My husband forbade me to come here ... I don't even know if he will take me back now. And my mother ... the woman I know as my mother has come

366

with me, and she is very frightened of what all this will mean. She is afraid that after all this time she will lose me.' There were tears in her eyes as she spoke to Hilary, and Megan was nodding with tears in her own eyes. Rebecca was terrified of what seeing her sisters would mean to her. They had talked for an hour on the phone the night before, and she had promised she would call as soon as possible to reassure her. 'You have lost more than any of us, Hilary . . . but you are not alone . . . we love you, even now. You cannot turn your back on us.' And then putting her arms around her again, she cried softly. 'I won't let you.' Hilary stood tall and straight for a long moment, and then her arms went around Alexandra . . . how could she know what her life had been like? But it wasn't her fault . . . or Megan's . . . or maybe even Arthur's. She hated to admit that now, but it was possible. He had been a fool and he had paid a high price for it. He looked at Hilary sorrowfully over Alexandra's shoulder.

'Can you ever forgive me, all of you?' But he was looking at the oldest of the three and she took a long time to answer.

'I don't know . . . I don't know what I feel . . .' But she held tight to Alexandra and her eyes reached out to Megan.

'I'm glad you came anyway. The three of you had a right to be together. And if I had been a different kind of man, I would have defied my wife and kept you all myself. I wanted to, but she had such strong feelings about it that I didn't dare go against her. I'm sorry now, but it's too late to make any difference.' He looked mournfully at Hilary, and then at the child he had turned away, who was his own daughter. 'I made a terrible mistake. But I've paid for it. I've been a lonely man all my life . . . ever since your mother died . . .' He couldn't go on. He only shook his head and then stood up shakily, as John Chapman and one of the nurses came to help him. 'I'm going upstairs now. We all have a lot to think about.' Hilary's revelation had shocked them all, particularly Megan and Arthur. In a strange way, Megan now wondered if she was responsible for her mother's death . . . if she hadn't been born, would Sam have killed Solange? But it was too late to think about that, too late to cry over what had happened thirty years before. It was time to move on, as best they could. And he turned to them again before he left the room. 'I want you all to stay for as long as you can . . . for as long as you want to. This will be your home one day; I am leaving it to all of you, so you have a place to come, a home together finally, and a place to bring your families and your children. I'll stay out of your way while you're here, but I want you to stay here and get to know each other.' Alexandra and Megan thanked him quietly, and Megan rose quickly to help him upstairs, as Hilary watched, saying nothing. And when he was gone, she turned to Alexandra and shook her head.

'I don't know if I'll ever stop hating him, Axie.' It was still so easy to call her that, even after all these years, and the younger of the two smiled.

'You will. You have to. There's nothing left to hate any more. He's almost gone.' Hilary nodded. It was clear that the man wouldn't live much longer. 'I'm only grateful that he brought us together in time. That he still cared enough to do that.' They walked slowly upstairs arm in arm, and Hilary walked into Alexandra's bedroom, thinking suddenly of the room they had shared in Jack and Eileen's house, and three of them in one bed, as she tried to keep the baby from crying so Eileen wouldn't beat them.

'What are your children like?' She sat down in the rocking chair. It was a comfortable room, but she hadn't decided yet to spend the night. She just wanted to sit and talk for a while with Axie.

Alexandra smiled at the question. 'Marie-Louise looks a lot like you. She has your eyes . . . and Axelle looks a lot like photographs of me as a little girl. She's six . . . and Marie-Louise is twelve. I lost a little boy in between them.' And with a slice of pain, Hilary remembered her own abortion for the first time in years. She had been so careful after that to avoid any contact with children, and now suddenly had two nieces. 'Do you still remember your French?'

'Some.' Hilary smiled. 'Not much, I guess.'

'Marie-Louise and Axelle speak English anyway, thanks to my mother.'

'What's your husband like?' Hilary was curious about so many things about her . . . her husband . . . her parents . . . her life . . . her children . . . her habits . . . She wanted to know if they were alike. If after all these years, they had anything in common. And marriage was certainly not one of them. Hilary had assiduously avoided it.

Alexandra sighed, feeling very honest. 'He's difficult. And intelligent. And demanding. He wants to run everything, from the house to the office and back again. And he expects nothing less than perfection.'

'Don't you mind that?' She looked intrigued, her green eyes watching Alexandra as she shrugged and smiled.

'Not really. I'm used to it. And underneath his gruff exterior, I know he loves us . . . or he did.' She sighed. 'I don't know what's going to happen now. He was shocked when I told him our story . . . I mean about our parents . . .'

'It's not very pretty, is it?'

'Especially for Megan,' Alexandra added softly, just as she came down the hall. Megan had put Arthur to bed. He

369

had been in terrible pain, and he was crying. And she had given him an injection to sedate him.

'He's not going to live much longer.' She spoke quietly as she walked into the room, and Hilary noticed as John had, how much she sounded like Alexandra. 'I suspect he's got metastases everywhere. But he's still very alert.'

'The old bastard.' Hilary spoke in an undertone and Megan turned on her with flashing eyes.

'Don't talk about him like that. He's repented for his sins . . . he brought us here. What more do you want from him?'

'Something he can't give us,' Hilary shot back at her. 'The past . . . something decent we could have shared, instead of the heartbreak of tearing us apart.'

'We survived in spite of that . . . even you, Hilary. Look at you, you're a big success. You have a fantastic job, a nice life.' But it was an empty one, as only she knew, and Alexandra suspected. There was no one she cared about, and no one who cared about her, no one she was aware of anyway. And as they talked, John Chapman appeared in the doorway. He had disappeared discreetly for a while, and he suspected they would be talking late into the night. They had a lot of things to resolve, and a lot to learn about each other. And his job was finally over.

'Will we see you again, John?' Alexandra was the first to ask, and he shook his head, with a bittersweet smile.

'Not unless you want to look for someone else sometime, and I hope you never have to. My job's all done.' And then in a soft voice, he added, 'I'm going to miss you.' He had been living with each of them for months, hunting them down, seeking them out, getting to know them. And it suddenly came to him that he would miss Hilary most of all. He had ached so much for her past, and he had been too late to help her. 'Good luck to all of you.'

'Thank you.' They each stood up and shook hands with him, and Megan kissed him gently on the cheek with a shy smile. She had really liked him.

'If you ever get to Kentucky, call me.'

'Will you be there long?' he asked, hating to leave them, and she smiled at him, with the red hair that was exactly her mother's, and Alexandra's.

'I'll be through with my residency in December, but I'm pretty sure I'll stay on. I haven't told my parents yet,' she shrugged with an easy laugh and she looked very young again, 'but I think they already kind of expect it. My Dad does anyway. He knows how crazy I am.' They exchanged a long warm smile, and then Alexandra hugged him.

'Take care of yourself.' She mothered everyone, and it touched him as she patted his shoulder afterwards. 'Thank you for everything.'

'Don't let anyone talk you into dyeing your hair again . . . you look beautiful . . .'

'Thank you,' she blushed and he smiled and Hilary held out a hand and gruffly thanked him.

'I'm sorry I gave you such a hard time in my office . . . I was fighting all this . . .' And then with great effort in a low voice. 'But I'm glad I came.' She looked at both of her sisters, and her eyes filled with tears again, and then she looked back at him and without invitation he gently pulled her into his arms and she nestled there as he held her, wishing he could keep her there forever. There was still so much life owed her.

'You're going to be all right now, Hilary . . . it's going to be just fine . . .' His voice touched a place in her that had been closed for a long time, and she was sorry when she pulled away and looked up into his eyes with a shy smile.

371

'Come and see me sometime at the network.'

'I'll do that. Maybe we can have lunch sometime.'

She nodded, unable to say anything, she had to turn away as the tears coursed down her face. After so many years of isolation, she was surrounded by people she cared about deeply, and who seemed to love her.

It was Alexandra who put her arms around her this time, and smoothed back her hair as they walked John Chapman downstairs and waved as he drove away. And she and Hilary walked back upstairs again to Hilary's room. She had been given a room adjoining Alexandra's and Hilary changed into her nightgown and came back to chat, as Megan and Alexandra talked about Paris and Kentucky and the south of France, and whether or not Megan ever wanted to have children. She wasn't sure if it would interfere with her career or not, but Alexandra was telling her it was her greatest joy, as Hilary sat down in the rocking chair and shook her head in amazement. It was extraordinary being back together after all these years, and talking as though they had always been there.

'I never wanted kids, and I never regretted it,' Hilary lied, thinking back for a flash of a moment to the abortion. 'Well, I don't know . . . maybe I did when I was younger. It's too late now anyway.'

'How old are you?' Megan frowned. She had momentarily forgotten. She was thirty, and Hilary was . . . almost eight years older.

'Thirty-eight.'

'These days most women don't even have their first child till then. In this part of the world at least.' She smiled. 'Where I work, I see them having their first babies at twelve and thirteen, younger than that even sometimes. It's amazing.' It was a whole other world from this comfortable old house in Connecticut, and the lives her sisters led in the places where they lived. And then suddenly she laughed. 'Isn't it amazing how different we all are, and yet how similar? I live in the hills of Kentucky,' she said, looking at Alexandra then, '. . . and you live in a fancy house in Paris, and a château somewhere else, and a villa in the south of France in the summer,' and then she turned to Hilary, 'and you practically run a television network. Isn't it amazing?'

'It would have been more so,' Hilary said quietly, 'if we could have seen each other twenty-five years ago. My life wasn't so pleasant then.'

'What was it like?' Megan finally asked what they both wanted to know, and little by little, over the next two hours, with tears streaming down her face, she told them. All of it. The uglier and the ugliest, and the tragic and the brutal. But it helped to share it with them, and whereas she had once been the one who protected them, they comforted her now, and Alexandra held her hand, as Megan told her story, of sit-ins in Mississippi, and the time her father had been shot on a rainy night in east Georgia, of what decent people they were, and how totally they believed in their causes, and how much she loved them. And then Alexandra told them about Margaret, and Pierre before he died, and her life with Henri, and how she was afraid that now he would divorce her.

'He'd be a damn fool if he did.' Hilary spoke up, as she flung her long black hair over her shoulder, in a gesture that struck a chord of memory for Alexandra as she watched her.

'He is so obsessed with his lineage, and you have to admit, ours is a bit exotic for someone like my husband.' The three of them laughed and the sun came up as they talked. They went to bed amidst yawns and kisses and hugs and promises to meet again in the morning. They all

373

slept until noon, and Alexandra was the first one to get up. She called her mother and the children at the hotel, but they were out, and she left a message that all was well and she would be home on Sunday night. And then she thought about calling Henri, but she didn't know what to say, so she went back upstairs and showered and dressed, and when she came back downstairs again, Megan was wearing a clean pair of jeans and a white blouse with a ribbon in her hair. And she looked more like a little girl than a doctor, and Alexandra said so. The two of them chatted over coffee and hot biscuits, and one of Arthur's nurses informed them that he had had a difficult night, so Megan went upstairs to check on him, just as Hilary came downstairs in shorts and a silk shirt, her black hair pulled severely into a bun, and her feet bare as she came to breakfast. She looked somehow much younger than she had the night before, and Alexandra realized that they all did. They were travelling back in time, and burdens that had aged them were falling from their shoulders. In her case it was the fear of what Henri would do to her, and that no one would love her any more if he divorced her. If he did, she still had Margaret, and the girls, and now she had these two women to support her. It didn't seem so terrifying any more. In fact, she felt good, and for the first time in a long time, she didn't feel frightened.

'Late night, last night, wasn't it?' Hilary smiled lazily over her coffee. 'What'll we do today? We could talk ourselves to death by tomorrow night, if we don't watch out.' She and Alexandra both laughed, and Alexandra looked at her thoughtfully. 'You're going back tomorrow night too?' The message she had left at the hotel said she would. She didn't want to abandon her mother and the girls for too long. She had promised to spend a week with them in New York, and she knew her daughters would wear her mother out eventually.

'I have to,' Hilary answered. 'I have some important meetings scheduled for Monday morning.' So what else was new? When didn't she? She grinned. 'When are you going back?'

'To New York, tomorrow night. I left my mother at the Pierre with Axelle and Marie-Louise. I think by tomorrow night she'll have reached her breaking point, even though she's very good with them. But they're a handful.' Alexandra paused, thinking of Margaret and how worried she had been about this meeting. 'I also feel like I should get back to reassure her. I think she was afraid I would stop loving her when I met my sisters, as though she wouldn't really be my family any more. I owe her a little reassurance.'

Hilary nodded and smiled. 'I could drive you in, if you like. We could go out to dinner this week . . . or lunch . . .' She looked at her hopefully, like a shy child with a new best friend, and Alexandra's eyes lit up in answer.

'I would love it. And you could meet the girls! We're going to be here for a week. And then,' she said triumphantly, Henri de Morigny be damned, 'you could come to visit us in Paris!'

'That's a great idea!' Hilary laughed, as Megan joined them.

'What are you two cooking up today?' She was smiling but her eyes were serious.

'Just a little mischief in New York,' Hilary smiled at her. She still thought of her as 'the baby'. 'Care to join us? You could stay at my place with me.'

'Or at the Pierre with us,' Alexandra offered, but Megan had already made another decision.

'I'd love to, and I'll come and visit both of you as soon

as I can. But I'm going to stay here for a few days. He seems much worse today.' Her eyes indicated Arthur upstairs. 'I'd like to be here if anything happens.' And it was obvious that it was going to very soon. It was the only thing she could do for him now, her first and last gift to him as his daughter, to be with him when he died. She tried to explain her feelings about it later to Alexandra, as they strolled in the garden. 'He seems so pathetic . . . and so frail . . . as though he's already gone. I know Hilary hates his guts, but I have no axe to grind with him. I had a good life. I love the only parents I've known . . . he's kind of like a late gift in life. Someone who might have meant something to me once, but it's too late now. It's too late to do anything but say goodbye and help him go. And if I can help him do that, it would make me happy.'

'Then that's what you should do, Megan.' Alexandra smiled at her. In an odd way, she reminded her of her daughters.

They had a quiet dinner that night. The housekeeper was extremely discreet and left them alone most of the time, and eventually they began talking about John Chapman.

'I thought he was going to attack me when he forced his way into my office.' Hilary laughed, and Alexandra smiled, and blushed as she often did.

'The first time I saw him I thought he was very handsome.'

'So did I,' Megan confessed, and the three women laughed like three young girls and speculated about his wife.

'I think he said he was divorced.' Alexandra frowned, trying to remember, but Hilary shrugged. She hadn't opened her heart to anyone in years, and it was enough to have done so to two sisters. It had been an exhausting twenty-four hours. But it was like coming home, to the warm, comfortable country house, their ship finally safe in the harbour.

Chapter 31

The next day, they sat on the porch and talked for a long time. They promised to visit, and to write, and all three of them cried as Hilary and Alexandra got in the car, and drove away, waving to Megan until they could no longer see her. She had promised to stop and have dinner with both of them in New York that week, before she flew back to Kentucky. And Alexandra had tiptoed into Arthur's room to say goodbye to him, but Megan had just given him a shot and he was sleeping. He had opened one eye, and smiled at her, as though seeing someone else, and then drifted off again, as Hilary stood and watched from the doorway. She had nothing more to say to him, and she looked at him for a long moment, before she turned and walked downstairs, and got in the car to leave with Alexandra.

'Do you think he will die soon?' Alexandra asked, as they drove back to New York. She was sorry for him. He was so alone and so lonely, and she was glad Megan had decided to stay with him.

'Probably. He'd done what he wanted to do.' Her voice held no tenderness for him, but at least it no longer held anger.

They got to the hotel just before dinner-time, and Alexandra insisted that she come upstairs and meet the girls and Margaret, and finally after some protest that she

377

wasn't dressed properly, it was late . . . when in truth, she was scared to meet Alexandra's family, what if they hated her? . . . she finally went upstairs with her. They looked like two girls returning from camp, slightly dishevelled, but relaxed and happy, and Alexandra opened the door of the suite with her key, and heard Hilary gasp as Axelle ran towards her.

'Hi, sweetheart . . . look who I brought! . . .' She acted as though Santa Claus had come home with her, and Axelle stopped in her tracks and stared at the tall, dark-haired woman who was openly crying.

'Who is she?'

'She's my sister,' Alexandra said as she began to cry too, and reached out for Hilary's hand. 'We haven't seen each other for a long, long time. And we have another sister named Megan . . . but she couldn't come tonight. This is your Aunt Hilary.' She spoke in a gentle voice and Axelle went to her cautiously as Hilary opened her arms and began to sob. All she could do was whisper the words of long ago . . . 'Oh, Axie . . .'

Marie-Louise came next and kissed her solemnly, and even Hilary could see how much they resembled each other. It was like having a daughter of her own, and they held hands as Alexandra introduced her to her mother.

'Maman, this is Hilary . . . Hilary, this is my mother. Margaret de Borne . . .' And suddenly all three of them were crying, and Margaret took Hilary in her arms, like another daughter.

'How are you? Are you both all right? I've been so worried about you!'

Alexandra smiled and wiped her eyes, and Hilary did the same, and looked down at the girls with a grin. 'Aren't we a mess? But I haven't seen your Mommy in a long, long time . . .'

'Why?' It was all a little confusing for the girls, and Alexandra sat down with Axelle on her lap as she looked from her to Marie-Louise to Hilary and her mother.

'A lot of very sad things happened to us a long time ago, and we never saw each other again after I was five years old, just a little younger than Axelle. And Hilary grew up in a lot of very sad places. And we missed each other very much, and we just couldn't get together till now.'

'Oh,' Axelle said, as though it all made sense to her now, and Marie-Louise nodded. And then Axelle added something important of her own. 'We went to the Bronx Zoo yesterday, and then we saw the Rockettes at Radio City Music Hall!' And everyone laughed, as Margaret ordered champagne for all of them. And when Alexandra put the girls to bed, Margaret told Hilary quietly how relieved she was that the meeting had gone well for them. She admitted that she had been very worried.

'Alexandra loves you very much.' Hilary comforted her, surprised by how much she liked her. She was a woman with warmth and courage and style, and a wonderful sense of humour. 'She told us all about you and her father. Nothing will ever change what she feels for you, and what you did for her. In her heart, you will always be her parents.'

Tears rolled down Margaret's cheeks at the words, and she patted Hilary's hand gratefully and then asked her a question. 'And Henri? Did she mention him?' Hilary nodded. 'He hasn't called since we left. He took all of this very badly. It was a great shock to him, and I think she was wrong to have told him.'

'She wants to be accepted as she is, I think. That's very important to her. And I can't disagree. He'll have to adjust. Just as we have.' She sounded matter-of-fact.

Margaret smiled ruefully at her. 'You don't know her husband.'

'What's all this about?' Alexandra had just come back from putting the girls to bed, in spite of their protests that they wanted to stay up with their aunt, but she had promised them that they would see her the next day. 'The girls want to have lunch with you tomorrow, by the way. Are you free?'

'For you? Hell, yes!' Hilary grinned. She could hardly wait to show the girls around the network, take them out to lunch, and to '21' for dinner. She was suddenly an aunt, and amazed at how much she liked it.

They made their plans for the following day, and Margaret smiled as she listened to them, and kissed Hilary as she would her own daughter when she left. And then she looked deep into Alexandra's eyes.

'You're happier, aren't you, sweetheart?'

Alexandra nodded. 'Yes, I am. It meant a lot to me to meet the two of them . . . even more than I thought it would. I'm so glad we came.' She threw her arms around Margaret and held her tight. 'And I'm so glad you came with me.'

'So am I.' The older woman had to fight back tears again. They had all cried a lot in the past few days. And then Alexandra told her about Megan. 'What a shock for Mr Patterson.' She looked horrified.

'It was. I thought it might kill him. Megan's staying with him for a few days. She doesn't think he'll live more than that.' It was sad to think about, but maybe Hilary was right. He had done what he had wanted to do, and now he could go in peace, holding the hand of his daughter.

Chapter 32

Their lunch with the girls the next day was great fun, and Margaret insisted on leaving them alone with the children. She said she had some errands to do on her own, and she wanted some time to herself, and Hilary and Alexandra had a marvellous time with the girls. After some major juggling, Hilary even managed to take the afternoon off, and they went to the park, and then to the Plaza for tea. And over the girls' heads, as they munched on *petits fours*, Hilary and Alexandra mused about what it would have been like if their parents hadn't died, and they had gone on living the good life in New York, living on Sutton Place, their father a star, and doing things like taking them to have tea at the Plaza.

'I guess we'll never know, will we, Axie? But this isn't so bad.' Hilary smiled as they strolled outside and crossed the street to the Pierre where Alexandra and the girls were staying. She had dinner with them that night, and when she went back to her apartment she was exhausted. She was not used to children, and as delightful as they were, they were much more tiring than a day at the office.

The phone was ringing when she got inside her front door and she was surprised to realize that it was John Chapman. Megan had called him an hour before. Arthur had died peacefully in his sleep, and the funeral was in two days in Connecticut. Megan was staying for that and then going back to Kentucky.

'I thought you'd like to know. I'd be happy to drive you out.' She thought about it for a long moment and then shook her head in the quiet apartment.

'I don't think so, John. I don't think it's my place to be there.' Although she had a suspicion Alexandra would go, but that was different, because Alexandra herself was very different.

'Are you still angry?'

'Maybe not. I'm not sure yet. And in any case it's over now. I just don't think I need to be there.' It was honest in any case, and John was embarrassed at how grateful he was for a reason to call her, even this one.

'How was the weekend?'

'The happiest in my life. It was wonderful. I spent the whole afternoon with my nieces today. They're terrific, and so is Alexandra. So is Megan ...' And then with embarrassment, 'Thank you for everything you did to bring us together, John.' She was much more grateful to him than to Arthur.

'Mr Patterson made it possible. All I did was find you.' ... and think about you day and night ... and worry about you and your sisters ... and spend sleepless nights ... 'I was wondering if ... if you'd like to have lunch sometime? Like maybe later this week, after I get back from Connecticut ...' He felt like a fifteen-year-old kid and he laughed. 'This probably sounds crazy, but I miss you ...' His voice trailed off and what he had said had touched her. She seemed so open suddenly to tenderness and pain and other people's feelings. And she sensed something very powerful and warm coming from him, and it aroused a host of new feelings in her. The weekend had given her something she'd never had before, not in thirty years. Love. And she was like a flower that had just been watered.

'I used to worry about you a lot.' It was easier saying things to her on the phone than it would have been in person.

'Why?' She sounded surprised. 'You didn't even know me.'

'Yes, I did ... in a lot of ways ... I knew you better than most people know their own children.' And he told himself he was crazy for telling her those things, but suddenly he couldn't stop now. 'You must think I'm nuts.'

'Sort of.' She laughed. 'But nice nuts. Sounds like you take your job to heart.'

'Not always ... but this time ... When can I see you for lunch?' He felt more than ever like a schoolboy, but at her end she was smiling. 'Is Thursday all right?'

'Sounds fine.' And if it wasn't, she'd cancel anything else she had, maybe even Alexandra. 'You know where my office is.' They both laughed.

'I'll pick you up at twelve-fifteen. And if I'm late, just relax. Sometimes I have a hell of a time getting out of the office.' But unlike Sasha, she understood that only too well. She frequently had the same problem.

'Don't worry. We'll both be lucky if I'm not stuck in a meeting. I'll do my best to get free by twelve, even if that means firing fewer people.' She laughed and he smiled to himself as they hung up. He could hardly wait to see her.

Chapter 33

As Hilary had suspected she would, Alexandra had gone to Arthur's funeral, mainly to be with Megan. And afterwards, she and Megan and John had driven back to New York in the limousine, and that night the three sisters had dinner together for the last time. Megan was flying back to Kentucky at midnight. She met Margaret, and the girls, and they had another pleasant evening, although Megan was a little subdued. It had been a strange week for her, discovering a father that she had never known and then watching him die in her arms only a few days later. But the greatest gift of all was that of the two sisters he had left her.

They talked about the house Arthur had left them, and what they would do with it. The housekeeper was going to stay on until everything was settled, and Arthur had left ample funds to care for it, and the remains of his estate were to be divided between the three women. He had no other relatives of his own. And Alexandra wanted all three of them to plan on spending some time there the following summer.

'We could do it every year! Make it a tradition!' She smiled at them, and Megan grinned.

'Can I bring some of my hillbillies when I come?'

'Why not?' Hilary added with a mysterious look. She was looking forward to lunch with John Chapman the next day, but she hadn't said anything to either of her sisters. It was a little embarrassing, and she was afraid they would suspect how much she liked him.

They drove Megan to the airport at eleven o'clock, and then Hilary and Alexandra drove back to town together. Hilary dropped her younger sister off at the hotel, and then went home. They were both exhausted. It had been an emotional week for all of them. And Alexandra was looking forward to her bed and an early evening.

The lights in her room were on. The door was closed, and Margaret had apparently gone to bed, but Alexandra could hear someone stirring in her room as she stood outside the door, and then someone pulled it open, and she found herself staring at her husband. He had just arrived a little while before. And Margaret had wisely retired, after greeting him. He offered no explanation as to why he had come, and acted almost as though his visit had been planned and he was expected.

'Henri?' Alexandra stared at him as though she'd seen a ghost.

'You were expecting someone else?' But this time it was not an accusation. He was smiling at her, and she stared at him in amazement. 'I certainly hope not. The children are well?'

'Very, thank you. We've had a lovely time.'

'So your mother told me. I saw her when I arrived.'

And then Alexandra could not stand the charade any longer. Why had he come? Why was he there? What threat was he going to make now? But it was odd, she was not nearly as frightened of him as she had been before. She stood eyeing him curiously from across the room, as he sat down and sipped a glass of champagne he had ordered while he waited for her. 'Would you care for some?' He was very nonchalant as he held out his glass to her, and Alexandra could not understand it.

'No, thank you. Henri, why did you come here?' she said coolly.

'I came to see you . . . and the children . . .' He spoke cautiously as though he wasn't quite sure what to say. 'I thought we needed to talk.' He looked at her with troubled eyes.

'You could have called me.' Her eyes were cold but she was protecting herself from the pain she knew he could cause her.

'Would you have preferred that?' He looked so sad, it tore at her heart, even though she was resisting the impulse to reach out to him. She was still afraid of possible rejection. Maybe he had come to tell her he was going to divorce her. And she wanted to know now.

'I just don't understand why you came here.'

He stood up and set down his glass, and then slowly walked toward her. 'To see you, *ma chérie*. Difficult as it may be to believe sometimes, I love you very much . . . no matter who you are . . .' He added carefully, '. . . Or who you've become.' He smiled almost shyly at her. 'I see you're a redhead again. It's not quite as loud as I remembered it.' He was watching her, looking into her eyes for something he hoped was still there, if he hadn't broken it this time forever. 'It was a great shock to me when you told me about . . . about your family. I think it might have been for anyone . . . and I can't come here now and tell you I've reformed, that I won't be demanding any more, that I'll stop dragging you to the Elysée for dinner . . . but I accept who you are . . . if you will accept who I am . . .' There were tears in his eyes as Alexandra looked up at him in astonishment. This was the man she thought hated her . . . and here he was, telling her he loved her. 'I love you

386

very much. And I want you to come home . . . in a few days . . . and if you'd like, I will stay with you here . . . He pulled her firmly into his arms and she knew with total certainty that he would never change, but he had come to her with open arms and she owed him a great deal for that. She owed him her life. And she turned her lips up to his with a gentle smile as he laughed softly.

'You know, I love your hair . . .' He ran his hands through the silky strands of red and they both laughed. Maybe things had changed just enough . . . perhaps . . . and if not, she had lived with him for fourteen years . . . for better or worse . . . and she had no intention of doing anything different for the rest of it.

He pushed the door closed and took his wife in his arms with a smile of expectation and pleasure. He was glad he had made the trip and as he felt her gentle hands on him, he was even more so.

Chapter 34

Their last night in New York was happy and sad and emotional. They had dinner at the Côte Basque, and Henri and Alexandra brought the girls, Margaret came, at Alexandra's insistence, and Hilary had said something about bringing a friend, which Alexandra thought was a little unusual, but she didn't dare question her sister. But she was secretly thrilled when the friend turned out to be John Chapman. She had always liked him, and she could tell Henri approved of John, looking very handsome in a dark suit, with his quiet ways, and obvious intelligence and good breeding. The group got on famously. Margaret entertained them all and Henri even let the girls drink champagne at dinner. It was a perfect culmination of the trip, and everyone hugged and kissed goodnight as though they might never see each other again. Although Hilary and John had insisted on coming to the airport the next day when the others left for Paris.

It was a classic scene with Axelle carrying an enormous doll under each arm and Marie-Louise clutching her new magic kit, from her Aunt Hilary of course. Alexandra's trophies from Bergdorf and Bendel's seemed virtually limitless, and Margaret's stack of Louis Vuitton seemed to have grown considerably in a mere ten days as Henri attempted to keep track of it all, hold the tickets, and rescue the passports from Axelle's busy little hands. And meanwhile Hilary and Alexandra were talking a mile a minute, promising to meet again as soon as possible. Hilary was thinking of spending Christmas with them in Saint Moritz, unless Megan came to New York, in which case she'd come in the spring instead, but in spite of all the words and the frantic talk, the final moment came anyway. Margaret shepherded the girls on to the plane, waving at Hilary every inch of the way, and Henri left the two women alone, standing apart from his wife, chatting with John, and suddenly Hilary looked into her sister's eyes and began to cry as she reached out to her.

'Axie, I can't leave you again . . .' She choked on the words, and Alexandra held her tight.

'I know . . . promise me you'll be all right.' They were crying again, and Hilary thought she would never let go this time. It was too much like the past, the red curls in her arms, the little girl she had loved. '. . . Axie . . . I love you . . . Axie, I . . .' The echoes of the past rang out in her ears as Alexandra held her tight. 'I'll see you soon and I'll call you all the time from Paris.' Henri was beckoning her towards the plane and she knew she had to go. They would be closing the door in a moment, but she couldn't let her go, couldn't leave her alone. And then John walked quietly up to them, and gently took Hilary from her, holding her in his powerful arms as she stood there with tears streaming down her cheeks.

'Have a good trip, Alexandra. We'll see you soon,' John said in his quiet voice. Alexandra slowly pulled away, her eyes blinded by tears as she looked at Hilary, her eyes huge, her face deathly pale, as John quietly held her. Alexandra waved for a last time with a tearful smile, and as Hilary stared after her and whispered the familiar words, 'Goodbye, Axie,' she waved and then smiled slowly through her own tears and Alexandra disappeared into the plane with her husband.

'It's all right, sweetheart . . .' John whispered to Hilary as he held her tight, and suddenly for the first time in her life, she felt safe. She looked up at him, and he smiled. 'It's all right, Hillie . . .' He held her tightly in his arms and she knew that he was telling the truth. 'Everything's going to be all right now.'

FAMILY ALBUM

To my family: With all my love
To Beatrix, Trevor, Todd, Nicholas,
Samantha, Victoria, and especially . . .
most especially, with all my heart . . .
to John.

d.s.

'God places the solitary in families,' comforting words from the Bible . . . families, by blood, by obligation, by necessity, by desire . . . and sometimes, if one is very lucky, by love. It is a word that implies solidity, a rock-solid foundation, a place to go home to . . . to grow out of . . . to grow away from, and yet to remember and hang onto . . . the echoes never leaving one's ears or one's heart, the memories carved like painted ivory, from a single tusk, delicately coloured in brilliant hues, and softer ones, faded sometimes, so dim as to be almost forgotten . . . and yet never to be totally forgotten or left behind. The place where one begins, and hopes to end . . . the thing one works hard to build on one's own . . . the pieces like building blocks reaching high into the sky . . . Family . . . what images that conjures . . . what memories . . . what dreams.

PROLOGUE 1983

The sun was so brilliant nearly everyone was squinting, though it was only eleven o'clock in the morning. The tiniest of breezes ruffled the women's hair. The day was so beautiful there was a kind of agony to it, an amazing silence, and all one could hear in the silences were birds, a quiet chirping, a sudden shrieking, and the overwhelming smell of flowers ... lily of the valley, gardenias, freesia, buried in a carpet of moss. But Ward Thayer saw none of it and he seemed to hear nothing at all. His eyes had been closed for several minutes, and when he opened them, he stared for the longest time, almost like a zombie, looking colourless, so unlike the image everyone had of him ... had had for the last forty years. There was nothing dashing or exciting or even handsome about Ward Thayer this morning. He stood immobilised in the brilliant sunlight, watching nothing. His eyes closed again; he pressed his eyelids tightly together, and for a moment he wanted never to open them again, as she had not, as she never would again.

There was a voice, droning softly in the distance, saying something, sounding no different than the hum of insects buzzing near the flowers. And he felt nothing. Nothing. Why? Why did he feel nothing, he asked himself? Had he felt nothing for her? Had it all been a lie? He felt a wave of panic wash over him ... he couldn't remember her face ... the way she wore her hair ... the colour of her eyes ... his eyes flew open brusquely, tearing the lids apart like hands that had been clasped, skin that had once upon a time been grafted. The sun blinded him in an instant, and he saw only a flash of light and smelled the flowers, as a bee hummed lazily past him, and the pastor said her name. Faye Price Thayer. There was a muffled popping sound to his left and the lightning of a camera flash exploded in his eyes, as the woman beside him pressed his arm.

He looked down at her, his eyes adjusting to the light again, and suddenly he remembered. Everything he had forgotten was reflected in his daughter's eyes. The younger woman looked so much like her, yet how different they were. There would never be another woman like Faye Thayer. They all knew that, and he knew it best of all. He looked at the pretty blonde beside him, remembering it all, and longing silently for Faye.

His daughter stood tall and sedate. She was plainer than Faye had been. Her smooth blonde hair was pulled tightly into a knot, and beside her stood a serious-looking man, who touched her arm often. They were on their own now, all of them, each one different, separate, yet part of a larger whole, part of Faye . . . and of him as well.

Was she truly gone? It seemed impossible, as tears rolled solemnly down his cheeks and a dozen photographers leapt forward to record his pain, to put on front pages around the world. The grieving widower of Faye Price Thayer. He was hers now, in death, as he had been hers in life. They were all hers. All of them. The daughters, the son, the co-workers, the friends, and they were all there to honour the memory of the woman who would never come again.

The family stood beside him in the front row. His daughter Vanessa, her bespectacled young man, and beside him, Vanessa's twin Valerie, with hair of flame, a golden face, a perfect black silk dress which clung to her breathtakingly, her success stamped on her unmistakably, and beside her an equally dazzling man.

They made such a beautiful pair one had to stare at them, and it pleased Ward to see how much Val looked like Faye. He had never noticed it quite so much before, but he saw it now . . . And Lionel, who looked so like her too, though more quietly. Tall, handsome and blond, sensual, elegant, and delicate, yet at the same time proud. He stood staring into the distance now, remembering the others he had known and loved . . . Gregory and John, lost brother, treasured friend. He thought too of how well Faye had known Lionel, better than anyone perhaps. She had known him better than he knew himself . . . and as well as he himself knew Anne, standing beside him now, prettier than she had been before, so much more confident, and still so young, in sharp contrast to the grey-haired man who held her hand.

They were all there in the end. They had come to pay homage to all that she had been. Actress, director, legend, wife, mother, friend. There were those who had envied her, those she had driven too hard and wanted too much from. Her family knew that best of all. She had expected so much of them, yet given so much in return, driven herself so hard, gone so far. Ward remembered it all as he looked at all of them, all the way back to that first time in Guadalcanal. And now here they were, a lifetime past, and each of them remembering her as she had been, as she once was, as she was to them. It was a sea of faces in the bright Los Angeles sun. All of Hollywood had turned out for her. A last salute, a final smile, a tender tear, as Ward turned to glance at the family he had built with her, all of them so strong and beautiful . . . as she had been. How proud she would have been to see them now, he thought, tears burning his eyes again . . . how proud they were of her . . . finally. It had taken a long time . . . and now she was gone . . . it seemed impossible to believe when only yesterday . . . only yesterday they'd been in Paris . . . the South of France . . . New York . . . Guadalcanal.

GUADALCANAL 1943

CHAPTER 1

The heat of the jungle was so oppressive that just standing in one place was almost like swimming through thick, dense air. It was a presence you could feel and smell and touch, and yet the men pressed forward wanting to see her . . . to get closer . . . to see more . . . Their shoulders were tightly compressed, as they sat there, side by side, cross-legged on the ground. In the front, way up front, they had folding chairs, but they had run out hours before. The men had been sitting there since sundown, baking, sweating, waiting. It felt like a hundred years that they'd been sitting here in the thick jungles of Guadalcanal and they didn't give a damn. They would have waited half a lifetime for her. She represented everything to them right now . . . mothers . . . sisters . . . women . . . girlfriends they had left behind . . . women . . . Woman. There was an almost audible purr after nightfall, as they sat there, talking, smoking, rivulets of sweat pouring down their necks and backs, their faces glistening, their hair damp, their uniforms sticking to their flesh, and all of them so young, children almost . . . and at the same time children no more. They were men.

By 1943, they had been here for longer than they cared to remember, and everyone wondered when the war would end – and if it ever would. But tonight no one thought about the war, only the men on duty had to worry about that. And most of the men waiting for her now had bought out of being on duty for the night with every kind of currency they could lay their hands on, everything from chocolate bars to cigarettes to cold hard cash . . . anything . . . anything to see her . . . they would do anything to see Faye Price again.

As the band began to play, the air wasn't thick so much as sultry,

3

the heat no longer oppressive but sensual, and they felt their bodies stir in a way they hadn't in a long, long time. It wasn't just hunger they felt for her, it was something deeper and more tender, something that would have frightened them if they had felt it for too long. They felt the first stirrings of it now as they waited ... waited ... every moment seeming an age as a clarinet began to wail. The music wrenched at the gut and was almost painful, and every face, every man, held his breath and was still. The stage was empty in the darkness, and then suddenly, dimly, they saw her, or thought they did ... it was impossible to be completely certain, a tiny spotlight sought her in the distance. It found her feet and there was a flash of silver, a sparkle in the distance, like falling stars in a summer sky ... the shimmer of her body as she approached them made their guts ache, and suddenly she stood there before them. Blinding perfection in a silver lamé gown. There was an audible sigh from the men who watched her, a perfect blend of desire and ecstasy and pain. Her skin was like the palest of pink velvet in the dazzling silver gown, the long, blonde hair was almost the colour of ripe peaches and she had worn it down. Her eyes danced, her mouth smiled, she held her hands out towards them as she sang, and her voice was deeper than any woman they remembered. She was more beautiful than any they had known. She moved and the gown revealed endless, exquisite flesh, the pink perfection of her thighs.

'Oh God ...' one voice murmured in a back row, and around him, half a hundred young men smiled.

They all felt that way about her, had for years. They hadn't believed it when they'd been told she was going to do a show for them. She had been doing shows like this halfway around the world. In the Pacific, in Europe, in the States. A year after Pearl Harbor, the guilt had overwhelmed her, and she'd been touring off and on now for more than a year. Recently, she had stopped to make another film, but she was back on the road now ... and tonight, she was here ... with them.

Her voice had grown mournful as she sang to them and, in the front row, the men who watched could see a pulse beating in her neck. She was alive ... she was human ... and if they had reached across the makeshift stage, they could have touched her ... felt her ... smelled her flesh. It made them almost keen just to watch her, and seeming to look each man in the eye as she sang, Faye Price let no one down.

At twenty-three years of age, Faye Price was already a legend in Hollywood. She had made her first film at nineteen, and from there had rushed headlong into success. She was beautiful, striking, and so damn good at what she did. She had a voice that ranged from molten lava to melted gold, hair that shimmered like a golden sunset, green eyes like emeralds in an ivory face. But it wasn't the features, or the voice, or the texture of the skin on her long narrow frame that belied the softly rounded hips and full breasts, it was the warmth that lit her from within, the brilliance that exploded in her eyes, the laughter in her voice when she wasn't singing that enthralled the world. She was a woman, in the best and purest meaning of the word. She was someone men wanted to cling to, women wanted to stare at, children loved to look up to. She was the stuff of which dream princesses were made.

From a small town in Pennsylvania, Faye had made her way to New York after graduating from high school, and had become a model. Within six months she was making more than any girl in town. The photographers all loved her, her face was on the cover of every major magazine in the country, but secretly she admitted to her friends that she was bored. There was so little to it, she insisted; all she had to do was stand there. She tried to explain it, and the other girls looked at her as though she were mad. But two men recognised what she was: the man who later became her agent, and Sam Warman, the producer, who knew a gold mine when he saw one. He had seen her pictures on the magazine covers and he thought she was pretty, but it was only when he met her that he realised how fabulous she was. The way she moved, the way she looked into his eyes when she talked to him, her voice, and he knew instantly that this one wasn't looking to get laid. She wasn't looking for a damn thing, not outside herself, Sam instinctively suspected. And everything Abe, her agent, said about her was true. She was fabulous. Unique. A star. What Faye Price wanted, she wanted from within. She wanted a challenge, she wanted to work hard, she wanted to try anything they'd let her . . . and he did. He gave her the chance she wanted. It wasn't difficult for Abe to talk him into that. Sam brought her to Hollywood and gave her a part in a film. It was a small part, and as it was written, it was not an

5

overly demanding role. But somehow she managed to get under the skin of the writer; there were times when he openly admitted she drove him nuts, but she had got what she wanted out of the part, and what she wanted was very, very good; good for the movie, and for her. The part had been small but gutsy, and a light shone through Faye Price's performance that took people's breaths away. There was something magical about her, half girl, half woman, from elf to siren, and back again, drawing on the full range of human emotions, sometimes only using her facial expressions and her incredible deep green eyes. That part had won her two others and her fourth film had won her the Oscar. Four years after her first role, she had done seven films, and in the fifth one, Hollywood had discovered she could sing. And that's what she was doing now, singing her guts out for soldiers halfway around the world. She gave her guts and her heart and her life to these men, just as she did with everything she attempted. Faye Price was no halfway person, and at twenty-three she was no longer a 'girl' in anyone's eyes, she was all woman. The men who watched her on the stage knew that about her. To watch Faye Price move, to hear her sing, to see her before you was to feel what God intended when he created woman. She was the infinite ... the ultimate ... and tonight every man who watched her longed to touch her, just for a moment ... longed to be within the circle of her arms, his lips gently pressed on hers, his hands in the silky blonde hair ... they wanted to feel her breath on their shoulders ... hear her moan softly. There was a sudden groan from one of the boys who watched her and his friends laughed at him. He didn't give a damn.

'Holy Moses ... ain't she fantastic?' The boy's eyes lit up like a child's at Christmas and the men around him smiled. For a long time they had watched her in total silence, but after the first half hour, they could bear it no more. They screamed, they hooted, they keened for her, they howled. And when the last song ended, they screamed so long and hard that she sang five or six more songs for them. Though they couldn't see it, when she left the stage there were tears in Faye Price's eyes. It was so little to do for them, a few songs, a silver dress, a flash of legs, a hint of womanhood shared among a thousand men in a jungle night, five thousand miles from home. And who knew how many of them would live to go home

6

again? The thought of it always tore at her heart. It was why she had come here, why she had to do this for them. And in the months she had done it, she allowed herself to appear more of a siren than she ever did back home. She would have died before wearing a dress slit almost to her crotch in L.A., but if that was what they wanted here, and it was clear they did, then that's what she would give them, what harm was there in giving them a little make-believe pleasure from the safety of a stage?

'Miss Price?' She turned quickly as one of the C.O.'s aides spoke to her as she came off the stage. They could still hear the men screaming for her, and she could barely hear the aide's voice even here.

'Yes?' She looked exhilarated and distracted. Her face and chest were wet with perspiration, and he thought her the most beautiful woman he had ever seen. It wasn't just that her features were perfect, it was that you wanted to reach out and touch her . . . hold her . . . she exuded something he had never felt before, at least not at such close range. A kind of magic mixed with glamour, a sensuality that made you want to kiss her, without ever stopping to ask her name. She was about to leave him and go back out to the men begging for her, and instinctively he reached out and touched her arm. He felt everything within him quicken, and then he felt foolish for his reaction. This was ridiculous. What was she after all? Just another film star, dolled up, done up, and if everything about her was so convincing, it was just that she was better than some of the others at the artistry she created. It was all an illusion, wasn't it? . . . But he knew it wasn't as his eyes met hers, and she smiled at him. There was nothing fake about the woman who stood there. She was precisely who she was. 'I've got to go back out there.' She waved towards the din, mouthing her words as she spoke carefully, and he nodded, shouting his.

'The C.O. would like you to join him for dinner.'

'Thank you.' Her eyes pulled away from his and she left him and went back to give the men another half hour. This time she sang songs that amused them, including two in which they joined her, and at the end a ballad that made them all fight back tears. When she left them, she did it with a look that seemed to envelop each one of them, like a goodnight kiss from their mothers . . . their wives . . . the girls back home . . . 'Goodnight, friends . . . God bless.'

Her voice was husky and suddenly the din had turned into silence. Almost no one spoke as they left their places, and quietly went home to bed. Her words rang in their heads for hours. They had screeched and applauded, but they had been ready when she left them, and now they wanted to go back to their bunks and think about her, letting the songs roam in their heads ... remembering her face ... her arms ... her legs ... the mouth that seemed to kiss them, and then exploded into laughter and then grew serious again. They all remembered the look in her eyes when she had left them. They would remember it for months. Right now it was all they had. And Faye knew that. It was her gift to them.

'She's some woman.' The words were spoken by a thick-necked sergeant, and were unlike him. But no one was surprised. Faye Price brought something special out in each of them. Their guts, their hearts, their hopes.

'Yeah ...' An echo voiced a thousand times that night by the men who had seen her, and the men who hadn't, who had been forced to be on duty, tried to pretend they didn't feel cheated. And in the end, they didn't have to pretend at all. Her request was unusual, but quickly granted, and the C.O. was obviously surprised when he heard of it. He had even assigned his aide to take her around. She had requested permission to tour the base, to meet the men on duty that night. By midnight, she had shaken hands with everyone. So that the men who hadn't seen her performance had met her face to face instead, looking into those incredible green eyes, feeling the strong, cool hand she extended, smiling awkwardly at her words. And in the end, each one felt he had been special ... those who had heard her singing, and those whom she had come to see instead. Suddenly, men were sorry they hadn't been on duty, so that she would have come to see them. But all in all, everyone was pleased. And at twelve-thirty she turned to the young man who had taken her around the base, and she saw something warm and friendly in his eyes. He hadn't looked that way at first. But slowly she had won him over, as she had everyone else. He had wanted to say something to her about it all night, but there had never been quite the right moment. He had been so sceptical about her at first, the cool Miss Faye Price from Hollywood ... who did she think she was, coming to show off to the men on Guadalcanal? They'd been through enough, they'd seen it all. They'd already survived Midway and the Coral Sea, and the hideous naval battles it had taken to win and keep Guadalcanal. What did she know about it? Ward Thayer thought to himself as he first looked at her. But after all these hours at her side, he had begun to see her differently. She cared. She cared a lot. He read it in her eyes. Watching her meet the men's eyes, totally oblivious of her own charms, reaching out only to them with something they had never felt before made you care about her as well. There was a kind of warmth and compassion about her that in turn enhanced her already incredible sexual appeal. There were a thousand things the young lieutenant wanted to say to her as the night wore on, but it was only after she had finished her rounds that she seemed to notice him at all. She turned to him with a tired smile, and for an instant he wanted to reach out and touch her hand, almost to see if she was real. He almost wanted to comfort her. She had had a long, hard night. But then again, they had had a long, hard year . . . two years.

'Do you suppose your C.O. will ever forgive me for not making it to dinner with him tonight?' She smiled tiredly.

'He may be heartbroken, but he'll live.' In fact, the lieutenant knew that an hour or two before, the C.O. had been called into a secret meeting with two generals who had arrived by helicopter that night. He would have had to leave Faye anyway. 'I think he'll be very grateful for what you did for the men.'

'It means a lot to me.' She spoke gently as she sat down on a large, white rock in the warm night air and looked up at him. There was something magical in her eyes, and there was a strange tug in his gut as he looked down at her. It almost hurt to look at her, she brought up feelings that he had wanted to leave behind him in the States. There was no room for that here, no time, no one to share the feelings with. Here there was only killing and misery and loss, and anger sometimes, but the gentler emotions were too painful now, and he looked away from her as she stared at the back of his head. He was a tall, handsome, blond man with broad shoulders and deep blue eyes, but all she could see of him now were the powerful shoulders and the wheat-coloured hair. There was something about him that made her want to reach out to him. There was so much pain here, they were all so damn lonely and sad and young . . . and yet with only a little warmth, a touch, a hand on

9

theirs they came alive, and they laughed and they sang . . . that was what she loved about these tours, no matter how tiring they were. It was like bringing new life to all of these men, even this young lieutenant, who was so tall and proud as he turned to face her again, obviously defending himself, or trying to, against all that he felt, and yet not quite able to shut her out after all. 'Do you know, after spending the whole evening with you,' she smiled up at him again, 'I don't know your name.' She knew only his rank, and they had never really been introduced.

'Thayer. Ward Thayer.' The name rang a distant bell, but she didn't know why and didn't really care. He smiled at her, and there was something cynical in his eyes. He had seen too much in the last year and she sensed that easily about him. 'Are you hungry, Miss Price? You must be starved.' She had performed for hours, and had been touring the base, shaking hands, for three hours since. She nodded now, with a shy smile.

'I am. Do you suppose we should go knock on the C.O.'s door and ask if there's anything left?' They both laughed at the thought.

'I think I can dig something up for you somewhere else.' He glanced at his watch, as she looked at him. What was there about this man? There was something about him that kept making her want to reach out, to ask him who he really was, to find out more. There was something one couldn't know, and yet which one sensed about him. But he smiled up at her now, and he looked young again. 'Would you be terribly offended if we check out the kitchen? I'll bet I can get you a real meal there, if you'd like that.'

She held up a graceful hand. 'A sandwich would be great.'

'Let's see what we can do.' They headed back to his jeep, and drove swiftly to the long quonset hut where the men's meals were prepared and, twenty minutes later, she was seated on a long bench faced with a plate of hot stew. It wasn't what she would have picked for a hot jungle night, but she was so hungry and it had been such a long night that the steaming concoction actually tasted good, and Ward Thayer had a plate of it too. 'Just like "21" eh?' He glanced at her with his cynical grin again and she laughed.

'More or less . . . except it's not hash . . .' she teased and he winced.

'Oh God, don't say that word. If the cook hears you, he'll be only too happy to oblige.' The two of them laughed again, and

Faye was suddenly reminded of midnight suppers after school proms back home and suddenly she began to laugh harder as she looked at him, and he cocked an eyebrow over the handsome blue eyes. 'I'm glad you're amused. This place hasn't struck me as funny in well over a year.' But he looked happier now. He was enjoying her company and it showed and, nibbling at the stew, she explained it to him.

'You know ... just like after the prom ... when you have breakfast in some diner at five am ... this is sort of like that, isn't it?' She looked around the harshly lit room and his eyes followed hers and then searched her face again.

'Where'd you grow up?' They were almost friends now. They had been together for hours, and there was something about being together in a war zone. Everything was different here. Faster, more personal, more intense. It was all right to ask questions one would never have asked anywhere else, and to reach out in ways that otherwise one wouldn't have dared.

She answered him thoughtfully. 'Pennsylvania.'

'Did you like it?'

'Not much. We were dirt poor. All I wanted was to get the hell out, which I did, the minute I graduated from high school.'

He smiled. It was difficult to imagine her dirt poor anywhere, and least of all in some hick town.

'What about you? Where are you from, Lieutenant?'

'Ward. Or did you forget my name again?' She blushed as he teased. 'I grew up in L.A.' He seemed loath to add more, and she wasn't quite sure why.

'You going back there after ... afterwards?' She hated the word 'war', and by now so did he. It had already cost him a lot, too much; there were wounds now that would never heal, even if they weren't the kind she could see. But instinctively she knew that they were there.

'Yeah. I guess so.'

'Are your folks there?' She was curious about him, this sad, cynical, handsome young man, with the secrets he didn't want to reveal, as they ate their stew in the ugly, brightly lit mess hall on Guadalcanal. There were stiff blackout covers on all the windows, so the impression was that there were no windows at all. They were both used to that.

11

'My folks are both dead.' He looked evenly at her, something dead in his own eyes. He had said the word too often by now.

'I'm sorry.'

'We weren't close anyway.' But still . . . her eyes searched his again as he stood up. 'More stew, or something more exotic for dessert? They tell me there's an apple pie hidden somewhere.' His eyes smiled and she laughed.

'No thanks. There's no room in costumes like this for apple pie.' She glanced down at the silver lamé dress, and for the first time in several hours, so did he. He was getting used to her looking like that. It was different from Kathy of course . . . so different in her starched white . . . and eventually, the fatigues she wore . . .

He disappeared for a moment and then returned with a small plate of fruit and a tall glass of iced tea. It was more precious than wine here, ice being almost impossible to make. But he had filled the glass with the precious ice cubes, and she had been on tour often enough to know what a rare gift this was. She savoured each mouthful of the chill drink as a few men came and went, staring openly at her. But she seemed not to mind. She was used to it. She smiled casually at them, always turning her eyes back to Ward, and now she had to stifle a small yawn, as he pretended to look crushed and shook his head, mocking her. He teased a lot, and there was something funny about him. And at the same time something sad.

'Funny, they always do that after talking to me. I put them to sleep every time.' She laughed and took another sip of the iced tea.

'If you'd been up since four o'clock this morning, you'd be yawning too. I suppose you officers hang around in bed until noon around here?' She knew it wasn't true, but she liked teasing him; it quenched some of the sadness in his eyes and she sensed that he needed that. And he looked at her oddly then.

'What makes you do this, Faye?' He suddenly dared to use her first name and he wasn't sure why, but it felt good on his lips, and she didn't seem to mind. She said nothing about it anyway.

'Some kind of a need I guess . . . to repay all the good things that have happened to me. I never really feel I deserve it all. And you have to pay your dues in life.' It was the kind of thing Kathy would have said and tears almost filled his eyes. He had never felt that kind of a need, to pay 'dues', to repay anyone for how fortunate he

12

had been. And now he didn't feel fortunate any more anyway. Not since . . .

'Why do women always feel a need to pay dues?'

'That has nothing to do with it. Some men do too. Don't you, in a way? Don't you want to do something nice for the next guy, if something good happens to you?'

His eyes grew rock hard as he looked at her. 'Nothing good has happened to me in a hell of a long time . . . at least not since I've been here.'

'You're alive, aren't you, Ward?' Her voice was soft beneath the bright lights where they sat, but her eyes bore into him.

'Sometimes that's not enough.'

'Yes, it is. In a place like this, that's a lot to be grateful for. Look around you every day . . . look at the boys wounded and crippled and maimed . . . the ones who're never going home at all . . .' Something about the tone of her voice bore straight to his heart and for the first time in four months, he had to fight back tears.

'I try hard not to think about that.'

'Maybe you should. Maybe it'll make you glad you're alive.' She wanted to reach him, to touch the place that hurt so much. She wondered what it was, as slowly he stood up.

'I don't give a damn any more, Faye. If I live or die, it's all the same to me and everyone else.'

'That's a terrible thing to say.' She looked shocked and almost hurt as she stared up at him. 'What could possibly make you feel like that?'

He looked down at her for an endless moment, silently begging himself not to say anything more, and suddenly wishing she'd go away. But he stared at her; she seemed not to move at all, and suddenly he didn't give a damn who he told. What difference did it make now? 'I got married six months ago, to an army nurse, and two months after that she was killed by a fucking Jap bomb. It's kind of hard to feel good about this place after that. You know what I mean?'

She sat frozen in her seat, and then slowly nodded her head. So that was it. That was the emptiness she saw in his eyes. She wondered if he'd always be like that, or if he'd come alive again. One day. Maybe. 'I'm sorry, Ward.' There wasn't much else one could say. There were other stories much like this, some worse.

13

But that was no consolation to him.

'I'm sorry.' He smiled a quiet smile. There was no point dumping it on her. It wasn't her fault. And she was so different from Kathy. Kathy was quiet and ordinary and he had been so desperately in love with her. And this woman was all beauty and flash, worldly right down to the tip of every brightly polished nail. 'I'm sorry, I didn't mean to tell you something like that. There are a thousand stories like that here.' She knew that there were and she had heard most of them before, but that didn't make them any easier to hear. She felt terrible for him, and as she followed him slowly back out to the jeep, she was glad she hadn't had dinner with the C.O. after all, and she told him so, as he turned to her with that quiet half smile of his that somehow appealed to her, more than any smile she'd seen in Hollywood, at least in the last year or two.

'That's a nice thing to say.'

She wanted to touch his arm, but she didn't dare. She wasn't just Faye Price the actress now, she was herself. 'I mean it, Ward.'

'Why? You don't have to feel sorry for me, Faye. I'm a big boy. I can take care of myself. I have for a long time.' But she saw more than that. She saw what Kathy had, and more. She knew how desperately hurt he was, how lonely, how shocked still by the pretty little nurse's death ... his wife ... it had happened two months after they got married, to the day, but he didn't tell Faye that bitter detail as he drove her back to the tent she'd been assigned. 'I still think it's damn nice of you to come out here to see the men.'

'Thanks.'

He stopped the jeep, and they sat looking at each other for a long time, each with a lot more to say, but no way to say it here. Where did one start? How did one begin? He had read about her affair with Gable years before, and he wondered if it was over now. She wondered how long he would pine for the army nurse he had loved.

'Thank you for dinner.' She said it with a shy smile and he laughed as he opened the door for her.

'I told you ... it's just like "21" ...'

'Next time I'll try the hash.' They were back to joking again, it seemed to be the only route open to them, but as he walked her to

14

the door of her tent, and pulled the flaps back for her, there was something more in his eyes, something quiet and deep and alive in a way he hadn't been a few hours before.

'I'm sorry I told you all that. I didn't mean to lay my troubles in your lap.' He reached out a hand and touched her arm as she looked at him.

'Why not, Ward? What's so wrong with that? Who else do you have to talk to here?'

'We don't talk about things like that.' He shrugged. 'Everyone knew anyway.' And suddenly the tears he had fought back before sprang into his eyes again, and he started to turn away, as she grabbed his arm and pulled him back.

'It's all right, Ward . . . it's all right . . .' And the next thing she knew, she was holding him tight, and they were both crying, he for a dead wife, and she for a girl she had never known, and a thousand men who had died and would continue to die long after she went home. They cried for the agony and the waste and the sorrow that was inescapable here, and then he looked down at her, and gently smoothed a hand over her silky hair. She was the most beautiful woman he had ever seen, and it struck him as odd that he didn't even feel guilty for thinking that. Maybe Kathy would understand . . . maybe it didn't even matter any more . . . she was never coming back to him . . . he would never hold her or touch her again . . . and he would probably never see Faye again after that night. He knew that too, and wished he could go to bed with her. Now. Before he died or she did, or time ended the spark they felt as surely as any bomb.

She sat down slowly on the room's only chair, and looked up at him, as he sat down on her sleeping bag, and they silently held hands, a lifetime of words unspoken but deeply felt, as the jungle roared to life in the distance somewhere.

'I'm never going to forget you, Faye Price. I hope you know that.'

'I'll remember you too. I'll be thinking about you over here . . . I'll be knowing that you're all right every time I think about you.' And he actually believed that she would. She was that kind of girl, despite the fame and the glamour and the silver lamé dress. She had called it a 'costume' and to her that was all it was. That was the beauty of her.

15

'Maybe I'll surprise you and drop in on you at the studio when I come home.'

'You do that, Ward Thayer.' Her voice was quiet and firm, her eyes still beautiful after the tears.

'Will you have me thrown out?' He seemed amused at the thought and she looked incensed.

'Of course not!'

'I may try it, you know.'

'Good.' She smiled at him again, and he could see how exhausted she was. She had given so much of herself that night. To the others, to him. And it was after four o'clock. She would have to be up again in less than two hours, in order to move on, to do the next show. She had been working nonstop for months now. Two months on tour, and three months before that, without a day off, on her biggest film so far. And when she went back, there was another film waiting for her. She was a big star, and she had a big career, but none of that seemed to matter here. She was just a pretty girl with a big heart, and given a little time, he could easily have fallen in love with her.

He stood up, almost regretfully, took her fingers in his own, and then lifted them to his lips. 'Thanks, Faye . . . if I never see you again, thank you for tonight . . .'

She left her fingers in his for a long moment, her eyes holding his. 'We'll meet again one day.' He wasn't as sure, but he wanted to believe her words. And then the weight of the moment was too much for him, and he needed to make light of it. 'I'll bet you say that to all the guys.'

She laughed and stood up as he walked slowly to the tent door. 'You're impossible, Ward Thayer.'

He turned and glanced over his shoulder at her. 'You're not bad yourself, Miss Price.' She was just Faye to him now, in his mind, it was difficult to remember who else she was . . . Faye Price . . . the film star . . . actress . . . singer . . . important personality . . . she was just Faye to him, now, for tonight. His face sobered slowly then. 'Will I see you again before you leave?' Suddenly that mattered a lot to him, and to her as well, more than he knew in fact. She wanted to see him again too before she left.

'Maybe we can catch a quick cup of coffee tomorrow morning before things get too crazy.' She knew the crew had probably been up all night, raising hell with the enlisted men, or the nursing staff, or preferably both, singing and playing the band's instruments. It was the same everywhere they went, but they needed to let off steam, and they never seemed to mind staying up all night. The crunch would come the next day when they had to get organised to leave, and then suddenly everything would be totally insane for two hours before they boarded the plane to the next base. She went through it almost every day, and then finally on the plane they would all sleep until the next stop, and then the magic would begin again. She would have a lot to do before they left, to help everybody load up, but maybe, just maybe ... there would be a spare moment for him ... 'I'll look for you.'

'I'll be around.'

But when she joined the others at the mess hall the next day at seven o'clock, he was not there. The C.O. had needed him, and it was almost nine o'clock before Ward found Faye standing with the others while their plane warmed up. There had been a faint look of panic in her eyes which pleased him as he shrieked up in the jeep, and jumped out to speak to her.

'Sorry, Faye ... the C.O. ...' The noise of the propellers drowned him out, and there were frantic orders being given by the stage manager to the rest of the group around her.

'It's all right ...' She smiled her dazzling smile at him, but he saw that she looked tired today. She couldn't have had more than two hours' sleep, and he had had half of that himself, but he was used to it. She was wearing a bright red jumpsuit today with platform sandals that made him smile. The latest fashions for Guadalcanal ... and then suddenly Kathy's face flashed into mind and he felt the old familiar pain again. His eyes met Faye's as someone in the distance shouted her name. 'I have to go ...'

'I know.' They were both shouting above the din.

He grabbed her hand for one moment and squeezed it hard. He wanted to kiss her lips but he didn't dare. 'I'll see you at the studio!'

'What?' She looked distressed; in all her travels among service men, no one had touched her as this man had.

'I said ... see you at the studio!'

She smiled at him, suddenly wondering if she would ever see him again. 'Take care of yourself!'

17

'Sure.' There were no guarantees here. For anyone. Even for her. Her plane could have been shot down on its way to their next stop. They all accepted that, realised it, until someone they cared about got hurt . . . a buddy, a roommate, a friend . . . Kathy . . . he shook the image from his mind again. 'You take care too.' What did you say to a woman like her? 'Good luck.' She didn't need much of that, she already had it all. Or did she? He wondered if there was a man in her life, but it was too late to ask now. She had begun to walk away with the others, looking back and waving at him. The C.O. had suddenly arrived for a last round of thanks, and Ward saw her shaking his hand, as he watched her go, and then she was in the plane, standing in the doorway for a last instant as she waved at him, and then the red jumpsuit disappeared from his life, probably for good, he thought. He hardened himself never to see her again. It was unlikely that he would, he told himself, as Faye told herself the same thing. She found herself looking down at him, wondering why he had hit her so hard. Maybe it was time to go home after all, maybe the men she met on tour were beginning to appeal to her, and that could be dangerous . . . but it wasn't that . . . it was something else about him . . . something she had never felt before. But she couldn't afford those feelings now. He was a stranger to her, she reminded herself, and she had a life to live. A life which didn't include him. He was fighting a war. And she had enough wars of her own . . . on tour . . . in Hollywood . . . Goodbye, Ward Thayer, she whispered to herself . . . good luck . . . and then she sat back and closed her eyes as the plane flew on . . . but his face haunted her for weeks . . . those deep blue eyes . . . it was months before he was completely out of her mind. And then he was. At last.

HOLLYWOOD 1945

CHAPTER 2

Everyone on the set stood in total silence, and tension was heavy in the air. They had waited for almost four months for this moment, and now that it was here they all wanted to stop it, to keep it from coming, to make it come on another day. It had been one of those magical films where almost everything went smoothly; what seemed like lasting friendships had been made, everyone was crazy about the star, and all of the women were more than half in love with the director. The male lead was Christopher Arnold, and everyone said he was Hollywood's biggest male star. It was easy to see why, the man was a pro. And now they all stood watching him, in his last scene, speaking softly, tears in his eyes. You could have heard a pin drop all the way to Pasadena, and Faye Price walked off the set for the last time, head bowed, real tears streaming down her cheeks. Arnold watched her go, devastated . . . that was it . . . the final scene . . . it was over.

'That's a wrap!' the voice shouted, and there was an endless instant of silence, followed by a shriek, and then suddenly everyone was shouting, laughing, hugging, crying. There was champagne for the entire crew, and it rapidly turned into a raucous party with everyone talking at once, wishing each other well, hating to leave. Christopher Arnold gave Faye a powerful hug, and pulled away a moment later to look deep into her eyes as he held her.

'It's been a joy working with you, Faye.'

'I've enjoyed it too.' They exchanged a long, knowing smile. They had been involved with each other once, almost three years before, and she had been hesitant about doing the film because of that. But it had worked out beautifully. He had been a perfect gentleman from beginning to end, and other than a glimmer of something more than recognition in his eyes on the first day, this was the first sign of their old liaison. It hadn't got in the way of their work at all during the entire three months of making the picture.

He smiled at her warmly as he took his arms from around her. 'I'm going to miss you all over again now. And I thought I was over all that.' They both laughed.

'So will I.' She looked around at the rest of the cast, happily raising hell, and the director, passionately kissing the set designer, who also happened to be his wife. Faye had enjoyed working with them both. Directing had fascinated her ever since she had started acting. 'What are you going to do now, Chris?'

'I'm leaving for New York in a week, and then I'm sailing to France. I want to spend a few days on the Riviera before this summer is entirely over. Everyone tells me it's too soon for France but what have I got to lose? I hear nothing's changed, except for a little rationing.' He looked rakish for a moment as he winked at her. He was twenty years older than she, but on him it looked more like ten. He was probably the best-looking man in town, and he knew it. 'Care to come with me?' As attractive as he was, he no longer appealed to her.

'No thanks.' She gave him an airy smile, and then wagged a finger at him. 'Now don't start that again. You've behaved yourself through this whole picture, Chris.'

'Of course, that was work. This is different.'

'Oh is that it?' She was about to say something to tease him, but suddenly the chaos around them seemed to heighten and a page ran onto the set screeching something Faye couldn't discern. For a moment, panic registered on a number of faces, and then shock, and then there were tears, and Faye still hadn't heard what had happened. She pulled at Chris Arnold's sleeve, her eyes anxious. 'What did he say . . .? What . . .?' Chris was speaking to someone to his right, and Faye was straining to hear above the din.

'My God . . .' He turned to her with a look of amazement. And then without thinking he pressed her to him in a huge hug again, and she could hear his voice tremble when he spoke to her. 'It's all over, Faye . . . the war is over. The Japanese have surrendered.' It had ended in Europe only months before, and now finally it was all over. Tears sprang to her eyes, and she was crying as she hugged

22

him back. Suddenly everyone on the set was crying and laughing, others had joined them, and fresh cases of champagne were opened. Everyone was shouting now. 'It's over! It's over!' No longer the film ... but the war.

It felt like hours before she left the set to go back to her house in Beverly Hills, and the pain of finishing the film was long since gone. It had been totally eclipsed by her joy that the war was over. It seemed amazing. She had been twenty-one years old when Pearl Harbor was bombed, and now here she was, twenty-five years old, grown up, a woman, at the summit of her career.

This had to be the summit; she told herself that every year. She couldn't imagine anything improving from this point on. How could it? And yet it had. The roles got better and bigger and more important, the praise more lavish, the money more unbelievable each year. The only blemish in it all came when her parents died. It made her sad that her parents were no longer alive to enjoy it with her. They had both died the previous year. Her father of cancer, her mother in a car accident on an icy Pennsylvania road near Youngstown. She had tried to get her mother to come out to live in California, after her father died, but she hadn't wanted to give up her home. So now she had no one. The little house in Grove City, Pennsylvania, had been sold the year before. She had no sisters or brothers. And other than the faithful couple who worked for her in the handsome small house she had bought in Beverly Hills, Faye Price was alone. She seldom felt lonely though; there were too many people around her for that. She enjoyed her work and her friends. And yet, it was odd not having any family now. No one she 'belonged' to. It still surprised her that she had become so successful, and her life had become so lavish, in such a short time. Even at twenty-one, when the war had broken out, her life had been different. But now, ever since her last USO tour two years before, things had settled down. She had bought the house, made six films in two years, and although she had intended to go on tour again she had never had the time. Life seemed to be an endless round of premières and publicity pictures and press parties, and when she wasn't doing that, she was getting up at five o'clock in the morning and going to work on a film. Her next picture was scheduled to start in five weeks, and she was already reading the script for hours every night before she went to sleep, and now that she had finished the film she'd been working on, she could really get down to work. The new one was a sure Oscar for her, her agent had told her. But she always laughed when he said that . . . it was a ridiculous thought . . . except that she had already won one, and been nominated two other times. But Abe insisted this film would be a big one, and Faye believed him. In an odd way, he had become a father figure to her.

She turned her car right on Summit Drive, past Pickfair and the Chaplins, and a moment later reached her own home as Bob, who spent his days in the little gate house, opening the gate for deliveries and friends, or for Miss Price herself, ran out with a smile for her.

'Have a nice day, Miss Price?' He was ancient and white-haired and grateful for the job. He had been working for her now for over a year.

'I sure did, Bob. Did you hear the news?' He looked blank. 'The war is over!' She beamed at him and tears came to his eyes. He had been too old to go to the First World War himself, but he had lost his only son. And now, in this war, it reminded him every day of the grief he and his wife had felt way back then.

'Are you sure, ma'am?'

'Positive. It's all over.' She reached out and shook his hand.

'Thank God.' His voice trembled and he turned his head to wipe his eyes. But he didn't apologise to her when he looked back into the lovely face. 'Thank God.' She wanted to kiss him for all that they both felt, but she smiled, and waited for him to open quietly the large handsome brass gates which he kept shined to perfection at all times.

'Thank you, Bob.'

'Goodnight, Miss Price.' He would come up to the house later for dinner in the kitchen with her butler and maid, but Faye wouldn't see him again until she drove out the next day. And if she chose to stay at home, she wouldn't see him at all. He only worked in the daytime, and at night, her butler, Arthur, drove for her, and would open the gate himself with his key. Most of the time, Faye preferred to drive herself. She had bought a beautiful Lincoln Continental with a convertible top, in a deep shade of blue, and she was perfectly content to drive around Los Angeles herself. Except at night when Arthur drove her out in the Rolls. It had seemed a shocking thing to buy at first, and she had almost been too embarrassed to admit it was hers, but it was such a beautiful machine that she hadn't been able to resist. And there was still a certain excitement as she stepped into it; the rich smell of leather everywhere, the thick grey carpeting beneath her feet. Even the wood in the magnificent car was totally unique, and finally she had decided what the hell. At twenty-five, her success no longer embarrassed her as it once had. She had a right to it, 'more or less', she teased herself, and she wasn't hurting anyone. She had no one else to spend her money on, and she was making so damn much of it. It was hard to know what to do with it all. She had invested some, on her agent's advice, but the rest just sat there and waited to get spent, and she was far less extravagant than most of the stars of her day. Most of them were wearing emeralds and diamonds to the floor, buying tiaras they couldn't afford, sable coats and ermine and chinchillas, to parade around in at openings of other people's films. Faye was far more restrained in what she wore, and what she did, although she did have some beautiful clothes which she enjoyed, and two or three very beautiful fur coats. There was a white fox coat that she adored; she looked like an exquisite blonde eskimo when she buried herself in it on a cold night. She had worn it just the winter before in New York, and she had actually heard people gasp as she walked past them. And then there was a dark chocolate sable she had bought in France, and a sensible mink she kept for 'everyday' ... 'Just my everyday mink,' she grinned to herself, as she pulled the Lincoln up outside the house. How life had changed since she was a little girl. She had always wanted to have a second pair of shoes, for 'dressing up', but her parents had been too poor back then. The Depression had hit them hard, and both of her parents had been out of work for a long, long time. Her father had wound up doing odd jobs, and hating everything about his life. Her mother had finally found a job as a secretary. But it all seemed so dreary to Faye. That was why the movies had always seemed so magical to her. It was the perfect escape for hours and hours and hours. She would save every penny she could lay her little fingers on, and then off she'd go to sit in the dark, gaping at what she saw. Maybe that was in the back of her head after all when she went to New York to find work as a model ... and now here she was, walking up the three pink marble steps to her own house in

Beverly Hills, as a serious-faced English butler opened the door to her, and in spite of himself smiled into her eyes. He couldn't resist the 'young miss', as he called her in private to his wife. She was the nicest employer they had ever had, they agreed, and certainly the youngest by far. And she had never acquired what they referred to as 'Hollywood ways'. She didn't seem overly impressed with who she was, and she was always pleasant and polite and thoughtful to them. The house was a pleasure to run, and there was very little to do. Faye seldom entertained, and she was working most of the time, so all they had to do was keep things neat and clean, and running smoothly for her, a task Arthur and Elizabeth both enjoyed.

'Good afternoon, Arthur.'

'Miss Price,' he looked extremely prim, 'excellent news, isn't it?' He assumed correctly that she would have heard, and he knew she had when she beamed.

'It certainly is.' She knew that they had no sons to fear for, but they still had relatives in England who had been hit hard by the war, and Arthur had always been deeply concerned for them. He spoke of the RAF as very near to God-like. They had discussed the Pacific theatre as well from time to time, but there would be no war to discuss any more. As she walked into her study, and sat down at the little English desk to open her mail, she wondered how many of the men she had seen were still alive, how many of the hands she had shaken were no more. It brought tears to her eyes as she thought of it, and she turned to look out into the perfectly tended garden and the pool house beyond. How difficult to imagine the holocaust that had existed over there, the countries that had been destroyed, the people who had died. She wondered, as she often had, if Ward was among them. She had never heard from him, but over the years, he had never quite left her mind. And thinking of him often made her feel guilty that she hadn't gone on tour again; but there had never been time. There never was. Not lately. Not after her parents' death, and the constant demands of her career.

She turned back to her desk now, glancing through a stack of mail from her agent, and assorted bills, trying to force the faces of the past from her mind, but there was so little in her present to occupy her thoughts, other than work. She had had a serious involvement with a director twice her age the year before, and she realised at the end of it that she had been more in love with his work than she was with him. She loved hearing about what he did, but after a while there wasn't much excitement left, and they had finally drifted apart, and there had been no one serious in her life since. She wasn't given to the usual Hollywood affairs, and she had never got involved with anyone unless she truly cared about him. She kept to herself most of the time, and avoided publicity as much as she could. For a major star, she led a remarkably quiet life, but she insisted to her friend and agent, Abe, when he scolded her for 'hiding' too much of the time, that she couldn't work as hard as she did unless she did stay home, to study and prepare for her roles, and that was just exactly what she was planning to do in the next five weeks, no matter how much Abe nagged her to get out, be seen, and have some fun with her colleagues.

Instead, she had promised to go up to San Francisco to visit a friend for a few days, an elderly actress, now retired, whom she had befriended at the beginning of her career. And on the way home she was planning to stop and see friends in Pebble Beach. After that, she had agreed to a weekend with the Hearsts at their vast country estate, complete with wild animals and a zoo, and after that she was coming home to rest and relax and study and read. She liked nothing better than lying around her own pool, soaking in the sun, smelling the flowers, listening to the bees. She closed her eyes now, just thinking of it, and never heard Arthur walk softly into the room. She heard him clear his throat some distance from her and opened her eyes. One never heard Arthur come in. For a man of his size and years, he walked with catlike grace, and now he stood before her, some eight or ten feet beyond her desk, in his tailcoat and striped trousers, wing collar, and carefully starched shirt and tie, holding a silver tray, bearing a single cup of tea. She had bought the china in Limoges herself and was especially fond of it. It was pure white, with a tiny blue flower here and there, as though put there almost as an afterthought, and she saw as Arthur set the cup down on her desk with the white linen napkin she had bought in New York, made in Italy before the war, that Elizabeth had sent in some cookies today as well. Normally, Faye wouldn't have indulged, but she had five weeks before the next picture after all, so why not? She smiled up at Arthur, and he bowed; and silently left the room. She looked around at the things she loved; the shelves lined with books, both old and new, some even very rare, the vases filled with flowers, the sculptures she had begun to buy a few years before, the beautiful Aubusson rug in dusty pinks and pale blues with scattered flowers all over it, the English furniture she had selected so carefully, the silver pieces that Arthur polished till they shone, and beyond her study she could see the lovely French crystal chandelier that hung in the hall, the dining room with its English table and Chippendale chairs and another chandelier beyond. It was a home that gave her pleasure every day, not just because of the beauty of its treasures, but also because of the contrast to the threadbare poverty she had grown up with. It made each object more precious, from every silver candlestick and lace tablecloth to each gleaming antique. Each was a symbol of her accomplishment and its rewards.

There was a handsome living room as well, with a pink marble fireplace, and delicately shaped French chairs. She had blended English with French, a few modern pieces with the old, two lovely Impressionist paintings that had been a gift from a very, very dear friend. And a small but elegant staircase led upstairs. Here, her bedroom was done entirely in mirrors and white silks, like the kind of fantasies she had had as a little girl, enamoured by the cinema. There was a white fox bedspread on her bed, fur pillows on the couch, a white fur thrown on the chaise longue, and a white marble fireplace identical to the one in her mirrored dressing room. Her bathroom was all done in white marble and white tile. And there was another small sitting room, which she often used late at night when she was studying a script, or writing a letter to a friend. And that was all of it. A tiny, perfect gem. Just the right size for her. There were servants' quarters behind the kitchen on the main floor, and a huge garage with a flat over it, where Bob, the gatekeeper, lived. Extensive gardens, a good-sized swimming pool with a small pool house and a bar, and dressing room for her friends. She had everything she wanted here, a world unto itself, she often said. She almost hated to go anywhere any more, and she was almost sorry she had promised to go to San Francisco the following week to visit her old friend.

Once she was there, she had a good time with her. The woman,

Harriet Fielding, had been a famous actress on the Broadway stage years before, and Faye had enormous respect for her. Harriet had taught her a great deal, and Faye talked to her about her new role now. There was no doubt it would be challenging. The leading man was said to be difficult, and a prima donna of the worst sort, everyone said. Faye had never worked with him before and wasn't looking forward to it. She hoped she hadn't made a mistake accepting the role, but Harriet insisted that she had not. The part had more meat to it, and required more expertise, than anything Faye had ever done before.

'That's exactly what frightens me!' She laughed with her old friend as they looked out across the Bay. 'What if I fall flat on my face?' It was like having a mother again, being able to talk to her, although Harriet was very different from how her own mother had been. She was more sophisticated, more worldly, more knowledgeable about Faye's work. Margaret Price had really never understood anything about what Faye did or the world she had moved into, but she had certainly been proud of her. She bragged to everyone, and Faye was touched to realise how much her mother cared about it all whenever she went home. But there was no home to go back to now, no one she still cared about in her home town. Instead, there was Harriet, who meant a great deal to her. 'I'm serious, what if I'm terrible?'

'In the first place, you won't be. And in the second, if you do fall on your face, and we all do from time to time then you'll pick yourself up and try again, and do better next time. Probably much better, in fact. What's the matter with you? You've never been cowardly before, Faye Price.' The old woman sounded annoyed, but Faye knew it was all an act. 'Do your homework and you'll be just fine.'

'I hope you're right.' The old woman growled at her in response, and Faye smiled. There was something so comforting about Harriet in many ways. They walked the hills of San Francisco side by side for five days and talked about everything from life to the war, from their careers to men. Harriet was one of the few people Faye really talked to. She was so wise and so bright and so funny. She was a rare, rare, woman and Faye was always grateful to have found her.

When the conversation turned to men, Harriet questioned her, and not for the first time, about why she never seemed to settle down with any one man.

'They're never quite right, I guess.'

'Some of them must be.' Harriet looked searchingly at her young friend. 'Are you afraid?'

'Maybe. But I really don't think any of them have been right. I can have anything I want from them: orchids, gardenias, champagne, exotic evenings, fabulous nights, entrée to some extraordinary parties, and in some cases expensive gifts, but that's never really been what I wanted. None of that seems real to me. It never has.'

'Thank God.' That was one of the reasons why Harriet liked her. 'It isn't real. You've always been smart enough to see that. But there are other men in L.A., not just the fakers and the pretenders and the playboys.' Although they both knew that because of Faye's looks, and her star status, she attracted hordes of what Harriet loved to call the 'glitter gluttons'.

'Maybe I just haven't had time to meet the right ones.' And the funny thing was that she could never imagine settling down with any of those men, even Gable. What she wanted was a slightly more sophisticated version of the men she would have met back home, in Grove City, the kind of guy who would shovel snow on a cold winter morning, and cut down a Christmas tree for the kids, and go for long walks with her and sit by a fire, or walk along beside a lake with her in summer . . . someone real . . . someone else she could talk to . . . someone who put her and the children ahead of all else, even his job . . . not someone who was looking to hitch his wagon to a star and get a great part in someone else's new film. Thinking of that brought her mind back to her new film, and she questioned Harriet again about some of the subtleties of the script and the techniques she wanted to try. She liked being adventurous about her acting – and creative. As long as she wasn't creating a home and a family for someone, the least she could do was put all her creative energies into her career, and thus far she had done that with enormous success, as the whole world knew. But Harriet was still sorry that the right man hadn't come along. She sensed that that would bring out a dimension of Faye that hadn't been touched yet, a dimension which would enhance her both as a woman and an actress.

'Will you come down and watch me on the set?' Faye turned to her with pleading eyes and she looked like a child to the older woman. But Harriet only smiled gently and shook her head.

'You know how I hate that place, Faye.'

'But I need you.' There was something lonely in Faye's eyes; it was the first time Harriet had seen it, and she patted her young friend's arm reassuringly.

'I need you too, as a friend. But you don't need my advice as an actress, Faye Price. You've got more talent than I ever had in my little finger. You're going to be just fine. I know it. And my being on the set would only distract you.' It was the first time in a long time that Faye had felt she needed moral support on the set, and she still felt shaky about it when she left Harriet in San Francisco, later than planned, and began her trip down the coast road to what the Hearsts modestly called their 'Casa'. All the way down, she found herself thinking of Harriet.

For some reason she herself didn't understand, she felt lonelier than she had in years. She found herself missing Harriet, her old home in Pennsylvania, her parents. For the first time in years, she felt as though there were something missing in her life, though she couldn't imagine what. She tried to tell herself that she was just nervous about the new part, but it was more than that. There was no man in her life just then, hadn't been in a long time, and Harriet was right, it was too bad she never did settle down, but with whom? She couldn't imagine a single face that appealed to her at the moment; there was no one she was anxious to see when she got home, and the revels at the Hearsts' estate seemed emptier than ever. There were dozens of guests, and as always, lots of amusing entertainers, but there suddenly seemed to be no substance to the life she led, or the people she knew and met. The only thing that made any sense was her work, and the two people she cared about most, Harriet Fielding, who lived five hundred miles away, and her agent, Abe Abramson.

In the end, after smiling interminably for days on end, it was a relief to head for Los Angeles. When she arrived, she let herself in with her key and walked upstairs into the white splendour of her own bedroom, feeling happier than she had in weeks. It was wonderful to be home. It looked better to her than the Hearsts' grand estate, and she lay across the white fox throw with a happy grin, kicking off her shoes, staring up at the pretty little chandelier, and thinking with excitement of her new role. She felt good again. So what if there was no man in her life? She had her work, and it made her very, very happy.

For the next month, she studied night and day, learning every line in the script, hers and everyone else's as well. She tried out different nuances, spent entire days walking the grounds of her home, talking to herself, trying it out, becoming the woman that she was to play. In the film she would be driven mad by the man she had married. Eventually, he would take their child from her, and she would attempt to kill herself, and then him, and slowly, slowly she would realise what he had done to her. She would prove it in the end, retrieve the child, and finally kill him. But even that final act of violence and vengeance was desperately important to Faye. Would the audience lose sympathy with her then? Would they love her more? Would they care? Would she win their hearts? It meant everything to her.

On the morning that filming was to begin, Faye was at the studio right on time, the script in a red alligator briefcase she always carried with her, her own makeup case made to match, a suitcase filled with a few things she always liked to have on the set, and she moved into her dressing room in a quiet and businesslike way that was a delight to some, and enraged those who could not compete with her. Above all, and beyond anything, Faye Price was a professional, and she was also a perfectionist. But she demanded nothing from anyone that she didn't demand from herself first.

A maid from the studio was assigned to take care of Faye, her clothes, and her dressing room. Some brought their own help, but Faye could never imagine Elizabeth here, and she always left her at home. The women provided by the studio did just as well. This time they assigned a pleasant black woman to her, who had worked with her before. Pearl was extremely capable, and Faye had enjoyed her comments and remarks before. The woman was sharp and had been working around the studio for years, and some of the stories she told made Faye laugh until she cried. So this morning, they were happy to meet again. She hung up all of Faye's own clothes, put her makeup out, did not touch the briefcase because she had made that mistake before and remembered that Faye didn't like anyone else handling her script. She served her coffee with exactly the right dose of milk, and at seven in the morning, when the hairdresser arrived to do Faye's hair, she brought her one soft-boiled egg and a single slice of toast. She was known for working miracles on the set, and taking exquisite care of 'her stars', but Faye never took advantage of it, and Pearl liked that.

'Pearl, you're going to have me spoiled for life.' She looked gratefully at her as the hairdresser went to work on her hair.

'That's the whole idea, Miss Price.' She beamed at Faye. She liked working with this girl. She was one of the best, and she loved talking about her to her friends. Faye had a kind of dignity that was difficult to describe, but she also had warmth and wit and, she grinned to herself, one hell of a pair of legs.

In two hours her hair was done, set exactly the way it was meant to be, and she had put on the dark blue dress that had been assigned to her. Her makeup was done just as the director had specified, and Faye was standing in the wings. The usual excitement had begun. Cameras were being pushed around, script girls were standing by, the director was conferring with light men, and almost all the actors had arrived, except for the other star. Faye heard someone mutter 'as usual', and wondered if this was the way he always worked, and with a quiet sigh, she sat down unobtrusively in a chair. If need be, they'd go on to a scene that didn't call for him, but it didn't bode well for the next few months, if he was late for the first day. She was staring down at the matronly blue shoes she had been assigned by the wardrobe mistress when suddenly she had the odd feeling that someone was watching her, and she looked up into the deeply tanned face of a strikingly handsome man with blond hair and deep blue eyes. She imagined that he was one of the actors in the film, and maybe he wanted to say hello to her before they began. She smiled casually at him, but the young man didn't smile.

'You don't remember me, do you, Faye?' For the flicker of an instant there was that sinking feeling all women get when confronted with a man who gives the impression that he knows one well, although one doesn't remember him at all. Did I really know this man? Did I forget his face? Could it be? ... but it couldn't have been serious ... He simply stood and stared, desperately intent, and he almost frightened her. There was a hint of memory somewhere at the very back of her mind, but she couldn't place this man. Had she acted with him before? 'I don't suppose there's any reason why you should.' His voice was quiet and calm, his eyes so serious as he looked at her, as though disappointed that she hadn't recognised him at once, and she was growing increasingly uncomfortable. 'We met in Guadalcanal two years ago. You did a show for us, and I stood in for the C.O.'

Oh my God ... her eyes grew wide ... and suddenly it came back to her ... all of it ... that same handsome face, their long talk, the young nurse he had married, and who had been killed ... the two of them stared at each other as the memories flooded back. How could she have so nearly forgotten him? His face had haunted her for months. But she had never expected to see him again. As she stood up and held out a hand, he smiled at her. He had wondered for so long if she would remember him.

'Welcome home, Lieutenant.'

He saluted smartly, as he had so long before, and did a little bow, the mischief slowly returning to his eyes. 'Major, now, thank you.'

'I apologise.' She was relieved that he was still alive. 'Are you all right?'

'Of course I am.' He answered her so quickly that she wondered if indeed he was, but he looked well enough; in fact he looked fabulous. She looked up at him, and then she remembered where they were, and the film that was about to begin, if her co-star ever arrived.

'What are you doing here?'

'I live in Los Angeles. Remember? I told you that ...' He smiled. 'I also told you I'd drop in on you at the studio one day.' She smiled in answer. 'I usually keep my promises, Miss Price.' It was easy to believe that about him. He was better-looking than she remembered, and there was something very dashing about him, and yet restrained. Like a magnificent stallion held in on a tight rein. She knew he must be twenty-eight by now, and he had lost his boyish look. He looked every inch a man. But she had other things on her mind ... like the star who hadn't yet arrived. It was awkward seeing him here again for the first time.

'How on earth did you get in here, Ward?' She still remembered his name. She smiled gently at him as she asked the question.

Suddenly the mischief in him came back again and he grinned

happily. 'I greased a few palms, told them I was an old friend of yours . . . the war . . . Purple Heart . . . medals . . . Guadalcanal . . . you know, the usual.' She was laughing at him now. He had bribed his way in, but why? 'I told you I'd like to see you again.' But he didn't tell her how often he had thought of her in the past two years. A thousand times he had wanted to write to her, but he hadn't dared. What if they threw her 'fan mail' away, and where would he send the letter to anyway? Faye Price, Hollywood, USA? He had decided to wait until he came home, if he ever did, and there were times when he doubted that. Many, many times. And now here he was. It was like a dream, standing there, looking at her, listening to her talk to him. He had remembered her voice in all his dreams, that deep, sensual voice that had lingered in his head for two years.

'When did you get back?'

He grinned again. He decided to be honest with her. 'Yesterday. I would have come by then, but I had a few things to take care of first.' His lawyers to see, papers to fill out, the house that still seemed too big to him. He was staying in a hotel.

'It's perfectly all right, I understand.' But suddenly she was glad he was here now, glad he had lived, glad he'd come home. He was like the one living example of all the men she had met on tour. He stood before her like someone in a distant dream, someone she had met in a jungle two years ago . . . and now here he was, smiling down at her, out of uniform, just like everyone else, except that there was something special about him, in a way she'd never run into before.

And then suddenly her co-star arrived and everything exploded on the set, and the director began roaring at everyone and she had to do her first scene with her leading man. 'You'd better go, Ward. I've got to go to work.' She felt pulled suddenly, for the first time in her life, between work and a man.

'Can't I watch?' He looked like a disappointed child as she shook her head.

'Not this time. First day is kind of tough for all of us. In a few weeks, when we've all relaxed.' He liked the sound of that. They both did . . . 'in a few weeks' . . . as though they had all the time in the world, and a future to share. Who was this man, she suddenly asked herself as he looked intently at her? He was only a stranger after all.

'Dinner tonight?' He whispered the words on the darkening set and she started to say something to him and shake her head, and then the director roared again and Ward tried to speak to her but she held up her hand. Her eyes met his and she could feel the man's strength. He had fought a war, he had come home, he had lost his first wife, and he had come to see her. Maybe that was all she needed to know about him. For now anyway.

'All right,' she whispered back, and he asked her where she lived. She smiled, and scribbled her address for him, embarrassed that he would see how grandly she lived. It wasn't nearly as lavish as it could have been, but surely by his standards he would be somewhat awed. But there was no time to arrange another meeting place. She just handed the slip of paper to him, and waved him off the set with a grin, and five minutes later, she was getting directions and an introduction to her leading man. He was a powerful, intriguing, and very handsome man. But Faye realised as they worked together for several hours that there was something lacking in him, something. Warmth ... charm ... she tried to define it to Pearl in the privacy of her dressing room later on.

'Yeah, I know what you mean, Miz Price. There's two things he ain't got. Heart and brains.' And suddenly, with a burst of laughter, Faye knew she was right. That was what was wrong with him, he wasn't bright. He was also terribly full of himself, which was tiresome after all. There was a fleet of valets, secretaries, and go-fers to attend to his every need on the set, from cigarettes to gin. And when they had finished work for the day, Faye saw him undressing her with his eyes. And then he asked her to dinner that night.

'Sorry, Vance, I've already got a date for tonight.' His eyes lit up like Christmas trees and she could have kicked herself. It wouldn't have mattered if she didn't have a date for the next ten years, she would never have gone out with him.

'Tomorrow night?'

She shook her head, and quietly walked away from him. It wasn't going to be easy working with Vance Saint George, but there were moments when she had thought his performance was actually very good.

And it actually wasn't Vance she was thinking of as she hurried back to her dressing room that night. It was already six o'clock, and she had been on the set for twelve hours, but she was used to that. After she changed her clothes she bid Pearl goodnight, and hurried out to where she had parked her car. She drove towards Beverly Hills as quickly as she could. Bob was still at the gate when she arrived; he let her in and she raced through, leaving the car out front, and not even taking the time to put up the top. She glanced at her watch again. He had whispered eight o'clock, and it was a quarter to seven now.

Arthur opened the door to her, and she raced upstairs. 'A glass of sherry, miss?' he called after her, and she stopped on the stairs for a moment with the smile that always warmed his heart. He was crazy about her, more so than he would ever have admitted to Elizabeth.

'There's someone coming for drinks at eight o'clock.'

'Very well, miss. Shall I send Elizabeth up to run your bath? She could bring a glass of sherry to you now.' He knew how exhausted she got on the set sometimes, but she didn't even look tired tonight.

'No, thank you, I'll be fine.'

'Do you wish your guest to be shown into the living room, miss?' It was a rhetorical question, he knew she would, and was surprised when she shook her head.

'My study, please, Arthur.' She smiled once more at him, and vanished, cursing herself for not arranging to meet Ward somewhere downtown. How ridiculous to play film star with him, poor kid. Well, at least he'd survived the war. That was the important thing, she told herself, as she ran into her dressing room, pulling open all the closet doors, and then dashing into the white marble bathroom to turn on the bath. She pulled out a plain white silk dress that suited her perfectly, and wasn't too showy. It had a grey silk coat that went over it, and she selected a pair of grey pearl earrings from her jewellery box, grey silk pumps, and a grey and white silk bag. All put together, it looked a little dressier than she thought, but she didn't want to insult him either by being too casual. He knew who she was after all. The only problem was that it was she who knew nothing about him. She stopped for a minute, staring into space, remembering him, as she turned off her bath. It was a good question. Who was Ward Thayer after all?

CHAPTER 3

At exactly five minutes to eight, Faye was downstairs in her study waiting for Ward. She was wearing the white silk dress, and the matching grey coat was tossed over the back of a chair. She paced nervously once or twice, regretting again that she hadn't arranged to meet him elsewhere, but it had been such a shock, his turning up on the set like that, after their brief meeting in Guadalcanal two years before. How strange life was. Here he was again, and she was having dinner with him, her heart was pounding, and she had to admit she was excited about it. He was a very attractive man and there was something a little mysterious about him.

The doorbell broke into her reverie and as Arthur went to answer it, Faye took a deep breath and tried to steady herself, and then suddenly she was looking into the deep sapphire eyes again, and she felt an exhilaration she hadn't felt in years. It was like riding a roller coaster just looking at him. She tried to sound cool as she offered him a drink, and noticed how well he looked in civilian clothes. He wore a simple pinstriped grey suit but it moulded his shoulders to perfection, and he seemed even taller than he had before. She still felt a little strange being here with him, this soldier from a war that was finally over. But it was a nice gesture after all, and if they had nothing in common, she wouldn't have to see him again. She was still impressed with the fact that he had bribed his way into the studio to see her, and there was a definite charm about the man. But she had felt that long before when she had met him in Guadalcanal.

'Please sit down.' The silence between them was awkward and she was struggling for something to say to him when she saw him smile. He was looking around with obvious pleasure, and he seemed to notice all the little details of the room: the small sculptures, the Aubusson rug; he even stood up to glance at the collection of rare books she had bought in an auction long since, and she noticed a sparkle in his eye.

'Where did you get these, Faye?'

'At an auction several years ago. That particular set is all first editions and I'm very proud of them.' In fact, she was proud of almost everything she had. It had all been hard earned and meant more to her because of that.

'Mind if I take them down?' He glanced at her over his shoulder and he looked more at ease, as Arthur walked into the room with a silver tray and their drinks. A gin and tonic for Faye and scotch on the rocks for Ward, in her pretty crystal glasses from Tiffany in New York.

'Of course, take a look at them.' Faye watched him from where she sat, as he gingerly removed two books, put one down, and opened the other, examining the fly leaf, and then the back pages of the old leather-bound edition. She saw him smile and then he looked at her with an amused expression.

'That's what I thought. These were my grandfather's. I would have known them anywhere.' He grinned, and handed her one of the books, pointing to an interesting handstamped logo on the back page. 'He put that in all his books. I have a number of them myself.' His words made her curious and reminded her of how little she knew about him, and she attempted to draw him out over drinks as they chatted. But somehow Ward remained vague; he talked about his grandfather's interest in ships, summers spent in Hawaii, and she learned only that his mother had been born there. He didn't say much about his father, and she was unable to learn more. 'And you, you're from the East, aren't you, Faye?' He always seemed to turn the conversation back to her, as though he thought the details of his life were unimportant. He almost seemed determined to remain a mystery to her. Handsome, poised, there was something terribly worldly about him and she was suddenly dying to know more. She would have to draw him out over dinner. He was watching her quietly, with an appreciative look in his eyes.

'I'm from Pennsylvania, but I feel like I've been out here forever.'

He laughed. 'Hollywood does that, I think. It's hard to imagine having another life.' He declined a second drink, glanced at his

39

watch, and stood up, reaching for her coat. 'I think we'd better go. I made reservations at nine.' She was dying to ask him where, but she didn't want to push, and let him help her on with her coat, as they walked slowly into the hall and once again he looked around. 'You have lovely things, Faye.' He seemed to understand the beauty and history of all that he saw and easily recognised a fine English table she had near the door. What he didn't know was the reason why her home meant so much to her: because of the poverty that had come before.

'Thank you, I collected them all myself.'

'That must have been fun.' But it had been more than fun. At the time, it had meant everything to her. Now the objects in her life seemed less important, less real. She was more secure now.

His eyes met hers, and he reached the door and opened it for her before Arthur could help them. He smiled at the English butler and seemed unperturbed by his disapproving stare. Arthur felt it was not proper for the young man to open the door himself, but Ward looked happy and carefree as they stepped outside. The night was warm and balmy, and he ran lightly down the marble steps to the car he'd parked out front. It was a bright red Ford convertible, with more than a few dents, but it had a certain rakish look to it, which amused her. 'What a great car, Ward.'

'Thanks. I borrowed it for tonight.' Which was true, he had. 'Mine is still up on blocks. I just hope I can get it running again.'

She didn't ask him what he had, and slipped into the little Ford as he held the door open for her. The car started easily and rumbled off towards the gate which Arthur had gone ahead to open for them, and Ward sped through with a friendly wave. 'Awfully serious houseman you've got, madam.' He grinned at her and she smiled. Arthur and Elizabeth were so good to her she wouldn't have given them up for anything in the world.

'I'm spoiled, I guess.' She looked faintly embarrassed and he smiled at her.

'There's no harm in that, Faye. You should enjoy it.'

'I do.' She blurted the words out and then blushed as the wind whipped her thick blonde hair into a froth about her shoulders and they both laughed as she attempted to keep it down.

'Do you want me to put the top up?' he asked her as they sped downtown.

'No, no . . . I'm fine . . .' And she was. She enjoyed racing along beside him. There was something wonderfully old-fashioned about what they were doing. Like a Saturday night date back home in Grove City. She didn't feel at all like a film star as she sat beside him. She just felt like a girl, and she liked it, even more than she had expected. The only thing that concerned her was that she had to get up at five the next morning, and she didn't want to stay out too late.

He stopped the car at Ciro's on the strip, and hopped out with ease as the doorman approached him. He was a tall, handsome black man, and his face lit up when he saw Ward. 'Mr Thayer! You're home!'

'I sure am, John, and believe me, it wasn't easy!' They exchanged a long fervent handshake and a warm smile, and then suddenly the older black man looked with horror at the car.

'Mr Thayer, what happened to your car?'

'Up on blocks for the duration. I'll have it out again next week, I hope.'

'Thank God . . . I thought you sold it for this pile of junk.' Faye was a little surprised at the rude remark about the car, and equally so that they seemed to know him so well at Ciro's, but it was more of the same when they went inside. The headwaiter almost cried as he shook Ward's hand, congratulating him on his return, and it seemed as though every waiter in the place knew him and came over to say hello. They were given the best table in the house, and after ordering drinks, he led her out on the floor to dance.

'You're the prettiest girl here, Faye.' His voice was soft in her ear, and his arms felt powerful around her.

She smiled up at him. 'I don't need to ask you if you used to come here often.'

He laughed at her remark and circled her expertly around the floor. He was the smoothest partner she had known, and she was growing more intrigued by the moment about who he really was. Just a young L.A. playboy? Someone important? An actor whose name she had never heard before the war? It was obvious that Ward Thayer was 'someone', and she was seriously beginning to wonder who he was. Not because she wanted something from him, but it was strange to be out with someone she barely knew, and had met in such a far-off place, in such an anonymous way.

'Something tells me you're keeping secrets from me, Mr Thayer.'

Her eyes sought his and he laughed and shook his head. 'Not at all.'

'All right, then. Who are you?'

'You know that much already. I told you. Ward Thayer, from L.A.' He reeled off his rank and serial number and they laughed again.

'That doesn't tell me a damn thing and you know it. And you know what else?' She pulled away slightly to look up at him again. 'You're enjoying this, aren't you? Making a fool of me, playing mystery man. I suddenly get the feeling that everyone in town knows who you are except for me, Ward Thayer.'

'No, just the waiters . . . that's it . . . I was a waiter . . .' But suddenly, as he said it, there was a flurry in the doorway, and a woman in a skintight black dress walked into the room, her hair an explosion of fiery red. It was Rita Hayworth, and she had come here as she always did, with her handsome husband. She and Orson Welles would dance around the floor so he could show her off and it was easy to see why he was so proud of her. Faye thought instantly that she was the most spectacularly beautiful woman she had ever seen. She had seen her once or twice in the past, though only from a distance, and as she brushed past her now, Faye's breath caught she was so impressed. And then, as though the woman had heard her, she stopped, and quickly turned around. Faye blushed furiously beneath her own mane of peach-coloured hair, and was about to apologise for being rude, when suddenly Rita Hayworth seemed to spring into her arms and the next thing she knew, Ward had been pulled from her, and he and Rita were hugging tightly. Orson was standing a few paces away watching them with interest, and eyeing Faye, and Rita squealed with delight as she pulled away from Ward.

'My God, Ward, you made it! You rotten boy. All these years and not a word if you were alive or dead. Everyone kept asking and I never knew what to tell them . . .' She threw her arms around him again, her eyes closed, her mouth smiling the smile that made grown men cry from desire, as Faye watched in awe. Rita hadn't even seen her she was so happy to see Ward. 'Welcome home, you bad boy, you.' She grinned and glanced at Faye, nodded, recognition dawning in her eyes, and then interest as she glanced back at Ward. 'Aha, I see . . .' she teased him. 'Does anyone know that piece of gossip yet, Mr Thayer?'

'Now come on, Rita, for chrissake . . . I've only been back for two days.'

'Fast work.' She grinned at him, and smiled openly at Faye. 'It's nice to see you again.' Polite empty words. The two women had never been friends. 'Take good care of my friend here.' She patted him on the cheek, and then rejoined Welles, who saluted Ward with a smile from the distance, and as they left for a table at the far side of the room, Faye almost exploded. Ward led her back to their table, and took a sip of his drink, as Faye grabbed his other arm.

'Okay, Major. That does it. The truth.' She was glaring at him in mock fury, and he laughed openly as he set the drink down. 'Before I make a complete ass of myself, I want you to tell me what in hell is going on. Who are you? An actor? A director? A gangster . . . did you used to own this place?' They were both laughing and he was enjoying the game much more than she was.

'How about a gigolo? How's that?'

'That's garbage, that's what that is. Come on, dammit, tell me. First of all, how do you know Rita Hayworth that well?'

'I used to play tennis with her husband. And actually, I met them here.'

'As a waiter, right?' She was amused now. This anonymous soldier she had met in Guadalcanal had a lot of spirit to him. But she was dying to know more. She forced him to look her in the eye and attempted not to laugh. 'Now stop it. Here I am feeling sorry for you taking me out to dinner, embarrassed at having you see my house, and you know lots more important people than I do.'

'That's not what I hear, pretty one.'

'Oh really?' She blushed, and tossed her hair off her shoulders. 'What about Gable?' The blush grew deeper.

'Don't believe everything you read in the papers.'

'Just some things. And that I heard from some of my good friends.'

'I haven't seen him in years.' She attempted to look vague and Ward was too much of a gentleman to press it. And suddenly she looked into his eyes again. 'Now don't try and sidetrack me, dammit. Who are you?'

43

He leaned towards her and whispered in her ear, 'The Lone Ranger.' She laughed at him and the headwaiter approached their table with a huge bottle of champagne and the menus.

'Welcome home, Mr Thayer. It's good to have you back.'

'Thank you.' He ordered dinner for them both, toasted her with the champagne, and proceeded to tease her for the rest of the evening, until finally they sat in the open Ford outside her front door, and he earnestly took her hand in his own. 'Seriously, Faye, I am an unemployed soldier. I don't have a job, and didn't have one before I left. I don't even have an apartment any more. I gave it up when I was drafted. And they know me at Ciro's because I used to go there a lot before the war. I don't want to pretend I'm anyone important. I'm not. You're the star, and I've been nuts about you since the day I met you, but I'd be lying to you if I pretended to be someone I'm not. I'm just who you think I am, Ward Thayer . . . a man with no home, no job, and a borrowed car.'

She smiled gently at him. If it was true, she didn't give a damn. She hadn't had as nice an evening in years. She enjoyed being with him. He was bright and fun and good-looking. He danced like a dream and there was something warm and virile and exciting about him. He was knowledgeable on subjects she had never dreamt of, and he was different from all the men she'd known over the years. He didn't have that empty Hollywood superficiality about him although everyone certainly seemed to know him. 'I had a wonderful time, whoever you are.' It was almost two o'clock, and she didn't even want to think about how she would feel in the morning. She had to get up in less than three hours.

'Tomorrow night then?' Ward looked hopeful, and suddenly very young as she smiled at him and shook her head.

'I can't, Ward. I'm a working girl. I have to get up at a quarter to five every morning.'

'Until when?'

'Until we finish the picture.'

He looked crestfallen. Maybe she hadn't had a good time after all. And after two years spent dreaming of her, he desperately wanted her to have a good time when she was with him. He wanted to take her out every night, and wine her and dine her, and sweep her off her feet as never before. He didn't want to wait patiently on the sidelines while she finished her movie.

44

'Hell, I'm not going to wait that long. How about you get a good night's sleep tomorrow night, and we go out again after that?' He glanced at his watch. 'And I won't keep you out so late next time. I didn't realise how late it had got.' His eyes sought hers and his voice was deep and gentle. 'I had a wonderful time, Faye.' He was head over heels in love with her and he barely knew her. But he had been dreaming of her for the past two years, just like a star-struck kid, and he had promised himself he would look her up when he got home. And now he had, and he wasn't going to let her go until she was just as desperately in love with him. And what Faye didn't know was that what Ward Thayer wanted he got. Almost always.

And now his eyes pleaded with her and she couldn't resist him. 'All right. But you have to have me home by midnight or I turn into a pumpkin. Is that a deal?'

'Cross my heart, Cinderella . . .' He sat staring at her, aching to kiss her, but he didn't dare. It was too soon. He didn't want it to be just like every other date she'd had, with someone pawing her because of who she was. There was so much more to it than that for him. He got out of the car, and came around to open the door, and she stepped out lightly, her hand in his.

'I had such a good time, thank you.' She looked up at him and then he followed her up the pink marble steps. She was half tempted to invite him in for a drink, but then she'd never get any sleep at all, and she needed at least a few hours' sleep before she went back on the set. He stood in the doorway, looking down at her, feeling like the boy next door, and his lips gently brushed the top of her head, as he tilted her chin up with one hand so he could look into the exquisite emerald eyes again.

'I'll miss you in the next few days.'

And then, without even wanting to say the words, she nodded. 'I'll miss you too, Ward . . .' Just as she had missed him in the beginning, after Guadalcanal. He had a way of getting under her skin, after these few meetings, as no man ever had before. It would have frightened her, except that she was having too good a time to be frightened. Especially by Ward Thayer.

CHAPTER 4

Faye was on the set on time the next morning, and Pearl brought her three cups of stiff black coffee.

'My hair may stand up straight for the rest of the day after this.'

'Yeah, honey, but if you don't drink it all, you may fall asleep in that big dummy's arms during a love scene.'

'That might happen anyway.' The two women laughed. It was no secret between them, even on the second day on the set, that they didn't think much of her co-star. He had arrived late for work again, and had behaved like a complete horse's ass. His dressing room was too hot, and when they set up fans for him, he complained that there was a draught. He didn't like the hairdresser or the makeup man they had assigned him, and he was still complaining about the lighting and the wardrobe, when in desperation the director told them all to break for lunch. And when she went back to her dressing room, Pearl had the paper open for her. Hedda Hopper's column told her everything she had wanted to know the night before. She read the words carefully and sat staring at them for a moment afterwards, as though to digest them, as Pearl stood watching her, wondering what was in her mind.

'. . . The playboy heir to the Thayer Shipyard millions, Ward Cunningham Thayer IV, is safely home from the war, and back at his old haunts, we're told: Ciro's last night, where he got a warm welcome from Rita Hayworth and her hubbie. And it looks like there's a lovely new lady on his arm. Faye Price, with one Oscar and a lot of handsome beaux to her credit already, one of our favourites (and yours) among them, as we all know. In fact, we've been wondering if the lonely widower would come back for more now, but it looks like Thayer has the inside track. Fast work, Ward.

He's only been home for three days! Faye, by the way, is working on a new film with Vance Saint George, and director Louis Bernstein will have his hands full with that combination, no thanks to Faye, we might add . . . and good luck, Ward! In fact, good luck to you both. And will there be wedding bells in their future? Let's wait and see! . . .'

'Boy, they work fast, don't they?' She smiled up at Pearl, half amused, half intrigued . . . 'Playboy heir to the Thayer Shipyard millions' . . . Now she recognised the name of course, though it hadn't rung any bells for her before. Playboy heir . . . she wasn't sure if she liked that. She didn't want him to think she was after his money, nor did she intend to be a notch on the belt of a notorious playboy. Suddenly he seemed a little less appealing than he had the night before, a little less ordinary, less 'real'. He wasn't like the men in Grove City after all. In fact he was extremely different. It bothered her more than she wanted to admit, and after mentioning it only once, Pearl got the hint and didn't mention it again. It was a difficult day anyway. Vance Saint George made a nuisance of himself all day, and when they all left the set at six o'clock, Faye was totally exhausted. She left her makeup on, slipped into a pair of tan trousers and a beige cashmere sweater, the honey-coloured hair flying loose around her face, and she started the Lincoln Continental, just as she heard an insistent horn behind her. She glanced in the windscreen mirror and saw a familiar red car, and sighed to herself. She was not in the mood to talk to anyone, let alone a 'playboy millionaire'. She was a working girl, she'd had two hours' sleep the night before, and she wanted to be left alone, even by Ward Thayer. No matter how attractive he was, she had her own life to lead. And now he was just a 'playboy'.

He hopped out and slammed the door of the little red car and ran over to see her with a smile, his arms filled with white tuberoses and gardenias and a bottle of champagne. She shook her head and grinned at him, almost in despair.

'Don't you have anything else to do with your time, Mr Thayer, except chase poor actresses after they finish a day's work?'

'Listen, Cinderella, don't get excited. I know you must be dead. I just thought these might cheer you up on your way home . . . unless, of course, I could steal you away to the Beverly Hills Hotel for a drink . . . any chance of that?' He looked like a hopeful little boy and she almost groaned.

'Who's your press agent, by the way?' She sounded a little bit annoyed, and his eyes looked worried as he watched her.

'I suppose Rita did that. I'm sorry . . . do you mind very much?' It was no secret that Hedda Hopper disliked Orson, but she had always been fond of Rita. And Ward, but Faye didn't know that.

She smiled. It was impossible to be annoyed with him. He was so ingenuous and generous and obviously happy to see her, and she had to admit that, even knowing he was a playboy, he still had enormous appeal. There was something overwhelmingly attractive about him. There had been, even in Guadalcanal. And now, in his own element, he was even more so. He exuded confidence and sex appeal, and Faye was far from immune to him.

'At least now I know who you are.'

He shrugged with a grin. 'None of that junk means very much, or is very accurate, as you know.' He made no comment about the 'beaux' mentioned in the piece, but he smiled at her in a way that touched her heart. He had a knack for doing that. 'Shall we follow their suggestion, Faye?' There was something funny in his eyes and she didn't know him well enough yet to know if it was serious or playful.

'What was that?' She was so tired she couldn't think and he watched her eyes carefully as he answered.

'Remember the bit about wedding bells . . . we could surprise the hell out of them and get married.'

'What a great idea,' she mocked, glancing at her watch and squinting. 'Let's see . . . it's six twenty-five . . . how about at eight o'clock tonight, that way it could make the morning papers.'

'Great idea.' He ran around to the other side of her car, and before she could object, he hopped in beside her. 'Okay, let's get going, kid.' He sat back against the seat matter-of-factly, and grinned at her, and suddenly she was amused at him too. She forgot how tired she was. Actually, she was happy to see him. More so than she meant to be.

'You mean you expect *me* to drive? What kind of marriage is this?'

'You read the papers. It said I was a playboy. Playboys don't drive. They get driven around.'

'That's gigolos. That is *not* the same thing, Ward Thayer.' They

48

were both laughing, and he had moved closer to her on the seat, but she didn't mind it.

'Why can't a playboy be driven too? I'm tired. I had a hard time today. I had lunch with three friends and we drank four bottles of champagne.'

'My heart bleeds for you, you lazy dog. I've been working since six o'clock this morning and you've been drinking champagne all day!' She tried to sound angry but all she could do was laugh as an enormous limousine pulled up for Vance Saint George.

'That's what you need, Faye.' He almost sounded serious and she laughed at him.

'A car like that? Don't be ridiculous. I enjoy driving myself.'

'It's not ladylike.' He assumed a prim expression, and glanced at her. 'Besides, it's not suitable for the victim of a playboy.'

'I'm your victim, am I?'

'Hopefully you will be.' He looked at his watch and then back at her. 'Now what time are we getting married? You said eight o'clock . . . we'd better step on it . . . or would you rather just stop for a drink after all?'

She shook her head, but she was less convincing than she had been before. 'No. I'd rather go home, Mr Thayer. Remember me, I'm the working girl, and I happen to be exhausted.'

'I can't imagine why. You probably went to bed at ten o'clock last night.'

'Nope.' She crossed her arms and grinned at him. 'I had a date with a playboy millionaire.' Now that it was out in the open they were both having a good time with it. It all seemed totally absurd, like a joke on them both, and Faye refused to take it any more seriously than he did.

'No, you didn't!' He attempted to look shocked. 'Who?'

'I can't remember his name.'

'Was he nice?'

'More or less. Terrible liar of course, but they all are.'

'Handsome?"

She looked him square in the eye.'Very.'

'Now you've picked it up from him, lying again. Come on, I've got some friends you ought to meet.' He put an arm around her and she could smell the spicy fragrance of his after-shave, which was masculine and sexy. 'Let's go have a drink.

49

I promise I'll get you home early tonight.'

'I can't, Ward. I'd fall asleep on the table.'

'Don't worry. I'll pinch you.'

'Were you serious about meeting friends?' That was the last thing she wanted to do tonight. All she wanted to do was go home. She had some new lines to study in the script, and with Saint George performing so poorly she felt an obligation to work even harder to compensate for him. Otherwise, they'd make a botch of the whole movie.

Ward shook his head. 'I was joking about seeing friends. Just the two of us. I'd take you to my place, if you'd come, but I don't have one.' He laughed. 'That makes it a bit difficult.'

'I'll say.'

'I was going to stay at my parents' place, but it's all closed up and it's too damn big. I've got a cottage at the Beverly Hills Hotel until I find something I like, so I'm afraid all I can offer you is the hotel bar, for the moment.' It would have been highly improper to suggest coming to his cottage for a drink, and he wouldn't have considered suggesting that to her. She wasn't that kind of girl, no matter how big a film star she was, or how many beaux she'd had. There was still more than a hint of the well-brought-up young lady about her, and he liked it that way. The papers weren't far off the mark as to his intentions. 'So what do you say? Half an hour and then I'll take you home. Okay?'

'Okay, okay . . . my God, you drive a hard bargain. I'm glad I don't work for you, Ward Thayer.'

'Ah, my little chickadee,' he pinched her cheek, 'that could be arranged. Now slide over and I'll drive.' He hopped out and got back in behind the wheel.

'Won't you need your car?'

'I'll take a cab and come back for it after I take you home.'

'That's not too much trouble for you, Ward?''

He looked at her, amused. 'Not at all, little one. Why don't you put your head back and rest on the way to the hotel? You look tired.' She liked the tone of his voice, the look in his eyes . . . the feel of his hand as he touched hers . . . she watched him through half-closed eyes as they drove along. 'How's work?'

'Vance Saint George is an awful pain in the neck. I don't know how he's got as far as he has.' Ward knew, but he didn't say anything to her. He had slept with everything that moved, woman or man, and collected favours from everyone in town, but it had to catch up with him someday.

'Is he any good?'

'He would be, if he'd stop worrying about draughts and how much makeup he wears and studied his lines for a change. It's difficult to work with him, he's never prepared, and it delays us for hours.' She sat up and looked out as they neared the hotel.

'I hear you're awfully professional, Miss Price.' He looked admiringly at her.

She smiled. 'Who told you that?'

'I saw Louis B. Mayer at lunch today. He said you're the finest actress in town, and of course I agreed.'

'A lot you know.' She laughed. 'You've been gone for four years. You've missed all my best films.' She sniffed primly and he laughed. He was happy with her. Happier than he'd been in years.

'Yeah, but don't forget, I saw you in Guadalcanal.' He glanced over at her tenderly and touched her hand again. 'How many people can boast of that?' and then suddenly they both laughed, thinking of the thousands of troops she'd entertained. 'All right, never mind . . .' He pulled up in front of the pink hotel, and jumped out, as a doorman rushed to his aid, touching his hat and murmuring Ward's name. And he went to open Faye's door himself, as she stepped out and looked down at her slacks.

'Can I go in like this?'

'Faye Price?' He grinned. 'You could go in wearing a bathing suit and they'd kiss your feet.'

'Would they now?' She smiled at him. 'Or is that just because I'm with Ward Thayer?'

'What a lot of nonsense that is.' But as usual, the headwaiter gave him the best table. This time, three people asked her for her autograph, and when they left the hotel an hour later, much to her dismay someone had called the press, and a flashbulb exploded almost in their faces.

'Damn. I hate that stuff.' She looked annoyed as they took refuge in her car, and the photographer had followed them all the way. 'Why can't they leave us alone? Why do they have to make a thing of it?' She liked her privacy and the same thing had happened to her before. And this time she wasn't even involved with Ward yet. It was only their second date.

'You're big news, kid. It can't be helped.' He wondered then if she objected to being paired off with him; maybe there was someone else. He hadn't thought of that before, but it made perfect sense. And as he drove her home, he brought it up gingerly. 'It won't . . . it won't mess up anything else for you, will it, Faye?' He looked concerned, and she smiled as she saw the worried look in his eyes.

'Not the way you mean. But I don't like to go around advertising how I spend my private hours.' She still looked annoyed and also tired.

'Then we'll have to be discreet about where we go.' She nodded, but they both seemed to forget the vow the following night when he picked her up in his own car, a custom-built Duesenberg he had bought before the war and had left up on blocks in his garage. It was the car the doorman at Ciro's had been referring to, and Faye could see why. It was the most beautiful car she'd ever seen.

He took her to the Mocambo that night, and Charlie Morrison, the grey-haired owner, had run up and almost kissed Ward as he hugged him and pumped his arm. Like everyone else, he was ecstatic over Ward's safe return, and another mammoth bottle of champagne appeared as Faye glanced around the room, wondering who was there. She had been there before of course, and it was the most glamorous place in town, with an entire wall of rare, live birds flying around, while couples danced, and big film stars drifted in and out, just as she did now with Ward.

'I don't suppose our being here will go unnoticed tonight. Charlie may call the papers himself, you know.' Ward looked concerned. 'Do you mind very much, Faye?' He suspected she hadn't been pleased with the photograph that had appeared on page four of the L.A. *Times* that day, showing them leaving the Beverly Hills Hotel after cocktails the night before and running for the safety of her car.

But she only smiled at him. 'I get the feeling, Ward, that you don't know how to be invisible.' They both knew it was the truth. 'And actually, I'm not really sure I care. Neither of us has anything to hide. It would have been nice to maintain our privacy, but it looks like that isn't in the cards for either of us.' She had thought about it a lot the night before, and decided what the hell, they had nothing to hide.

'I've never worried about it much before.' He sipped the sparkling wine. He always drank gallons of champagne, it seemed to be almost a trademark with him. 'That's just the way things are' ... if you're the heir to a shipyard fortune, she thought, and drive a custom-built Duesenberg ... And suddenly she laughed.

'Little did I know, when I met that nice young lieutenant in Guadalcanal, that he was spoiled rotten to the core, and used to hanging out in a lot of fancy watering holes and drinking rivers of champagne ...' She teased him and he didn't seem to mind, it was all true, yet there was a great deal more to him. In some ways, he knew that the war had done him good. They were the hardest four years of his life, and he had proved something to himself, that he could survive almost anything: hardship, danger, misery, discomfort. For all four years, he had never once traded on his connections or his name, although of course there were those who knew who he was.

And then there had been the girl he had married. At first, he had thought he would never recover when she'd been killed. It had been a reality he had never faced before, and a grief almost beyond bearing. And now there was Faye with all her magic and her glamour, and underlying it her keen sense of reality, and her enormous talent. He was glad Faye hadn't known who he was at first. She might have felt differently if she had, might have thought he was frivolous. And he was at times, he liked to have fun. But he was capable of seriousness too, as Faye was beginning to discover. There were so many dimensions to the man, as there were to her. And together they were quite a combination. They each liked the other for what they were, not for what they had. They were a good match in a lot of ways, as Hedda Hopper and Louella Parsons both quickly noticed.

'What are your lifetime goals, Miss Price?' Ward teased her over their fourth glass of champagne, although he seemed to be feeling no effect from it, but Faye knew she'd have to slow down or she'd get drunk, and that was something she never did. 'What do you want to be doing ten years from now?' He seemed serious as he asked and she knit her brows and looked at him. It was an interesting question.

'Do you mean it?'

'Of course.'

'I'm not sure. When I think about things like that, I always see two possibilities, like two roads with two very different destinations, and I'm never sure which one I'll take.'

'And where do those two roads go?' He was intrigued by what she said, he was intrigued by everything about her now, even more so than he had been before.

'One road represents all this,' she looked briefly around the room before glancing back at him, 'the same people, places, things . . . my career . . . more films . . . more fame,' she was being very honest with him, 'more of the same, I guess . . .' Her voice trailed off.

'And the other road?' He gently took her hand. 'Where does that one go, Faye?' The room faded around them as he spoke and she looked into his eyes. There was something there she wanted very much, and she wasn't sure yet what it was. 'The other road . . .?'

'It goes to a very different place . . . a husband . . . children . . . a life far, far from all this . . . more like the life I had as a little girl. I can't really imagine it any more, but I know the possibility is there, if I wanted to make that choice. But that's a hard choice to make.' She looked honestly at him.

'You don't think you could have both?'

She shook her head. 'I doubt it very much. The two don't mix. Look at the way I work. I'm up at five, gone by six. I don't come home until seven or eight o'clock at night. What man would put up with that? And I've seen Hollywood marriages come and go for years. We all know what that's like. That's not what I want if I settle down.'

'What do you want, Faye . . . if you settle down, I mean?'

She smiled at him. It was a funny conversation for them to have on their third date. But she was beginning to feel she knew him well. They had seen each other three times in three days, and something strange had happened to them in Guadalcanal so long ago. It was as though a bond had formed and strengthened silently over the years, and it was still between them now, holding them fast, bringing them closer than they might have been had they just met. She thought about his words again.

'I guess I'd want stability, a marriage that would last for years and years, with a man I'd love and respect, and children of course.'

'How many?' He grinned at her and she laughed again.

'Oh, twelve at least.' She was teasing now.

'As many as all that ... good lord ... how about five or six?'

'That might do.'

'Sounds like a good life to me.'

'It does to me too, but I still can't imagine it.' She sighed.

'Is your career that important to you?'

'I'm not sure. I've worked awfully hard at it for six years. That might be difficult to give up ... or maybe not ...' Suddenly she laughed. 'Enough films like the one I'm working on and maybe I'd give it all up like that.' She snapped her fingers and then he took her hands in his again.

'I'd like to see you give it all up one day.' His face was suddenly so serious that it startled her.

'Why?'

'Because I'm in love with you, and I like that second road you described. That's the fulfilling one. The first road is a road to loneliness. But I think you already know that.' She nodded slowly and stared at him. Was he proposing to her? He couldn't be. She wasn't sure what to say, and slowly she drew her hand away.

'You just got home, Ward. Everything looks different to you right now. You're going to be very emotional for a while ...' She wanted to discourage him. It was only right. He was moving too quickly ... for heaven's sake, she barely knew him, and yet it felt like a time which might never come again, and they were both still under the spell of his surviving the war. The magic of wartime was still there for them both, and yet this was very real. And very special.

He retrieved her hand again and kissed her fingertips. 'I'm serious, Faye. I've never felt like this in my life. And I knew it the minute we met in Guadalcanal. I just didn't know what to say to you there. For all I knew I'd be dead the next day. But I'm not, and I'm home, and you're the most incredible woman I've ever known ...'

'How can you say a thing like that?' She looked upset and he wanted to hold her in his arms, but he didn't dare, not in the middle of the restaurant, with the photographers possibly lurking nearby, and everyone anxious to report what they'd seen. 'You don't even know me, Ward. You saw me perform for two hours in Guadalcanal ... we talked for half an hour afterwards ... we've seen each other twice since you got back ...' She wanted to discourage him now, before it was too late but she wasn't even sure why. It's just that it all seemed to be going so fast, and yet she had this incredible feeling about him, as though she could have walked off into the sunset with him that night, hand in hand, and everything would have been all right for the rest of their lives. But it didn't happen like that. Did it? It couldn't ... or maybe it did ... maybe that was 'the real thing' that everyone talks about. 'It's too soon, Ward.'

'Too soon for what?' He looked matter-of-fact. 'Too soon to tell you I'm in love with you? Well, maybe it is. But the fact is, Faye, I am. I've been in love with you for years.'

'Then it's an illusion.'

'No, it's not. You are exactly who I sensed you were. You are smart and realistic and practical. You are modest and warm and funny and beautiful. You don't give a damn who the press agents say you are. As far as you're concerned, you like what you do, you work hard. You are the most decent woman I've ever met, and what's more you're good at what you do, because of all of the above ... and if I don't drag you out of here and kiss you in the next five minutes, I'm going to go nuts, Faye Price, so just shut up, or I'll kiss you right here!'

Her eyes were worried, but she couldn't help smiling at him. 'What if you figure out that you hate me in six months?'

'Why should I?'

'I probably have habits you'd detest. Ward, I'm telling you, you don't know who I am. And I don't know you.'

'Fine. Then we'll get to know each other.' But he had already tipped his hand to her and he didn't care. 'But I'm going to glue myself to you and drive you nuts till you say yes.' He looked completely satisfied with what he had just said, and drained his glass of champagne with a contented look, and then set it down and looked at her. ' All right with you?'

'Would it make a difference if I said no?'

'Not a bit.' It was the grin she had already come to love, the mischievous spark in the deep blue eyes. He was difficult to resist, and she wasn't even sure she wanted to. She just wanted them both to be sensible. She had had romances with other men before, though admittedly none was quite like him. But she didn't want to be one of those women the press wrote about constantly, in love with this one, engaged to that one, and in the end it all amounted to their being used up, like tired old Hollywood whores. She still cared about things like that, which was another thing he liked about her. In fact, he was convinced that he liked everything, and she suspected the same about him, but she wasn't about to give in, certainly not after three days.

'You're impossible.'

'I know.' He looked pleased with himself, and then suddenly concerned as he leaned toward her. 'Does it bother you that I don't work?' Maybe that was it, the work ethic was bothering her.

'Not if you can afford not to, I suppose. But don't you get bored, Ward?' She was intrigued with what he did with his spare time. She worked so hard, and had for years, it was difficult to imagine just playing tennis and going out to lunch. It sounded deadly to her, but he certainly didn't seem unhappy with it.

'Faye.' He sat back and looked at her. 'I love my life. I've had a good time ever since I was a kid. And when my father died, I told myself that I would never work myself into the ground like he did. He was forty-six when he died, of a heart attack. My mother was forty-three. I think she just worried herself to death about him. They never took a minute to do what they wanted to, to have a good time, hell, they never even spent any time with me. And I swore to myself that when I had kids one day, and even long before that, I wouldn't live like that. There's no reason to. I couldn't spend all that money if I tried, to be vulgar about it,' which he seldom was, as Faye knew, but he was being honest with her and she valued that. It gave her a good insight into him. 'My grandfather did the same damn thing, died at fifty-six of overwork. So what? Who cares how hard you worked when you die. I want to enjoy life while I'm here and I am enjoying it. Let them say what they want to. Let them call me what they want. I'm not going to drop dead from a heart attack at forty-five, or be a stranger to my wife and kids. I'm going to be right there, enjoying life with them, knowing who they are, and letting them know me. I never even knew who my father was, Faye. He was a stranger to me. Like you, I see life divided in two roads. The life they lived that I don't ever want to live, and the one I'm living now, and this one suits me just fine. And I hope to hell it doesn't bother you.' He looked deep into her eyes and took a deep breath. 'Of course, if you want me to, I could always get a job.'   She looked at him in shock before she answered. He was serious about all this. But how could he be after just three days? 'You don't have to get a job for me, Ward. What right could I possibly have to ask you to do that?' And if he could afford his lifestyle, why should he do anything differently? He wasn't hurting anyone with the way he lived. She looked at him and spoke softly. 'I can't believe you're serious about all this.' Their eyes held for a long time as he nodded, and then silently he led her to the floor and they danced for a long time, without saying a word. And when he led her back to the table, he watched her, wondering if he had upset her and praying that he hadn't.

'Are you all right, Faye?' She was suddenly very pensive, and he was concerned that he had frightened her by telling her what was on his mind.

'I don't know.' She looked at him honestly. 'I think you've taken my breath away with all that.'

'Good.' He put an arm around her and squeezed her shoulders, admiring again the navy satin backless dress she wore. She had a flair for dressing with subtle sensuality in a way that pleased him immensely, and he was dying to buy her clothes and jewellery and furs. For the rest of the evening, they kept to lighter subjects, Faye trying to pretend to herself that he hadn't bared his heart already, and he seemed even happier than before to know that she knew what he felt for her. After dinner, he drove her back to her place, and this time she invited him for a glass of cognac, although she was almost afraid to. She knew his thoughts now, and she wondered if it was dangerous to let him inside. And then as she poured his drink, she laughed at herself. Hell, he wasn't going to rape her. She handed him the glass and he wondered at her smile.

'You're so lovely, Faye ... even more beautiful than I remembered.'

'You need to have your eyes checked.' His praise embarrassed her at times, it was so lavish, and his adoration of her was so clearly written in his eyes. He was a carefree, happy man, with few disappointments and no current worries, and he was clearly very much in love. 'What are you doing tomorrow?' She said it just to have something to say and he laughed.

'I'll tell you one thing I'm not doing. I'm not working.' In some ways, he was shameless about it and it amused her. He had certainly told her all he felt on the subject at dinner, but it was almost as if he were proud of not working. He didn't even mind being called 'the playboy millionaire'. 'I wish you weren't working on a film just now, Faye. We could go out and play.' She could just imagine the trouble they would get into. Lazy afternoons on the beach, days of expensive shopping, maybe a trip or two. She had to admit, the prospect was almost appealing, but she wouldn't even let herself dream about that yet. 'I'd like to take you to the Casino at Avalon Bay one of these nights, but we'd have to spend the night on Catalina Island. I don't suppose you'll have a weekend off, will you?'

Sadly, she shook her head. 'Not till the film is over.' She smiled at him over their cognac, smelling the heady aroma, and thinking of all the fun things they had in store.

'There are a lot of places I'd like to take you . . . Paris . . . Venice . . . Cannes . . . Now that the war is over, we can go anywhere we want.'

She laughed at his words and shook her head as she set down her glass. 'You really are spoiled, my friend, aren't you? One of us has to work at least. I can't just go off halfway around the world.'

'Why not?'

'The studio wouldn't let me. After this film, my agent is going to renew my contract, and I'm sure they'll keep me pretty busy for a long, long time.'

Ward's eyes lit up like Christmas and he stared at Faye. 'You mean after this film, your contract is over?' She nodded her head, amused at his reaction. 'Hallelujah, baby! Why don't you take a year off?'

'Are you crazy? I might as well give it up for good, Ward. I can't just do that.'

'I don't know why not. You're one of the biggest stars they've got, for heaven's sake. You don't think you could take a year off and pick up exactly where you left off?'

'I doubt it.'

'Don't believe that for a second, Faye Price. You could walk out and come back any time you wanted.'

'That's quite a risk, Ward. I wouldn't play games like that with my career.'

He watched her with serious eyes. Things were happening much faster than either of them had expected. 'It's the fork in the road again, isn't it, Faye? . . . Which road do you really want to follow? The old one? Or the other one we talked about . . . marriage and babies . . . stability . . . and a real life . . .' She walked away from him and stared out into her garden, saying nothing, and when she turned around, he saw that there were tears in her eyes. But more than anything she looked angry, and he was startled.

'I want you to stop that, Ward.'

'Stop what?' He hadn't intended to upset her and he was shocked at her reaction.

'Stop torturing me with this nonsense. We hardly know each other. We're strangers. For all I know, by next week, you'll be involved with some little starlet, or Rita Hayworth, or someone else. I've worked like a dog to get where I am, and I'm not ready to give it up yet. Maybe I never will be. But I'm sure not going to do it for some half-crazy ex-GI fresh off the boat from the war, who thinks he's been in love with me for two years because he talked to me for a while when I was on tour. You don't throw your whole life away for that, Ward Thayer. And I don't give a damn how rich you are, or how carefree, or if you've never worked a day in your life. I have. I've worked every day of my life since I turned eighteen, and I don't intend to stop now. I got here, and I'm staying here, until I know it's safe to walk away from it.' He was interested in the work she had chosen . . . 'safe' . . . and she was right. She had worked hard to get where she wanted, and now that she was there she would have been crazy to throw it all away. But in time he would show her that he meant everything he was saying . . . if she would listen. 'I don't want to hear that stuff any more.' The tears were spilling down her cheeks now. 'If you want to see me, fine. Take me to dinner. Dance with me. Make me laugh. But don't ask me to throw away my career for a stranger, however much I might like him, however much I may care . . .' and with that a sob broke from her and she turned her back to him again, her shoulders shaking in the exquisite evening dress by Trigère. He went quickly towards her and put his arms around her, holding her close to him, her back against his chest, his face nestled in her silky hair.

'You'll always be safe with me, babe . . . always . . . I promise. But I understand what you're saying. I didn't mean to scare you. I just got so excited . . . I couldn't help it.' He turned her slowly to face him, and his heart tore when he saw her face wet with tears. 'Oh Faye . . .' He crushed her to him, and then crushed his lips on hers, and instead of pulling back, every inch of her reached towards him. She needed the comfort he had to offer, needed something she saw in him, wanted him more than she had ever wanted any man before.

They kissed for what seemed like hours, his hands caressing her back, his lips seeking her mouth, her face, her eyes, her hands on his neck, and then touching his face as she kissed him, feeling relief from the fear and anger she had felt only moments before. She was crazy about this man, and she was not yet sure why. Except that perhaps she believed what he told her, that she would be safe with him . . . always . . . he offered her a protection she had never had. Not with her parents during the Depression, or on her own, or with the other men she had known. And it wasn't just the money. It was his outlook, his lifestyle, his certainty that he lived in a perfect, carefree world. And it was obvious that he adored her. They had to tear themselves from each other an hour later, in order to avoid something that neither of them wanted yet. He knew that Faye was not yet ready, and would always have regretted succumbing to him so soon. And he had to leave her, for fear that he might lose control. He wanted to take her on the floor of her study, in front of the fire, or upstairs in the silky white bedroom, or in her bathtub . . . or on the stairs . . . anywhere . . . his whole body keened for her, but he knew he couldn't have her so soon. And when they met the next night, the agony was even sweeter, as their lips met instantly, and they spent an hour in his Duesenberg, beyond her gates, kissing like two children, and then laughing as he drove her to the Biltmore Bowl.

There was a big party being held there, and the photographers went wild when they saw him. But this time, Faye didn't seem to resist it. In four brief days, she knew that there was no running away from Ward Thayer. She didn't know where their romance would lead, but she wasn't going to fight it any more. She had worn her floor-length white fox coat to the party, over a black and white satin gown. She looked absolutely exquisite as they walked in, with her hand tucked into Ward's arm. She looked up at him warmly for an instant, and he smiled at her, just as the photographers approached them, and they had a field day with Ward and Faye for the rest of the night. But as promised, he got her home early. The late nights were beginning to wear on her in the morning. But Vance Saint George arrived on the set so late every day that she usually had time to take a nap.

'Did you have fun?' He looked down at her, as she rested her head on his shoulder while they drove home. 'I thought it wasn't a bad party.' It had been to promote a new film, and all the big names had been there.

'I thought it was fun too.' She was beginning to enjoy their nightly outings even more than she had at first. 'If I didn't have this damn film to do, I could really have some fun.'

He laughed at her and tugged at a lock of the golden hair. 'See, that's why I told you not to renew your contract the other night. This is fun, isn't it?'

'It's habit-forming. But I'm a working girl, Ward.' She tried to look at him disapprovingly, but they both laughed.

'That's your choice, but you can choose differently any time you decide to.' He looked meaningfully at her and she didn't answer, and when they reached her house, he kissed her passionately on the lips again, and this time he had to fight himself not to carry her upstairs. 'I'm going.' He said it in a voice of anguished desperation, and she kissed him once more in the doorway. The delicious torture went on for weeks, until finally late one Sunday afternoon in October, a month after their courtship had begun, they were walking in her garden, talking about the war, and other subjects. She had the afternoon off from shooting, and Arthur and Elizabeth were off for the weekend. There was a feeling of peace between them as they wandered. She had begun telling him about her childhood, her parents, her desperation to leave Pennsylvania, the initial excitement of modelling in New York, and then finally the boredom, and then she confessed that at times it was still that way for her now.

'It's as though there's something more I could be doing . . . with my mind . . . not just my face or my lines. I don't want to just memorise other people's lines for the rest of my life.'

It was an interesting confession and it intrigued him. 'What would you rather do, Faye? Write?' As usual, he was aching for her body, but there was nothing he could do about it. At least they were alone for a change. She wasn't rushing to or from work, Arthur wasn't hovering in the doorway with tray in hand, and they weren't going to a party. They were growing hungry for time alone and she had offered to cook him dinner that night. They had spent a lovely afternoon, lazing around the pool, and then walking in the garden. 'Would you like to write a screenplay?' He turned to her and smiled at her expression. She looked frightened at the thought as she shook her head.

'I don't think I could do that.'

'What then?'

'Directing . . . one day . . .' She barely breathed the words. It was quite an ambition for a woman, and he didn't know of any who had directed films before.

'Do you suppose anyone would let you?'

She smiled and shook her head. 'I doubt it. Nobody believes a woman could do that. But I know I could. Sometimes when I watch Saint George on the set these days, I just want to scream, I know what I want to have him do . . . how I would direct him . . . the instructions I would give him. He's such a simple-minded fool, you have to bring it down to the kind of emotions he can relate to, and believe me,' she looked painfully at Ward and rolled her eyes, 'they're damn few.'

Ward smiled at her and picked a bright red flower to tuck behind her ear. 'Have I told you lately that I think you're amazing?'

'Not for at least an hour.' She smiled appreciatively up at him. 'You spoil me, you know. No one's ever been as good to me as you are.' She looked genuinely happy and he couldn't resist the urge to tease her. They had a comfortable, easy way about them that they both enjoyed. 'Not even Gable?'

'Stop that.' She made a face at him and ran past him, as he chased her, and then suddenly he caught up with her and grabbed her, and they were kissing in an arbour, and suddenly all the breathlessness they both felt overwhelmed them, and Ward felt he couldn't bear to take his hands or lips from her again. It was almost painful when at last he tore himself away.

'It's not easy, you know.' He looked agonised as they walked slowly back to the house and she nodded. It wasn't easy for her either. But she didn't want to make a mistake with Ward. He had made his intentions clear to her right from the beginning, and it was too dangerous to play games with that. He wanted everything from her, her life, her career, her body, her children. He wanted her to give everything up for him ... and at times it was almost tempting to her. Lately she had even told her agent not to rush into the next contract, although he thought she was crazy. But she said she needed time to think, and it was growing more and more difficult to think when Ward was near her.

'You make me crazy too, you know,' she whispered as they went up the pink marble steps into her study, but it looked so bleak there, so stuffy and much too formal. She went to make them both a cup of tea and then suggested they move to her sitting room upstairs. It was small and warm and cosy, and Ward lit a fire, although they didn't really need it. But it was pretty, and they sat side by side admiring the blaze. 'I've had an offer to do a wonderful film,' she told him, but there was no excitement in her voice as she said it, and she wasn't sure she wanted to do it at all. In fact her agent had been furious at her indecision.

'Who's in it?'

'No one yet, but they have some awfully good possibilities.'

'Do you want to do it?' He didn't sound upset, he was only asking but she took a long time to answer as she stared into the fire.

'I just don't know.' She looked up at him, feeling contented and at peace with life. 'You make me awfully lazy, Ward.'

'What's wrong with that?' He nuzzled his face into her neck, and began to kiss her with one hand lazily sculpting her breast. She gently touched his hand, wanting to push away his fingers, but it felt too good. She had no desire to push him away, hadn't since they'd met, and yet it seemed wiser ... wiser ... suddenly all she could feel were those delicious burning fingers, their mouths met, and a passion rose in them both that was difficult to quell. They never seemed to come up for air, as her skirt rose slowly past her knees, and his hand found her thighs. Her whole body trembled as his hand moved up, and then suddenly he moved away. Breathless, anguished, he looked at her, and held her face in both his hands. 'Faye ... I can't ... I've got to go ...' He couldn't stop himself any longer, he wanted her too badly, had for much too long. He looked at her with tears in his eyes, and then he kissed her, just once more, and it was the moment that decided both their futures. The way she kissed him told him that she didn't want him to go, and then silently she stood up and led him across the hall to the spectacular white bedroom, and without waiting a moment longer, he laid her across the white fox-covered bed. He peeled her clothes from her, devouring her flesh, murmuring to her in whispers, as her fingers gently disentangled him from his clothes, and moments later they lay side by side, naked, enveloped in the rich white fur, and then suddenly they were engulfed in each other's bodies, and neither of them thought of resisting or being sensible any more. Faye shouted out for him with a passion that overwhelmed her, and Ward lay within her, his excitement far beyond control. They spent themselves in what would have looked like agony to strangers, and was the purest passion either of them had ever known. And as she lay silent at last, in the circle of his arms, the white fur bedspread soft beneath them, he looked down at her with a love he had never known before.

'Faye, I love you more than life itself.'

'Don't say that . . .' His passion frightened her sometimes. He loved her so much . . . what if one day it stopped? She couldn't have stood it. She knew that now.

'Why not? It's true.'

'I love you too.' She looked up at him with a sated smile, and he bent to kiss her once more, and it amazed him how quickly his body begged for her again, and how hungrily she reached for him, and they made love in her bed for hours, never able to get enough, to make up for the years when they had done without each other. It was as though they had waited for this for much, much too long.

'Now what, my love?' He sat on the edge of her bed at midnight, smiling at her as she rose slowly, stretched, and smiled down on the man she so richly loved.

'How about a bath?' And then suddenly she remembered, and covered her mouth with a look of horror. 'Oh my God, I forgot to give you dinner.'

'No, you didn't.' He pulled her towards him again. 'This suited me just fine.' She blushed faintly and he smoothed the long, blonde hair back from her face, and then followed her to the white marble bath. She filled the tub with warm soapy water, and they slid in together, his feet tickling her in subtle places, as he nibbled on her toes. 'I asked you a question a little while ago.'

She frowned slightly, unable to remember. 'What was it?'

'I asked you, "now what?".'

She smiled at him, mysteriously. 'And I said, "a bath".'

'Cute. But you know what I mean. I don't just want to have an affair with you, Faye.' He looked faintly troubled, and at the same time extremely pleased with the evening they had just spent together in her bed. 'Although, I must admit, it's tempting. But I think you deserve more.' She said nothing. She only watched him, her heart beating faster. 'Will you marry me, Miss Price?'

'No.' She suddenly stood up, and he looked shocked. It was a rapid refusal as she stepped out of the tub.

'Where are you going?'

She turned to look at him, magnificent in her naked beauty in the centre of the white marble bathroom. 'I will not tell my children that their father proposed to me in the bathtub. How can I tell them something like that?' He began laughing as he looked at her in amusement.

'No problem.' He leapt out of the tub, swept her up in his arms, and deposited her soaking wet on the white fox bedspread once more, as he knelt at her feet and looked up at her with blatant adoration. 'Will you please marry me, my love?'

She grinned at him, impish, happy, yet at the same time terrified at what she was doing. But she knew she had no choice now. It was not just because she had slept with him; but it was what she wanted, 'the other road' . . . the good life . . . marriage and babies with him . . . and with him, she was brave enough to do it. For her, it meant giving everything up, but she didn't care. 'Yes.' It was the merest whisper, and he crushed his lips on hers before she could change her mind, and when they came up for air they were both laughing with delight and excitement.

'Do you really mean it, Faye?' He had to be sure . . . had to . . . before he went totally berserk and gave her the world.

'Yes. I do . . . yes . . . yes . . . yes . . .yes!'

'I love you. Oh God, I love you.' He crushed her to him, and she laughed as he held her close to him. She was happier than she had ever been before, and then suddenly he looked at her, grinning, his blond hair tousled, his eyes the purest sapphires as he smiled. 'Tell me something, do you have to tell your children what you were wearing when I proposed? If you do, you're in big trouble, Mrs Thayer.'

'Oh dear . . . I didn't think of that.' She laughed as he held her, and a moment later, he was beside her on the bed again. It was hours before they reached the bathtub again, and they had to fill it with more hot water. By then it was almost four o'clock in the morning and Faye knew she wouldn't sleep before she went to work. Instead, they sat in the bathtub for an hour, talked about their plans, their lives, their secret, when they would make the announcement. They giggled over how shocked everyone would be, not that they were getting married, but that she was giving up her career. And as she said it, she felt a tremor, but it was more excitement than panic. She realised now that secretly, deep within, she had thought about this a great deal. She had always known what Ward wanted from her, and how much he wanted to give her. She regretted nothing now, and suspected that she never would. What was she giving up? A career she had enjoyed, but she had already reached the summit. She had won one Oscar, considerable acclaim, and had made a dozen interesting films. It was time to go now. She had another life to live. A life she wanted more than making films. She lay back in the bathtub, smiling at her future husband, feeling something she had never felt before. A confidence, a peace, a certainty that she had chosen the right road.

'You're sure you won't regret it?' He looked faintly worried, but more happy than anything else. He wanted to start looking for houses with her that afternoon, but she pointed out to him that she had to work, for another month or so at least.

'I won't regret it for a minute.' She was absolutely certain.

'When do you think you'll finish this film?'

'I would think by the first of December if Saint George doesn't screw things up too badly before.'

'Then we'll get married on December fifteenth. Where shall we honeymoon? Mexico? Hawaii? Europe? Where do you want to go?' He beamed at her, and her heart swelled with the love she felt for him.

'How did I get lucky enough to find you anyway?' She had never been as happy in her life as she was now. With him.

'I'm the lucky one.'

67

They kissed and reluctantly left the bath, and a few minutes later, she went downstairs. She made coffee for them both, and brought it up, reminding herself to clear up the bedroom and to leave the empty cups in her sitting room when they left, and he drove her to work in the Duesenberg, as they both almost shouted with delight. The next two months were going to be difficult for them, but they would have a lot to do ... a lot to look forward to ... so much to plan for their future.

BEVERLY HILLS

CHAPTER 5

The wedding took place at the Hollywood Presbyterian Church on North Gower Street, near Hollywood Boulevard, and Faye slowly walked down the aisle in an exquisite ivory satin gown. It was encrusted with the tiniest of pearls in delicate designs and she moved with measured grace, her head held high, her hair piled into an ivory satin crown encrusted with the same miniature pearls, a whisper of a veil floating around her for what seemed like miles. Her hair looked like spun gold as it cascaded over the sides of the pearl-encrusted crown, and around her neck sparkled a diamond choker the height of her swanlike neck. It had been a wedding present from Ward, and a favourite piece of his maternal grandmother's.

Faye had walked down the aisle on the arm of her agent, and Harriet Fielding had come to be matron of honour. Faye had overcome her ferocious protests and her old friend was there, with tears streaming down her face as Abe handed Faye to Ward at the altar. The young couple had beamed at each other, and been more beautiful than any two people in a film. And when they emerged from the church arm in arm, there had been hundreds of well-wishers standing outside to greet them. Fans throwing handfuls of rose petals and rice, young girls screaming for Faye's autograph, women crying, and even men smiling tenderly as they watched them. The couple disappeared into the new Duesenberg Ward had bought several weeks before to celebrate the wedding, as a kind of nuptial gift to himself and his bride, and they drove on to the reception at Biltmore, where they were met by Abe, Harriet, and four hundred friends they had invited. It was the happiest day of Faye's life, and the papers had a field day with the pictures.

But there was even more coverage three weeks later, when they returned from their honeymoon in Acapulco. Faye made the announcement she had decided on two months before, but she had wisely decided to keep the news to herself until then, and even Abe was shocked when she told him. The headlines that night told it all in few words: 'Faye Price Gives Up Career for Millionaire Husband'. It was blunt, and the piece was overdone, but in essence that was her decision, not so much because of Ward's 'millions', although obviously that eliminated any need for her to work, but she felt strongly that she had 'done it', and now she wanted to devote herself entirely to her husband and her future children. And Ward certainly wasn't complaining about her decision. He was thrilled to have her all to himself, to lie in bed with him until noon, make love any time they wanted, eat breakfast on trays in their room, and even lunch if they so desired, dance all night at Ciro's or Mocambo or the homes of their friends. And Ward was having a wonderful time shopping with her, buying her fabulous new clothes to add to her already copious wardrobe. Her three fur coats looked meagre in comparison to the wonders he bought her, two floor-length sable coats in slightly different shades and styles, a fabulous silver fox, a red fox, a silver raccoon; she had every imaginable fur, and more jewellery than she thought she could wear in a lifetime. A day hardly went by that he didn't disappear for an hour or two and return with a box from a fur shop or dress store or jeweller. It was like Christmas every day of the year, and Faye was overwhelmed at his generosity and the love he lavished on her constantly.

'You have to stop this, Ward!' She was laughing as she sat naked in the new red fox coat with a string of enormous pearls around her neck and nothing else on the exquisite young body he adored.

'Why?' He sat down to watch her with a happy grin and a glass of champagne. He seemed to drink rivers of it, but he never appeared drunk so Faye didn't really care. And she smiled tenderly at him now.

'You don't have to do all this. I would love you in a grass shack, if we had to wear newspapers to keep warm.'

'What a disgusting thought . . .' He made a grimace and then squinted as he looked at the long, shapely limbs. 'On second thoughts . . . you might look fabulous wearing the sports page, and nothing else.'

72

'Silly.' She ran over to kiss him again and he pulled her onto his lap and set down his glass. 'Can you really afford all this, Ward? We shouldn't be spending all this money, with neither of us working.' She still felt faintly guilty about no longer going to work, but it was so heavenly spending all her time with Ward that she never really missed her career. As she had told the papers when she retired, she had 'done it'. But she looked at Ward with concerned eyes. He had spent an absolute fortune on her in the three months since they'd been married.

'Darling, we can spend ten times this.' It was a generous thought, though not exactly what he had been hearing from his attorneys. But he knew how conservative they were. They had no flair, no style, no sense of romance. It annoyed him to listen to their petty warnings that he should be more cautious. He knew how large his fortune was, and there was plenty of leeway for a little fun. He could afford what they were spending, for a while at least, and then they'd settle down to a more 'sensible' life, and neither of them would ever have to work. And at twenty-eight, he had no intention of starting. He was having too much fun, he always had had, and now his life with Faye was sheer perfection. 'Where do you want to go tonight for dinner?'

'I don't know . . .' She hated to admit it, but she loved the corny exotic decor of the Coconut Grove with its palm trees and the projections of white ships passing each other in the distance. It always made her feel as though they had sailed away, and the palm trees reminded her faintly of Guadalcanal, where she had first met Ward. 'The Grove again, or are you too tired of it?'

He laughed again, and called the majordomo downstairs to have him make a reservation. They had hired an army of new people to care for their house.

In the end, Ward had decided not to move into his parents' old mansion after all. Instead, he had bought Faye a fabulous new estate that had belonged to a silent movie queen. It had grounds that could almost be called a park, a lake with swans, several lovely fountains, long walks, and a house that looked like a French château. They could easily have the ten children here that he always threatened he wanted. They had filled it with Faye's pretty antiques from her own house, which had sold almost the day she put it up for sale, and they had taken the pieces they liked best from

73

his parents' place, and the rest they had bought together, at auctions and antique stores in Beverly Hills. The new house was already almost fully furnished. And Ward was talking about putting his parents' house on the market. It was too big and dark and old-fashioned for their taste and there was no point in keeping it any longer. His lawyers had always urged him to keep it for a while, lest when he married one day he would want it, and he was sentimental about it anyway, but it was obvious they would never live in it now. And his lawyers were anxious for him to get rid of it. They wanted him to reinvest the money in something that would bring in more income for him and his bride, although Ward wasn't too concerned about that.

He and Faye took a stroll in the gardens that afternoon, and sat by the little lake kissing and talking. They never seemed to tire of each other and these were golden days as they talked about the sale of his parents' house and a dozen other things. Faye looked up with a dreamy smile when Arthur brought them two glasses of champagne on a tray. She was pleased that Ward had let her keep Elizabeth and Arthur and they seemed happy in their new life. Arthur seemed to approve of Ward, most of the time, although at times there was no denying that he behaved like a crazy boy. One day he had even bought her a coach and four white horses to drive around the estate, and there were six shiny new cars in the garage, being constantly polished by one of their two chauffeurs. It was a lifestyle Faye had never seen before, let alone lived, and at times she felt more than a little guilty. But Ward turned everything into such a delight that it didn't seem naughty any more, just fun, and the days flew by faster than she could count them.

'You're not drinking your champagne.' Ward smiled at her. She had never been prettier than she was now, even at the very height of her career. She had put on a few pounds, and there was a glow in her cheeks, and her eyes were the most brilliant green he had ever seen, especially in the sunlight. He loved kissing her in the gardens . . . in the bedroom . . . while going for a drive. He loved kissing her anytime . . . anywhere. He adored his bride and she was crazy about him.

More than anything she was content, and it showed in her face as she looked at him and declined the proffered champagne. 'I think I'd rather have lemonade.'

'Ugh.' He made a terrible face and she laughed, and hand in hand they walked slowly back to the house, to make love lazily before they bathed and dressed for the evening. It was an idyllic life, and in a way Faye knew that these days would never come again. One day they would have children, they would have to grow up themselves, they couldn't spend their life playing forever. But it was fun while they could, and it made their honeymoon days seem to go on forever.

That night at the Grove, Ward gave her a magnificent ring with three huge pear-shaped emeralds in it, and Faye gasped when she saw it. 'Ward! Good heavens ... but ...' He always loved her amazement, her delight, at the things he bought her.

'It's for our third anniversary, silly girl.' It had been three months that day, and they were the happiest months of Faye's life, and Ward's. There was not a single cloud on their horizon to worry them. He slipped the ring on her finger, and they danced for hours, but he noticed that tonight she looked a little tired when they went back to their table. They had been up late for several nights, several months in fact, he acknowledged with a small smile, but it was the first time he had noticed it taking a toll on her. 'Do you feel all right, sweetheart?'

'Fine.' She smiled, but she also ate very little, drank not at all, and by eleven o'clock she was yawning, which was usually not her style.

'Well, I guess this is it. The honeymoon's over,' Ward pretended to look crushed, 'I'm beginning to bore you.'

'No ... how awful ... I'm sorry, darling ... I just ...'

'I know ... never mind. Don't try to explain.' He teased her mercilessly all the way home, and when he went into the bathroom to undress and brush his teeth, he returned to find her sound asleep, cosy in their big double bed, and appealing in her pink satin nightgown. But he attempted to rouse her to no avail, she was dead to the world, and it was obvious why the next morning. She awoke and was desperately ill immediately after eating breakfast. It was the first time he had seen her sick, and he was frantic and insisted on calling the doctor to the house, despite all her protests.

'For heaven's sake ... it's just the flu or something. You can't drag the poor man all the way out here. I'm fine.' But she didn't feel it.

'The hell you are. You're absolutely green. Now go to bed and stay there until the doctor comes.' But when he arrived, he saw no reason whatsoever for Mrs Thayer to stay in bed, not unless she intended to stay there for another eight months. According to his calculations, the baby was due in November. 'A baby? A baby! Our baby!' Ward was absolutely beside himself with excitement and relief, and Faye laughed at him as he danced around the room when the doctor left. He was quick to come to her side, begging her to tell him what she wanted, needed, or what he could do to make her feel better. She was delighted at the news and his reaction, and of course as soon as word was out, it made headlines. 'Retired Movie Queen Expecting First Child'. Nothing in their life remained a secret for long, but Ward couldn't have kept it to himself anyway. He told anyone who would listen, and treated Faye like the most delicate piece of glass, and if he had lavished gifts on her before, it was nothing to what he did for her now. She didn't have enough drawers and jewel boxes to keep all the outrageously expensive baubles he bought her.

'Ward, you have to stop! I don't even have room to keep it all any more.'

'Then we'll build a cottage just for your jewels.' He laughed mischievously and all her scolding was for naught. If he wasn't buying jewels for her, he was buying prams and pony carts and mink buntings and teddy bears, and he even had a full-scale carousel built on the estate. He allowed Faye to ride slowly around on it in October when she walked across the grounds to see it for herself.

She had been feeling remarkably well since the first few queasy months, and her only complaint was that she was so large she felt like a balloon about to take off. 'All I need is a basket attached to my heels and they could rent me out for sightseeing trips over L.A.,' she told a friend one day and Ward was outraged. He thought she looked beautiful, even in her swollen state, and he was so excited, he could barely stand the remaining month to wait. She had reservations in the finest hospital in town, and she was being attended by the fanciest doctor.

'Only the best for my darling and my baby,' he always said as he attempted to ply her with champagne, but she had no taste for it any more, and there were times when she wished he didn't either.

It wasn't that he got drunk when he drank, it was just that he drank so much of it when he did, and he seemed to drink it all day long, moving on to scotch when they went out in the evening. But she hated to complain. He was so good to her in so many ways, how could she object to a little thing like that? And she knew he meant well, when he ordered a case of their favourite champagne sent ahead to the hospital, so it would be waiting for them when the big moment arrived. 'I hope they keep it chilled.' He ordered Westcott, the majordomo, to call the hospital and instruct them exactly how to cool it, and Faye laughed.

'I suspect they may have a few other things on their minds, my love.' Although the hospital she would be going to was used to such requests; it was where all the big stars gave birth to their babies.

'I can't imagine what,' he said. 'What's more important than keeping the champagne cooled for my love?'

'Oh, I can think of a few things . . .' Her eyes told him all he wanted to know, and he held her gently in his arms, and they kissed as they always had. He was hungry for her, even now, but the doctor had said that they couldn't make love any more. And Faye could hardly wait until they could again. It seemed an eternity to wait, and his hands roved over her full belly, night after night, loving even that, and wanting her desperately.

'This is almost as bad as before we made love for the first time,' he complained with a wry smile as he climbed out of bed late one night and poured himself a glass of champagne. Her due date was only three days away, but the doctor had warned them that the baby could be several weeks late. First babies often were, so they were prepared for a late arrival, and it was beginning to seem like forever to both of them.

'I'm so sorry, love.' She looked tired now, and for the past few days any kind of movement at all had been exhausting. She hadn't even wanted to walk in the gardens with him that afternoon, and when he told her about the miniature pony he had bought, even that hadn't got her outside. 'I'm just too damn tired to move.' And that night, she insisted that she was too tired even to eat dinner. She had gone straight to bed at four in the afternoon, and now at two in the morning she was still there, looking like a giant pink silk balloon with maribou feathers around her collar.

'Want some champagne, sweetheart? It might help you sleep.'
She shook her head, her back hurt, and she had been feeling
queasy for the past several hours. On top of everything she thought
she might be coming down with the flu.

'I don't think anything will help me sleep any more.' One thing
might have, she suggested lasciviously a moment later, but that
was forbidden them.

'You'll probably be pregnant again before you leave the
hospital. I don't think I'll be able to keep my hands off you for
more than an hour after the baby's born.'

She laughed at the thought. 'At least it's something to look
forward to.' She looked doleful for the first time in nine months,
and he kissed her gently and went to turn off the lights, but as he
did he heard a sharp cry from the bed, and turned in surprise to see
her face contorted by pain and then suddenly the pain was gone,
and they both looked at each other in amazement.

'What was that?'

'I'm not sure.' She had read a couple of books, but she was still
hazy about how to be absolutely certain when labour began. And
everyone had warned her that in the last few weeks there could be
endless false starts and false alarms, so they both knew that this
wasn't likely to be 'it'. But the pain had certainly been sharp, and
Ward decided to leave the lights on and see if it happened again.
But twenty minutes later, when it hadn't, and he went to turn the
lights off again, she gave another sharp cry, and this time she
seemed to writhe in their bed and he noticed a film of perspiration
on her face when he approached her.

'I'm calling the doctor.' He could feel his heart pound in his
chest, and his palms were damp. She looked suddenly very pale
and very frightened.

'Don't be silly, darling. I'm fine. We can't call the poor man
every night for the next month. It probably won't be for weeks.'

'But you're due in three days.'

'Yes, but even he said it would probably be late. Let's just relax
and wait until morning.'

'Shall I leave the lights on?' She shook her head, and he turned
them off and slid gingerly into bed beside her, as though he were
afraid that by shaking the bed too much he would cause her to
explode then and there and have the baby. She giggled at him in

78

the dark, and then suddenly he heard her breath catch, and she reached for his hand and held it tight. She was almost fighting for air when the pain had passed, and she sat up in bed when it was over.

'Ward . . .' He was lying very still, wondering what to do, and the sound of her voice touched him to the core. She sounded so vulnerable and frightened and instinctively he took her in his arms.

'Sweetheart, let's call the doctor.'

'I really feel silly bothering him at this hour.'

'That's his job.' But she insisted that they should wait and see what happened until morning. But by seven o'clock there was no doubt in Ward's mind. This had to be the real thing. And he didn't give a damn what anyone had told her about false alarms, the pains were coming five minutes apart, and she was fighting not to scream as each pain lunged through her. In desperation, he left the room, and called the doctor they had engaged. He seemed satisfied with what he heard, and suggested Ward bring her in at once.

'It'll probably take a while from this point on, Mr Thayer, but it's a good idea to get her into the hospital, and settled in.'

'Can you give her something for the pain?' Ward was desperate after seeing her suffer for the past five hours.

'I'll have a better idea once I see her.' The doctor was noncommittal.

'What the hell does that mean? For chrissake, she can hardly keep control now . . . you've got to give her something . . .' Ward himself was desperate for a drink, something a lot stronger than champagne this time.

'We'll do what we can for her, Mr Thayer. Now just keep calm, and bring her to the hospital as soon as you can.'

'I'll have her there in ten minutes, five if I can.'

The doctor didn't say anything, but he had no intention of getting to the hospital himself in anything less than an hour. He had to shower and shave, he hadn't finished reading the paper, and he knew the ways of obstetrics well enough to know that she wouldn't deliver for hours, maybe even for another day, so there was no point rushing in, no matter how panicked the young father was. He'd say all the right things to him when he arrived, and the nurses could keep him at bay after that. They'd had one man force his way into the delivery room the week before, but the security people had dragged him out and threatened to put him in jail if he didn't behave. But he didn't anticipate any problems with Ward Thayer.

And the doctor was pleased to be delivering her. It was another feather in his cap to be delivering Faye Price Thayer.

But Ward was horrified when he walked back into their room and found her doubled over a pool of water on the white marble bathroom floor, with a look of shock mingled with pain. 'My water just broke.' Her voice was huskier than usual, her eyes wide open and afraid.

'Oh my God, I'll call an ambulance.' But at his words she laughed and sat down on the edge of the tub.

'Don't you dare. I'm fine.' But she didn't look all that fine to him and she looked scared, almost as scared as he was. 'What did the doctor say?'

'To bring you in right away.'

'Well,' she looked into her husband's eyes, 'I'll say one thing. I don't think it's a false alarm.' She looked a little more relaxed then, and he put his arms around her and helped her back to her dressing room. 'What'll I wear?' She stared at the open closets and he groaned.

'Oh for chrissake, Faye . . . anything . . . just make it quick. How about a dressing gown?'

'Don't be ridiculous. What if there are photographers there?' Ward looked at her and smiled.

'Don't worry about it. Come on.' He pulled a dress out of the closet, helped her into it, and gently led her downstairs. He wanted to carry her but she insisted she could walk. A couple of minutes later, she was comfortably tucked into the Duesenberg, the sable lap robe tucked around her legs, as she cautiously sat on a thick pad of towels. The driver pulled up in front of the hospital, and Ward let her out. She was instantly put in a wheelchair and whisked away, and he was left to pace the hall for the next six hours. His demands to see the doctor when he arrived were all in vain, until finally at half past two he saw him striding down the hall, his surgical cap still on, swathed in a blue gown, the mask hanging loosely around his neck, and he met Ward with an out-stretched hand.

'Congratulations, you have a fat, handsome son!' The doctor smiled and Ward looked shocked, as though he hadn't quite expected it, even after all these hours of going half mad, pacing the halls. He thought he wouldn't have been able to stand it for another half hour. 'He weighs eight pounds nine ounces, and your wife is doing fine.'

'Can I see her?' Ward could feel his whole body go slack at the news. He was so relieved that it was over, Faye was well, the baby was fine.

'In a few hours. She's sleeping now. It's hard work, you know, pushing these little fellows into the world.' The doctor smiled again. He didn't tell him how hard on Faye it had been, or how close they had come to doing a Caesarean. And he hadn't wanted to give her gas until the head was out. They had waited until the very end and then, put her out, once the baby was born. It made sewing up easier for him, and there was no reason for her to be awake now. Her work was over.

'Thank you, sir.' Ward pumped his hand, and almost ran out of the hospital. He had a present waiting at home for her, a huge diamond brooch with a matching dinner ring and bracelet, all lying in a blue velvet box from Tiffany's. He wanted to get it and bring it back, but more importantly, he needed a drink. Desperately, in fact. He had the chauffeur drive him home as fast as he could, and he almost raced into the house. What an incredible day it had been. With a double scotch straight-up under his belt, he sat down and relaxed, took a deep breath, and realised finally that he had a son. He wanted to shout it from the rooftops he was so pleased, and he couldn't wait to see his wife. He tossed off his drink, and poured a second one, before rushing upstairs to look at the present he had waiting for her. He knew she would be pleased with it, but more than anything he was pleased with her . . . a baby boy! . . . A son! . . . his firstborn. As Ward showered and shaved and dressed to go back and see Faye at the hospital, he thought of all the things he would do with him one day, the trips they'd go on, the mischief they'd get into. His father had never been willing to do anything with him, but everything was going to be different with him and his son. They'd play tennis, polo, go on deep-sea fishing trips in the South Pacific, travel together, have a grand time. He was beaming radiantly when he arrived back at the hospital at five o'clock, and asked the nurse to bring the champagne into Faye's room. But when he tiptoed in, he found her still dozing groggily. She opened her eyes and seemed not to know who he was at first, and then she smiled, the strawberry blonde hair looking like a halo around her pale face. She looked almost ethereal as she stared sleepily at him.

'Hi ... what did we have?' Her voice drifted off and her eyes closed again, as Ward kissed her cheek and whispered to her.

'You mean they haven't told you yet?' He looked shocked, and the nurse quietly left the room. Faye shook her head. 'A boy! A little boy!' She smiled sleepily at him, and declined the champagne. She didn't seem able to sit up and she still looked kind of green to him, and he was desperately worried about her, even though the nurses insisted everything was fine. He sat for a long time with her hand in his. 'Was it ... very ... difficult, sweetheart?' He stumbled on the words and something in her eyes told him that it was terrible but she bravely shook her head. 'Have you seen him yet? Who does he look like?'

'I don't know ... I haven't seen him ... I hope he looks like you.' He let her go back to sleep after that. He had showed her the spectacular gift he'd bought for her, and she looked appropriately awed but she was definitely not herself and he suspected she was in a lot of pain but didn't want to admit it to him. He tiptoed down the hail by himself to look at his son. The nurse held him behind the glass window in the nursery, and the baby looked like Faye; he was big and round and beautiful with a fluff of blond hair like hers. And as Ward watched he gave out what looked like a healthy wail, and Ward thought he had never been so proud in his life as he strutted out of the hospital and into the Duesenberg. He went to dinner at Ciro's alone, knowing he would run into all his friends, and he bragged to everyone, handed out cigars, and got extremely drunk on champagne, while in her hospital room, Faye slept, trying to forget how awful it had been.

She left the hospital in less than a week, and by the time she got home, she looked more like herself. She wanted to nurse the baby, but Ward had convinced her that it wasn't practical. She needed her sleep. They had hired a nurse, who took over while Faye regained her strength, but within two weeks, Faye was on her feet again, with the baby in her arms most of the time, and looking more beautiful than she ever had before, Ward said.

They named the baby Lionel, and christened him on Christmas Day at the church where they'd been married.

'He's the perfect Christmas gift.' Ward beamed down at his son as he held him in his arms on the way home, and Faye laughed. Lionel was almost two months old. 'He's beautiful, sweetheart, and he looks so much like you.'

'He's pretty cute, whoever he looks like.' She gazed down at the sleeping infant happily. He had barely cried during the brief ceremony. And once at home, he woke up and didn't seem to object when he was passed from hand to hand. Everyone wanted to have a look at him. All the illustrious and celebrated of Hollywood were there, all the big film stars, producers, directors, from Faye's old life, and Ward's more social friends. It was a dazzling list of names, and the Hollywood people all teased Faye about giving up her career for 'all this' . . . 'Are you just going to go on having babies forever, Faye?' She said she was, and Ward stood at her side and beamed. He was so proud of Faye and Lionel and the champagne flowed like the Seine all day. And that night Ward and Faye went dancing at the Biltmore Bowl. She had made a remarkable recovery. She already had her figure back, and felt well. And Ward thought she had never looked more beautiful. The photographers concurred.

'All set to do it again?' Ward teased. She wasn't quite sure she was. The memory of how painful it had been still lingered with her, but she was crazy about Lionel. It might not be so terrible to do it again, she thought now, though only weeks before she would have shrieked at the idea. 'How about a second honeymoon in Mexico?' he proposed, and she loved the idea. They left shortly after New Year's Day, and had a fabulous time in Acapulco for three weeks. They ran into a number of their friends, but spent most of their time alone, they even rented a yacht and spent two days fishing blissfully. It was the perfect holiday, and would have been even more so if on the last week of their trip, Faye hadn't begun feeling ill. She blamed it on the fish, the heat, the sun, and couldn't imagine anything else. But when she got back, Ward insisted she go to the doctor to check it out, and when she did, she was stunned. She was pregnant again.

Ward was thrilled, and so was she. This was exactly what they had both wanted from the first, and everyone teased them mercilessly this time. 'Can't you leave the poor girl alone, Thayer? What's the matter with you two? Can't you leave her alone long enough to comb her hair?' But they were both happy about it, and this time they made love almost until the end, doctor's advice be damned. Ward said that if she was going to spend nine months out of every ten pregnant, then he wasn't giving her up, and he barely did this time. She went into labour five days late, and it was easier this time. She recognised the symptoms of labour more easily, and it began one hot September afternoon. They barely had time to make it to the hospital, the pains came so hard and fast, and Faye was clenching her teeth with tightened fists when they arrived at the hospital. The boy was born less than two hours after that, and when Ward saw her late that night, he wasn't as upset this time at how sleepy she was. This time he had bought her sapphire earrings with a matching thirty-carat ring. It was another boy, and they named him Gregory, and Faye bounced back just as quickly this time. But this time she vowed to be a little more careful, at least 'for a while'.

When the baby was three months old, she and Ward went to Europe on the *Queen Elizabeth* for a nice long trip. They took the nurse and both boys along, with a separate stateroom for them, and huge suites of rooms in every city where they went. London, Paris, Munich, Rome. They even went to Cannes for a few days in March and the weather was pleasant and warm, and then finally back to Paris and from there home again. It was a wonderful trip for all of them, and Faye was as happy as could be with the husband she adored and her two sons. She was stopped for autographs once or twice, but that happened much less often now. People seldom knew who she was. She was still very beautiful, but she looked different somehow. More matronly perhaps, slightly less glamorous, except when she went out in the evenings with Ward. But she was perfectly content to wear trousers and a sweater and a scarf around her golden hair, and go out with her two little boys. She couldn't imagine a more perfect life, and Ward was so obviously proud of them.

They found all well when they went back, but the gossip in Hollywood was ugly these days. The Hollywood Blacklist had come out months before, and countless actors, directors, writers, and other people they had known could no longer find work.

Suddenly the word 'commie' was on everyone's lips, fingers were all too anxious to point in all directions, even towards old friends. It was a sad time for many people, and in a way, Faye was glad she was no longer a part of it. The saddest thing of all was that those who had been blacklisted suddenly found themselves with no friends, as well as no work. People were afraid to be seen with them.

Warner Brothers had put up an enormous billboard outside the studios, 'Combining Good Pictures with Good Citizenship', which told everyone where they stood.

The House Committee to Investigate UnAmerican Activities had been in operation for ten years, but it had never taken itself so seriously, and when in October 1947, the 'Hollywood 10' were given prison sentences for refusing to testify, it was as though the whole town had gone mad, and it made Faye sick to hear the stories that were going around about old friends, people they all knew. By 1948, talented people they had all loved were being forced to leave Hollywood and get jobs as plumbers, carpenters, anything they could. Their Hollywood days were over, and Faye looked pained whenever she spoke to Ward of it.

'I'm glad I'm out of all that. I never thought it would get as ugly as this.'

Ward looked at her carefully. He had to admit, she seemed happy with her present life, but he wondered sometimes if she didn't miss the old days of her film career. 'You sure you don't miss it, babe?'

'Not for a minute, my love.' But he had noticed that she was restless lately, as though she needed something more to do. She had begun doing volunteer work in a local hospital, and she spent a lot of time with the boys. Lionel was almost two years old, and Gregory was ten months old, a precious baby with a happy smile and dancing curls. But Faye was happiest of all when she announced to Ward just days before Greg's first birthday that she was pregnant again.

This time it was more difficult for her. She felt less well than she had, right from the first, and she was much more tired this time. She never seemed to want to go out, and Ward noticed that she was much bigger this time. Although the rest of her looked even thinner than usual, her stomach was enormous almost at once, and by Christmas the doctor suspected why. He examined her carefully, and as she sat up, he smiled at her.

'I think the Easter bunny might have quite a surprise for you this time, Faye, if he waits that long.'

'What's that?' She felt as though she could barely move, and she still had three months to go.

'I have a suspicion, just a faint one, that it might be twins.' She stared at him in astonishment, the possibility had never even crossed her mind. She just thought that she was more tired this time, but now that she thought about it, she was much bigger too.

'Are you sure?'

'No. We can do an X-ray in a while, and we'll certainly know at the delivery.' And that they did. Two beautiful little girls popped out of her, nine minutes apart, and Ward was so beside himself when he saw the two baby girls that he went completely berserk. It was matching ruby and diamond bracelets this time. Two ruby rings. Diamond and ruby earrings, two of everything. And even Greg and Lionel looked surprised when they came home with two babies instead of one.

'One for each of you,' Ward said, lovingly putting one tiny pink bundle into the arms of each little boy. The twins were a big success with everyone. They weren't identical technically, but they might just as well have been they looked so much alike. They called the older one Vanessa, who looked incredibly like Faye: the same green eyes, the same blonde hair, the same tiny perfect features, yet she was the quiet one. It was the younger twin who screamed the loudest whenever she wanted to eat, who smiled first. The same tiny perfect face and huge green eyes, but Valerie had fiery red hair, right from birth, and a personality to match.

'My God, where did she get that?' Ward looked shocked as her red hair began to grow, but as she grew older, her hair, like the rest of her, grew more and more beautiful. She was a startlingly pretty little girl and people often stared at her. At times, Faye worried that Valerie eclipsed her twin. Vanessa was so much quieter, and she seemed to accept living in the shadow of the twin sister she adored. Vanessa was a pretty child too, but quieter, more ethereal; she was happy looking at her picture books, or watching Valerie torment the boys. Lionel was always particularly patient with her, and Greg would grab fistfuls of the bright red hair. It taught

Valerie the art of self-defence at an early age, if nothing else. But on the whole, the children had a good time with each other, and people said they were the prettiest lot anyone had ever seen. Two beautiful little girls, toddling around the grounds of the estate, playing with the miniature pony their father had bought several years before, and the two boys cavorting all around, climbing trees, and reducing their beautiful little silk shirts to shreds with glee.

They all enjoyed the carousel now, the pony rides, all the treats their father had bought for them. And he adored playing with them. At thirty-two, he seemed hardly more than a boy himself, and Faye was content with her family. Four children seemed perfect to both of them. She didn't want any more, and Ward was content to stop at four, although he teased her sometimes about still wanting ten. But Faye would roll her eyes at the mention of it. She had her hands full as it was, and she liked spending time with all of them. They went on wonderful holidays; Ward had bought a house in Palm Springs the year before, and they spent part of every winter there. Faye loved going to New York with him to visit friends. They had a good life, in all possible ways, far, far, from the poverty of her early life, and the loneliness of his childhood years.

Eventually, he had confided everything to her. He had led the life of a 'poor little rich boy' as a child. He had had everything materially, but his parents were never around. His father had been working all the time, his mother had been constantly involved with various committees as a volunteer, and in between they had taken extensive trips, but always leaving Ward behind. As a result he had sworn that he would never do the same thing to his own family. He and Faye took all four children everywhere, on weekends in Palm Springs, on trips, even to Mexico. They enjoyed their company and the children flourished with the attention lavished on them, each in their own way. Lionel had an inclination to be quiet, perceptive, serious, and close to Faye. His seriousness unnerved Ward at times, he was less rough and tumble than Greg, who played football for hours on the lawn with Ward. Greg was more like he himself had been as a child, happy go lucky, athletic, carefree . . . or more as he would have been, had he had the same amount of attention lavished on him. And Valerie only grew more beautiful. She was the most demanding of the four, the most aware of her own charms, and because of that, Vanessa seemed to demand nothing at all. Valerie took her dolls, her toys, her favourite clothes, and Vanessa didn't even seem to notice it. She was happy to give anything up for her twin. She cared about other things, the look in her mother's eyes, a warm word from Ward, a trip to the zoo, holding Lionel's hand, and her own secret life of dreams, as she glanced through a picture book or stared up at the sky as she lay beneath a tree. She was the dreamer of the family. She could lie on the grass for hours, looking up at the sky with her own thoughts, sometimes singing a little song to herself as Faye smiled at her.

'I was like that when I was her age,' Faye said softly to Ward as he glanced at the pretty little blonde girl.

'And what did you used to dream about, my love?' He kissed her neck and took her hand, his eyes as warm as the morning sun. 'Did you dream of being a film star?'

'Sometimes, but I was a lot older than that by then.' Little Vanessa didn't even know what films were.

He smiled happily at his wife. 'And what do you dream of now?' He was so happy with her. She had taken all the loneliness out of his life. And she was fun. That was important to him. His parents had never seemed to have a good time. All his father did was work, as far as Ward could see, and his mother did the same with her endless charities. He had sworn to himself long before that he would never live like that. He wanted to enjoy his life. Both his parents had died young, without ever really enjoying themselves. That was not the case with Ward and Faye. They had a wonderful time. He looked at her again now, so peaceful and beautiful, she almost looked like a painting as she pondered the question he had asked.

'I dream of you, my love . . . and the children. I have everything I want in this world . . . and more.'

'Good. That's the way I always want it to be.' And he meant every word of it, as the children grew up, and time passed by.

Ward still drank too much champagne sometimes but he was harmless and good-humoured, and Faye loved him enormously, even with his occasional boyish flaws, of liking to have too much fun, or drinking a little too much. There was no harm in it.

The lawyers came to see him more than they used to do, about his parents' estate and what was left of it, but she didn't concern herself with it. It was his money after all, and she had enough to do with Lionel, Gregory, Vanessa, and Val. But she noticed around the time that the twins turned two that Ward was drinking more, and it was less champagne and more scotch, which worried her.

'Anything wrong, sweetheart?'

'Of course not.' He smiled, feigning unconcern, but there was something frightened in his eyes these days and she wondered what it was. But he persisted in insisting nothing was wrong, and still the lawyers came, and often called. She wondered what they said to him. And then somehow, it all seemed less important again. The earlier decision was forgotten late one night, and in the throes of passion after going to the Academy Awards with him in April of 1951, they threw caution to the winds, and by late May, Faye was sure.

'Again?' Ward looked surprised, but not displeased, although he was less interested this time. He had too many other things on his mind, although he did not tell Faye that.

'Are you mad at me?' She was concerned, and he pulled her into his arms with a broad grin.

'Only if it isn't mine, you silly girl. Of course I'm not mad. How could I be mad at you?'

'Five children is an awful lot, I suppose . . .' She was faintly ambivalent about it this time too. The family seemed so perfect as it was. 'And if I have twins again . . .'

'Then that'd make six! It sounds fine to me. We might even reach our original goal of ten one of these days.' But as he said it, all four of the children they had ran into the room, shrieking with excitement, falling all over each other, laughing and shouting and pulling hair, and Faye shouted over their heads at him, 'God forbid!' He smiled at her, and all went well and in January, Anne Ward Thayer was born, the smallest child Faye had borne, and she looked so tiny and frail one was almost afraid to hold her. In fact, she was so tiny and delicate that Ward refused to take her in his arms, but he seemed pleased with her. He bought Faye an enormous emerald pendant this time, but somehow he seemed less excited than he had before, and Faye told herself that she could hardly expect him to hire a brass band for their fifth child. But still, she was disappointed that he didn't seem more pleased.

But within days, she knew exactly why. The lawyers didn't even try to talk to Ward this time. They talked to her, feeling it was high time she knew what was going on . . . Seven years after the end of the war, Thayer Shipyard hadn't seen a profit in almost four years. It had been running in the red for years, despite all their pleading with Ward to pay some attention to it, cut down the scale of operations, and face what was happening. They wanted him to go to work in the office at the yard, as his father had. And he had flatly refused. Instead, he had ignored their pleas and not only allowed the shipyard to run itself into the ground, but he had bankrupted the estate as well. He had insisted that he wasn't going to ruin his life by working night and day. He wanted to be with his family. And now there was nothing left, hadn't been in almost two years. And suddenly, as she sat in shocked silence listening to them, Faye looked back remembering when he had begun to seem pre-occupied, concerned, drinking more, but he had never admitted anything to her. And for the past two years, without saying a word to her, he had been running on 'empty'. There was no money left at all, there were only monumental debts which he had accumulated with their extravagant lifestyle. Faye Price Thayer sat listening to what they had to say, her face pale, features taut, a frown between her eyes, and she looked as though she were in shock. In a way she was. She almost staggered out of the room when they left her. And when Ward came home later that afternoon, he found her sitting upright in a chair in the library, silently waiting for him.

'Hi, babe. What are you doing downstairs so soon? Shouldn't you be resting?' Resting? *Resting?* How could she be resting when they had no money left, when she should be out looking for a job? All they had left were debts, and as she raised her eyes to his, he knew that something terrible had happened. 'Faye? . . . Darling, what's wrong?' There were tears trembling in her eyes and she didn't even know where to begin. The tears spilled onto her cheeks and she began to sob. How could he have played this game? What was he thinking of? When she thought of all the jewellery he had bought, the cars, furs, the house in Palm Springs, the polo ponies . . . it went on forever . . . and God only knew how bad the debts were. 'Darling, what is it?' He knelt beside her and all she could do was sob, until finally she took a deep breath and gently touched his face with her hand. How could she hate this man? She had never faced it until now, but he was only a child, a boy pretending to be a man. At thirty-five, he was less mature than their six-year-old son. Lionel was already practical and wise . . . but Ward . . . Ward . . . there was the sorrow of an ended life in Faye's eyes as she attempted to calm down and talk to him about what she had heard that afternoon.

'Bill Gentry and Lawson Burford were here this afternoon, Ward.' There was nothing ominous in her voice, only sorrow, for him and for all of them, and Ward looked instantly annoyed. He spun around and walked to the bar, and poured himself a stiff drink. He'd had fun that afternoon, until now. He glanced over his shoulder at his wife, searching her eyes.

'Don't let those two upset you, Faye. They're both a pain in the ass. What did they want?'

'To talk some sense into you, I guess.'

'What's that supposed to mean?' He looked nervously at her as he sat down in a chair. 'What did they say?'

'They told me everything, Ward.' His face went white, as hers had hours before. 'They told me that you don't have a dime left. The shipyards have to be closed down, this house has to be sold to pay our debts . . . everything's going to change, Ward. We're going to have to grow up and stop pretending we live in a fairy land and aren't subject to the same pressures as everyone else in the world.' The only difference between them and everyone else was that he'd never worked a day in his life and they had five children to support. If only she had known. She would never have had this last child. She didn't even feel guilty at the thought, no matter how sweet the new baby was. Their very lives were at stake right now, and she knew in her gut that Ward wasn't going to do a damn thing about it. He wasn't capable of it, but she was. And if he couldn't row the boat to shore, then she would, and that's all there was to it. 'Ward . . . we have to talk about this . . .'

He jumped up and stalked across the room. 'Some other time, Faye. I'm tired.' She leapt to her feet, not caring how weak she still felt. All of that was forgotten now. That was a luxury. Another luxury they could no longer afford.

'Dammit! Listen to me! How long are you going to play games with me? Until they put you in jail for bad debts? Until they throw us out of this house? According to Lawson and Bill, we don't have a dime left, or damn few anyway.' They had been brutally honest with her. They would have to sell everything. They had just to pay their debts. And then what? That was the question she was asking herself.

Ward stood and faced her then. 'And what do you suggest I do about it, Faye? Start selling my cars? Put the children to work?' He looked horrified; his world was coming down around his ears and he was equipped for no other way of life than this.

'We have to face reality, no matter how frightening it is.' She walked slowly to him then, her eyes alight with green fire, but she wasn't angry at him. She had thought of it all afternoon, and she understood how he was, but she couldn't let him pretend to himself any more, or to her. He had to face the changes that had to be made. 'We have to do something, Ward.'

'Like what?' He slumped slowly into a chair like a deflated balloon. He had thought about it before, and it was beyond his ken. Maybe he had been wrong to keep it from her, but how could he possibly tell her how desperate things were? He never had the heart. So he always bought her a new piece of jewellery instead, and the stupid thing was that he knew she didn't really care about those things. She loved the children and him . . . she did love him, didn't she? That was what always frightened him about telling her. What if she walked out on him? He couldn't bear the thought. And now finally he was looking at her, and he saw hope in her eyes. She wasn't going to desert him after all and suddenly tears filled his eyes and he bent to her and buried his face in her lap, sobbing at what he had done. She stroked his hair and spoke softly to him for what seemed like hours, and when he stopped she was still there. She wasn't going to go away after all, at least not yet, but she also wasn't going to let him run away from it any more.

'Ward, we have to sell the house.'

'But where will we go?' He sounded like a frightened child, and she smiled at him.

'We'll go somewhere else. We'll fire the staff. Sell most of this expensive stuff, the rare books, my furs, my jewellery.' It pained her to think of that, only because he had given her all of it and all of it for important events in their life. She was sentimental about it, but she also knew that the jewellery was worth a great deal and they couldn't hang onto anything now. 'How bad do you suppose the debts are?'

'I don't know.' His face was muffled in her thighs, and she pulled his face up to hers with her hands.

'We have to find out. Together. We're in this together, sweetheart, but now we have to bail out.'

'Do you really think we can?' It was terrifying facing it, even with her.

'I'm sure of it.' At least she told him so, but she was no longer sure of anything.

He felt relief sweep over him at the tone of her voice. Once or twice, between cases of champagne, he had actually contemplated suicide. And he knew exactly how weak he was. He was totally unprepared to face what he had to face now. Without Faye, he couldn't have faced it at all. And with her, it was hardly easier. She forced him to go to the lawyers with her the next day. The doctor had told her not to go out yet, but she totally ignored the rules. After her fifth child, she wasn't as impressed with all that as she might have been after her first, and she wasn't going to let Ward squirm out of it. She stood beside him all the way, but in that sense she was merciless. It had to be faced, by both of them. According to the lawyers, they were three and a half million dollars in debt. She almost fainted when she heard the words, and Ward's face as he listened was a deathly chalk white. The lawyers explained that they would have to sell everything, and if they were lucky they would have a little money left, which they could invest, but they could no longer live on it as they once had. In fact, Bill Gentry looked pointedly at Ward; they would have to go to work, or at least one of them would. They wondered if Faye wanted to go back to her old career, but it had been seven years since she'd done her last film, no one asked for autographs any more, and the papers no longer ran headlines about her as they once had. She was old news. At thirty-two she could certainly make a comeback if she wanted to, but it wouldn't be quite the same thing, and it wasn't what she had in mind anyway. She had another idea, but it was too early to think of that.

'What about the shipyard?' Her questions were intelligent and blunt and Ward was relieved not to have to ask. Somehow it all embarrassed him, and he desperately wanted a drink as Faye pressed on. The lawyers were firm.

'You'll have to declare bankruptcy.'

'And the house? How much do you think we'll get for that?'

'Half a million, if you find someone who falls in love with it. Realistically, probably less.'

'All right, that's a start ... then we've got the house in Palm Springs ...' She pulled a list out of her bag. The night before, after Ward had gone to sleep, she had made a list of absolutely everything they owned, right down to the dog. She figured that with a little luck they might collect five million dollars for everything they had. Or at least four.

'And then what?' Ward looked at her bitterly for the first time. 'We dress the children in rags and go begging in the street? We have to live somewhere, Faye. We need servants, clothes, cars.'

She shook her head. 'Car. Not *cars*. And if we can't afford that, we take the bus.' Something in his face suddenly frightened her. She wondered if he could successfully make the change. But he had to, they had no choice, and she was going to help him make it. The only thing she was not willing to give up was him.

At the end of two hours, the lawyers stood up and shook their hands, but Ward's face looked grim. He seemed to have aged ten years in the past two hours, and he hardly spoke a word as they drove home in the Duesenberg. He almost had tears in his eyes realising that it might be the last time they went out in it.

As they walked in the door, the baby nurse was waiting for them. Little Anne had a fever. The nurse was sure that she had caught cold from Val and she was concerned. With a distracted look, Faye went to the phone and called the doctor for her, but she didn't take the baby from the nurse's arms, and when she offered the baby to Faye later on, Faye waved her away with a distracted look and uncharacteristically brusque words. 'I don't have time.' She had other things on her mind. 'Other things' being the demise of their current way of life. The prospect of what she had in store for her was exhausting just to think about. But it had to be done, and she was the one who was going to have to do it all. Ward couldn't cope with it. She would have to do everything, and he was grateful to her when she began tackling it the next day. She called all the estate agents in town and made appointments for them to come to see the house. She called the lawyers again, made appointments with several antique dealers, and began to make lists of what they would keep and what they would sell. Ward watched her stupefied as she sat at her desk at noon the next day, businesslike, matter-of-fact, a frown on her face, and he shook his head, unnerved by it all.

She looked up at him, still wearing a frown, but it wasn't meant for him. 'What are you doing today?'

'Having lunch at the club.' That was another thing that would have to go, all his club memberships, but she didn't say anything to him now. She merely nodded her head, and a moment later he left the room. He didn't come back until six o'clock and when he did he was in a very good mood. He had been playing backgammon all afternoon and had won nine hundred dollars from one of his friends. But what if you'd lost? Faye thought the words silently and said nothing to him, as she went upstairs quietly. She didn't want to see him playing with the twins, knowing he was drunk, knowing all that she knew now. And there was so much to do. Tomorrow she would have to begin firing the help . . . they still had the cars to sell . . . and after everything was done here there would still be the house at Palm Springs . . . tears filled her eyes at the thought of it all, not so much with regret, but more with the sheer weight of it all, and the weight was resting entirely on her. There was no avoiding it. It was like a nightmare, or a very, very strange dream. In a mere twenty-four hours, their entire life had fallen apart; she could barely allow herself to think of it. If she did, she might scream. It was so strange, only days ago, her head had been filled with other things . . . the new baby being born . . . another spectacular gift from Ward. They were thinking of spending a few weeks in Palm Springs, and now suddenly it was over . . . forever . . . gone. It was totally incredible. As she walked up the stairs with a heavy heart, wondering what they would do, the nurse waylaid her again, as she had already done several times that day. But Faye had no time for the baby now. There was just too much going on. The woman in white stood at the head of the stairs looking at Faye ominously, a bottle of formula in one hand, as she clutched the newborn babe to her breast, wrapped in an embroidered pink receiving blanket Faye had bought for the twins.

'Would you like to feed the baby now, Mrs Thayer?' The fancy British nanny stared malevolently at her, or at least that was how

Faye saw her now, thinking of her salary and also of how she had attempted to make her feel guilty all day.

'I can't, Mrs McQueen. I'm sorry . . .' She turned away, feeling the knife of guilt slice at her heart. 'I'm too tired . . .' But it wasn't that. She wanted to go through her jewellery before Ward came upstairs. She had made an appointment with Frances Klein the following day, and she had to decide now what she wanted to sell to them. She knew that she would get a fair price from them. And there was no turning back now . . . and also no time for little Anne, poor tiny frail child. 'Maybe tomorrow night,' she murmured to the nurse, as she hurried to her room, averting her eyes. It would be easier if she didn't see the child, so recently sprung from her womb. And a week or two before, that was all she had to think about. But not any more . . . not now . . . With the tears spilling from her eyes, she hurried into her room and closed the door. Mrs McQueen watched her go, shook her head, and headed for the nursery upstairs.

CHAPTER 6

Christie's picked up the furniture in February. They took all the significant antiques, the six sets of fine antique china Faye and Ward had bought in the last seven years, all the crystal chandeliers, the Persian rugs. They took everything except the bare necessities. And Faye arranged it all so that the children would be in Palm Springs with their nurse, and she urged Ward to go away as well.

'Trying to get rid of me?' He looked at her balefully over the standard glass of champagne he always seemed to hold, except that the glasses were larger nowadays.

'You know better than that.' She sat down next to him with a sigh. She had been labelling furniture all day. Red tags for everything that went, blue for what stayed, and there wasn't much of that. She wanted to sell everything valuable they had. The simpler things they could use when they moved on. It was depressing for everyone, but it had to be faced. They were words Ward had come to hate, but she was merciless. Now that she knew the truth, she wouldn't let him hide from it any more. She was doing everything she could to help, but she wouldn't allow him to lie to himself or to her. It was Faye who dealt directly with the lawyers now, and privately it worried her. She knew that what she was doing was, in some hidden way, emasculating him. But what could she do? Let him go on living the lie? Running up more debts? She shuddered at the thought. To her, it seemed better to face the music now, and then build a new life again. They were still young enough. They had each other, and the kids. Now and then, she was as terrified as Ward. It was like climbing a steep mountainside, but she rarely allowed herself to look down. That was another luxury they could no longer afford. They just had to move on. 'I sold the carousel yesterday.' It was the only subject they talked about any more, what had been sold, what had not. The house still hadn't moved, and it was beginning to worry her. 'I sold it to a hotel, for a decent price.'

'How wonderful.' He got up suddenly and went to fill his glass again. 'I'm sure the children will be thrilled with the news.'

'I can't help that' . . . but you could have, she thought suddenly, and then forced the words out of her mind. It wasn't her fault that they were losing everything. But she wouldn't allow herself to blame Ward either. He had never known any other way of life. No one had taught him to be responsible. And he had always been wonderful to her. In spite of everything, she still loved the man, but sometimes it was difficult not to blame him for what was happening now. It had all been such a sham, for so long . . . if only she had known . . . She found him staring at her, a look of despair in his eyes as he held his glass. For an instant, just an instant, she could glean what he would look like as a very old man. Most of the time, he still looked like a boy, a very handsome, debonair, carefree young man, but now suddenly, in the past two months, he seemed to have taken on the weight of the world and it was ageing him. She had even noticed a few grey hairs mixed in the blond, and there there were new lines around his eyes. 'Ward . . .' She looked across the room at him, wondering what she could say to ease the pain, to make them both better able to live with the truth. And the questions and terror roared through both their minds like trains. Where do we go from here? What do we do now? What happens when the house is sold?

'I wish I'd never dragged you into this.' He sat down, feeling sorry for himself, guilty towards her. 'I had no right to marry you.' But he had wanted and needed her so desperately, especially after the war, after his first bride's death two months after marrying her . . . and Faye had been so remarkable. And she still was. That made it even harder now. He hated what he was doing to her.

She walked slowly to him and sat on the arm of his chair. She was thinner than she had been before Anne, thinner than she had been for years. But she was working hard these days, up at dawn, packing boxes, sorting through mountains of things. She did some of the housework herself, with one of the two remaining maids. The huge staff was reduced to two women who cooked and cleaned for all of them, the nurse who had been with the children for the past six years since Lionel was born, and the baby nurse who had been hired to care for Anne. Eventually, Faye planned to reduce their numbers further to two, but for the moment she still needed these, to help her pack up and close the house eventually. The rest of the staff was long since gone. Arthur and Elizabeth had retired tearfully some six weeks before, leaving Faye after so many years. Both chauffeurs had been fired, the majordomo, and half a dozen maids. Eventually perhaps they wouldn't need anyone at all, if they found a house that was small enough. She hadn't even begun to tackle that yet. She had to sell this one first. And Ward was letting her do it all.

'Wouldn't you rather just have a divorce?' He stared at her, his glass empty in his hand once again. But not for long. Never for long any more.

'No.' She said it loud and clear in the half-empty room. 'I would not. As I recall, the man said "for better or worse", and if things are tough right now, then okay, that's the way it is.'

'"That's the way it is"? We have the rugs sold out from under our feet, the roof from over our head, our lawyers are lending us money to buy food and pay the maids, and you're just going to shrug it off? And just how do you think we're going to eat after this?' He poured himself another drink, and she had to fight herself not to ask him to stop. She knew he would eventually. Everything would be normal again. One day. Maybe.

'We'll figure something out, Ward. What choice do we have?'

'I don't know. I suppose you think you'll go back to your film career, but you're no spring chicken any more, you know.' She could tell from the way he was beginning to slur his words that he was drunk by now, but she didn't cringe at his words.

'I know that, Ward.' Her voice was painfully calm. She had been thinking about it herself for weeks. 'Something will work out.'

'For who? For me?' He advanced on her menacingly, which was unlike him. But they were both under such strain that anything was possible now. 'Shit, I've never worked in my whole life. What do you think I'm going to do? Get a job at Saks selling shoes to your friends?'

'Ward, please . . .' She turned away so he wouldn't see the tears in her eyes, and he grabbed her arm and pulled her back viciously.

'Come on, tell me your plans, Miss Reality. You're the one who's been so busy making us face up to it all. Hell, if it hadn't been for you, we'd still be living the way we were before.' So that was it, he blamed her and not himself, or maybe he only wished he did. She knew him well, but it didn't stop her from lashing out at him.

'If we were, we'd have five million dollars in debts instead of four.'

'Christ . . . you sound just like those two old maids. Gentry and Burford. They don't know their ass from a hole in the ground. So what if we were in debt?' He shouted the words and walked away from her. 'We had a decent life, didn't we?' He glared at her in fury from across the room, but it was fury at himself, not her, and suddenly she shouted at him.

'It was a lie goddammit! It was only a matter of time before they took the house out from under us and carted the furniture out of here.'

Ward laughed bitterly. 'Oh, I see. And just what do you think is happening now?'

'We're selling it ourselves, Ward. And if we're lucky, we'll have some money left at the end of it. Money we can invest if we're sensible, and maybe live on for a while. And you know what? All that really matters is that we still have each other and the kids.'

But he didn't want to hear what she had to say. He slammed out of the room, and the door shuddered in the frame from the impact as he left. Her hands shook for half an hour after he had left, but she went on packing their things. And three weeks later, they sold the house. It was a sombre day for them, but it was the only way out. They got less than they had hoped for it, but the buyers knew that they were desperate, and it didn't look as good as it once had. The gardeners were all gone and the grounds were already a little run down, the disappearance of the carousel had left some ugly scars. All the really fine furniture was gone, the huge rooms looked barren without the chandeliers or curtains. They got a quarter of a million dollars for the place from a well-known actor and his wife. He wasn't particularly pleasant to Faye, and they never even met Ward. They just strutted around the house, and made comments to their estate agent, as though Faye weren't there. The offer came in the next day, and it took a week of negotiation just to get them up as high as they did. And Burford, Gentry, and Faye all pressed

Ward to agree to it. They insisted he had no choice, and finally in desperation, he agreed with them, signed the offer himself, and then locked himself into his study with two bottles of champagne and a fifth of gin. He sat there staring at the photographs of his parents on the wall, and crying silently, thinking of his father's life and the life that now faced him. Faye didn't even see him until late that night when he finally came upstairs. She didn't dare speak to him as he came into the room. She just watched his face, and she wanted to cry just looking at him. It was the end of his whole way of life, and suddenly she was frightened for him, wondering if he could survive the change. She had been poor before, although admittedly not in a very long time, but she still remembered the realities of it. And it wasn't as terrifying to her as it was to Ward. She felt now though as if she had been running for months, and wondered if she was ever going to be able to stop, if they were ever going to be able to find each other again. It was like the worst nightmare of her life, and all their idyllic moments were gone. They were left with the shock of reality, the tragedy of what he'd done, and the dreary ugliness of the rest of their life. But she refused to let it be like that, refused to let him let go and give up, to become a hopeless drunk.

He stood staring at her, as though reading her thoughts, and he looked heartbroken as he walked into the room and sat down. 'I'm sorry I've been such a sonofabitch about all this, Faye.' He sat staring at her and she felt tears in her eyes as she tried to smile at him.

'It's been hard on all of us.'

'But it's all my fault . . . that's the worst part of it. I'm not sure I could ever have turned the tide, but I could have slowed things down a little bit.'

'You could never have revived a dying industry, Ward, no matter how hard you tried. You can't blame yourself for that.' She shrugged and sat down on the edge of the bed. 'As for the rest . . .' She smiled sadly at him. '. . . it was fun for a while . . .'

'What if we starve?' He looked like a frightened little boy. For a man who had lived on credit for all these years, it was an amazing thing to ask. But he had finally faced those thoughts tonight and the one thing he realised was that no matter how angry he was, he desperately needed her. And she didn't fail him now.

She looked calm when she spoke to him, far calmer than she felt. But she wanted to give him something she knew he didn't have. Faith. Confidence. It was what she could do best for him now. And to her that was what it meant to be his wife. 'We won't starve, Ward. You and I can handle this. I never starved before, even though I came pretty close at times.' She grinned tiredly at him. Her whole body ached from the packing and pushing and moving things around.

'There weren't seven of you then.'

'No.' She looked at him tenderly for the first time in weeks. 'But I'm glad there are now.'

'Are you really, Faye?' His own misery had sobered him hours before. He just couldn't seem to stay drunk tonight, and now he was just as glad. 'Doesn't it frighten you to have all of us pulling on your skirts, and me most of all, I'm more frightened than the kids.' She walked slowly towards him and touched the thick sandy blond hair. It was strange how much he looked like Gregory, and sometimes he seemed even more a little boy than their son.

'It'll be okay, Ward . . . I promise you that.' She spoke in a whisper as she kissed the top of his head, and when he turned his face up to her, there were tears pouring slowly down his cheeks and he had to gulp down a sob.

'I'm going to help you now, babe. I promise . . . I'll do whatever I can . . .' She nodded, and he pulled her face down towards his, and for the first time in what seemed like years, he kissed her lips. Moments later, he followed her to bed, but nothing happened there. It hadn't in a long time. There were too many things on both their minds. But at least the love was still there, battered but not gone. It was all they had left now. Everything else was gone.

CHAPTER 7

They moved out of the house in May with tears streaming quietly down Faye's and Ward's cheeks. They knew that they were leaving a world and a life that would never come again. Lionel and Gregory were crying too. They were old enough to understand that they were leaving the house for good. It had been their childhood home, and it was beautiful and safe and warm. And there was something frightening about the look in their parents' eyes. Everything was suddenly different somehow, but the children weren't entirely sure how. Only Vanessa and Val seemed less affected by the move. They were only three years old and didn't seem to mind as much, although they felt everyone else's uneasiness too. They thought it was exciting that they were all going to the house in Palm Springs.

Ward drove them all down in the only car they had left. It was an old Chrysler station wagon they had kept for the help, but it served the purpose now. The Duesenbergs were all gone, Faye's Bentley coupé, the Cadillac, and the rest of the fleet of cars they had had.

For Faye and Ward it was like leaving their youth behind them for good. The house in Palm Springs had to be vacated by June. But in the meantime, it gave Faye and Ward a place to leave the children for a few weeks. She had leads to several houses to rent, and the furniture would wait in storage until then. She was going to drive down to Palm Springs with all of them, and then go back to Los Angeles alone to find a house, while Ward oversaw the packing up of the house in Palm Springs. He insisted that it was the least he could do, after all she had tackled things alone in L.A. She didn't have to touch a thing this time, she just had to find them a decent place to live. And she knew it wasn't going to be easy to do. With the sale of the shipyard, the house in Beverly Hills, all

103

their furniture, their art, the collection of rare books, the cars, and the house in Palm Springs with most of its contents too, they would have just enough to pay off all of their debts, with about fifty-five thousand to spare, which, carefully invested, would eke out barely enough to support them all. They were going to rent a house, and Faye was hoping she could find something cheap. And as soon as they were all settled in, and the children went back to school in the fall, she was going to see about getting a job. Of course Ward was talking about getting one too. But she had more faith in her own ability to find work, and it would be easier for her. She had worked before, and even if she was thirty-two, she certainly wasn't over the hill yet, not for what she wanted to do. Lionel would be starting first grade, Greg would begin kindergarten, the twins would be in nursery school, so she would have plenty of free time. She was keeping only their nurse to keep an eye on all of them, and the baby as well, and help with the housework and cook. Baby Anne was only four months old and not much trouble yet. It was a perfect time for Faye to leave home. And as she thought of it on the drive to Palm Springs, she suddenly felt guilty about the baby again. The others had all spent so much time with her at the same age, but this time she hadn't had a moment to spare. She had barely seen the baby since she'd been born. But disaster had struck so immediately after her birth, it was impossible even to think of her more than now and then, she had so many other things on her mind. Ward glanced over at her several times as they drove, noticed the frown and patted her hand. He had promised her he would drink less once they got to Palm Springs, and she hoped he would keep his word. The house was smaller there and the children would be much more aware of it if he was drunk all the time. Besides, he had a lot to do, and Faye hoped it would keep him occupied.

She went back to Los Angeles two days later, by train, and moved into a small room at the Hollywood Roosevelt Hotel when she arrived. The houses she saw were depressing beyond words. In bad neighbourhoods, with tiny backyards and small ugly rooms. She combed the papers, and called all the agencies, and finally, desperate, by the beginning of the second week, she found a house that was not quite as ugly as the rest, and was large enough for all of them. It had four good-sized bedrooms on one floor. She had already decided to double up the boys, and the twins, and the nurse and Anne could also share a room. The fourth bedroom would be for her and Ward. Downstairs there was a large, somewhat gloomy, cheaply panelled living room, a fireplace that had not worked in years, a dining room that looked out on a bleak little garden, and a big old-fashioned kitchen, big enough to put a big kitchen table in. The children would certainly be closer to her than they ever had before, and she tried to tell herself that it would be good for them, that Ward wouldn't hate it and refuse to live in it, and that the children wouldn't cry when they saw the dreary rooms. The best thing about it was the rent, which was an amount they could afford. And it was in a family neighbourhood in Monterey Park which was a long, long way from their old life in Beverly Hills. There was no kidding anyone about that, and when she returned to Palm Springs, she didn't really try to. She told them all that it would be 'for a while', that it was an adventure they would share, that they would all have chores to do, and they could plant pretty flowers in the garden. And when Ward faced her when they were alone, he stared at her openly and said the words she feared:

'How bad is it really, Faye?'

She took a deep breath. The only thing she could do was tell him the truth. He would find out soon enough for himself. There was no point lying to him. 'Compared to what we had?' He nodded. 'It's grim. But without looking back at that, if we can make the effort not to for a while, it's not so bad. It's freshly painted, it's reasonably clean. The little bit of furniture we have left will fit. And we can make it prettier with curtains and bright flowers. And,' she took another breath, trying not to see the look of devastation on his face, 'at least we have each other. It'll be all right.' She smiled at him but he turned away.

'You keep saying that.' He was angry at her again, as though it were all her fault. And secretly, she was beginning to believe it was. Maybe she shouldn't have forced him to face it all. Maybe she should have let him go on living in debt until they couldn't any more. But it would have all had to be faced sooner or later anyway . . . wouldn't it? She didn't have the answers any more. At least he had kept his word, and packed up the house in Palm Springs, and he hadn't started drinking again until she returned. Then he knew she would take over and he could relax. At least for a while . . . until they moved.

When they closed up the house and drove to Los Angeles all together on a Tuesday afternoon, it felt terribly hot. Faye had already made a little headway in the Monterey Park house before rejoining them in Palm Springs. She had unpacked what she could by herself, hung a few pictures in everyone's rooms, filled vases with flowers, made beds with clean sheets. She had done everything possible to make it look like home, and the children were intrigued when they arrived, like puppies sniffing out their new home, and delighted when they found their rooms and their toys and their own beds. Faye watched them hopefully, but Ward looked as though he were going to faint as he walked into the dark, ugly, wood-panelled living room. He said not a word as Faye watched his face, and fought back tears. He glanced out into the garden with narrowed eyes, glanced around the dining room, noticed a table they had kept from an upstairs den, and instinctively looked up, expecting to see a familiar chandelier that had been sold months before, and then shook his head as he looked at Faye. He had never seen anything like it before. He had actually never been in a home this poor, and instantly it cut him to the quick.

'So much for that. I hope at least it's cheap.' He felt guilt overwhelm him again at what he was doing to her, and all of them.

Her eyes were gentle, as they stood facing each other in their new home. 'It's not forever, Ward.' That was what she had told herself years before, as she longed to escape the poverty of her parents' home. But that had been much worse than this. And this wouldn't be forever either. This time, she was sure of that. Somehow, they would dig their way out.

Ward looked around again sorrowfully. 'I don't think I can take too much more of this.' And at his words she felt anger bubble up inside of her for the first time in months, and when she spoke she roared.

'Ward Thayer, everyone in this family is making the best of this, and you'd damn well better too! I can't turn the clock back for you. I can't pretend this is our old house. But this is our home, *ours*, mine, the children's and yours too.' She was trembling as she stood staring at him and he looked at her eyes. She was determined to make the best of it, and he respected her for that, but he wasn't sure he had the strength to do it too, and when he went to bed that night, he was almost sure he did not. The room smelled of old rot, as though the beams had been damp for years, there was a musty smell about the whole house, and the curtains Faye had hung were from their old servants' quarters and didn't fit. It was like becoming servants in their own home, it was all like an incredible, surrealistic, ugly dream. But it was theirs, and it was real, and she knew they had to make the best of it. He turned to say something to her, to apologise for how badly he was taking it all, but she was already fast asleep, curled into a little ball, huddled onto her own side of the bed, like a frightened child, and he wondered if she was scared too. He was terrified most of the time these days – even the drinking didn't help any more – and he wondered what would happen to the rest of their lives. Was this it for good? They certainly couldn't afford more than this, and he wondered if they ever would again. She said that it was just a stepping stone, an interim place, that one day they would move on, but when and how and to where? In his wildest dreams, as he lay in the ugly, musty bedroom, painted pale green, he couldn't even imagine it.

HOLLYWOOD ... AGAIN 1952-1957

CHAPTER 8

It had been years since he had represented her, and her hand trembled as she dialled. It was entirely possible that he had retired, or perhaps wouldn't have time to speak to her. He had called her when Lionel had been born, and tried to convince her once again to pick up the threads of her career before too much time had passed and it was too late. And it was surely too late now, seven years after she had abandoned her career. She didn't need him to tell her that. But she needed his advice. She had waited until September. The children were all in school, as planned, except, of course, Anne. And Ward was out seeing old friends, trying to get a job, he said, but most of the time he just seemed to be having long lunches at his favourite restaurants and clubs; 'making contacts', he told her when he came home. Maybe he was, but she could see it going on for years and getting them nowhere, not unlike this call . . . if he wouldn't talk to her. She prayed he would, as she gave the secretary her name. There was an interminable pause and she was asked to hold the line, and then suddenly there he was . . . just like the old days, long before this.

'My God . . . a voice from the distant past. Are you still alive?' His voice boomed in her ear as it had years before and she laughed nervously. 'Is it really you, Faye Price?' She was suddenly sorry she hadn't seen more of him over the years, but she'd been so busy with Ward and the kids, and Hollywood was part of another life.

'It's me, the same Faye Price Thayer, with a few grey hairs now.'

'That can be changed, although I don't suppose that's why you called me. To what do I owe the honour of this surprise, and do you have ten children yet?' Abe sounded as warm as he had before, and she was touched that he still had time to talk to her. They had been such good friends once upon a time. Her agent for all the years

111

of her stellar career, he had faded from her life, and now she was knocking on his door again. But she smiled at what he had said.

'Not ten children, Abe, only five. I'm only halfway there.'

'Christ, you crazy kids. I knew from the light in your eye, you meant it way back then, that's when I gave up on you. But you were great while you were up there, Faye. And you could have stayed there for a long, long time.' She wasn't sure she agreed with him, but it was nice to hear. She would probably have started to slip one day. Everyone did eventually, and Ward had spared her that, but now . . . she had to get up the courage to ask what she wanted from him, although he must have suspected the moment he heard her name. He read the papers, just like everyone else, and had heard how much trouble they were in, the house sold, their goods auctioned off, the shipyards closed. It was a quick trip down, just like for some of his stars. But it never changed the way Abe felt about the people he liked. He felt damn sorry for Faye now, with no money, a husband who had never worked a day in his life, and five kids to support.

'Do you ever miss the old days, Faye?'

She had always been honest with him. 'I never have, to tell you the truth.' Not till now anyway, and even then, she had something else in mind.

'I don't suppose you have had time with five kids on your hands.' But she'd have to go out and work again now. He knew that only too well and decided to get to the point, and spare her the embarrassment of crawling to him.

'To what do I owe both the honour and the pleasure of this call, Mrs Thayer?' Though he could guess . . . a part in a play . . . a small part in a film. He knew her well enough to know she wouldn't ask the moon of him.

'I have a favour to ask, Abe.'

'Shoot.' He had always been direct with her and if he could, he would help her now.

'Could I come and see you sometime?' She sounded like an ingenue again and he smiled.

'Of course, Faye. Name your day.'

'Tomorrow?'

He was startled at how soon she wanted to come in. They really were desperate then. 'Fine. We'll have lunch at the Brown Derby.'

112

'That would be wonderful.' For just an instant, she thought longingly of the old days. It had been years since she had thought of that. And after she hung up, she walked upstairs with a secret smile. She just prayed he wouldn't tell her she was out of her mind.

When she met him the next day, he didn't say that, but he sat very quietly, thinking of what she had asked. He had been shocked to hear the details of what had happened to their life, and that they were living in Monterey Park. It was so far from where they had begun, light-years away in fact, but she seemed to be holding up. She was one hell of a gutsy girl, always had been, and she was smart enough to do what she had in mind. He just wondered if anyone would give her the chance.

'I read somewhere that Ida Lupino directed a film for Warner Brothers, Abe.'

'I know. But not everyone is going to give you that chance, Faye.' He was honest with her. 'In fact, few will.' And then, 'What does your husband have to say about all this?'

She took a deep breath and looked her old agent in the eye. He hadn't changed much over the years. He was still rotund, grey-haired, sharp, demanding, but kind, and honest to a fault. And best of all, she sensed instantly that he was still her friend. He would help her if he could. 'He doesn't know yet, Abe. I thought I'd talk to you first.'

'Do you think he'll object to your coming back to Hollywood?'

'Not like this. He might if I tried to act again. But the truth is I'm too old now, and I've been gone for too long.'

'At thirty-two, that's a lot of crap. You're not too old, but it would be hard to make a comeback after all these years. People forget. And the young kids have their own stars today. You know,' he sat back and drew pensively on his cigar over dessert. 'I like your idea a lot better. If we can sell it to a studio, it would really be something else.'

'Will you try?'

He pointed the cigar at her. 'Are you asking me to be your agent again, Faye?'

'I am.' She met his eyes and he smiled.

'Then I accept. I'll sniff around and see what I get.' But she knew him better than that. She knew he would turn over every rock and stone until he found something for her, and if he didn't find anything, it would be because there was nothing there. And she was right about him. He didn't call her for six weeks, and when he did, he asked her to come in to see him again. She didn't dare ask him on the phone. She just took the bus from Monterey Park to Hollywood, bumping along nervously, and then running up the steps to his offices. She was breathless when she arrived, but still beautiful he noticed as she sat down. She was wearing a striking red silk dress with a lightweight black wool coat. She had kept some of her clothes from their better days and she looked wonderful. She almost trembled as he watched her face, and he reached across the desk and took her hand. He knew just how anxious she was.

'Well?'

'Relax. It's nothing fabulous, but it's a start. Maybe. If it appeals to you. It's a job as assistant director, at pathetic pay, at MGM. But my friend Dore Schary liked the idea. He wants to see what you can do. And he's well aware of what Lupino is doing at Warner Brothers. He likes the idea of having a woman in his stables too.' Schary had long since had the reputation of being the most forward-thinking of the studio heads, he was also the youngest of all of them.

'Will he be able to tell if I'm any good, if I'm working for someone else?' She was worried about that, but on the other hand, no one would just let her direct by herself for the first time. She knew that too.

Abe nodded his head. 'The director is someone he has under contract, and Dore knows he's no good. If this film turns out halfway decently, it'll be due to you. And the guy is so lazy and drinks so much, he won't even be on the set half the time. You'll have a free hand; what you won't get is much money or much glory out of this. That comes the next time around, if you do a good job this time.'

She nodded. 'Is the picture any good?'

'It could be.' He was honest with her again, outlined the script, told her who the stars would be. 'Faye, it's a chance and that's what you want. If you're serious about this, I think you should give it a try. What have you got to lose?'

'Not much I guess.' She looked at him pensively, thinking over all that he had said, and she liked the sound of it. 'When would I

114

start?' She wanted time to study the script, and she could almost see Abe gulp. He knew how she liked to work, how thorough she was, how studious. He grinned sheepishly.

'Next week.'

Faye rolled her eyes with a groan. 'My God.' It also didn't give her much time to break Ward in to the idea. But this was what she wanted, it was all she knew how to do. She wasn't even sure she knew how to do it, but she desperately wanted to try. She had secretly been thinking about it for months. She looked Abe Abramson in the eye and nodded her head. 'I'll take it.'

'I haven't told you how much.'

'I'll take it anyway.'

He told her the pay, and they both knew it was ridiculous, but the important thing was that she was being given a chance.

'You'll have to be on the set by six o'clock every day, earlier if they want you to. You may work till eight or nine o'clock at night. I don't know how you'll manage with the kids. Maybe Ward can help you out.' Although Abe couldn't imagine that. Ward wasn't that kind of man. He was too used to having an army of help to fulfil his every need. And Abe wondered how much he helped Faye now.

'I still have one woman to help me out.'

'Good.' He stood up. It was just like the old days . . . almost . . . sort of . . . she grinned.

'Thank you, Abe.'

'Never mind that.' His eyes said that he felt sorry for her, but he respected her. She'd bail herself out yet. She was just that kind of girl. 'Come back tomorrow and sign the contract, if you can.' It meant another long bus ride into town, but nothing compared to the ride she would have now every day, getting all the way across town from east to west, to Culver City, and MGM. But she would have walked over ground glass for this job, or for Abe. She knew he would take ten percent from her, and ten percent of what she would be making was hardly worth looking at for him, but he didn't seem to mind. And neither did she. She was thrilled.

She had a job! She wanted to shout as she ran down the stairs. And she smiled to herself all the way home on the bus, and burst into the house the way one of her children would have.

115

She found Ward sitting in the living room, obviously feeling the effects of another champagne lunch with one of his friends, and she dropped onto his lap and threw her arms around his neck.

'Guess what?'

'If you tell me you're pregnant again, I'll kill myself . . . but only after I kill you!' He laughed at her and she shook her head with a smug look he hadn't seen her wear before.

'Nope. Guess again.'

'I give up.' His eyes were red and his words were slurred but she didn't even mind that now.

'I have a job!' He looked shocked and she went on. 'As assistant director on a film that starts next week at MGM.' He stood up so quickly that she had to scramble to her feet so as not to fall on the floor, as he looked down at her.

'Are you out of your mind? What the hell did you do that for? Is that what you've been out doing? Looking for work?' He looked horrified, and she wondered how he thought they were going to support themselves. Fifty-five thousand in bonds was hardly going to do the job for two adults, five children, and a maid. 'Why the hell did you do a thing like that?' He was shouting at her and the children were staring at them from the stairs.

'One of us has to, Ward.'

'I told you, I've been making contacts every day.'

'Great. Then something will turn up for you soon. But in the meantime, I want to do this. It could be a wonderful experience.'

'For what? Is that what you want? Hollywood again?'

'Only like this, not like the old days.' She fought to keep her voice calm, and she wanted to be honest with him. She also wanted the children to go upstairs and stop staring at them, but when she waved them away, they didn't budge, and Ward paid no attention to them at all, these days he rarely did. 'I think we should talk about this when we're alone.'

'To hell with that. We'll talk about it now.' His good looks seemed to vanish as he raged. 'Why didn't you ask me before you did this?'

'It came up suddenly.'

'When?' He was throwing words at her like rocks.

'Today.'

'Fine. Then tell them you changed your mind. You're not interested.'

Suddenly something in her snapped and she could feel fury mounting in her. 'Why should I do a thing like that? Ward, I want this job. I don't give a damn how badly it's paid, or what you think. This is what I want to do. And one day you'll be glad I did. Somebody has to bail us out of this mess we're in.' Instantly, she regretted the words.

'And you're it. Is that it?'

'Maybe so.' She might as well go on now, the damage was done.

'Great.' His eyes blazed at her as he grabbed his jacket off the back of the chair. 'Then you don't need me around here, do you?'

'Of course, I do ...' But the words weren't out of her mouth before he had slammed out of the door and Valerie and Vanessa began to cry, as Gregory looked sadly down at her.

'Is he ever coming back?'

'Of course he is.' She walked up to meet them, suddenly feeling tired. Why did he have to make everything so difficult? Why did he have to take it all so personally? Probably because he drank too much, she told herself with a sigh, as she kissed Lionel and Greg's hair, and then reached down to pick up the girls in her arms. She was strong enough to carry both of them. She was strong enough to do a lot of things. Maybe that was the problem with Ward. He didn't like knowing that and it was getting harder and harder to keep that fact from him. She wanted to ask him why he was doing this to her, but she already knew the answer to that. He couldn't cope with what had happened to them, and his choices were to blame her or himself. Either way she paid the price. As she did that night, lying awake until four o'clock, waiting for him to come home, praying that he hadn't smashed up the car and got hurt. He walked in at four-fifteen, reeking of gin and barely able to crawl into bed in the darkened room. There was no point even talking to him now. She would wait until morning and tell him her plan. But when she did, he was not impressed.

'For Heaven's sake, Ward, listen to me.' He was so hung over he could barely see, and she was in a hurry to get to Abe's office in Hollywood, to sign the contract and pick up the script.

'I don't want to listen to that shit. You're as crazy as I used to be. Pipe dreams. That's all they are. You're nuts. You don't know any more about directing than I do, and I don't know a damn thing about any of it.' He looked at her furiously.

'Neither do I. But I'm going to learn. That's the whole point of this job, and maybe the next one after that . . . maybe the next ten films, for all I know. But after that at least I'll know something about it, and what I'm suggesting to you isn't all that insane.'

'Horseshit.'

'Ward, listen to me. Producers are people with a lot of contacts, people who know other people with money. They don't have to have a dime themselves, and they don't even have to like the film, although it helps if they pretend they do. They're go-betweens. They put together the deal. What better job for you? Look at the people you know, the contacts you have. Some of your friends would love to invest in films and get a little bit involved in Hollywood. And one day, if we do this right, we could be a team. You produce, I direct.' He looked at her as though she were out of her mind.

'Why don't you just sign us up for vaudeville? You're goddamn nuts, and you're going to make a fool of yourself.' Finally, she pulled away from him. He didn't want hope yet. He couldn't even begin to see the possibilities, but she could. She could see it all, if he'd only get off his backside and try. She picked up her coat and handbag and looked down at him.

'Laugh at me if you want, Ward Thayer. But one day you'll admit I was right. And if you ever get the guts to be a man again, you might even try my idea. It's not as crazy as you'd like to think. Think about it sometime, if you have time, between drinks.' And with that, she walked out and closed the door.

And for the next two months, she barely saw Ward at all. He was sound asleep when she left the house for the long bus ride she took to get to work every day. She had to leave the house just after four, and the bus took forever to get to MGM. And by the time she got home at night, it was after ten o'clock, the children were sound asleep, and most of the time Ward was out. She never asked him where he went at night. She just fell into bed after a hot bath, a snack, and a glance at the script, and the next day it would begin again. It would have been enough to kill anyone, but she wouldn't give up. The director she was working for hated everything she did, and gave her a hard time whenever she was on the set, but

fortunately he was almost never there. And she didn't give a damn
what he did; there was pure magic between the actors and herself,
and she got something from them that no one else could. It showed
in the daily rushes, and more than that it showed in the print they
finally showed to Dore Schary. Abe called her at home late in
January, a week after they had wrapped up the film and she'd come
home to find Ward gone for several days this time. He had told the
maid he was going to Mexico 'to see friends', and she hadn't heard
a word from him. A small chill ran up her spine as the message was
delivered to her, but she forced herself to think that everything was
all right and concentrate on the children she'd barely seen since
she began working on the film. Abe's call came as she was playing
with Anne.

'Faye?' The familiar voice boomed in her ear, and she smiled.

'Yes, Abe.'

'I've got good news.' She held her breath. Please, God, let them
like her work. She had been dying over it, waiting to hear. 'Schary
says you're fabulous.'

'Oh God . . .' Tears stung her eyes.

'He wants to give you another shot at it.'

'On my own this time?'

'No. As assistant director again, but for more pay. And this
time, he wants you to work with someone good. He thinks you'll
learn a lot from him.' He mentioned a name that took Faye's
breath away. He had directed Faye herself years ago, and she knew
what Dore Schary said was true. She would learn a lot from this
man. She wanted to direct a film herself, but she knew she had to
be patient now. She reminded herself of that as Abe outlined the
new deal, and it sounded very good to her. 'What do you think?'

'The answer is yes.' They needed the money anyway, and God
only knew where Ward was. This Mexican trip was really the last
straw and she intended to tell him that when he came back. That,
and a lot of other things too. She wanted to tell him about this new
deal. It was wonderful, and there was no one else she could tell.
She had been so desperately lonely without him. 'When do I
start?'

'Six weeks.'

'Good. That'll give me some more time with the kids.'

He noticed that she didn't mention Ward, and hadn't for quite a while, but he wasn't surprised at that. He wouldn't have given ten cents for the chances that their marriage would survive. Ward was apparently not adjusting to their circumstances, from the little Faye had said, and sooner or later, Faye would dig her way out and leave him behind. It was easy to read the handwriting on the wall, or at least Abe thought so. He had never fully understood how deeply attached to Ward she was. Without family or many close friends, and having given up her old life as a star for him and the kids, she had been totally dependent on him for years and still was. She needed him, just as much as he needed her, or so she thought. It came as an enormous shock when she saw him return from Mexico. He was tanned, healthy, happy, with a long, thin Cuban cigar in his teeth, an alligator suitcase in his hand, and wearing one of his old white linen suits. He gave the impression that the Duesenberg would still have been parked outside if she'd looked. And he only appeared slightly sheepish when he looked at her as he came in. He had expected her to be in bed at that hour. It was well after midnight, but she was studying the new script.

'Have a good trip?' The chill in her voice hid all the loneliness and pain she had felt since he'd left. But she was too proud to let him see that . . . yet.

'Yes . . . sorry I didn't write . . .'

'I imagine you didn't have time.' Something in his face made her feel sudden anger at him. There was sarcasm in her voice, and anger and bitterness. He wasn't sorry he had gone at all. She could see it instantly, and she rapidly sensed the reason why. 'Who were you with?'

'Some old friends.' He set his bags down, and sat across from her on the couch, aware that this was more delicate than he had told himself it would be.

'How interesting. Funny you never mentioned it before you left.'

'It came up pretty suddenly.' Something nasty lit in his eyes. 'And you were busy with your film.' That was what it was really all about. His revenge for her finding a job when he had not, and she knew that too, but it wasn't fair of him.

'I see. Of course then I understand. Next time you leave for three weeks, you might try calling me at work before you go. You may be surprised at how easy I am to reach by phone.'

'I didn't know that.' He was growing pale beneath the tan.

'I guess not.' She looked deep into his eyes and knew the truth. She just didn't know how to confront him with it. But the papers made it easy for her the next day. It was all there. All she had to do was throw it across the bed at him. 'Your press agent's pretty good, and your travel agent must be too. I just don't happen to think much of your taste in girls, or your judgement about who you take along on trips.' There was a gash in her guts that felt as though it would kill her on the spot. But she refused to show him that. She didn't want him to know how much pain he'd caused her with this flagrant affair. And she knew too that it was his way of coping with all that had happened to them, of pretending that he was still part of the world he had just lost. But no matter how hard he pretended all that, it was over for them . . . unless he married that world again.

Ward almost gasped as he read the words. 'Bankrupt millionaire Ward Thayer IV and Maisie Abernathie should be back from Mexico any day. They've been lolling on her yacht outside San Diego for three weeks, and went down to Mexico to meet friends and play with the fish. They look awfully happy and everyone is wondering what he did with his retired movie queen . . .' Faye stared at him with terror and hatred in her eyes for the first time in her life. 'You can tell them I quit. It won't make headlines any more, but at least it'll clear things up for you and Miss Abernathie, you sonofabitch. Is that how you're going to handle what happened to us? By running around with people like her? You both make me sick.' Maisie Abernathie was a spoiled, self-indulgent heiress who had slept with almost every man they knew . . . 'except me', he used to tease. And now the list included him as well.

Faye walked out of the bedroom and slammed the door, and when he came downstairs, he found that she had left to take the four older children to school. She had been spending most of her time with them for weeks, to make up for the months she'd worked and would work again now. She missed them terribly when she worked, but she wasn't thinking of them as she walked back into the house and found Ward waiting for her, downstairs, in a blue silk dressing gown he'd bought in Paris years before.

'I have to talk to you.' He looked terrified as he stood up, and she brushed past him on her way upstairs. She was going to do her reading at the public library.

'I have nothing to say to you. You're free to go whenever you want. I'll find a lawyer, and he can call Burford.' She was beginning to convince herself that Maisie Abernathie was not only for real, but for good.

'It's that simple, is it?' He grabbed her arm as she swept by, avoiding his eyes. But now she looked him full in the face and it almost frightened him. He had never seen such contempt, let alone felt it, and it almost broke his heart as he realised what he'd done. 'Faye, listen to me . . . it was all a stupid mistake. I just had to get out of here . . . the children screaming all the time . . . you gone . . . this depressing house . . . it was more than I could take.'

'Good. Then you're out of it permanently. You can move back to Beverly Hills with Maisie. I'm sure she'll be happy to take you in.'

'As what?' He looked at his wife bitterly. 'Her chauffeur? For chrissake dammit. I can't even get a job, and you're at work all the time, what the hell do you know about what I feel? I can't stand this life. I wasn't brought up for this . . . I don't know . . .' He let go of Faye's arm and she stared unsympathetically at him. This time he had gone too far. The drinking, the self-pity, the inability to work, the lies as he wasted the last of his money before she found out, she could forgive him all of it, but not this. This was it. But he looked pitifully at her anyway. 'I can't help it. You're stronger than I am. You have something inside you that I don't. I don't know what it is.'

'It's called guts. And you've got them too, if you'd just give yourself a chance, and stay sober long enough to get on your feet.'

'Maybe I can't. Has that occurred to you yet? It has to me. Every day, in fact, until I went away. And maybe that's something I should do for good.'

'What?' She looked blank, but she felt terror crawl up her spine again.

He looked strangely calmer now, as though he knew what he had to do. 'I mean get out of your life, Faye.'

'Now? That's a stinking thing to do.' In spite of what she had said she was horrified, she didn't want to lose this man. She still loved him. He and the children were all that mattered to her. 'How can you do a thing like that to us?' There were tears in her eyes and he forced himself to look away, just as he had forced himself not to think of her in the last few weeks. He couldn't stand the guilt any more. What had happened was all his fault, and there was nothing he could do to help. He had nothing to offer her and she seemed to be doing fine on her own. At least that was what he told himself, and what he was telling himself now, without looking at her. Had he looked, he'd have seen the agony in her eyes as she stared back at him. 'Ward, what's happening to us?' Her voice was husky and hoarse, and he sighed deeply and walked across the room to look out the window at the nonexistent view of their neighbour's unpainted house, and the rubbish in his yard.

'I think it's time for me to get out of here, find a job on my own, and let you forget we ever met.'

'With five kids?' She would have laughed except that she wanted to cry. 'Are you planning to forget them too?' She stared at the back of his head in disbelief. This couldn't be happening to them, except it was. It was like a nightmare or a very bad script.

'I'll send you everything I can.' He turned slowly to face her from across the room.

'Is it Maisie? Are you serious about her?' It was hard to believe, but anything was possible now. Maybe he was that desperate for their old life, and Maisie was certainly part of it. But Ward shook his head.

'It's not that. I think I just need to get out of here for a while.' He looked almost bitter as he said it. 'I feel as though I ought to leave you alone to build a new life for yourself. You could probably wind up married to some successful film star.'

'If I'd wanted that, I could have had it years ago. But I didn't want that. I wanted you.'

'And now?' He felt the first surge of courage he had felt in years. It was all out now. There was no place left to go but up. He had nothing left to lose, if in fact he had lost her.

She stared at him with sad, empty eyes. 'I don't know who you are any more, Ward. I don't understand how you could go to Mexico with her. Maybe you'd better go back to her.' They were words of false bravado, but he snapped at the bait.

'Maybe I will.' He stalked upstairs then in a rage, and a moment later, she could hear him crashing around their bedroom, packing his things. She sat in the kitchen, staring blindly into a coffee cup, thinking of the last seven years and crying bitterly, until it was time to pick the children up at school again.

And when she came home with the kids, he was gone. The children had never realised he was back, so she had nothing to explain to them. She fixed dinner for them that night, lamb chops that were overcooked, baked potatoes that remained like rocks, and spinach that she burned. She wasn't at her best cooking for them, but at least she tried, and all she could think of that night was where he was – with Maisie Abernathie undoubtedly – and had she been wrong to blow up at him? She lay in bed that night, thinking all the way back to Guadalcanal, the good times they had shared . . . the tenderness, the dreams, and she cried long into the night, and finally cried herself to sleep, aching for him.

CHAPTER 9

The second film Faye worked on was far more difficult than the first; the director was constantly there, making demands on her, giving her orders, criticising what she did. There were times when she would have dearly loved to throttle him, but when all was said and done, he gave her a rare and very special gift. He taught her all the tricks she so desperately needed to know for her new trade; he demanded the utmost from her and got far more than that, and at times he let her take the reins and then corrected her. When they finished the film, she had learned more than she might have otherwise in ten years and she was grateful to him. He paid her an enormous compliment before walking off the set for the last time and there were tears in her eyes as she watched him go.

'What did he say to you?' one of the grips whispered and Faye smiled.

'He said he'd like to work with me again, but he knows he won't. That I'll be directing my own film next time.' She sighed deeply and looked at the actors hugging and kissing and celebrating the end of their hard work. 'I hope he's right.' And he was. Two months later, Abe offered her her first job as director at MGM again, without being assistant to anyone. Dore Schary had given her her big chance, and she had lived up to it.

'Congratulations, Faye.'

'Thanks, Abe.'

'You deserve every bit of it.' The new film would begin in the autumn. It was an enormous challenge and she was pleased. The children would be back in school by then. Lionel was going into second grade, Greg into first, the twins were still in nursery school for this final year, and Anne was not yet two years old, straggling behind the others, anxious to keep up, and somehow always outrun by them. Faye always meant to spend time with her, but somehow she never had enough time. The others clamoured for her; now she would have the script to study and read for several months, eventually the film to do. It was difficult to stop everything and spend time with a baby again. Anne was different from the others; not only younger, but also so much less able to communicate. It was always easier to leave her with the nurse, who loved her so much, and Lionel who had always been especially attached to her.

Faye was excited about the new film, except that day in, day out, she still thought of Ward and wondered where he was. Since the day he'd walked out, they'd never heard from him. She'd read about him in Louella Parsons once, but the piece told her nothing at all. At least it hadn't mentioned Maisie Abernathie.

In light of that, the film gave her something to do. She had been anxious to keep her mind occupied since finishing the other film. She had asked Abe for a lawyer's name several months before, but somehow she had never got around to calling him, although she promised herself that she would. Something always came up, and the memories would flood her again.

Then suddenly, one day in July, Ward appeared at her front door. The children were playing in the back, in the yard they had all so carefully planted with flowers. The nurse had built a swing for them, proud of their accomplishment and ingenuity. Suddenly, there he was, in a white linen suit and a blue shirt, looking more handsome than he ever had before. For an instant, she felt the old familiar pull towards him, but she reminded herself that he had walked out on her, and Lord only knew who he was involved with now. She felt shy as she looked at him, and lowered her eyes before glancing up at him again.

'Yes?'

'May I come in?'

'Why?' She stared at him nervously and he looked uncomfortable, but it was obvious he wouldn't go away until she let him in to talk to her. 'It'll upset the children if they see you here.' They had only recently stopped asking for him and she assumed that Ward was planning to disappear again.

'I haven't seen my children in almost four months. Can't I at least say hello to them?' As she hesitated, she noticed that he was thinner than he had been before. It made him look younger than he had in years. She hated to admit to herself how handsome he was. There was no point falling in love with him all over again. 'Well?' He wasn't backing off and finally she stepped back and held the screen door open for him. The house looked even uglier to her than it usually did, seeing it again through his eyes, as he stepped inside and looked around. 'Well, nothing's changed here.' It was a simple statement of fact and it riled her immediately.

'I suppose you're living in Beverly Hills again?' There was a sharp edge to her voice that cut through him like a knife, just as she had intended it to. He had hurt her terribly when he left, and he was probably just coming back to torment her again. She instantly assumed the worst.

He turned to her quietly. 'I'm not living in Beverly Hills, Faye. Do you really think I would leave all of you in a place like this and go back to Beverly Hills myself?' He looked horrified and Faye just stared at him. Somehow that was exactly what she had assumed.

'I don't know what you'd do, Ward.' She certainly hadn't noticed the cheques rolling in from him, but they had been managing on the income from their small fund and her salary. Actually, she wondered what he'd been living on for the past few months, but she had no desire to ask.

And at that point, the children came running in. Lionel stopped in the garden doorway, shocked to see him there, and then advanced slowly towards him with wide eyes. But when Greg saw his father, he thundered past Lionel and hurled himself into his arms. The twins followed suit. Anne simply stood staring at him, with no idea who he was. She didn't remember him and she looked up at Faye and held her hands out to be picked up. Her mother obliged, watching the other four climb all over Ward, laughing and screeching now as he tickled them. Only Lionel seemed more cautious than the other three, and he looked towards Faye again and again, as though needing to know what she thought of it. 'It's all right, Lionel.' She said it gently. 'You can play with your Dad.' But he remained on the fringe, watching them. And at last, Ward talked them all into getting cleaned up, with the promise of taking them out to lunch for a hamburger and an ice-cream cone.

'Do you mind?' he asked her after the children had gone upstairs.

'No,' she looked at him cautiously. 'I don't.' She looked nervous as she faced him now, but he seemed equally so. Four months was a hell of a long time. They were almost strangers again.

'I have a job, Faye.' He said it as though he expected trumpets to play and she resisted the urge to smile.

'Oh?'

'In a bank ... it's not a very important job. I got it from one of my father's friends. I just sit at a desk all day and collect a cheque at the end of the week.' He looked surprised, as though he had expected it to be more painful than that, like surgery.

'Oh?'

'Well, aren't you going to say anything, dammit?' He was angry at her again. Suddenly, she was so damned hard to please, and she had never been like that. Maybe going back to work had taken its toll on her. He knew she didn't just sit at a desk all day waiting for her cheque on Friday afternoons. He took a deep breath and tried again. 'Are you working these days?' He knew she couldn't be, or she wouldn't have been at home playing with the kids, at least it hadn't been that way when he was around.

'No, not for another month. I'll be doing my own picture this time.' She was instantly annoyed at herself for saying too much. It was none of his business any more what she did, but it felt good telling him anyway. It had always felt good telling him everything.

'That's great.' He seemed to hop from one foot to the other, watching her, not sure what to say to her. 'Any big stars in it?'

'A few.'

He lit a cigarette. He had never smoked before. 'We haven't heard from your lawyer yet.'

'I haven't had time to take care of it.' But that wasn't entirely true. She had been free for several months, not that he could know that. 'You will.'

'Oh.'

And then the children came thundering down. He took all four of the older ones to lunch, offering to drive them in his new car. A 1949 Ford. It still looked practically new and Ward glanced apologetically at her. 'A Duesenberg it's not, but it gets me back and forth to work.' She resisted the urge to tell him she still took the bus. The station wagon had finally died the month before, leaving them with no transportation at all. 'Would you like to come to lunch with us, Faye?'

She started to say no, but the children begged her so loudly that it was easier just to give in and go, and part of her was curious about him; where he had been, what he had done, where he was living now. She wondered if he was still involved with Maisie Abernathie, but she told herself she didn't care any more, and almost convinced herself until she saw the way the waitress looked at him and then she felt herself flush. He was still a very handsome young man, and women certainly seemed to notice him, more than men ever noticed her. But then, she still wore her wedding band, and everywhere she went, she dragged five children along.

'They're wonderful.' He praised her on the way home, as the four children pushed and shoved each other on the back seat of the dark blue Ford. 'You've done a good job with them.'

'It isn't as if you've been gone for ten years, for heaven's sake, Ward.'

'It feels like it sometimes.' He was silent for a little while and then glanced at her when they paused at a red light. 'I sure miss all of you.'

She wanted to blurt out, 'We miss you too,' but she forced herself to say nothing at all, and was surprised when she felt his hand on hers. 'I've never stopped regretting what I did, if that counts at all.' His voice was so low the children couldn't hear, and they were making such a ruckus they wouldn't have heard anyway. 'And I've never done it again. I haven't gone out with another woman since I walked out of our house.' 'Our house', strange words from him, referring to that awful place, and what he said touched her heart as her eyes filled with tears, and she turned to look at him. 'I love you, Faye.' They were the words she had longed to hear for four months and instinctively she reached out her arms to him. They were at the house by then and the children tumbled out of the car. Ward told them to go inside, and he would be there in a moment. 'Babe ... I love you more than you'll ever know.'

'I love you too.' Suddenly she began to sob, and pulled away to look at him with ravaged eyes. 'It's been so awful without you, Ward ...'

129

'It was just as terrible for me. I thought I'd die without you and the kids. Suddenly, I realised all we had, even without our old life and a big house ...'

'We don't need all that.' She sniffed and smiled. 'But we do need you.'

'Not as much as I need you, Faye Thayer.' He looked at her hesitantly. 'Or is it Faye Price again?'

She laughed through her tears. 'Not a chance!' And at the same time noticed that he was still wearing his wedding band too. At that exact moment, Greg was calling to him from the house.

'I'm coming, son! Just a minute.' He shouted back. There was so much left to say, but Faye slid slowly out of the car.

'Go ahead. They've missed you too.'

'Not half as much as I've missed them,' and then, with a look of desperation in his eyes, as he reached out and grabbed her arm, 'Faye, please ... can we try again? I'll do anything you want. I stopped drinking as soon as I left. I realised what a complete jerk I had been. I've got a lousy job, but at least it's something ... Faye ...' Tears filled his eyes and suddenly he couldn't contain his feelings for her any more. He bowed his head and began to cry. After a moment he looked at her honestly. 'I didn't know what to do with myself when you went to work. I felt as though I wasn't a man any more ... as though I never had been ... but, oh God, I don't want to lose you, Faye ... please ... oh babe, please ...' He pulled her into his arms, and Faye felt as though her heart had found its home again. She had never really given up on him. She wasn't even sure she ever could. She put her head on his shoulder and the tears began to flow again.

'I hated you so much for a while ... or at least I wanted to ...'

'I wanted to hate you too, but I knew I was the one who was wrong.'

'Maybe I was too. Maybe going back to work wasn't the right thing, but I didn't know what else to do.'

He shook his head. 'You were right,' and then he smiled at her through his own tears, 'you and your crazy ideas about making me a producer one day ...' He smiled tenderly at her. What a good woman she was, how lucky he was to have her back in his arms, even for an hour or two.

She was shaking her head at him. 'That wasn't a crazy idea. It's possible, Ward. I could teach you everything you need to know. You could hang around the set on this next film.' She looked hopeful but this time he shook his head.

'Can't. I'm a working man now. Nine to five and all that.'

She laughed. 'All right, but you could still be a producer one day, if that's what you want.'

He sighed and put an arm around his wife. 'Sounds like pipe dreams to me, my friend.'

'Maybe not.' She looked up at him, wondering what life would bring. At least it had brought him home to her again.

He stood in the doorway to the ugly house in Monterey Park, looking at her. 'Do we give it another try? ... No ... more correctly, will you give me another chance, Faye?'

She looked at him long and hard, and slowly a small smile dawned in her eyes. It was a smile born of wisdom and disappointment and pain. She was no longer a young girl. Life was no longer the same as it had been a few years before. Her whole world had turned upside down, and she had survived. Now this man was asking her to walk along beside him again. He had hurt her, deserted her, cheated on her, betrayed her. And yet, deep inside, she still knew that he was her friend, that he loved her, and she him, and that she always would. He didn't have the same instincts that she had, and was not nearly as well equipped to survive. But perhaps, side by side, hand in hand ... maybe ... just maybe ... in fact, she was sure of it. More important, she was sure of him again.

'I love you, Ward.' She smiled up at him, feeling suddenly young again. It had been an endless few months without him. She never wanted to live through that again. She could survive anything but that, even poverty.

He stood kissing her then, as the children looked on, and suddenly they all began to laugh. Greg pointed at them, laughing the hardest of all, as Ward and Faye began laughing too. Life was sweet again, as it had been long before, only better now. They had both been through hell and back, not unlike Guadalcanal in some ways. But they had won the war. Finally. And now life could begin again. For all of them.

CHAPTER 10

Ward gave up his furnished room in West Hollywood, without ever staying there again, and he moved back into the ugly house he had hated so much in Monterey Park, without ever noticing this time how dreary it was. It looked wonderful to him as he carried his bags up the stairs to their room.

They had three idyllic weeks before the children went back to school, and Faye began her new film. And when she did, he insisted that she take the car, while he took the bus to work, which saved her hours on the bus at 4 and 5 am, and she was grateful to him. He was nicer to her than he had ever been before. And if it was no longer emerald pendants and ruby pins, it was dinners he had prepared for her with his own hands, and then kept warm until she came home, little presents he bought when he got paid, like a book, or a radio, or a warm sweater for her to wear on the set. It was messages he left for her when she was so tired she wanted to cry, and the hot baths he ran with bath oil he had bought. He was so good to her, at times it almost made her cry. Month after month he proved to her how much he loved her, and she proved the same to him, and from the ashes of their old life emerged a stronger relationship than they had ever had before and memories of the ugly months began to fade. Still they rarely allowed themselves to reminisce about the old days. It was too painful for both of them.

In many ways Faye enjoyed her new life. Her first job as director went very well, and she was given three pictures to do in 1954, all with major stars. Each of them was a major box-office hit. She had begun to make a name for herself in Hollywood again, not as a pretty face or a big star, but as a director with a fine mind, a great gift, and amazing power with her stars. She could get a heart-rending performance out of a rock, Abe Abramson said, and Dore

Schary didn't disagree with him. They were both proud of her, and when the first offer of 1955 came in, Faye demanded what she had wanted from them for years. She had been grooming him ever since he came back, and she knew he was ready now. Her agent almost fell off his seat when she explained her conditions to him.

'And you want me to tell Dore that?' He looked shocked. The guy didn't know a damn thing about pictures and Faye was out of her goddamn mind as far as Abe was concerned. He had thought she was crazy when she took him back. It was the first time he had ever disagreed with her, but he never told her what he thought. Not then. But he did now. 'You're nuts! They'll never buy a package like that. He has no background at all. The guy is thirty-eight years old, Faye, and he has no more idea how to be a producer than my dog.'

'That's a disgusting thing to say, and I don't give a damn what you think. He's learned something about finance in the last two years; he has a sharp mind, and he has some influential friends.' But more importantly than that, Ward had finally grown up, and Faye was enormously proud of him.

'Faye, I just can't sell a package like that.' Abe was sure of it.

'Then you can't sell me, Abe. Those are my terms.' She was as hard as rock, and Abe wanted to reach across his desk and strangle her.

'You're making a big mistake. You're going to blow everything. If you screw this up, no one will ever touch you again. You know damn well how hard it was to sell a woman director at first. And everyone is just waiting for you to fall on your face. No one else will give you the chance Dore gave you, not again . . .' He was running out of arguments, and she held up a hand, bare of rings except for her simple gold wedding band which she hadn't taken off since her wedding day. All the other jewellery Ward had given her had been sold long ago. She didn't even miss it any more – it was part of another life, another time.

'I know all of that, Abe. And you know what I want.' She stood up and looked down at him. 'You can do it if you try. It's up to you. But those are my terms.' He wanted to throw something at the door after she left.

But he was even more stunned when MGM accepted her terms. 'They're even crazier than you are, Faye.'

'They said yes?' She was in shock as she clutched the phone.

'You two start next month. At least he does. He starts first and then you come into it once the film gets under way. Producer, director, with your own offices at MGM.' He still couldn't get over it, and he sat at his desk shaking his head. 'Good luck . . . and listen, you'd both better get your asses in here and sign the contracts right away before they come to their senses and change their minds.'

'We'll come in this afternoon.'

'Damn right,' he growled. And when they did go in Faye was proud of Ward again.

It was a terrible thing to say, but the hard times had been good for him. There was an air of quiet maturity about him now, and intelligence. Abe began to think he might just pull it off after all, and he knew she'd do everything to help. He wound up shaking hands with both of them and kissing Faye's cheek, wishing them luck, and shaking his head once they had left. You never knew . . . it was possible . . . just possible . . .

The film was a huge box-office hit, and their career took off after that, producing and directing two to three films a year. In 1956 they were finally able to leave the house Ward had hated so much, although now neither of them had time to notice it. They rented another house for two years. And in 1957, five years after they had left, they were in Beverly Hills again. Not in the grandiose splendour they once had known, but in a pretty, well-kept house with a garden front and back, and five bedrooms, which gave them an office at home, and a modest swimming pool. The children were enchanted with it, and Abe Abramson was happy for them. But not as happy as Ward and Faye Thayer were. They had made it back. It was like returning from the war all over again, and they clung to their careers for dear life, appreciating every moment of it.

BEVERLY HILLS ... AGAIN
1964-1983

CHAPTER 11

His office at MGM looked out at nothing in particular, and he glanced out without much interest, while giving dictation. When Faye walked in, she looked across the room at her husband's profile, and smiled to herself. At forty-seven years of age, he was as handsome as he had been twenty years before. More so perhaps – his hair had turned white and his eyes were the same wonderful deep blue. His face was lined, but his body was still long and lean and sinewy, and he was holding a pencil as he measured his words. It was about their next film, slated to go into production in three weeks, and almost on schedule this time. He was fearsome about that. Ward Thayer Productions went out on time, and were expected to come in on time too. And God help those who didn't cooperate with him. They never worked for him again. He had learned a lot in the last ten years. Faye had been right. He was a genius at producing films, more so than anyone had suspected at first. He learned to budget everything well in advance, and came in with investment money from sources that boggled everyone. He tapped the resources of his friends at first, but after that he became ingenious at going out to corporations for funds, conglomerates looking to diversify. As Abe Abramson had said about Ward, 'He could charm the birds off trees,' and he had again and again. He and Faye had worked long into the night for months, figuring it all out together for the first few years. But after the first half-dozen films, Ward was really on his own. She stuck to her directing. He put the packages together long before she got involved in the directing and together they produced hit after hit. They were often called Hollywood's Golden Team. And although they had their flops, most of the time they could do no wrong.

Faye was so damn proud of Ward. She had been for a long time.

The drinking had stopped, there had been no other women in his life since that distant interlude when they had been separated in 1953. He had worked hard, done well, and she was happy with him. Happier even than they had been in those early fairy-tale years. Those years no longer seemed real to her, and Ward seldom mentioned them any more. She knew he still missed that life, the easy life, the trips, the estate, dozens of servants ... the Duesenbergs ... but they had a good life now. Who could complain? They enjoyed their work, and the kids were almost grown up.

She smiled quietly at Ward now, and glanced at her watch. She would have to interrupt him soon. And as though he had sensed her in the room, he turned and smiled at her, their eyes met and held, in the way that people still envied them after all these years. There was something very special about Ward and Faye Thayer, a love which still burned brightly and was the envy of all their friends. Their life hadn't been without pain. But there had been rich rewards too.

'Thanks, Angela, we can finish the rest this afternoon.' He stood up and came around the desk to kiss his wife. 'Time to go?' He pecked Faye on the cheek and she smiled up at him. He still wore the same after-shave after all these years, and it was always like an announcement that Ward had been in the room. If she closed her eyes, it still conjured up the same romantic images of long before, but there was no time for that today. Lionel was graduating from Beverly Hills High. They had to be there in half an hour, and the other children were waiting to be picked up at home.

Faye glanced at the handsome sapphire and gold Piaget watch he had given her the year before. 'I think we should go, sweetheart. The troops are probably hysterical by now.'

'No,' he grinned at her, as he grabbed his jacket and followed her out, 'only Valerie.' They both laughed. They knew the children well, or thought they did. Valerie was by far the most high-strung, ebullient, excitable, with the worst temper coupled with the most strident demands. She lived up to her red hair, most of the time, in sharp contrast to her more subdued twin. And Greg had lots of energy too, but he used it differently; all he thought about were sports, and lately girls. And then there was Anne, their 'invisible child', as Faye referred to her sometimes. She spent most of her time in her room, reading, or writing poetry. She always seemed separate from the rest. She always had. And it was only when she was with Lionel that a different side of her came out, that she laughed and joked and teased, but if the others pushed her too hard, she would retreat again. It seemed to Faye that she was always saying to the others 'Where's Anne?' and sometimes they even forgot to ask. It was difficult to know the child, and she was never quite sure she did, which seemed an odd thing to say about one's own child, but it truly seemed to apply to Anne.

Ward and Faye waited for the elevator at MGM. They had their own complex of offices now, handsomely decorated all in white and bright blue and chrome. Faye had redone it all herself two years before, when Thayer Productions Inc. officially established permanent offices at MGM. In the early days they had had temporary offices there, and then they had set up shop halfway across town, and as a result, spent half their lives in cars driving to meetings with the MGM staff. But now they were both independent and at the same time part of MGM, subcontracting to them for two years at a time, working on their own projects as well as those they undertook for MGM. It was an ideal position to be in, and Ward was satisfied with the way things had worked out, although he privately thought it was all because of Faye. He told himself that, and once confessed it to her, although she disagreed violently with him, insisting that he didn't appreciate his own worth. And he didn't of course. She had always been so much more the star, so much more in control of everything. She had known everyone in the industry for years and they respected her. But they respected him too now, whether he admitted it to himself or not, and Faye wished he would. It was difficult to convince him of how important he was. Somehow he was never quite sure. But in another way, that was part of his charm, the boyish ingenuousness that had followed him into middle age, and still gave him the appearance and the sweetness of youth.

Their car was parked in the car park, a black convertible Cadillac they'd had for two years. They kept a huge station wagon at home for when they went out with the kids, and Faye had a small bottle-green Jaguar she loved to drive. But somehow, even at that, they never seemed to have enough cars. Now that both Lionel and Greg could drive, they were always fighting over the station wagon, a situation which was about to end, unknown to Lionel, that afternoon. As a combination graduation and birthday gift, they were giving him one of the new little Mustangs that had just come out. It was bright red, convertible, with white sidewalls and red upholstery. Faye had been even more excited than Ward when they picked it up the night before, and they had sneaked it into their neighbours' garage. They could hardly wait to give it to the boy that afternoon. They were all going to lunch at the Polo Lounge to celebrate, and there was to be a party for him at the house that night.

'It seems incredible, doesn't it?' Faye looked over at Ward as they drove home, and she smiled nostalgically. 'He's going to be eighteen ... and graduating from high school ... it seems like yesterday doesn't it, when he was just a little thing learning to walk?' Her words conjured up images of the old days, and Ward was thoughtful as they drove along. All of that had changed forever twelve years before, and it still saddened him sometimes when he thought of it. That had been such a good life, but so was this, and that didn't even seem real any more. It was a lost world, and he glanced at Faye now.

'You haven't changed a bit since then, you know.' He smiled appreciatively at her. She was still beautiful, her hair was still almost the same peachy blonde, and she coloured the grey so it didn't show. At forty-four, her figure was still good, her skin clear and smooth, and the green eyes still danced with emerald fire. He looked older than she did now, by quite a bit, but it was because of his white hair. His blond hair had turned early, but it suited him. It was in sharp contrast to the youthful face, and she often thought that she liked him better like this. He looked more mature. She leaned over to kiss his neck as he drove.

'You lie beautifully, my love. I look older every year, but you're still pretty dashing, you know.'

He chuckled with a look of embarrassment and pulled her closer to him. 'You're going to be cute thirty years from now, you know that? Necking with me as we drive along ... pulled over maybe ... catching a quickie in the back seat ...' She laughed at the thought, and he noticed the long, graceful neck he had always loved, amazingly still free of lines. He often thought that she should have stayed in films herself. She would still have been beautiful, and she knew so much about the art. He was reminded of it every time he saw her direct, but she was so damn good at that too. There was very little Faye Thayer couldn't do. The realisation of that used to bother him, but he was proud of her now. She was just one of those people who could do many things well. But the odd thing was that he was too, although he didn't recognize it, and would have argued, and often did, when Faye told him that. He didn't have the self-confidence she had, even now, or the drive, or the assurance that let her cast herself at anything, sure that she could accomplish it.

She glanced at the Piaget watch again now. 'Are we late?' Ward frowned as he looked at her. He didn't want to let Lionel down. He wasn't as close to him as he was to Greg, but Li was his oldest son after all, and this was his big day, and when he saw the car . . . Ward smiled again.

'We're not late yet. What are you smiling at?' Faye looked at him curiously.

'I was just thinking of Li's face when he sees the car.'

'God, he's going to die!' She giggled to herself again, and Ward smiled. She was so crazy about that boy, always had been, almost too much so, he thought sometimes, and too protective of him. She was never willing to let him take the physical risks Greg took, or be exposed to as many things. He didn't have Greg's physical strength, she always said, or his ability to take hard knocks, emotionally or otherwise, but Ward was never as sure. Maybe he would have been tougher, if Faye had given him a chance. In other ways he was so much like her, he was as quietly stubborn as Faye herself had always been, as determined about what he wanted to do, at all costs, as certain. He even looked like her; if you squinted they could almost have been twins, and spiritually, they were, to the exclusion of everyone else sometimes. If Ward had been honest about it, he would have been jealous of the boy sometimes. She was so close to him as he grew up, they confided in each other so much, that it left everyone else out, especially Ward, who resented it. Lionel was always polite to him, pleasant, but he never went out of his way to seek him out, to go anywhere with him . . . not like Greg, who bounded up to Ward the moment he came home, every night for the last sixteen and a half years, or ever since he could walk anyway. Sometimes Ward even found him asleep on his side of the big double bed when he got home at night. Greg would have some urgent adventure to relate to him and wanted to be sure he woke up when they got home. The sun rose and set on his Dad, and Ward had to admit that that kind of passionate approval was hard to beat, and it made Lionel's shy aloofness seem even more difficult to penetrate. Why even try when you had a child like Gregory panting at your feet? But he knew he owed something to his oldest son. He had just never been quite sure what.

Even the car had been Faye's idea. It would make his commute to UCLA in the autumn so much easier, and his summer job too. He was working at Van Cleef & Arpels, the jewellers, on Rodeo Drive, doing errands and odd jobs, and he was thrilled. It wasn't the kind of job Ward would have wanted for him, and Greg would have hated doing something like that, but Lionel had got the job for himself; he had gone in for the interview with his hair freshly cut, dressed in his best suit, and he had obviously impressed them despite his age, or maybe they had known who his parents were. But whatever it was, he had got the job, and when he announced it to the family that night, it was one of those rare times when he had seemed almost childlike in his excitement, instead of more composed and mature. Greg had looked nonplussed, and the twins had been none too excited at the news. But Faye had been especially pleased for him; she knew how badly he had wanted the job, and he had got it all on his own. She had urged Ward to congratulate him too, and he had, but he had to admit he hadn't been all that pleased.

'You sure you wouldn't rather go to Montana in August with Greg?' He was going to work on a ranch for six weeks, and before that he was going camping in Yellowstone Park with a group of boys and teachers from school, but that was exactly the kind of thing the elder boy hated most.

'I'd be a lot happier here, Dad. Honest . . .' His eyes were as wide and green as Faye's, suddenly terrified they wouldn't let him take the job, and he had tried so hard . . . but his father had backed down rapidly at the look on his face.

'I just thought I'd ask.'

'Thanks, Dad.' Lionel had disappeared into the solitude of his room. Ward had built on to the house several years before; they had no guest room any more, and the maid slept in a tiny

142

apartment built over the garage, but now each of the children had their own room in the main house, even the twins, who had been relieved finally to sleep apart, although they didn't admit it at first.

Ward and Faye drove into the driveway on Roxbury Drive, and the twins were already waiting on the front lawn. Vanessa was in a white linen dress with a blue ribbon on her long, blonde hair. She was wearing new sandals, and carrying a white straw bag, and both parents thought instantly how pretty she looked, as did Val, but in a far more striking way. She was wearing a bright green dress that was so short it was closer to her crotch than her knees. It was low-cut in the back, and defined her lush figure perfectly, and unlike her twin, she did not look anywhere near fifteen. She was already using makeup most of the time, her nails were freshly done, and she was wearing cute little green French heels, but Faye sighed and glanced at Ward as he stopped the car.

'Here we go again ... our resident siren on the march ...'

Ward smiled benevolently and patted his wife's hand. 'Let it go, babe. Don't get into an argument with her today.'

Ward squinted at her appraisingly, still from the safety of the car and then laughed. 'Just tell people she's your niece.' He looked gently at his wife then. 'She's going to be a beauty one day.'

'I'll be too old and senile by then to appreciate it.'

'Just let her be.' He always said that. It was his answer to everything, except Lionel of course. In Lionel's case, he always had to be told, reprimanded, made to conform. Ward expected everything from him. Always too much according to Faye. Ward had never been able to understand how different the boy was, how creative he was, how sensitive, how totally unique were his needs. But Val ... she was something else ... headstrong, demanding, belligerent. She was surely their most difficult child ... or was it Anne, so constantly withdrawn? ... sometimes Faye couldn't decide which was worse. But as she stepped out of the car, Vanessa came bounding towards her with that clear easy smile, and she decided to be grateful for the easy one today. It was simpler that way. She told her how pretty she looked, put an arm around her and kissed her cheek.

'Your brother's going to be so proud of you.'

'You mean Alice in Wonderland here?' Val sauntered up, seething inwardly as she noticed her mother's arm around her twin; she had been watching intently when she kissed Vanessa's cheek. 'Don't you think she's a little old for that look?' Valerie was everything mod, and in contrast, Vanessa looked like innocence itself. And now that she had come nearer, Faye could see a thick black line on Val's upper eyelid that made her physically cringe.

'Sweetheart, why don't you take some of that makeup off before we go? It's a little early in the day for all that, isn't it?' It was easier to blame it on the hour, rather than her age. Fifteen seemed more than a little young for Cleopatra eyes to Faye, and this sort of thing had never been her style anyway. But Valerie had adopted absolutely none of her mother's ways, or Ward's. She seemed to have her own ideas about everything, and God only knew where they came from; surely not from any of them, she told herself. She was straight out of a teenage film about Hollywood, with some of its worst features exaggerated until her mother wanted to scream. But Faye attempted to remain calm now, as Val stood in front of her and visibly dug in her little green heels.

'It took a lot of time to put this on, Mother. And I'm not taking it off now.' 'Make me' were the only words she forgot to add, and Faye wasn't sure she could have anyway.

'Be reasonable, sweetheart. It looks a little overdone.'

'Who says?'

'Come on, squirt, go take that shit off.' Greg had bounded out, wearing khaki slacks and a blue oxford shirt, a tie that was more than slightly askew and looked as though it might have spent the night under the bed for several years. His loafers were all banged up, and his hair wasn't quite lying down the way he wanted it to. But despite his obvious contrast to his father's far more debonair style, he was clearly a carbon copy of him, and Faye smiled as he glanced at Val with a shrug. 'It really looks dumb.' But his words only enraged Val more.

'Mind your own business . . . you're nothing but a dumb jock anyway.'

'Well, I can tell you one thing. I wouldn't go out with a girl with all that goop on her face.' He looked her over and it was obvious that he didn't approve. 'And your dress is too tight. It makes your boobs stick out.' She blushed faintly but was instantly furious with him. She had wanted them to, but she didn't want her hateful brother to point it out. 'Makes you look like a tart.' He said it matter-of-factly but her eyes flew open wide and she took a swing at him, just as Ward came out of the house again and shouted at them both.

'Hey, you two! Behave! This is your brother's graduation day.'

'He called me a tart!' Valerie was furious with him, and Vanessa looked bored. They went through it all the time, and she secretly thought he was right – not that that would influence Valerie anyway. She was so headstrong and determined, she'd do exactly what she wanted anyway, or make their lives miserable for the rest of the day. They'd all been through it before, at least ten thousand times, with her.

'She looks like one, doesn't she, Dad?' Greg was defending himself against her ferocious swing, and standing nearby, Faye heard the wrinkled blue oxford shirt rip.

'Stop it!' It was useless, but they exhausted her when they behaved like this. They usually did it when she was bone-tired, after a bad day on the set. Gone were the days of quietly reading them stories at night by the fire, but she hadn't been home for most of that anyway. The baby-sitters and the maids had taken her place over the years, and sometimes she wondered if this was the price she had paid for it. There were times when they were completely out of control, like now. But Ward stepped in and grabbed Val's arm, speaking to her firmly in a voice that quieted her down.

'Valerie, go and wash your face.' There was no ambiguity to what he said, no space for argument, and she hesitated for a moment, as he looked at his watch. 'We leave in five minutes, with you, or without, but I think you should be there.' And with that, he turned his back on her and looked at Faye. 'Where's Anne? I couldn't find her upstairs.' She didn't know any more than he did; she had come home from the office with him.

'She was here when I called. Van? Do you know where she went?'

Vanessa shrugged. It was impossible to keep tabs on that kid, she came, she went, she didn't talk to anyone, most of the time she was reading in her room. 'I think she was upstairs.'

Greg gave it a moment's thought. 'I thought I saw her go across the street.'

'To where?' Ward was beginning to get impatient with them all. It was begining to remind him of those unbearable family holidays

145

they used to take, to places like Yosemite, until they could finally afford to send them all to camp and have a little peace. It wasn't that he didn't enjoy his family, he did, but there were times when they all drove him nuts, and this was one of them. 'Did you see where she went?' He noticed silently that Val had disappeared into the house, hopefully to take some of the makeup off, or maybe even the dress, although that seemed too much to hope, and it was. She emerged while they were still hunting for Anne, the thick black line on her eyelids had diminished by slightly less than half. The dress was just as tight and green. 'Valerie, do you know where Anne went?' He looked at her exasperatedly, ready to kill them all.

'Yeah. She went to the Clarks'.' Simple. Finally. That child was always getting lost. He remembered the time he had spent three frantic hours hunting for her in Macy's in New York, only to find her outside, sound asleep in the back seat of their rented limousine.

'Would you mind running over to get her please?' He could see that the mod beauty queen was about to object, but after one look at her father's face, she didn't dare. She nodded, and ran across the street, the tiny miniskirt clutching her shapely rear. He glanced at Faye with a groan. 'She could be arrested in an outfit like that.'

Faye smiled at him. 'I'll go and start the car.' And out of the corner of her eye, she saw Valerie escorting their youngest child back across the street. She was dressed more appropriately than the rest in a pretty pink shirtwaist dress, perfectly pressed, the right length. Her hair was shining clean, her eyes bright, her red shoes were freshly shined. She was a pleasure to look at, in sharp contrast to her far more flamboyant older sister. She piled into the station wagon into the farthest row of seats, not because she was angry at anyone, but because it was where she liked to sit.

'What were you doing over there?' Greg asked as he got in, in front of her with one of the twins on either side. Anne was sitting alone, although usually Lionel or Vanessa sat next to her. It was no secret that she didn't get along with Val, and she didn't have much in common with Greg. It was Lionel whom she adored, and Vanessa who took care of her when no one else was around. Those were always Faye's orders to them. 'Vanessa, see to Anne.'

'I wanted to see something.' She said nothing more, but she had seen it . . . the graduation gift . . . the beautiful little red Mustang . . . and she was so happy for him. She didn't say anything to

146

anyone all the way to the school. She wanted it to be a surprise, and when they got out, Faye wondered if she knew. But she said nothing at all, just followed the others into the auditorium, and sat down at the end of the row. It was one of the happiest days of her life, and one of the saddest too. She was happy for him, but she was sad for herself. She knew that in the autumn, Lionel would be moving to an apartment he would share with friends on the campus of UCLA. Mum had thought he was too young, but Dad had said it might do him good. She knew why he had said that, because he was jealous that Li was so close to Mum. But now he would be gone. She couldn't imagine not living with him any more. He was the only person she could talk to. He always had been. It was always Li who took care of her, even made her lunch for school, and made it with things she liked to eat, not dried-up old bologna, or rotten leftover cheese. That's what Vanessa or Valerie would have done. But Lionel made her things like egg-salad sandwich, or roast beef, or chicken or turkey. He brought her books she loved to read. He talked to her late at night, explained how to do her maths. He was her best friend. He always had been ... and he tucked her in at night when Mum and Dad were at work. He had been more like a mother and father to her than they had ever been. And suddenly as she saw him on the stage, in his white mortar board and white robe she felt tears in her eyes. It was like watching him get married ... almost ... just as bad in some some ways. He was marrying a new life. And one day soon, he would be leaving her.

Greg watched him with envy, wishing he were the one graduating this year, if he ever did. His grades hadn't been good all junior year, but he had promised Dad he would pull them up next year ... lucky creep ... going to college ... although Greg didn't think much of his choice. He thought UCLA was a dumb school. He wanted to go to some place like Georgia Tech where he could be a big football star, even though Dad was talking about somewhere like Yale, if he could get in, of course he could play football there ... he almost drooled at the thought ... and the girls ...!

Valerie was watching a boy in the third row. Lionel had brought him home a few weeks before and he was the best-looking guy she had ever seen. With smooth jet-black hair, dark eyes, he was tall, had clear skin, and he danced like a dream. He was also going steady with some stupid senior girl. But Val knew she was a lot better-looking than his steady girl, if she could just talk to him a couple of times . . . but of course Li wouldn't cooperate. He never fixed her up with anyone. And then there was John Wells, Greg's best friend. He was cute, but he was so shy. He blushed every time she talked to him. And he was going to UCLA eventually too. That would really be a coup to land a college boy, but for the moment her only success had been with three boys in her own sophomore class and they were all drips, and all they wanted was to feel up her boobs. She was saving the rest for a college man! Like the guy in the third row . . .

Vanessa was watching her twin, almost reading her mind. She knew her too well. She even knew which boys she would like. It was really a pain how boy crazy she was, and she had been like that since seventh grade. Vanessa liked boys too, but it wasn't an obsession with her; she was more interested in writing poetry and reading books. Boys were okay, but there had been no one special yet. And she was beginning to wonder if Val had already gone all the way. She hoped not. It would ruin her life if she did. Of course there was the pill . . . but you couldn't get it unless you were over eighteen, or something, or engaged. She knew that one of the girls in the junior class had got it by pretending she was twenty-one, but she couldn't imagine doing that, or wanting to.

Faye would have been relieved if she could have read her thoughts. She worried about those things too. But her mind wasn't on Greg, or Anne, or the twins, it was entirely concentrated on her older son, standing so beautiful and innocent and tall, singing the school song, his diploma in his hand, as the sunlight streamed into the room. She looked at him, knowing that this moment would never come again, he would never be this young, or this pure. Life was just beginning for him and she wished so many things for him as the tears poured down her cheeks and Ward silently handed her his handkerchief. She turned and looked at him with a bittersweet smile. How far they had come, and how dear they all were to her . . . especially Ward . . . and this boy . . . she wanted so badly to protect him from all the pain in life . . . all the disappointments, the sorrows, and instinctively, Ward put an arm around her shoulders and pulled her closer to him. He was proud of the boy but he wanted very different things for him.

'He looks so sweet,' she whispered to Ward. In her eyes, he was still a little boy.

Ward whispered back, 'He looks like a man.' Or at least he hoped that one day he would. For the moment, he still had the slightly effeminate look of youth, and sometimes Ward wondered if he always would. He looked so much like her . . . and just as he thought that, he saw Lionel look out and into the crowd until he found Faye's eyes, and the two of them stared at each other lovingly, to the exclusion of all else. It made Ward want to pull her back, for her own sake as much as the boy's, but the two of them were beyond anyone's reach. They had always shared something that no one else could touch.

'He's such a wonderful boy.'

It made Ward doubly glad that Li would be moving out in the fall. He needed to get away from her. And he was even more sure of it when Lionel raced to hug Faye tight after the ceremony. The other boys were all standing around, holding hands with awkward-looking girls.

'I'm free, Mum! I'm not a high school kid any more!' He had eyes only for her, and she was so excited for him.

'Congratulations, sweetheart.' She kissed him on the cheek and Ward shook his hand.

'Congratulations, son.'

They all hung around for a while, and then went to lunch at the Polo Lounge at the Beverly Hills Hotel. And just as Anne knew he would, he sat with her in the very last seat on the way there. No one thought it strange. He had sat next to her back there for years, just as Faye and Ward had sat in front, and then Greg and the twins in between.

The crowd at the Polo Lounge was the same as it always was at lunch, showy, dressed in silks and gold chains and miniskirts, directors and writers and film stars, people asking for autographs and phones being rushed from one table to the next, as people pretended to get important calls. Faye went outside at one point and called Lionel to congratulate him, and everyone laughed, except Ward. They acted like lovers sometimes, and it always bothered him. But the boisterous group had a good time anyway. And after lunch, they all went home and swam in their pool. Some of the kids' friends dropped by, so no one noticed when Ward and Faye sneaked away stealthily and went next door to the Clarks'. Ward drove the car almost up to the pool, honking frantically as Faye laughed, sitting on a towel in the front seat, in her wet bathing suit, as the kids stared, not understanding any of it at first, except that obviously their parents had gone berserk. And then Ward hopped out, walked over to his son, and handed him the key as tears filled the boy's eyes, and he threw his arms around his father's neck, crying and laughing all at once.

'You mean it's mine?'

'Happy graduation, son.' There were tears in Ward's eyes too. He was touched by the boy's delight, it was a special moment that would never come again. With a shriek, Lionel hugged him again, while from the sidelines Anne watched him and beamed.

He invited everyone to pile into it, and Ward and Faye stood back as the children did, sitting on each other, on the seats, on the back of the car with the top down. 'Take it easy, Li,' Faye admonished him, and Ward took her hand, and led her a few steps back.

And for an instant, just an instant, before he started the car and drove away, he paused, and met his father's eyes, perhaps in just that way for the first time, and the two men exchanged a smile. There was no need for any more thanks than that. And as they drove away, Ward felt as though he had just made contact with his son for the first time, finally.

CHAPTER 12

That night there were a hundred people, most of them kids, invited to celebrate Lionel's graduation with a barbecue. And Ward and Faye had arranged for a rock band to play under a tent in the backyard. It was the biggest party they'd given in years, and the whole family was excited about it. Greg was wearing a wrinkled striped T-shirt and jeans. His blond hair looked uncombed, and his feet were bare. Faye was about to send him back upstairs but he escaped, and when she said something to Ward, he said what he always did, 'Let him be, babe, he's all right.'

His wife looked at him disapprovingly. 'For a man who used to spend his time changing shirts three times a day and wearing white linen suits, you certainly don't seem to expect much of your son.'

'Maybe that's why. That was twenty years ago and it was outdated then. People don't live like that any more, Faye. We were practically dinosaurs, albeit lucky ones. Greg has more important things on his mind.'

'Like what? Football? Girls? The beach?' She expected more of Greg, like the kind of things Lionel did. But Ward seemed happier with their jock than with their more intellectual child. It didn't make sense to her, and it always seemed unfair that he expected so much less of Greg, and never appreciated Lionel's outstanding accomplishments, but the matter couldn't be resolved in one night. It was a difference they had always had, sometimes more vociferously, but this was a special day and she didn't want to fight with him. It was funny, they actually fought very seldom, but occasionally about the children they disagreed violently and exchanged harsh words . . . particularly about Lionel . . . but not tonight . . . please not tonight she thought to herself, and decided to give in about Greg.

151

'All right . . . never mind . . .'

'Let him have a good time tonight. It doesn't matter what he wears.'

'I hope you feel the same way about Val.' But it was a real challenge to both of them not to say anything to her. She was wearing a skintight white leather minidress with a fringed skirt with matching boots that she had apparently borrowed from a friend.

Ward leaned over and whispered to Faye as he poured her a drink at the bar, 'What street corner does her friend work on? Did she say?' Faye laughed and shook her head. It seemed to her that she had had teenagers for so long that almost nothing surprised her any more. It prepared her well to deal with the actors at MGM. None of them could be more impossible, more difficult, more unpredictable, more argumentative than any teenage kid, although many of them tried.

'I think poor Vanessa tries to counteract Val's effect,' Ward said to Faye. She had worn a pink and white party dress that looked more suitable for a ten-year-old, and pink ballet shoes, with her hair done Alice in Wonderland style again. The two couldn't have been more opposite and Faye suspected it was no mistake. And looking around at all of them, Lionel in a light tan summer suit, looking handsome and dignified with a pale blue striped shirt and one of his father's ties, working at looking extremely grown up, the new car prominently parked on the front lawn, Greg in his wrinkled clothes . . . Valerie in the white leather dress . . . Vanessa in her childish garb . . . all of them individuals certainly, it reminded Faye of something again, and she looked at Ward over the drink he had handed her. 'Have you seen Anne?'

'She was around the pool with some friends a while ago. She's all right. Lionel will keep an eye on her.' He always did, but tonight was a big night for him, and Ward had even looked the other way when he saw him pouring himself a glass of white wine. He had to allow the boy let off some steam for a change, and if he got roaring drunk on graduation night, what harm could it do? It might dent his impeccable image for a change and that might do him good too. He just had to keep Faye busy enough not to keep an eye on him, and eventually he invited her to dance. Valerie watched them, horrified, Vanessa was amused, and eventually Lionel cut in and danced with Faye himself, and Ward went around to chat with friends, and make sure that none of the kids were getting too desperately out of line. A few of them were pretty drunk, but they were all Lionel's age, and this was their graduation night too. Ward felt that they had a right to get a little crazed, as long as none of them drove home, and he had given stern instructions to the parking valets. No one got the keys to his car if he appeared inebriated, and that applied to adult as well as child.

He spotted Anne sitting by the pool talking to John Wells, Greg's best friend. He was a sweet boy who worshipped the ground Greg walked on, and Ward suspected that Anne had a crush on John, but he wasn't likely to return her sentiments, considering that she was only twelve. She had some growing up to do, although Lionel treated her as though she already was. It was amazing how mature she could be sometimes. Far more than the twins, or even Greg at times. He wondered what she was saying to John, but she was so skittish and shy that he didn't dare approach them now, for fear that he would scare her off. She seemed to be having a good time, and a little while later, Lionel joined them, and Ward saw John look up with a smile, his admiration for Li matching Anne's ... the wonder of kids ... Ward smiled to himself, and went to retrieve Faye from a group of neighbours and friends. He wanted to dance with her again. He still thought she was prettier than any girl there, and it showed in his eyes as he slipped an arm around her waist.

'Care to dance?' He tapped her on the shoulder and she laughed when she saw who it was.

'I certainly would.'

The band was good. The kids were all having a good time. And Anne was enjoying herself with Lionel and John. They both treated her like an adult, which was more than most of the other kids did. She was tall for her age, and she had the same ripe peach-coloured hair that Faye had had in her youth. One day she would be a beautiful girl, but she never quite felt like one. She thought she wasn't as pretty as Faye, or as spectacular as Val, and she thought Vanessa had quietly distinguished good looks. But Lionel always told her that she was the best-looking of them all and she told him he was nuts. She pointed out her knobbly knees, what she described as 'wimpy, weird hair', because it framed her face in a soft fluff. She was just starting to develop breasts and she felt awkward about that too. She felt awkward about everything, except when she was with Lionel. He made her feel wonderful about everything.

'How do you like your new car?' John was smiling at the older brother of his friend, secretly admiring how neatly he tied his tie. He loved the way he dressed, but he would never have dared say that to him.

'Are you kidding?' Lionel grinned boyishly. 'I'm crazy about it. I can't wait to get it out tomorrow and really go for a spin.' He smiled at Greg's friend. John had been hanging around their house for years, and he had always liked him. He was more interesting than most of Greg's jock friends, although he had discovered that by accident one day when he'd talked to John when Greg was out. Most of the time, John pretended to be like the rest of them, but Lionel correctly guessed that it was camouflage he wore, and there was a lot more to him than just football and bikes, and the rest of it, which had never interested Lionel very much. 'I start work next week, and it's going to be great having my own car.'

'Where are you going to work?' John sounded interested, and Anne watched the exchange, saying nothing, as usual. But she was listening to her brother, and watching John's face. She had always thought he had beautiful eyes.

'Van Cleef & Arpels. It's a jeweller in Beverly Hills.' He felt a need to explain it to him. None of Greg's friends would have had any idea what that was.

But John laughed and, watching him, Anne smiled. 'I know that. My mother goes there all the time. They have pretty stuff.' Lionel looked both surprised and pleased. John hadn't gagged at the thought of Lionel working there. 'Sounds like a nice job.'

'It is. I'm looking forward to it.' He beamed, glancing in the direction of the car again. 'Especially now.'

'And UCLA in the fall. You're lucky, Li. I'm sick to death of high school.'

'It won't be long now. You've only got a year to go.'

'It feels like an eternity.' John groaned and Lionel smiled.

'And then what?'

'I don't know yet.' That wasn't unusual. Most of his friends hadn't figured that out.

'I'm doing cinematography.'

'That sounds wonderful.'

Lionel shrugged modestly. He had won photography awards ever since he was fourteen, and he had started getting into films two years before. He was ready for everything UCLA could offer him, and excited about going there, in spite of what his father said. His father had wanted him to go to a gung-ho school in the East. And he had the grades, but it had absolutely no appeal for him. He could sell that line to Greg.

He looked at John with a friendly smile. 'Come and see me at school sometime. You can have a look around while you're making your mind up about schools.'

'I'd like that a lot.' John looked at him intently, and for a moment the boys' eyes met and held, and then quickly John turned away, and a moment later he spotted Greg. He seemed anxious to leave them then, and Lionel invited Anne to dance. She blushed furiously at the thought and refused to dance with him, but after he had insisted for a while, she relented and followed him onto the floor.

'What's that?' The boy who had wandered into the house with Val had followed her into the den, and he was determined to get a hand up her skirt, which didn't look too hard. But a coveted object pushed onto a shelf in the bar had caught his eye. 'Is that what I think it is?' He was impressed. This was the first house he'd been in that actually had one of those, even though you sure heard about them a lot in L.A.

'Yeah. So what? Big deal.'

'It sure is.' He stared at it in awe, and then reached a hand out to touch it so he could tell his Dad when he picked him up. 'Whose is it? Your Mum's or your Dad's?'

It seemed to cost her something to admit it to him. 'My Mum's. You want a beer, Joey?' And then he almost fainted. There was another one. They had two!

'My God! She's got two of them. What for?'

'Oh for chrissake. I don't remember. Now do you want a beer or not?'

'Yeah. Yeah. Okay.' But he was much more interested in hearing what her mother had won the Oscars for. His Dad would ask him later, and so would his Mum, but Val didn't seem to want to talk about them. 'She used to be an actress, didn't she?' He knew she was a director now. Everyone knew that. And her Dad was a big producer at MGM. But Valerie sure didn't talk about it much. She was more interested in booze and boys. At least that was the reputation she had, and he could almost see up her white leather skirt when she sat down. But actually all he glimpsed was a long expanse of inner thigh.

'Did you ever smoke dope?' He hadn't but he didn't want to admit it to her. He was fifteen and a half years old, and he had met her in school that year, but he'd never taken her out. He hadn't had the guts. She was beautiful, and terrifyingly mature.

'Yeah. Once.' And then he couldn't help himself. He had to ask again. 'Let's talk about your Mum.'

That was it. She jumped to her feet, her eyes blazing with rage. 'No, let's not!'

'Don't be so uptight for chrissake. I'm just curious, that's all.'

Val looked at him with contempt as she strode to the doorway and looked back. 'Then ask her, you creep!' And with a flash of her red mane, she was gone, and he stared at the empty doorway in despair and whispered to himself:

'Shit.'

'Oh?' Greg stuck his head in to see who was there, and the boy blushed and jumped to his feet.

'Sorry ... I was just relaxing in here ... I'll go back outside.'

'That's okay. I do that here all the time. No sweat.' He grinned and disappeared, in hot pursuit of some dark-haired girl, and Joey went back outside. And eventually they all wound up in the pool late that night, in clothes, in bathing suits, in suits, in dresses, in sneakers and bare feet and shoes. They had a wonderful time and it was 3 am before the last guest went home, and when they were all gone, Lionel walked upstairs with Ward and Faye, and all three of them yawned sleepily as Faye laughed.

'We're a lively bunch ... good party though, wasn't it?'

'The best.' Lionel smiled, and kissed his mother goodnight, and when he sat down on his bed in the terry robe he had put on to cover his bathing suit, he sat and stared at the wall for a minute, thinking of the day . . . the diploma . . . the white gown . . . the car . . . the friends . . . and the music . . . and funnily enough, he found himself thinking of John, and what a nice kid he was. He liked him better than even some of his own friends.

CHAPTER 13

The day after the graduation party dawned like any other working day for Faye and Ward. The kids could sleep it off until noon, but they had to be at the studio by nine. Their next film would be starting soon and the two of them had mountains of work on their desks. It always seemed to require so much discipline to go on, to work, no matter how tired they were, especially when Faye was actually directing the film. Then she was always at the studio before six o'clock, often before the actors were there. But she had to be there, to breathe the air, to get the feel of it. In fact, while they were shooting, it was always difficult to force herself to go home, and sometimes she did not. Sometimes she slept in a dressing room, eating, sleeping, and thinking the script, making it become almost a part of her, until she knew every character as though she had been born in their skin in another life. It was what made her so demanding of the actors who worked for her, but she taught them a kind of discipline they never forgot, and most of the actors in Hollywood talked of Faye Thayer with awe. Her kind of talent was a gift, and she was so much happier than when she had been acting herself. This was the fulfilment she had been looking for, and Ward loved seeing that light in her eye, the light that came only when she was thinking of her work. It made him a little jealous sometimes because he liked what he did, but not with the same determination, the same fire, as she seemed to feel. She breathed her very soul into her work. And he was thinking of that now. In a few weeks he was going to lose her to their new film, but they both thought it was the best one they had ever done. They were both extremely excited about it, and more than once Faye had said how sorry she was that Abe Abramson was no longer alive. He would have loved this film. But he had died some years before. He had lived long enough to see their success, to see her win the second Oscar of her life, this one for directing, but he had died after that, and she still missed him sometimes, as she did now. She lay back against the seat, looking at Ward and thinking of the night before.

'I'm glad the kids had a good time.'

'So did I.' He smiled at her, but he was painfully hung over, and these days that was rare. He often wondered how he used to drink as much as he did. He couldn't take it any more, without paying a tremendous price for it. Youth . . . he smiled to himself . . . a lot of things changed when you added a few years and a few grey hairs . . . and other things did not. In spite of the hangover, he and Faye had made love that morning after he got out of the shower. That always got his day off to a good start, and he gently put a hand on her thigh now. 'You still drive me wild, you know . . .'

She blushed faintly and looked pleased. She was still in love with him. Had been for nineteen years, longer if you counted the time they had met in Guadalcanal in '43 . . . that would make it twenty-one . . . 'It's mutual, you know.'

'That's good.' He looked pensive as he pulled into the MGM car park. The guard at the gate had smiled as he waved them in. You could set your clocks by those two, he thought to himself . . . nice people . . . with nice kids . . . and they worked hard. You had to hand it to them. 'Maybe we should put a communicating door between our offices, and a lock on my door,' Ward suggested.

'Sounds good to me,' she whispered in his ear, and then playfully nipped his neck before sliding out. 'What have you got going today, love?'

'Not a hell of a lot. I think almost everything is squared away. What about you?'

'I'm meeting three of the stars.' She told him who. 'I feel like I need to do a lot of talking to all of them before we start, so that everyone's prepared. So that they all know where we're going with this thing.' It was the most challenging film she'd done. It was about four soldiers during the second world war, and it wasn't a pretty film in that sense. It was brutal and painful and tore your guts out, and most studio heads would have assigned a male director to it, but Dore Schary still trusted her, and she wasn't going to let him down. Or Ward. It hadn't been easy for Ward to raise the money for this film, in spite of their names. But people were afraid that no one would want to see a depressing film. After the assassination of John Kennedy the year before, everybody wanted comic relief, not serious film, but both Ward and Faye had agreed from the start, when they read the script, that this was it. It was a brilliant film, the screenplay was magnificent, as the original book had been, and Faye was determined to do right by it. Ward knew she would, but he also knew how nervous she was.

'It's going to be okay, you know.' He smiled at her just outside her office door. They both knew it would be, but he also knew that she needed reassurance from him, and he knew that even more certainly as she answered him.

'I'm scared to death.'

'I know you are. Just relax and enjoy yourself.' But she didn't do that until they started the film, and then she plunged into it even more fully than she usually did. She never got home before midnight or one, was gone again by five am, and often didn't come home at all. Ward knew it would go on for months that way, and he had promised her he would keep an eye on the children for her, and he tried. She had always worked that way. When she was directing a film she was totally involved, and when she was finished she spent her life folding shirts, doing laundry, driving car pools. She took special pride in it, but right now, even the children were far, far from her mind.

Ward came back to the studio to pick her up late one night; he didn't trust her to drive when she was that tired, or that wrapped up in her work. He was afraid she'd wind up in a tree off the motorway somewhere, so he came to pick her up, and she collapsed on the front seat of his car like a little rag doll. He leaned over and kissed her cheek. She opened one eye sleepily and smiled at him. 'I may not survive this one . . .' Her voice was deep and hoarse. She had drunk gallons of coffee all day long, and talked endlessly, urging them on, begging for more from them, and her actors hadn't disappointed her. She looked at Ward and he smiled.

'It's going to be great, babe. I've been watching the dailies all week.'

'What do you think?' She had seen them herself, and she kept seeing what was wrong and never what was right, but in the last

160

two days she had seen a ray of hope. The actors were really working hard, as hard as she was, to give it their all. 'Think it'll fly?' She looked terrified as she asked. His judgement was better than anyone else's she knew and she trusted him implicitly, but he was smiling at her.

'It'll fly right over the moon, love. And that Oscar is going to fly into your hands again.'

'Never mind that. I just want it to be good. I want us to be proud of it.'

'We will.' He was sure of that, and he was always proud of her, just as she was of him. He had come so far, for a man who had never worked a day in his life until he turned thirty-five. It was miraculous what he had done with himself, and she never lost sight of that. She was always proud of him, more so than he knew. Much, much more.

She laid her head back on the seat again. 'How are the kids?'

'They're okay.' She didn't need the petty aggravations now. The cleaning woman was threatening to quit, Anne and Val had had a major fight, and Greg had put a dent in the car, but they were all minor problems he could handle himself. Still, he was always grateful when she finished work and went back to running the house. He often wondered how she stood the daily irritation of it all. It always drove him nuts, though he didn't tell her that. 'They're all busy. The twins have been baby-sitting every day, Greg leaves for the ranch next week.' He didn't add aloud, Thank God. At least it would be quieter without the phone ringing, and doors slamming, and half a dozen of Greg's friends playing catch with a favourite vase. 'We hardly see Lionel now that he has a job.'

'Does he like it?' She opened her eyes. She would have asked him herself but she hadn't seen him in weeks.

'I think so. He hasn't complained anyway.'

'That doesn't mean much. Li never complains.' And then she thought of something else. 'I should have lined something up for Anne. I just didn't think we'd get going so soon.' But the money had come in, the set had been free. Everything had fallen into place, and instead of late September, they had started in June. That was unusual, and Faye didn't want to make trouble by saying that she wasn't free to start, but it meant deserting her kids for the summer, which was complicated, and Anne had steadfastly refused to go to

161

camp. 'What's she doing all day?'

'She's all right. Mrs Johnson is there till I come home. She has friends over and they hang around the pool. I told them I'd take them to Disneyland next week.'

'You're a saint.' She yawned and smiled at him at the same time, and she leaned heavily on him as they walked into the house. The girls were still awake. Val's hair was set in giant curlers, and she was wearing a bikini that would have made Faye gasp if she had had the strength. She made a mental note to say something to her the next day, if she had time, and saw the child. They were listening to music in the den, and Vanessa was in a nightgown and talking to a friend on the phone, oblivious to the noise that Valerie was making.

'Where's Anne?' Faye asked Val and she shrugged, mouting the words to the song. She had to ask again before Valerie answered her.

'Upstairs I guess.'

'Is she asleep?'

'Probably.' But Vanessa shook her head. She had the uncanny knack of listening to several conversations at once and often did. Faye went upstairs to kiss her youngest child goodnight. She already knew that Greg was out with friends, and a note in the kitchen had said Lionel was having dinner with some people from work, which accounted for everyone. She liked knowing where all her children were, and she often worried about that on the set. Ward was more relaxed than she was about letting them do what they wanted, and she wanted him to keep a tight rein on them, but he never did. He would have gone mad if he had, that and run the house.

She gently opened the door, and as she came up the stairs, she could have sworn she saw a light, but the room was dark now, Anne was curled up in her bed, her back to the door, and Faye stood there for a long moment, and then walked to her, and gently touched the soft halo of hair. 'Good night, little one,' she whispered and then bent to kiss her cheek. She closed the door again and walked on to her own room with Ward, telling him about the film again and sinking into a hot bath before going to bed. A few minutes later she heard the girls come upstairs; they pounded on her door and yelled goodnight, and she didn't see Vanessa go to her younger sister's room. The light was on again, and Anne was reading *Gone With the Wind*.

'Did you see Mum?' Vanessa searched her face and saw something strange in her eyes, something hidden and distant that was almost always there, except with Li. Anne shook her head. 'How come?' She didn't want to admit that she had turned off the light and pretended to be asleep, but Vanessa guessed. 'You played possum, didn't you?' There was a long hesitation again and the girl shrugged. 'Why?'

'I was tired.'

'That's bullshit.' It made her angry. It was infuriating and so typical of her. 'And it's not nice. She asked for you the minute she came in.' Anne's face didn't give an inch, and her eyes said nothing at all. 'I think that was crummy of you.' She turned and started to leave the room, and Anne's voice reached her as she got to the door.

'I don't have anything to say to her.' Vanessa looked at her and walked out, never understanding the truth that Lionel understood so well. Anne was afraid that her mother had nothing to say to her. She never had. She had never been around when she was a little girl. It was always nurses or baby-sitters or maids, or one of the other children baby-sitting for her, while her mother worked, or went out or did something else. She was always 'tired' or 'had something on her mind', or 'had to read this script' or had to 'talk to Dad'. So what was there left to say now? Who are you? Who am I? It was easier to talk to Lionel and avoid her . . . just as she had avoided Anne for so long. Now she had to pay the price for it.

CHAPTER 14

Faye was still deep into the film when Lionel moved into an apartment with four friends, and began classes at UCLA. He stopped in to see her the following week on the set just to catch up. He stood by waiting patiently for a break. He always enjoyed watching her work, and finally, after an hour of three retakes on a very gruelling scene, she dismissed them all for lunch, and glanced up to see her son. She had been so intent before that she hadn't even noticed him arrive. Pleasure instantly warmed her face and she hurried over to give him a kiss.

'How's everything, sweetheart? How's the apartment, and school?' She felt as though she hadn't seen him in years, and she was suddenly lonely for all of them, especially him. She hadn't felt the full blow of his absence yet. She was so used to having him around, to having those wonderful chats with him and now he was gone. But she had been so busy at work that she hadn't had time to notice it yet. 'Do you like your place?'

His eyes lit up enthusiastically. 'It's pretty nice, and the other guys are fairly neat. Thank God there's no one like Greg.' He grinned , and she laughed, thinking of the familiar chaos of Greg's room. Nothing had changed.

'Have you been home at all since you moved out?'

'Just once or twice to pick some stuff up. I saw Dad, and he said you were okay.'

'I am.'

'It looks great.' He nodded toward the stage she had just left, and she was pleased. Like his father, he had a good eye for successful films. She got too caught up in details to see the whole, and they were better at that. They could stand back and see it differently. 'That was some scene.'

She smiled. 'We've been working on it for a week.' And as she spoke, their big star, Paul Steele, whose scene it was, wandered over towards them, casting a glance at Lionel, and looking more seriously at Faye. He was as much a perfectionist as she, and she loved working with him. This was the second picture they'd done and she was very pleased with him. He was one of the up and coming stars of Hollywood. Paul sat down next to Faye.

'What did you think?'

'I think we got it the last time.'

'So do I.' He was glad that she had felt it too. 'I was getting worried by yesterday. I didn't think I'd ever get this scene right. I stayed up all last night working on it.' She was, as always, impressed with him.

'It showed. Thanks, Paul. That kind of dedication is what makes it work.' But damn few actors were willing to work like that. He was. And he stood now, and looked at Lionel with a smile.

'You must be Faye's son.' People always noticed and both Faye and Lionel laughed.

'How'd you guess?'

Steele squinted with a grin. 'Oh, let's see ... the hair ... the nose ... the eyes ... Listen, kid, all you need is the same hairdo and a dress and you could be twins.'

'I'm not sure I'd approve of that,' Faye laughed. 'In fact, I can tell you right now, I wouldn't.'

'So much for that.' Paul laughed.

'I was very impressed by your last scene, Mr Steele.' Lionel was deeply respectful of him, and Steele was touched.

'Thank you.' Faye introduced them formally, and Paul shook his hand. 'Your mother is the toughest director in town, but she's so good it's worth all the blood, sweat, and tears.'

'My my, such compliments.' All three of them laughed and Faye glanced at her watch. 'We have about an hour, gentlemen. Can I invite you both to lunch in the commissary?'

Paul made a grisly face. 'Christ, torture yet. Can we do better than that? My treat. My car is right outside the studio.' But they all knew there wasn't much outside the studio, and they didn't have much time. 'All right, all right. I give in. Indigestion, here we come.'

'It's not that bad.' Faye tried to defend it to no avail. Paul and

Lionel both disagreed with her vociferously and the threesome walked to the commissary. Paul inquired if Lionel was in school, and he explained that he had just started at UCLA, majoring in cinematography.

'That's where I went. Have you had time to figure out if you like it yet?'

'It seems great.' Lionel grinned happily, and Paul was amused. He was so young, but as they talked over lunch, it was obvious that he was a bright kid. He was intelligent and sensitive, knew a great deal about his chosen field, and talked intensely with Paul until Faye said they had to get back. And once they did, Lionel seemed to linger, wanting to absorb the atmosphere. Paul invited him into his dressing room, while he put his makeup on again and the studio hairdresser did something different to his hair. He was a prisoner of war in the next scene, and Lionel was dying to stick around but he had to get back to school. He had three more classes that afternoon.

'That's too bad. I've enjoyed talking to you.' Paul looked at him with a genuine smile. He was sorry to see him go. He liked the boy . . . too much perhaps . . . but he wasn't going to let it show, out of respect for Faye, and this very young boy. He wasn't in the habit of corrupting anyone, and virgins weren't quite his thing. But Lionel seemed anxious to see him again, much to Paul's surprise.

'I'd like to come back and watch some more. I have a free afternoon at the end of the week.' He looked at Paul Steele hopefully, like a child waiting for Santa Claus, and Paul wasn't quite sure if it was the film he was excited about, or something else, so he proceeded carefully. 'Maybe I could come back then?' Lionel's eyes searched his, and Paul was no longer sure what he saw, boy or man.

'That's up to your Mum. She runs this show. She's my boss too.'

They both laughed and Lionel agreed. 'I'll ask her what she thinks.' Paul worried for a moment that she would think he had put him up to it; he made no secret of his preferences. 'See you Friday, I hope . . .' Lionel looked at him hopefully, and Paul turned away. He didn't want to start anything . . . he did . . . but it wasn't right . . . and he was Faye Thayer's son . . . Christ, life was complicated sometimes. He lit a joint after the boy left, hoping to calm down again but it only made him long for him more.

When he went back to the set there was a hunger and loneliness in him that was almost an ache, and it came across in the film. They got the scene on the first take this time, an almost unheard of victory, and Faye congratulated him. But he was cool to her, and she wondered why. She thought nothing of his being pleasant to Lionel. She knew Paul well enough to know that she had nothing to fear from him. He was a decent man, and whatever he did with his spare time, he wouldn't take advantage of her son. She felt sure of that, and she wasn't upset when she saw Lionel on the set again on Friday afternoon. When he was younger, he had often dropped in to watch her work. Lately, he hadn't had as much time, but it was no secret that he loved the making of films. And now he would be making a career of it. She was actually pleased to see him there, and although he didn't show it at first, so was Paul Steele.

'Hello, Paul.' Lionel said the words hesitantly, and the moment they were out, he wondered if he should have called him Mr Steele. Paul was only twenty-eight years old, but he commanded great respect in the industry and Lionel was eighteen, and felt like a kid around him.

'Hi.' Paul looked casual as he walked past, on his way to someone's dressing room, praying that their paths wouldn't cross again. But late that afternoon, Faye offered him a glass of wine when they took a break. Lionel was standing there, obviously in awe, and Paul couldn't resist the urge to smile at him.

'It's nice to see you again, Lionel. How's school?' Maybe if he pretended to himself the boy was just a child, it would be easier. But nothing was easy when he looked into those eyes. They were impossible to resist. They were so much like hers, but deeper, more compelling, sadder and wiser in some ways, as though he were keeping some terrible secret inside him. And instinctively, Paul knew what the secret was. At his age, he had had the same secret himself. It was a lonely place to be until someone held out a hand to you. Until then you were a freak living in a lonely hell, frightened of your own thoughts and what other people would think if they knew. 'What did you think of today's take?' There was no point treating him like a child. He was a man. They both knew that. And Paul looked him in the eye.

'I thought it was very, very good.'

'Would you like to see the dailies with me?' Paul liked to see them whenever he could, so that he could correct his mistakes. They were important to his work, and Lionel was flattered beyond words that Paul should invite him into such a special world. His eyes were huge with awe, and Faye and Paul laughed. 'Now, listen, if you look like that, I won't let you watch. You've got to realise most of what you'll see is crap. Embarrassing crap, but that's how we learn.'

'I'd love to see the dailies with you.'

They watched them at around six o'clock, and as they took their seats and the lights went off, Paul felt Lionel's leg inadvertently touch his knee. He felt a thrill rush through him that was almost painful to refuse. But he carefully moved his leg away and forced himself to concentrate on what was on the screen, and afterwards when the lights came up, Lionel discussed what he'd seen with him, and amazingly they felt the same way about the same scenes. The boy was brilliant about film; intelligent, intuitive, and he had an instinct for style and technique. It was hardly surprising, he had grown up with it. But Paul was still impressed. He was dying to talk about it with him some more as Faye got ready to leave the set. She had to leave early tonight. For her seven-thirty was midafternoon and she glanced at them both, amused, as they rattled on.

'Have you got your car with you, love?' Faye asked him. She looked tired tonight and was longing to go home and unwind; it had been a gruelling week, and they were doing a scene at dawn the next day. She had to be up before three.

'Yes, Mum. I drove here.'

'Good. Then I'll let you boys talk yourselves out. This old lady's going home. Before I fall on my face from sheer exhaustion. Good-night, gentlemen.' She kissed Lionel's cheek, waved goodbye to Paul, and hurried outside to her own car. Ward had gone home ahead of her to have dinner with the kids. Paul was stunned when he looked at his watch after that. It was almost nine o'clock, and they were the last ones on the set. He hadn't had anything to eat since lunch, and from something he had said he knew Lionel hadn't either. What harm could there be in having a bite to eat?

'Do you want to go out for a hamburger, Lionel? You must be starving.' It seemed harmless enough to ask, and Faye's son looked pleased.

'I'd like that, if you don't have anything else to do.' He was so young and humble it was embarrassing, and Paul smiled and put an arm around his shoulder as they walked to their cars. There was no one else around, so it couldn't be misconstrued.

'Believe me, talking to you is the most fun I've had in weeks, maybe even months ...'

'That's a nice thing to say.' He smiled at Paul as they reached his car. Paul was driving a silver Porsche, and Lionel had the red Mustang he was so proud of.

'What a great car!'

'I got it for graduation in June.'

'That's some gift!' Paul looked impressed. At his age, he had bought a clunker for seventy-five dollars, but his parents weren't Ward and Faye Thayer, and he didn't live in Beverly Hills. He had come to California from Buffalo when he was twenty-two, and life had been beautiful ever since, especially in the past three years. His career had taken off meteorically, at first thanks to one fortuitous romance with a major producer in Hollywood. But after that, the breaks he got were thanks to his own strengths and abilities. There was no denying it, and few did. No matter what you thought of Paul Steele, he was damn good. Most of the people who had worked with him didn't have ugly things to say about him. He was a decent man, fair to work with, he kept to himself most of the time, and if you got to know him well, he could be fun. Between films, he was a wild man sometimes, smoking a lot of dope, snorting a little cocaine, he was into poppers, and there were rumours about orgies at his place, and kinky sex, but he took advantage of no one; no one got hurt, and working as hard as he did, he had to do something to let off steam, and he was still young after all.

He took Lionel to Hamburger Hamlet on Sunset, and had him follow him there in his car, driving carefully. For some reason, he found himself anxious about the kid. He didn't want him to get hurt, physically or in any other way. He liked him, more than he'd liked anyone in a while. It was just a damn shame that he was only eighteen. That was rotten luck. He was so damn beautiful and so fucking young. He couldn't take his eyes off him as they ate, and afterwards they stood outside, Lionel not even sure how to thank him for the honour and the rare treat, Paul dying to invite him up to his place, but afraid of how it would sound so they stood there, awkwardly, as Paul looked at him. He wished he knew what Lionel knew of himself, but he still wasn't sure of that. If the boy knew, maybe it would be different, but if he didn't suspect as yet . . . just looking at him, Paul was already sure, but was Lionel? And then suddenly, as they stood there in the car park, Paul knew he had to take the bull by the horns, so to speak. Maybe he'd even ask him eventually. Maybe he was wrong. Maybe they could be friends. But he couldn't let him go . . . not yet . . . not now . . . not quite so soon.

'I know this sounds dumb, but would you like to come to my place for a drink?' He was almost embarrassed to say the words, but Lionel's eyes grew wide with delight.

'I'd love it.' Maybe he did know . . . Paul was going crazy trying to figure it out, and there was no way to guess.

'I live in Malibu. You want to follow me again, or leave your car here? I could drive you back afterwards.'

'Wouldn't that be a lot of trouble?' Malibu was an hour from there.

'No, not at all. I never go to bed very early. And I may not go to bed tonight at all. We shoot at four am tomorrow, and I work better on calls like that without going to bed.'

'Will my car be safe?' They looked around, and decided that it would. The hamburger place was open all night, so people would come and go, and no one would dare break into it with people around. That decided, Lionel slid into the passenger seat of Paul's Porsche and instantly felt that he had died and gone to heaven. It was like being lifted into another world. Sitting on the smooth black leather seats, the dashboard looked like the panel of a plane and with a shift of gears they took off. Paul turned the stereo on as the music of Roger Miller singing 'King of the Road' filled their ears. It was almost a sensual experience getting to Malibu. Paul was dying for a joint, but he didn't want to smoke dope in front of the boy, and he was a little bit afraid of what he might do if he did, so he refrained, and they talked from time to time on the brief drive, listened to the music as they flew along, and by the time they reached the house on the beach, Lionel was totally relaxed with his new friend.

Paul put his key in the lock, and let them in, and the house just continued the same mood. There was a full ocean view with soft lights, a sunken living room filled with couches and soft cushions, huge plants and recessed lights that highlighted a few pieces of art Paul loved. There was a handsome bar, a wall of books, and a stereo that seemed to fill the whole world with soft music as Lionel sat down and looked around. Paul threw his leather jacket on the couch, poured them each a glass of white wine, and came to sit down with him.

'Well,' he smiled, 'you like?' He had to admit, he was proud of it. For a poor boy from Buffalo, he had come a long, long way, and he was happy here.

'My God . . . it's so beautiful . . .'

'It is, isn't it?' He didn't disagree. They could look out at the beach, the sea. The whole world seemed to lie at their feet, and when they finished their wine, Paul suggested a walk. He loved to walk on the beach late at night, and it was only eleven o'clock. He kicked off his shoes, and Lionel did the same. They walked out onto the smooth white sand, and Lionel thought he had never been as happy as this. He felt something he had never felt before, and he felt it each time he looked at this man. And it was confusing to him. He fell silent after a while, and on their way back, Paul stopped and sat down on the sand. He looked out at the ocean, and then at Lionel and suddenly the words just came. 'You're confused, aren't you, Li?' He had heard his mother call him that and wondered if he'd mind the familiarity, but Lionel didn't seem to object, and he nodded his head, almost relieved to admit what he felt to this man who was becoming his friend.

'Yes . . .' He wanted to be honest with him, maybe then he'd understand what he felt himself. He felt both very old and very young. 'I am.'

'I used to feel like that too. Before I came out here from Buffalo.' He sighed in the night air. 'I used to hate it there.'

Lionel smiled. 'It must be very different from this.' They both laughed, and as the laughter subsided, Paul looked at him.

'I want to be honest with you. I'm gay.' Suddenly he was terrified. What if Lionel hated him for that? . . . What if he jumped up and ran away? . . . It was the first time he had been afraid of that kind of rejection in years and that frightened him. It was like taking a giant step back . . . back to Buffalo . . . to being in love with

171

Mr Hoolihan at baseball practice in the spring and not being able to say anything ... just watch him in the shower and want so desperately to touch his face ... his arm ... his leg ... to touch him anywhere ... to touch him there ... he turned to Lionel with frightened eyes. 'Do you know what that means?'

'Yes, of course.'

'I don't mean just that I'm a homosexual. I assume you'd understand that. I mean do you know the special kind of loneliness that can mean to a man?' Paul emptied his soul into his eyes and Lionel nodded, never taking his eyes from him. 'I think you do know, Lionel ... I think you've felt the same things I have. Haven't you?'

Tears slowly ran down Lionel's cheeks as he nodded his head, and suddenly he couldn't bear looking into those eyes any more; he dropped his face into his hands and began to cry, and a thousand years of loneliness welled up in him. Paul took him in his arms and held him there until he stopped, and then he lifted his chin until he looked into his eyes again.

'I'm falling in love with you. And I don't know what to do about it.' He had never felt as free as he did just then. It felt wonderful to admit it to him, and Lionel felt his whole body turn to fire. Suddenly he understood things he had never understood before about himself ... things he had never wanted to know ... or was afraid to think about ... he knew them all as he looked into this man's eyes. 'You're a virgin aren't you?'

Lionel nodded and his voice was hoarse. 'Yes, I am.' He was falling in love with him too, but he didn't know how to say it yet. He prayed that in time he would, that Paul wouldn't send him away ... that he would always, always let him be with him ...

'Have you ever slept with a girl?' He shook his head silently. That was how he had known. He had never wanted to. Ever. It just wasn't there. 'Neither had I.' He sighed and lay back on the sand with a sigh, gently taking Lionel's hand and kissing the palm over and over again. 'Maybe it's easier like this. The choice was made for us a long time ago. I've always believed that about people like us. I know we have nothing to do with the choice, and it's there even when you're a very little boy. I think I knew it way back then, but I was afraid to know.'

Lionel felt braver now. 'So was I ... I was afraid somebody

would find out . . . would know . . . would see my thoughts . . . my brother is this all-out jock, and my father wanted me to be like that. And I just couldn't be . . . I couldn't . . .' Tears filled his eyes again, and Paul held his hand tight in his own.

'Does anyone in your family suspect?'

Lionel quickly shook his head. 'I never really even admitted it to myself until tonight.' But now he knew. He knew for sure. He wanted it to be like this. With Paul. And no one else. He had waited for him all his life and wasn't going to lose him now.

But Paul was watching him carefully. 'Are you sure you're ready to admit it now? You can never go back again. You can't really change your mind . . . some do, I guess, but I always wonder how convinced they are . . . I don't know . . .' He looked up at Lionel as they lay on the the sand side by side. He was propped up on one elbow and looking down at him, and there was no one around for miles. The houses were lit up behind them like jewels, a thousand engagement rings he was offering him . . . a crown . . . 'I don't want to do anything you're not ready for.'

'I am . . . I know I am, Paul . . . it's been so lonely until now . . . don't leave me out there again . . .' Paul took him in his arms and held him tight, and he couldn't bear it any more. He had done what was right. He had offered him a choice. He had never taken advantage of anyone and he didn't intend to start now with this boy.

'Come on, let's go home.' He stood up gracefully on the sand, and held out a hand to Lionel, who sprang up beside him easily. With a carefree smile, Lionel followed him home, hand in hand, as they talked, suddenly more animatedly. Suddenly he felt as though a thousand-pound weight had been lifted from him. He knew who and what he was, and where he was going now, and suddenly it was all right. It wasn't as frightening any more. They reached the house a few minutes later, and walked back inside, feeling invigorated by the night air. Paul poured them each another glass of wine, took a sip of his, and lit the fire, and then he disappeared into another room, and left Lionel with his own thoughts and his wine, and when he returned, the lights were dim, the room was dark, the fire was lit, and he stood naked in the centre of the room, beckoning to him. He said nothing, and Lionel didn't hesitate. He stood up and followed him.

CHAPTER 15

Paul drove Lionel back to his car at the hamburger place at four in the morning, and they stood in the car park, looking at each other. It seemed odd to be back here. So much had happened since they had eaten here. It was remarkable. Lionel felt as though he had wings. It had been the most beautiful night of his life, and he felt a relief he had never experienced before. He finally knew what he was, and Paul had made it seem all right ... more than that he had made it beautiful. And Lionel didn't know how to begin to thank him now.

'I don't know what to say ... how to thank you ...' he said, shifting from one foot to the other, smiling shyly at his friend.

'Don't worry about it. Do you want to see me tonight?'

Lionel could hardly breathe, and he felt excitement stir in him again. He hadn't known how incredible it would be, but with Paul it was. 'I'd like that a lot.'

Paul narrowed his eyes, thinking of where they could meet. 'How about meeting me back here again at eight? Just wait in your car, and then you can follow me out to the house. If I'm not too wiped out, we can make something to eat, or stop on the way. Sound okay?' It wasn't the way he usually liked to woo his men, but he was working long hours just then on the film.

'Sounds great.' Lionel beamed and then yawned sleepily as Paul laughed and tousled his hair.

'Go home and get some sleep ... lucky boy. I'm going to be working my ass off all day.'

Lionel looked at him sympathetically. 'Say hi to my Mum.' And then suddenly he looked shocked at what he had said.

Paul laughed. 'I don't think I'd better do that just yet.' If ever. He wasn't at all sure how Faye would react to knowing that her older son was gay. 'If she asks, I'll just tell her we had a hamburger and you went home. Okay?'

Lionel nodded. What if he slipped? What if he himself said something to someone one of these days? It was a frightening thought, or was it? . . . Eventually people would have to know. He didn't want to live in hiding for the rest of his life. But on the other hand, he didn't want to tell anyone just yet . . . not yet . . . he wanted it to be his secret with Paul. 'Have a nice day . . .' He wanted to reach out and kiss him right here in the car park, but he didn't dare, and Paul gently touched his cheek with warmth in his eyes.

'Take care of yourself today . . . get some rest, love.'

Lionel felt the power of his loving in his words, and his heart tugged as he watched him go. He waved as the silver Porsche drove away, and slipped into his own car, with his own thoughts. He could hardly wait until that night came, and when it did, he was waiting in his car, in a clean shirt and sweater, impeccable suede slacks, his hair neatly combed and a new brand of after-shave he had bought just that afternoon. Paul recognised all the preparations as he stepped out of the car, and he was touched. He hadn't even had time to shower before leaving the set, but he didn't want to be late. He put an arm around Lionel and they hugged, and it was obvious that the boy was happy to see him again. Li was thrilled.

'How was your day, Paul?'

'Great. Thanks to you.' He smiled generously and the boy beamed. 'I remembered all my lines, sailed right through everything, but we worked our asses off this afternoon.' He looked down at himself. He was still wearing fatigues from the set, but no one had said anything when he left. 'Let's go home, so I can clean up and change.' He would have liked to take him to a gay bar afterwards for dinner, or at least a drink, but he wasn't ready to introduce him to the gay world yet. Instinctively, he sensed that Lionel wasn't ready. He wanted this to be special, something that existed only between them, and Paul was willing to play the game for a while, staying away from his usual friends to be alone with him. Lionel decided to ride in the car with him again, and they stopped at a market on the way to Malibu. They bought a six-pack of beer, some wine, the makings of a salad, a bag of fresh fruit, and two steaks. It was a wholesome dinner for two, and Lionel said he knew how to cook.

As it turned out, he was as good as his word, and when Paul stepped out of the shower with a towel wrapped around his waist, Lionel handed him a glass of wine with a smile. 'Dinner will be ready in five minutes.'

'Great. I'm starving.' But then, Paul set the wineglass down, and reached over to give Lionel a kiss. As they parted, their eyes held, and Lionel's heart soared. 'I missed you today.'

'So did I.'

The towel slipped slowly from around Paul's waist, and he whispered at the boy as he fumbled hungrily with his belt. 'Will the steaks burn if they wait?' Not that he really cared . . . he didn't care about anything just now except this young flesh . . . Lionel was one of the most exciting lovers he had had in a long time. He was so enthusiastic and new, every inch of him smelled sweet and good, his body was so young and firm. He tore the suede trousers down until he found what he sought, and Lionel groaned as Paul's mouth found him there. A moment later, they were tangled on the wet floor, dinner forgotten, their bodies locked in passion.

CHAPTER 16

The affair went on through the fall, and Lionel had never been happier in his life. He was doing well in school, and Paul was still working on the Thayers' film. Once in a great while, Lionel dropped by the set, but it was too hard to pretend with Paul right there. He had to fight to keep his eyes away, and he was afraid that his mother would see.

'She doesn't know everything, you know,' Paul teased him once. 'Even if she is your Mum. And I think she could take it if she knew.'

Lionel sighed. 'I think so too . . .' But when he thought of Ward '. . . My Dad couldn't though. He'd never understand.'

Paul nodded, agreeing with him. 'I think you're right there. I think it's hard for fathers to accept their sons.'

'Did your parents know about you?'

Paul shook his head. 'They still don't. And I'm still young enough that they can understand why I stay single out here. But ten years from now, they'll really be on my back.'

'Maybe you'll be married and have five kids by then.' They both laughed at the absurd possibility. It appealed to Paul not at all. He had no bisexual leanings whatsoever. Women had never turned him on. But Lionel did. They spent most of their nights making love in his huge bed, or on the couch in front of the fire . . . or the floor . . . or the beach. It was an entirely sensual, erotic relationship, and everything about each of them turned the other on. Lionel had the key to the Malibu house now, and sometimes he went there straight from school, or else he'd go back to his own place and meet Paul in Malibu when he finished working later on. But he hadn't spent a night in his own apartment in months, and his roommates teased him every chance they got.

'Okay, Thayer . . . who is this broad? What's her name? When are we going to lay eyes on her, or is she one of these easy dames you hide from your friends and just screw all the time . . .?'

'Very funny.' He tried to fob them off, he put up with their jokes, their admiration, their jealousy, wondering what they would say if they knew the truth. But he knew the answer to that. They would call him a fucking filthy little faggot and probably throw him out.

'Have you told any of your friends?' Paul asked him one night, as they lay naked in front of the fire, having just made love.

Lionel shook his head. 'No.' All he could think of were the boys he shared the apartment with. Typical freshmen jocks, or young intellectuals, all dying to get laid and working hard at it all the time. Their sex lives were far less active than Lionel's, but in a totally different vein. They would have been horrified if they could see him now. Yet he was so happy like this. He looked tenderly at Paul, who was watching him carefully, as though trying to read his mind.

'You going to hide all your life, Li? It's the shits. I did myself for a long time.'

'I'm not ready to come out yet.' They both knew that.

'I know.' And Paul hadn't pushed. He didn't take him anywhere, although the boy was absolutely beautiful and his friends would have all drooled enviously, but he didn't want word to get out. It was only a matter of time, once he did go out with him, before people found out who he was. Faye Thayer's son . . . and then the shit would hit the fan. Paul wanted to spare them both that, and that seemed wise for both of them. Particularly for Paul, whose career could have been jeopardised if Faye or Ward went berserk when they heard, and they might well. The boy was only eighteen after all, and Paul had just turned twenty-nine. It could make a real stink, and it wouldn't do Paul any good. His PR agent still linked his name with actresses whenever possible. People cared about that stuff. No one wanted to hear that their idol was gay.

At Thanksgiving, Lionel spent the day with his family, feeling separate and grown up and strange and different from them now. He didn't have anything to say, he discovered, listening to them. Greg was so childish, and the girls seemed as though they came from another world. He couldn't talk to his parents now, and only

178

Anne was bearable as he waited for the day to tick by. He was relieved when, after dinner, he could finally leave and go back to Paul. He had told his parents that he was going up to Lake Tahoe with friends, though of course he was spending the weekend quietly with Paul. Paul only had another few weeks of shooting left, and they were both relaxed.

It seemed only moments later when Christmas had arrived. Lionel did all his Christmas shopping as soon as he got out of school for the holidays and he dropped in on the set one afternoon, while Paul was in his dressing room.

He didn't see his parents anywhere, so Lionel just drifted into the little room he knew well by now and flopped down in a chair. Paul was smoking a joint, and he offered it to Li, but he had never enjoyed it as much as Paul said he did. He took a quick hit, and gave it back, and the two men sat back and smiled at each other. Paul touched Lionel's thigh. 'If we weren't here, I'd have a great idea.' The two men laughed. They were so easy with each other sometimes they forgot there was something to hide. Paul leaned forward and they kissed.

Neither of them heard the door or the single step, but Lionel was sure he heard a sharp gasp and he pulled away to see Faye standing there, her face frozen with shock and tears in her eyes. Lionel jumped to his feet instantly, and slowly Paul stood up, as the three of them stared at each other.

'Mum, please . . .' Lionel held out a hand to her, tears also in his eyes. He felt as though he had just put a knife to her heart, but he didn't move and neither did she. She just looked at them both, and then she sank slowly into a chair. She didn't feel as though her legs could hold her any more.

'I don't know what to say. How long as this been going on?' She looked from Lionel to Paul.

Paul didn't want to make things worse for either of them. And it was Lionel who spoke up, as he dropped his hands to his side with a defeated look. 'A couple of months . . . I'm sorry, Mum . . .' He began to cry, and Paul's heart went out to him. He stood up and went to his side, looking down at Faye. He owed it to him to stand by the boy now, but he knew how great the cost might be. She could destroy his career if she chose . . . it had been an insane thing to get involved with her son. He regretted it now, but it was much,

much too late. The damage was already done.

'Faye. No one's been hurt. And no one knows. We haven't gone anywhere.' He knew she would be relieved to know that and she lifted her eyes to him now.

'Was this your idea, Paul?' She wanted to kill him, but part of her told her that she was wrong, that it wasn't entirely his fault. She looked sorrowfully up at her son's tear-stained face.

'Lionel . . . is this . . . has this happened before?' She wasn't even sure what questions to ask, or if she had a right to know after all. He was a man, and if Paul had been a girl, would she have asked for the details? But the facts of this affair actually frightened her. She knew very little about homosexuality, and she wanted to know even less. There were plenty of gay men in Hollywood, but she had never made it her business to research exactly who did what to whom, and now suddenly it was her son standing there . . . her son had just been kissing a man . . . she wiped the tears from her cheeks, and looked at them both again, as Lionel sighed and sank into the chair across from her.

'Mum, this was the first time . . . I mean with Paul. And it isn't his fault. I've always been like this. I think in my heart I've known it for years, I just didn't know what to do, and he . . .' He faltered, glancing up at Paul almost gratefully, and Faye thought she felt sick. '. . . he introduced me so gently to all this . . . I can't help it. This is what I am. Maybe it's not what you want, and you'll never be able,' he gulped down a sob, 'to love me again . . . but I hope you will . . .' He went to her and put his arms around her, burying his face in her dress, and there were tears in Paul's eyes too as he turned away. He had never been involved in anything like this, even with his own family. Lionel looked up at Faye again then. 'I love you, Mum . . . I always have . . . I always will . . . but I love Paul too . . .' It was the most grown-up moment of his entire life, and perhaps he would never have to be this grown up again. But right now he had to stand up for who and what he was no matter how much pain it caused her. She put her arms around her son and held him close kissing his hair, and at last she took his face in her hands and looked hard at him. He was the same little boy he had been for the past eighteen years, to her, and she loved him just as much.

'I love you just as you are, Lionel Thayer. And I always will. You remember that.' She looked deep into his eyes. 'No matter what happens to you, or what you do, I'm behind you all the way.' She glanced at Paul, as Lionel smiled through his tears. 'I just want you to be happy, that's all. And if this is what your life is, then I accept it. But I want you to be careful and wise about what you do, who you see, how you handle yourself. You've chosen a difficult life. Don't fool yourself about that.' He already suspected it, but it was less difficult with Paul, and less difficult than hiding from himself all these years. She stood up again then and stood looking at Paul, her eyes bright with tears.

'I only want one thing from you. Don't tell anyone about this. Don't ruin his life. He may change his mind one day, give him that chance.' Paul nodded silently, and she looked back at her son. 'And don't say anything to your father about this. He won't understand.'

Lionel visibly gulped. 'I know he won't . . . I . . . I can't believe how great you've been, Mum . . .' He wiped the tears off his face again and she smiled through her own.

'I happen to love you a lot. And your father does too.' She sighed sadly, looking at the two men. It was difficult for anyone to understand. They were both so handsome, so virile, so young. It was a terrible waste, no matter what anyone said, and she had never thought it a happy life. Certainly not for her son. 'Your father will never understand, no matter how much he loves you.' She hit the hardest blow then. 'It'll break his heart.'

Lionel choked again. 'I know.'

CHAPTER 17

They finished the film five days after New Year's Eve, and the wrap party was the best Paul had ever seen. It was a major event that went on almost all night, with everyone leaving at last with the usual kisses and hugs and tears. For himself, he was relieved. No matter how understanding she had been, it had been difficult working with Faye for the last few weeks, and he knew the strain had shown in the quality of his work, although most of the important scenes had been in the can long since.

He suspected that she had felt the tension too, and he wondered nervously, as he had several times recently, if she would give him a part again. He loved working for her, but he felt as though he had betrayed her this time. And maybe he had. Maybe he should have walked away from the kid, but he had been so damn beautiful, so fresh, so young, and he had convinced himself that he was falling in love with him. He knew differently now. He was a sweet boy, but he was just too damn young for him. Unsophisticated, naïve, he would be fabulous in ten years, but just then there wasn't enough substance for a man of Paul's age. He felt like his father most of the time, and he was missing his old friends, the gay scene, the parties and orgies he went to, to let off steam, from time to time. It was an awfully sedate little life staying home night after night, staring into the fire. The sex was good, particularly lately with the help of a little amyl nitrate, but he knew that it wouldn't last long. It never did with him. And then he'd have to live with the guilt of that. Life was just too damn complicated sometimes, he thought to himself as he drove home. But when he found Lionel, looking like a sleeping god, curled up in his bed, he had second thoughts about it ending for a long, long time. He quietly peeled off his own clothes, and sat down at the edge of the bed, running a finger down the endless length of Lionel's leg as he slept, and then stirred, and finally opened one eye.

'You look like a sleeping prince ...' It was a whisper in the darkened room, lit only by the moonlight from the beach, and Lionel smiled and held out his arms to him sleepily. It was more than any man could want, Paul thought to himself as he abandoned himself to the pleasures of the flesh. They slept late the next day and went for a long walk on the beach. Afterwards, they talked about life. But it was in those moments he realised again how young Lionel was. He smiled at him in a certain way he had, and Lionel looked annoyed.

'You think I'm just a baby, don't you?'

'No, I don't.' But he was lying to him. He did.

'Well, I'm not, and I've seen a lot.'

Paul laughed and it enraged Lionel more, and eventually it led to one of their rare fights, and that night Lionel went back to his own place. As he slid into his own bed for the first time in weeks, he wondered if things were going to be different now, with Paul out of work. He would be free all the time, and Lionel had to go to school. He was diligent about that, despite his affair with Paul.

Within weeks, it became obvious that it did complicate things somewhat. Paul was restless much of the time; he was reading scripts, trying to decide what he wanted to do next; he was still nervous about Faye, and by spring he was tired of his schoolboy love. It just didn't give him enough. It had lasted six months, which was a long time for him. Lionel sensed it before Paul said anything. It was painful for both of them when it ended, but Lionel finally confronted Paul with it. He couldn't stand the strained silences between them any more, and suddenly the house in Malibu seemed oppressive to both of them.

'It's over, isn't it, Paul?' He didn't look quite so young any more, but he was, Paul reminded himself. He wasn't even nineteen. Christ. They were eleven years apart. Eleven years. And he had just met a forty-two-year-old man who had turned his legs to mush. He had never had an older lover before, and he was anxious to spend some time with him. But he couldn't with Lionel hanging around his neck. He looked at the boy now, and he had no regrets for what they'd done. He wondered if Lionel did, but he had never seemed to in all these months. He seemed to have found his niche in life. He was happy, his grades had soared. He seemed to have found himself. Maybe it was worth it after all. Paul smiled sadly at him. It was time to be honest and call it a day.

'I think it might be, my friend. Life is like that sometimes. And we've had a good run, wouldn't you say?'

Lionel nodded, looking sad. He didn't want to let go. But it hadn't been good for a while, except in bed. It was always good there, but they were both healthy and young, there was no reason for it not to be. And now he wanted to know the truth. 'Is there someone else?'

Paul was honest with him. 'Not yet.'

'But soon?'

'I don't know. And that's not the point.' Paul got up and walked around the room. 'I just know I need to be free for a while.' He turned back to look at Lionel. 'It's not like the other world, Li. People don't fall in love and get married and live happily ever after with thirteen kids. It's a lot harder for our kind. It's pretty rare for people to stay together for a long time. It happens, sure, but most of the time it's a one-night stand, or a couple of days, or even a week, or if you're lucky six months like us . . . and then, there's nowhere to go, and that's it.'

'That's not good enough.' Lionel looked upset. 'I want more than that.'

Paul smiled. He was wise to his way of life. 'Good luck. You may find it, but most of the time you won't.'

'Why not?'

Paul shrugged. 'Not our style maybe. We're all too interested in good looks, beautiful bodies, a tight little ass, a body as young as yours . . . and all of us know we won't be young any more one day.' He was already starting to feel like that. He was envious of Lionel sometimes, which made him bitchy with him. But this older man made him feel beautiful and young, as Lionel was to him.

'What do you want to do now?'

'I don't know. Travel for a while maybe.'

Lionel nodded. 'Can I still see you sometimes?'

'Of course . . .' And then he looked up at the boy. 'It's been wonderful for me, Lionel . . . I hope you know that . . .'

But Lionel looked far more intensely at him. 'I'll never forget you, Paul . . . never . . . for the rest of my life . . .' He went to him, and they kissed. Lionel stayed there that night. But the next day Paul drove him home, and without being told, Lionel knew that he wouldn't be seeing him again. Not for a long, long time anyway.

CHAPTER 18

In June 1965, the entire Thayer family found itself sitting in the same row of the auditorium of Beverly Hills High as it had the year before. But it was Greg graduating this time, and it characteristically lacked the solemnity of Lionel's graduation the year before. Faye didn't cry this time, although both she and Ward looked deeply moved, and Lionel was there looking very grown up in another new suit. He was going into his sophomore year at UCLA and loving it. The twins looked far more grown up than they had at fifteen, too. Vanessa had given up looking like Little Bo Peep. She was wearing a red miniskirt and Louis heels with a red and white blouse Faye had bought for her in New York, and had a little red patent-leather shoulder bag. She looked young and fresh, with her hair hanging down her back in a sheet of gold. Only Valerie had made a negative comment on what she wore, but she always did, grumbling that she looked great, if you didn't mind looking like a peppermint stick. She had chosen to look more subdued, she felt, and was also wearing a miniskirt, but hers was black, and her sweater was too tight once again this year. There remained about her a look of startling maturity. The lush figure, the makeup more subtly done now, the red hair in a breathtaking mane that eclipsed all else but her dress. She actually looked very pretty, or would have for cocktails in Beverly Hills. She was just somewhat overdressed for a high school auditorium at 9 am, but they were all used to that by now. Faye was just grateful she hadn't chosen to wear something with a plunging décolletage, and the miniskirt was, remarkably, one of her most modest ones. 'Thank God for small favours,' she had whispered to Ward as they got in the car, and he had grinned. They were quite a bunch, and they were all growing up. Even Anne had matured. She had grown breasts and softly rounded hips, was thirteen now, and mercifully hadn't got lost this year before they had to leave for the ceremony. Greg's graduation gift had been no surprise. He had badgered them so badly for it, that Ward had given in and presented it with a flourish the week before. It was a yellow Corvette Stingray convertible, and he was even more excited than Lionel had been about his, if that was possible. It was actually a fancier car than Lionel's little red Mustang but that had been Ward's idea. And Greg roared up and down their street, and then vanished to pick up all his friends for a ride. Ward had been certain that he would either crash or be arrested within the hour, but somehow they had all survived, and nine of his closest friends had arrived whooping and screeching as they careered down the street, burning rubber as they turned into the drive, and then all of them had leapt out of the car outside the house and headed for the pool. Ward wondered if he'd made a terrible mistake. Greg certainly didn't have Lionel's calm ways, and Ward just prayed that he would drive sensibly when he got to the University of Alabama. He had won a football scholarship, and he could hardly wait to leave. He was going back to the ranch in Montana to work for a month again. But then he was going to the university on August 1st to begin football practice with the team and their famous coach 'Bear'. Ward could hardly wait to fly down and see him in his first game. Faye knew she was going to be doing a lot of that this year, but she didn't mind. She had promised to go whenever she could, although they'd be winding up a film in the autumn, and starting another after the first of the year, but she'd do what she could.

They watched Greg receive his diploma, as Lionel had last year, but Greg merely grinned sheepishly – unlike his more poised brother. He waved to his family and friends, and then took his seat again, his broad shoulders almost knocking his friends off their seats. He was the big hero in school for getting a football scholarship, and Ward was so proud he could hardly see. He had told everyone he knew, and he had looked at Lionel almost reproachfully when he heard the news. Lionel was currently doing an experimental film on ballet and the dance, and there were times when Ward wondered what went through the boy's mind. He was certainly different from their younger son, but at least he was doing well in school. And Faye seemed to see a lot of him at lunch.

187

He hadn't had much time himself. He'd been putting together the package for another big film deal, and he had a lot on his mind. But the boy looked all right. At least none of their brood had gone haywire with this flower child nonsense, and none of them were into drugs, although he frequently warned Faye to keep an eye on Val. That child was too damn seductive by far, and she seemed to have a knack for hanging out with older boys. She had turned up with some character in May who admitted to being twenty-four, and he had squashed that romance fast enough. But there was no denying she was hard to control. There was one in every brood, he'd been told, and Val was theirs. But so far, despite the wild garb, the makeup, and the older boys, she seemed to have stayed within the bounds of some kind of propriety.

The party they gave Greg that night differed radically from Lionel's the year before. By midnight everyone was not only drunk on beer, but most of them were naked in the pool. Faye wanted to have them all thrown out, but Ward prevailed and told her to let them have their fun. He wanted to send Anne and the twins to bed, and Faye said that was impossible. You either had to close the whole show down or let them be, but the police made the decision for them shortly after two o'clock. They told them to turn the music off and tone it down. Every neighbour on their street had complained, especially the couple next door, when a chorus line of twelve hefty young men had appeared on the front lawn, and mooned them before leaping into their pool. Ward had thought the whole thing in good fun, but he was amused by almost everything Greg did. Faye was slightly less amused. There had been no complaints at all over Lionel's party the previous year. By the time the police came, Greg was sprawled out on a chaise longue, a towel wrapped around his naked waist, and an arm draped across his date, both of them drunk on beer and sound asleep. Neither of them woke up when the rest of the guests left, talking about what a great party it had been. Faye was just grateful that none of them had come into the house. Only one couple had wandered in and had been necking heavily in Greg's room, but Faye had seen them tiptoeing in and had asked them to go outside immediately. Sheepishly they had, and they had left early with a few others, who wanted to do some serious groping before going home. But for the most part they were more interested in pushing each other into the pool and consuming as much beer as they could before they had to leave.

And when the last guest left, Lionel and John Wells were still sitting a little distance from the pool, in a comfortable old double swing, under a tree. They were talking about UCLA, and Lionel was telling him which classes he liked best, and about his projects in film. John had got his dream fulfilled, and he had been accepted there too.

The swing moved slowly back and forth as they watched the revellers beyond. Lionel had escaped quite a while before, and John had found him sitting in the swing. 'I've been thinking about fine arts a lot,' John said. He was still Greg's best friend, officially, but in the last year they seemed to spend less and less time together. John was still on the football team too, but he didn't care about it as much as Greg did, and he was relieved to be free of it now. He never wanted to play football again, no matter how well suited to it he was. Greg had told him he was nuts. He had been offered a football scholarship at Georgia Tech, and had actually turned it down. Oddly enough, the friendship hadn't been as close after that. Greg just couldn't understand his giving up an opportunity like that. He had stared at his childhood friend in disgust and disbelief, and every time they met now, John felt as though he had to explain it again, as though he had committed an unpardonable sin. And in Greg's eyes he had. But Lionel didn't seem to care. And he had always been fond of John.

'They have a good fine arts department. And a great drama department of course.' Lionel knew he hadn't chosen his major yet.

'I don't think that's my style.' John smiled shyly at the older boy. He had always admired him.

'Are you living on campus next year?'

John looked hesitant. 'I'm not sure. My mother thinks I should live in the dorm, which doesn't appeal to me much. I think I'd rather live at home.'

Lionel looked pensive for a time as they moved gently on the swing. 'I think one of my roommates is moving out.' He looked thoughtfully at John, wondering how he would fit in. He was still very young, but he was a decent kid. He didn't smoke, didn't drink, didn't seem to raise too much hell, certainly nothing like Greg. He was a lot like Li's roommates, most of whom Lionel liked. Occasionally, they got rowdy on Saturday nights, but they weren't completely wild, and unlike a lot of other freshmen and sophomores, they didn't choose to live like pigs. They kept the apartment fairly clean, two of them had girlfriends who slept there a lot, but they didn't bother anyone, and Lionel came and went as he pleased. No one asked him a lot of questions any more. Sometimes he wondered if they knew, but no one said anything, and no one asked. It was a good group, and John Wells might just make a good fifth. 'Would you be interested, John? The rent is pretty cheap.' He looked at him. 'How would your parents feel about your living off campus first year? Actually, it's just across the street, but it's not the dorms.' He grinned, and looked just like Faye as he did. He had grown from boyhood into manhood that year, and he was a beautiful young man. People often stared at him in the street with his graceful build, long limbs, big green eyes, and golden hair. And he wore quiet clothes that set off his good looks in a casual way. He could have been in films if he'd wanted to, but that end of the camera had never appealed to him. He looked at John now, and the younger boy felt something stir in him. 'What do you think?'

His eyes lit up with quiet excitement as he glanced up at Lionel. 'Boy, I'd love to find a place like that. I'll ask them tomorrow, first thing.'

Lionel smiled. 'No rush. I'll just tell the others I know someone who's interested. I don't think anyone is worried about it yet.'

'How much is it? My Dad'll want to know.' John's parents were comfortable, but careful. He was the oldest child of four, and they were going to have four in college in the next four years, not unlike the Thayers, although Lionel's Dad worried less than John's. But Ward had two or three successful films under his belt every year, and John's did not. He was a plastic surgeon in Beverly Hills, and his mother did a little decorating for her friends when she had time. She looked great though. She had had her eyes done the year before, her nose bobbed several years before that, and that summer she was going to have implants done in her breasts. Besides, she looked great in a bathing suit. His sisters were pretty nice-looking too, he always thought. Greg had gone out with two of them, and one of them had had an eye on Lionel for years. But he had never seemed interested, and John had never wondered why.

'Divided by five, the rent only comes to sixty-six dollars a month, John. It's a five-bedroom house in Westwood, and the landlady is pretty good about staying off our backs. There's no pool, and there's only room for two cars in the garage. You'd have a good-sized bedroom, looking out on the front, and you share a bath with two other guys. The room comes with a bed and a desk. You'd have to supply the rest yourself, unless Thompson wants to sell his junk. He's going East to Yale for the next two years.'

'Wow!' John's eyes were all alight with excitement. 'Wait till I tell my Dad!'

Lionel smiled. 'Want to come by tomorrow and have a look at it? There are only going to be two of us there this summer, which will make the rent pretty steep. But it's too much trouble to move back in here,' he shrugged and looked vague, 'and I don't know . . . it's easier. Once you move out, I think it would be hard to come home again.' Especially in his case; there would be so many questions asked that he didn't have to contend with now. And he liked the freedom he had. With only one other boy that summer, it would almost be like his own place. He was looking forward to it.

'Yeah, I know . . . can I come and see it tomorrow?' It was Saturday and Lionel didn't have any plans. All he was going to do was sleep late and do some laundry. He had been invited to a party that night, but he was free all day.

'Sure.'

'Nine o'clock?'

John looked like a five-year-old kid waiting for Santa Claus to come, and Lionel laughed. 'How about noon?'

'Great.' They abandoned the swing then, and Lionel gave John a ride home. After he dropped him off at the miniature French mansion where he lived in Bel Air, with the regulation Cadillac and Mercedes parked outside in plain view, he drove slowly home, thinking about John. He felt something he couldn't deny, but he didn't know if it was appropriate in this case. He suspected not, and he had no intention of taking advantage of him. The offer of the room in his house was sincere. He wasn't setting John up, but he had to admit, having him so close could be difficult, or . . . and as his thoughts whirled around while he pulled up in front of the house he shared with the four other boys, he suddenly wondered if Paul had felt that way about him. There was an odd kind of responsibility to reaching out to someone like John . . . especially if it was the first time . . . and Lionel suspected it would be. . . . He almost shook himself then. What was he thinking of? What if John didn't feel that way at all? He'd be crazy to make a pass at him. He reminded himself of that several times as he brushed his teeth and went to bed. He was crazy to even consider it, he told himself as he lay in the dark, trying not to think of him again. But John's innocent young face kept coming to mind again and again . . . the powerful legs . . . broad shoulders . . . narrow hips . . . he could feel himself becoming aroused, just thinking of him. . . . 'No!' He said it aloud in the dark, and turned over, instinctively stroking himself, as he tried to force John out of his mind. But it was impossible, and his whole body shuddered with desire, as he thought of John diving into the pool earlier that night . . . and all that night, as he slept, Lionel dreamt of him . . . running on a beach . . . swimming in a deep tropical sea . . . kissing him . . . lying at his side . . . He awoke with a dull ache that refused to go away, and he took his bike out and went for a long ride before anyone else got up, anxiously waiting for noon, and promising himself that he was going to tell John the room had been rented to someone else. That was the only way out. He could have called, but he didn't want to. He would tell him when he came to the house at noon . . . he would . . . that was the best way . . . tell him to his face . . . that was the only way.

CHAPTER 19

When Greg woke up the morning after his graduation bash, he had the worst hangover of his life, and he had already had quite a few. His head throbbed, his stomach was upset. He had woken up twice during the night and thrown up, once on his bathroom floor, and he thought he would die when he tried to stand up at eleven o'clock the next day. But his father saw him staggering downstairs, and handed him a cup of black coffee, a piece of toast, and a glass of tomato juice with a raw egg in it. Just looking at it made him feel sick again, but his father insisted that he force it down.

'Make an effort, son. It'll do you good.' He seemed to speak from experience, and Greg trusted him, so he did his best, and was amazed when he felt a little better afterwards. Ward handed him two aspirins for his head and he gulped them down, and he felt almost human by noon, as he stretched out in the sun at the pool. He glanced over at Val, her lush figure poured into a bikini Faye didn't like her to wear when there was anyone else around, but with family it was all right. It was barely more than a piece of string, but Greg had to admit, it looked great on her.

'Great party, wasn't it, Sis?'

'Yeah.' She opened an eye and looked at him. 'You sure got drunk enough.'

He looked unconcerned. 'Were Mum and Dad mad?'

'I think Mum would have been, but Dad kept telling her it was your graduation night.' She grinned. She had had quite a few beers too, and the music had been good. They had all danced a lot before passing out.

'Just wait till it's your turn. You'll probably go nuts.'

'It's my turn next.' Except that she would have to share it with Van. That was the one thing she hated about being twins; you

193

always had to share everything with someone else. And Faye had never understood that she wanted to be separate, to do things by herself, to have her own friends. She always treated them as though they were one, and Valerie had spent her whole life fighting that, making a point of how different they were, at all costs. And still nobody understood. It ruined everything. But not for much longer.

Only two more years at home, and then she was moving out. Vanessa said she was going to college in the East, but she knew exactly what she was going to do. She was going to take classes at acting school. Not UCLA drama school – the real thing, the kind working actors went to between jobs, and she was going to start looking for work. She'd get her own apartment. She wasn't going to waste her time going to college. Who needed that? She was going to be an actress, and a bigger one than her mother had ever been. She had set that goal for herself years before, and she had never swerved from that desire.

'What are you looking so uptight about?' Greg had been watching her, and she was wearing an ominous frown. She usually looked like that when she was plotting against some poor slob she had the hots for. But she only shook the long red hair back now, and shrugged. She hadn't told anyone what she was going to do. They would just give her a hard time. Greg would try and talk her into being a physical therapist, or an acrobat, or getting a dumb athletic scholarship somewhere, Vanessa would try and talk her into going to school in the East with her, Lionel would have some other dumb idea, like going to UCLA because he did. Mum would make speeches about education, Dad would tell her how bad makeup was for her skin, and Anne would look at her as though she were a freak. She knew all of them too well after sixteen years of living with them.

'I was just thinking about last night,' she lied and he lay back in the hot sun again.

'Yeah ... it was the best.' It occurred to him then to ask what had happened to his date. 'Dad took her home. She almost threw up in his car.' Val grinned and he laughed.

'Christ, he didn't say a word.'

'Lucky it wasn't one of us, he'd have had a fit.' They both laughed and Anne wandered by on her way to the swing with a book.

'Where are you going, squirt?' Greg squinted at her in the sun, noticing what a trim figure she was getting in a bathing suit. Her waist seemed to be shrinking by the hour and he could have got both hands around it, and her breasts were almost as big as Val's. Their little sister was getting all grown up, but she wasn't the kind of kid you could say something about it to. She was the most restrained of all of them, and she never gave him the impression that she liked any of them much, except Lionel of course. It seemed to Greg that they had barely heard her speak since their older brother moved out. 'Where are you going, kid?' He repeated the question as she walked past them expressionlessly. She never had anything much to say to Greg. She had never liked sports and she always thought his girlfriends were dumb. And she had her worst fights with Val, who glared at her ominously now. She thought Anne's bathing suit looked suspiciously like one of her own, but she wasn't quite sure, and Anne could feel her eyes examining her.

'Nowhere.' She walked past them without saying another word, holding tight to her book. Greg whispered to Val once she was past:

'She's a weird kid, isn't she, Val?'

'Yeah, I guess.' Val wasn't interested. She had just figured out that the bathing suit wasn't hers. Hers didn't have a yellow stripe down the sides.

'Growing up a lot though. Did you see those tits?' He laughed. 'They're almost as big as yours.'

'Yeah? So what?' Val sucked in her already flat stomach as she stood up and pushed out her breasts. 'She's got short legs anyway.' She didn't look like any of them. Her looks had never been as striking as the other four. Val looked at her own legs now, trying to decide if she had taken enough sun for one day. If she took too much, she'd burn, although she had more tolerance than most redheads. She noticed that Greg was already starting to fry. 'You better watch out. You're turning red.'

'I'll go inside in a little while. John said he'd come by, and I want to go downtown to get extra floor mats for my car.'

'What about Joan?' She was the little blonde her father had had to escort home the night before. She had the biggest boobs Val thought she'd ever seen. They were almost gross, and everyone in school said she was an easy lay. And that seemed to suit Greg perfectly.

'I'm seeing her tonight.' He had been sleeping with her for the last two months, ever since they'd heard about his football scholarship to the University of Alabama.

'Are you doubling with John?' She knew he had no special girlfriend and she was always hoping to be asked to be his date, but Greg had never suggested it, and neither had John.

'No. He said he had other plans.' He glanced at Val. 'Why? You got the hots for him, little Sis?' He was the worst tease of all, and in years past they had had some almost lethal fights. He loved to bait her, and she always went for it, as she was about to now.

'Hell, no. I just wondered. I've got a date,' she lied again.

'With who?' He knew her better than that.

'None of your business.'

'That's what I thought.' He lay back with a grin and she wanted to strangle him. Anne watched them silently from her distant hiding place in the old swing. 'You don't have a date with anyone, smartass.'

'The hell I don't. I have a date with Jack Barnes.'

'Bullshit. He's going steady with Linda Hall.'

'Well.' Her face was bright red and not from the sun. From the distance, Anne could tell she had just told a lie . . . she knew them all so well, better than they knew her. 'Maybe he's cheating on her.'

Greg sat up and stared at his sister carefully. 'Not unless you're putting out the way she is, Sis. Which brings up a question I've been meaning to ask . . . are you?'

Val's face looked like it was on fire. 'Screw you.' She wheeled on her heel and flounced into the house, and he laughed again as he lay down in the sun. She was a hot number, his little Sis, he had heard it from a couple of his friends whose younger brothers had gone out with her. But supposedly she would do anything except the real thing. He knew she was still a virgin, at least he thought she was, and he also knew she had lied about Jack Barnes. He suspected too that she had always had the hots for John Wells, but John had never seemed interested in her, and he was just as glad. That was a little close to home for his taste, and she wasn't John's type. He went for quieter, less showy girls. He was still pretty shy, and Greg was almost sure he hadn't done it yet either. Poor kid.

He'd better hurry up. He was probably the last guy in their class who hadn't got into someone's pants yet, at least that was what they said. And it was getting embarrassing for Greg to have a friend like that. Hell, people would start to think John was queer, and worse yet, if they hung out together, they would say it about him. But he smiled to himself then. With what he'd been up to with Joan, there was no chance of that.

'Boy, this is a nice place.' John was looking around the house in Westwood rapturously, as though it were Versailles, or a Hollywood set, instead of a shabby student house across from UCLA. My Dad thought the rent was cheap. Mum was a little nervous about my not living in the dorm, but Dad said that as long as you were here, you could keep an eye on me.' He blushed, feeling stupid for what he had just said. 'I mean . . .'

'That's okay.' Lionel was fighting to repress his dreams of the night before, and he had the oddest feeling of reliving a film he had seen once before, only this time he was cast as Paul. It was like a variation of *déjà vu*, and he couldn't seem to escape his thoughts as he showed John around. Lionel's own room would be across the hall from John's, but he was sure that if he was willing to give up the only room in the house with its own shower, he could have the room adjoining John's. The other guys would have killed to have his room, and he would have been willing to give it up if . . . he pushed the thought out of his head, and forced himself to concentrate on John, and the tour of the house he was giving him. 'There's a washing machine in the garage. No one uses it for weeks, and then everyone wants to use it all in one night.' Lionel smiled.

'My mum said I could bring my laundry home.' Lionel couldn't help thinking how unlike Greg he was, it was most odd that they were friends, except that they had gone to school together for thirteen years, and he suspected that it was habit more than anything else. Had he thought about it, John would have admitted he was right. He and Greg hadn't had much in common for the last couple of years, and especially in the last few months. They seemed to disagree about everything, from the football scholarship to the class whore Greg was sleeping with. John couldn't stand being around her, and as a result he had been seeing less and less of Greg. He had been spending more time alone, and it was almost a relief to be talking to Lionel, someone sensible, who even went to the same school he'd be going to. 'I really love this place, Li. It's great.' It could have been a barn and he would have fallen in love with it. It was all so grown up, so collegiate, and so cool, and it was comforting knowing Lionel would be there. He felt shy about starting out in a new school, and he had hated the idea of the dorm, after living at home with four sisters for eighteen years. It was all going to be so foreign to him, but not now, not with Lionel, not here.

'Would you want to stay here this summer, John? Or move in in the autumn before school starts?' Lionel could feel his heart pound and he hated himself. What difference did it make when the kid moved in? Leave him alone, he wanted to shriek, and he was suddenly sorry he had suggested it at all. It was just going to make things difficult for him. It had been a stupid idea, but he couldn't back out now, and he had told two of the boys that morning before John arrived. They were pleased he had found someone. It saved them the trouble of placing an ad, or calling friends.

'Could I move in next week?'

Lionel was momentarily shocked. 'So soon?'

'Oh no ...' John blushed nervously '... not if that's inconvenient for you. I just thought that since Tuesday is the first, it would be easier from the standpoint of the rent ... and I have a summer job at Robinson's. I could live here while I work.' It was a department store, and Lionel was faintly reminded of his job the year before at Van Cleef & Arpels. He had enjoyed that and was sorry he couldn't do it again, but he wanted to work in film this year. It made more sense for him, and if he was lucky he would get credit from UCLA for the work, if the project turned out well.

'No, no ... you're right, John. I hadn't thought of that. And the room is free. I just thought you'd want to think about it for a while ...' It was too late, he had offered the room to John and now he wanted it. He would have to live with what he'd done, no matter what the cost to himself.

'I don't need to think about it, Li. I think the room is great.' Shit. Lionel stared at the tall dark-haired boy, with the exquisite body that had tormented him the night before, and there was nothing left to say.

'Fine. I'll tell the other guys. They'll be thrilled. It saves them a lot of headaches.' And then, in an attempt to make the best of it, 'Do you want help moving in?'

'I don't want to bother you . . . I thought I'd borrow Dad's car and move some stuff in tomorrow.'

'I'll come pick you up.' John's face lit up like a child again.

'I really appreciate it, Li. You're sure it's not too much trouble?'

'Not at all.'

'Mum said she had a bedspread and some lamps and some other stuff.'

'Great.' Lionel could feel his heart sink, as he wondered what he had got himself into. John looked up admiringly at him.

'Can I take you to dinner tonight, Li, to thank you for all this?'

Suddenly Lionel was embarrassed by the boy's sincerity, and he was touched. 'That's all right, John. You don't have to do anything like that. I'm glad it worked out.' But he wasn't. He was scared. What if he lost control? If he did something dumb? If John found out he was gay? But suddenly he felt John's hand on his arm and a chill ran down his spine. He wanted to tell John not to touch him again, but he'd think he was nuts.

'I can't thank you enough, Li. It's like a whole new life.' He was so relieved to get away from the kids at Beverly Hills High. He just didn't feel like them any more. He hadn't in years, and he had hidden it for so long. Now he could start a new life somewhere else. He wouldn't have to try as hard, or listen to the jocks, or run away from the girls, or pretend to get drunk on Saturday nights . . . even the locker room had become a nightmare for him . . . all those boys . . . all those jocks . . . even Greg . . . especially him . . . and he knew he was different from them. And yet with Lionel he didn't feel as though there were something wrong with him. He was so quiet and understanding, and he felt so comfortable with him. Even if he didn't see him much at the new house, it was nice to know that he'd be there once in a while, that their paths would cross, that he could talk to him sometimes. He looked into his eyes now and he wanted to cry with relief. 'I've hated school so much, Li. I can't wait to get out.'

Lionel was surprised. 'I thought you liked it, John. You're a big football star.' They wandered into the kitchen, and Lionel handed him a Coke, which he took gratefully. He was even more grateful it wasn't a beer. It would have been if it had been Greg.

'I've hated that for the last year. I'm just sick of all that shit.' He took a sip of the Coke, and sighed with relief. It really was a whole new life. 'I hated every moment I spent on that damn football team.'

Lionel was stunned. 'Why?'

'I don't know. I just never gave a damn about it. I was good at it, I guess, but I didn't really care. You know they actually used to cry in the locker room when they lost a game. Sometimes the coach cried too. As though it really mattered that much. All it is is a bunch of big guys beating each other up on a field. It just never turned me on.'

'Then why did you play?'

'It meant a lot to my Dad. He played in college before he went to med school. And he always used to kid me that if they smashed up my face, he'd fix it for me, for free.' John looked disgusted at the thought. 'That didn't increase the appeal much.' He smiled slowly at Lionel. 'Being here is going to be like a dream.'

Lionel smiled at him. 'I'm glad you like the room. It'll be nice having you around, although I'm not here much. But if there's anything I can do . . .'

'You've done enough, Li.'

True to his word, Lionel went to pick him up the next day, put the top down on the little red Mustang, and made three trips to help him move in his stuff. He seemed to have mountains of it, but he performed miracles and Lionel hardly recognised the room by Sunday night. He stopped in the doorway and stared.

'My God, what did you do?' He had stapled fabric to one wall, hung plants, put up simple curtains and a handsome painting over the bed. Two lamps provided warm light, there were posters on the other wall. It looked like an apartment in a magazine, and there was a small white flokati rug on the floor. 'Did your Mum do this for you?' Lionel knew she was a decorator and he couldn't imagine John doing all that in a matter of hours. There were even orange crates with the same fabric stapled on them, with magazines in baskets, and cushions giving the impression of a window seat. It was a small haven, and Lionel was impressed beyond words and it showed.

'I did it myself.' He looked pleased at the effect on Lionel. Everyone said he had a talent for interior design, he had always been able to take a room and change it in a matter of hours, using whatever materials were at hand. Even his mother said he should do something with his innate ability – he was better than she was, she claimed. It took her months to achieve the effects she struggled for. 'I love doing stuff like that.'

'Maybe one of these days, you can wave a magic wand over my room. It still looks like a jail cell, and I've lived here for a year.'

John laughed. 'Anytime.' He glanced around. 'Actually, I had two extra plants, and I was going to ask you if you wanted them.'

Lionel smiled at him. 'Sure. But they'll probably die the first time I walk into the room. I don't exactly have a knack with anything green.'

'I'll take care of them for you. I'll water them when I do mine.' The two young men exchanged a smile and Lionel looked at his watch. It was seven o'clock.

'Want to go out for a hamburger?' The very words had a ring of *déjà vu* again, and he was reminded of Paul. It was even more eerie when John agreed and suggested they go to the very place he had gone with Paul the first time. It made Lionel silent and moody for the first part of the meal. He was thinking of that first night when he had gone to Malibu with Paul. He hadn't heard from him in months, but had seen him drive past once, on Rodeo Drive, in the passenger seat of a beige and brown Rolls with a handsome, older man at the wheel. They had been talking animatedly as Lionel watched, they were smiling at each other, and Paul had laughed at something the other man said. And now here he was again, with John . . . his younger brother's best friend. It felt odd. Even more so when they went back to the house they now shared. The other two living there just then were both staying at their girlfriends' that night, and the others had already moved out at the end of the school year.

'Thanks for dinner.' John smiled at him as they sprawled comfortably in the living room and Lionel put a record on. Two of the bulbs were burned out in the room's main lamp, and the light was unintentionally dim. John lit a candle on the coffee table and glanced around. 'This room could use a little help too.'

Lionel laughed. 'You're going to have this place in shape in no time, but I think the other guys will discourage you a little bit. When they're here, this place always looks like someone just threw a bomb into the room.'

John laughed too. 'My sisters keep their rooms like that.' His face grew more serious. 'I've never lived with men before, except my Dad of course. I'm so used to having girls around all the time, this is going to be weird at first.' And then he smiled. 'That must sound crazy to you.'

'No, it doesn't. I've got three sisters too.'

'But you've had Greg around too. I've always been so close to my Mum and the girls. I'll bet I miss them for a while.'

'It's good training for when you get married, to have that many women around.' Lionel smiled again and wondered to himself if he was testing him. He told himself that wasn't fair. John was just a kid . . . but he was the same age he had been when he met Paul . . . but Paul was so much more experienced . . . and he was the experienced one now. Not as much as Paul had been, but more so than this boy. But where did you start? How did you ask someone something like that? He tried to remember what Paul had said to him, but the words escaped him now . . . he remembered that they had gone for a long walk on the beach . . . and Paul had asked him something about being confused. But there was no beach here, and John didn't look confused to him. He was a trifle shy, and he was far less rowdy than Greg, but he was a happy, pleasant, young man . . . yet Lionel could never remember seeing him seriously involved with a girl.

They chatted on for a while, and finally Lionel got up and said he was going to take a shower. John said he'd do the same. It was ten minutes later, when John knocked on the bathroom door and apologised, shouting into the shower where Lionel stood, trying not to think of him, as rivulets of hot water purified his mind and his flesh.

'I'm sorry, Li . . . do you have any shampoo? I forgot mine.'

'What?' Lionel pulled aside the curtain so he could hear and saw John standing there, naked save for a towel wrapped around his waist. He felt his body stir, and pulled the shower curtain closed again so John couldn't see.

'I said, do you have any shampoo?'

'Sure.' He had already used it and his hair was wet and clean. 'Here.' He handed it to John, who disappeared with a thanks and a smile, and he returned with it in a little while, wearing his towel again, his hair wet and dark, his body rippling with the muscles football had built for him, and Lionel was wandering naked around his room, putting things away and humming to himself. He had the radio on, and Lennon and McCartney were singing 'Yesterday', as John handed the shampoo back to him.

'Thanks.' He seemed to linger in the door, and Lionel turned away, wishing he would go. He didn't want to start anything, and he didn't want anyone to get hurt. His way of life was his own and he wasn't looking to drag anyone else into it, when suddenly he felt John's hand on his back, and it was as though his whole body was electrified. It was going to be agonizing having the boy around and hiding his secret from him. Without turning, he grabbed a white terry-cloth robe from a nail on the wall, struggled into it, and turned around, but he had never seen a more beautiful face than John's, there was sorrow and pain and honesty there. And their faces were only inches apart, as John looked at him. 'I have to tell you something, Li. I should have told you before.' There was anguish in the boy's eyes, and Lionel ached for him, wondering what it was.

'Something wrong?'

The younger boy nodded and sank down slowly on the edge of the bed, looking sadly up at him. 'I know I should have told you before I moved in, but I was scared you wouldn't . . . you'd be pissed.' He looked up at him, frightened, but honest. He came right to the point. 'I think you should know I'm gay.' He looked as though he had just admitted he had just killed his best friend, and Lionel's jaw almost dropped he looked so stunned. How simple it all was. How brave he was to speak up, not knowing what Lionel would do or say. His heart went out to the boy and he sat down on the bed next to him and started to laugh. He laughed until tears came to his eyes, and John looked at him nervously. Maybe he was hysterical, or maybe he just thought it was so disgusting it was ridiculous. It was a relief when he finally stopped laughing long enough to speak, and he was stunned when Lionel put his hands on his shoulders as he did.

'If only you knew the things I've been telling myself since you moved in . . . I've been torturing myself . . .' It was clear that John didn't understand. 'Baby, so am I.'

'You're gay?' John looked appalled and Lionel started laughing

203

again. 'You *are*? But I never thought . . .' And yet that wasn't true, there had been a faint, hesitant current between them for the last year and yet neither could accept the possibility that the other understood. They talked about it for the next two hours, lying on Lionel's bed, friends at last. Lionel told him about Paul. And John confessed to two brief, terrible affairs. There had been no love in either of them for him, just terrible, anguished, tortured, guilt-ridden sexual release, one with a teacher from his school, who had threatened to kill him if he talked, the other with a stranger, an older man, who had picked him up on the street. And the only purpose the two affairs had served was to show him what he was. He had suspected it for a long time, but he had always thought it was the worst thing that could ever happen to him. People like Greg Thayer would never have talked to him again. But Lionel was so different, he understood it all, and he looked at the younger man sympathetically now, from his vantage point of nineteen. And John was curious about one thing.

'Does Greg know?'

Lionel was quick to shake his head. 'Only my Mum. She found out last year.' He told John how. It still hurt thinking of how shocked she had been, but she had been wonderful to him since then, understanding, compassionate, she accepted him as he was. 'Everyone should be lucky enough to have a mother like her.' She had far exceeded his hopes and dreams.

'I don't think my Mum could accept it . . . and my Dad . . .' He almost cringed at the thought. 'He always wanted me to be such a jock. I played football for him, and I kept thinking, I'm going to get my teeth kicked out doing this, and I hate it, I hate it.' His eyes filled with tears as he looked at Li. 'I did it for him.'

'I wasn't as good as you were. But my Dad had Greg to pin his hopes on. I always let him carry the ball, so to speak.' He smiled gently at the new friend he had known for years. 'It took the heat off me in some ways, but I paid the price I guess. My father has never approved of me. And if he knew . . . he'd die.' They had so much guilt for so many years, for what they were not, for what they could never be, and in the past year, for what they had done. It was almost too much to bear at times. Lionel thought of it now as he looked into John's eyes. 'Did you know about me?'

John shook his head. 'I don't think I did. I wished a lot though sometimes.' He smiled honestly up at Li and they both grinned, as Lionel tousled the damp black hair that framed his face.

'You little shit. Why didn't you say something?'

'And have you knock my teeth down my throat, or call the cops, or worse yet . . . tell Greg?' He shuddered at the thought, and the thought of something else. 'Are all the guys in this house gay?'

Lionel was quick to shake his head. 'None of them, and I'm pretty sure of that. You get a feel for that when you live with people. And they all have girls stay here pretty regularly.'

'Do they know about you?'

Lionel looked at him pointedly. 'I'm damn careful that they don't suspect, and you'd better be the same, or they'll throw us both out.'

'I'll be careful. I swear.'

Lionel found himself thinking again of changing rooms to the one that shared the bathroom with John, but he forgot the room and looked up at John instead, lying across his bed, and suddenly he felt relief and desire wash over him, as he remembered his dreams of the night before. He reached out to touch John, lying back on the bed, waiting for Li's lips and his hands and his touch, his youthful flesh rippling with excitement and begging for him. Lionel found him with his mouth, and his tongue danced hot fire up John's thighs, as he groaned, and discovered something at Lionel's hands that he had never had before. This time there was nothing clandestine, nothing frightening, nothing embarrassing about the love that Lionel lavished on him for the next couple of hours, until, satisfied and peaceful, they lay in each other's arms and slept. They had each found something that they had been looking for, for a long time, without ever knowing it.

CHAPTER 20

School began in the autumn without event. Lionel and John had never been happier, and no one at the house knew. Lionel had changed rooms before the others came back from their summer plans, and the arrangement worked out perfectly. John and Lionel both locked their doors at night, and no one had any idea who spent the night in whose bed, as they tiptoed back and forth stealthily, whispering late at night, and keeping their moans of ecstasy dimmed. It was only on the rare nights when no one was there at all, sleeping at girls' houses, or going skiing over a long weekend, that they allowed themselves a little more liberty. But they were cautious that no one should know, and for once Lionel didn't even say anything to Faye. He just said that school was going well. He didn't offer any romantic news, and she didn't to pry, although she suspected there was someone in his life from the happy look in his eyes. She just hoped it was someone decent who wouldn't make him unhappy eventually. From what she knew of the homosexual world, there seemed to be so much unhappiness, promiscuity and infidelity, it wasn't a life she wanted her eldest child condemned to. But she knew that there was no alternative for him, and she accepted that.

In November, whe invited Lionel to the Première of their latest film. He accepted with delight, and she wasn't surprised to see John Wells with him. She knew that John was renting a room in the same house as Lionel, and going to UCLA as well, but at the end of the evening when they went to Chasen's for supper and champagne with the twins and a number of business associates and friends, she suddenly wondered if she didn't see something special pass between their eyes. She wasn't quite sure of it, but she sensed something, and she thought John looked much more

206

mature than he had in June, as though he had grown up a lot in the last few months. She suspected something, but she said nothing to anyone, of course. She was startled when Ward questioned her as they got undressed that night. She was talking to him animatedly about the film, the audience response, the favourable reviews they hoped to get, and she was stunned when he interrupted her with a worried frown, standing in his trousers with a bare chest.

'Do you think John Wells is queer?'

'John?' She looked amazed, but in her heart she knew she was stalling for time. 'My God, Ward, what a thing to say . . . of course not, why?'

'I don't know. He looks different to me suddenly. Didn't you notice something about him tonight?'

'No,' she lied.

'I don't know . . .' He walked slowly to his closet and hung up his jacket, still wearing the same frown. 'I just get a funny feeling about him.' Faye felt her whole body grow cold. She wondered if he had the same suspicions about their son. And like Lionel, she wasn't at all sure he could survive knowing the truth, although maybe he would have to one day. In the meantime, she was dedicated to keeping the truth from him. 'Maybe I should say something to Lionel. Warn him . . . he may think I'm nuts, but if I'm right, he may thank me some day. Greg thought there was something wrong with him when he turned down that scholarship at Georgia Tech. Maybe he was right.'

Faye looked suddenly annoyed. 'Just because he doesn't want to play football doesn't mean he's gay for chrissake. Maybe he's interested in other things.'

'You never see him with girls.' They didn't see Lionel with girls either, but Faye didn't point that out to him. And she knew Ward just assumed that Lionel kept his love life to himself. He did not assume he was carrying on with men, just because he didn't see the girls. But she didn't point that out to him either.

'I think you're being unfair. It's like a witch hunt, for God's sake.'

'I just don't want Lionel living with some damn queer, and not realising it.'

207

'I'm sure he's old enough to figure it out for himself. If that's the case.'

'Maybe not. He's so wrapped up in those crazy films of his. Sometimes I think he's completely lost in his own world.' Well, he had noticed that much about his eldest son at least, she told herself.

'He's a remarkably creative boy.' She was anxious to get Ward off the subject of John. And she had to admit, there had been something different about him tonight. But instinctively, she felt a need to protect him. She suspected that he was involved with Lionel. Lionel still didn't look gay, and John was only just beginning to, and he had talked a lot about decorating and interior design. Maybe it was time she said something to Lionel about him. 'Have you seen Li's last film, sweetheart? It's beautiful.'

Ward sighed and sat down on their bed in his shorts. He was still a beautiful man, and at forty-eight he was as well built as his sons. 'Just between us, Faye, I have to tell you it's not my cup of tea.'

'It's a whole new wave, sweetheart.'

'It still isn't something I understand.'

She smiled at him. He was so good at what he did, but he was rarely open to new ideas. He put packages together for her films, but he was interested in none of the new and more exotic trends in films. He had hated the Cannes film festival that year. But he loved the Academy Awards and had been disappointed when she hadn't won another one. He had bought her a beautiful emerald ring to make up for it, and it reminded her of the old days before 1952 when everything changed for them. 'You ought to give Li's films a chance, love. One of these days he's going to surprise the hell out of you and win an award for one of those odd little films.' She was convinced of it but Ward didn't look impressed.

'Good for him. Did you hear from Greg today? He said he'd call about the weekend he wants us to come down.'

'No, he didn't call and I'm not sure I can. I've got meetings with the new script writer every day for the next three weeks.'

'Are you sure?'

'More or less. Why don't you ask Lionel to go with you?'

Ward didn't look sure, but in the end he did, and it gave him the perfect opening to ask him about John when he extended the invitation to him.

'You don't think he's a fag, do you, Li?'

Lionel forced himself to keep a blank look in his eyes. He hated that word and it took every ounce of restraint not to lash out in defence of his friend. 'For heaven's sake, what makes you say a thing like that?'

Ward smiled. 'You look just like your mother when you say that.' But then his face sobered rapidly. 'I don't know. He looks different to me suddenly and he talks about decorating all the time.'

'That's ridiculous. That doesn't make him gay.'

'No, but chasing men would. Watch out he doesn't go after you. And if you sense anything weird about him, throw him out of that house. You don't owe him a thing.' For the first time in his life, Lionel had to fight the urge to punch his father out, but he managed to appear calm until he left his parents' house. He drove all the way back at eighty miles an hour, wanting to kill somebody, mainly his Dad. When he reached the house, he slammed the front door, and a moment later, slammed the door to his room and locked it. It was one of the few times his roommates had ever seen him out of control, and everyone looked shocked. A while later, John wandered into his own room and locked his door as well. He walked quickly through the bathroom that now joined their two rooms.

'What's wrong, love?' Lionel looked up at John with fire in his eyes, and he had to admit to himself that John *was* beginning to look gay. In spite of the well-muscled physique, there was something smooth and pure about his face, he was wearing his hair differently, and his clothes were almost too perfect, too stylish, too neat, but he loved the boy, loved his talent, his warm heart, his giving ways, his body, his soul, he loved everything about him, and if he were a girl, they would already have been engaged and no one would have been surprised. But he was not, so everyone called him queer. 'What's wrong?' He sat down in a chair and waited for Lionel to unload.

'Nothing. I don't want to talk about it.'

John looked at the ceiling quietly and then back at his friend. 'That's a dumb way to handle it. Why not get it off your chest?' And then, suddenly he suspected it had to do with him. 'Did I do something to upset you, Li?' He looked so worried and hurt, that

Lionel walked over to him and gently touched his cheek.

'No ... it has nothing to do with you ...' But it did, and he didn't know how to explain to him. 'It's nothing. My father just pissed me off.'

'Did he say something about us?' He had correctly sensed that Ward had been staring at him the other night. 'Does he suspect?'

Lionel wanted to be vague, but John was too sharp. 'He might. I think he's just feeling around.'

'What did you say?' John looked concerned. What if he said something to the Wells? They had so much to hide. What if they had him arrested or sent away, or ... it was terrifying thinking of it all, but Lionel kissed his neck and spoke to him soothingly. He knew how worried he got.

'Relax. He's just talking off the top of his head. He doesn't know anything.'

John had tears in his eyes. 'Do you want me to move out?'

'No!' Lionel almost shouted the word. 'Not unless I go too. But we don't have to do that.'

'Do you think he'll say something to my Dad?'

'Stop being so paranoid. He just made some cracks and he pissed me off, that's all. It's not the end of the world.' But to pacify Ward, Lionel went to Alabama with him, to watch Greg play ball, and it was the most boring weekend he had ever spent in his life. He hated football almost as much as John, and he had nothing to say to Greg. Worse yet, there were endless painful silences with his Dad, who went berserk when one of their star players suffered an injury and the coach put Greg in his place, just in time for Greg to score a touchdown in the last two and a half seconds of the game and win for his team. Lionel tried to feign the same excitement as Ward felt but it just wasn't there, and he was desperately relieved on the flight home, as he talked about films to him, and tried to explain what he was working on. But as he had felt that he might as well have been on the moon as he watched Greg play, so his father looked at him as he described his latest avant-garde film.

'Do you really think you can make money with something like that one day?' Lionel looked at him, stupefied; it was a goal that had never entered his mind. They were trying out new techniques, stretching the language of film to its utmost. Who gave a damn about making money on it? This was much more important than that, and the two men stared at each other in confused disbelief, each convinced that the other was a fool, yet feeling the burden of pretending that they respected the other's views. It was a terrible strain for both of them, and they both looked relieved to see Faye waiting for them at the gate. Ward talked endlessly about Greg's extraordinary touchdown, crushed that she hadn't watched it on TV, and Lionel looked at her as though he couldn't have stood a moment more. She laughed to herself, knowing them both so well and how different they were, yet she loved them both, just as she loved her other son, and the girls. They were just all very different people, who needed different things from her.

She dropped Ward off at home first, and then said that she would run Lionel home, and come back in time for a drink with Ward. It gave her a few minutes to talk to her eldest son, and commiserate over the boring weekend he had had.

'Was it terrible, love?' She smiled at the look on his face, and he groaned as he leaned his head back against the seat after they dropped his father off at home. He had never felt so exhausted in his entire life.

'Worse. It was like going to another planet and trying to talk their language all weekend long.' She wondered if it was just the boredom of the sport, or the strain of pretending to be straight, but she didn't ask.

'Poor thing. How was Greg?'

'The same.' He didn't need to say more to her. She knew how little they had in common. Sometimes it was hard to believe that they were both her sons. And then she asked him what she had worried about all weekend long.

'Did your father ask about John?'

Lionel's face went tense and he sat up again. 'No. Why? Has he said anything else to you?' He sought her eyes, he still hadn't admitted anything to her, but he knew that she knew without being told, and he wasn't sure what she thought. He had a feeling that she thought it was too close to home, and in some ways she was right.

'I think you ought to be careful, Li.'

'I am, Mum.' He sounded very young and her heart went out to him.

211

'Are you in love with him?' It was the first time she had asked, and he nodded with serious eyes.

'Yes.'

'Then be careful, for both your sakes. Do the Wells know about John?'

Lionel shook his head, and Faye felt a ripple of fear course up her spine as she drove home alone again. One day it would all come out, and someone would get hurt ... maybe a lot of people would ... John, Lionel ... the Wells ... Ward ... she didn't care so much about John and his family, although she was fond of them ... but she was terrified about what it would do to Ward ... and Lionel ... She thought that Lionel could probably weather the storm. He was growing up, unconsciously preparing himself to face that one day, not just from his father, but from everyone. Lionel wasn't the kind of man to hide for the rest of his life. But Faye wasn't sure if Ward would survive the shock. It would destroy a part of him, she knew that, and it terrified her. But there was nothing she could do. Lionel had promised her to be discreet. At that moment, he had just locked his bedroom door, and was quietly kissing John and then sighed as he told him how lonely the weekend had been.

CHAPTER 21

On Christmas Day, Lionel joined his family for their traditional Christmas dinner. Greg was home for a few days, although he had to go back early to play another game, and Ward was going with him. After that, they were flying to the Super Bowl. Ward wanted Lionel to come too, but he insisted that he had other plans. Ward looked annoyed, but Faye distracted them all with an enormous turkey, and champagne for all. Valerie drank a little too much, and everyone teased Van. She looked absolutely beautiful in a new hairdo and a new dress. She was in love for the first time, with a boy she had met at a school dance several weeks before, and she suddenly looked grown up. Even Anne had changed remarkably this year. In the past few months, she had sprouted up, and she was as tall as the twins, though she hadn't come into her own yet, but she was getting there. Lionel reminded them all as he toasted her, and she blushed, that she would be fourteen in a few weeks. After dinner, Lionel and Anne sat by the fire and talked. He saw her less than he would have liked to these days, not so much because he was living out of the house, but because of his work on the film, but it was clear that he still adored her, and it was mutual. And then she surprised him by asking about John, and there was an odd look in her eyes when she did, as though she had a crush on him, and he was surprised that he hadn't realised it before. But everything about her was so hidden and so clandestine, it wasn't surprising that he hadn't noticed it.

'He's fine. I guess he's doing all right in school. I don't see him very much.'

'He's still living at your house though, isn't he? I saw Sally Wells the other day, and she said he loved it there.' Sally Wells was Anne's age, but she was far more mature, and he prayed that Sally hadn't figured things out and told Anne, but it didn't look as though she had. Anne still had that light of innocence and hope in her eyes.

'Yes, he's still there.'

'I haven't seen him in a long time.' She looked at Lionel wistfully and he wanted to laugh she looked so sweet, but he didn't say anything.

'I'll tell him you said hello.' She nodded and the others came in. Ward lit a fire, and they were all pleased with their gifts, and Ward and Faye looked over each other's heads and smiled. It had been a good year all around.

Lionel was the first to leave, as was John at the Wells' home. The other boys were all gone for the holidays. They had the whole house to themselves, so they didn't have to hide and lock their bedroom doors. It was wonderful being able to relax and be themselves. It was a strain being careful all the time, especially for John, who seemed to be growing more obviously effeminate day by day. Now he could fill the house with flowers, and spend long hours in bed every afternoon with Lionel, who was taking a break from his film over the holidays. The two boys took long walks, and talked a lot, and came home to cook and drink hot toddies or white wine by the fire.

It was almost like being grown up, John teased, so much so that they didn't even bother to lock the front door, and never heard Lionel's father walk in the day after Christmas Day. He had stopped in to see if he could talk Lionel into flying South with him after all, and watching Greg play, before all three of them went to the Super Bowl. But the thought went right out of his head, as he walked quietly in after no one had answered his knock. He found the two boys lying near the fire, fully dressed, but with John's head nestled in Lionel's lap, Li's head bent low, saying something endearing to him. Ward stopped and uttered an almost animal groan, as the two boys jumped and looked up. Lionel's face went white. They both scrambled to their feet, and without thinking, Ward advanced toward John angrily, and took a vicious swing at him, making his nose bleed at once, and then he swung at Lionel, but Li grabbed his arm and stopped the blow before it reached his face. There were tears in his eyes, and his father was crying with rage, screaming obscenities at both of them.

'You little sonofabitch ... you whore ...!' The words were meant for John, but he was shouting them at his son, too, his eyes blinded by fury and tears. He couldn't believe what he had just seen. He wanted them to take it back, to tell him it wasn't true, but it was, and there was no hiding from it now. Lionel felt physically sick as he held his father away from him, and John had begun to cry. It was a nightmarish scene and Lionel was attempting to keep calm. He felt as if his whole life was in question now, and he had to explain it to him. Maybe he would understand ... he had to try desperately to explain how different he had always been from Greg ... from all of them ... how he had felt ... he didn't even feel the tears pouring down his cheeks, or the blow when his father finally freed his hands and slapped his face.

'Dad, please ... I want to talk to you ... I ...'

'I don't want to hear any of it!' He was trembling from head to foot and Lionel was suddenly terrified he would have a heart attack. 'I never want to see you again! You two fag bitches!' He looked at them both. 'You scum!' And then at Lionel. 'You're not my son any more, you little queen. I never want to see you in my house again. I won't pay another dime for your support. You are out of my life from now on, is that clear? And stay away from my family!' He was sobbing and shouting and he advanced menacingly on John again. All his dreams had been shattered at once. His elder son was queer. It was more than he could bear, more than losing his fortune years before or the threat of his losing his wife shortly after that ... in his eyes, this was even worse than a death. It was a loss he would never understand, and in some ways a loss he was inflicting on himself, but he didn't realise that. 'You're through! Is that clear?' Lionel nodded his head numbly and, staggering towards the door he had come in only moments before, Ward almost fell blindly down the stairs as he left. The shock was too much for him. He went straight to the nearest bar, had four scotches straight up. At eight o'clock Faye called Lionel with a worried voice. She hated to bother him, but it didn't make sense. They had been expecting guests at six o'clock and Ward hadn't come home. They said he had left the studio early that afternoon, and she couldn't imagine where he'd gone.

'Darling, did your father call you today?' Lionel was still numb. John had been sobbing on the couch for hours, aghast at what had been said, the end result, and the fear that Ward would tell his parents too. Lionel had tried to calm him and had forced him to put an ice pack on his swollen cheek and nose, and he felt an anguish in his own heart that no one could soothe now. His voice was still trembling when he answered the phone, and he couldn't answer at first. And then suddenly, with an icy chill, she realised something was wrong. 'Li . . . sweetheart, are you all right?'

'I . . . yuh . . . I . . .' The words were unintelligible, and suddenly he began to sob too. John sat up and stared at him. He had been so calm, so strong, and suddenly he was falling apart. 'Mum . . . I . . . can't . . .'

'Oh my God . . .' Something terrible had happened to him . . . maybe Ward had got hurt and they had called Lionel. She felt panic rise in her throat. 'Calm down. Now come on . . . tell me what happened . . .'

'Dad came . . . by . . .' There were great terrible gulping sobs locked in his chest and they were begging to come out. 'He . . . I . . .' And then suddenly she knew.

'Did he find you and John?' She imagined the worst, that he had found them in bed and she felt faint at the thought. She herself wouldn't have enjoyed that scene no matter how tolerant she was of her son. And Lionel was beyond being able to reassure her as to what his father had seen.

He could only force out a single word before collapsing totally on the phone. 'Yes . . .' It was moments before he could speak again. 'He said he never wanted to see me again . . . that I wasn't his son . . .'

'Oh my God . . . darling, calm down. You know none of that is true, and he'll come to his senses eventually.' She talked to him for over an hour, their guests having gone home after several cocktails some time before. She offered to go over and talk to them, but he wanted to be alone with John, and she was just as glad. She wanted to be home when Ward returned.

When he did, she was horrified by the condition he was in. He had stopped at several bars after the first one, and he was drunk and staggering, but he still remembered having seen Lionel and John and what he now knew of them. He looked at Faye with hatred and despair. He had turned on her too.

'You knew, didn't you?'

216

She didn't want to lie to him, but she didn't want him to feel there had been a conspiracy to keep it from him for years. 'I suspected about John.'

'Fuck that little sonofabitch . . .' He reeled toward her and she saw that there was blood on his shirt. He had fallen and cut his hand on the way out of the last bar, but he wouldn't let her come to him. 'I mean you knew about our son . . . or should I call him our daughter now?' He reeked of booze and she fell back as he approached and grabbed her arm. 'That's what he is, did you know that? Did you know?'

'Ward, he's still our child, no matter what he does. He's a decent human being and a good boy . . . it's not his fault if that's the way he is.'

'Whose fault is it then? Mine?' That's what he was really worried about. Why had Lionel turned out that way? He had tortured himself over it from one bar to the next, and he didn't like any of the answers that came to mind . . . he had let Faye have too much of a hand with him . . . he hadn't spent enough time with him himself . . . he had frightened him . . . he hadn't loved him enough . . . he had always favoured Greg . . . the reproaches were legion, but they all amounted to the same thing. His son was queer. Where had he learned? How had it happened? How could it happen to him? It was a personal affront to his own manhood . . . his son was a fag . . . the words burned through him like fire, and he looked into Faye's eyes with tears in his own eyes again.

'Stop blaming yourself, Ward.' She slipped her arms around him and led him to their bed, where they sat side by side, as he leaned heavily against her.

'It's not my fault.' It was the whine of a frightened child, and she felt sorry for him. She had asked herself the same questions too the year before, but maybe it was harder for him. She had always known it would be. He wasn't as strong as she was, as sure of herself, or what she had given their kids.

'It's not anyone's fault, not yours, not mine, or his, or even John's. It's just the way he is. We owe it to him to accept that.' But as she said it, he pushed her away from him and stood up unsteadily, grabbing her arm until she winced.

'I will never accept it. *Never!* Do you understand? That's what I told him. He's not my son any more.'

217

'Oh yes, he is!' Now she was furious too and she wrenched her arm away from him. 'He is *our* son, whether he is crippled or maimed or impaired, or deaf or dumb, or mentally ill, or a murderer, or whatever he is ... and thank God, all he is is a homosexual for chrissake. He is my son until my dying day or his, and he is your son until then too, whether you like it or not, or whether you approve of him or not.' She was crying now too, and Ward was shocked at her words and the vehemence with which she spoke to him. 'You can't banish him from your life or mine. He is not going anywhere. He is our son, and you'd damn well better accept him as he is, or you can go to hell, Ward Thayer. I'm not going to let you put that boy through any more misery than he's already been through. It's hard enough on him as it is.'

Ward's eyes blazed into hers. 'That's why he's the way he is. Because you've protected him all his life. You make excuses for him, you let him hide in your skirts.' He sat down in a chair and began to cry again, as he looked up at her. 'And now he's wearing your skirts, damn you. We're lucky he isn't walking around in a dress for chrissakes.' The way he spoke of their son tore at her heart so terribly that she reached out and slapped him hard across the face, and he didn't move from where he sat. He just looked at her with eyes so cold and hard that they frightened her. 'I never want to see him in this house again. And if he comes here, I will throw him out myself. I told him, and I'm telling you, and I will tell everyone else, and if any of you disagree, you're welcome to leave too. Lionel Thayer no longer exists. Is that clear?' She was speechless with rage, and she would have liked to kill him with her bare hands. For the first time in her life, even with all that had happened to them before now, for the first time she was sorry that she had married him and told him so, before slamming out of the room.

She slept in Lionel's room that night, and the next morning at breakfast Ward broke her heart again. He looked as though he had aged ten years overnight, and she remembered now what she had said to Lionel before. She had been afraid then that the truth would kill Ward, and it looked now as though it might, but by the time she was finished, she wished it would. He drank a cup of coffee in silence, stared at the paper without picking it up, and then spoke up in a numbed, flat voice to all of them. Oddly enough, it was one of the few times that they had all had breakfast together in months. But Greg home for another day before going back for his big game, the twins were both up, which was miraculous, and Anne had come downstairs only moments after them. They all sat there now staring at Ward, as he told them that, in his eyes, Lionel would no longer exist from that day forth, that he was a homosexual and having an affair with John Wells. The girls sat and stared at him in open horror and Vanessa began to cry, but Greg looked as though he might throw up. He jumped to his feet, shouting at his Dad as Faye gripped her chair.

'That's a lie!' He said it more in defence of his old friend than his brother, who was, in some ways, a stranger to him. 'That's not true.' His father looked as though he might hit him and pointed at his chair.

'Sit down and shut up. It is true. I walked in on them yesterday.' Anne's face turned to ash, and Faye felt as though her entire family, her whole life, were being destroyed. She hated Ward for it, for what he was doing to all of them, and most of all their firstborn. 'Lionel is no longer welcome in this house. As far as I'm concerned, he doesn't exist. Is that clear? You are all forbidden to see him again and if I find out you have, you're welcome to leave too. I will not support him, or see him, or speak to him ever again. Does everyone understand?' They all nodded woodenly, and all eyes were damp, and a moment later he was gone. He got in his car, and drove to Bob and Mary Wells, as Faye sat at the breakfast table staring at them all, and they stared back at her. Greg was fighting back tears, and he kept thinking of what his friends would say when they found out. It was the worst thing he could think of, and he wanted to die. Most of all he wanted to kill John Wells, the phony little shit . . . he should have known when he wouldn't take the scholarship to Georgia Tech . . . fucking fruit . . . he clenched his fists and looked at them all helplessly as Vanessa searched Faye's eyes.

'Is that how you feel, Mum?' Vanessa asked. There was no point asking if it was true, no matter how unbelievable it was. Their father had said he had walked in on them, and none of them could imagine anything worse. It sounded mysterious and frightening and terrible, and they all imagined obscene acts going on before his eyes, instead of two boys in front of a fire, with one's head in the

219

other's lap. But it had all been very clear, and there was no argument now.

Faye looked at them all and then at Vanessa again. She spoke in a measured, quiet voice, and she thought she had never known such pain. He had destroyed everything she had built for almost twenty years. What would happen to these children now? What would they think of Lionel? Themselves? Their father for banishing their eldest brother from their lives, their mother for letting him do it? . . . She had to speak up. To hell with Ward. 'No. That is not how I feel. I love Lionel, just as I always have, and if that is how he feels, and what he is, and he is a decent upstanding man, no matter what his sexual preferences are,' it was time to be honest with them, 'I will always stand by him. And I want you all to know that right now. Whatever you do, wherever you go, whatever mistakes you make, and whatever you become, whether it be good or bad, or something I approve of or not, I will always be your mother and your friend. You can always come to me. I will always have a place in my heart and my life and my home for you.' She went then and kissed each of them as they cried, all four of them, for the brother they had just lost at their father's hands, for the disappointment they felt, the shock of the secret revealed. It was all a little beyond their ken, but their mother's message was clear.

'Do you think Daddy will change his mind ?' Val's voice was subdued, and no one had noticed Anne slip away a moment before.

'I don't know. I'll talk to him. And I suppose in time, he'll come to his senses, but he just can't understand it right now.'

'Well, neither can I.' Greg slammed a fist into the table and stood up. 'I think it's the most disgusting thing I ever heard.'

'How you feel about it, Greg, is up to you. I don't give a damn what they did. As long as they don't hurt anyone, as long as that's the way they are, I accept them as they are.' She looked her son in the eye and saw the distance between them now. He was too much like Ward. His mind was closed, and now so was his heart. He ran upstairs and slammed the door, and once he had left, Faye noticed that Anne was gone. She knew what a blow it would be to her, and she resolved to go upstairs and talk to her, but when she did, the child's door was locked and she wouldn't answer her. The twins went to their rooms too, and the entire family acted as though someone had died. Faye called Lionel a little while later, and he and John knew by then that Ward had gone to the Wells.

They were all hysterical and Bob and Mary Wells had called. There had been rivers of tears, and after the phone call, John had gone to the bathroom and thrown up. But for all the shouting and screaming and reproaches they directed at both boys, they wanted John to know that he was still their son, that they did not share Ward Thayer's view, that they still loved him, and they accepted Lionel as well. It brought tears to Faye's eyes when she heard, and she was secretly pleased when Lionel told her that Bob Wells had thrown Ward out of their house.

Faye went to see both boys that afternoon. She wanted Lionel to know again how strongly she supported him, and mother and son stood holding each other for a long time, and then she turned and hugged John. It wasn't easy to accept, and it wouldn't have been her choice for her son, but it was what he was. And she also wanted him to know that he would always be welcome in their home, that he was still part of the family no matter what his father said, and that from now on, she would be supporting both his school career and his living expenses. If his father wanted to cut him off, that was up to him, but Faye would always be there for him. She would take the responsibility on now, and Lionel cried as she told him, and promised to get a job to help support himself. And John did too. His parents had already told him earlier that they would continue to support him as long as he was in school, that nothing was going to change for him.

But Ward stuck to the same party line, when he returned that night. He had disappeared all day, and Faye could tell from the way he looked when he got home that he had been drinking all day. He reminded everyone at dinner that night that Lionel was no longer welcome in his house, that he was dead as far as he was concerned, and as he said the words, Anne rose and stared at him with hatred in her eyes.

'Sit down!' It was the first time he had ever spoken harshly to her, and she stood up to him, much to everyone's surprise. It was a time in their family that no one would forget soon.

'I won't. You make me sick.'

He walked around the table and grabbed her arm, forcing her into her seat, but she wouldn't touch her food, and then with measured tones she stood up at the end of the meal and glared at him.

'He's better than you are.'

'Then get out of my house.'

'I will!' She threw her napkin onto her plate, which was still full, and disappeared into her room. They heard Greg's car roar away moments after that. He was having trouble coping with it all. Vanessa and Valerie looked at each other with concern. They were both frightened for Anne and what this could do to her.

That night she slipped out of the house, and hitched a ride to Lionel's house. She rang the bell, and knocked on the door. She could see lights upstairs, but they wouldn't answer her and when she went to the corner and called on the pay phone there, no one answered the phone. They had heard it ring, and they were sitting quietly in the living room. But it had been such a nightmarish twenty-four hours for them that they couldn't take any more. John thought that maybe they should answer the door. But Lionel disagreed.

'If it's one of the guys coming home early, they've all got the key. It's probably my father drunk again.' They'd been through enough. They both agreed about that. They didn't even look out the window to see who it was. And downstairs Anne fished a pencil out of her coat pocket, and tore a piece of newspaper off the garbage can, scribbling a note to Lionel. 'I love you, Li. I always will, A.' Tears filled her eyes. She had wanted to see him again before she left, but maybe it didn't matter now . . . she slipped the piece of paper into the mailbox. That was all he needed to know. She didn't want him to think she had turned on him too. He had to know she never would. But she couldn't stand it any more. It had been unbearable ever since he moved out, and now it would be worse. She would never see him. She had only one choice, and she was surprised at how relieved she felt.

That night as they all slept, she quietly packed a small duffle bag, and slipped out of her bedroom window, as she had done when she had gone to see Li. There were easy footholds all the way down the side of the house. She had used them before, plenty of times. And she slipped quietly down now, wearing sneakers and jeans, her hair in a long blonde braid, a warm parka on. She knew it would be cold up there. She had everything she cared about in the one small bag. She didn't even look back as she left the house. She didn't give a damn about any of them, any more than they did about her. She stealthily crept down the road, and walked all the way into L.A., and there she hitched a ride on the motorway heading north. She was surprised at how easy it was. She told the first driver that she went to Berkeley and had to get back after the Christmas holiday. He didn't ask her anything else, and drove her all the way to Bakersfield before dropping her off.

And by then, Faye had found her note. She had left the door unlocked, and the note on her bed.

'That makes two of us you're rid of now, Dad. Goodbye, Anne.' No word to anyone else. Nothing to Faye. Her heart almost stopped when she found the piece of paper left on Anne's bed, and they called the police immediately. She called Lionel too, and he had found the scrap of newspaper by then. It was the worst time in her life Faye could ever recall, and she wondered if she'd live through it, as she waited for the police to arrive. Ward was sitting, stunned, in a chair in the den, the note still in his hand.

'She couldn't have gone very far. She's probably at a friend's.'

But Valerie took care of that hope. 'She doesn't have any friends.' It was a sad statement about Anne, but they all knew it was true. Her only friend had been Lionel, and her father had banished him. Faye sat watching him with unspoken rage, as the bell rang. The police had come. She just prayed they would find Anne before something happened to her. There was no telling where she had gone, and she had already been gone for hours.

CHAPTER 22

After the first driver who picked her up left her in Bakersfield, it took Anne several hours to catch another ride, but this one took her straight up to Fremont, and she caught another ride easily from there. It took her a total of nineteen hours to get to San Francisco, but on the whole she was surprised at how easy it was, and all of them had been nice to her. They thought she was just another college kid, 'a flower child' two of them had teased. None of them would have guessed that she was a few weeks shy of being fourteen years old. And when she reached San Francisco, she walked down Haight Street, feeling as though the streets were paved with gold. There were young people everywhere, in bright, homemade clothes. There were Hare Krishnas in soft orange robes with shaved heads, boys with hair to their waists in jeans, girls with flowers braided into their hair. Everyone looked happy and pleased with life. There were people sharing food on the streets, and someone offered her an acid tab for free, but she smiled shyly and refused.

'What's your name?' someone asked, and she whispered softly, 'Anne'. This was the place she had longed to be for years, free of the strangers she had been related to and hated for so long. She was glad, in a way, that it had come to this. Lionel had John now, and maybe soon she would have someone too. Lionel would know that she loved him no matter what, and as for the others . . . she didn't care. She hoped she'd never see them again. On the way north, she had thought seriously about changing her name, but once on the streets of the Haight-Ashbury, she realised that no one would care. There were others who looked even younger than she, and no one would suspect she'd come here. She had said nothing to anyone.

224

And a girl named Anne was as anonymous as anyone could be. Her looks were plain, her hair an ordinary blonde, unlike Vanessa's pale golden hair, or Val's which looked like flame. The twins couldn't have got away with this, even if they wanted to. But she knew she could. She could fade into any crowd. She had been doing it at home for years. No one knew when she was there, when she was not, when she arrived, or when she disappeared, and she was so used to everyone asking 'Where's Anne?' that she knew that she could easily do the same thing here.

'Hungry, Sister?' She looked up to see a girl in what looked like a white bedsheet wrapped around her spare frame, with a tattered purple parka over it. The girl was smiling at her and held out a piece of carrot cake. Anne suspected it might be laced with acid or some other drug, and the girl in the parka saw her hesitate. 'It's clean. You just look like you're new here.'

'I am.'

The girl with the carrot cake was sixteen and she'd been here for seven months, having come from Philadelphia in late May. Her parents hadn't found her yet, although she'd seen their ads in the 'Personals', but she had no inclination to respond. There was a priest who roamed the streets, offering advice, and to make contact with their parents, if they wished. But not too many did, and Daphne wasn't one of them. 'My name is Daff. Do you have a place to stay tonight?'

Hesitantly, Anne shook her head. 'Not yet.'

'There's a place on Waller. You can stay for as long as you like. All you have to do is help keep it clean, and help cook the food on the days they assign.' They had also had two outbreaks of hepatitis recently, but Daphne didn't tell her that. Outwardly everything was beautiful and loving here. The rats, the lice, the kids who died from overdose were not something one discussed with a neophyte. And no matter, those things happened everywhere, didn't they? This was a special time in history. A time of peace and love and joy. A wave of love to counteract the useless deaths in Vietnam. Time had stopped for all of them and all that mattered was the here and now, and love and peace, and friends like this. Daphne gently kissed her cheeks and took her hand, leading her to the house on Waller Street.

There were roughly thirty or forty people living there, mostly in

Indian garb of rainbow hues, although there were some in patched jeans too, and outfits with feathers and sequins sewn on. Anne felt like a plain little bird in her jeans and an old brown turtleneck she'd worn on the trip, but a girl who met her at the door offered to lend her a dress, and she found herself suddenly wearing a costume in faded pink silk. It had come from a thrift shop on Divisadero Street, and she slipped her feet into rubber thongs, unbraided her hair, and wove two flowers into it. By that afternoon she felt and looked like one of them. They ate an Indian dish, and someone had baked bread, she took a few hits on someone's joint, and she lay back on a sleeping bag feeling full and warm and content, looking around at her new friends, feeling a warmth and acceptance she had never felt before. She knew she would be happy here. It was a lifetime away from the house in Beverly Hills, her father's angry edicts about Lionel . . . the perfidies of the people she knew . . . the stupidity of Gregory . . . the selfishness of the twins . . . the woman who called herself her mother that she had never understood . . . this was where she belonged now. Here on Waller Street, with her new friends.

When they initiated her three days after she arrived, it seemed suitable and right and loving. It was a supreme act of love in a room filled with incense, as a fire blazed warmly in the hearth, and the hallucination carried her from heaven to hell and back again. She knew she would be a different person when she woke up again. They told her that before she ate the mushrooms, followed by the tiny tab of LSD absorbed into a sugar cube. It took a little while for it to take hold on her mind, but when it did, there were friendly spirits there, and a room full of people she knew. Later, there were spiders and bats and terrifying things, but they held her hands while she howled and screamed, and when she felt her body racked with pain, they sang her songs, and cradled her as her mother never had . . . even Lionel had done nothing like this for her . . . she crossed a desert on her hands and knees, and then at last she came to an enchanted forest, filled with elves, and she felt their hands on her, and felt the spirits singing to her again. And now the faces that had hovered over her all night, and waited for her to be free of the evil of her past life, came forward towards her.

Already, she felt purified, and knew that she was one of them. The evil spirits had been killed, they had left her, and now she was pure . . . now they could complete the ritual with her. Gently, they peeled away her clothes, and washed her with oils, each one gently massaging her tender flesh . . . she had come far that night, and parts of her were sore, but the women gently massaged her, getting her ready now, reaching slowly into her, and stretching her as she screamed. She fought them at first, but they whispered so gently to her, and she could hear the music now. They had her drink something warm, and poured more oil on her, as her two guardians tenderly massaged her most secret place and she writhed beneath their hands, howling with agony and joy, and then her new brothers came, the spirits who would belong to her now, to replace the others she had left behind, and each of them knelt beside her as the sisters crooned, and one by one the brothers entered her, as the music grew louder, and birds flew high overhead . . . there were sharp arrows of pain at times, and waves of ecstasy, and again and again they came into her, and held her there, and left again, until the sisters returned, kissing her now and reaching far far into her until she could feel no more, and heard no sound. The music had stopped. The room was dark. Her past life was gone. She stirred, wondering if it had all been a dream but when she sat up and looked around, she saw them there, waiting for her. She had been gone for a long, long time, and she was so surprised at how many there were. But she recognised each one of them, and crying, she held out her arms and they came to her, embracing her. Her womanhood was complete, her sisterhood was sure. They gave her another acid tab as a reward, and this time she soared with them as one of the flock, dressed in a gown of white, and when the brothers and sisters came to her again, she was one of them this time, kissing them too . . . touching the sisters as they had touched her. This was her privilege now, they explained, and this was an expression of her love for them and theirs for her. She was to participate often in the ritual in the next few weeks, and when a new face arrived in the house on Waller Street, it was Sunflower who greeted them, with her blonde hair woven with flowers and her gentle smile . . . Sunflower who had once been Anne . . . she lived mostly on LSD, and she had never been as happy in her life.

Three months after she had come to them, one of the brothers took her as his own. His name was Moon, and he was tall and thin and beautiful, with silver hair and gentle eyes. He took her to bed with him every night, and cradled her, and in some ways he reminded her of Lionel. She went everywhere with him, and often he would turn to her with his mystic smile.

'Sunflower . . . come to me . . .' She knew the magic of what pleased him now, knew best how to warm the herb potions he drank, when to bring him drugs, when to touch his flesh. And now, when a newcomer arrived, and they performed the ritual, it was Sunflower who went to the sisters first, gently pouring the warm oil over them, welcoming them to their tribe, and letting her swift fingers prepare them for the rest of the tribe. Moon was always very proud of her, and gave her extra acid tabs because of it. It was strange how different life was now from what it had once been. It was filled with bright colours and people that she loved, people who loved her too. There was nothing left of the lonely ugliness of her life. She had forgotten all of them. And when, in the spring, Moon felt her belly and told her she was with child, and could no longer participate in the ritual, she cried.

'Don't cry, little love . . . you must prepare for a much greater ritual than that. We will all be there with you when this tiny moonbeam pierces the skies and comes to you, but until then . . .' He cut down on her acid tabs, although he let her smoke as much marijuana as she wished. And he laughed at her when it increased her appetite.

The baby was just beginning to show when she walked down Haight Street one day, and saw a face she knew she recognised from the past, but she wasn't quite sure who it was. She returned to Moon in the house on Waller Street with a pensive air.

'I've seen someone I know.'

It didn't particularly worry him. They all saw people they knew at times, in their minds and hearts, and occasionally in more concrete ways. His wife and child had died in a boating accident just before he had walked out of his house in Boston one day and come here. He saw them in his mind's eye, much of the time, especially during the ritual. For Sunflower to see someone she knew now surprised him not at all. It was a sign of her rising to a higher state, and that pleased him. This child, who was part his, would bring her even higher before it came. 'Who was it, child?'

'I'm not sure. I can't remember his name.' He had let her have one of the rare acid tabs he allowed her the night before, and the name Jesus kept coming to her mind, but she was sure it wasn't him.

Moon smiled at her. Later, she would have more mushrooms and acid again, but she had to remain pure for the coming child, she could have only just enough to keep her in an enlightened state. But she could not soar too high now, or it would frighten the child. And this baby belonged to all of them after all. They had all shared in it, the brothers and the sisters. Moon felt certain that it had been conceived during her first night, when she was the centre of the ritual. The child would be specially blessed and as he reminded her of that the name John came into her mind, clearly, and then suddenly she remembered him.

CHAPTER 23

'Are you sure?' Lionel stared at him disbelievingly. John had done this to him twice before. They had both dropped out of school three months before, much to everyone's despair, and they had come to San Francisco to search for Anne. Ward had refused to hear about it from Faye, and Bob Wells was afraid they were using it as an excuse to drop out of school, go to San Francisco, and join the gays living freely there.

But Lionel insisted that Anne would go there. It was a haven for runaway kids, and though he didn't tell his parents, he felt certain that the runaways could live there for years without being recognised or turned in. There were thousands of them, crushed into tiny apartments, living like ants in the houses of the Haight-Ashbury, the houses painted a riot of colours, with flowers and rugs and incense and drugs and sleeping bags everywhere. It was a place and a time that would never come again, and Lionel instinctively felt that Anne was part of it. He had felt it from the first moment he'd arrived. It was just a question of finding her, if they could. He and John had combed the streets for months without success, and there wasn't much time left for them. They had promised to return to school by June for the summer session to make up for the time they'd lost.

'If you don't find her in three months,' Bob Wells had said, 'then you have to give up. You can only search for so long. She could be in New York, or Hawaii, or Canada.' But Lionel knew he was wrong. She would come here to search for the love she felt she'd never had from them. John agreed with him, and now he was certain that he'd seen her walking in a daze near Ashbury, wrapped in a purple bed sheet, with a crown of flowers on her hair, her eyes so glazed he almost wondered if she had seen him at all. But for an instant, just an instant, he had been certain that she had known who he was, and then she had drifted off again. He had followed her to an old broken-down house that seemed to be housing an entire colony of obvious druggies and runaways. The smell of incense wafted right out into the street, and there must have been twenty of them on the steps, singing an Indian chant, and holding hands, crooning and laughing softly and waving at friends. And as she came to the stairs, they parted like the Red Sea for her, helping her up the stairs through their midst, as a grey-haired man waited for her in the doorway, and then carried her inside as John watched. It was the strangest sight he had ever seen and he tried to explain it to Lionel, describing her again.

'I have to admit, it sounds like her.' But the others John had found had too. Every day they split up and wandered through the Haight-Ashbury looking for her. If she was there, it was amazing they hadn't found her yet. And at night, they went back to the hotel room they had rented with the money Lionel had borrowed from Faye. They usually ate a hamburger quietly somewhere; they never went to a single gay bar. They kept to themselves.

In the mornings, they started all over again. It was a labour of love, the like of which Faye had never seen. She had flown up several times to join them in their search, but as Lionel finally explained, she only hampered them. She stood out in the crowd of flower children; her shirts were starched, and even with her jewellery reduced to a minimum it was still too much – her jeans were too clean. She looked exactly what she was, the mother of a runaway from Beverly Hills, looking for her child, and they ran from her like rats. Finally, Lionel had told her straight out. 'Go home, Mum, we'll call you if we see anything. I promise.' She had gone back then to work on a film. She had urged Ward to take a co-producer on this one, because he was drinking so heavily, and things had gone from bad to worse with them. He still refused even to speak to Lionel. And when Lionel called her to report on what he had seen in the Haight-Ashbury, the moment Ward heard his voice, he hung up on him. It made communication with Faye extremely difficult for Lionel and Faye was furious. Eventually, she put in a separate phone for Lionel to call her on. But she noticed that the children avoided their brother as well; they were afraid of what their father would do if they talked to him. The twins

231

never answered the phone Lionel called her on, as if Ward would know if they had talked to him. They had taken him at his word, and Lionel was abandoned by all save Faye, who loved him more than ever before, out of compassion, her own loneliness, and for what he was doing to find Anne. She spoke to Mary Wells as often as she could and expressed her gratitude for John's help. They seemed to have accepted the situation gracefully. They loved their son, and they accepted hers as well. It was far more than she could say for Ward, who had never spoken to the Wells since the morning Bob had thrown him out, the day he'd broken the news to them.

Things were no longer the same between Ward and Faye either. He had actually gone to the Super Bowl with Greg despite Anne's running away. He had insisted that the police would find her eventually, and when they did he would punish her, and put her on restriction for the next ten years if that was what it took to put some sense into her. But it was as though he couldn't cope with anything more, and he left with Greg, and had a great time at the Super Bowl. He seemed surprised to learn that the police had not located Anne when he came back, and in the ensuing weeks, he began to pace the floor at night, pouncing on the phone the moment it rang. He finally understood that it was serious, and the police had told them bluntly that it was possible that their daughter was dead, or that she was alive and they would never find her again. It was like losing two children at once, and Faye already knew that they would never recover from it. She had buried herself in her work to ease the pain, to no avail, spending whatever time she could with the twins when they were free. But they felt it too. Vanessa was quieter than she had ever been before, her big romance died shortly after it began, and even Valerie was more subdued. She hardly seemed to wear makeup any more or go out. Her miniskirts were less intentionally shocking and her wardrobe hadn't grown. It was as though they all waited to hear something that they might never hear again, and as each day passed Faye grew more fearful that her youngest child was dead.

She began going to church, which she hadn't done in years, and she said nothing at all to Ward when he didn't come home at night. At first, he came home at one or two o'clock, when the bars closed, and it was easy to see where he'd been, but eventually he began not to come home at all. The first time it happened, Faye felt sure he had been killed. But when he walked in at six o'clock the next morning, tiptoeing in with the newspaper under his arm, there was a look on his face which frightened her. He wasn't drunk, he was not hung over, he offered her no explanation at all, and suddenly she remembered a name she hadn't thought of in years . . . Maisie Abernathie . . . she remembered when Ward had gone to Mexico with her for five days fourteen years before, and Faye knew that although it obviously wasn't the same girl, it was the same look on his face . . . the same way of avoiding her eyes, and suddenly she completely withdrew from him. He came home less and less, but she was so numbed by pain and tragedy that she felt nothing any more. She was barely hanging on to her own sanity. Her days were filled with work, her nights were filled with guilt, and in between she did whatever she could for the twins – but their entire family had fallen apart in a few brief moments.

Eventually she heard the rumours at MGM. He was involved with the star of an important daytime TV show, and according to rumour, the affair was serious. She just prayed that it wouldn't turn up in the columns so she wouldn't have to explain it to the girls. She had enough on her hands just then, and just when she thought she couldn't stand any more Lionel called her. He had gone out with John that afternoon and followed the girl John had been so sure was Anne, and he was sure of it now too. She looked drugged and completely dazed, and she was heavier than she had been before, and wrapped up in what looked like a purple sari, but they were both sure it was Anne.

Tears rolled down Faye's cheeks as she listened. 'Are you sure?'

Lionel said that they almost were, as sure as they could be. She was so dazed-looking and so wrapped up in her strange garb, surrounded by the members of her odd little sect, it was difficult to get close enough to her to find out if it was Anne. It wasn't as if one could yell 'Anne' and have her wave back. Lionel hated to raise his mother's hopes and then disappoint her. 'No, we're not sure, Mum. And we wanted to know what you want us to do now.'

'The police told us to call them.'

'What if it's the wrong girl?'

'Apparently, it happens all the time. She'll probably turn out to be another runaway they're looking for. They said not to hesitate to call if we think we know where she is, and there's a Father Paul

Brown up there who knows every kid there. He helps them out all the time.' The boys knew who he was, and agreed to contact him as well as the police. 'Do you think I should fly up tonight?' She had nothing else to do at night now once she left work. She never saw Ward. He made almost no pretence about coming home at night, and he seemed to be waiting for her to confront him about it, but she didn't have the strength. She wondered if the rumours were true, that it was serious. It seemed incredible after all these years to get divorced, except that that looked extremely likely now ... if they could just find Anne ... and get Lionel back in school first ... then she could deal with Ward's affair ... and a divorce ... Her private line for Lionel rang at midnight that night, and she knew it could only be he. Ward never called any more when he wasn't coming home and he would call her on their usual line.

She picked the phone up and held her breath. 'Li?'

'The police think it's her too. We pointed her out to them today. They have half a dozen undercover cops working narcotics details out there, and looking for runaways. And they have been to talk to Father Brown. Apparently her name is Sunflower. He knows who she is. But he doesn't think she's as young as Anne.' Anne would be fourteen and a half by now, but she had always looked older than her years, as they all knew, especially recently. He also didn't tell Faye the rest of what Father Brown had said, that she was living in a sect that indulged in strange sexual and erotic practices that involved group sex. They had all been busted several times, but it seemed impossible to prove either what went on, or that any of them were in fact minors. Everyone claimed to be over eighteen, and it was impossible to prove differently. He had also told them that LSD was involved heavily in what they did, and 'magic mushrooms', as peyote was called. The worst of it was that this girl they were following was with child. But he didn't dare tell Faye that yet. If it was the wrong girl, there was no point worrying her about that. 'Mum, do you want her arrested, or just questioned?' They had never come this close before, and Faye felt her heart sag as she thought of her child. It had been five months since she had seen Anne, and God only knew what had happened to her in that time. She didn't dare think of it, and forced herself to concentrate on what Lionel had asked.

234

'Can't they just take her away, and have you have a good look at her?'

Lionel sighed. He'd been over that all day with them. 'They can, if it turns out to be Anne. But if not, and if the girl isn't a runaway, and is of age, she can sue them for false arrest. Most of those hippies won't, but they're pretty cautious about that. I guess they've been burned a couple of times.' He sounded so tired, her heart went out to him, and Faye sighed. She wanted Anne back, at all costs.

'Tell them to do whatever they have to, sweetheart. We've got to know if it's her.'

He nodded at his end. 'I'm meeting the undercover guys at ten o'clock tomorrow morning. They're going to stake out the house, and follow her again. If we can just talk to her, we will. If not, they'll bust her for being under the influence, or something like that.'

Faye sounded shocked. 'Is she on drugs?'

Lionel hesitated as he looked at John. They were both sick to death of the Haight-Ashbury, the filth, the drugs, the scum, the scams, the kids. They were almost ready to give up, but now . . . if it could be her . . . 'Yeah, Mum. It looks like she is. If that's Anne. She doesn't look too great.'

'Is she hurt?' There was such anguish in Faye's voice that it tore at his heart.

'No. Just spaced out. And she's living in a pretty strange place. It's some kind of Eastern sect.'

'Oh Christ . . . ' Maybe she had shaved her head. Faye couldn't imagine it. The whole place had been beyond her when she had gone up to meet Lionel and John to look for her before. She had actually been relieved when they had sent her away. But now she wanted to go back. She suddenly sensed that it could be Anne this time, and she wanted to be there too. She could still envisage her as she had been the day she was born. It was hard to believe it was so long ago.

'We'll call you tomorrow, Mum. As soon as we know something.'

'I'll be in the office all day.' And then, 'Should I make a reservation on an afternoon flight, just in case?'

He smiled into the phone. 'Just hang on. I'll call you either way, whether it's Anne or not.'

'Thank you, sweetheart.' He was the dearest son a woman could want, and so what if he was gay. He was a better son to her than Greg had ever been, although she loved them both, but Greg lacked his sensitivity. He would never have dropped out of school for three months to look for Anne. In fact, when he had come home at Easter, he had said that he thought Lionel was nuts. Ward had glared at him instantly for speaking the forbidden name, and she had to control herself not to lash out at him in front of Greg. She had had all she could take, and maybe it would be a relief to get a divorce from him. But she couldn't think of that now. All she could think about was Anne.

She lay awake long after speaking to Lionel, thinking of Anne when she had been a little girl, the things she had done, the funny things she'd said, the way she'd hidden so much of the time, the way she'd clung to Lionel. The timing of her birth had been unfortunate, Faye realised now, but that was no one's fault. Disaster had struck only weeks after she'd been born, and Faye had had her hands full selling the house, their antiques, her jewellery, moving them all into the hideous little house in Monterey Park, and then Ward leaving them, and her trying to support them all herself. Anne had more or less got lost in the shuffle of it all. The others had been just old enough not to need her quite as much, and she had given all her time to them before that. But not to Anne . . . never to Anne . . . she had worked ever since then, and Anne had got tossed in with the pack. Faye could remember moments now when the nurse had come to her, months after Anne had been born, asking if she wanted to hold the child, or give her her next bottle, and Faye had told her, 'Not now . . . I don't have time.' She had brushed her off again and again, and Anne had paid the price for it. How could you tell a child like that that you *did* care, that you always had, but that you just hadn't had the time . . . what right did one have to the child if one had no time for it? And yet, when she had been conceived, their life had been so easy, and she had had all the time in the world. Bad timing, bad luck . . . bad mother, she told herself again and again as she lay in the big empty bed, thinking about Anne, and wondering if it was too late, if Anne would hate her for the rest of her life. It was possible, she recognised that now. Some things could never be mended again, like her relationship with Ward . . . and with this child . . . and his with Lionel . . . the fabric of their family seemed to have been irreparably rent in the past few months, and it weighed on her like a rock.

She got up at six o'clock, having slept not a wink all night. But she couldn't sleep now, wondering if the girl Lionel had seen was Anne. She showered, and dressed, waited for the twins to leave for school, and then went to her office at MGM. It amazed her that Ward was making no pretence at all. He didn't even call her, or try to explain where he had spent the night. Once in a while he came home, and she asked no questions of him. And now, when he did show up, he slept in Greg's room, and they spoke not at all.

She caught a glimpse of him as she walked down the hall later that morning, but she said nothing to him. She didn't want to say anything about Anne yet. There was no point until she was sure she had been found, and it wasn't sure at all. Not until she got the call just after noon and her heart almost stopped. Her secretary told her Lionel was on the line, and she hit the button hurriedly on her phone.

'Li?'

'It's okay, Mum, relax.' He was shaking from head to foot, but he didn't want her to know that.It had been hairy getting her out of them, but the police had handled everything, and no one was hurt, not even Anne. She was a little dazed. But she didn't even seem upset to have been removed, although the old guy had been. He had waved a staff at them and said the gods would punish them for stealing his child. But she had just let them carry her away, and she had smiled at Lionel, and now she seemed to know who he was. But she was also very high on dope, and it was possible that when she came down, she would be mad as hell. They were prepared for that. The cops were used to it and there was a doctor standing by.

Faye held her breath, and then her words exploded on the phone. 'Is it Anne?' She closed her eyes.

'Yes, Mum, it is. And she's all right. More or less . . .' They had found her at last.

He looked at John again. The last months had formed a bond between them that they both knew would last for the rest of their lives. It was as though they were married to each other by now. But Lionel forced his mind back to his mother at the other end of the line. 'She's fine, Mum. We're at Bryant Street, with the police, and they'll remand her into my custody, if you want. I'll bring her home in a day or two when she's had a chance to adjust.'

'Adjust to what?' He had a lot to tell her, which he couldn't tell her yet. Not over the phone at least. She was going to have to get prepared.

'She's been away from us for a long time, Mum. It takes a little adjustment to get used to the real world again. She's led a very different life for the last few months.' He was looking for a tactful way to say it to her, but he hoped she never heard the tales the police had told him. They knew the sect well, and their rituals. She would have died if she knew what Anne had been through, although Anne looked none the worse for wear. In fact, Lionel thought she looked happier than she had in years, except that most of that was probably the drugs, and she was probably not going to be nearly as happy when she came down from them. The police had discussed the possibility of bringing charges for being under the influence, but since she was fourteen years old, and had probably been coerced, they had decided not to press any charges at all. They wanted to know if the Thayers wanted to press any charges against the members of the sect for abducting or seducing her, and Lionel knew his parents would have to decide that. Faye was still trying to decipher what Lionel was telling her.

'Is she on drugs?'

He hesitated, but the truth had to be told. 'I'd say so, yes.'

'Hard drugs? Like heroin . . .' Faye's face went pale at her end. Her life would be over if that was the case, people never got off heroin, but Lionel was quick to put her mind at rest.

'No, no, more like marijuana, and probably some LSD and other hallucinogens.' He was becoming very expert about all that, and Faye sighed.

'Are the police holding her?'

'No. I thought I'd take her back to our hotel, let her take a bath and unwind . . .' (ie, come down . . .)

'I'll catch the next plane up.'

Lionel gritted his teeth, He wanted desperately to clean her up before Faye arrived, and the 'next plane' didn't give him much time, also there was something else that Faye would have to know, and it was easy to see now. 'Mum, there's something you ought to know . . .' She had known instinctively that there was something he wasn't telling her. Anne had been hurt . . . something . . . 'Mum?'

'What is it, Li?'

'She's pregnant, Mum.'

'Oh my God.' At that, Faye burst into tears. 'She's fourteen years old.'

'I know that. I'm sorry, Mum . . .'

'Do they have the boy?'

He didn't have the heart to tell her that the child had probably been fathered, not by a 'boy', but by the thirty or so male members of the sect. Instead, he was vague and said they'd have to leave that to Anne. It was difficult for Faye to regain her composure after that, and she made a hasty note on her office pad, 'Call Dr Smythe'. He would arrange an abortion for her. He had taken care of the star of one of her films the year before, and if he wouldn't do a child of Anne's age, she'd take her to London or Tokyo. She didn't have to go through with this. She'd probably been raped. Somehow, the idea that Anne was pregnant was more horrible than the rest of this whole grim affair and she had to remind herself to be grateful that the girl had been found at all. She was still crying when she hung up the phone, and buried her face in her hands for a moment before taking a deep breath, blowing her nose, and straightening her shoulders to go down the hall to see Ward. He had to be told. Anne was his child too, however little he and she had in common now. She wondered how they would handle the division of their business life. So far they had gone on as before, but that couldn't go on forever either. And now that Anne had been found, Lionel would be coming home. And she had no excuses left not to confront Ward. She stopped outside his office, and his secretary jumped nervously.

'Is Mr Thayer in?' But she knew he was. She had seen him only moments before.

The secretary looked at her anxiously, dropped a pencil on the floor, and then tried to avoid Faye's face. 'No . . . he's not . . .'

'That's a lie.' Faye wasn't in the mood to listen to garbage from anyone. 'I happen to know he's in.' It was a guess, but it worked.

'He's not . . . well, he is . . . but he asked not to be disturbed.'

'Fucking on his office couch again?' Faye's eyes blazed. She

239

knew exactly what was going on, and in their offices. He had one hell of a nerve. 'I didn't know we used the casting couch here quite so much.' She advanced towards his office door and the secretary gasped as Faye turned towards her. 'Don't worry. I'll tell him I overpowered you.' And with that, she opened the door and stepped in. And the scene which met her eyes was reasonably sedate. He and Carol Robbins, the star of 'Follow my World', the daytime soap, were both fully dressed and talking across the desk, but he was holding her hand, and everything about them suggested that they were deeply involved. She was a pretty blonde with long legs and enormous tits. She played a nurse on the show, and the men loved to watch her buttons strain. Faye looked directly at Ward as he let go of the girl's hand, and looked at his wife nervously. She never acknowledged the presence of the girl, and kept her eyes directly on his.

'They found Anne. I thought you'd want to know.'

His eyes grew wide, and it was obvious that he cared a great deal. For a moment, he completely forgot the girl in the room, and looked only at his wife. 'Is she all right?'

'Yes.' She didn't tell him about the drugs or the pregnancy. She didn't want the girl to know. It would have been all over Hollywood by dinnertime. 'She's fine.'

'Who found her? The police?'

Faye shook her head. 'Lionel.' There was a look of victory in her eyes as she watched his face go taut. 'I'm going up there in two hours. If I can, I'll bring her home tonight. You can stop by and see her tomorrow when she's had some sleep.'

He looked surprised at what she said. 'Is there any reason why I can't come home tonight?'

Faye smiled a small bitter smile at that, and finally allowed her gaze to drift to the full-breasted girl sitting across from him.

'That's up to you. Tomorrow seems plenty of time to me.' She looked back at him then and he blushed beneath his white mane, and as she looked at him, she saw how much he had aged in the past six months. He was going to be fifty years old soon, but he looked older than that. He had been carousing with this girl, and drinking heavily for the last five months, and before that he had had two severe shocks. It had all taken a toll, but she didn't feel sorry for him. She had aged too, and he had done nothing for her. He had deserted her, and sought solace with this girl. She was almost sorry she hadn't done something like it herself, but she had been too worried about Lionel and Anne. She would have enjoyed an affair just then. But she'd have plenty of time for one now, and at forty-six she wasn't completely over the hill. She looked at him now with utter contempt. 'I'll have Anne call you when we get back, if she wants to talk to you.' He looked horrified at the tone of her voice, the look in her eyes, and he glanced nervously at the buxom blonde, as Faye walked out of his office and closed the door. Outside, his secretary was shredding a Kleenex waiting for him to come out and murder her, but Faye looked perfectly calm as she walked out and nodded to her and hurried down the hall. She had to be at the airport in an hour, and she was just throwing a toothbrush she kept in her desk into her handbag when Ward stormed in.

'Just what do you mean by all that shit?' His face was red, and she couldn't know that he had just told Carol to go home. She had left in tears, accusing him of dumping her, which he was considering seriously. He was still married to Faye, as far as he was concerned, although she seemed to have forgotten it. And the affair had been begun for 'fun' supposedly and had got out of hand in the last few weeks.

Faye looked up at him uninterestedly. Part of it was an act, although part of it was for real. 'I don't have time to talk to you. My flight is at three o'clock.'

'Fine. Then we can talk on the plane. I'll come up with you.'

'I don't need your help.' Her eyes were cold and his were sad.

'You never did. But she's my child too.' Faye was momentarily silenced by that.

She looked up at him finally, unable to resist the urge to hurt him again, he had already hurt her so much recently. 'Are you bringing your friend?'

He looked down at his wife. 'We have to talk about that one of these days.' She knew it too, and she nodded at him, but they didn't mean it quite the same way.

'I wanted to get things settled with Anne and Lionel, before I tackled you on that. But I guess in a few weeks, everything will be relatively normal again, as much as it ever will be. I'll have time to talk to a lawyer then.'

'Have you already made up your mind?' He looked depressed, but he wasn't surprised. He hadn't done anything to prevent her from deciding that, and it was probably too late now. He felt defeated by life. His marriage was over, his son was a queer, his daughter had run away from them, and God only knew what had happened to her since she had. It was devastating to contemplate it all, but Faye seemed unswayed by all of it. She was remarkable. She never drowned. She just kept swimming until she reached the shore again, and she looked as though she just had. He was happy for her. 'I'm sorry it's come to this.'

She spoke quietly as she stood up. She was ready to leave. 'So am I. And I would assume that you're the one who's made up his mind. You don't even call to make excuses any more. You just don't come home at all. I'm surprised you haven't just moved your clothes out yet. I keep coming home at night, expecting to find your things gone.'

'Nothing has reached that point, Faye.'

'I don't see how you can say that. You've walked out, you just haven't bothered to explain it yet.' It seemed wrong to be fighting when Anne had just been found. They should have been shouting with relief, except that there was so much bitterness between them now. And they had avoided each other for so long.

'I haven't known what to say to you, Faye.'

'Apparently. You just walked right out of our lives.'

He knew it was true, and it was the second time in their life he had done that, but he didn't have the strength she had. Carol had come along, and it had made him feel like a man again. It softened the blow of his son turning out to be gay ... it was no longer a reflection on him ... he was okay ... but in the process he had walked right over Faye. He saw that now. But how could he explain it to her? There was no way that he could. She walked past him to the office door.

'I'll call you as soon as we're back.'

Ward looked at her sheepishly. 'I made a reservation on the three o'clock flight too. I figured that was the one you'd be on.'

'There's no point in both of us going up.' She really didn't want him along. She had enough on her mind, especially with Lionel saying Anne might be on drugs, and the pregnancy they'd have to get rid of as soon as possible. All she needed was Ward making

242

excuses for what a sonofabitch he'd been. She didn't want to hear it now. It just wasn't the time. She looked at him in exasperation and he begged with his eyes.

'I haven't seen her in five months, Faye.'

'Couldn't you wait another day?' He didn't move from where he stood, and she looked at him and sighed. He was just making this more difficult. She looked suddenly resigned. 'Fine. I have a studio car downstairs.' She turned and walked out the door, and he followed her. He said not a word to her on the way to the airport; it was clear that she had no desire to talk to him. Their seat assignments were not together on the flight, and when the man at the desk attempted to do them a favour and shift some other people around, she discouraged him. There was no doubt in Ward's mind as they boarded the plane separately, that his marriage to Faye was over. And the bitch of it was that the other girl didn't mean a damn to him. She had just been a way of confirming his own masculinity to him and soothing the pain, but it was too late to try and explain that to Faye. She agreed to share a cab to Lionel's hotel with him, although she looked him straight in the eye and laid down the law to him.

'I just want to make things clear to you, Ward. Those two boys have just devoted five months of their lives to finding her. They gave up a term in school, and they've gone looking for her every day. If it were up to the police, we still wouldn't know where she was. So if you say one ugly word to either of them, I am never ever going to see you again, and I will sue you for every dime you've got, just to get even with you. If you want a friendly divorce, my friend, be decent to your son and John Wells. Is that clear?' Her eyes were rock hard, and his wore the same look of sorrow she had seen in them all day. He looked like a beaten man these days, but it was his own damn fault as far as she was concerned.

'And if I don't want a friendly divorce?'

'Then don't even try and ride into the city with me, Ward.' She raised an arm to hail a cab for herself and he pulled it down harder than he had meant to, but he was desperate now.

'That isn't what I meant. Why are you so sure I want a divorce? I haven't agreed to that. I haven't said anything at all about that.'

She laughed bitterly at him outside the airlines terminal. 'Don't be ridiculous. I've hardly seen you for the last four months, you

243

never even come home at night, and you expect me to stay married to you? You must take me for an even bigger fool than I am.' Besides which he had caused damage which she suspected could never be repaired.

'You're not the fool, Faye, I am.'

'I completely agree with you. But this is neither the time nor the place to discuss it.' She looked at him with immeasurable irritation. 'I really don't know why in hell you came along.'

'To see Anne . . . and talk to you . . . it's been so long, Faye . . .'

'That's not my fault.'

'I know that. It's mine.' He seemed perfectly willing to take the blame. As though he had come to his senses at last. But it was too late. For both of them.

She looked at him sceptically now. 'What happened, did your little soap-opera nurse call it quits this morning when I walked in on you in your office?'

'No. As a matter of fact, I called it quits with her.' More or less. She had left in a rage because he said he was going to San Francisco with Faye, and he had told her he'd talk to her about it when he got back. But he had every intention of telling her it was over between them, whether Faye wanted to stay married to him or not. She was twenty-two years old, and he was beginning to feel ridiculous with her. It was all over. It had been foolish and insane, but it was what he had needed at the time. What he needed now was Faye. He knew now that he always had, yet she had been so locked in her own pain that he couldn't reach her any more. They had had nothing to give each other for a short time, yet all he wanted now was another chance – if she'd listen to him, but she was showing no sign of it now. She had hailed a cab, yanked open the door, and was staring at him.

'Are you coming, Ward?'

'Did you hear what I said? I told you, it's over with that girl.'

'I don't give a damn.'

'Fine. Just so you know where we stand.'

'And just so you know where we stand, Ward; we stand finished. Over. Finito. Through. Is that completely clear?' She gave the driver the address and sat back against the seat.

'I don't happen to agree with you.'

She was so furious she wanted to punch him, but she had to

244

restrain herself. She attempted to lower her voice so the driver wouldn't hear, and went on arguing with him. 'You've got one hell of a fucking nerve. For half a year, you abandon us, shit all over me, and make a fool of yourself with a girl almost thirty years younger than you are, and now magnanimously you decide to come back. Well, go fuck yourself, Ward Thayer. I want a divorce.' She saw the driver glance in the windscreen mirror, but Ward took no notice of him.

'I want to be married to you.'

'You're a sonofabitch.'

'I know I am. But we've been married for twenty-one years and I don't want to quit now.'

'Why not? You had no trouble quitting five months ago.' But they both knew why. The shock of Lionel had been too great for him. She had always known it would be, and she felt a stirring of compassion for him now.

'You know what that was all about.'

'That's no excuse for walking out on me.'

'I had no other way to prove my masculinity again.'

'That's a miserable excuse.'

'But it happens to be true.' He stared out the window and then back at her again. 'You'll never know what that did to me.'

'And now? Are you going to punish him again?'

'I'm grateful that he found Anne.' But his voice told its own tale.

'But you'll never forgive him, will you?'

'I can never forget what he is.'

'He's your son, Ward. And mine.'

'It's different for you.'

'Maybe. But I love him anyway. He's an extraordinary young man.'

Ward sighed. 'I know that ... I don't know what I feel any more. I've been hurting and confused for so long, it's not easy to sort out now ... and there's Anne ...' Faye frowned, thinking of what Lionel had said. She wondered if she should warn Ward, if that would be too much of a shock for him too.

Her voice was gentle for the first time in months when she spoke to him again. 'Lionel thinks she's on drugs.' He immediately looked up at her with a worried frown.

'What kind?'

'He's not sure yet. Marijuana, LSD . . .'

'It could be worse, I guess.'

'It is.' Faye went on. 'She's pregnant too.' Ward closed his eyes and then opened them again and looked at her.

'What's happened to us all in the last six months? Our whole damn life has fallen apart.'

She smiled gently at him. What he said was true. But in time, they would put it together again, they'd crawl out of it. They had before. He looked at her, and took her hand.

'We've both been through hell.' She didn't disagree with him, and she didn't pull her hand away. They needed each other now, if only for the next few hours, and she was suddenly glad he had come along. Even if they never saw each other again after this.

The cab hurtled into town, as they both sat, lost in their own thoughts, thinking of their little girl.

CHAPTER 24

They arrived at the San Marco Hotel shortly after five o'clock. It was a small unassuming hotel off Divisadero Street, and had been John and Lionel's home for more than four months. Faye looked up at it for an instant before hurrying inside with Ward on her heels. She knew that their room was on the third floor, from her last trip up, and she headed quickly up the stairs before the desk clerk could say anything to her. She didn't want to talk to anyone now. She just wanted to see Anne. She even forgot that Ward was with her, as she rapped softly on the door. A moment later Lionel appeared. He looked at her through the narrow opening, seemed to hesitate, and slowly opened the door. And from where she stood, Faye could see the still form lying there, her back to her. She was wearing Lionel's bathrobe, her hair had grown long and her feet were bare, and for an instant Faye thought she was asleep. Then she turned slowly to see who it was, her face tear-stained, her eyes dark-rimmed and huge in the suddenly narrow face. Faye was instantly taken aback, but she didn't want to let on. Anne had completely changed in the five months she'd been gone. She was thinner, looked more grown-up, and there was something so different about her face that Faye wasn't even sure she would have recognised her. She was almost sure she would not have from a photograph and was grateful that John had.

'Hello, sweetheart.' Faye advanced slowly towards the bed, almost afraid she'd frighten her away, like a wounded bird. Anne gave a soft moan and huddled further into a ball as she turned away again. She was coming down from the hallucinogens she had taken on and off for so long, and Lionel and John had been feeding her orange juice and candy bars to keep up her strength. And a while before they had forced her to eat a hamburger they had brought in.

She had thrown up after eating it, but she looked better now; at least to John and Li. They had seen what she looked like when the police first picked her up several hours before, and Lionel had cringed at the thought of his mother seeing her then. He looked from her to his parents now, and he was stricken by the look in his mother's eyes. He didn't dare look directly at Ward. It was the first time he had seen him since that terrible day when he had walked in on him with John. But at least he had come, if not for them, then for Anne.

'She's not feeling too hot, Mum.' He spoke to her in a soft voice and Anne didn't turn around as John handed her another candy bar which she took in a trembling hand. She felt hungry and sick all at once, and she didn't want to be here. She wanted to go back to them ... to the Haight ... to Moon ... to the ritual ... she belonged with them ... Tears choked her throat as she tried to swallow a bite of the candy bar, and she lay back and closed her eyes.

'Is she sick?' They spoke of her as though she weren't there, and Lionel hated to explain it all to them.

'She's just coming down from some of the stuff she's been on. She'll be all right in a few days.'

'Can we take her home tonight?' Faye was anxious to get her home, to have her seen by the doctor who had taken care of her for years, and to get her to Dr Smythe before it was too late for him to take care of the other problem. She hadn't seen Anne from the front yet and didn't know how far along she was, but she assumed that it wasn't too late. There was no reason to think it was. But Lionel was shaking his head in answer to what she had said, and Faye frowned.

'I don't think she's up to travelling yet, Mum. Give her a day or two to adjust.'

'To what?' Faye looked shocked. 'To us?'

Ward stepped forward for the first time, and avoided his son's eyes while speaking to him. 'Has she seen a doctor yet?' Lionel shook his head. 'I think she should.' He walked slowly around the bed, and looked down at his youngest child. She was still filthy, caked with dirt, her face stained with tears, and the eyes were huge in her face. He gently sat down and stroked her hair, feeling tears sting his own eyes. What had brought this child to that? How could she have run away from them? 'It's so good to see you again, Anne.' She didn't shrink from his hand, but she watched him like a frightened animal. He let his eyes rove slowly down her limbs, and they stopped midway and moved on. He tried not to register the shock he felt. It was much too late to do something about the pregnancy. He turned towards Faye with a look of despair and then stood up, and glanced at Lionel again. 'Do you know a doctor in town?'

'The police gave us a name. He thought they should examine her anyway. And they want to talk to you and Mum.' Ward nodded; at least he was able to speak to the boy, but he couldn't bring himself to look at John. The room's only bed, a double that looked barely that wide, on which Anne lay now, spoke for itself and he tried not to think of it. One drama was enough, and he wanted to speak to the police now. He took out his pen and jotted the names down of the men who had cooperated in finding her, and particularly the two who had brought her in. Lionel said they would have all the details, and Ward shuddered at the prospect of hearing them. But he knew they would have to know eventually.

Faye went over and sat on the bed next to Anne, as Ward had, but this time the girl flinched. It was like having a desperately sick child and visiting her in the hospital. Faye's eyes were riveted to her face and Anne started to cry.

'Go away ... I don't want to be here ...'

'I know, sweetheart ... but we'll all be going home soon ... to your own house ... and your own bed ...'

'I want to go back to Moon and my friends.' She sobbed. She was a fourteen-year-old girl and she sounded like she was five. Faye didn't ask who Moon was. She assumed that he was the father of the child. As the thought came to mind, she glanced down at Anne's belly, assuming it would still be flat, and she gasped in shock as she saw it sticking out. Faye knew from experience she was at least four or five months gone. She decided to ask right away, much to Ward's chagrin. He didn't want to push her yet. Lionel was right. She needed time to adjust to all of them again. She had gone far, far away, and she had been away from them for a long time.

'How pregnant are you, Anne?' She wanted her voice to sound gentle when she asked, but she instantly knew it did not. It sounded nervous and harsh and sharp and Lionel looked at them in despair.

'I don't know how pregnant I am,' Anne answered her with closed eyes. She refused to look at her any more. She hated her. She always had. And she hated her even more now. It was her fault that they had taken her away, her fault they wouldn't let her go back. She had always ruined everything for all of them, pushing them all around, doing everything her way. But she wouldn't this time. They could take her anywhere, and she would escape again. She knew how easy it was now.

'Haven't you seen a doctor yet?' Faye sounded shocked. Anne shook her head again, her eyes closed. And then slowly she opened them.

'My friends took care of me.'

'How long has it been since you had a period?' It was just like talking to the police, only worse, Anne thought. At least they didn't ask her questions like that. She knew she didn't have to answer her. But she always did. Faye just had that kind of way about her. As though she expected everyone to do what she said, and Anne did now.

'Not since I left home,' Faye knew only too well that was five months before, and she cringed at the thought. It must have happened almost as soon as she left.

'Do you know who the father is?' It was an outrageous thing to ask so soon, and Lionel glanced at Ward, wishing he would stop Mum from asking her those things. Anne wasn't ready to be pushed, and he was afraid she would run away again before they got her home. And maybe this time they wouldn't find her. Lionel was afraid of that, but Anne only smiled at the memories.

'Yes.'

'Is it Moon?'

Anne shrugged. But Faye was in no way prepared for what came next.

'Yes. It's all of them.'

Faye's breath caught. That couldn't be right. There had to be some mistake. 'All of them?' She stared uncomprehendingly at the child who was a child no more. She was a woman now, a twisted broken one, but nonetheless she was no longer a little girl, and she was expecting a baby of her own. Suddenly Faye understood and a look of horror came into her eyes.

'Do you mean to tell me that the entire commune fathered this child?'

'Yes.' Anne looked sweetly at her, and sat up for the first time. As she did the room reeled, and she looked to Lionel for help. He came to her and supported her as John handed her a glass of orange juice. They had both suspected something like that from what the police had told them about the sect, but Faye and Ward were not prepared, and now that Anne was sitting up, she looked even more pregnant than she had lying down.

Ward took over now, thinking of what had happened to his innocent child. He looked firmly at Lionel, ignoring Anne. 'I'm going to call those inspectors now.' He had every intention of seeing all those sonsofbitches in jail, and Faye was crying softly as they left the room. She clung to Ward when they got downstairs, and she didn't care who was looking at them now.

'My God, Ward, she'll never be the same again.' He was as afraid as she, but he refused to admit that to her. He was going to help her now, just as Faye had helped him so long ago, given him a career he could never have found himself, taught him everything he knew until he could fly on his own. He would do everything he could, and if she still wanted a divorce afterwards, he would accept it gracefully. She had a right to that after what he'd done. He still felt shaky now, looking at Lionel and John, but he couldn't allow himself to think of that now. They both had to stop blaming themselves, he for Lionel's homosexuality, and Faye for what had happened to Anne. He knew that they were both consumed with guilt, but to what end? It did neither child any good. 'She'll be all right, Faye.' He wished he believed his own words, but above all, he wanted to convince her.

'She's got to get rid of that child, and with the drugs she's been on, God only knows what it will be. It'll be a vegetable.'

'Probably. Do you think it's too late for an abortion?' He looked at his wife hopefully and she laughed bitterly through her tears.

'Did you see her, Ward? She's five months pregnant, at least.' It suddenly dawned on her that she might have even been pregnant when she left home. She didn't think she was, although who knew any more with Anne.

They went to the police station at Bryant Street immediately, and then went upstairs to speak to the juvenile authorities. There were apparently hundreds of cases like this one now. Children were migrating from all over the States, coming to the Haight-Ashbury. Some of them did a lot worse than losing their virginity – some of them lost their lives. There were stories of eleven-year-olds overdosing on heroin or jumping out of windows on LSD. There were illegitimate children being born to thirteen- and fourteen- and fifteen-year-olds, delivered in hallways as their friends sang. One girl had bled to death only six weeks before, and an ambulance had never been called. As they listened, Faye was deeply grateful they had found her at all. She steeled herself to hear the tale they told about the sect Anne had been living with. She wanted to kill them all when she'd heard all of it, and Ward was insistent that he wanted the entire sect put in jail, but the police were discouraging. It would be difficult to bring charges against all of them, and it was impossible to accuse an entire tribe of statutory rape on one girl. Above all, was this what they wanted for Anne? Wasn't it just easier to take her home, get her good psychiatric help, and let her forget the whole thing, instead of subjecting her to a lengthy trial, which wouldn't even come up for a year or two, if not longer than that, and which they probably wouldn't win? The kids would have disappeared by then, their own families, many of them moneyed and influential, would bail their children out. It just didn't make sense. In a year or two, it would all seem like a distant dream, the police said. A nightmare she would soon forget.

'What about her pregnancy? What about this Moon?' Faye wanted to know. And they told her that nothing concrete could be proved against him. He held none of them against their will, and none of the members of the sect would ever testify against him. They doubted that Anne ever would herself, and later they discovered the police were right. She had an unreasoning love for the man, and she refused to talk about him to anyone, even Lionel. It was hopeless, Faye and Ward finally agreed. And as wrong as it seemed, the police were right perhaps. It was best to take her home, get help for her, deliver her safely of the monstrous child, and let her forget it all, if only she'd be willing to. Lionel thought she would, in time, and John said nothing at all. He was still terrified of Mr Thayer, and frightened he would lose control and hit him again, although Lionel swore he wouldn't let that happen again. Ward showed no sign of losing control, except when he spoke of Moon or one of them. His rage was directed at them now, much to John's relief.

They took turns staying with Anne that night, and the next morning the three Thayers discussed the trip home, while John sat with her. Faye was anxious to get her back, and maybe even check her into a hospital, though Lionel thought they should wait a few days. She was fairly clear now, but she was extremely paranoid. He thought she should have a few more days to come down. Ward agreed with Faye, but he couldn't imagine getting her on a commercial airline in the dishevelled, disorientated condition she was in. Eventually, a compromise was reached. Ward called MGM and chartered the studio plane for all of them. It was to pick them up in San Francisco at six o'clock that night and fly them back to Los Angeles. He wanted to see the police once more, and after that he talked to his lawyer, who basically agreed with them. No charges were brought, and at four-thirty that afternoon, they bundled Anne up in a bathrobe Faye had bought for her on Union Street, and they took a cab out to the airport. She sobbed all the way. The four of them felt like kidnappers as the young cab driver stared at them all angrily. Hardly a word was said, and she didn't have the strength to walk, so Ward carried her onto the plane. For the first time in two days, he had a stiff drink once they boarded the plane, and the two boys and Faye all had a glass of wine. It was a difficult trip for everyone and Lionel and John were feeling the strain of being with Ward. He never really spoke to them. Whenever possible he addressed Faye and let her pass the message on, as though he was afraid to contaminate himself by speaking directly to either of them. When the MGM limo dropped the boys off at their place on the way to the Thayer house, John heaved an enormous sigh of relief.

'I just don't know what to say to him.' He took a big gulp of air and looked apologetically at Lionel, who understood perfectly.

'Don't feel badly. Neither do I. But he's just as uncomfortable with us.' It had been an uneasy truce, and Lionel felt sure that he hadn't changed his mind, and wouldn't rescind the family ban on them. Lionel felt no more welcome in the family home than he would have three or four months before, and he was right.

'He acts like being gay is a contagious disease and he's afraid to catch it from us.'

Lionel grinned. It was good to be home, or so he thought. Faye had continued paying for their rooms at the house at UCLA for all these months, and they hadn't seen their roommates since they had dropped out in January. But they couldn't go to Lionel's parents' house or the Wells'. They would have been upset by the tales about Anne. So they walked up the steps now, home for the first time in months, anxious to unpack and settle in.

They were talking about starting the summer sessions in a few weeks. They could both go back to real life now, whatever that was, but they had forgotten what it was like to pretend and hide, and suddenly as they walked into a room full of sophomore and junior boys, drinking beer, they both remembered the agony they had forgotten, after five months of living in the hotel while they looked for Anne. They had to go back into hiding now, and it depressed them both as they put their things away. Lionel wandered into John's room, and they exchanged a look. Suddenly, they wondered if everyone knew about them. They felt as though it could be clearly seen, and Lionel wasn't even sure he cared any more. Yes, he was gay. Yes, he was in love with John. He adopted an almost belligerent air as he went to the kitchen and helped himself to a beer, but no one said anything. Those who knew were glad he had found Anne. One of the others had a runaway sister too, a twelve-year-old, and they hadn't found her yet. Her parents were afraid she was dead, and her brother was convinced she was in San Francisco too. They talked about it for a little while, and Lionel thought there was a funny look in the boy's eyes, as though he wanted to ask him something but didn't dare.

At the Thayer house, everyone was subdued. The twins had been shocked when they had seen Ward carry Anne in. They didn't realise she would look that sick, and when she stood up on shaky legs and they saw her belly sticking out, Vanessa had actually gasped, and Valerie couldn't believe her eyes.

'What's she going to do?' they questioned Faye later that night, who thought she had never felt so tired in her life. She didn't have the answer to that herself.

They took her to the doctor the next day, and were relieved to hear that he could find no evidence of abuse on her. Whatever she had done, she had done willingly, and there were no marks, no scars. He estimated that the baby was due on October 12, suggested that she recuperate for six weeks after that, assuming the baby came on time, and could comfortably be back in school after the Christmas holiday. She would have lost exactly one year from the time she left, and she could finish eighth grade after the baby came, and go on to high school the following year. They made it sound so easy as Anne stared at them and, with the doctor standing by, Faye brought up what she had discussed with him. It was too late for an abortion of course, which would have been the easiest solution for her, assuming she would have agreed, though Faye would have seen to that. And it was impossible to tell just how many drugs she had taken since she'd conceived, or what effect they'd had. But even if the baby had minor disabilities as a result, there were plenty of childless couples who would be happy to adopt, even with some small defect. The Haight-Ashbury culture had been a real boon for them. There were dozens of babies being put up for adoption now, babies born of girls who would never have got pregnant a few years before. These were mostly girls from middle-class homes, sleeping with boys of the same ilk, in communes that had sprung up. And once the babies came, they weren't interested in them. Some were, of course, but most were not. They wanted to be free, to enjoy their days of sunshine and peace and love, without the burden of responsibility. The doctor would be happy to help, he explained. Why, just in Los Angeles, he knew four couples anxious for such a child. All of them would give the baby a good home, and it would be a blessing for Anne. She would go back to the life of a fourteen-year-old girl, and forget it ever happened. Faye and the doctor smiled and Anne looked at them, horrified, struggling not to scream.

'You want to give my baby away?' She started to cry, and Faye tried to put an arm around her, but she fought her off. 'I'll never do that! Never! Do you hear me!'

But there was no doubt in Faye's mind. They would force her to give the child up. She didn't need to drag some little mongoloid around for the rest of her life, to remind her of a nightmare they all wanted to forget. No, absolutely not. She and the doctor exchanged a speaking look. They had four and a half months to convince her of what was best for her.

'You'll feel differently about it later on, Anne. You'll be happy you gave it up. And it may not be normal anyway.' Faye tried to keep her voice matter-of-fact, but she was panicking inside. What if she ran away again? If she insisted on keeping the child? The nightmare refused to end, and all the way home, Anne huddled on the far side of the car, looking out the window with tears running down her cheeks. When Faye stopped the car at home she tried to reach for her hand, but Anne pulled it away and refused to look at her. 'Sweetheart, you can't keep that child. It would ruin your life.' Faye was sure of it, and Ward agreed with her she knew.

'Yours or Dad's?' She glared at her mother now. 'You're just embarrassed I got knocked up, that's all. And you want to destroy the evidence. Well, what are you going to do with me for the next four months? Hide me in the garage? You can do anything you want, but you can't take my baby from me.' She ran out of the car and Faye lost control, screaming at her as she went. The last few days had been too much for her. The last few months in fact.

'Yes we can. We can do anything we want! You're not even fifteen years old!' She hated herself for saying the words, and by that afternoon, Anne was gone again. But she only went to Lionel's this time, and sat sobbing out her tale to him and John.

'I won't let them take it away from me . . . I won't . . . I won't!' She looked like such a baby herself, it was hard to imagine her with a child. And even though she had grown up in the Haight, she was still so young. Lionel didn't know how to tell her, but he agreed with their mother. As did John. They had talked about it the night before, as they lay in bed, whispering so the other boys wouldn't hear. It had been so much better in the hotel, but now they had to face real life too, not unlike Anne.

'Baby,' Lionel looked at her compassionately, and gently took her hand in his. He looked just like their mother when he did, but Anne never wanted to see the resemblance between the two of them. If she had, she might have loved him less than she did. The fact that he did look so much like Faye was the one thing that brought him a little closer to Ward, though not much any more. 'Maybe they're right. It would be a terrible responsibility, you know, and it's not really fair to impose that on Mum and Dad.'

She hadn't even thought of that. 'Then I'll get a job and take care of it myself.'

'And who'll take care of it while you work? See what I mean? Baby, you're not even fifteen years old . . .'

She started to cry. 'You sound just like one of them . . .' And he never had before. She couldn't stand it from him too. She looked up at him with heartbroken eyes. 'Li, it's my baby . . . I can't give it up.'

'You'll have others one day.'

'So what?' She looked appalled. 'What if they'd given you away because one day they'd have me?'

He had to laugh at the example, and he looked at her so tenderly. 'I think you ought to give it some thought. You don't have to make your mind up right now.'

She agreed to that at least, but when she got home, she got into a huge fight with Val, who demanded that she stay inside the house whenever her friends came around.

'I'll be the laughing stock of school if everyone knows you're knocked up. And you'll be going there in a year yourself, you don't want everyone knowing that.'

Faye admonished her that night for being unnecessarily cruel, but it was already too late. Anne had gone to her room after dinner and packed her bags, and at ten o'clock she was standing in Lionel's living room again.

'I can't live with them.' She told him why, and he sighed. He knew how difficult it was for her, but there wasn't much he could do for her. He gave her his bed that night, and told her they'd figure it out the next day. He called Faye to tell her where she was. She had already called Ward, and Lionel got the impression that he was going to spend the night at home, but he didn't ask. He told his roommates that he was going to sleep on the floor, but of course he slept with John, and reminded Anne to be careful of what she said, because his roommates didn't know that they were gay. The next day, when the three of them went out for a walk, he was embarrassed at the questions she asked, but he tried to be honest with her. 'Do you and John really sleep together every night?'

He started to say something and then changed his mind. 'Yes. We do.'

'Like husband and wife?'

Lionel saw John blush out of the corner of his eye. 'Sort of.'

'That's weird.' She didn't say it meanly and Lionel laughed.

'I guess it is. But that's the way things are.'

'I don't know why people get so upset about that, I mean like Dad. If you love each other, what difference does it make what you are, I mean a man and a woman, or two girls or two men?' He wondered just exactly what she had seen in the commune, and remembered what the police had said. She had probably had numerous homosexual experiences now too, but he didn't ask her that, and hers would have been drug-induced, and as part of a large group probably, given the sect's practices. Lionel didn't want to ask anyway. She might not even have remembered what she'd done. It was very different from what he and John shared, which was a genuine love affair. But he looked at her now. It was odd how she floated between being a woman and a child.

'Not everyone sees it that way, Anne. It's frightening to some people.'

'Why?'

'Because it's different from the norm.'

She sighed. 'Like me being pregnant at fourteen.'

'Maybe.' That was a tough one. And it brought to mind what they were going to do about her. He and John had talked about it for half the night, and they had an idea. Lionel had talked to Faye about it. In some ways it would be easier for Faye and Ward too.

Lionel had been right of course. He had always been an intuitive child, and he wasn't wrong this time. Ward had spent the night. His father answered Faye's phone, but he said not a word to Lionel, and they were back on their old terms of his no longer existing in the Thayers' life. Now that he had found Anne, they could dispense with him again, or at least Ward could. He handed the phone to Faye, and she proposed the idea to Ward when she hung up.

'Lionel wants to know what we think of their taking an apartment near school, and letting Anne stay with them until the baby comes. And after that, she can move out, come back here, and they'll find a roommate to rent her room. What do you think?' She looked at him carefully over coffee. It was nice to have him back in a way, even if it was for one night, or two. He gave her some support in these difficult times. He frowned now, thinking of Lionel's idea.

'Can you imagine what she'd be exposed to with those two?'

The thought made him sick and Faye bridled instantly.

'Can you imagine what she did herself in that disgusting commune, Ward? Let's be honest about this.'

'All right, all right. We don't have to go into that.' He didn't want to think about things like that with his little girl. Nor did he want her with John and Lionel, in a fag nest somewhere. But it was obvious that she was not going to come home to them, and it might take some of the strain off him and Faye for a while. The only ones home now were the twins, and they were never there. They were always out with their friends, especially Val. He looked at Faye. 'Let me think about it.'

He still wasn't sure he liked the idea, but the more he thought it over, the more he had to admit that it wasn't such a bad idea. The boys were relieved when Faye told them that. They had come to realise how impossible it was living with the other boys in their old house, and neither of them wanted to pretend any more. At twenty, Lionel was ready to admit he was gay, and John was too.

Faye helped them find a small but attractive apartment in West-wood, not far from where they'd been living with the rest of their friends, and offered to decorate it for them, but John worked his magic in a matter of days, with whatever he had at hand, and Faye couldn't believe how pretty it was. He had bought yards of pale grey flannel and pink silk, and transformed the place, putting fabric on the walls, upholstering two couches they bought for fifty dollars at a garage sale, finding prints in back streets, reviving plants that had looked beyond hope. It looked like a sophisticated apartment done by a professional decorator, and John was thrilled with her praise. His mother was even more proud of him, and bought them a beautiful mirror for over the fireplace. She felt sorry for poor little Anne, and was grateful it wasn't one of her girls.

Anne had never been happier in her life than she was with them. She kept the apartment clean for them. It was even better than the commune she said one night, as John taught her to make roast duck. He was a fabulous cook, and made dinner for them every night. Lionel had gone back to school, for the summer session in cinematography, to make up for the time he had missed, and he'd be caught up by autumn. But John had taken a big step. He knew he didn't want to go to UCLA. He dropped out permanently and got a job with a well-known decorator in Beverly Hills. The guy had the hots for him and it was a pain in the neck rebuffing his advances every day, but the decorating experience he got was fabulous. He got none of the credit and did all the work, but he loved the homes he got to work on, and he told them both about his job every night. He had had it since July, and by late August the guy had finally got the message and was leaving him alone. He had told him about Lionel and that it was serious, and the older man had laughed, knowing it was only a matter of time. 'Kids,' he had laughed. But he was pleased with John's work, so he let him be.

Faye dropped in on them from time to time. Ward had moved back in with her, and they were trying to put the pieces together again. She spoke to Lionel about it when they were alone, but not in front of Anne, and she inquired if he had made any progress about getting her to promise to give up the baby when it came. It was less than two months away now, and the poor thing looked huge. She was uncomfortable in the heat, and the apartment wasn't air conditioned, though John had bought them all fans. He was insisting on paying for half of the apartment now, since he had a job and Lionel was in school, and Faye was touched by how hard he worked and what good care he took of all of them. She looked at her son tenderly one day.

'You're happy, aren't you, Li?' It was important to her to know that. He meant so much to her. And she was fond of John; she always had been, but she was more so now, after him helping to find Anne.

'Yes, I am, Mum.' He had grown up beautifully, even if he wasn't what she and Ward had expected him to be. Maybe that didn't really matter after all. She asked herself a lot of questions about that at times, but it was still impossible to discuss it with Ward.

'I'm glad. Now what about Anne? Will she give the baby up?' The doctor had a couple who were definitely interested. She was thirty-six and he was forty-two; they were both sterile, and the agencies said they were too old to adopt. She was Jewish and he was Catholic, and with all of that there was absolutely no hope, except this way. They didn't even mind the risk of the baby's possible defects from drugs. They were desperate and insisted they would love him or her anyway. And in September, Faye insisted that Anne at least meet them, to give them a chance. They were very nervous and very sweet, and they almost begged the child to give her baby to them. They promised her that she could come to visit him sometimes, although the doctor and their lawyer discouraged that. It had led to some terrible incidents once or twice, and a kidnapping once, after the papers had been signed. It was better to make a clean break, they said, but they would have agreed to anything. The woman had shining black hair, and beautiful brown eyes, a good figure, a bright mind. She was a lawyer, originally from New York, and her husband was an ophthalmologist with features similar to Anne's. The baby could even have looked like them, if it looked like Anne at all, and not the rest of the commune, Faye thought to herself. They were lovely people and Anne felt sorry for them.

'How come they can't have kids?' Anne asked as they drove away and her mother took her back to Lionel's.

'I didn't ask. I just know they can't.' Faye was praying she would be reasonable. She wanted Ward to talk to her too, but he was away. He had begged Faye to come with him, he thought they needed a 'honeymoon' as he put it, now that they were back together again. She had been touched, but she just didn't feel comfortable leaving Anne until after the baby was born. If something happened to her, if she delivered early, which the doctors said teenagers sometimes did . . . and he had warned her that girls in their teens had the hardest time, even harder than women her age, which surprised her. She was forty-six years old now, and babies were the farthest thing from her mind. But she was frightened that Anne would have a hard time, and she refused to go away with Ward. They had some time between films, but she was trying to spend as much of it as she could with Anne. Instead, Ward went to Europe with Greg. Faye thought it would do them both good to get away.

Anne hadn't agreed to anything by the time the baby was due. She was so enormous she looked as though she was having twins, and Lionel felt desperately sorry for her. She seemed to be having pains all the time, and he suspected that she was scared. He didn't blame her at all; he would have been terrified. He just hoped he was home from school when the baby started to come. If not, John had promised to take a cab home from work and get her to the

261

hospital. It was a lot easier to reach him than Lionel. She had had some crazy idea about having it at home, like they did at the commune, but they had squashed that, and Faye had made them swear that they would call her right away. Lionel had promised, but Anne had begged him not to.

'She'll steal my baby, Li.' The big blue eyes pleaded with him and his heart went out to her. She was frightened all the time now, of everything.

'She won't do anything of the sort. She just wants to be there with you. And no one is going to steal the baby. You have to make up your own mind.' But he was still trying to influence her. He thought his mother was right. At fourteen and a half, she didn't need the burden of a child. She was still a baby herself. And he was even more sure of it the night she began to have labour pains. She panicked and locked herself in her room, sobbing hysterically, and he and John had alternately threatened to break down the door. Eventually, while he talked cajolingly to her, John went out on the roof, slipped in through the window, unlocked the door, and let her brother in. She was sobbing hysterically on the bed, convulsed with pain, and there was water all over the floor. Her waters had broken an hour before, and the pains had grown severe. She threw her arms around Lionel's neck and sobbed, clutching him with each pain.

'Oh Li, I'm so scared . . . I'm so scared . . .' No one had told her it would hurt this much. On the way to the hospital in the cab, she moaned and dug her nails into his hand, and refused to go away with the nurse. She hung on to him and begged him to stay with her, but when the doctor came, he told her to be a good girl, and two nurses wheeled her away while she screamed.

Lionel was visibly shaken and John was pale as they spoke to the quiet older man. 'Can't you give her a sedative?'

'I'm afraid not. It may slow her labour down. She's young, she'll forget it all afterwards.' That seemed difficult to believe and he smiled sympathetically at them. 'It's hard on girls her age, they're not really prepared to go through childbirth, physically or mentally. But we'll get her through and she'll be just fine.' Lionel wasn't as sure. He could still hear her screaming from down the hall, and he wondered if he should be with her. 'Have you called your mother yet?' Li shook his head nervously. It was eleven o'clock at night, and he wasn't sure if they'd be asleep. But he knew she'd be furious if they didn't call, so he dialled his old home number with trembling hands. Ward answered and Lionel spoke at once.

'I'm at the hospital with Anne.'

Ward didn't waste time handing the phone to Faye. For once, he spoke to Lionel himself. 'We'll be right there.' And he was as good as his word. In ten minutes, they were at UCLA Medical Center, looking slightly rumpled, but wide awake. The doctor made an exception, and let Faye stay with Anne, at least as long as she was in the labour room. None of them were prepared for how long it would take. Even the doctor didn't know, although he was usually good at predicting that, but again with teenagers, nothing was sure; she could race through it or it could take three days. She was dilating well, but she would stop at each stage for long hours, begging for release, for drugs, for anything, clutching at her mother's hand, trying to sit up to leave and then collapsing with the pain, clawing at the walls, and begging the nurses to let her go. It was the worst thing Faye had ever seen, and she had never felt so helpless in her life. There was nothing she could do to help the child, and she only left her once to go outside and say something to Ward. She wanted him to call the lawyer first thing the next morning, in case Anne agreed to give the baby up after it was born. They would have her sign the papers immediately. They had to review them again in six months, to make them permanent, but by then the baby would be gone, and hopefully she'd have started a normal life again. Ward agreed to call him the next morning, and she suggested he go home since it could take hours. The three men agreed. Ward dropped Lionel and John off, without saying much to them, and the two boys went upstairs. They were surprised to realise that it was already 4 am and Lionel never got to sleep that night. He crept stealthily out of bed and called the hospital several times, but there was no news of Anne. She was still in the labour room, and the baby had not been born. And she was still there the following afternoon when John came home from work, and found Lionel still sitting by the phone. It was six o'clock and he was amazed.

'My God, hasn't she had the baby yet?' He couldn't imagine it taking so long. She had gone into labour around eight o'clock the night before, and had already been in terrible pain when they got her to the hospital. 'Is she all right?'

Lionel looked pale. He had called the hospital what seemed like a thousand times, had even gone there for a few hours, but his mother didn't even want to come out to talk to him. She didn't want to leave Anne. He noticed a couple waiting nervously in the waiting room with the Thayers' lawyer, and he correctly guessed who they were. They were even more anxious for the baby to come than the Thayers were. And the doctor was guessing only a few more hours now. They had seen the head all afternoon, and she was ready to push, but it was going to be a while. And if there was no progress by eight or nine o'clock that night, he was going to do a Caesarean.

'Thank God,' John said, and both of them found they couldn't eat. They were too worried about her. At seven, Lionel called a cab. He was going back to the hospital.

'I want to be there.'

John nodded. 'I'll come too.' They had spent five months looking for her, another five living with her now. John felt as though she were his little sister too, and the house didn't seem the same without her clothes and her books and her records spread around. He had threatened to put her on restriction once, if she didn't pick up her clothes, and she had laughed and teased him and said she'd tell the whole neighbourhood he was queer. He was desperately sorry for her now. It sounded like a grisly ordeal and when he saw Faye Thayer's face shortly after nine o'clock, he could only begin to imagine what the child was going through.

'They just can't get it out,' Faye reported to Ward, who was back at the hospital too. 'And he doesn't want to do a Caesarean on a child her age, unless he absolutely has to.' What Anne was going through was worse than anything Faye had ever seen. She was shrieking and begging, half delirious with the pain. There was absolutely nothing they could do for her, and the nightmare went on for another two hours, while Anne begged them to kill her . . . the baby . . . anything . . . and then finally, the little head emerged, and as the rest of him came, slowly, tearing his mother wickedly and causing her as much grief as possible right till the end, they all understood why it had been such agony for Anne. The child was huge, just over ten pounds, and Faye couldn't think of worse punishment for her narrow frame. It was as though each man who had entered her had contributed to this child, and he had emerged full grown, a composite of all of them. Faye stood watching him, with tears in her eyes, tears for the pain he had caused Anne, and for the life which would never touch theirs again.

Hours before, Anne had agreed to give him up. She would have agreed to anything then. And the doctor slipped a gas mask on her face now. She never saw the child, never knew how big he was, never felt them sewing her up, and Faye silently left the delivery room, feeling sorry for her own child, for the pain she had borne, for the experience she would probably never forget, the child she would never know, unlike her own, who had caused her joy and pain over the years, but none of whom she regretted having. And now her first grandchild was to be given away, and she would never see him again. He was put in a polyethylene basket and rolled away to the nursery, to be cleaned up, and given to someone else.

Half an hour later, as she and Ward left the hospital, she saw the woman with the dark hair holding him, with tears streaming down her face and a look of love in her eyes. They had waited fourteen years for him, and they accepted him as he was, not knowing who his father was, or what damage the drugs had done. They accepted him with unconditional love, and Faye held tightly to Ward's hand as they left, and took a deep gulp of the night air. The doctor had said that Anne would sleep for several hours. She would be heavily sedated now, thank God, and that night, as she lay in her bed, Faye cried in Ward's arms.

'It was so horrible . . . she screamed so terribly . . .' She sobbed uncontrollably now. It had been almost unbearable watching her, but it was all over now. For all of them. Except the couple with Anne's child. For them it had just begun.

CHAPTER 25

They kept Anne in the hospital for a week, in an attempt to let the wounds heal, both physically and mentally. The doctor told Faye that they would heal with time. They kept her on Valium, and Demerol for the pain. She had been torn badly by the baby's head because he was so large. But more than that, they all recognised that she would have emotional scars from this. A psychiatrist came to talk to her every day, but she would say nothing at all to him, she just lay in bed and stared at the ceiling or the wall, and every day after an hour he went away. She said nothing to Faye, or Ward, or the twins, or even Lionel when he and John came, carefully, at a different time from Faye and Ward. Lionel brought her an enormous stuffed bear, and he hoped it didn't remind her of the lost child. The baby had left the hospital three days after it was born. His new parents took him away in an elaborate blue and white outfit by Dior, and two blankets his new grandmother had made. They had sent an enormous arrangement of flowers to Anne, but she had them given to someone else. She wanted no reminder of them. She hated herself for what she had done, but in those first few hours after she woke, she felt so terrible that she never wanted to see him again. It was only now that he was gone that she wished she could have seen his face, just once . . . so she would remember him . . . her eyes filled with tears at the thought. Everyone said she had done the right thing, but she hated them all, and herself most of all. She told Lionel that now, as John fought back tears. If it had been his sister, he would have died for her, and he tried to cheer Anne up now. Even if the jokes were in bad taste, they were heartfelt. He felt terrible for her.

'We could always redo your room in black. I have some great black corduroy at the shop . . . we could drape black tulle over the

266

windows, a few little black spiders here and there.' He squinted artistically, and for the first time in a week she laughed. But when it was time to go home, it was Ward and Faye who came for her. They had talked to Lionel earlier that day, or at least Faye had, and explained that they were taking Anne home now. He and John were free to rent her room to a friend, or do whatever they liked with it. The purpose had been served, and now Anne had come home to resume her life with them.

Anne was even more depressed when she found that out, but she didn't have the strength to argue with her parents now. She sat in her room for the next few weeks, refusing to eat most of the time, telling the twins to get the hell out when they stopped in to say hello to her, which admittedly they seldom did, although Vanessa really did try more than once. She wanted to reach out to Anne, with records, and books, and a bunch of flowers once or twice. But Anne steadfastly refused to be wooed by the gifts. She kept her heart closed to all of them. And it was Thanksgiving before she joined them for dinner again. Lionel was conspicuously not there, nor was Greg, who was playing a big game at school, and Anne returned to her room as soon as possible. She had nothing to say to any of them, even Vanessa, who tried so hard, and Faye, whose grief still showed in her eyes. Anne hated them all. All she could think of was the baby she had given up. He was exactly five weeks old now. She wondered if for the rest of her life she would remember exactly how old he was all the time. She could almost sit down now, which was at least something, Lionel reminded her when he stopped by, when he knew for sure their father was out. Ward knew he was coming to see Anne, and he didn't say anything, just so he didn't have to see him himself, or John. He hadn't changed his mind about any of that, and at Christmas, Faye begged him to let her invite Lionel to share Christmas dinner with them, but Ward refused to bend.

'I've taken a position, and I intend to stick by it. I disapprove of his way of life, and I want the rest of the family to know that, Faye.' He was totally intractable, but she argued with him day and night about it. He hadn't always been a saint. He had betrayed her more than once. But Ward was outraged that she would dare to compare his heterosexual indiscretions with Lionel's homosexuality.

'I'm just trying to point out that you're human too.'

'He's queer, dammit!' He still wanted to cry when he thought of it.

'He's gay.'

'He's sick and I don't want him in my house. Is that clear once and for all?'

It was pointless. She couldn't budge him an inch. And sometimes, she was almost sorry he had come back. Their marriage was definitely not what it had once been, and the issue of Lionel didn't help anything. It was a constant source of friction and despair between them. Mercifully, they had started another film, and she was out most of the time. And she was grateful for Lionel stopping by. Someone had to talk to Anne. She had been through such an ordeal, and Lionel had always been able to talk to her. It seemed so wrong to her to close the door on him and she hated Ward for it. She looked at him angrily now. And yet, always beneath the anger, was the love she had always felt for him. Ward Thayer had been her world and her life for so long that, sinner or saint, she could never imagine a life without him.

On Christmas Day, Lionel was not there, and as soon as the family left the table, Anne left and went to their house. The Wells had made an excuse for not inviting Lionel although they would have welcomed their son, but somehow inviting his lover made too much of a reality of it, even for them. So John and Lionel had chosen to celebrate Christmas alone. They were joined after dinner not only by Anne, but also a few of John's friends from work and a gay friend of Li's from school.

Anne found herself surrounded by a dozen gay young men, and she didn't feel the least bit uncomfortable. She was far more comfortable with them than the rest of her family. She was looking more herself again now. She had lost all the weight she had gained, and her eyes were a little brighter. She looked older than her years, and far more mature. She would turn fifteen in a few weeks, and go back to her old school to finish eighth grade. She was dreading it. She was going to be a year and a half older than everyone, but Lionel said she just had to grit her teeth and go, and in a way she was doing it for him.

They let her have half a glass of champagne, and she stayed with them until after nine o'clock. She had saved up and bought Li a cashmere scarf, and a beautiful silver pen from Tiffany's for John.

They were the best friends she had, and the only family she cared about. John drove her home that night in his secondhand VW bug, while Lionel stayed with their friends. She knew the party would go on for several hours, but Lionel had wanted her to go home. He didn't think she belonged at evenings like that. Sometimes they talked pretty openly, and some of their friends weren't as discreet as John and Li were. She had hugged her brother when she left, and she kissed John's cheek before she got out of the car.

'Merry Christmas, love.' He smiled at her.

'Same to you.' She gave him a quick hug and hopped out, and ran upstairs to her room to try on their gifts to her. They had given her a beautiful soft pink angora sweater with a matching scarf from Li, and little pearl earrings from John. She could hardly wait to put them on and when she did, she preened in front of the mirror with a happy smile. She was so happy with the gifts that she hadn't even heard her sister come in. It was Val, watching her admire herself. She was annoyed and in a rotten mood. Greg had promised to take her out with his friends, and at the last minute, he had backed out. Vanessa had a date with a serious beau she had, and Val was left at home to cool her heels. Even Ward and Faye had gone to friends' for a drink and Valerie and Anne were left alone. Val stared at her.

'Where'd you get the sweater and scarf?' She would have liked to try them on, but she knew Anne would never offer them. Valerie helped herself to most of Vanessa's clothes, but Anne kept her door locked most of the time, and never offered them anything, nor did she ask anything of them. She kept to herself, as she always had, even more so than before.

'Li gave them to me.'

'Playing favourites, as usual.'

Anne was hurt by the remark, but it didn't show. It never did. She was a genius at hiding what she felt. She always had been. 'It's not as though you and he have ever been close.' It was a grown-up remark and the honesty of it took Valerie by surprise.

'What does that have to do with anything? He's my brother, isn't he?'

'Then do something for him some time.'

'He's not interested in me. He's all wrapped up in his fags.'

'Get out of my room!' Anne advanced on her menacingly, and

she took a step back. There were times when the intensity in Anne's eyes frightened her.

'Okay, okay, don't get all worked up.'

'Get out of my room, you whore!' But she had said the wrong thing. Val froze in her tracks and looked viciously at Anne.

'If I were you, I'd watch that. I'm not the one who got knocked up and had to sell my kid.'

It was more than Anne could bear. She swung at Val and missed, and Valerie grabbed her arm and slammed it into the door. There was a sharp crack, and both girls looked shocked, as Anne freed her arm, and swung at her again. This time she didn't miss. She punched Val squarely in the face and stared at her, holding her arm. 'The next time you talk to me, I'm going to kill you, you bitch, is that clear?' She had hit a nerve so painful and raw that she might almost have lived up to her words, but just then Faye and Ward walked in. They saw Val's face, saw Anne clutching her arm, and they easily guessed that the two had exchanged words. They reproached them both, and Ward made ice packs for both girls, but Faye insisted on driving Anne to the hospital for an X ray. As it turned out the arm was badly strained but not cracked after all, and they bandaged it for her. By midnight, they were home again, and they had hardly come in the door when the phone rang. It was Mary Wells and she was hysterical. At first, Faye couldn't understand what she was saying . . . something about a fire . . . and the Christmas tree . . . and then a chill ran down her spine . . . had it been at their home or John's? She began to shout into the phone, trying to find out what had happened to her, but eventually Bob came on the line. He was crying openly, as Ward picked the extension up, and they heard the words at the same time.

'The boys' Christmas tree caught fire. They left it on when they went to bed. John is . . .' He could barely go on, and they could hear his wife sobbing in the background, and somewhere far, far in the distance, there were Christmas carols. They had had friends over when the news came, and no one had thought to turn the music off. 'John is dead.'

'Oh my God . . . no . . . and Li?' Faye whispered the words into the phone as Ward closed his eyes.

'He's badly burned, but alive. We thought you should know . . . They just called us . . . the police said . . .' Faye couldn't follow the rest of it, she sank into a chair as Anne watched her with terrified eyes. They had forgotten all about her as she stared at her mother now.

'What happened?'

'There's been an accident. Li's been burned.' She could hardly absorb it all and her breath was coming short and fast. That had never happened to her before, but for a moment, she had thought they were going to tell her Li was dead . . . but it was John . . . John . . . poor child . . .

'What *happened*?' Anne was crying now, and the twins had come to the top of the stairs. Faye looked up at them in disbelief. It wasn't possible. She had talked to him only hours before.

'I don't know . . . Li and John's Christmas tree burned . . . John was killed . . . Lionel was taken to the hospital . . .' She leapt to her feet as the girls began to cry, Vanessa instinctively taking Anne in her arms, and the younger girl letting her. Faye turned to see Ward crying softly as he grabbed his car keys again. They left a moment later, as Anne lay on the couch and sobbed, and Vanessa stroked her hair with one hand, while holding Val's hand with the other.

In the hospital, Faye and Ward found Lionel being treated for severe burns on his arms and legs. He sobbed uncontrollably as he tried to explain it to Faye.

'I tried . . . Mum, I tried . . . Oh God, Mum . . . but the smoke was so thick . . . I couldn't breathe . . .' As they both sobbed, he told her of the fumes, of how he had tried to give John mouth-to-mouth after dragging him outside, but it was too late and he could barely breathe himself. The fire department had arrived as he collapsed. He had woken up in the hospital, where a nurse inadvertently told him that John was dead of toxic fumes. 'I'll never forgive myself, Mum . . . it's my fault . . . I forgot to turn the lights off on the tree . . .' The enormity of the loss engulfed him again, as Faye sat and cried with him, reassuring him, holding him as best she could with his bandages and salves, but he seemed to hear none of it. He was so hysterical about John that he didn't even feel the pain from his burns. Ward stood by helplessly, watching them as Faye and the boy cried, and for the first time in months, he felt something for his son. He looked down at him gently, and suddenly he remembered him as he had been so long ago . . .

running on the lawn ... playing with the pony cart at their old house, before everything had changed ... it was the same boy he was looking at now, except that he had become a man, and they didn't understand each other any more. But it was hard to remember that as he lay in his bed and cried, thrashing the bandaged arms, and at last Ward took him in his arms and held him close, the tears running down his cheeks, as Faye watched them both, heartbroken at what had happened to John ... and feeling guilty at how grateful she was that it had not been her son.

CHAPTER 26

The funeral was devastating. It was the most painful thing Faye had ever seen. Mary Wells was hysterical, and Bob cried even harder than she did. John's four sisters looked as though they were in shock, and as they rolled the casket away, Mary tried to throw herself on it and had to be restrained. Lionel stood so tall and thin and pale in a dark suit Faye didn't know he owned that she thought he would faint where he stood, and on his one unbandaged hand, she noticed for the first time with a shocked glance that he wore a narrow gold wedding band. She didn't know if Ward had ever noticed it, but she knew what it meant. As she stared at it, she knew what John had meant to her son, and she looked at his face. It was the greatest loss of his life so far, and possibly one of the worst he would ever endure.

Anne stood as close to him as she could, crying softly into a handkerchief, looking up at him to make sure he was all right. There was no question about what would happen afterwards. Ward and Faye had discussed it the night before. Lionel was coming home to stay with them for a while. After the funeral he and Ward took a walk. Greg had escaped almost the moment they got back to the house. John had been his friend for most of his life, but he didn't seem to feel the pain so much.

'What can I say?' He shrugged to Val after the funeral. 'The guy was a fucking fag.' But he had also been his friend, and Valerie remembered the crush she had had on him, to no avail. They all knew why now.

Faye kept a discreet eye on Anne, she had been through a great deal in the past few months, but she seemed to be all right now . . . unlike Lionel, who walked along woodenly at his father's side unable to think of anything but his fight through the flames and his inability to get to John. He had thought of it again and again and again in the past three days. He would never allow himself to forget . . . never . . . it was all his fault . . . he had forgotten to turn the Christmas-tree lights off when they went to bed . . . they had drunk too much wine . . . and those damn little fucking blinking lights . . . why hadn't he remembered them . . . it was all his fault . . . he might as well have killed him with his bare hands.

He said as much to his father now. He had nothing in common with Ward any more, but he had to talk to someone. He wondered if John's parents blamed him.

'They should, you know.' He looked at his father with broken eyes and Ward felt his heart melt towards the boy he had tried so hard to hate for the past year. Now one of them was dead, and it had to end. Faye was right. They were lucky it hadn't been Li. These moments with him now were like a gift.

'We blamed you both for a lot of things in the past year. And we were wrong.' Ward sighed and looked out at the trees as they walked along. It was easier than looking his son in the eye, something he hadn't done in almost exactly a year, even after Li and John had rescued Anne. 'I didn't understand what made you the way you are. I thought it was my fault, so I took it out on you . . . and I was wrong. . . .' He looked at Lionel, and saw tears coursing slowly down his cheeks, tears mirrored by his own. 'I was wrong to blame myself. Just as you're wrong to blame yourself now. You couldn't have done anything, Li. . . .' They stopped walking and he took the boy's hands in his own. 'I know how hard you must have tried,' his voice broke, 'I know how much you loved John.' He didn't want to know but he did. And now he pulled Lionel close to him, their cheeks touching, their hearts beating against each other's chests, their tears falling on each other's shoulders as they cried and Lionel looked at him, seeming like a little boy again.

'I tried, Daddy . . . I did . . . and I couldn't get him out fast enough. . . .' Great sobs broke from him, and Ward held him tight, as though to keep him safe from harm.

'I know you did, son . . . I know. . . .' There was no telling him it was all right. For John, it would never be all right again. And Lionel felt he would never recover from it. It was a loss that none of them would ever forget, a lesson dearly learned.

When they went back to the house, the others were waiting for them. It was a quiet dinner that night, and afterwards they all went to their own rooms. Almost everything Lionel owned had been destroyed in the fire, except a few things he had forgotten which were still at his parents' house; some jewellery that had been darkened by the smoke, but not lost, and his car, which was parked outside now. He was sleeping in his old room. Quietly Faye went about shopping for him in the next few days, and bought a few things she knew he'd need, and he was touched. Ward lent him some things, and the two men spent more time together than they had in a long time.

Greg went back to school, and the day of her birthday, Anne went back to school too, for the first time in a year. It was painful and difficult but it was what she had to do. Anyway, it distracted her. A few weeks later, the bandages came off Lionel's arms. The scars were there, scars they could all see, unlike those he wore deep inside. And no one had mentioned the fact that he had not gone back to school. He wasn't ready yet.

He took them all by surprise when he asked Ward to lunch one day. He looked across the table from him at the Polo Lounge, and he looked far older than his years, Ward thought as he watched him quietly. He didn't understand his way of life any better than he had before and he was sorry that that was what he preferred, but he respected him now. He liked his values and his views and his reasoning and it disappointed him all the more when Lionel told him he wouldn't be going back to school.

'I've thought about it a hell of a lot, Dad. And I wanted you to be the first to know.'

'But why? You only have a year and a half left. That's not so bad. You're just upset right now.' At least he hoped it was that. But Lionel shook his head.

'I can't go back, Dad. I don't belong there any more. I've had an offer to work on a film, and I want to get out there and do that now.'

'And then what? In three months you're through with that and you're out of work again.' It was a business he knew well.

'Just like you, huh, Dad?' he teased. Ward smiled, but he still wasn't pleased with the news, although he respected him for telling him man to man. 'I've just had it with school. I've got to try my wings.'

'You're only twenty years old. What's your rush?' But they both knew he had lived a lot for his age, in part because of John. He had suffered, and lost someone he dearly loved. He couldn't go back to being a child again, no matter how much Ward wanted him to, and although he resisted admitting it, Ward knew it too. John's death had changed all of them, it had allowed him to form a bond with his son again. But Lionel would never be as young, or as carefree, as he had been before. Maybe he was right to give up school, but Ward was sorry anyway. 'I'm sorry to see you do it, son.'

'I knew you would be, Dad.'

'Who's offering you the job?'

Lionel grinned. 'Fox.' The competition of course. And Ward laughed and put a hand to his heart as though he had been shot.

'What a blow. I wish you'd stay out of this damn business.' He meant what he said but Lionel shrugged.

'You and Mum seem to like it a lot.'

'And sometimes we get good and tired of it.' He had been feeling that way for a while, and he wanted to talk Faye into taking a trip with him. She had finished a film and would be free for a while, and she had no excuses now. Then as he looked at Lionel, he had an idea. 'You're not moving out right away, are you?'

'I thought I'd start getting organised one of these days and look for a place to stay. I don't want to get in your way.'

'Not at all.' Ward smiled apologetically at him, remembering how harsh he had been. 'Would you be willing to stay for another month and keep an eye on the girls?'

'Sure.' Lionel looked surprised. 'How come?'

'I want to take your mother away. She needs a break, and so do I.' They hadn't had five minutes alone since he had ended his affair and moved back into the house nine months before, and it was high time they went on a trip together. Lionel smiled at the thought.

'I'd be happy to do that, Dad. It would do you both good.'

Ward smiled at him as they left the restaurant. They were friends again. Friends as they had never been. Man to man . . . no matter how odd that seemed. And that night Ward told Faye about his plans. 'And I don't want to hear any arguments. No excuses. Nothing about work or the kids, or the actors you have to talk to about the script. We're leaving two weeks from tonight.' He had ordered the tickets that afternoon. They were leaving for Paris, Rome, and Switzerland, and instead of arguing, her eyes lit up.

'Are you serious?' She looked at him, amused, and put her arms around him.

'I am. And if you don't come willingly, I'll kidnap you. We're going to stay away for three weeks, and maybe four.' He had checked her production schedule secretly that afternoon and knew she could stay away for that long.

She followed him upstairs that night with a lighter step, and pirouetted in her nightgown as he teased her about Paris and Rome.

'It's been too long since we did something like that, Faye.'

'I know.' She sat down quietly on the bed and looked at him. They had almost lost each other twice; they had almost lost two children ... a daughter ... and a son ... they had given up a grandchild and their son's lover had died. It hadn't been an easy time for any of them. And if anyone had asked her a year before if her marriage could have been saved, she would have told them no. But now, as she looked at him, she knew she still loved the man, with all his faults, with his affair, with the times he had failed her, even with the anguish he had inflicted on their son. She loved Ward Thayer. She had for years, and probably always would. She had few illusions about him after twenty-two years, but she loved the man he was. And that night, when they went to bed, they made love as they had done years and years before.

CHAPTER 27

Paris was exquisite that spring. They wandered along the Seine, went to Les Halles for onion soup, strolled down the Champs Élysées, went to Dior, and then lunch at Fouquet's and dinner at Maxim's and the Brasserie Lipp. They had drinks at the Café Flore and the Deux Magots and they laughed and cuddled and hugged and kissed over cheese and wine. It was exactly what Ward had wanted it to be – a second honeymoon, a place to forget all the sorrows of the past year or two, the children, the films, the responsibilities. When they reached Lausanne, Faye sat looking out at Lac Léman and smiled at him.

'You know, I'm glad I married you.' She said it matter-of-factly as she sipped her coffee and ate a croissant, and he laughed at her.

'I'm awfully glad to hear that. What made you decide?'

'Well,' she mused, staring out at the lake, 'you're a nice man. You make a mess of things sometimes, but you're smart enough and decent enought to go back and straighten things out.' She was thinking of Lionel, and she was relieved that he and the boy were friends again. And she was thinking of his affair too.

'I try hard. I'm not as smart as you are sometimes, Faye.'

'Bullshit.'

'You sound like Val.' He looked disapprovingly at her and she laughed.

'Well, I'm no smarter than you are. Just more stubborn sometimes.'

'I don't always have the guts to hang on the way you do. Sometimes I want to run away.' He had done it twice so far, but she had taken him back both times and he was grateful for that. But he was surprised at what she said next.

'Sometimes I want to run away too, you know. But then I worry about what would happen if I did ... who would keep an eye on Val ... make sure Anne was all right ... Vanessa ... Greg ... Li ...' She smiled at him. 'You. Somehow, I'm so damn egocentric that I figure none of it would run right if I disappeared, which isn't true, but it keeps me hanging in.'

'I'm glad.' He smiled at her and took her hand. They still had romance between them after all these years. 'Because you're right. None of it would run right if you disappeared, and I'm glad you never have.'

'Maybe one day I will. I'll run off and have some wild affair with a grip on the set.' She laughed at the thought, but Ward did not look amused.

'I've worried about that a few times. There are some actors I'm not crazy about you working with.' It was the first time he had admitted that to her and she was touched.

'I always behave myself.'

'I know. That's why I keep such a good eye on you.'

'Oh it is, is it?' She tweaked his ear, and he kissed her, and a little while later they went inside, forgetting Lac Leman and the Alps, and their children and careers. They only thought of each other for their remaining days abroad, and they were both sorry when they boarded the plane to go home. 'It was a beautiful holiday, wasn't it, love?'

'It was.' He smiled at her, and she slipped a hand into his arm, and leaned her head on him.

'I'd like to spend a lifetime doing that one day.'

'No, you wouldn't,' he laughed, 'you'd go stark staring mad. By next week, you'll be knee deep in your new picture, and telling me how impossible everyone is, that none of the costumes fit, the scenery stinks, the locations are no good, no one knows their lines. You'll be tearing your beautiful blonde hair out by the roots. Without that, you'd be so bored you couldn't stand it ... could you?' She laughed at his accurate description of her business life.

'Well, maybe I'm not quite ready to retire yet, but one of these days ...'

'Just let me know when.'

'I will.' And she looked as though she might.

But he was right. Two weeks later, life was just as he had described; she was going totally nuts, her biggest star was giving her a rough time, two others were on drugs, another drank on the set and showed up drunk every day after lunch, an entire set had burned to the ground, the unions were threatening to walk out. Life was back to normal again, but all the same they were both revived after their trip. Lionel had the girls well in hand when they got back. Anne seemed to have settled back into school; the twins were behaving, more or less; the news from Greg was good; and a month later, Lionel moved out again. He had found a place on his own, and although Faye knew he would be lonely without John, she thought it might do him good. He was doing the film for Fox, and it was going well, he said, whenever he called. The only problem they had was with Anne, who had wanted to move in with him. Lionel had discouraged her. He told her that she didn't belong with him now. That he had to live his own life, and so did she, that it had been right for a time, but no more. Now she had to make a life for herself in school again, make new friends, revive old friendships if she wished. She belonged with Ward and Faye, he told her.

Anne watched him in tears as he moved out one Saturday afternoon and she spent the rest of the day in her room. But the next day, she went to the cinema with one of her friends, and Faye decided there was hope for her. She hadn't mentioned the pregnancy in a long time, and she never mentioned the baby she had given up. Faye prayed that she would forget it all if that was possible.

And Faye tried to forget it herself as she dived into her film, stopping only for the Academy Awards, which were at the Santa Monica Civic Auditorium that year. She persuaded Lionel and the twins to come. She thought that Anne was too young, so she stayed home in lonely isolation, as usual, refusing to even watch the awards on TV.

Faye didn't think she'd win, and she kept telling Ward all that night as she got dressed that it was ridiculous to get worked up about it, they didn't mean anything any more . . . not like when she was young . . . when she was acting . . . when it was the first time. 'And after all,' she looked at him, as she fastened pearls around her neck, 'I've already won two.'

'Show-off.' He teased her and she blushed.

'That's not what I meant,' she replied. She looked ravishing in a black velvet dress that showed off the still firm perfectly rounded breasts and he slipped a hand inside her dress now until she shooed him away. She wanted to look perfect tonight. Everyone would be so beautiful and young, and she was forty-seven now ... forty-seven ... how did it all happen so fast? It seemed like only last year when she was twenty-two ... and twenty-five ... and she was madly in love with Ward Thayer ... and they were dancing at Mocambo's every night. She looked dreamily at Ward, remembering the distant past, and he kissed her gently on the neck.

'You look beautiful tonight, my love. And I think you're going to win.'

'Don't say that!' She didn't even want to think of it. Things had been wonderful between them ever since they got back from their trip. There was an aura of romance which shut out everyone else sometimes, but she didn't mind. She loved being alone with him, in spite of the children they loved so much. They needed just each other at times. As they left the house that night with the twins, all dressed up in long gowns and the strings of pearls Faye had lent each of them, Faye saw Anne standing in her room and stopped in to kiss her goodnight. She looked like a lonely lost child and Faye was sorry they hadn't invited her too, but she was so young, just fifteen ... and it was a Monday night after all, she had told Ward. Anne had school the next day. Yet, she reproached herself for not taking her. 'Goodnight, sweetheart.' She kissed Anne's cheek nervously, and her youngest looked up at her, still with that puzzled air that always seemed to be asking her who she was. She had hoped that after she had sat through childbirth with her, they would be friends, but it hadn't worked out that way. Secretly, Anne blamed her for causing her to give up the child, and as soon as she had come home from the hospital, the doors had closed again. There was no getting close to her. Except for Lionel, of course. He was both mother and father to her.

'Good luck, Mum.' She called it out carelessly as they left, and then helped herself to something to eat.

They picked up Lionel at his place on the way. He looked very handsome in an old tuxedo of Ward's, and he jabbered with the twins in the back seat of Faye's Jaguar. Ward complained all the way that it wasn't driving well again; he didn't understand what she did to it. It was one of those nervous nights, when you pretend you're not thinking what you really are.

Everyone was there, Richard Burton and Liz, both of them nominees for *Who's Afraid of Virginia Woolf?*, and she was wearing a diamond the size of a fist. The Redgrave sisters were there, both of them nominated as well ... Audrey Hepburn, Leslie Caron, Mel Ferrer. Faye was up against Antoine Lebouch, Mike Nichols, and more for best director. Anouk Aimée, Ida Kaminska, the Redgraves, and Liz Taylor were vying for best actress. Scofield, Arkin, Burton, Caine, and McQueen for best actor. Bob Hope kept everyone amused as emcee, and then suddenly it seemed they were calling Faye's name ... she had won the best director award again. She flew towards the stage with tears in her eyes, still feeling Ward's kiss on her lips, and suddenly there she was, looking at all of them, the golden statue clutched in her hands, just as she had held it so long ago when she had won the best actress award for the first time in 1942 ... a hundred years ago, it seemed and only last night ... twenty-five years ... The thrill was still there for her.

'Thank you ... all of you ... my husband, my family, my co-workers, my friends ... thank you.' She beamed and left the stage, and she could hardly remember what happened for the rest of the night.

They came home finally at 2 am, and though she knew it was too late for the twins to be out, it was a special night. They had called Anne from the Moulin Rouge but she hadn't answered the phone. Val had suggested that she was probably asleep, but Lionel knew better than that. It was her way of shutting them out, of getting back at them for not including her. And, like his mother, he knew they had made a mistake by not bringing her.

Long afterwards, they dropped Lionel off on the way home, and he kissed his mother's cheek again. The twins were strangely silent for the rest of the drive home. Vanessa was half asleep, and Val hadn't said anything to Faye all night. She was seething with anger over her mother's award. Lionel and Vanessa were well aware of it, but Faye seemed not to realise how jealous Val was of her.

'Did you have a good time, girls?' Faye turned to look at them in the car, thinking of the Oscar she had won. They had taken it away to be engraved, but she felt its presence as though she still held it in her hands. It was impossible to believe it had happened to her again. Now she had three. She beamed at Val, and was startled to see something chilly in her eyes, something she had never recognised quite that clearly before. It wasn't just anger this time, it was jealousy.

'It was all right. You must be pretty pleased with yourself.' They were unkind words, and no one else seemed to hear them quite the way Faye did, but they were aimed straight at her heart, and Val had hit her mark.

'It's very exciting. It always is, I guess.'

Val shrugged as she looked at her. 'I hear they give them out of sympathy sometimes.' The comment was so outrageous that Faye laughed.

'I don't think I'm quite over the hill yet, although you never know.' And of course it was true, sometimes they passed one up and then made it up the next year, although they denied that it worked that way, but everyone felt that it did. 'Is that what you think this was, Val?' Her mother searched her eyes. 'Sympathy?'

'Who knows?' She shrugged indifferently and looked out of the window again as they drove up to the house. It irked her that Faye had won and she made no secret of it. She was the first to leave the car, to reach her room, to close the door, and she never mentioned the Oscar again, not even to Anne the next day. Or when her friends mentioned it in school, and congratulated her. That seemed strange, she had nothing to do with it after all and what did she care anyway? So she just shrugged and said, 'Yeah, so what? Big deal.' And changed the subject to something that interested her like the Supremes. She was sick of hearing about Faye Thayer. She wasn't so hot. And one day, she would show all of them, she would be an actress who would make Faye Price Thayer look pale by comparison. She only had a few months left before she could get out there and show them her stuff, and she could hardly wait. She'd show them all. To hell with her mother ... three Oscars? Bullshit. So what anyway?

CHAPTER 28

The twins graduated from high school two months after Faye won the Academy Award, and Greg came home for the summer just in time to attend the graduation ceremony at his old school.

This year their eyes were dry. Ward leaned over to Faye halfway through the ceremony to say 'I feel as though they should be giving *us* a diploma by now.' Faye giggled softly and rolled her eyes. He was right, and they would be back again four years from now, for Anne. It seemed to go on forever. In two years, Greg would be graduating from the University of Alabama. They seemed to be spending half their life watching young people line up in gowns and mortarboards. But it was touching when the twins got theirs, in spite of how many times they'd seen it before. They wore simple white dresses beneath their gowns, Vanessa's totally plain with a high neck and embroidered hem, Val's a slightly too dressy organdie with a pair of very sexy high heels that showed off her legs. But the shoes weren't Faye's biggest disagreement with her. Valerie had staunchly refused to apply to any college, East or West. She was going to model, act, and in her spare time go to acting school, and not the drama department at UCLA, but the kind where 'real actors' went between jobs, to perfect their skills. She was sure she would find herself in classes with Dustin Hoffman and Robert Redford and she was equally sure that she was going to set the world on fire, despite everything Ward and Faye said to her.

It had been a heated argument for the past several months, and she was more stubborn than either of them. In desperation, Ward had told her he wouldn't support her if she didn't go to school, and that seemed to suit her fine. Someone had told her about a coven of young actresses in West Hollywood; for only a hundred and eighteen dollars a month, she could have a bed and share a room. Two of the actresses had jobs on soaps, one of them did porno films (though Val didn't tell her parents that), one was a big star in a horror film the year before, and there were four others who modelled regularly. It sounded like a whorehouse to Faye, and she told Val so, but the twins were nearly eighteen now, and Valerie reminded her of it constantly. It was an argument which they couldn't win. A week later, they knew that she would be moving out. Vanessa had done exactly as she planned. She had applied to a handful of schools in the East, been accepted by all of them, and was going to Columbia in the fall. She was staying at home until the end of June, and then she was going to New York to work for two months before starting school. She had got a job as a receptionist in a publishing house and she was very excited about it. Meanwhile Greg was going to Europe with friends. Only Anne was staying home this year. They had tried to talk her into going to camp, but she insisted that she was too old. She wanted to go camping with Lionel for a week or two, but he was working on a new film for Fox and didn't have time. Ward and Faye were starting a biggie too. Ever since the Academy Award, the offers had been rolling in with even greater regularity than before. Faye had three projects lined up back to back for the next year, and no spare time at all. Ward reminded her that it was a good thing they'd made the trip to Europe when they had, and she agreed.

The twins' graduation party was the rowdiest of all, and Faye looked at Ward in exhaustion as the last guest left at 4 am. 'Maybe we're getting too old for this.'

'Speak for yourself. Personally, I think seventeen-year-old girls are a lot more attractive than they used to be.'

'Watch out for that.' She wagged a finger at him, and lay down on their bed, before leaving for work at five. There was a big scene she wanted to set up, and Ward was going to spend the day with Lionel and Anne. Val had a hot date, Vanessa had her own plans. God only knew where Greg was, or with whom, but undoubtedly it involved sports, beer, or girls, and he seemed relatively well able to take care of himself, so Faye went to work happily just as Ward fell asleep.

The summer seemed to whiz by. Valerie moved into the apartment she loved so much. There were actually nine girls living there when she moved in. It was a huge house, and half the beds had no sheets on them at all. In the kitchen there were six bottles of vodka, two lemons, three bottles of soda, and no food at all in the fridge, and she hardly ever saw any of the other girls. They had their own lives, boyfriends, some of them had their own phones. Val had never been happier in her life, she told Vanessa just before she left.

'This is just what I've always wanted to do.'

'How's acting school?' Vanessa asked, wondering how they could have shared the same womb, same life, same house. Two people couldn't have been more different than they.

Val shrugged. 'I haven't had time to enrol yet. I've been busy going to go-sees.' But in August she struck oil. Vanessa was already long gone, staying at the Barbizon in New York, and looking at apartments with a friend from work. The job at Parker Publishing was actually pretty dull as all she did was answer phones, but she was looking forward to Columbia. Valerie called her late one night to tell her that she had a walk-on in a horror film. 'Isn't that great?'

It was three o'clock in the morning and Vanessa yawned, but she didn't want to take the wind out of Val's sails. She was pleased she'd called. 'What do you get to do?'

'I walk across the set, oozing blood from my eyes and nose and ears.'

Vanessa repressed a groan. 'That's wonderful. When do you start?'

'Next week.'

'That's great. Have you told Mum?'

'I haven't had time. I'll call her this week sometime,' but they both suspected Faye wouldn't be quite so thrilled, although they didn't voice it. She never seemed to understand anything Val did, or so Val felt, and she was never pleased for her, and probably wouldn't be about this. But *she* had started small too. Hell, she had done soap ads in New York for a year before they discovered her. And this was straight into film, as she said to Van, who didn't remind her that their mother had never had to walk across a set bleeding from the nose and eyes and ears. 'How's your job, Van?' She was feeling magnanimous, usually she didn't really care about anyone but herself, as Vanessa knew only too well.

'It's okay.' Vanessa yawned again. 'Actually, it's pretty dull. But I met a nice girl from Connecticut. We thought we'd try and find a place together near Columbia. She's going there too.'

'Oh.' Val already sounded bored, and decided to hang up. 'I'll let you know how things go.'

'Thanks. Take care.' They were oddly close, and yet not; linked to each other somehow, but with nothing in common at all. It was a bond Vanessa had always felt and never quite understood. She envied other sisters who seemed so close. She was close to neither of hers, and had always longed for a sister she could talk to and confide in, which was what was so nice about the girl from Connecticut.

In California Anne was discovering that too. She had discovered a girl walking down Rodeo Drive one day eating an ice-cream cone, and swinging a bright pink purse from her arm. She looked like an ad in a magazine, and she had smiled at Anne. Anne thought she was beautiful, and had noticed her an hour later, eating lunch at the Daisy, sitting by herself, as Anne stopped there for a hamburger. Her mother had given her money for two new pairs of shoes, and she had been wandering along Rodeo Drive, watching the people stroll in the bright sun. It was a hot day, but there was a nice breeze, and she found herself sitting at the next table from the girl with the pink purse. They smiled at each other again, and she spoke up easily. She had soft brown hair, which fell almost to her waist, and big brown eyes, and she looked about eighteen Anne thought; but she was surprised to learn they were the same age, almost to the day.

'Hi, I'm Gail.'

'I'm Anne.' The conversation would have ended there, left up to her, but Gail seemed to have lots to say. She told her that she had seen this neat skirt at Giorgio's, it was white leather, and real soft, and they had great boots too. Anne was impressed at the places where she shopped and told her about the shoes she'd seen further up the street. They discussed the Beatles, Elvis, jazz, and eventually got around to schools.

'I'm going to Westlake next year.' She looked unimpressed and Anne's eyes grew wide.

'You are? So am I!' It was another happy coincidence, in addition to their age. She told Anne honestly that she had had

287

glandular fever, and then a bout of anorexia, and all in all she'd missed a year of school. She was fifteen now, and she was a year behind, she shrugged. Anne felt as though good fortune had just walked into her life for the first time.

She was honest with her too, to a point; there were some things she intended never to tell anyone, like about the baby she'd given up, but there were other things she could say. 'I dropped out for a year, and I'm a year behind too.'

'That's fabulous.' Gail looked thrilled and Anne grinned. No one had ever reacted that way before, and she knew instantly she liked this girl. She was ready for a friend. And she was bored around the Thayers' pool alone every day. Maybe Gail would like to come by some time. 'What did you do when you dropped out?' She looked fascinated by her adventurous new friend, and Anne tried to look blasé.

'I went up to the Haight-Ashbury for a while.'

Gail's eyes grew huge. 'You did? Wow! Did you take any drugs?'

Anne hesitated for a fraction of an instant and shook her head. 'That stuff's not so hot.' She knew differently, but she also had experience of the price you paid, and she realised that this girl knew nothing of that life. She looked clean and neat and pretty and well dressed and a little spoiled. She was what some people described as a Jewish American princess, and Anne was intrigued by her. All the girls at her old school were so dull, and practically no one had even talked to her when she came back from the Haight, but this girl was nothing like them. She had style and looks and obviously a great personality, and they were attracted to each other instantly. By the end of lunch, they were giggling and having a great time, and the maître d' was giving them angry looks for tying up two tables outside, until, finally, Gail suggested they take a walk back up Rodeo Drive.

'I'll show you the boots at Giorgio's if you want.' Anne was even more impressed when she discovered that Gail had a charge account there, and everyone seemed anxious to help her buy something. Usually, when kids went into places like that, the salespeople were anxious to get rid of them, but not Gail. Everyone called her by name, they even offered Anne a Coke from the bar. They had a great time even though Gail had decided she didn't like the boots that much after all and they were giggling again when they left.

'I'll show you the shoes at the place I went.' It was the most fun she'd had in years, ever probably. The two had hit it off, and they were having a wonderful afternoon, with nothing else to do. 'Your Mum must buy a lot of stuff at Giorgio's for them to be so nice.'

Gail was quiet for a minute, staring into space, and then she looked at Anne. 'My mother died of cancer two years ago. She was thirty-eight years old.' They were such shocking words that Anne just stared at her. It was the worst thing she had ever heard, much worse than anythng that had happened to her in some ways. Even though she and Faye weren't close and there were times when she hated her, still to have her die that way would be terrible, and she could still see the pain in Gail's eyes now.

'Do you have sisters and brothers?'

'No. Just my Dad.' She looked at Anne honestly as they walked along. 'That's why he kind of spoils me, I guess. It's like I'm all he has left. I try not to take advantage of that, but it's hard sometimes.' She smiled and Anne noticed that there were freckles dusted across her face. 'I like getting my way, and he gets so upset when I cry.'

Anne laughed. 'Poor man.'

'What are your parents like?'

Anne hated to even talk about them, but after Gail's confidence it seemed unfair not to share something with her. 'They're all right.'

'Do you get along with them?'

Anne shrugged. The truth was that she did not, and never had. 'Sometimes. They weren't too crazy about it when I took off.'

'Do they trust you now?'

'I think so.'

'Would you do it again?' Gail was curious about her new friend. But Anne shook her head. 'No, I wouldn't.'

'Do you have sisters and brothers?' They had reached the shoe shop and were wandering inside, as Anne nodded her head. 'Two of each.'

'Wow!' Gail smiled the dazzling smile which showed how she could have been a child actress if she'd wanted to. 'Lucky you!'

'That's what you think!' Anne knew better and rolled her eyes.

'What're they like?'

'My older brother, Lionel, is neat. He's going to be twenty-one.' She didn't tell Gail he was gay. 'He dropped out of school too, and he's making films for Fox.' She said it like a pro and Gail was impressed again. 'My other brother is a jock and goes to the University of Alabama on a football scholarship. He'll be a junior this year. And my sisters are twins. One of them just went East to go to Columbia, and the other one is trying to be an actress here.'

'Wow! That's neat!'

'Lionel is . . . we've always been close . . . the others are . . . well,' she shrugged again, dismissing them at one blow, 'a little strange at times.' It was what they said about her too, but she didn't care what they said now. She had a friend of her own now.

Gail bought two pairs of the same shoes in different colours. A few minutes later, she looked at her watch.

'My Dad's picking me up at four, in front of the Beverly Wilshire. Do you want a ride somewhere?'

Anne hesitated. She had taken a cab from home, but it would be fun to ride with Gail. 'You don't think he'd mind?'

'Not at all. He loves doing stuff like that.' Giving strangers rides? Anne laughed. Gail was naïve in some ways but she liked that about her. They crossed Wilshire Boulevard, and stood in front of the sumptuous hotel, waiting for the car to arrive. Anne was impressed when she saw his car. He was driving a two-toned grey Rolls, and Gail waved frantically until he stopped. Anne thought she was kidding at first, because of the fancy car, but a stocky, thick-shouldered man, with features much like hers, leaned over and opened the door. Gail hopped in and beckoned to Anne, explaining her instantly to the man at the wheel of the Rolls. 'Hi, Daddy, I made a new friend. She's going to the same school as me next year.' He didn't look upset that she was hitching a ride, and warmly shook her hand. He wasn't a handsome man, but he had a kindly face, Anne decided. His name was Bill Stein, and Anne gathered that he was a lawyer in the entertainment world. She was sure he would know who her parents were, but she didn't offer their names. She was just Anne.

He took them to Will Wright's on Sunset Boulevard for ice cream. And he had a surprise for Gail that night, he said. They were going to dinner at Trader Vic's and then to a film with some friends. The funniest thing of all was that the film was one of Ward and Faye's, but Anne only said that she had seen it and liked it a lot, and then they talked of other things. All the time, she felt his eyes on her, as though he were trying to figure out who she was, but more as though he were trying to draw her out. The odd thing was that she felt safe with him, and comfortable in a way that she rarely did with anyone. When they dropped her off, she hated to see them go, and she watched the grey Rolls disappear, anxious to see Gail again. She had given her her phone number on the drive home, and Gail had promised to call the next day and come over to swim in the pool. Anne could hardly wait. She wondered if Mr Stein would drop her off. She was surprised to see her own father at home when she walked in, until she glanced at the clock and saw that it was almost six o'clock.

'Hi, sweetheart.' He looked up at her from the glass of wine he was pouring himself. Faye wasn't home yet, and dinner wouldn't be for a couple of hours. He wanted to relax and watch the news, maybe take a swim, and enjoy his glass of wine. He didn't drink much any more, only wine. He was surprised to see Anne looking so pleased with herself, he couldn't imagine over what. Most of the time, she still hid in her room. 'What did you do today?'

She looked at him for a long moment and then shrugged. 'Nothing much.' And then she disappeared upstairs, as usual, and closed her bedroom door, with a smile this time, thinking of her new friends.

CHAPTER 29

The Barbizon for Women had provided a pleasant home for Vanessa since she had arrived in New York. There were only women living there, it was a nice neighbourhood at Sixty-third and Lexington, there was a swimming pool, and a coffee shop downstairs. It met all her needs, and she was hardly there anyway. Louise Matthison lived there too. They went to Long Island at weekends, to people Louise knew, and eventually they found an apartment to share. It was on 115 Street on the West Side, and she knew her parents would have died if they'd seen the neighbourhood. But it was close to Columbia, and all the kids lived up there. She didn't like it as much as the Barbizon, but there was more freedom there. They moved in a month before school began, and took turns buying groceries and doing household chores.

It was Vanessa's turn to do the shopping, and she struggled up the stairs one day with a bag in each arm. There was an ancient elevator which never worked, and she was afraid she'd get stuck in it anyway. It was easier just to stagger up the stairs to the third floor, but as she did so on a hot August afternoon, after work, she found someone staring down at her. He was tall and he had auburn hair, a pleasant face, and he was wearing a T-shirt and shorts, and carrying a stack of papers in one hand.

'Do you need help?' She looked up at him and was about to decline, but she liked the look of him. There was something matter-of-fact and intelligent about the man that appealed to her instantly. He was the kind of man she had hoped to meet at Parker when she took the job. But she never seemed to meet anyone there who excited her, and this young man had something that appealed to her now. She wasn't sure what it was, maybe it was just the stack of papers he held. It looked like a manuscript to her, and she wasn't far wrong. That was exactly what it was, he explained, as he set her bags of groceries down outside her door. 'Just moved in?' He had never seen her before, and he'd been living there for years. He had moved in when he'd gone to graduate school, which he'd finished the year before. But he'd been too lazy to move out; he had too many papers lying around. He was doing research for a thesis on philosophy, and he was thinking about writing a play, but he forgot about it all now, as he looked at the slim girl with the long, blonde hair. She nodded in answer to his question, and dug her key out of her bag.

'I moved in with a friend two weeks ago.'

'Starting graduate school next month?' He knew the type. He'd been dating them for years. He'd been at Columbia since 1962, and five years, almost six in fact, was a long time. But she was smiling at him, amused. Lately, people had begun to think she was older than she was. It was a refreshing change after years of people thinking her less sophisticated and much younger than her twin.

'No. Undergraduate, but thanks for the compliment.'

He smiled ingenuously. He had nice teeth, and an attractive smile. 'Not at all. Well, see you sometime.'

'Thanks again for the hand.' He clattered down the stairs with his manuscript in hand, and Vanessa heard a door slam on the second floor. She mentioned him to Louise that night, who grinned as she set her hair in rollers for work the next day.

'He sounds cute. How old do you think he is?'

'I don't know. Old, I guess. He said he was working on his thesis, and he was carrying a manuscript.'

'Maybe he was just putting you on.'

'I don't think so. He had to be pretty close to twenty-five.' Louise immediately lost interest in him; she had just turned eighteen, and she thought nineteen was old enough. Twenty-five wasn't even fun. They just wanted to climb into bed the first time around, and Louise wasn't ready for that.

As it turned out, Vanessa was right, or pretty close. He was twenty-four, and they met each other again one Sunday night as the girls came home from a weekend in Quogue. They were juggling suitcases and tennis rackets, Louise's oversized hat, and Van's camera, and they were climbing out of the cab that had just brought them from Penn Station all the way uptown. He had parked his battered MG across the street and was watching them. He thought Vanessa had great legs in the shorts and sandals she wore. She looked a lot like Yvette Mimieux, right down to the turned-up nose, and she had fabulous green eyes, he had noticed that the day they had met on the stairs. He sauntered across the street, wearing shorts and a T-shirt again, and loafers without socks.

'Hi, there.' They hadn't introduced themselves and he didn't know her name, but he volunteered to help with the bags. He was juggling both tennis rackets, a suitcase in each hand, and his own briefcase, which was no small feat, and Vanessa was awkwardly attempting to help and thanking him, as everything fell in a heap in front of their door and he looked at her. 'You guys sure drag a lot of stuff around.' And then in a soft voice, as Louise stepped inside, 'Want to come down for a glass of wine?' Vanessa was tempted to, but she had the feeling he was putting a fast move on her. She didn't go to men's apartments, and she didn't really know who he was. He could have been the Boston Strangler for all she knew, but he seemed to read her mind. 'You won't get raped, I swear. Not unless you agree.' He looked her over appraisingly and she blushed, as he wondered exactly how old she was. She looked about twenty-one but she had said she was an undergraduate. Maybe twenty, or even nineteen. She had a calm, tranquil air, and a healthy blonde beauty which appealed to him. He was dying to spend some time with her.

Instead of going downstairs with him, she invited him in to join her roommate and herself for a beer. It wasn't what he would have preferred, but since he seemed to have no choice, he accepted gracefully, put the rest of their stuff inside the hall, closed the door, and looked around at what they'd done to the place. It had all been painted pale yellow and there were plants and magazines, and a lot of rattan, and some Indian prints, and there was a photograph of a large family on the wall. A massive group standing next to a swimming pool. It looked very Californian to him, and he inquired who they were, and then suddenly recognised Van, standing next to Valerie, with Lionel next to her.

'Those are my folks.' She said it simply and he didn't question her about who they were, and then suddenly Louise laughed as she strolled by with a beer can in her hand.

'Aren't you going to ask her who her Mum is?'

Vanessa blushed to the roots of her hair and she could have killed her friend. She hated talking about that, but Louise had been impressed ever since she had discovered that her mother was Faye Thayer. She had seen all her films, including the ones she had acted in years before.

'Okay.' The tall young man with auburn hair looked at her with an obliging smile. 'Who's your Mum?'

'Dracula, who's yours?'

'Cute.'

'Want another beer?'

'Sure.' He liked the way her eyes danced when she smiled, and he was curious now, as he glanced at the photograph again. There was something familiar about all of them, but nothing specific came to mind as he looked at Vanessa again. 'Are you going to tell me, or do I have to guess?'

'Okay, big deal. My Mum is Faye Thayer.' It was easier to get it over with than to play coy. It wasn't all that important to her, and she hadn't bragged about it since third grade. In fact, she had learned to keep her mouth shut most of the time. It wasn't easy being the child of a celebrity, let alone one who had won three Academy Awards. Somehow, it made people expect more of you, or else they were quick to criticise. And Vanessa liked getting by quietly in life. The boy was looking at her now, with narrowed eyes, as he nodded his head.

'That is very interesting. I like her films. Some of them.'

'So do I.' She smiled. At least he hadn't fallen over himself the way some people did. 'What did you say your name was again!' He had never really said. It had all been pretty casual as he carried their bags upstairs.

'Jason Stuart.' He smiled at her. She certainly didn't seem stuck up about who she was. Her friend was a lot more impressed. He glanced at the picture again. 'Who are all the other kids?'

'My brothers and sisters.'

'That's quite a mob.' He was impressed. He was an only child, and large families had never appealed to him much. He liked his life the way it was. His parents were older and had retired to New Hampshire, and everything would come to him one day, not that there was much. His father was a lawyer, with a small country practice now, though he wasn't really interested in pursuing it any more, and he did as little as he could. Jason had thought he might like to go into law too, but when he thought of it seriously, writing had a lot more appeal to him. He was going to write a play, after his thesis, he told Vanessa over their third beer. It wasn't so much that he liked to drink, but the heat was killing them. The whole building seemed to be baking after a day of it, and after Louise went to bed, they went outside to get some air. They walked along Riverside Drive for a while, he telling her about New England, and she talking about Beverly Hills.

'I'd say they're worlds apart, wouldn't you?' He smiled down at her again. She seemed mature for her age, and quiet, and unassuming. She laughed a little later on and told him about her twin.

'We're worlds apart, too. All she wants to do is be a big star. She just got a part in a horror movie with blood streaming out of her ears.' He made a face and they both laughed. 'I'd like to write a screenplay one day, but you couldn't pay me to act.' And then, for no reason in particular, she thought of Lionel, and she had a feeling he would like this man, and that Jason would like him. Both of them were honest, unpretentious, and bright. 'My brother's making films too.'

'You people must be quite a group.' Overwhelming at best.

'I suppose we are. I'm used to us. And everyone's going their own way now. There's only one left at home.' Poor little Anne with her runaway days in the Haight, and the baby she'd had to give away. Vanessa felt sorry for her sometimes, although she didn't understand her now any better than she ever had. They all seemed so far away now, as though they were part of another world. She wondered when they would all be together again, or if. It seemed unlikely now, although she had promised them she would try to come home for Christmas this year. But who knew what would happen between now and then, or where Lionel or Val or Greg would be.

'Do you like your family?'

'Some of them.' For no reason in particular, she was honest with him, though she had no reason not to be, as long as she didn't tell him too much, about Lionel or Anne, but she had no intention of doing that. 'I'm closer to some than others. My older brother is really neat.' She had come to respect him more and more for standing up for what he was. She knew how difficult it had all been for him.

'How old is he?'

'Twenty-one, his name is Lionel, and my other brother Greg is twenty, then there's Val, my twin, she's eighteen too, obviously, and Anne is fifteen.'

'Your folks sure didn't lose any time.' He smiled and Vanessa smiled back, and they walked slowly home, as the river drifted nearby. And he walked her to her door. 'Want to have lunch tomorrow?'

'I can't. I have to work.'

'I could come downtown.' The idea didn't really appeal to him much. He wanted to stay uptown and write, but she appealed to him a lot.

'Wouldn't that be too much trouble for you?'

'Yes.' He looked at her honestly. 'But I like you. I can spare an hour or two.'

'Thanks.' She left him then.

He picked her up at the reception desk at Parker's the next day, and they went for a long walk, and wound up eating avocado sandwiches in a health-food restaurant he knew. He was interesting to talk to, he took himself seriously in some ways, and he thought Vanessa should too. He thought writing screenplays was junk, and he suggested she think about writing a serious play.

'Why? Because that's what you want to do? Films don't have to be junk, you know.' He liked the way she stood up to him, and he invited her to dinner that night too, though she turned him down. 'I promised I'd meet Louise with some friends.' He was dying to come along, but he didn't let on. He wondered if there was another man involved, which there was. But the boy was Louise's date. Vanessa just didn't want to look too anxious to him. But she liked him just as much as he liked her. She thought of him all that night, as they ate spaghetti and clams on Houston Street, and it seemed hours before they came back uptown. When they did, she noticed that his light was still on. She wondered if he was writing or just hanging out, and she made as much noise as possible clattering up the stairs and slamming their door, hoping he'd call. He didn't call for two days. He had decided to play it cool, and when he did, she was gone for the weekend. They didn't meet again until the middle of the following week, when he saw her coming home from work one night, looking hot and tired, after an endless ride on the bus uptown.

'How've you been?' He smiled and she looked pleased. She thought that he had forgotten her.

'Pretty good. How's your play?'

'I haven't done a thing. I've been working on that damn thesis all week.' He told her that he was going to do substitute teaching at a boys' school that autumn, to make ends meet. He wasn't too excited about it, but it would leave him plenty of time to write, and that was what mattered to him most. Vanessa was impressed by how serious he was. But he was serious about a lot of things, and he was developing a serious interest in her.

This time when he asked her out, she was free. They went to a little Italian restaurant uptown, and they drank a lot of red wine, and talked until almost one o'clock, and then took a leisurely walk home, with Vanessa glancing over her shoulder now and then, hoping they wouldn't be mugged. She wasn't used to New York yet, and it was hardly a lovely neighbourhood. But Jason put a powerful arm around her, sensing her fears, and she felt safe with him. He walked her slowly upstairs, and seemed to hesitate on the second floor, but she began the next flight up, and he gently touched her arm. 'Want to come in for a drink?' She had drunk enough, and she suspected what he had in mind. It was almost 2 am, and she was asking for it if she went to his place. She wasn't ready to make that kind of commitment yet, to anyone, not even to him, and she liked him a lot.

'Not tonight, Jason, but thanks.' He looked disappointed, as he walked her to her door, and she felt just as disappointed when she went inside. For the first time in her life, she really wanted a man. She had always had fun playing with boys before, but she wasn't like Val. She didn't need conquests, or ache with desire for anyone. There were boys that she liked, but never that much. Until now. Suddenly, she knew from the unfamiliar stirrings she felt that she wanted to sleep with him.

She tried to distract herself for the next few days. She went out with Louise and her friends. She even had lunch with her boss at Parker, and she could see that he had the hots for her but she couldn't even stand his touch on her arm. As she went home at night all she could think of was the tall boy with auburn hair on the second floor, and it was almost a relief when she ran straight into him that weekend. She was going to the laundromat with her things. Louise had gone to Quogue again, and she was alone for a change. But she didn't tell Jason that. She didn't want to encourage him.

'How've you been, kid?' He tried to make her feel very young, and ashamed for not going to bed with him. And she did. But she didn't let on.

'Fine. How's the play?'

'Okay. It's been kind of hot to work.' She could see that he had a tan, and had probably been spending time on the roof. His parents had wanted him to come to New Hampshire for a few days, but he liked it better in New York. It was so damn dull up there, and there was an additional lure to town now. He could almost feel a throbbing pulse being in the same building with her. No one had turned him on that much in a long time, and he almost resented it. It made him curt with her now. 'See you, kid.' It was obvious where she was going, and he could calculate how long she'd be gone, and when he heard a step on the stairs an hour later, he swiftly opened his door. And he had guessed right. She was carrying a bag of clean laundry upstairs and she turned to look at him as she heard his door open. 'Hi. Want some lunch?'

She felt her heart pound as she met his eyes, wondering if that was all he meant, or if he meant more. 'I . . . okay . . . sure . . .' She was afraid to turn him down again, for fear he wouldn't ask her again. It wasn't easy being young and in New York for the first time, even worse if you were a virgin and he was an older man of twenty-four. She followed him into his apartment, and dropped her bag of laundry near the door, glad that she had put her personal things near the bottom where they wouldn't fall out.

He made tuna sandwiches for them both, and cold lemonade, which she liked. She was surprised at how relaxed she was, as they sat and talked and munched potato chips from the bag.

'Do you like New York?' She could feel his eyes bore into her and she had to concentrate on his words. There was something intense happening between them, but oddly enough it didn't frighten her. She felt as though she were almost floating on a wave of his thoughts, and the air beneath them was soft, warm, and sensual. The air around them was deathly still, and it felt as if there was a thunderstorm brewing that afternoon, but the only world that seemed to exist was in that room between them.

'I like New York a lot.'

'Why?' His eyes dug deep into her soul, as though he were looking for someone, for something that she had brought with her, and she met his eyes now.

'I don't know yet. I'm just glad I'm here.'

'So am I.' His voice was soft and sensual, and she felt herself physically pulled towards him, unaware of his hands pulling her close, his hands reaching for her thighs, touching them, caressing her, kneading her flesh, and then suddenly she felt his lips on hers and his hands on her breasts, and desire exploding from beneath her legs as his fingers moved deftly there, and she was breathless as they lay back on his couch, and then suddenly she was begging him to stop. He seemed surprised, and sat up, looking down at her where she lay.

'Don't, please . . .' He had never raped anyone before, and he had no intention of starting now. He looked almost hurt, and didn't understand what was happening, as tears sprang to her eyes. 'I don't . . . I've never . . .' And yet she wanted him, and suddenly he understood and he held her close to him, and she could feel his warmth and smell the sweetness of his flesh, it had the smell of lemon spice and she wasn't sure if it was soap or eau de cologne, but she liked the smell, and she knew she liked him, and he was looking down at her gently now, having understood everything, but it only made him want her more.

'I didn't realise . . .' He leaned away from her and gave her room to breathe and think. He didn't want to overpower her. Not now, not the first time. 'Would you rather wait?' She was embarrassed for her honesty but slowly she shook her head. She didn't want to wait at all, and a moment later, he was carrying her to his bed, as though she were a little rag doll, and he laid her gently down, and peeled away the few clothes she wore, her shorts, the sleeveless shirt, the underpants, the bra. She felt like a little girl beneath his hands, and he slid into bed next to her, turning away after he shed his clothes, so he wouldn't frighten her. He thought of everything, and he touched her everywhere, and she lay in bed with him in ecstasy as the thunder and lightning came. She was never quite sure if the storm were real or part of what he made her feel. But when they were spent, he lay next to her and the rain beat on the windowpane, and she smiled at him. There was blood on his sheets but he didn't seem to care, he said her name again and again, and touched her face with his hands, and her body with his lips and then he parted her legs again and let his tongue play with her until she screamed. Then he entered her again, and this time the storm was not in the sky, but only in her head as she shouted his name in ecstasy, and she felt herself drift away in his powerful arms.

CHAPTER 30

'Action!' The director screamed for the eleventh time, and Valerie had to dash across the set again with red paint streaming from her ears and down her cheeks, and from her nose. And each time she had to wash it off, in order to start again. It was the most tedious thing she had ever done, except that after this she would be a big star . . . she just knew it . . . someone would discover her . . . and she would end up playing a role with Richard Burton, or Gregory Peck, or Robert Redford . . . even Dustin Hoffman wouldn't be bad. . . . The director shouted 'Action' for the nineteenth time and she did it again. The paint kept running into her hair and he was yelling at the makeup man that it was the wrong consistency. And when he yelled 'Cut' again, Faye tiptoed off the set. Valerie had never known she was there, and Faye was embarrassed for her. It was a pathetic little role, as she told Ward that afternoon. In fact, it was worse than that, it was embarrassing.

'I wish she'd do something decent with herself like go to school.'

'Maybe she'll make something of herself, Faye. You did.'

'That was almost thirty years ago for God's sake. Times have changed. She can't even act.'

'How can you tell in a role like that?' He was trying to be fair, and he thought Faye was being unduly harsh.

'Let's put it this way, she doesn't even walk across a stage well.'

'Would you, with paint pellets shoved up your nose, and into your ears? Personally, I think she's a hell of a good sport.'

'I think she's a damn fool.'

But she got another role like the first, as soon as she completed that, and she was thrilled although Faye was worried about it. Faye tried to ask her tactfully if she was happy doing films like that, but

Valerie took it as a slur and there had been pure hatred in Val's eyes when she had answered her.

'You started with soap flakes and cereal, I'm starting with blood, but basically it's the same. And one day, if I want to, I can be right where you are.' It was an ambitious goal, and as he watched the two women spar, Ward was sorry for Val. She so desperately wanted to compete with Faye that she forgot to be herself sometimes. Unlike Anne, who seemed to have come into her own finally, in the last few months. She seemed quieter, more mature, and she seemed to love her new school. She had a new friend, whom she spent time with constantly, a child whose mother had died a few years before apparently. The two girls went everywhere as a team. The father doted on his child, and seemed willing to chauffeur them everywhere, take them to every possible kind of show and game, drop them off, pick them up. It was a blessing for Ward and Faye. Since the last Academy Award, they had had no free time at all. They were grateful to Bill Stein for taking such good care of Anne. Ward knew vaguely who he was, their paths had crossed once or twice, but in a strictly friendly way. He seemed like a nice man, and if he spoiled his child, it was understandable, she was the only one he had, and he had no wife. He had no one else to spoil, except now Anne, and of course Gail.

He was always giving Anne nice things, a sweater when he bought one for Gail, a little red Gucci bag, a yellow umbrella from Giorgio's on a day when it was pouring with rain, and he wanted nothing in return from her. He just had a sense of how lonely she was, and how little time Faye and Ward spent with her. It made him happy to do little things for her, just as he did for Gail.

'You're always so nice to me, Bill.' He let her call him that, in fact he wanted her to, he had said so several times, and she finally did, still feeling a little shy with him.

'Why shouldn't I be? You're a nice person, Anne. We enjoy your company.'

'I love you both too.' The words had poured out of her starved little soul, and his heart went out to her at times. He suspected that there was a sorrow there that no one knew, and he didn't know what it was, but it never left her eyes, no matter how much love you lavished on her. He knew she had run away to the Haight almost two years before, and he wondered if it was something that had happened there. He asked Gail about it once, but she didn't seem to know.

'She never talks about it, Dad. I don't know . . . I don't think her parents are very nice to her.'

'I suspected that too.' He had always been honest with Gail.

'It's not that they're mean to her or anything. They're just never there. No one is. Her brothers and sisters are all grown up and gone, and she's always alone there with the maid.' Most nights she even ate dinner alone, but she was used to it by now.

'Well, she doesn't have to be any more.' The Steins took her under their wing, and Anne basked in the warmth of the love they gave. She was like a little flower in full bloom, and Bill loved to watch her play with Gail. They did homework together sometimes, or just sat and talked, and sometimes they dived into the pool, or giggled for hours at some private joke. He loved to buy them both pretty things, and make them smile. Life was short, he had learned that when his wife died. He was thinking of her one day, as he sat by the pool with Anne. It was a warm autumn day, and Gail had just gone inside to get them something to eat.

'You look so serious sometimes, Anne.' She was comfortable with him now, and she didn't look frightened at what he said, although she had sometimes at first. She was afraid he would ask her something she didn't want to tell anyone. 'What do you think about then?'

'Different things . . .' My brother's friend who died . . . the baby I gave up . . . already at fifteen, there were ghosts that haunted her, but she didn't tell him any of that.

'Your days in the Haight?' He had wondered about that and she didn't run away from him. Her eyes met his, and he saw something there that broke his heart. There was a pain in her which no one could reach. He hoped he would one day. She was like another daughter to him, and he was surprised at how much she had come to mean to them in a few months. They were deeply attached to her, and she to them. Other than Lionel and John, they were the first people who had ever taken care of her, or given a damn, or so she thought.

'Sort of . . .' And then she surprised herself by opening up more than she'd planned to him. 'I gave up something once that I cared about very much . . . sometimes I think of it, even though it doesn't

304

change anything.' There were tears in her eyes and he reached out and touched her hand, with tears in his own.

'I didn't give up something, but I lost someone I loved very much. Maybe that's a little bit the same thing. A kind of loss. Maybe it's even worse if you give it up willingly.' He thought she was referring to someone she had loved, and wondered how someone so young could have cared so much. It never crossed his mind that she had given up a child. She and Gail still seemed so innocent to him, and he cherished that. But her eyes reached out to him now with wisdom far beyond her years.

'It must have been terrible for you when she died.'

'It was.' It surprised him that he could say the words so easily to her. But she seemed so understanding as they sat holding hands by the pool, like old friends. 'It was the worst thing that ever happened to me.'

'That's like what happened to me.' She had a sudden urge to tell him about the baby she'd given up, but she was afraid he would never let Gail near her again. There were things better left unsaid, and she stopped herself now.

'Was it terrible, sweetheart?'

'Worse than that.' Every day she wondered where he was, whether she had done the right thing. Maybe he was sick, or he had died, or the drugs she had taken had affected him after all, although there was no sign of it at the birth, they said. . . . Her eyes met Bill's now, and he looked so sadly at her.

'I'm so sorry, Anne.' He held her hand tight, and she felt warm and safe. In a little while Gail came out with lunch for all three of them. She thought Anne slightly subdued, but she got that way sometimes. It was just the way she was. She didn't see anything different in her father's eyes that day, though he seemed to watch Anne a lot after that. Anne noticed it sometimes, as he sat looking at her, and one day when they were alone, waiting for Gail to come back from a friend's, she got a chance to talk to him again. She had arrived a little bit before the time she had arranged with Gail, and Bill had just come out of the shower and was wearing a robe. He told her to make herself at home, and she stretched out in the den with a magazine, but then she saw him watching her. She put the magazine down and felt everything she had held back for so long. Without saying a word, she stood up and walked to him. He took her in his arms, and kissed her hard, and then he forced himself to pull away from her. 'Oh, God, Anne, I'm so sorry . . . I don't know what . . .' But she silenced him as she kissed him again, and he was stunned. He knew instinctively that she was no novice at this, and as her hands sought him beneath the robe, he knew that there were secrets about Anne that no one knew. He gently took her hands away and kissed her fingertips. His body was straining for her, and she had stroked him so enticingly, he felt half mad, but not so crazed that he would let her get hurt or do something insane. She was just a child, in his eyes. And he knew this was wrong. She was a fifteen-year-old girl, almost sixteen, but still . . . 'We have to talk about this.' He sat down on the couch next to her, turned towards her, pulling the robe tight, and looked into her eyes. 'I don't know what happened to me.'

'I do.' She spoke the words so gently that he thought he had dreamed what she said. 'I'm in love with you, Bill.' It was the truth, she was, and he was in love with her. It was madness for them. He was forty-nine years old and she was fifteen. It was wrong . . . wasn't it? He had to remind himself of that as he looked at her, and he couldn't help himself. He kissed her again. He felt tortured by the waves of passion that he felt and he took her hand in his.

'I love you too, but I won't let this happen to us.' He sounded anguished as he spoke. There were tears in Anne's eyes. She was terrified he would send her away. Maybe even for good. And she couldn't have lived through that.

'Why not? What's wrong with it? It happens to other people too.'

'But not at your age and mine.' They were thirty-three years apart, and she wasn't even of age. Maybe if she had been twenty-two and he fifty-five and not the father of her best friend. Anne was shaking her head frantically. She wouldn't lose him now. She refused. She had already lost too much in her short life, and she wouldn't lose him too, no matter what he said.

'That's not true. It happens to other people just like us.'

He smiled at her. She was so earnest and so sweet, and he loved her so much. He realised that now. 'I wouldn't care if you were a hundred years old. I love you. That's all. I won't give you up.' The melodrama of it made him smile again, and he kissed her lips to silence her. They were so sweet, and her skin in his hands was like velvet to the touch. But this was wrong. Technically, it was statutory rape, even with her consent. He knew that, and he looked at her now.

'Have you ever done this before, Anne? Honestly. I won't be angry at you.' He had a gentle way of bringing out the truth, and it was always easy for her to be honest with him.

She knew what he meant, more or less. And they were both grateful Gail was late. 'Not like this. When I was . . . in the Haight . . .' It would be so difficult to explain to him, but she wanted to now. 'I . . .' She sighed horribly and he was sorry he had asked.

'You don't have to tell me anything you don't want to, Anne.'

'I want you to know.' She tried to make it brief and clinical, but it still sounded terrible to her. 'I lived in a commune, and I took LSD. I took other things too, but mostly that, some peyote . . . a lot of dope, but mostly acid. And the group I lived with had strange practices . . .'

He looked horrified. 'You were raped?'

Slowly, she shook her head, her eyes never leaving his, she had to be honest with him at all costs. 'I did it because I wanted to . . . and I did it with all of them, I think. I don't remember much any more. It was like being in a trance and I don't know what's memory and what's dream . . . but I was five months pregnant when my parents brought me back. I had a baby thirteen months ago.' She knew now that she would remember the date for the rest of her life. She could have told Bill how many days past thirteen months. Five to be exact. 'And my parents made me give him up. It was a boy, but I never saw him. It was the worst thing I ever went through.' There was no way to describe to him what she had been through. 'And giving him up was the worst mistake I ever made in my life. I'll never forgive myself. Every day, I ask myself where he is, if he's all right.'

'It would have ruined your life, sweetheart.' Gently, with one hand he stroked her face, so desperately sorry for her and the pain she had been through. She was so different from Gail. She had seen so much of life. Too much, at her age.

'That's what my parents said,' she sighed. 'I don't think they were right.'

'What would you do with a baby now?'

'Take care of him . . . just like his other mother does . . .' Her eyes filled with tears and he held her close. 'I should never have given him up.' He wanted to tell her he'd give her another baby one day, but it seemed an outrageous thing to say, and then they heard Gail's key in the lock. Bill moved quietly away from her, with a last look, a last touch, an ache of desire, as he pulled his robe close, and they both smiled for Gail.

For the next two months, Anne met him whenever she could, just to talk to him, to go for walks, to share her thoughts with him. Gail knew nothing of it, and Anne hoped she never would. It was forbidden fruit for both of them, and yet they couldn't stop. They needed each other too much now. He confided in her too. The relationship was chaste, but they couldn't hold out for much longer, and when Gail's grandmother invited her for the Christmas holidays, they made a plan. Anne would tell her parents that she was going to stay with them. And from Christmas Day until Gail returned, Anne would stay with him. It was thought out ahead of time and planned. Almost like a honeymoon.

CHAPTER 31

Louise had long since figured out what was going on between her roommate and the man on the second floor. She didn't disapprove, although she thought he was too old for Van. Twenty-four was already a man. And she was sorry she didn't see more of Vanessa now, but she had her own friends too, and Columbia kept them more than busy enough with assignments and projects and homework and exams. The months flew by and it was hard to believe that the Christmas holidays had already rolled around. The weather was cold and crisp, and just after Thanksgiving, they had had their first snow.

Vanessa was enchanted with it and she and Jason had thrown snowballs at each other in Riverside Park. There was always so much for them to do, the Cloisters, the Metropolitan, the Guggenheim, the Museum of Modern Art, the opera, the ballet, concerts at Carnegie Hall, and always the lure of Off Broadway for him. Jason led a full cultural life, and now he always took Vanessa along. She hadn't seen a film with him since she'd arrived, except some old ones at a festival at the Museum of Modern Art. He continued to disapprove of all that, and he worked on his thesis while she studied for exams. Somehow she loved his seriousness, and his purism about his philosophies. To her, it made him not rigid, but more lovable.

'I'm going to miss you a lot over the holidays.' She was lying on his couch with a book on her lap. As she looked at him, he appeared terribly serious with his glasses on. He peered over them with a smile.

'It'll probably be a relief to get back to Plastic Land,' which was what he called L.A., 'you can go to the cinema with your friends every day, and eat tacos and french fries,' he had a horror of those things too, 'before you have to come back here again.' She laughed at his visions of Los Angeles. According to him, people were running everywhere with hamburgers and tacos and pizzas in their hands, wearing curlers in their hair, dancing to rock, and going to trashy films. It made her laugh even more to think of what he would have thought of Val. She was making another horror film, and in this one she was covered in green slime, hardly his idea of what fine cinema should be. But it would be fun to see them all again too. Sometimes she thought Jason took himself too seriously, but she was enjoying their affair, and she had told the truth. She would miss him over the holidays.

'What are you going to do?' He still hadn't decided the last time they'd talked about it. She thought he should go home, but he didn't seem keen on the idea. She noticed that his parents never called, and that he rarely mentioned them. She didn't call home that often either, but she still considered herself close to all of them. As Vanessa looked up, she saw Jason smiling at her. There was a tender side of him that she really loved and she could see it now. She reached out a hand to where he sat at his desk, and he kissed it and smiled.

'I'm going to miss you too, you know. And it'll probably take me weeks to straighten you out again.'

'One of these days, you'll have to come to California with me.' But neither of them was ready for that. Her family sounded terrifying to him, and the prospect of bringing him home frightened her too. That would mean that it was serious, or so her parents would think, and it was not. It was just a lovely first affair. She expected nothing more of it than that or so she told herself. 'I'll call you, Jase.'

She repeated exactly the same words to him as they stood at the airport on December 23. He had decided not to go home, but to work on his thesis instead, which sounded like a lonely way to spend the holidays to her. But he said he'd be fine, and she promised to call every day. He kissed her long and hard before she boarded the plane, and then she was gone in the huge silver bird in the air, and he dug his hands into his pockets, and wrapped his scarf around his neck, and went back out into the cold air. It was snowing again. It frightened him to realise how much he had fallen in love with her. He had wanted it to be a casual affair, even the convenience of living in the same building appealed to him. That had nothing to do with it now. He liked everything about her; she was serious, intelligent, beautiful, kind, and wonderful in bed, and his apartment seemed like a tomb as he unlocked the door, and sat down at his desk and stared. Maybe he should have gone home after all. But it was so depressing for him. Life in their small town was so limited, and his parents always smothered him, he couldn't stand it any more. As much as he loved them, he wanted to be free. His father drank too much. His mother had become so old, he knew it would depress the hell out of him, and he was happier in New York alone. It had been almost impossible to explain to Vanessa before she left, her family was so different from his. She had actually been happy to go back. And he could hear it in her voice when she called him that night. She called almost as soon as she got off the plane.

'Well, how's Plastic Land?' He tried to sound less glum than he was and she laughed.

'Still the same. Except you're not here, and that's what's wrong with it.' She loved L.A., but now she had come to love New York too. Because of him. 'Next time you have to come out.' He almost shuddered at the thought. He couldn't face a family like that, high-powered, shiny, totally involved in the film world. He could imagine Faye cooking breakfast in gold lamé high heels, and the image of it made him laugh as he talked to Van.

'How's your twin?'

'I haven't seen her yet. I thought I'd drop by tonight. It's only eight o'clock here.'

'That's because they don't know how to tell the time,' he teased, and his face looked youthful and sad as he did. He missed her so much. The next two weeks were going to be unbearable. 'Give her my best.' They had talked to each other on the phone several times, and she sounded like fun, although totally different from Van.

'I will.'

'Let me know if she's turned green.' He had teased her merciless-ly about the green slime film, telling her that that was typical Holly-wood and probably the best they could do. Except Vanessa had taken umbrage at that. Her mother had made beautiful films in her life, and one day they'd probably be in the archives of the Museum of Modern Art too. She was still eighteen, and they were her family. He went easy on it after that. But he would have been horrified, Vanessa thought, if he could have seen the place where Val lived.

She borrowed her father's car and drove to the place Val shared with at least a dozen other girls. Vanessa thought she'd never seen such chaos and filth in her entire life. There was stale food left on plates in the living room from God knew when, and unmade beds in every room, some even without sheets; an empty tequila bottle lay on the floor; there were stockings hung in the bathroom in all shapes and hues, and everywhere hung the rancid smell of too many perfumes. In the midst of it all sat Val, happily doing her nails and telling Vanessa about her part in the film.

'And then I come out of this swamp . . . I hold out my arms like this,' she did so, almost knocking over a lamp, 'and I scream . . .' She demonstrated that too, and Vanessa covered her ears. It seemed to go on for hours, and she was actually impressed. She grinned at her twin. It was good to see her again, even here.

'You've developed quite a range with that in the last few months.'

Val laughed. 'I get plenty of practice every day.'

Vanessa looked around again. 'How do you stand this place?' Between the smell, the filth, the disorder, and the girls, Vanessa knew she would have gone mad in two days, but Valerie seemed oblivious to it all. In fact she seemed happy there, happier than she had been at home by far, and she said as much to her twin.

'I can do whatever I want here.'

'And what does that include?' Vanessa was curious about what she'd been up to the last three months. Val knew about Jason, although Vanessa hadn't gone into details about her affair, and she didn't intend to now. 'Any big new heart throbs since I left?'

Valerie shrugged. There were a number of men in her life, one she cared about, and three she was sleeping with, but she knew her sister would be shocked so she didn't say anything. It didn't mean that much to her. A little dope, a little booze, a terrific piece of ass in some boy's apartment or rented room. There was so much going on in Hollywood that it didn't seem so terrible to be a part of it, and all of them in her apartment passed the pill around like after-dinner mints. There was always an open box somewhere in the house. Someone had told her not to mix brands, but they seemed to work anyway. And if there was a slip, she could always get rid of it. She wasn't as dumb as her little sister, Anne. 'What about you?' Valerie turned the tables on her, as she started on the nails on the other hand. 'What's that guy like you're with all the time?'

'Jason?' Vanessa feigned innocence and Val laughed.

'No. King Kong. Is he cute?'

'By my standards yes, but probably not by yours.'

'That means he has a harelip and a club foot, but he's cute and you think he's serious.'

'More or less. He's working on his PhD.' Vanessa sounded proud of him and Valerie stared at her. He sounded horrible to her. She hated intellectuals, she liked all the Hollywood types, especially long hair, open shirts, the California beach-boy look.

She looked at Vanessa suspiciously. 'How old is this guy?'

'Twenty-four.'

'You think he wants to marry you?' That horrified her, but Vanessa was quick to shake her head.

'He's not that type and neither am I. I want to finish school, and come back here to write screenplays.' She and Jason argued about that all the time. He thought she had too much talent to write 'junk', but she insisted that some films were very good. 'It's just nice for now.'

'Well, watch out you don't get knocked up. Do you take the pill?' Vanessa was embarrassed by the directness of her twin, and shook her head. She hadn't even admitted that she was sleeping with him, but Val knew her better than anyone. "You're not?" Valerie was appalled at her naïveté.

'Jason takes care of it.' She blushed beet red and Valerie laughed as a girl in a red satin G-string walked through the room. And with that she glanced at Val again. 'Has Mum seen this place?' She couldn't imagine that she had, or she would have had Valerie out of it in two hours, or possibly less.

'Just once. And we cleaned it up pretty good before she came. No one was here that day.'

'Thank God. She'd have your head for this, my friend.' But that would have applied to just about anything Val was doing these days, from the little snorts of cocaine, to the pipes filled with hashish, to the men she was experimenting with, to the roles she played in horror films. As she said to Van bitterly, 'She never wants me to have any fun.' Someone had just offered her her first porno role but she had turned it down. She had been terrified her mother would hear of it. But as Vanessa drove back to the house, she had the feeling that Valerie was going bad. She was way out of control, and she was just eighteen. But she knew her well enough to know that there was no stopping her. She was rolling wildly down a hill, and it would all end somewhere. Vanessa just hoped she didn't get hurt on the way.

'How was Val!' Her father glanced at her as she came in, and read something in her eyes that she wouldn't have said to him.

'Okay.'

And then, 'Just how bad is that place?' They couldn't have known how bad it really was. But she wondered. If they knew other things. Hollywood was a small town, and if she was sleeping around, they were liable to hear of it.

'It's not that bad. Just a lot of girls running around making a mess, and leaving dirty dishes on the floor.' That was the least of it, but it was all she felt safe telling them. She tried to make it sound better than it was, for Valerie's sake. 'Just a magnified version of our rooms.'

'As bad as that?' He laughed, and reported that Greg was coming home the next day. And a little while later, Anne came in with a glow in her eyes that Vanessa had never seen before.

'Hi, kiddo.' She stood up and kissed her cheek, and she could have sworn that she smelled a man's after-shave in her hair, though she wasn't sure. Little Anne was growing up. She was about to turn sixteen after the holidays, and Vanessa noticed that she was becoming beautiful. Her dress was short, her legs were long and slim, and she was wearing beautiful little red shoes and a ribbon in her hair. Vanessa smiled at the image that had developed in three short months. She looked as old as Vanessa herself. 'When did you get so grown-up?' Ward glanced at her admiringly too. She had settled down beautifully in the last few months, and she had made new friends in her new school. Especially Gail Stein, who seemed like an awfully nice girl, even if she was a little spoiled. So what if she wore Vuitton bags and Jourdan shoes, she was a nice, decent, wholesome girl, and her father took good care of her. It was a pleasant change from the agony of what had happened in the Haight, and he and Faye were both grateful for that.

Anne didn't waste much time with them and disappeared quickly into her room. She did the same thing on Christmas Day, after they ate, but they were all used to it. Anne had been hiding in her room for years, but tonight she was packing a bag. The next day she was moving in with Bill for the holidays.

CHAPTER 32

Anne had explained to her mother weeks before that Gail had invited her to spend ten days with them until they went back to school. At first Faye had balked, but Anne had preyed cunningly on her maternal sympathies, reminding her that Gail was an only child, without even a mother to keep her company. Since her mother's death, the holidays were hard for her. That had done the trick with Faye, eventually.

'She only lives a few miles from here, Anne. Why can't you both stay here! Why do you have to sleep over at her house?'

'It's too confusing here. And you and Dad are out all the time anyway. What difference does it make?' There had been panic in her eyes and Ward saw it too. He didn't want her going wild on them again. They'd all been through enough two years before. Maybe it was better to give in to her on small things like this.

'Let her go, babe. There's no harm in it. Gail's father seems to sit on her like an egg about to hatch. They'll be fine. And she can always come home, if you want.'

'Will anyone else be there?' Faye never trusted anyone, not where her children were involved, and this time she was right.

'Just the cleaning lady and the cook.' He also had a gardener but that didn't count, she knew. And in fact, none of them did. Both women were leaving for the holidays as soon as he put Gail on a plane to her grandmother's in New York. But Faye had no way of knowing that. When Anne left the house with her small valise, it was filled with her prettiest clothes, and her frilliest nightgowns, including two new ones she had bought just for this. She called a cab after everyone left the house, and left a note, 'See you on the 3rd. I'll be at Gail's.' The cab pulled up on Charing Cross Road in Bel Air ten minutes later, and Anne felt her heart pound. He was waiting for her in the living room. Gail had left only hours before, and the maids were gone. They were finally alone. They had planned it for months, and now suddenly they were both terrified. All morning, he had asked himself if he was insane. He was practically raping a fifteen-year-old girl, and he had long since resolved to take her home as soon as she arrived.

He tried to explain it as they sat in his cosy den. There was a tiger skin on the floor, and photographs he had taken of Gail over the years hung on the walls, Gail in first grade . . . Gail in a funny hat . . . Gail eating an ice-cream cone when she was four . . . but his eyes were riveted to Anne's now, and they saw nothing in the room. She only saw him, this man she so deeply loved, who wanted to send her away now.

'Why do I have to go? . . . Why? We planned it for weeks.'

'But it's wrong, Anne. I'm an old man. You're a fifteen-year-old girl.' He had thought about it all night as he tossed and turned, and he had finally come to his senses. He wasn't going to let her change his mind now.

'I'm almost sixteen.' There were tears in her eyes, and he smiled as he smoothed her hair back from her face. But just that small touch electrified him again. This was forbidden fruit of the sweetest kind, and he mustn't let her stay even an hour, or he couldn't be responsible for what he would do. He knew himself too well. He had never felt this way for anyone – it was just one of life's cruel jokes that she was a fifteen-year-old girl. 'I'm not even a virgin, Bill.' She said it sadly with heartbroken eyes. She loved him so much; he was all she wanted in life. He was the reward for all the loneliness and pain she had had.

'That's beside the point, sweetheart. Your other experiences don't count. They were drug-induced, hallucinating dreams. You don't even have to think about them any more. That's all behind you now. It's not like making a decision to become involved with a man. This is something neither of us could handle for very long. And then what do we do? Someone would get hurt, and I don't want it to be you.' He didn't tell her that it could also be him, that he could wind up in jail for sleeping with her, if her parents found out. And they might, no matter how carefully they had planned. She had told Gail not to call her at home, that she couldn't talk anyway, with all the brothers and sisters around for the holidays.

And she was going to call Gail herself every day, so that she wouldn't have a reason to call. They had thought of everything. He was breaking her heart now: she didn't care if she got hurt, she didn't care if she died, as long as she could be with him.

She looked at him with deep, sad eyes. 'If you make me go, I'll run away again. You're all I have to live for, Bill.'

It was a terrible thing to say and it tore at his heart. She had been through so much and she was so young, and in some ways she was right, she was far more mature than most girls her age, certainly more than Gail; but she had also been exposed to more. The Haight-Ashbury, the commune, the baby she had given birth to, her difficulties with her parents. It seemed unfair to hurt her again, but this was for her own good, he told himself as he stood up, her hand gently held in his. He was going to drive her home himself – but she wouldn't move. She just sat looking at him, with that broken look, those heartrending eyes. 'Baby, please . . . you can't stay . . .'

'Why not?'

He sank down on the couch next to her. He could only fight her for so long, and if she didn't go soon . . . it wasn't fair to him . . . he was only a man after all. 'Because I love you too much.' He took her gently in his arms, and kissed her, with every intention of taking her home after that. But his iron resolve began to melt as he felt the hot molten lava of her tongue reaching into his mouth, and instinctively his hand went between her legs. They had been getting bolder and bolder for weeks now, each time they were alone. 'I want you so much, little one . . .' he whispered hoarsely into her neck, '. . . but we can't . . . please . . .'

'Yes, we can,' she whispered back. She was melting into the couch, pulling him down with her, and all his arguments began to drift away . . . maybe just this once . . . just once . . . they would never do it again . . . and then suddenly he came to his senses, and pulled away from her. His legs were shaking when he did, but he shook his head and stopped.

'No, I won't do this to you, Anne.'

'I love you with all my heart.' She looked like a stricken child.

'And so do I. I'll wait for the next two years for you, if that's what we have to do. And then I'll marry you. But I will not ruin your life.'

317

Suddenly she laughed, and it was the laugh of a very young girl as she kissed his cheek. 'I love you so much. Do you mean you'd really marry me?' She was stunned and delighted and pleased and happier than she'd been in a long time.

'I would.' He smiled gently at her. It had been a difficult hour for him, for both of them, but more so for him, and he hadn't slept all night. But he meant what he said to her now. He had thought of it before. He even thought that Gail might approve of it one day. Other men had married girls less than half their age. It wasn't the worst thing he could do. 'If you were crazy enough to marry me, that is. In two years, you'll be eighteen and I'll be fifty-one.'

'Sounds great to me,' she grinned.

'How about when you're thirty and I'm sixty-three?' He was testing her now and watching her eyes. He was serious about proposing to her. He could think of nothing else in life he wanted more, but there was no reason why they couldn't have both, his happiness and hers. He wanted to take care of her, to keep her from sorrow for the rest of her life. He sensed that her parents had done precious little for her since the day she was born, certainly less than he did for Gail. But Gail was an only child, and Anne was the last of five, and from what he had heard, she had been born into their lives at a difficult time. Still that was no excuse. He would spend the rest of his life making it up to her. Everything. Even the baby she had given up.

'That sounds fine to me.' She was responding to his second question about the difference in their ages, and she looked genuinely unimpressed. 'I can count too, you know. And when I'm sixty, you'll be ninety-three. How does that sound to *you*? You sure you won't want someone younger by then?' She was teasing him now and they both laughed as he began to relax. It had been a nightmarish morning, filled with terror and guilt, but this was more like the easy moments he had known with her before, although he had never proposed to her.

'Shall we call it definite then? We're engaged?' He smiled at her and she smiled back at him, and then leaned forward to kiss him again.

'We're engaged, and I love you with all my heart.' He kissed her so tenderly in answer to what she said that their bodies seemed to become almost one, and he had to remind himself to pull away again, though he didn't really want to any more . . . and if he was going to marry her one day . . . wouldn't it be all right now . . . just this once? . . . to seal their vow, as it were. He sat back, looking into her eyes, knowing he couldn't think straight any more.

'You make me crazy, you know.'

'I'm glad.' She looked like a woman as she said the words, and her eyes bored deep into his. 'Can I stay for a while?'

There was no harm in that. They had done that before, when Gail had other plans and the maids were off weekends. The only difference was that then they knew everyone was eventually coming back, and now they were totally alone. He offered to heat the pool so they could swim, and she thought it a fine idea. She didn't bother with a bathing suit, and dived neatly in from the diving board. He watched the smooth velvet of her flesh stretched over her long, graceful limbs. She was a beautiful girl, although no one in her family seemed to have noticed it yet. She was just 'little Anne', the quiet one who hid in her room. But she wasn't hiding now. He shed his clothes and dived in after her, and they swam like porpoises beneath the surface of the pool, and then leapt high, catching each other by the waist, and slowly he brought her to him. He couldn't stand it any more. He wanted her too much. Their bodies met and held as he caressed her back and neck and kissed her tenderly. He led her from the pool, wrapped her in a towel, and then carried her inside the house. There was nothing left to say. He couldn't fight it any more, she looked like a delicate princess as he laid her on his bed, and smiled down at her, his own body still firm, his muscles hard, his legs strong. They would have beautiful children together one day, he thought to himself, though he wasn't thinking of babies now. He was thinking only of her, as he touched every inch of her, caressing and kissing and letting his tongue dance over her, and from some distant part of her, she remembered a kind of loving she had never really known before, and she gently caressed him until he could bear it no more and their bodies joined as one. Her whole body arched with pleasure at his touch, and they seemed to dance there together for hours, sailing high into the sky, until at last they exploded like the sun.

319

CHAPTER 33

Their days together were the most idyllic either had ever known. There were no drugs this time, no hallucinogens, no rituals, no make-believe, only Bill and the tenderness and beauty he brought to her life, and the joy she brought to his. For ten days they allowed themselves to forget how difficult it would be for the next two years. They stayed within the confines of the house and grounds, but they ran and they played, they listened to music, and he gave her a glass of champagne, only one, on what he called their wedding night. They took long baths in his tub, and he read to her, and at night in front of the fire he combed her hair, and he loved her in ways she had never been loved before. It was the kind of fatherly love he had always had for Gail, enhanced now by the love he had once had for his wife and yet had no one to share with for several years. He poured his soul out to Anne, and she gave hers to him. She was happier than she had ever been in her life. She cried on their last night. She had dutifully called Gail every day, who reported that she was having fun in New York. But she had never bothered to call home. They knew she was all right, and they knew where she was. They had no idea what she was up to, but that was her secret now, and they would have to live with it for the next two years.

'What if Gail ever found out?' she asked as they lay in bed. She had hardly worn clothes for the past ten days, they made love all the time, and he seemed unable to get enough of her. He had made love more in ten days than he had in the past ten years. He sighed now, thinking of what she had asked.

'I don't know. At first, I think she'd be shocked, but I think she'll accept it in time. I think the best thing is if she doesn't find out for a year of so, she'll be older then and more mature, and

320

better able to accept what we feel.' Anne nodded, agreeing with him. She agreed with him about almost everything. 'I think the most important thing is that she know eventually that our love can be shared with her too, that it won't shut her out. I love her just as I once did. But I also love you now. I have a right to get married again one day, after all . . . it just may surprise her a little when it's one of her friends.' Anne suddenly envisaged herself in a white veil with Gail as the maid of honour, and she smiled to herself. It was a lovely dream, but it was still a long, long way off. A lot could happen in two years.

She knew that better than anyone. She had told him about Lionel and John, about their being gay, and taking her in until the baby was born, and how nice they had been . . . and John dying in the fire, and how heartbroken Li still was. It had been a year and he still wasn't the same. He lived alone, and except for work, he never went out. He took her to lunch now and then, but he was so quiet it frightened her. Bill understood what she described. He had felt that way when his wife died, but he had had Gail of course to cheer him up. He began to feel he knew everything about Anne now, all her secrets, her fears, the way she felt about Faye; she was convinced that her parents had never loved her at all, and it saddened him for her. 'We're going to have to be very careful, little one. Not just with Gail. But with everyone.'

'I know that. I've kept secrets before.' She looked mysterious and he laughed and kissed the tip of her breast, which hardened instantly.

'Not like this, I hope.'

'No,' she smiled, and a few minutes later, they made love again. He didn't even feel guilty about it any more. This was what was, and it was his, and he wouldn't lose it now. He would never give her up. He would stand by her for the rest of their life together and he promised that as he took her home the following afternoon. They both looked tired, they had stayed up all night to make love and talk, and he had to pick Gail up at the airport in two hours, and that night, the maids would be back. The fairy-tale honeymoon was over now; now they had to walk carefully, hand in hand, and into what their life would be like for the next two years. But there would be moments like this again. Holidays they could go on, stolen weekends, a night here and there. He had promised her that, and her eyes were still alight with his love as she walked in her front door, carrying her suitcase in one hand. She stopped, listening, as she heard the Rolls Royce purr as it drove off.

'You sure look tired.' Her mother glanced at her as she came in. They hadn't filmed that day. It was a Sunday afternoon and she looked at Anne's eyes. She looked happy enough though. 'Have a good time, sweetheart?'

'Mm hmm . . .'

'It was probably one long pyjama party for ten days.' Ward smiled. 'I don't know what it is about girls your age, they never want to get dressed.' She smiled and disappeared into her room without saying anything, but as Vanessa glanced at her she saw something more than her parents did, though she wasn't sure what it was. It made her uneasy about the girl, and she wanted to talk to her before she left. But there was never time. Anne went back to school the next day. There were some friends Vanessa still wanted to see, and the next night she had to pack, and then she was gone, without ever finding out what had lit Anne's eyes up like that.

CHAPTER 34

Everyone went back to their own lives, Val to her life with her horror films, a smattering of drugs, a new man in her bed whenever possible, and Vanessa back at school in New York. Greg was having trouble with his grades, but promising to pick up, and Anne didn't seem to give anyone any trouble. She spent most of her time at her friend's, but everyone was used to it by now. They never saw her any more. She had turned sixteen, and barely had a night to spare for her family to celebrate it. Gail and her father had taken her to the Bistro for a celebration with them the next day, but Faye didn't see anything wrong with it. They were awfully nice to her, and she reminded Anne to buy a gift for Gail now and then, just to show that she appreciated it.

In Febuary, Lionel called Faye at the studio and asked if he could have lunch with her and Ward. It was unusual for him to do something like that, and she hoped it meant good news in his life, like an exciting film or even a job change, or an announcement that he was going back to school. But neither of them were prepared for what he announced to them instead.

He seemed to hesitate, as though afraid to cause them pain, and Ward suddenly felt sick. Maybe he was going to tell them that he was in love with another man, and he didn't want to hear about it. But Lionel dived in quickly, there was no way to ease the words. 'I've been drafted.' They both stared. Vietnam was in full swing and it was on everyone's minds. Ward looked horrified. As much as he loved his country, he didn't want to sacrifice either of his sons for a war which stank, in a place he didn't give a damn about, and Faye's jaw almost dropped at the first thing Ward said.

'Tell them you're gay.' It was the first time he had used the word and Lionel smiled and shook his head.

'Dad, I can't.'

'Don't be shy, for chrissake. It may save your life.' This was exactly why he had told Greg to pull up his grades. All he needed was to get kicked out of school and sent to Vietnam. But Lionel had the perfect excuse. He hadn't really worried about him. 'Be sensible, boy. Either that or go to Canada.'

'I don't want to run away, Dad. It just wouldn't be right.'

'Why not, for chrissake?' He pounded the table in the commissary but no one looked. There was so much action and noise that no one noticed anyone, no matter what they wore or did or said. You could have walked in naked, screaming at the top of your lungs, and everyone would have figured you were practising for a part. But Ward was serious with him now. 'You have to get out of it, Li. I don't want you to go.'

There were tears in her eyes, as Faye listened to the two men. 'Neither do I, sweetheart.'

'I know, Mum.' He gently touched her hand. 'I'm not happy about it either, but I don't feel like I have a choice. I talked to them yesterday, and I think they know what I am, they also know my film background, and they'd want me to do something with film.' Ward and Faye both looked relieved.

'Do you know where?'

He took a breath. 'Probably in Vietnam for a year, and maybe in Europe for a year after that.'

'Oh my God.' Ward's face went white and Faye started to cry, and it was a dismal two weeks while Lionel wrapped up the details of his life, gave up the small apartment he had, left his job, and moved in with Faye and Ward for a few days before he left for boot camp. They were grateful to have the time with him and they both left work early every day. But the last night was rough. Everyone cried as they toasted him. They all stood in the doorway and waved the next day at 6 am as the cab drove away, and Faye collapsed in Ward's arms and sobbed. She was afraid she would never see him again, and as he held her, Ward cried just as hard. It was a heartbreaking time for all of them. Anne and Bill went for a long, long walk, and Anne voiced to him what her parents were afraid to say; that he had never recovered from John's death and maybe he had gone to Vietnam to let himself be killed. It was a sobering thought.

'I'm sure that's not true, sweetheart. He's just doing what he thinks he has to do. I went to war once too, you know. Not everyone gets killed. And if he's working in film, I'm sure he'll be pretty safe.' It wasn't entirely true. He knew that those boys often got hit, riding low in helicopters to get the best shots. He just prayed that her brother would be sensible, and that her assessment of his psychological state was wrong. But Ward and Faye were secretly afraid of it too.

Only Val seemed certain that he'd be fine. She was so involved in her own life, it was difficult for her to think of much else. She had just landed a part in a monster film being made outside Rome. It was an international cast and the whole thing was being dubbed, but she had no lines in it anyway. There were a number of old stars in it, all of them failing badly and long since out of work.

'Isn't that great?' She had called Vanessa to tell her she'd be coming through New York. Only for one night, but it would be fun anyway. Vanessa had invited her to stay to meet her 'friend'.

Valerie hurtled off the plane wearing a red leather skirt and purple tights, a purple fur, and suede boots that looked like neon signs. The sweater she had on was cut almost to her waist, and her hair was still the same wild mane. Suddenly as Vanessa glanced up at Jason in his subdued forest greens and charcoal grays, she coughed and wondered what she had done.

'My God, is she for real?' he whispered to Van, but her beauty was undeniable, no matter how ridiculous her clothes were, and Vanessa grinned.

'Plastic Land at its best.'

She threw herself into Vanessa's arms, kissed Jason a little too lovingly for a first time. Her perfume was too heavy and as they kissed, Vanessa could smell marijuana in her hair. They went to Greenwich Village that night, to listen to some jazz, and then came back and talked in Jason's apartment until four o'clock. He poured tequila until they ran out, and Valerie pulled out a box of joints.

'Help yourselves.' She lit one expertly as Jason watched, and he followed suit, but Vanessa hesitated. She had only tried it once before and she didn't think much of it. 'Come on, Sis, don't be a square.' Vanessa did it to be a good sport, and insisted it had had no effect, except that they all found themselves combing the yellow pages for an all-night pizza joint, and settled for emptying Louise and Van's refrigerator instead, laughing and giggling as Jason stared at Val. He couldn't get over how different she was from Van, and he was still staring at her the next day as she got back on the plane, this time in a lime-green leather suit her parents had never seen. She had borrowed a lot of her wardrobe for the trip from the girls she roomed with and no one seemed to care. No one knew what belonged to whom any more, and she was only going to be gone a few weeks, unless she got more work, once she was over there.

'Ta ta, guys. Take care of yourselves.' And then she winked at Van. 'He's okay.'

'Thanks.' The two young women kissed, and Jason waved as she boarded the plane. It was like having been hit by a cyclone for two days.

'How on earth did she wind up like that, with you the way you are?' He couldn't figure it out and Van laughed at him. He looked as though he were in shock.

'I don't know. We're all different I guess, even if we are one family.'

'Apparently.'

'Want to trade me in for Val?' She was always afraid of that. Valerie was so much more spectacular, and outrageous, with her box of joints, her loose morals, her wild red hair. She got the feeling that she would have gladly slept with Jason, if Vanessa would only have disappeared, but she knew her sister too well, and was careful of that. She had lost too many boyfriends to her over the years to ever trust her again with a man, though she didn't hold a grudge for it. It was just the way Val was, and it didn't mean anything to her.

'Not yet.' Jason looked enormously relieved to have found the quieter twin.

But he did not look relieved when Vanessa made a suggestion several months after that. Their affair had been continuing comfortably. In fact, she had moved in with him downstairs, and Louise had found another roommate in no time at all. The deal they made was that if her parents called, they would cover for her, tell them to hold on, and come downstairs and bang on the door so she could run up and talk to them. But they seldom called. And if they had come to town, Vanessa would have moved back in for a few days, but so far they hadn't come. They were too busy with their latest film. Lionel was still in Vietnam, but miraculously thus far all had gone well, and Valerie still hadn't returned from Rome. She had got another bit part once there, this time in a cowboy film, which was new for her, and she had modelled a few times in Milan, she'd said on the phone. What she didn't tell Faye was that it was without clothes.

But whatever the case, they were spread all over the world now, and the only one left in L.A. was Anne. Ward wanted to rent a house in Lake Tahoe for two weeks, and he wanted to know if Van could be there. Lionel would be on leave, Greg would be through with his summer job, Val said she'd be home from Rome by then, and Anne said she'd go if she could bring Gail. What he wanted was a commitment from Vanessa, who wanted to bring Jason along. Jason looked horrified at the thought.

'To Plastic Land? For two weeks?'

'Come on, you'll be finished with your thesis by then, and Lake Tahoe's for real. Besides, I want you to meet my family.' That was precisely what he feared. He imagined that they all looked like Val and he would be devoured by the enemy. He was a small-town boy and he had no defences against them. 'You already know Val, so they won't all be strangers to you.'

'Oh God.' He did everything to talk her out of it in the next few weeks, but she absolutely refused. She had taken a summer job in a bookstore downtown, and she bugged him about it when she came home every day. 'Isn't there something else we can talk about? Robert Kennedy's been killed, the politics in this country stink, your brother is in Vietnam. Do we have to talk about holidays now?'

'Yes.' She knew he was scared but she couldn't imagine of what. They were a harmless bunch, at least in her eyes. 'We are going to talk about it, until you agree to come.'

'Shit!' He had shouted at her because he really loved her a great deal. 'All right! I'll come!'

'Christ, was that a big deal!' It had only taken two months. When she called her parents, they were stunned. Other than Anne's little friend Gail, Vanessa was the first one to ask to bring 'someone' along.

'Who is he, sweetheart?' Faye tried to sound casual as she

frowned at her desk at MGM. She was suddenly frightened that he wasn't good enough, or didn't have Vanessa's best interests at heart. How could she know if the guy was decent or not? Vanessa was still so naïve about everything. She had run into Valerie the week before with some character who looked like a hairdresser and he had been so stoned Val was practically holding him up. She was going to have to spend some time with that girl. Ever since she'd been in Rome she had gone totally wild, and rumours were beginning to reach Faye that she didn't like at all, mostly about the people she ran around with. But she knew herself that it was almost impossible to control Val. Now she turned her mind to Vanessa again, and this mysterious friend she wanted to bring out, knowing that Vanessa's taste in men was far more sedate than Val's. She didn't even know what Ward would say, although the place he had rented was certainly big enough. There were a dozen bedrooms, and it was right on the lake. Actually, it sounded like a nice idea to her too, and it would be wonderful to have them all around again. 'Who is this boy again? Is he at Columbia with you?' She didn't want to nag, but she knew it probably sounded like it to her child.

'Not any more. He's just finishing up his Ph.D.'

'How old is this boy?' Now Faye was really upset.

'Sixty-five.' She couldn't resist teasing her mother but Faye was not laughing with her. 'Come on, Mum. Relax. He's only twenty-six. Why?'

'Isn't that a little too old for you?' She was fighting to keep her voice relaxed, but without much success.

'Not that I've noticed. He still walks pretty well. He can dance . . . ride a bike . . .'

'Stop being cute. Is it serious? Why do you want to bring him home with you? How involved are you with this man?' The questions came faster than Vanessa could answer them, and she was glad she had called when Jason was out.

'No, it's not serious. He's just a good friend' . . . I live with him, Mum . . . She would really have been thrilled at that. 'Why don't you ask Val questions like that and get off my back?' Why did she always have to take the brunt of it? They had always done that to her. They let the boys do what they wanted, they couldn't control Val, and Anne wouldn't talk to them, although she suspected that all of them had deeper secrets than hers. Greg had been banging everything in skirts for the past three years; God only knew what Val was into now; and Anne had had that secret look . . . but the heat wasn't on them, it was on her, because she was decent to them. It wasn't fair. But the gentleness of her mother's voice touched her heart, with the next question.

'Are you in love with him, sweetheart?'

Vanessa hesitated. 'I don't know. I just like him very much, and I thought he'd get along with everyone.'

'Is he your steady beau?'

Vanessa smiled at the term and they were friends again. 'More or less, I guess.'

'Well, I'll speak to your father about it, and see what he says.' But after asking fewer questions than Faye, of course, he said yes, and told Faye to relax, which was easy for him to say. She had five children to think about, and to her that's what they still were.

CHAPTER 35

They arrived at Lake Tahoe separately. Ward wanted a few days alone with Faye, and he was pleased that the house they had rented was even better than they'd hoped. There was a small tower at each end, a huge living room downstairs, a dining table that seated eighteen in a panelled room with an enormous fireplace. Upstairs there were twelve bedrooms, which was more than enough for all of them. The decor was rustic and cosy, with quilts and antlers and pewter plates everywhere. There were Indian baskets and bearskins on the floor, and it was exactly what Ward had had in mind, he noted, as he arrived with Faye. They took over what was obviously the master suite, with a huge old-fashioned bathroom and a dressing room. They sat looking out over the lake the next day, holding hands and remembering their holiday a year before in Switzerland.

Faye looked wistful thinking of it, and turned to him. 'I'd like to retire to a place like this one day.'

'My God, you?' He smiled. He couldn't imagine anything more incongruous than his beautiful, worldly, elegant wife, winner of three Academy Awards, most important female director in the world, and trend-setter of sorts, giving it all up to sit staring at a lake for the next forty years. She was only forty-eight years old after all and he just couldn't imagine it. 'You'd go stark staring mad in three days, if not two.'

'That's not true, sweetheart. One of these days I'm going to surprise you and give it all up.' There was so little left that she hadn't done, that she still wanted to do. More and more often now she thought that she might like to give it all up. She had been directing films for more than fifteen years and that was almost long enough. He was surprised at how serious she looked.

'You're too young to retire, babe. What would you do?'

She smiled at him and nuzzled his neck. 'Stay in bed with you all day.'

'Sounds good to me. Maybe you *should* retire if that's what you have in mind.' He smiled, thinking of the next two weeks they had ahead of them. 'Think you can survive two weeks with our brood?' He was looking forward to it, especially to spending some time with Lionel and Greg. It had been years since he'd been outdoors with his sons, and he was relieved to know that Lionel was surviving Vietnam. There were tears in his eyes, as Li hopped out of his rented car two days after that. He was the first to arrive, and Ward embraced him with both arms. 'My God, you look tall and tanned, boy.' He looked wonderful to him. And he seemed to have grown up overnight. At almost twenty-two he looked five or six years older than that, and Ward couldn't help noticing that he didn't look gay at all. He wondered if maybe he had changed his mind, but that was too much to ask and when he hinted around at it later that night, Lionel laughed at him. It was the first time they had talked as friends in years. But Ward respected the films he was making in Vietnam, and the constant danger he was in.

'No, Dad.' He said it very gently, with kind eyes. 'I haven't "changed my mind".' Ward looked embarrassed and Lionel smiled. 'It doesn't work that way. But there hasn't been anyone since John if that's what you mean.' His face sobered thinking of his lost love. It had been a year and a half, and he still missed him terribly. In some ways, it was easier being in Vietnam. He didn't have to see the places where they had once been. It was a whole new life. And Ward could see how painful it still was for him.

They had a pleasant day and a half before the others began to arrive. First, Jason and Vanessa from New York. They flew to Reno and rented a car, reaching the house in the late afternoon. Vanessa got out and stretched, and Jason looked around, surprised at how beautiful it was. As Lionel came across the lawn to them, Jason was surprised. He spotted instantly what Van's brother was, and he wondered why she hadn't told him he was gay.

'Hello.' He had warm eyes, and he looked a little bit like Van. 'I'm Lionel Thayer.'

'Jason Stuart.' The two men shook hands, commenting on how

pretty the place was. There was a spectacular view of the lake, and a moment later, Faye and Ward came up from the beach in bathing suits. He with a fishing pole but no visible results and Faye teasing him all the way, in a black maillot that set off her still-beautiful shape. Now he could see where the real resemblance was. Lionel looked exactly like Faye. And although Jason wouldn't have admitted it to Van, it was impressive meeting her. She was beautiful and intelligent, and her eyes danced with a million ideas. She made everyone laugh, and she had a deep sexy voice. He thought she was one of the most interesting women he'd ever met, as they sat deep in conversation that night. She was quizzing him about his thesis, his plans, his ideas, and he suddenly realised how difficult it must have been to have grown up with her. She was so damn beautiful, and so bright, it would have been impossible to compete with her. It explained to him now why Vanessa was so quiet and subdued and her twin sister so wild. Van had obviously chosen not to compete at all, but to lead her own quiet life, and Val was still fighting every inch of the way, but in a way that ensured she would never win. She was trying to be more spectacular, more beautiful; she was trying to beat her at her own game, and she could only lose at that. Lionel had gone into film, but in a totally different vein, and he was curious to meet the other two now. Greg arrived next, talking constantly of playing ball, drinking beer, chasing girls. It was almost exhausting to be in the same room with him, but whenever Jason watched Ward talk to him, he saw his eyes light up. This was his adored son, his hero, his jock. And he could only begin to imagine the pain it must have caused Lionel for most of his life. He attempted to talk to Greg once or twice, the day he arrived, but he had nothing much to say, and he always seemed to have something else on his mind.

And then finally Val arrived with Anne. She had stayed in town as long as she could, and agreed to drive her sister up, although she wasn't in the mood to leave town just then. There was a new horror film being cast, and she didn't want to get passed up. But she couldn't do everything, and she knew there would be another one being cast in two weeks. They were practically a speciality with her now, and she didn't care how much her friends made fun of her. She was working almost all the time, and she was making regular money.

'Come on,' everyone teased once they'd all arrived. Lionel turned off the lights in the living room, 'Let's hear it, Val, the famous Valerie Thayer scream.' She had done dozens of them now, and everyone begged as she laughed, and then finally, standing up in the dark, near the fire, she began to clutch her throat, made a hideous face, and let out a long piercing scream. It was so convincing that they all watched her, horrified, thinking she was choking at first, and then realising what she had done. She was doing it for them, and she seemed to go on for hours and then suddenly, collapsed in a heap. The audience was thrilled and they clapped and cheered, Jason loudest of all. He and Van had gone canoeing with her that afternoon, and she'd been funny as hell. He was rapidly becoming one of her most ardent fans. And to prove that it was mutual, she had calmly handed him a frog on the way back to the house. He had jumped, Van had screamed, and Val had accused them both of being ridiculous.

'Hell, I worked with two hundred of them at once on the film I did in Rome.' Then suddenly all three of them started to laugh, and they raced each other back to the house. It was like being kids again. Lionel, Ward, and Greg had gone off fishing somewhere that day, and returned with several which they tried to convince Faye to cook, but she told them it was their treat instead. Lionel thought that Greg was a little quiet, and he wondered if there was anything on his mind. But all in all, everyone was having fun. Faye had spent a quiet afternoon, lying on the beach with Anne. Anne hadn't wanted to go canoeing with Jason and the twins, or fishing with the boys, and Faye wasn't even sure she wanted to lie on the beach with her. But she had nothing else to do, so she stuck around, and read a book. In the end, her friend Gail had decided not to come along. She didn't want to intrude on their family reunion, and had gone to San Francisco with her father instead, which left Anne felling lonely again. She wrote a letter, and went quietly into the house at one point, and Faye had glimpsed her on the phone. Faye suspected that she was just at the age when she didn't want to leave her friends, and she wasn't thrilled about the trip, but it was doing them all good. By the second week, they were all relaxed and brown. Ward and Jason were great friends, the twins hadn't enjoyed each other as much in years, and Greg seemed to have relaxed finally. Even Anne was having fun, and she went on a long walk with Vanessa one day, when Jason had driven Faye into town. Vanessa glanced at her, thinking again how grown up she looked now. She was sixteen and a half, but her experiences seemed to have matured her far more than her years.

'I like your friend.' She said it quietly, and Van was reminded of how withdrawn she had always been.

'Jason? So do I. He's a nice guy.'

'I think he likes you a lot too.' They both nodded. It was obvious that he did, and that he even enjoyed her family now. He had been so frightened of what they would all do to him. He had finally confessed that he thought it would be like being in a line-up, or being interrogated by each of them, and instead they all had foibles and weird traits of their own. He liked them all, even shy little Anne, who was looking at her big sister curiously now. 'Think you'll marry him?' Vanessa knew that everyone was wondering that, but she was only nineteen and she didn't want to think about that now. Not for several years.

'We never talk about it.'

'Why not?' Anne looked surprised.

'I still have a lot to do. I want to finish school . . . do my own thing . . . try to write. . .'

'That could all take years.'

'I'm not in a rush.'

'I'll bet he is though. He's a lot older than you. Does that bother you, Van?' She wondered what her sister would think of the thirty-years between her and Bill. Their difference was nothing compared to that.

'Sometimes. Why?'

'Just curious.' They had sat down on a rock, and were dangling their feet in a stream. Anne was staring into the water, dreamy-eyed, and Vanessa saw something in her eyes that made her wonder what went on the younger girl's head. They were only three years apart, but sometimes it felt more like ten, and it felt as though Anne were the older of the two, almost as if she had lived too much and felt too much pain. She turned to Vanessa then as though reading her thoughts. 'I'd marry him if I were you, Van.' She looked old and wise and Vanessa smiled.

'Why?'

'Because you may not find one as nice as him again. A good man is worth anything.'

'Is that what you think?' Vanessa looked at her, seeing something unreadable in her eyes again, and she suddenly sensed that there was a man in her life, possibly an important one. It was hard to tell with Anne. She gave so little away, but there was something there that was more than any young girl knew, and she turned her face away, as though to keep Vanessa from seeing what was there. 'What about you? Anyone special in your life?' She tried to keep her voice light and sound casual, but Anne instantly shrugged, almost too fast.

'No, nothing much.'

'No one at all?'

'Nope.'

Van knew she lied but there was nothing she could say, and eventually they put their sneakers back on and walked back. That night she said something to Li; he knew her so well.

'I think Anne is involved with someone.'

'What makes you say that?' He wasn't in touch with her doings any more. He had been in Vietnam for six months by then, and she didn't confide in him now.

'Just a feeling . . . I can't tell you why . . . but she looks different . . .' She couldn't put her finger on it and her brother laughed, and looked into her eyes instead.

'What about you, Sis? How serious is your attachment to this guy?' She wondered if they would all ask her before they left, and she grinned.

'Relax. Anne asked me the same thing today. I told her it's just for now.' She was being mostly honest with him. How could she know now what the future would bring?

'Too bad. I think he's nice.'

She looked at him and grinned, teasing him for the first time in years. 'You can't have him, he's mine.'

He snapped his fingers and grinned. 'Aw shit.'

Greg came up behind them just then, and looked from Lionel to Van. 'What's this all about?' But Vanessa didn't explain it to him. She just said something nonchalant, and went off to find her much-talked-about, apparently popular friend. She found him with Val, who was teasing him mercilessly about how straight he was. Ward and Faye were sitting on the porch drinking wine, and Anne was probably somewhere, inside, on the phone, calling a friend again.

'Probably Gail.' Her mother smiled at Ward, and he shrugged. All was well. There was no need to pry. They were seeing plenty of all of them, and he was happy to say he liked them all. Not all of them were turning out the way he'd planned. He'd had other hopes for Lionel, of course, and he would have liked to see Val going to school instead of learning how to scream, but Anne was back on the right track, Vanessa was certainly doing well, and Greg was their star of course. Although less than Ward thought, as he was admitting to Lionel at that particular point, down near the beach, as they sat on a log, watching the sun go down. Lionel had finally discovered what Greg had been worrying about ever since they'd arrived. It had spilled out like a hundred dollars' worth of groceries from a torn paper bag.

'I just don't know what to tell Dad, Li . . . if I get kicked off the team . . .' He closed his eyes, unable to finish the thought, but Lionel's face looked grim. It would be a terrible disappointment to Ward, but there was more to it than that, as he knew only too well. He saw boys like Greg every day, lying dead on the ground, their guts spilling through bullet wounds as his camera whirred.

'What the hell did you do a dumb thing like that for?' They had caught him smoking dope in the spring, and benched him, unbeknownst to Ward, who thought he'd hurt his foot. But his grades were so bad that there was a possibility they might not even let him back on the team.

'Christ, they could even throw me out of school if they wanted to.' There were tears in his eyes, but it felt good to talk about it at last. It had been killing him for weeks.

Without thinking, Lionel grabbed his arm and looked intensely in his eyes. 'You can't let that happen. You've got to go back and work your ass off to get those grades up. Hire a tutor if you have to, do anything . . .' He knew what he spoke of, though Greg had no idea of what was out there. But he was scared anyway.

Greg looked at him in utter despair. 'I may have to cheat.'

Lionel groaned and shook his head. 'No, you dumb ass.' It was like being kids again, and at least the confidence felt good now.

They had never really been friends, not in years, not since they had begun to grow up and Lionel had sensed the difference in himself. And certainly not since Greg had known the truth about him. But funnily enough, Lionel had been the one he had come to know. He had wanted to talk to him for days. He didn't know Jason well enough, and he couldn't tell his Dad, but he had to tell someone what was happening to him. Lionel was glaring at him furiously now. 'If you cheat, you asshole, they'll throw you out for sure. You have to do everything by the books. Because if you don't, and they throw you out, they're going to grab you up so fast for Vietnam that your head will spin. You're exactly what they want. Young, healthy, strong, and dumb.'

'Thanks.'

'I mean that. And when I say dumb, I mean a lot of things. I mean you're not old enough to be out there in the jungle worrying about your wife and kids. You'll just watch your buddies die and want to go out there and kill Charlie Cong. And you're healthy and young . . .' Lionel's eyes filled with tears. 'I watch kids like you die out there every day.' He hated to go back, but in a few weeks he would have to, and Greg looked at him now with new respect. He was surviving it somehow, and he had become a man, if you could call it that. He was still confused about why Lionel was the way he was, but he listened to him now. He knew he was right, and he was scared to death.

'I've got to get back on that team.'

'Just keep your grades up so they don't throw you out of school.'

'I'll try, Li. I swear.'

'Good.' He ruffled his hair as he had when they were kids, and the two brothers smiled as the sun went down. Greg put an arm around Lionel's shoulders, and it reminded them of their days at camp.

'I hated you then,' Greg said and they both laughed at the memories. 'And I really hated Val and Van.' He started to laugh then. 'I guess I hated everyone. I was jealous of all of you. I wanted to be an only child.'

'You were in some ways. You were always the closest to Dad.' Greg nodded, not denying it. 'But I didn't realise it then.' It impressed Greg that Lionel was so philosophical about that. In recent years, that closeness to Ward sometimes embarrassed him, and he quickly changed the subject now. 'At least I never hated Anne.'

Lionel smiled. 'None of us did. She was too little to hate.' But she wasn't little now. She was all grown up, or almost.

Anne had just hung up the phone from talking to Bill again. It was agony being without him, and she called him collect three or four times a day. Everyone had noticed it, but they all thought she was calling Gail. Only Vanessa continued to think Anne was involved with a man, but there was no way to find out, she wasn't telling anyone.

On the whole, they had all had a wonderful time, and on the last night, Valerie sat on the floor next to her door, lying in wait for Jason and Van. Every night, she had heard Vanessa scurrying down the hall to him, and tonight when she heard the patter of feet scampering past, she waited two minutes and then ran and knocked on Jason's door. She could hear a giggle, then a gasp, and then Jason's baritone said, 'Come in.' She stepped inside, and advanced on him with an amorous air, and as he stared at her in surprise, she pounced on the bed, almost killing her twin, who screamed. And then suddenly, they knew she was teasing them, and everyone laughed, and they talked long into the night. Eventually, they went to find Lionel and Greg and everyone went downstairs to raid the ice box and drink beer. It was the perfect end to a perfect holiday and as they all went their separate ways the next day, they took with them the memory of what fun it had been.

CHAPTER 36

Much to her amazement, Vanessa was able to convince Jason to spend a few days in L.A. Having met her family already, and come to know them fairly well, he had nothing to fear from them, and he was curious to see the place he had maligned for so long. He only agreed to stay for two days, and Valerie saw to it that he had a wonderful time. She took them everywhere, to every studio, every party, every 'in' restaurant, every set. Vanessa had never seen as much of Hollywood in her life as she did in those two days.

Faye and Ward were already back at work on the packaging of a new film, and Anne disappeared into her own life. Lionel flew back to Vietnam, via Hawaii and Guam. After two days, Jason and Vanessa flew back to New York, and everyone picked up the threads of their real lives again.

Vanessa went back to Columbia for her sophomore year, and Greg to Alabama for what should have been his senior year. But it didn't last long. As soon as he returned he knew he was off the team, and after staying drunk for a week to recover from the blow, he missed two important make-up exams he had left over from the previous term. By October 15, he'd been called in to see the dean. He was being 'invited to leave'. They were sorry to see it happen to such a fine boy. They suggested he go home and think about it for the rest of the school year, and if he was ready to settle down after that, they would be happy to see him come back. But six weeks after that, coming home with his tail between his legs, and seeing heartbreak in Ward's eyes, he found the army had a different invitation for him. He was being drafted.

He sat home, all one afternoon, stupefied, and was still sitting there when Anne arrived. She came home later and later now, always going after school with Gail to do homework at her house, and then Bill would drive her home when he got in from work. It gave them a few minutes alone, and was a routine she counted on. Generally, when she came back to the Thayer house at night, there was no one there except the maid anyway. But since Greg had come home, things had changed a bit.

She let herself in with her key, and saw him sitting there looking as though someone had died. She stopped and stared at him. She was tall and beautiful and grown up now, but he didn't notice that. He simply looked at her unseeingly.

'What happened to you?' She had never been close to him, but she was sorry he'd been kicked out of school. She knew how much the football team meant to him, and he'd been depressed ever since he got back, but he looked worse today, and something major had to be wrong.

He raised frightened eyes to her. 'I got my draft notice today.'

'Oh no . . .' She sat down across from him, realising instantly what it meant. It was bad enough having Li there. They were still sitting there talking about it, when Ward and Faye walked in. It was early for them and they were in a good mood. Things were going well and the cast was taking shape beautifully. Ward stopped and looked at them as soon as he walked in the door. He could see instantly on Greg's face that something was wrong and he was afraid that it was Lionel.

'Bad news?' He said the words as fast as he could, so they could answer him just as fast.

Greg nodded his head. 'Yeah.' He handed the notice to him wordlessly, and reading it, Ward sank into a chair. A moment later he handed it to Faye. All they wanted was for Lionel to end his tour there, but now they would have Greg to worry about too. It didn't seem fair to have both of them there.

Faye looked at Ward. 'Isn't there some kind of law against that?' Ward shook his head and looked back at Greg. It said he had to report in three days. They certainly weren't wasting any time, and it was already December 1. He thought of Canada again. But it seemed wrong with Lionel there. As though Vietnam were good enough for him to risk his life, but not for Greg. It was clear that he had to go.

He reported to Fort Ord just as the paper said, on December 4, and was sent to Fort Benning, Georgia, for basic training for six weeks. They didn't even let him come home for Christmas Eve, and it was a bleak holiday this year. Val had gone to Mexico with a group of friends; Vanessa had gone to New Hampshire with Jason finally; Greg was in basic training; Lionel in Vietnam; and Anne straining to run out of the door. She had made the same arrangement with Bill this year, and in a few weeks she would turn seventeen with only one more year to go, they told each other constantly.

Greg was shipped out on January 28, and sent straight to Saigon, and from there he went to Bien Hoa Air Base north of Saigon. He didn't even have a chance to touch base with Lionel, who had only three more weeks to serve there. He was being sent to Germany after that, and he could hardly wait. He'd had enough of that stinking war to last a lifetime – if he survived. Too damn many men he knew were killed the day before they went home. He was holding his breath until the plane touched down in Los Angeles and not before. But he also knew that Greg was in Vietnam, and he tried several times to contact him, to no avail. His C.O. had lost no time at all, sending all the fresh recruits to combat areas the day they arrived at Bien Hoa. It was a hell of a welcome to Vietnam.

And he stayed there for exactly two weeks. On February 13 the Army I Corps staged several actions and rocket attacks against the Viet Cong, destroying two villages, and taking prisoners for several nights. Greg had his first taste of blood and death and victory. The best friend he'd made in basic was shot in the gut, but the doctors said he'd be all right. The only good thing about it was that he'd be going home. Dozens of other boys died, seven disappeared, which frightened everyone, and Greg himself had the opportunity to shoot two old women and a dog, which he found both frightening and exhilarating, like running across the goal line with the ball in your arms. And then at 5 am, with the jungle rustling to life, and birds hooting and cackling all around, Greg was sent ahead with a party of other men, and he stepped on a mine. There wasn't even a body to reclaim after that. He disappeared in a cloud of blood as his buddies watched and most of them were wearing him as they headed back to camp. They staggered in, two of them badly maimed, all of them in shock. The news reached Lionel later that day. He sat staring blankly at the words on the paper someone had handed him. Regret. Gregory

Ward Thayer was killed by a mine today. Killed in action. And then only the name of the C.O. A ripple went down his spine, as it had as he looked down at John's face outside their charred apartment when the fire engines had arrived. He had never loved Greg as he'd loved John. He would never love anyone like that again. But he and Greg were brothers, and now suddenly he was gone. He thought of his father's pain too when he would hear the news, and suddenly a shaft of agony pierced through him.

'Sonofabitch.' He screamed the words outside his hotel, and then he leaned against the wall and cried, until someone came and peeled him away. He was a good guy, even though people knew what he was. But he didn't bother anyone. They felt sorry for him now. They all knew that his brother had been killed that day. Someone had seen the telegram from the front lines, and news travelled fast in Saigon. Everyone knew everything that was happening. Two boys sat up all night with Lionel, watching him drink and cry. And the next morning, they put him on the plane. He had survived a year in Vietnam, made more than four hundred short films to show in the States, many of them on the news all over the world. And his brother had only lived nineteen days. It wasn't fair – but nothing about the place was, not the rats or the disease or the wounded children screaming everywhere.

Lionel stepped off the plane in L.A. looking shell-shocked. He would never see his brother again. He had a three-week leave before going to Germany. Someone drove him home, he remembered later on. He felt the way he had when John had died, and that was only two years before . . . twenty-six months in fact . . . he had the same terrible numb feeling now.

He rang the doorbell because he no longer had a key, and his father stood there staring at him. They had got the news the night before. Everyone was there, except Vanessa, who was flying home that afternoon.

There would be no burial, because they weren't sending him home. There was nothing to send, except their fucking telegrams. And Lionel stood staring at Ward, as the older man let out a groan of agony. The two men fell into each other's arms, partly out of relief that Lionel was still alive, and the grief that Greg was gone. Eventually, Ward led him inside, and together they cried for a long time. Lionel held him in his arms like a little child, as Ward keened for the boy he'd loved so much, the boy he'd pinned all his hopes on, their football star. Now he was gone and there was nothing to send home. Nothing at all. They had only their memories.

They moved like wooden people for the next few days. Lionel was vaguely aware that Van was there and Val was staying with them, Anne . . . but no Greg . . . there would never be a Greg again. There were only four of them now.

They had a memorial service for him, at First Presbyterian Church of Hollywood. All his high school teachers came. Ward sat thinking bitterly that if those bastards in Alabama had let him stay on the team, or at least kept him in school, he would still be alive. But hating them didn't help anything. It was Greg's own fault for flunking out. But whose fault was it that he'd been killed? It had to be someone's fault, didn't it? The minister's voice droned on, saying his name, and none of it seemed real. Afterwards, they all stood outside, shaking people's hands. It was hard to believe that Greg was gone, that they would never see him again. Ward glanced at Lionel a thousand times, as though to be sure he was still there. And the girls were there too. But it would never be the same again. One of them was gone. For eternity.

CHAPTER 37

A few days after the memorial service, Vanessa went back to New York, and Val moved back to her own place again. Lionel spent most of his time alone in the house. His parents and Anne were never there. They were at work, she was in school, and he felt a hideous magnetic attraction for Greg's room. He remembered the days when he and John had been friends, and now they were both gone . . . together again somewhere. It all seemed so unfair, and he wanted to scream all the time.

A couple of times he went out for a drive, just to get some air. His old Mustang was still at the house. He had left it there when he went to Vietnam. Greg's car was there too, but he didn't want to drive it now. It was sacred, and just looking at it hurt his soul.

He took the red Mustang out one afternoon, a week before he was due to leave for Germany, and he decided to stop for a hamburger before he went home. It seemed like the first time he'd been hungry in weeks, and as he parked the car and walked inside, he noticed a two-tone grey Rolls Royce and thought that he had already seen it somewhere, but he wasn't sure where, and he wasn't really interested. He sat down at the counter and ordered a hamburger and a Coke, then glanced in the mirror ahead of him, and as he did he sat up straight. Behind him, reflected in the mirror that he faced, was his youngest sister with a much older man. They were holding hands and they had just kissed. She was drinking a milkshake, and he looked as though he were teasing her. They were laughing and then he saw them kiss again. He was horrified, the man looked as old as Ward. He wanted a better look, but he was afraid to turn around. Then suddenly he remembered who he was. It was the father of her friend . . . what was her name? . . . Sally? . . . Jane? . . . Gail! That was it!

As the couple left, the older man had an arm around the girl and they kissed once more, outside, without ever noticing him. The couple sat in the car for a long time, and Lionel could see their lips meet again, and finally they drove off. He stared, his hamburger forgotten, his appetite gone. He left his money on the counter, and drove home rapidly. When he got there, she was upstairs, the door to her room closed, and Faye and Ward had just got home. Lionel looked as though he had just seen a ghost, but none of them looked very well these days; they were all still mourning Greg. Ward looked and felt like an old man suddenly. At fifty-two, one of his brightest hopes was gone, and Faye looked tired and pale. But Lionel looked worse than either of them. Faye noticed it as he entered. He was fighting with himself about whether to tell them or not. They had enough on their minds, but he didn't want her getting into trouble again. They had all been through that once before, especially Anne, and she didn't need that again.

'Is something wrong, sweetheart?' Faye asked him gently as he sat down in the den. But everything was these days. Ward glanced at him despairingly, and Lionel decided it was unfair to say anything. He would talk to her himself first . . . but what if she ran away again? This time he couldn't stay to help them out. He couldn't spend five months looking for her with John. There was no time to waste. He sighed deeply and sat back in the chair, looking at them both, and then got up and closed the door. When he turned around and faced them again, they could both see that something was wrong. 'What is it, Li?' Faye looked at him with frightened eyes. Had one of them got hurt? Vanessa in New York? . . . Val on a set? . . . Anne? . . .

He decided to come right to the point. 'It's Anne. I saw her this afternoon . . . with a friend of hers . . .' His heart turned over as he thought of it. He was older than Ward. And he could just imagine what he'd been doing to her.

'Gail?' Faye looked even more nervous now. They hadn't monitored the friendship much. She seemed all right, and her father seemed very nice too, and the girls went to the same school. But Lionel totally stunned her with his next words.

'Not Gail, her father, Mum. They were at a hamburger joint where I went, kissing and holding hands.' Ward looked as though he'd been punched. He couldn't take much more now. And Faye stared at him in disbelief.

'But that can't be. Are you sure it was Anne?' He nodded slowly. There had been no question of it. 'But how is that possible?'

'Maybe you should ask her that.'

Faye's heart almost stopped, thinking of all the times she had stayed there, and they had never questioned it. What if Gail hadn't even been there? Or worse yet, if she had . . . if the man was really sick . . . Faye began to cry. They couldn't go through any more, and most particularly not with her. God only knew what her involvement was with this man. Faye jumped instantly to her feet. 'I'm going to get her down here right now.' But Ward reached out and touched her arm.

'Maybe we should all calm down first. It could all be a big mistake. Maybe Lionel misinterpreted what he saw.' He looked apologetically at his son, but he didn't want it to be true. He couldn't handle another tragedy, and God only knew what the child was into now. She was seventeen now. It would be harder to control her than it was at fourteen, and that had been hard enough.

Faye turned to her husband with a determined look. 'I think we should talk to her.'

'Fine. Then talk to her, but don't accuse.' Faye had the best possible intentions when she knocked on Anne's door, but the moment Anne saw her face, she knew that disaster had struck, and when she followed her mother downstairs to the den, she was stunned when she saw her brother there.

'Hello, Li.' But there was nothing friendly about them, or even about him. He nodded at her, and Ward was quick to take the floor.

'Anne, we'll get right to the point. No one's accusing you, but we want to know what's going on. For your own sake of course.' A premonition of disaster gnawed at her, but she held firm, and her eyes gave nothing away. She just searched their faces. She couldn't believe that even if Lionel had seen anything, he would actually betray her, but she was wrong. To her mind, he had. She would never forgive him, she told herself afterwards. 'Your brother thinks he may have seen you somewhere today. You may not even have been there, sweetheart,' and in his heart of hearts, he was begging her not to have been. He didn't want to have to deal with it, to face some man his own age, and accuse him of rape, which was what it was with a seventeen-year-old girl. 'It was a hamburger place.' He turned to Lionel. 'Where was it, son?' Lionel filled in the address and Anne felt her heart stop. 'But the important thing is that he thought he saw you with a man.'

'So? Gail's father took me for a milk shake on the way home.' She turned on Lionel angrily, and she looked beautiful when she did. This was no child any more. She was a woman now. Lionel was singularly aware of it that afternoon. It explained everything for the past year, why she had adjusted so well to her new school, why she was never at home. 'You have a filthy mind.' She spat the words at him.

'You were kissing him.'

She stared furiously at the boy who had once saved her life. 'Then at least I'm not gay.' It was a vicious thing to say, but he didn't give a damn. Without saying a word, he reached out and grabbed her arm, as her parents watched horrified.

'He's thirty years older than you, Anne.'

'Thirty-three to be exact.' Her eyes blazed. To hell with all of them. They couldn't do anything to her now. It was too late. She belonged to Bill. She always would. And she turned on all of them now. 'And I don't give a damn what any of you think. Not one of you has been decent to me over the years,' she hesitated for only an instant, glancing at Li, 'except you, but that was a long time ago. But you,' she glared at her parents hatefully, 'you've never been here for me. He's been there for me more in the last two years than you ever were, with your films, and your business deals, and your romance with each other and your friends. You never even knew who I was . . . and neither did I. Well, I do now, and I have since I met Bill and Gail.'

'Is it a *ménage à trois*?' Lionel was prepared to be just as vicious with her, as their parents looked on.

'No, it's not, as a matter of fact. Gail doesn't even know.'

'Thank God for that. You're a fool, Anne. You're an old man's tart. It's no different from what you did in the Haight, except for the hallucinogens. You're an old man's whore.' There had been an older man there too, Moon. She remembered him still. But this was nothing like that. She struck out at her brother, freed her arm and swung at him, but he stopped it before it reached his face.

Suddenly Ward and Faye were on their feet as one, and Faye was shouting at them.

'Stop! This is disgusting. For chrissake, stop it, both of you!'

'What are you going to do about her, Mum?' Lionel was furious. She had fucked up her life again. Why did she keep doing that? But she was adamant.

'You can all go screw yourselves. I'll be eighteen years old in ten months, and there isn't a damn thing you can do to me then. You can torture me all you want now, you can even keep me from seeing him. But in ten months, mark my words, I'll be married to him.'

'You're out of your mind if you think he'll marry you. All you are is a piece of ass to him.' The funny thing was that it felt good to shout at her, as though he could shout at the fates that had killed Greg and John. At least he could let some of the feelings out now, and besides, he was furious with her.

'You don't know Bill Stein.' Anne said the words in a calm measured way, as Faye watched her face, and suddenly she was afraid. She was serious about this man, and Faye couldn't help asking her.

'You're not pregnant again, are you?'

She looked at her with hatred. 'No, I'm not. I learned that lesson once. The hard way.' No one disagreed with her. And now Ward came forward with a set face and a frown.

'I just want you to know that in ten months or ten years, you are not marrying this man. I am calling my lawyer, and the police tonight, and I'm bringing charges against him.'

'For what? Loving me?' She looked at her father derisively. She had no respect for either of them. They had done nothing for her, and she knew she meant nothing to them. Maybe they were just angry that someone did love her, she told herself. But her father went on to explain his plans.

'It is statutory rape to have sexual intercourse with a girl your age, Anne.' Her father's voice was cold. 'He can go to prison for that.'

'I'll testify against all of you.' She looked panicked now.

'It won't change anything.'

She was suddenly frightened for him. What if he was right? Why had Bill never said that to her? She had to protect him now. She looked at her father desperately. 'Do anything you want to me, but don't hurt him.' The words struck Faye like a blow, she cared enough about this man to sacrifice herself. It was frightening that she loved him so much, and what if they were wrong? But they couldn't be. He had obviously taken gross advantage of her. But Faye looked at Ward.

'Why don't we talk to him first, and see what he says. If he promises never to see her again, maybe it would be simpler not take any legal action against him.' Ward was difficult to convince, but eventually Faye got through to him. They forced Anne to call, and demand that he come over immediately. She had to tell him why, and he could hear her crying on the phone.

He entered the Thayer house, to find a kangaroo court waiting for him. Ward let him in and he had to control himself not to attack him then and there. Lionel was standing by. Bill recognised all the players in the piece, especially Faye. He had come alone, and he faced Anne sobbing hysterically across the room. Instantly, he went to her, smoothed her hair, dried her cheeks, and then realised that they were all staring at him.

He had no excuses to make. He admitted it all. He sympathised totally with Ward, and told him he had a daughter the same age, but he also tried to tell them some things about Anne, about how lonely she had been, how marked by giving up her child, how guilty over what had happened in the Haight-Ashbury. He explained how her earliest memories of their seeming indifference went back to when she was a tiny child, and she had felt rejected by all of them all her life. He made no excuses for himself, but he explained to them who Anne Thayer was, and her parents sat there, realising what a stranger she had been to them. This unknown child, who had come to reject them eventually too, had found Bill Stein, and sought everything from him, and in his own loneliness he had nurtured her. Perhaps it was wrong, he admitted with damp eyes, but it was sincere. He echoed exactly what Anne had said to them, though in a kindlier tone. In less than a year, he planned to marry her, with or without their consent, or even Gail's, once she found out. He would have preferred everyone to wish them well, but this had gone on long enough, and if he could have married her sooner, he would. She could continue school, she could do anything she wanted to, but when her eighteenth birthday came, he would be waiting for her, whether they would continue to let him see her now or not.

As he quietly said the words, she sat there and beamed at him. He hadn't let her down, and he was willing to risk anything for her. He was exactly what she had always believed him to be, and the three other Thayers were shocked, most of all Ward, who stared at this unexciting-looking man and couldn't understand what his daughter saw in him. He wasn't beautiful or young, handsome or debonair. He was actually rather banal, and his looks were very plain. But he had offered something to their child that they had never been able to give her. Whether they wanted to see it or not, she was happy with him. She sat there now, blooming quietly in the sunlight of his love. They really didn't care what was done to them in the next year. Both were willing to wait, and after that it was clear what their plans were. Suddenly both Ward and Faye believed they would. One couldn't fight them at all, no matter how wrong it might be, or how great the age difference, or how big a fool they thought Anne was.

After he left, and they had lectured Anne, Ward and Faye talked quietly in their room. They didn't know what to make of him, and they had told her they didn't know if there would be charges or not. Bill had gone home to make a clean breast of it with Gail, and would be happy to speak to them at any time. He wasn't really apologetic with them. After two years of loving her, he felt he had relatively little to apologise for. He hadn't hurt her or abandoned her, used her, or done anything terribly wrong. By now she was almost eighteen, and it didn't seem shocking to be lovers any more. He suspected Gail would be stunned at first, but she would get over it too. And they had their lives to lead, Anne and Bill. Both had made that perfectly clear to everyone.

'What do you think?' Faye sat in a chair and looked at Ward. He still couldn't see what she saw in the man, and she was only seventeen years old. It was mind boggling.

'I think she's a damn fool.'

Faye sighed. This was worse than some of the films she'd done. 'So do I, but that's our opinion, not hers.'

'Apparently.' He sat down across from his wife, and took her hand. 'How do they get themselves into these things? Lionel with his damn inclinations to something I don't understand, Val with her crazy career, Vanessa living with that boy in New York, and thinking we don't know about it.' Faye smiled, they had talked about it before. She thought she was so exotic and unusual, and it was so transparent, they all knew what was going on, but they didn't really mind. She was twenty-years old and he was a nice boy. 'And now Anne with this man ... Good God, Faye, he's thirty-three years older than she is.' It still wouldn't sink in.

'I know. And he isn't even beautiful.' Faye smiled. 'If it was someone who looked like you, I'd understand at least.' At fifty-two he was still as handsome as he had been twenty years before, though in a different way. He was still long and lean and elegant, as was she. This man had none of that. It was difficult to see his appeal, except that he had kind eyes, and he seemed to care a great deal for her. She looked up at her husband then. 'Do we have to agree to this, Ward?' She didn't mean legally, she meant practically for the next ten months.

'I don't see why we should.'

'Maybe we'd be smarter if we did. You can't fight City Hall.' They had learned that again and again, with Lionel, with Val ... Vanessa ... now Anne. They did what they wanted to ... except poor Greg. And Ward looked at her now.

'You mean agree to her having an affair with him openly?' He looked shocked. 'She's only seventeen years old.' But they both knew that she was far older than that, in her soul, she had been through a lot, and it had weathered her.

'She's been doing it for the last year or so anyway.'

Ward narrowed his eyes at his wife. 'What makes you so liberal suddenly?'

She smiled tiredly at Ward. 'Maybe I'm just getting old.'

'And wise.' He kissed her again. 'I love you babe.'

'I love you too, sweetheart.' They agreed to think about it for a few days, and that night they had dinner with Lionel. Anne stayed in her room and no one urged her to come down.

There was enough strain on them as it was, and in the end, they decided to give in. They urged her to be discreet, not to become the talk of the town. Bill Stein was moderately well known in the entertainment industry. He was a respected lawyer and had several well-known clients, and they were sure he wasn't anxious for the publicity either. The whole idea was to keep it as quiet as possible, and then marry, as they planned to, after the first of the year. He gave her an enormous engagement ring, which she only wore when she went out with him. A pear-shaped solitaire that she called her Easter Egg. It was ten and a half carats, and she had been embarrassed when she showed it to Gail. Gail had been very decent to them. It had been a shock to her too at first, but she loved them both a great deal. She wished them well, and they both decided to go to summer school, so that they could graduate before the Christmas holidays. That way Anne wouldn't have to go to school, once she married Bill. And then Gail thought she should leave them alone, at least for a while. Besides, it would be embarrassing to live with them at first. And she wanted to go to the Parsons School of Design in New York.

Lionel was still angry with Anne when he left for Germany. He didn't approve of the man, no matter what anyone said.

'You got off easy, if you ask me,' he told her the day he left, and she'd looked coldly at him. She would never forgive him for turning her in, she said.

'You're a fine one to be making judgements about someone else.'

'Being gay doesn't impair my mind, Anne.'

'No. But maybe your heart.'

He almost wondered if she was right, as he left. He didn't feel the same way about anything any more, ever since Vietnam. He had seen too many people die, lost too many people he cared about . . . and two he deeply loved . . . John and Greg. It was difficult to imagine loving anyone again. He had no desire to in fact, and wondered secretly if that was why he was so angry with her. He couldn't understand her happiness, because his was long gone, with John, and could never come again, and her life stretched ahead of her, with promise and excitement and as much sparkle as her enormous engagement ring.

CHAPTER 38

On January 18, 1970, Anne Thayer and Bill Stein stood at Temple Israel on Hollywood Boulevard, with their families and a handful of friends watching them. Anne hadn't even wanted to go that far, but Bill had urged her to anyway.

'It'll be easier for your parents, sweetheart, if you let them plan a little something.' But Anne had no interest in it. For almost two years she had felt like his wife, and she needed no fanfare now. Gail thought it was silly of her. She was so unlike girls her age. She wanted no wedding dress, no veil.

It looks so barren, Faye thought to herself, remembering the magnificence of her own wedding day. Anne wore a simple white wool dress with a high neck and long sleeves, simple pumps, her blonde hair in a single braid with baby's breath in it, and she carried no bouquet. She came to him simple and stark, wearing no jewellery save the large diamond he had given her. The wedding ring was a wide band of diamonds too. She looked so innocent and young that it looked almost incongruous on her hand. But she noticed none of that. She saw only Bill. It was all she had wanted since the day they met, and she came quietly to him now, on her father's arm, and then Ward stepped back, feeling again how little any of them had known her in the last eighteen years. It was as though she had slipped through their lives too quickly, too silently, living behind a locked door, always disappearing. Suddenly, it seemed as though his entire memory of her childhood was saying, 'Where's Anne?'

They had a small luncheon at the house, which was all Anne would allow them to do. There were flowers everywhere, and the champagne was very fine. Faye looked quiet and restrained in a green silk suit that set off her eyes. But somehow she didn't feel like the mother of the bride. It all felt like a charade, as though they were playing games, and eventually Gail would go home with her Dad. But when they left in the grey Rolls that night, Anne went with them, and she turned to kiss Faye and Ward goodbye. Faye had an overwhelming urge to ask her if she was sure, and yet when she saw her daughter's eyes, there was no question there. She had given herself to the man she loved, and she was a woman now.

Gail was more subdued than usual, but she was happy for Bill and Anne. She and Anne had both graduated a few weeks before, and the couple would fly to New York with her now. She was going to Parsons School of Design, and would live at the Barbizon as Vanessa once had. After they dropped her off, Bill and Anne were flying on to San Juan, and then to St Thomas and St Martin's from there, ending up in St Croix. They would be gone for several weeks, and were in no hurry to come back. Bill wanted to take her shopping in New York too. There were several jewellers whose wares he wanted her to see: Harry Winston, David Webb, a few others he liked, and then there was other shopping too. 'Bergdorf's, Bendels, Bloomingdale's,' the two girls shouted in unison that night.

'You spoil me too much!' She smiled and kissed his neck, she wanted nothing more from him than his love. He wanted to buy a few pretty things for Gail too.

'Well, Mrs Stein, how does it feel?' He smiled at her that night as they lay on his big bed, legally this time, for the first time in two years.

'It feels wonderful.' She grinned like a little girl, still wearing her braid, and now a lacy nightgown that had been a wedding gift from Val, although it was clear she didn't approve of them. None of them did, but more than that they didn't understand. They never had . . . except Li . . . once upon a time. He hadn't been at the wedding though. He was still in Germany, waiting to be released in a few weeks. Van had been back in New York, deep in her junior year. It didn't really matter to Anne, the only one she had wanted there was Bill, and she looked happily at him now, pondering the past. It was as though none of it had ever been real, only this. 'I feel as though I've been married to you all my life.' And the funny thing was he felt that way too.

'So do I.' His friends had all made comments of course. But eventually they pretended to understand. There were lots of hits on the shoulder, slaps on the backs, surreptitious winks. 'Cradle robbing, eh, old man?' They all envied him; some of them said unkind things behind his back, but he didn't give a damn. He was going to take care of his little gem for the rest of his life, and as she looked up at him with trusting eyes, she knew he would.

They slept locked in each other's arms that night, grateful again that they could do anything they wanted now. They had a lazy breakfast with Gail, and that afternoon they all packed, and flew to New York, as planned, that night. Anne thought briefly of calling Ward and Faye to say goodbye and then somehow she never got around to it. She had nothing to say to them anyway, she told Bill, as the plane took off.

'You're awfully hard on them, love. They did their best. They just never understood very well.' In her eyes, that was the understatement of the year. They had robbed her of her child, threatened to bring charges against Bill, they had passed her over, passed her by, they would have totally destroyed her life, if it hadn't been for him. She looked gratefully up at him again, as they sat in first-class, he with 'his two girls' as he called them. Anne sat in the middle, and while Bill napped on the flight, she chatted with Gail. They were looking forward to the two days they would share in New York, before Gail moved into the Barbizon, and she and Bill flew on to their honeymoon. Meanwhile, they would share a suite at the Pierre.

For the next two days, they did nothing but shop. Anne had never seen so many beautiful things in her life, except in her mother's films. He bought Gail a beautiful little mink coat, in a sporty cut, with a matching hat. He told her she'd need it to keep warm, and a mountain of ski clothes, a new pair of skis, half a dozen dresses from Bendel's, six pairs of Gucci shoes, and a gold bracelet she'd been crazy about at Cartier's, with a little screwdriver to put it on, which the girls loved. Anne loved it so much, he surprised her with one too. But there were even more goodies for his young bride: a full-length mink coat for evening wear, a short one for day, dresses and suits and blouses and skirts, boxes and boxes of beautiful shoes, Italian boots, an emerald ring, a beautiful diamond pin, huge pearl earrings from Van Cleef that she loved, and two more gold bracelets she had admired, and on the last day of the trip, he gave her a splendid piece from David Webb. It was a lion embracing a lamb, all in a single massive hunk of gold, and it was so beautiful that one could only stare at it as it dangled from her arm.

'What am I going to do with all this?' She pranced around their hotel room in her underwear, waving at the beautiful furs and clothes hanging everywhere, the shoe boxes, the handbags, the fur hats, and in her suitcase were half a dozen jewellery boxes. It was almost embarrassing, except that he enjoyed it all so much too. He bought a few things for himself too, like a fur-lined raincoat, and a new gold watch, but he was far more interested in shopping for her. Even Gail thought it was fun. She had so many pretty things he'd given her over the years that she begrudged Anne nothing now. They were almost sisters anyway, and her father would still have bought her anything she desired, perhaps even more so now. He was far too generous, both girls told him on their last night, but they enjoyed every minute of it, and Vanessa's eyes almost fell out of her head when she and Jason met them in the Oak Room for drinks. Anne glided gracefully across the room in beautifully cut red slacks and a creamy silk shirt, a red alligator Hermès handbag to match, and a mink coat that people stopped and stared at, even in New York. As she approached, the diamonds sparkled on her hands; you could see the Webb bracelet in all its glory on her arm, and two small rubies in her ears. She looked so lovely and so poised that Vanessa barely recognised her as the same girl.

'Anne?' Her jaw almost dropped as she stared at her. She was wearing her hair in a simple braid again, with soft wisps of blonde fluff framing her face, her makeup was simple and in good taste, but everything she wore, from her jewellery to her boots looked like something out of *Vogue*. Vanessa hadn't imagined her that way, as she laughed and sat down. Vanessa could see that Jason was impressed too.

'We've been shopping an awful lot.' Anne's voice was as soft as it had always been, and she looked at Bill quickly with a shy glance, as he laughed. 'He's been spoiling me too much.'

'I can see that.'

She ordered a Dubonnet, which was the only drink she liked. Vanessa and Jason had already ordered scotch. Bill had a martini on the rocks, and Gail had white wine. They all chatted amiably about nothing much. The young people reminisced about Lake

Tahoe almost two years before, and Anne asked Jason about his job. He had timed it all perfectly. He received his Ph.D. weeks after he turned twenty-six. He had successfully evaded the draft for more than eight years, and now he had a job teaching literature at NYU. It didn't excite him very much, and he'd been doing it for the past year. He was still working on his play, but he was getting nowhere with it.

'I keep trying to get Vanessa to collaborate on it with me, and she won't.'

'I can hardly keep up with school,' she explained to Bill, whom she thought pleasant and fatherly. She still had another year to go at Columbia. It was all she could think of now. She wanted to finish and get a job herself. She seemed inclined to stay in New York, but Anne suspected it was because of Jason. They had been together for two and a half years, and she wondered if she'd ever marry him. Gail asked the same thing after dinner that night and Anne shrugged pensively. She didn't quite understand the relationship they had, she had the feeling they were just moving along parallel tracks, pursuing their own lives. They had no desire for a permanent bond; more important than that, no need. And neither of them mentioned having kids. All they talked about was their work, their jobs, their writing, his play.

'Sounds pretty boring to me,' Gail suggested, 'though at least he's cute.' He was that, but not in a way that appealed to Anne. She thought Bill the most handsome man in the world. As they went home in a cab that night, Vanessa talked to Jason about it.

'I don't understand that kid at all. She's practically a child, and there she is married to that old man, running around in diamonds and mink coat.'

'Maybe those things are important to her.' Jason couldn't understand it either but he had always thought she was a nice girl. Not as intelligent or interesting as Van, but maybe that was hard to say. She was so young and so withdrawn it was hard to know what she was.

But Vanessa was shaking her head. 'I don't think they are important to her. I don't think she gives a damn about any of that stuff. He just wants to give her all that, and she probably wears it to please him.' She was right on that score, she knew her sister that well, the only one in the family who would have loved the glitter and the furs was Val. Eventually Greg would have liked the good life, if he'd lived. The others had simpler tastes, and their parents did now too, contrary to their early life. But it had no importance for them any more, hadn't for years, Van knew. 'I just don't see what she sees in a man his age.'

'He's awfully good to her, Van, and not just materially. He can't do enough for her. If she's thirsty, she has a glass of water in her hand before she can speak up; if she's tired he takes her home; if she's bored, he takes her out to dance, to Europe, to see friends . . . you can't beat that.' He smiled at the girl he loved, suddenly wishing he did more for her. 'A guy his age thinks of all that stuff, he's got nothing else to do,' he teased, and she laughed.

'That's no excuse. You mean I don't get a diamond ring the size of an egg?'

He looked at her soberly as they walked into the house. 'Is that what you want someday, Van?'

'Nope.' She sounded sure of it and she was. She wanted other things in her life. Like him. Maybe a couple of kids one day, eight or ten years down the road. Stuff like that.

'What do you want?'

She shrugged pensively as she threw her coat on a chair. 'Maybe to publish a book one day . . . good reviews . . .' She couldn't think of anything else, and she didn't want to tell him that she might want him and a baby or two. It was too soon to think of that, let alone talk about it.

'That's all?' He looked disappointed.

She smiled at him, softening, 'Maybe you too.'

'You've got that now.'

She sat down on the couch and he lit a fire. They were comfortable here, with their books and papers all around, the Sunday *Times* still spread out on the floor tangled with his sneakers, and her shoes, his glasses on the desk. 'I really think this is all I want, Jase.'

He looked pleased. 'You have mighty simple tastes, my friend.' He held her close, and then, 'Are you serious about the book?'

'I hope so. After I finish school and get a job.'

He sighed. 'It's so damn hard to write them.' He knew that only too well. 'I still think we should collaborate on a play.' He looked at her hopefully and she smiled. He had always felt that their styles would mesh well.

'Maybe one day.' They kissed and he laid her back on the couch and slipped a hand into her blouse. It was a far cry from the scene between Bill and Anne at the Pierre. She was lying on the satin bedspread wearing a marabou-trimmed peignoir and his tongue ran lazily up her thigh. The diamonds on her hand sparkled in the dim light. He touched her where she liked it most, and she arched her back with a moan, as he pulled the peignoir from her. It drifted slowly to the floor. The feelings were the same as Jason and Vanessa. The love, the desire, the commitment to each other through thick or thin. It was all the same, in sneakers, or marabou.

CHAPTER 39

In May, Bill and Anne went back to New York for a few days.
Anne wanted to see Gail, and he had business there. They stayed at
the Pierre again, and he took her to the jewellers he liked best, and
insisted on buying her some new things. The weather was
beautiful, and she had just bought a beautiful white dress and coat
at Bendel's which she wore to lunch with him at Côte Basque. He
was very proud of her as she walked into the room. She was still
totally unaware of herself, and she moved like a doe as she
approached him across the room, seeing no one stare at her, seeing
only his eyes smiling at her. But he saw something else; that same
empty, nervous look that had been there for months. He hoped it
happened soon, and he knew why it was so important to her. He
wanted a baby too, but not as desperately as she did.

'How was Bendel's today?'

'Pretty good.' She still talked like a child sometimes, but she
didn't look like one any more. She was wearing her hair down, and
he had had a woman he knew in L.A. teach her how to put makeup
on. Suddenly she looked more like twenty-five than eighteen. Gail
had noticed it too, and had obviously approved. She had a new
boyfriend now, and was loving New York. Bill insisted that she
stay at the Barbizon, but she was threatening to move out by the
autumn and get her own place, and Anne had been assigned to
work on him. 'I just bought this today.' She waved at the dress and
coat with a perfectly manicured hand, and he noticed that she was
wearing the new pearls he had just bought her in Hong Kong.
They were huge and almost didn't look real. 'You like?'

'I love.' He kissed her gently on the lips, and the waiter took
their order for drinks. He had wine, she had Perrier, and they both
ate a light lunch. She loved the quenelles at the Côte Basque, and

he had a spinach salad and a steak. They weren't really doing justice to the exquisite cuisine, but he had another meeting to attend, and she was off to Bloomingdale's, and then she was going to meet Gail at school.

Bill wondered sometimes if she should be going to school too; she needed something more to do than get her nails done and shop and wait for him to come home at night. She needed something more than keeping her temperature chart every day. She had to think of something else, but he was afraid to tell her that. He just kept reassuring her it would happen soon. They had both had one child, so they knew they were each capable of it, it was just a matter of time, the doctor had told her that too. 'Have you called your sister yet, sweetheart?' She shook her head vaguely, playing with the cookie she had taken from the tray. 'Why not?' She still avoided most of the Thayers, even Lionel, whom he knew she had once loved so much. It was as though she wanted to shut them all out of her life now. She had him, and she wanted nothing else, but he didn't think it was right. It would have broken his heart if Gail had done that to him, although he knew that the Thayers had never been as close to her as he was to Gail.

Anne shrugged. 'Mum said she had exams when I talked to her last week.' It was obvious she had no interest in calling Van. And she never called Valerie in L.A., she hadn't talked to her in months.

'You can still give her a call. She might have time for a quick drink.'

'I'll call her tonight.' But he already knew she would not. She would lie around, thinking, counting forward and back ... fourteen days from ... and the next morning she would wake up at the crack of dawn and take her temperature again. He wanted her to stop and just relax about it all. She was getting so uptight about it she was losing weight. He was thinking of taking her to Europe in July to take her mind off things, and he wanted Gail to come too, but she had a summer job with Pauline Trigère, and she refused to go anywhere.

'What do you think, sweetheart?' They were strolling up Madison Avenue towards his meeting place, and he was trying to interest her in the European trip. He had to interest her in something. What if a baby never came, or it took years? She couldn't spend her whole life waiting for that, and it was beginning to dim the pleasure they had shared. It was all she could think about, all she could talk about sometimes, as though she could replace the baby she'd given up. He didn't dare tell her that she never would, no more than he could replace his wife. He loved Anne just as much, but it was all different now, and once in a great while, there was still that empty ache of missing her, just as he knew that Anne would always regret that child. There would always remain a lonely void for her, a void which no one could fill, no husband, no child. He looked at her tenderly. 'St Tropez would be fun. We could rent a boat.' She smiled at him then, he did so much for her, and she was always aware of it.

'I'd love that. And I'm sorry I've been such a drip. I guess we both know why.'

'Yes, we do.' He stopped right on Madison Avenue and took her in his arms. 'But you have to let Mother Nature take her own sweet time, and besides, it's fun trying, isn't it?'

'Yes.' She smiled at him. But he still remembered how she had cried when she got her last period, and the angry scene they'd had when she told him it was all Faye's fault. That if it hadn't been for her she would have had a three-and-a-half-year-old son now, and Bill had looked so hurt . . . 'Is that what you want?' he had asked, and she had screamed, 'Yes, it is.' He felt so sorry for her, he had even suggested they adopt a three-year-old boy, but she wanted their own. She wanted to have 'her own baby' again. It was pointless to try and tell her she could never replace the one she'd given up. She was determined to have a baby by Bill, immediately, if possible. Her mother suspected that when they had lunch one day, and the veiled look in her eyes accused Faye just as they had for years. She had never forgiven her, and possibly never would.

Now, on Madison Avenue, she looked sadly at Bill. 'Do you think it'll ever happen?' She had asked him that a million times since January, and it had only been four months since their wedding day. They had used precautions until then, no thanks to her, he reminded her several times. But he knew why she wanted to be careless. It was the same thing again. That desperation to have a child, to fill the void, to relive the past differently this time. She had never forgiven herself for giving that child up, or Faye for making her . . .

'Yes, I think it will happen, little love. Six months from now you'll be wallowing around like a whale, telling me how miserable and uncomfortable you are, and hating me for it.' They both laughed and he kissed her again and left for his meeting, as she headed for Bloomingdale's, and it tore at her heart when she passed the racks of baby clothes. She stopped for just a moment and fingered them wistfully, wanting to buy something just for good luck, and then afraid it would jinx her instead. She remembered when she had bought little pink shoes when she'd been pregnant before. She had been so convinced it would be a girl, Lionel and John had teased her about it.

The memory was still painful now, as she walked away, and it hurt to think of John. She wondered how Lionel was. They seldom spoke any more. Things had never been the same since he had told her parents about Bill, and she seemed to have nothing to say to him now. The last she'd heard, he was still looking for a job at one of the studios, anxious to get back into film. She sighed, and took the escalator downstairs. There was a riot of colour everywhere, silk flowers, patent-leather bags, bright suede belts in rainbow hues. She couldn't resist, and came home with bags of it, most of which she knew she'd never wear, unlike the diamond bracelet Bill gave her that night to ease the pain. He knew how unhappy she was about not getting pregnant yet. But he was sure she would. She was healthy and young and just trying too hard, and the doctor had told her as much. He told her so again the week before they went to St Tropez. 'Just relax and don't think of it,' he said, which was easy for him to say. He was fifty-eight years old, and had learned to be more philosophical about life.

Deep down she was still upset but for the three weeks that they played on the beach at St Tropez, Anne had never looked happier in her life. She wore blue jeans and espadrilles, bikinis and bright cotton shirts, and she let her hair go wild, in a haze of blonde bleached even paler by the sun. She was a beautiful girl, and growing prettier by the day. He was pleased to see she had even gained a little weight, and when they went to Cannes to shop, she didn't fit into her usual size, she had to move up one. He teased her when she had trouble zipping up her jeans again. He told her she was getting fat, but a question dawned which he didn't even dare voice to her. In Paris he was sure of it when she was too tired to walk along the Seine, fell asleep on the way to Coq Hardi for lunch, and turned green when he suggested a Dubonnet. He didn't say a word to her, but protected her like a mother hen with a chick, and when they got back to L.A., he reminded her that she hadn't had a period since they left a month before. For the first time in six months, she hadn't even thought of it, and suddenly her jaw dropped as she made rapid calculations in her head, and then grinned nervously at him.

'Do you think . . .?' She didn't even dare say the words and he smiled gently at her. It hadn't taken so long after all. Six months wasn't long at all, except it had been to her, so anxious to conceive.

'Yes, I do, little one. I've thought it for the last few weeks but I didn't want to get your hopes up, so I didn't say anything.' She squealed and threw her arms around his neck, and he tried to calm her down. 'Let's wait till we're sure, and then we'll celebrate.'

She went for the test the next day, and when she called them breathlessly that afternoon for the results, they were positive. She was so stunned, she just sat there and stared at the phone. When Bill came home she still looked dazed, and he whooped with delight. He noticed, as she wandered around in her bathing suit, that she had already subtly changed shape. She wasn't as angular as usual, everything seemed softer and more round.

'I am . . . I am . . . I am . . .' She was so excited she danced with glee, and he took her out to celebrate at the Beverly Hills Hotel, but she fell instantly to sleep, as he found himself dreaming of the baby they would have. He was caught up in it too, and he was thinking of transforming the guest room into a nursery. They could put another maid's room over the garage, and put one of the maids there . . . then put the nurse in what was now the maid's room . . . his mind whirled around all night as she slept, and the next day he came home for lunch to see how she was and celebrate again. It seemed to make no dent at all in their sex life, and she had never looked happier than she did then. She constantly spoke of their 'little boy', as though it had to be a boy, to replace the one that was gone . . . he would have been almost four years old by then, Bill knew . . .

They spent Labor Day weekend quietly with friends. People were getting used to her now, and although they envied Bill, they didn't make as many cracks as they once did. She looked more grown up than she had nine months before. Especially now – the pregnancy had given her a certain maturity.

They were planning to go to New York in the next few weeks, to see Gail, and the doctor said it was all right for Anne to go, but the day before they left, she began spotting lightly, and he put her to bed to rest. She was terrified of what it meant, but the doctor insisted that it happened all the time. Most women had some spotting in the first few months, it meant nothing at all, he said, except that after three days it hadn't stopped, and Bill was growing anxious now. He called another doctor he knew, who said the same thing. But Anne was strangely pale under her tan, mostly from fright. She barely moved from her bed all day long, except to go to the bathroom, and Bill came home for lunch every day to see how she was, and he left the office earlier than usual. They would just have to wait and see, both doctors said, but neither of them was concerned, until after a week of consistent bleeding, late one night she began to have terrible cramps. She woke with a start, and grabbed Bill's arm. She was barely able to speak she was in such pain, and she felt as though a hot poker were forcing its way through her, pushing everything down between her legs and on her lower back. Bill called the doctor, frantically wrapped her in a blanket, and took her to the hospital. Her eyes were wide with fear, and she held his hand tightly, as she lay in the emergency room. She begged him not to leave her, and the doctor let him stay, but it wasn't a pretty sight. She was in terrible pain and bleeding copiously, and within two hours, she lost the baby she had wanted so desperately. She sobbed in Bill's arms.

They put her out and wheeled her away to do a quick D and C and when Anne woke up in the recovery room, Bill was there again, with grief-stricken eyes filled with concern as he held her hand. The doctor had said there was no explanation for it, some foetuses were just wrong and the body eliminated them. It was best that way he said. But Anne was inconsolable as she lay in bed at home for weeks. They told her she could get up, but she had no desire to at all. She lost fifteen pounds, looked like hell, and refused to talk to anyone or go anywhere. Eventually, Faye got word of it in a roundabout way. Lionel called Anne to say hello, and Bill told him. He called Faye, who in turn called Anne to see how she was, but she wouldn't speak to anyone, Bill said in despair. And she flatly refused to see Faye. She got hysterical when Bill even mentioned it, screaming again that it was all her fault, that if she hadn't made her give the other baby away, she would have him now. She hated everyone, even Bill at times, and it was November before he could get her to travel with him again, or go anywhere, Gail was upset at how drawn she looked when she finally came to New York with Bill.

'She looks terrible.'

'I know.' He worried about her all the time, but there was nothing he could do except get her pregnant again, and that could take time. 'She took it very hard.' It had already been two months and she never talked about it, but it was easy to see how the miscarriage had ravaged her, and even the jewellery he bought didn't excite her very much. Nothing did. Not even the trip to St Moritz at Christmastime.

Finally, in January, she began to revive. It had been a terrible time for her, and the six weeks' depression the doctor had predicted for her had turned into three months. At least now she was over it, for the most part. She was back to her old life, of shopping and seeing a few friends. She called Gail in New York more often again, and she had set up her temperature charts again. This time it paid off in two short months. She found out she was pregnant on Valentine's Day.

The baby only lasted six weeks – she lost it on the first of March, two weeks after she found out. Bill braced himself for what she would go through again, but she was quieter about it this time. Silent, withdrawn, she rarely mentioned it, even to him, and in some ways that worried him more. He would rather have seen her cry all the time, at least she would have got it out of her system. Instead, there was something closed and dead in her eyes. She put the temperature charts away for good, threw the basal thermometer away, and talked about redoing the guest room in green or blue. It tore at his heart even more than the time before, but there was nothing he could do for her. Late one night, she confessed to him in the dark that she thought it might be because of all the drugs she took several years before. But that was five years ago, he reminded her, and he was convinced it had nothing to do with it. But she clung to her guilts and her regrets, and the memory of the relinquished child. It was obvious she believed she would never have one now, and he didn't even dare argue with her. It put a terrible silent pressure on him now whenever they made love, but at least she wasn't still taking her temperature. That was a relief of sorts.

She continued to avoid her parents like the plague, particularly Faye, and Bill brought her news of them from time to time. He had heard they were putting together an enormous package, and looking for a star.

'Maybe they'll give Val the part,' he said to distract her one day as they ate lunch by the pool. Even if he hadn't given her a child, she reminded herself constantly, he had given her a beautiful life, and happiness. She was cared for as never before. And it was she who had failed him, she felt, not being able to give him a child. But it didn't seem to matter as much to him as it did to her, and she laughed now at his suggesting Val for her parents' film.

'Only if they're doing a horror picture and need a star with a fantastic scream.' She described Val's famous scream to him, and he laughed as he listened to her. She was coming out of it more quickly this time and he was relieved.

But the suggestion he had just made to his wife was not as outlandish as it seemed. In their offices, Faye and Ward had a hundred résumés spread around, and there was another fat stack of rejects on the floor. They had thought of everyone and no one was right for the part. They wanted someone new and fresh, and beautiful. Someone who seemed real. And Ward looked at Faye with the same idea Bill had had, only he was serious.

'Val?' Faye sighed deeply and looked intensely at Ward. 'I don't think that's a good idea.' She had never put her own children into any of her films. For two decades she had kept her two worlds separate and now they were threatening to collide. Besides which, Val wasn't easy, and she and Faye seldom got along. Also, she had no experience with quality films. Yet, what a great gift to give her. 'I don't know, Ward . . .'

'Well, we've thought of everyone else in this town. And unless you want to start looking in Europe or New York, we're going to have to start looking under flat rocks. Why don't you give it a try?'

'What if it doesn't work?'

'Then you fire her.'

'My own child?' She looked shocked.

'I don't think you'll have to.' Ward wouldn't let go of his idea. 'This could change her whole life, Faye. It could be the chance she needs. The fact is that she's got the ability, she just hasn't had the vehicle.'

Faye smiled at him ruefully. 'You sound like her agent. Baby, don't do this to me, Ward. She's not right for the part.' It wasn't true, but it would have been easier if it were.

'What makes you say that?' He took a framed photograph off his desk and handed it to Faye. 'She has exactly the look you want, doesn't she?'

Faye smiled at her husband. 'All right. I give up.' But she looked happier than she had in a very long time. Ward smiled in answer. He was proud of her, and they both knew it wasn't going to be easy. He was convinced that this was right, and he would do everything possible to help them.

And the truth was that he was right. Val did have exactly the look she wanted for the star, but what a challenge it would be to work with her own daughter. On the other hand, it could be the chance of a lifetime. For Val anyway.

Faye stood up with a smile, and Ward walked towards her.

'You're terrific, do you know that?' He said it with a smile and Faye looked at him ruefully.

'Just be sure you tell that to your daughter.'

CHAPTER 40

'You want me to do *what*?' Val shrieked at her agent through the phone. She'd been sitting at home doing her nails, wondering whether to go out to eat that night or not. There was nothing in the refrigerator as usual, but three of the girls had been talking about stopping at Chicken Delight on the way home, and Val didn't feel like going out. She was sick of the men she'd been seeing lately. All they wanted was to get laid. And after a while it was all the same. She had given up her virginity six years before, and she couldn't even remember all the men she'd slept with any more.

'I want you to read for Faye Thayer,' her agent repeated again.

She started to laugh. 'Do you realise who you called?' He had made a mistake obviously. 'This is *Val* Thayer.' She wanted to add 'you jerk', but she restrained herself. She was going to read for another part later that week, in a film about drugs. It wasn't much of a part, but it would pay the rent and it was something to do with herself. She wasn't ready to admit defeat yet. She had been acting for four years, and she knew she'd get a big break one of these days, though not reading for her Mum. That was the funniest thing she'd heard in months.

'I'm serious, Val. Your mother's office just called.'

'You're out of your mind.' She put the bottle of nail polish down. 'This is a joke. Right? Okay, so ha ha. Now why did you call?'

'I'm telling you why I called.' He was beginning to sound desperate. Faye Thayer's office didn't call him every day, and it made him nervous too. He was a small agent on Sunset Strip, and he supplied actors and actresses and models for B films and horrors, soft porn, and live topless shows. Faye had been furious when Val said she had signed up with him. 'She's serious, Val. They want you there tomorrow at nine o'clock.'

'What for?' She could feel sweat break out under her arms. Why would they call her agent and not her?

'They want you to read cold.' He had offered to pick up the script so Val could study it that night but they had refused, at least the secretary had. And she said that Mrs Thayer wasn't available. Val was to report at 9 am the next day, that was it. Were they interested or not? He had pounced on it of course, but now he had to convince Val.

'What am I supposed to read?'

'All I know is it's a part in her new film.' It was the strangest thing she'd ever heard, and she finally agreed to show up there the next day, but she couldn't resist calling home that night. Her parents were out, as it turned out, and the maid must have been off, because no one was there. It made her sad to call the house, there used to be so many people there, and now they were all gone. It was the same way Faye felt when they came home late at night. But all Val could think of tonight was the mysterious part she was supposed to read for the next day. She hardly slept all night, and she was up at six o'clock the next day, washing and drying her hair, doing her face, checking her nails again. She decided to wear a plain black dress, just in case they were serious. It was a little dressy for nine o'clock and it was very low-cut, but her breasts were creamy and full, and her legs were long. It was the kind of outfit she would have worn to read for anyone else, so she decided not to do anything different for Faye Thayer. She tried to tell herself that this was no different from reading for anyone else, as she drove to the studio. Her hands were shaking as she pushed open the door, and she had taken so long to touch up her makeup and do her hair once more that she was half an hour late when she arrived. The secretary looked at her disapprovingly, and she saw Faye check her watch as she walked in, and then glance at the low décolletage, but she looked at her daughter with a smile, and she seemed as nervous as Val was. Ward and two other men were sitting in another part of the room, conferring quietly, with tables spread all around, and photographs of other actresses that they were checking out. They glanced up once and she saw her father wink at her. But it was her mother she had to concentrate on now. Her mother, the woman she had always resented, who was finally giving her her big chance now.

'Hello, Valerie.' Her voice was gentle, and her manner more professional than Valerie was used to. It was as though she were trying to tell Val something without saying the words, and giving her all the encouragement she could. As she watched her, Valerie began to feel calm. She forced herself not to think of the three goddamn Academy Awards and only the script at hand. Suddenly it meant everything to her. She hadn't had a big break yet, but she knew she could act, and if this killed her, she was going to do it. Faye Thayer watched her face, and examined every inch of her, wishing her well, almost praying for her. 'We'd like you to read for a part today, Val.' As she said it, she handed the script to her.

'That's what my agent said. What kind of part is it?'

'It's a young woman who . . .' She went on to describe the part, and Val wondered again why she had called her. She wanted to ask her why she had called, but she decided not to say anything.

'Can I have a few minutes to study it?' Her eyes were intense. She had always been so jealous of Faye, of her looks, of her past, her success, the acting career she had walked away from as a young girl. And now here she was, reading for her. It was the strangest development of her entire career. Her mother nodded now. Val saw that she was getting old. She was only fifty-one, but the last few years had taken their toll.

Suddenly she wanted the part, wanted it more than anything in the world. She wanted to show this woman she could act. She knew Faye didn't think she could, and she wondered whose idea it had been to give her a chance. Probably her Dad's.

'Take ten minutes in the other room and then come back in.' The voice was warm, the eyes worried. What if she couldn't do it? Val read her mother's fears clearly. This was a side of her that her children never saw, the consummate professional, the director who demanded guts and heart and flesh, the woman who had given her whole life to her work. And suddenly Val saw it all, who she was, what she did, how demanding she could be. But it didn't frighten her. She was sure she was equal to the task. She almost went into a trance as she studied the lines, feeling the role, making it part of her. And when she walked back into the room, she looked like a different girl. Ward and the other men glanced up at her, and watched her act. She didn't read. She raged and she stormed, and she spoke, and she never glanced at the paper once. Ward's heart went out to her. He knew how hard she had worked, and how badly she must want this now. There were tears of joy and pride streaming down Faye's cheeks when Val finished. The two women exchanged a long glance, and suddenly Val began to cry too, and the two women hugged and laughed and cried, as Ward watched them. And then finally, laughing through her tears, Val looked at them both. 'Well? Do I get it?'

'Hell, yes!' Faye was quick to answer and was stunned when Val gave her now famous scream.

'Hallelujah!'

CHAPTER 41

Val started work on the film in May, and she had never worked so hard in her life. Her mother worked herself and everyone else to the bone, demanding the utmost from them, working for long, gruelling hours, demanding everything Val had in her guts. But it was no more than she asked of herself, or the other actors who worked for her. That was how she worked, and why her work was so good, it was why she had won the Awards Val had sneered at for so many years. She wasn't sneering now. She was loving it. She could barely crawl home every night, and she ended most of her days on the set in tears. At twenty-two years of age, she had never worked so hard in her life, and wasn't sure she ever would again. And if she did, it would be because she wanted to. No one would ever demand so much from her . . . or teach her so much . . . she knew that too. And she was happy and proud and grateful.

She had been working for three weeks when her co-star, George Waterston, offered her a ride home. She had seen him around Hollywood before, and she knew he hadn't been pleased when he'd heard who would be playing opposite him. He had wanted a big star, and Faye had to work hard to convince him to give her a try. The deal had been that if she was no good, she'd be canned. Val knew all of that, from the scuttlebutt on the set, and she knew it now, as she saw Waterston looking into her eyes. She wondered if he was her enemy or her friend, and she found she didn't really care. She was too tired to give a damn, and she really needed a lift. Her car had been in the shop for weeks, and she had taken a cab to work. So she looked up at him gratefully.

'Sure . . . thanks . . .' She didn't even have the energy to talk on the way home, after she gave him the address, and she was horrified when she fell asleep and he woke her up outside her house. She gave a sudden start as he touched her arm and stared at him, mortified. 'Did I fall asleep?'

'Guess I'm not as interesting as I used to be.' He had brown hair and blue eyes, a strong, somewhat weathered face. He was thirty-five years old, and Val had admired him for years. It was all part of the dream that her life had become, starring in a film with this man. People were already saying that she had got the part because of who her mother was. But she didn't give a damn. She was going to prove them all wrong. She was going to knock them dead as Jane Dare, the woman she played, and she looked apologetically at her co-star now.

'I'm so sorry . . . I've been so tired . . .'

'My first film for Faye, I was like that too. I even fell asleep behind the wheel of my car once, and woke up just before I hit a tree. By the end of it, I was even afraid to drive. But she gets something out of you that no one else does, a piece of your soul. . . or your heart . . . by the time it's all over, she doesn't even have to pull it out of you any more. You want to give it to her.' It was exactly what Val was already beginning to feel, along with a whole rainbow of new feelings of love and respect for her mother.

'I know . . . I still can't believe she gave me the part.' She looked up at him honestly. 'She's never liked anything I've done before, and I haven't done much. I mean, I've had a lot of roles in films, but nothing as big as this.' He already knew that, and for the first time in weeks, he felt sorry for her. He hadn't liked her at all at first. She looked like a little tart, and he figured Faye was playing favourites with her, but he soon saw that he was wrong, and now he saw that the poor kid was so scared. It must have been hell for her working for Faye, and with him as a co-star. She was in a world of pros, and she was still a kid, he realised now, feeling something entirely new for her.

'She used to scare me to death.' He laughed, relaxing with Val. She didn't look as cheap as she had at first. She hardly wore any makeup any more, and she wore sweatshirts and jeans. There was no point wearing anything low-cut or dressed-up, she just took it off the moment she arrived, and she was beginning to live the role of Jane Dare, who was very different from Val. 'Your mother is something else, Val.' It was the first time he had called her by name, and she smiled at him.

374

'You know, I forget she's my mother when I'm on the set. She's just this woman screaming at me, making me so mad I want to kill her sometimes.'

'That's good.' He approved. He knew Faye well, and how she made him feel too. 'That's what she wants you to feel.'

Val sighed, comfortable in the big roomy car. It was a white Cadillac convertible with a red interior, and she hardly had the strength to open the door to go home. Then, feeling nervous, she turned to him. 'Do you want to come in for a drink or something? I don't know what there is to eat, maybe nothing at all. But we can call out for a pizza if you want.'

'How about going for a pizza somewhere?' He looked at the Rolex watch on his arm and then glanced back at her. 'I could have you back in an hour. I want to study tomorrow's scene again tonight.' And then he had an idea. 'You want to work on it together?'

She smiled at him disbelievingly. It couldn't be true. She studying lines with George Waterston for a film they were in? It had to be a dream. She decided to answer him quickly, before the dream disappeared. 'I'd love that, George. If I don't fall asleep again.' He laughed at her and he was as good as his word. They had a quick pizza on the way, went to his house in Beverly Hills, and read their parts together for two hours, trying different intonations, different moods, until they reached one they liked. It had the same feeling as the drama classes she had loved so much except that this was for real. And at exactly ten o'clock, he drove her home. They both needed their sleep for the next day. He waved casually at her as she let herself into her house, floating on a cloud. It was a pleasure not to be mauled by some kid, or some guy who looked like a pimp. She wondered why she had never met anyone like George before. And then she laughed at herself. Half the women in the world wanted to meet a man like him, and she was working with him every day.

The picture was going well, and Val had worked at his place several times. She would have had him to hers, but there was too much chaos there. He told her he thought she should move out and get a decent place. He was becoming almost a big brother to her, introducing her to his friends, and teaching her the ways of the upper echelon in Hollywood. 'It looks like hell to live in a place like

375

that, Val.' He could say anything to her now. They worked together twelve hours a day, and studied for two or three hours every night. 'Guys will think you're cheap.' It was exactly what had been happening to her for years, until this reprieve.

'I could never afford anything better than that.' She was telling him the truth and he looked surprised. The Thayers were certainly among the more important people in Hollywood, and it seemed strange that they wouldn't subsidise her. He said as much and she shook her head. That wasn't her style. 'I haven't taken anything from them in years. Not since I moved out.'

'Stubborn little thing, aren't you?' he said, smiling at her. Lately she had noticed a warmer bond between them. She was coming to rely on him. Almost too much, she warned herself. The film they were working on was an unreal world, and sooner or later it would end. But he was so easy to be with, so friendly, so warm, and he knew so much. He even had a fourteen-year-old son whom she liked. He had married at eighteen, divorced at twenty-one, and his ex-wife was married to Tom Grieves, the big baseball star. He saw his son on weekends and occasional Wednesday nights, and he had asked Val to join them a couple of times. She got on well with the boy, whose name was Dan. George told her he had wanted to have lots of kids, but he had never remarried, although she knew from the gossip around town that he had lived with several big stars. It was in early June that they wound up in the papers together for the first time.

Faye saw it too, and showed it to Ward before they left for work. 'I hope she's not getting involved with him.'

'Why not?' Ward suspected they were; he had always liked George. He thought he was one of the more decent people around town.

But Faye was looking at it from a different view. She had a single-minded goal in her mind when she was working on a film. 'It will distract her from her work.'

'Maybe not. He might teach her something.' Faye grunted something unintelligible, and they left for work. As usual, she was worried about Val. Ward had been right of course, she was fabulous in the part, though she didn't want to say too much to Val yet, it might throw her off. She was almost sorry they were all going to Vanessa's graduation in a few weeks. She didn't like socialising with her stars during a film, but it couldn't be helped in this case. She would keep as far away from her as she could, and hoped she'd understand. She was coming to love the child more and more, but right now she was also her director. And that mattered more. Right now.

When George heard Val was going to New York, he wanted to come too. 'I haven't been there since last year. And hell, I could bring Dan.' It was the strangest relationship. They went everywhere together now, and he had never laid a hand on her. She was sorry about it too. Yet they were becoming friends and she didn't want to spoil what they had. 'I could bring Danny too. I usually stayed at the Carlyle.'

'I think my mother's staying at the Pierre with my brother and sister and brother-in-law.' Bill had suggested it to them, and Faye had let him reserve the room. They were slowly becoming friends, and Ward had played tennis a few times with him.

But now George had an idea. 'What about staying uptown at the Carlyle with us? Faye won't want to hang around you too much anyway.'

Val knew that, and her father had explained it, so George's suggestion was perfect.

'She never talks to her stars. She says it confuses her. She can only deal with one identity at once. And right now, in her head you're Jane Dare, she doesn't even want to see Valerie Thayer or George Waterston.' The character he played was a man named Sam, and Val nodded now, understanding better. And she liked the idea of staying at the Carlyle with them.

'You're sure Danny won't mind having me around?'

'Hell, no. He's crazy about you.' And he certainly seemed to be as the three of them flew to New York, first-class. George signed several autographs as Val and Danny watched, and eventually they started teasing him, begging him for one too. She played cards with Dan while George slept, and they all watched the film, elbowing each other ferociously. It was one of George's recent films.

There was a limo waiting for them at the airport in New York, and it drove them straight to the Carlyle, where George had reserved a three-bedroom suite. There was a kitchenette, and a piano, and an airy living room with a view of the park. It was on the thirty-fourth floor, and Danny looked thrilled with it all. They ordered room service instantly, and went to dinner at '21' that night.

'Well, kid.' He spoke softly to her later that night in the bar after Danny had gone upstairs. 'It's going to be all over the world that you're having an affair with me. Think you can take the heat?' She laughed and said yes, and the crazy thing was that they were just friends. A little while later, they sat and listened to Bobby Short make magic on the piano at the Carlyle, and then they went upstairs to their rooms. She knew the rest of her family was in New York by then too, and the next morning Vanessa called, wanting to have lunch with her. She was excited about Val's film and wanted to hear all about it. They had had dinner with Ward and Faye the night before and she wouldn't say a thing.

'So you have to tell all.'

'Okay. Can I bring George to lunch?' She didn't feel right abandoning him and the boy, but Vanessa didn't understand.

'George who?'

'George Waterston.' She said it so casually that Vanessa almost fell off her seat at the other end.

'Are you kidding? Is he here with you?'

'Yup. We flew in together, with his son. He thought it would be fun to be here for a few days while I watch you graduate. Speaking of which, congratulations! At least one of us is educated now!' Vanessa had no interest whatsoever in her education now.

'George *Waterston*! Val, I can't believe you!' She covered the phone with her hand and told Jason the news, whispering loudly to Val after that. 'Are you involved with him?'

'No. We're just friends.' But Vanessa didn't believe a word of it, as she told Jason when she hung up. If he had come all the way to New York with her, they had to be more than just friends.

'You never know. You guys out in Plastic Land are weird. I've always said that.' He smiled at her then. They were moving the following week. They had found a loft in Soho, and they could hardly wait to move there. They had promised to show Ward and Faye, and there was no longer any pretence about where Van lived. She lived with him, and intended to continue doing so. Faye had questioned her about it the night before, hoping to hear that they were planning to get married one of these days, but they seemed to have no intention of it. Jason accused Van of torturing her after they went back to the Pierre and he and Vanessa were alone again. 'Poor woman, she's so anxious for you to be respectable. We could at least get engaged, you know.'

'That would spoil everything.'

'You're nuts.'

'No, I'm not. I don't need a piece of paper with you. There's a lot of stuff we both want to do first,' she reminded him, his play, her book, she had to look for a job now. But he was finished with school now and thinking of settling down. Vanessa was in no rush. She was still young enough to feel as though she had forever. Although she was in an enormous rush to meet Valerie's friend.

They made a date for lunch at PJ Clark's and promptly at one o'clock, Valerie and George Waterston, and his son Dan walked in. George was wearing jeans, a T-shirt and Gucci shoes with no socks, and Danny looked like any kid anywhere, in a blue shirt and khaki slacks. He was dressing up a lot these days, ever since he had developed an interest in girls. He had a huge crush on Val, who was wearing a red leather gypsy dress. But Vanessa had eyes only for George and she practically drooled. Valerie teased her about it halfway through lunch. Jason and George were getting on like a house on fire, and Jason had talked endlessly to Dan about sports, and promised to take him to a Yankee game before he left for the Coast again. It was an entirely congenial group, and Vanessa couldn't help but notice the change in her twin. She was calmer, more confident, more subdued, not so loud. She looked peaceful and happy and fulfilled, and it was difficult to believe she wasn't in love with this man. He certainly looked as though he were in love with her, and they talked about the film a little bit. Valerie still couldn't believe she'd got the part, as she told Van about the horrifying interview with her mother and how terrified she had been.

'That woman has always scared me to death.' It was the first time in her whole life she had admitted it, and Vanessa looked at her, surprised. She really had changed. It was almost as if she had finally grown up and become herself, and Van found herself liking her better than she had for years.

'I always thought you were jealous of her, not scared.'

'Both, I guess.' Valerie sighed, with a smile at George. 'She still scares the shit out of me at work, but I don't resent her as much. I see how hard she works. I guess she's deserved everything she's got. I could never admit that to myself before.'

'I'm impressed.' Vanessa spoke softly to her, and the two men exchanged a glance. It was extraordinary to think that these two young women were twins. Vanessa was so quiet, so intellectual, so hell bent on success in a totally different field. She didn't even want to go back to Los Angeles any more. Her life was in New York, with Jason and her friends, the publishing world she wanted to break into. She wasn't even talking about writing a film any more, just her book. And Valerie, with her flaming red hair and brilliant good looks was so much a part of the film milieu, but the best part of Hollywood now, not the rubbish. Without realising it, her whole outlook had changed in the past two months. The days of screams and green slime were gone for good. And one could already sense about her the aura of a big star. Faye saw it too. It was the same aura she had once had herself. Or very close to it.

At the graduation the next day, she looked at all of them, quietly. Anne, so impeccably dressed in her expensive clothes, with little diamonds sparkling at her ears, her arm tucked in Bill's; Vanessa so pretty and serious in her cap and gown; Valerie so incredibly beautiful it was startling except that she seemed unaware of it, which was wonderful; and Lionel, who looked happier than he had in two years. Faye wondered if there was a new man in his life, but she never wanted to ask, and of course neither did Ward. What he did was his own business now, he was twenty-five years old after all, and they had accepted him, as they had all of them, though some of that acceptance was still unilateral, Faye knew. She knew that Anne was still angry at her for the child she had given up . . . Val still jealous of her success . . . Vanessa had grown away from her now . . . and Lionel had his own life . . . poor Greg was gone. She missed him now, as she so often did, that shock of red hair, the passion for sports, the girls he loved to chase. He had been closer to Ward than to her, but he was her son too, and she tightened her hand on Ward's arm, knowing that he would be thinking of him too, and it was painful for both of them.

But it was all laughter and smiles that afternoon when they went to the Plaza to celebrate. Faye had arranged for a table covered with white flowers in the Edwardian Room, and Vanessa was stunned beyond words when Ward handed their graduation gift to her. They had debated about it long and hard, and they finally decided to include Jason too. It was a way of giving their approval to her way of life. They had given her two tickets to Europe, with a fat cheque to cover all their fun, and reservations at some of the finest hotels. It was going to be a fabulous trip for both of them, and Faye was relieved to hear that Jason could get away too, as soon as they moved to Soho the following week. He had quit his job to work full-time on his play.

'Well, you two, that ought to keep you out of trouble for a while.' Ward smiled at them. He still wished they would get married, but it didn't seem to be on the cards. At least not yet. And he was also wondering about George Waterston and Val. George had gone off with his son for the afternoon, but Ward was aware that Valerie was staying with them, and he was curious about how far the involvement went, and he hadn't said a word about it all day. Then of course there were Bill and Anne. And Bill seemed to get on very well with the rest of the mob. Vanessa had invited Gail, and she sat chatting with Lionel. She was crazy about her studies in design, her summer job with Bill Blass this year. Lionel was talking animatedly about the film he was working on. Everyone was happy and young. It warmed one's heart to look at them as he said to Faye, as they strolled slowly back to the Pierre. He tucked her arm in his, and pulled her to one side, spoke to a man standing next to a hansom cab, and the next thing she knew, she was driving around Central Park, with Ward holding her hand. He kissed her gently once or twice and she smiled. She was still crazy about him after a lifetime. 'I must say, that's quite a group we've got.' His mind ran over them again as they clomped along through the park, and Faye didn't disagree with him. She hadn't said much to Val, and she hoped that George would explain it to her. He knew her methods of working well. 'You're better-looking than all of them though, babe.'

'Oh my love.' She kissed him and smiled. 'Now I know you're as crazy as I always thought.'

'Just crazy about you.' He kissed her again then, and they held hands together for a long time, happy with each other and their lives. They had come a long, long way side by side.

CHAPTER 42

'Do you want to go to dinner tonight, sweetheart?' Anne shook her head as she lay on the bed at the Pierre. It had gone well after all, even though she really hadn't wanted to come, but Bill thought they should, and it was a good excuse to see Gail. Seeing Gail had been what finally convinced her. He even offered her a trip to Europe, with New York as a stop on the way, but she wasn't in the mood, and she was very tired again. She had been for months, ever since the first miscarriage. She never really seemed to have bounced back, and Bill worried about her.

'Why don't we order room service and eat here?' She knew that Gail was going somewhere with Lionel. She enjoyed his company and she had a lot of gay friends, but Anne hadn't wanted to go along. She thought that Bill would be bored, and she knew she would too. Jason and Vanessa were going to celebrate, Val had her film star, and she had no desire to see her parents. Once in a day was more than enough for her. But Bill thought it a shame to waste a night in New York.

'Are you sure?'

'I really don't feel up to going out.'

'Do you feel sick?' It was beginning to remind him of when Gail's mother had first been sick, and he wanted her to go back to the doctor.

But when they got back the next week, she resisted him. 'I don't need to see the doctor. I feel fine.' She looked at him stubbornly and he wouldn't give in to her this time. Some things were just too important to him, and she was the most important of all. He never wanted to lose her. Ever.

'You don't feel fine. You feel like hell. You wouldn't even go out with me in New York.' She had ordered room service and gone right to sleep, and she was doing almost the same thing every night. He had the feeling she was sleeping all day too. 'If you don't make an appointment yourself, I'll do it for you, Anne.' And in the end, that was exactly what he did. He made the appointment, pretended to pick her up for lunch, and took her to his doctor in Beverly Hills. She was furious.

'You lied to me!' It was one of the few times she had screamed at him, but he led her inside like a little girl, and she glowered at them both. The doctor found nothing wrong with her. Her glands seemed fine, her chest was clear, her blood count was all right, and then without saying anything to them, he had an idea. He did the test with the blood he had taken from her arm, and he called Bill with the results that night, and he was stunned when he heard. Stunned and thrilled and afraid. She was pregnant again. This time he hadn't even thought of it. And he was afraid to put her through another disaster again.

'Just have her do what she's doing now. Her body knows what she needs. She needs lots of rest, good food, as little stress as possible. All she has to do is lie low for a couple of months and she'll be fine.' Bill nodded, and went into the other room to talk to her. She was watching TV, and she was thinking of calling Gail, and he encouraged her to now, with a quiet smile.

'I think you should, sweetheart.'

'How come?'

'To tell her the news.'

'What news?' Anne looked blank.

He leaned over and kissed her tenderly on the lips, 'The news that you're pregnant again.'

Her eyes grew wide. 'I am? Who told you that?'

'The doctor just now. He just called. He didn't even tell us he was running the test, but you are.'

'I am?' She looked stunned and then suddenly she threw her arms around his neck, fighting back tears. 'Oh Bill . . .' She didn't even dare say the words this time. She didn't even tell Gail. She didn't tell anyone, until the ominous three-month period had passed, and this time all went well. By September, the doctor was no longer concerned, and the baby was due in February, possibly on Valentine's Day. Her other child would have been five and a half years old by then, though neither of them mentioned that.

They just talked about this child, and Bill knew how badly she wanted it. He treated her as though she were walking on eggs. They took no trips, barely went out, Anne rested constantly, and Bill spoiled her even more than he had before.

Faye called her several times, and said she hoped it was all going well, but Anne's voice was cold on the phone. She and her mother had been through this before, and she remembered the pressure she had put on her then. She hated talking to her now, because it reminded her of it. She even hated talking to Lionel, because it reminded her of living with him and John, waiting for her first baby to be born.

Gail called them as often as she could from New York, and asked how big she was. Anne laughed and claimed she was huge, and when Val saw her one day on Rodeo Drive, she laughingly agreed. It was November by then, and they had finished the film a month before. It was being edited day and night, because Faye wanted it released over the Christmas holidays. Everyone was working on golden time by then, but they wanted it eligible for the next Academy Awards so it just had to be out by year's end. And when Anne ran into Val, she noticed that George Waterston was parked in his Cadillac at the kerb, waiting for her. She couldn't help wondering if they were still 'just friends', as Val claimed. But one thing was sure, Val looked even more beautiful than before, and she was picking up a dress at Giorgio's for a party that night. Anne had just been in to pick up a few things to wear over the holidays. Bill wanted her to get out a little bit and she had outgrown everything she owned, even her maternity clothes.

'How do you feel?' Val asked, seeming genuinely concerned. All of them knew how much the baby meant to her, and why. Anne laughed. She was enjoying her pregnancy, in spite of the discomforts of it.

'I feel fat.'

'You look great.'

'Thank you. How's everything with you?' They rarely called each other any more. It was difficult to believe they had grown up in the same house once. But they hadn't really. Val had grown up only recently, and Anne had grown up at Bill's.

'I just got an offer for another role.'

'Not with Mum again, is it?'

Val was quick to shake her head. Working with her mother had been an experience she would never forget, and she would always be grateful for it, but she wasn't anxious to do it again soon. Most of the actors who worked for her said that, even George. 'Once in three years is about it with her,' he had said, and Val figured it was true. 'No, with someone else.' She named the director and the stars and Anne was impressed. 'I haven't decided yet. There are a couple of others I might do.' Her career had finally taken off 'overnight', after five years of screams. Anne was pleased for her. That night she told Bill.

'She's going to be the hottest thing in Hollywood one day. Just like your Mum was once.' It was easy to believe now; she was talented and beautiful and she had that smell of success about her. You could just see she was someone when she jumped out of a car, not like the old days in a tight black dress and sequined high heels. She had come a hell of a long way, and Anne thought George was responsible for the happiness she saw in Val's eyes.

'I think they're more than just friends, don't you?' She was trying to get comfortable in a chair but it was impossible until he put some pillows behind her. She thanked him with a kiss.

'I think so too. But I think they're smart to keep it quiet. He's a big star, and they don't need the headache of all that publicity.'

In fact, they had kept it from everyone, even Dan, for as long as they could. But eventually, they had had to tell him, and now Val was quietly living with them in the Hollywood Hills, in a beautiful house that was entirely walled in, surrounded by thick trees. Even the *papparazzi* hadn't caught onto them yet, and it had been going on for three months. Val had never been so happy in her life. When they'd come back from New York and gone back to work on the film, something different seemed to have happened between them. They were so close they understood every breath, every pause – it was like magic on the set every day, and Faye felt it too and was thrilled by it.

She didn't interfere with them, she just let it roll, and by August, when Dan went away with his Mum, Val quietly moved in with George. They explained it to Danny when he came back, and George was even talking about getting married, although neither of them was in any rush. They wanted time to be sure. Val was sure it was going to come out one of these days, but they were ready now. In fact, they were waiting for it.

'Do you think you could stand living here forever, with an old man, and a young boy?' He was kissing her neck the afternoon she had run into Anne, and told him how huge she was.

'It sounds like the good life to me . . . of course,' she put on a wistful face that convinced even him, 'it's not as nice as where I used to live before I moved here.'

George gave a roar and tousled the wild red hair. 'You mean that whorehouse full of old hens? It's a wonder you didn't get arrested just living there!'

'George, what a thing to say!'

'It's true!' She had finally even told her parents she was living with him, and she was relieved that they were pleased. She was all grown up now, but somehow it still mattered to her, especially now, after working with Faye. She had new respect for her after what she had seen, and for the first time in her life she felt as though her mother respected her. Faye had even helped her find a new agent, and they had had a long talk one day after the film was wrapped up.

'Val, you are very, very good. You know, your father thought that all along. He told me so. I have to admit, I had my doubts, but you're one of the best and you're going to go a long, long way.' Those words meant everything to her, and she couldn't believe she was hearing them from Faye Thayer.

'I used to hate you, you know.' It was a terrible thing to say and there were tears in her eyes as she did. 'I was so jealous of you and those damn Oscars in the den.'

'They don't mean anything, Val.' Faye's voice was soft, but Valerie shook her head. 'You five wonderful people are my Oscars.'

'I used to say they didn't matter, but they do. They mean how hard you've worked, how good you are. And you're wonderful, Mum . . . you really are the best.' The women had both cried then, holding each other close, and Val was still warmed by the memory. She had finally made peace with her. It had taken a long time, but she had. And she hoped that Anne would one day too. The ghosts would never leave her eyes until she did, and she said that to George too. She told him everything. He had become more than just her lover, he was her very best friend.

'You know, I kind of envy your brother-in-law.' He said it as they were stretched out in front of the fire that night, and Val looked at him, surprised.

'Bill? Why? You have everything he has and more. Besides,' she grinned, 'you have me, what more could you want?'

'Of course.' He smiled back at her, but there was a longing in his eyes she hadn't seen before. He was a quiet man, with values she liked, ideals that were easy to respect, and a stable way of life, all of which was very unusual for a Hollywood idol, which he was. 'I envy him that kid.'

'The baby?' She was startled by his words, children were something that she rarely thought of. She thought of having them one day, but not for a long, long time. Her career was important to her, she had worked hard for it, and she was just beginning the exciting climb to the top. She was nowhere near ready to step down yet, unlike Faye at almost her age. Faye had been twenty-five when she retired, Val was almost twenty-three. 'Would you really want a baby now, George?' He was at the height of his career too. It would have been difficult for both of them, although the idea appealed to her for a later date.

'Maybe not now, but someday soon.'

'How soon?' She rolled over on her stomach, propped her face on her hands, and looked worriedly at him.

'How about next week?' He was teasing her and he laughed at the worried look in her eyes. 'I don't know, a year or two. But it's something I'd like to do again one day.' Dan was a nice boy, and Val was fond of him too.

'I wouldn't mind that.'

'Good.' He looked pleased, and a little while later, in front of the fire, he peeled her clothes slowly from her, and said something about practising, as he made love to her.

CHAPTER 43

'How do you feel, sweetheart?' Bill looked at her solicitously, and she laughed.

'How would you feel, if you looked like this? Like shit. I can't move, I can't breathe. If I lie down the kid strangles me, if I sit up, I get cramps.' It was already February 9, and she was five days from her due date, but despite the complaints, she seemed to be enjoying it. She wanted the baby so much that she didn't seem to really care how big she got, or how uncomfortable she was. She just wanted to hold him in her arms and finally see his little face. She still thought it was going to be a boy, but Bill was secretly hoping for a girl. He claimed he was more used to them.

'Do you want to go out for something to eat?' She laughed and shook her head. Nothing fitted, not even her shoes, and she only had three ugly dresses she could wear. She had stopped going to Giorgio's to buy dresses to go out, because she never wanted to go out, and she didn't now. She was too uncomfortable to go anywhere. She just wanted to wander around the house barefoot and in the loosest things she owned, preferably a nightgown. And that night, after they ate some soup and a small soufflé, which was all she had room for now, they went for a walk near the house, but even that was too much for her. She huffed and she puffed and she had to sit down on a huge rock outside someone's house. He almost wondered if he'd have to go and get the car for her, but she insisted that she could get home again. She looked so vulnerable and so huge that he felt desperately sorry for her, but she seemed to accept it as the way things were, and the next day she even got up and made him breakfast before he left for work. She seemed to be brimming with energy and she said something about cleaning the baby's room again, which he thought unnecessary, but she seemed

388

hell-bent on it when he tried to discourage her, and as he left, she was dragging the vacuum across the floor. He was worried about her, so much so that he decided to drop by again before lunch, and when he did, he found her quietly lying on the bed with his stopwatch in her hand, timing contractions as she did the Lamaze breathing she had learned this time. She looked at him with a distracted look and he hurried to her side.

'Is this it?'

She smiled peacefully at him. 'I wanted to be sure before I dragged you home from work, or lunch at the Polo lounge.'

He looked suddenly nervous as he took the stopwatch from her hand. 'You shouldn't have vacuumed the baby's room.'

But she only laughed. 'I have to have this kid sometime, you know.' Her due date was only four days away now. He cancelled his lunch and called the doctor for her, and then told his secretary that he wouldn't be in for the rest of the day. But try as he would, he couldn't make her go to the hospital yet. Even the doctor said she could wait a while, but Bill was afraid they'd wait too long at home.

She remembered her last experience only too well, when it had taken days for the baby to be born. There was no reason to rush now, and the breathing was helping her control the pain. Bill made her a little cup of soup, and sat quietly in the bedroom with her, and now and then she got up and walked around. Then at four o'clock, she looked at him with a distracted frown. She couldn't stand up any more, or talk through the pains. She knew it was time to go, and he hurried to her dressing room to get her bag, and then rushed back again. As she changed her clothes her water broke all over the white marble bathroom floor, and then suddenly the pains were coming hard and fast and the breathing hardly helped. Bill looked as though he were going to panic and she was trying to reassure him while he helped her get dressed at the same time. But the pains were coming too hard and fast now.

'I told you we shouldn't have waited this long.' He was terrified. What if she had it there? What if the baby died . . .

'It's all right.' She tried to smile at him, and he kissed her hair, and finally they got her dress on and he swept her off her feet, and carried her barefoot to the car. 'I need shoes.' She almost laughed, but the pains were too sharp. She clutched at him instead, and he ran back for the sandals she wore all the time now, and drove to Cedars Sinai Hospital with his foot solidly on the gas, barely stopping for lights. The Rolls had never been used as an ambulance before, but he was desperate now. She was giving little sharp screams with each pain, and she said she could feel the head. He left the car doors open as he rushed her inside, and the nurse went out to lock his car up for him, as Anne panted and tried to breathe, and he tried to help. They called for her doctor to come downstairs. There was no time to get her to maternity, and Anne was half crying now as she lay on the gurney in the emergency room.

'I can feel the head ... oh God ... Bill ...' The pressure was unbearable, and it felt as though a bowling ball was tearing her apart as she looked desperately at him. He winced every time another contraction came. He had never seen his first child born; it wasn't done in those days, and he wasn't sure he was ready to see it now. He hated seeing Anne in such agony but the nurse said it was too late to give her anything. She had told him how awful it had been for her last time, and he didn't want it to be that way again, but she was half sitting up, and the nurse told him to hold her shoulders as she groaned horribly.

'You can push now, Anne,' the nurse said as though they had been friends for years. 'Go on ... as hard as you can.' Anne's face grew red and he felt her strain with every ounce of strength she had and she was crying when she stopped.

'It hurts too much ... I can't ... I can't ... oh God ... Bill. The pains ...!' And then suddenly, she was pushing again, and the doctor was there, in cap and gloves and gown. He swiftly took an instrument, and helped Anne make room for the head that emerged triumphantly on the next push. The baby was born in the emergency room, with his parents looking on. He wore a startled look and Bill thought he looked blue at first, but within seconds, he was bright and pink and wailing angrily as Anne cried and laughed all at once and Bill kissed her face and her hands, and told her how wonderful she was. 'He's so beautiful ...! He's so beautiful ...!' It was all she could say again and again as she looked from the baby to Bill, and a moment later, wrapped in an emergency-room blanket that was much too big for him, she was holding him in her arms. She hadn't seen the first child she had borne, and she couldn't see enough of this one. She insisted he looked just like Bill, and a little while later, with Bill walking proudly at her side, they rolled her upstairs to a private room in maternity.

'And next time, I'll thank you to come in right away, so I don't have to deliver you at the front door.' The doctor pretended to look stern and they all laughed. Bill was immensely relieved. It had looked so terribly painful and he had been so frightened for her. And now there she was laughing and smiling, with her baby in her arms. She didn't even want to give him up to send him to the nursery for a bath, but the nurse talked her into it, and a little while later they cleaned her up too. Then she and Bill called Gail and she cried when she heard the news. Anne wanted her to be godmother, just to confuse things a little more. And after that he wanted her to sleep a little bit, but she was too high on the news. The baby she had wanted so much had finally been born, and she felt a warmth in her heart she had longed for, for years. She could barely wait for them to bring him back from the nursery, and she rang for the nurse, who brought him back with a smile, looking very pink and clean, and she put him at Anne's breast, showing her what to do, as Bill watched with tears in his eyes. He had never seen anything so beautiful and knew he would remember it for the rest of his life.

Anne called Valerie that night, and Jason and Van, and Lionel, and finally her parents, although she had hesitated about that, and everyone was excited for her. They were naming him Maximilian, and would call him Max Stein, and Faye was just so happy for Anne. She had known only too well how desperately she wanted this child. When she came to see her the next day, she came hesitantly, with a huge teddy bear for Max, and a bed jacket for Anne. It looked like one she had worn in the hospital herself when Lionel was born.

'You look beautiful, sweetheart.'

'Thank you, Mum.' But there was always a gulf between them which nothing could bridge, it was an irremediable gap, and Bill felt it too when he came back from the house, where he had made sure everything was the way Anne wanted it. She was going home the next day.

Max was brought in, and they all oohed and ahhed, and Faye agreed that he looked like Bill. Val and George dropped by, and the nurses wanted George's autograph, and Val's too. The film was a huge hit, and posters of Val were plastered all over town. Everyone knew her now. Faye smiled as she sat back in the hospital room, and watched the two girls chat. Val was laughing about something Anne had said, and she was telling her what having the baby was like, as Bill and George stared wondrously at little Max.

Bill drove them proudly home the next day, and they settled Max in his nursery. He seemed happy and content, and he nursed a lot. Bill took a few days off just to be with them. 'You know,' she looked at Bill happily a few days after they got home, 'I'd do it again.' He stared at her and groaned. He wasn't sure he would. He was still impressed by the hideous pain she'd been in, even for such a brief time. It hadn't seemed all that brief to him, and it wasn't something he'd want to put her through again.

'Are you serious?' He looked shocked.

'I am.' She looked down at the baby, cosily tucked in at her breast, and she smiled up at Bill. 'I would, you know.' He realised it was the price of having a twenty-year-old wife, and he leaned over and kissed first Anne, and then Max.

'You're the boss.'

She laughed and her eyes looked different now. It wasn't what she had thought. The pain of the past was not completely gone, and she knew now that it never would be. But there was someone else now, someone else she could love. She would never know where that other baby was, what he was like, who he would be when he grew up, unless he sought her out. He was gone forever from her life, irretrievably lost, but she could move on now. The pain was finally dim, and no longer acute. She had Max now . . . and Bill . . . and even if they never had another child, she thought to herself, she was glad to have them. They were enough.

CHAPTER 44

The night of the Academy Awards, Anne turned to Bill with a worried look, asking him if she looked fat. She was wearing a pale blue and gold dress, with sapphires and diamonds on her hands and ears and throat, and he thought she had never looked more beautiful. She didn't look quite as gaunt as she once had, and she had lost that beaten look. She looked peaceful and content, and everything about her glowed.

'You look better than any film star.' He helped her on with a white mink wrap, and they hurried out to the car. They didn't want to be late. They had promised to meet Faye and Ward at their place and give them a ride. Valerie was going separately, with George, and Lionel had said he would meet them there. And once united at the Music Center, where the awards were held, they were definitely a striking group, the men in black tie, the women in jewel-coloured gowns, all of them looking faintly alike, not in their dress, but their allure. Valerie was wearing a dazzling emerald-green dress, her hair done high on her head, and emeralds she had borrowed from Anne sparkling in her ears. Faye looked resplendent in a shimmering grey gown from Norrell. They were quite a group. And in New York, Vanessa was curled up in jeans, watching it on television with Jason, wishing she was there.

'You just can't imagine how exciting it is, Jase.' Her eyes lit up as she saw people she knew, and again and again as the camera swept Val's face. And this year he felt it too. He had never really cared about the Academy Awards before, and before Vanessa came into his life, he had never even bothered to watch. But now, they were prepared to sit there all night. They sat through the boring ones, the special effects, the humanitarian awards, the sound effects, the screenplays, the songs.

Clint Eastwood was host for that portion, Charlton Heston having been delayed by a flat tyre. The award to the best director went to a friend of Faye's this year, and although George was nominated, he didn't win, and neither did their film. But then Faye was introduced to give the next award. 'The Best Actress', she said, qualifying it, reeling off the names of those who had been nominated by the Academy. And as Van and Jason watched they saw each tense face, and then finally a composite on the screen of each of them, Val sitting stone still, clutching George's hand, as they both seemed to hold their breath, and Faye looked out at her.

'The winner is . . . Valerie Thayer for *Miracle*.' The screams in the Soho loft could have been heard all the way to L.A. as Vanessa danced around, overwhelmed by the news. She screamed and cried, and Jason pounded the bed, tossing all the popcorn in the bowl onto the floor, and in Hollywood, Valerie was shrieking too. She ran headlong towards the stage with a last look over her shoulder at George, and a thousand cameras took her photograph as she looked at him, blew a kiss, and then joined her mother on stage. The Oscar was handed to her, and tears streamed unabashedly down Faye's face. She approached the microphone for an instant and said, 'You'll never know how much this girl deserves this award. She had the meanest director in town,' and then, as everyone laughed, she stood back, and hugged Val, and Valerie cried copiously, and thanked everyone for all they had done for her, and then crying harder still, she attempted to thank Faye.

'A long time ago, she gave me life, and now she has given me even . . .' she could barely go on '. . . more than that. She's taught me how to work hard . . . to do my best . . . she gave me the biggest chance of my life. Thank you, Mum.' The entire audience smiled through their tears as she held the coveted Oscar aloft. '. . . and Daddy, for believing in me . . . and Lionel and Vanessa and Anne for putting up with me for all these years . . .' She choked hard, but forced herself to go on, '. . . and Greg . . . we love you too . . .' And then, triumphantly, she left the stage, and flew into George's arms. It was the last award and they all went out to celebrate after that. She called Vanessa and Jason, the first chance she got, and everyone talked to them, although no one made much sense. Everyone was hugging her and shouting, kissing George, squeezing

Val, hugging Ward and Faye. Even Anne was beside herself with glee and at Chasen's afterwards, Lionel had his new friend join them. He was someone George had acted with once a few years before, and had liked, and he fitted into the group easily. He was about George's own age, and he and Lionel appeared to know each other well. Faye realised then that this was the man responsible for the look in Lionel's eyes these days. It was the first time she had seen that look since John and she was glad for him. She was glad for all of them . . . Val, of course . . . Anne with her baby . . . Li . . . Van . . . they were just fine. And that night she stunned Ward by suggesting something he hadn't heard from her in a few years.

'What do you say we retire one of these days, kid?'

'That again?' He laughed. 'I think I've figured it out. Every time you don't get an Academy Award, you want to retire. Is that it, my love?' She laughed at the thought and shook her head. She was so happy for Val, she didn't begrudge her anything. She had earned every bit of it.

'I wish it were as simple as that.' She sat down on the bed and unclasped her pearls. They were the first gift Ward had ever given her, and the only pearls she hadn't sold when they lost their fortune years before, and they were very dear to her, as he was, as their life together had been. But she was ready for a change now. She had known it for a long time. 'I just think I've done everything I want to do, love. Professionally anyway.'

'That's terrible.' He looked upset. 'How can you say something like that at your age?'

She laughed, and she was still so damn beautiful it amazed him sometimes. 'I happen to be fifty-two years old, I've made fifty-six films, had five children, one grandchild,' she refused to count the other one, he was gone to them all and had been for more than five years, 'have a husband I adore, have made lots of friends. In brief, that's it, folks. I think I want to go and play now. All our kids are all right, they seem happy, we've done our best. This is when they write, "The End" across the screen, dear.' She smiled at him and for the first time in their life together he thought she was serious about it.

'What would you do if you retired?'

'I don't know . . . spend a year in the South of France maybe. Go play somewhere. We don't have anything in the works.' She hadn't liked anything she'd seen lately, and maybe this was what she had been waiting for, Val's Academy Award so she could leave. There was something sweet about ending with that film, the film that had begun Val's career in a big way, like a legacy she could leave her child, a special gift.

'You could write my memoirs,' Ward teased.

'You do that. I don't even want to write my own.'

'You should.' They had certainly had a full life. He looked at her quietly. It had been a long, exciting night, and she might not mean what she said, although he suspected that she did. 'Why don't we think about this for a while, and see if you still feel that way in a month or two. I'll do anything you want.' He was almost fifty-six years old and he wouldn't have minded playing in the South of France. In fact, it sounded pretty good to him, like the old days almost, and they could afford it again now, although they no longer spent money as they once had. No one did any more. 'Let's think about this.'

When they discussed it again, they decided to leave in June. They agreed to make it a year off at first, to see how it felt. They rented a house in the South of France for four months, and after that they rented an apartment in Paris for six. Faye made a point of seeing each of their children before they left. Her suspicions about Lionel had been correct, this new man in his life was one he cared about a great deal. It seemed to be a good match for him, and they were living quietly together in Beverly Hills. It was the man Faye had met the night of the Academy Awards, and Faye liked him very much.

Valerie was deeply engrossed in preparing for a new role, and she and George were talking about getting married sometime that year, after George finished his new film too. Faye made her promise to come to France for their honeymoon. Val insisted they wouldn't make a fuss and would just sneak away to tie the knot, but they'd come to France for their honeymoon afterwards, and probably bring Danny too. The visit with Anne was more difficult, Faye always found it so hard to talk to her, but she went to see her one afternoon, and found her happily taking care of little Max. Faye thought she didn't look terribly well, and wondered why until Anne confessed that she was pregnant again, which startled Faye.

'Isn't that awfully soon?'

Anne smiled at her. How soon they forgot. 'Li and Greg were a year apart.' And then suddenly Faye smiled. It was true. You wanted them to be different, to be happier, better, safer, and always wise, and instead they did half the things you did yourself and had forgotten about . . . Val's acting . . . Anne's passion for a big family . . . the others had struck out on different paths, but they took parts of their parents with them too. Greg would have been just like Ward as a young man, had he lived . . . and now here was Anne, repeating history too.

'You're right.' The two women's eyes met, in a different way from how they had in a long, long time. It was as though Anne were facing her now, as though it had to be done, before Faye left. Perhaps they would never have quite this chance again. One could never be sure. 'Anne . . . I . . .' She didn't know where to begin. There were twenty years to unfold . . . or maybe five . . . a lifetime of never quite reaching a child that she loved, and she didn't want to miss her now. 'I made a lot of mistakes with you. I don't suppose that's a secret to either of us, is it?'

Anne looked at her honestly, with her child in her arms, and there was no anger in her eyes now. 'I don't think I ever made it easy for you . . . I never understood what you were all about.'

'Nor I you. My biggest mistake was that I never had time. If you had only been born a year or two before you were . . .' But who could have changed all that? It was history now. Along with everything else that had happened to her . . . the Haight . . . the pregnancy . . . the child she had given away. Their eyes met again, and Faye decided to say what was on her mind. She reached a hand out to Anne, and took the hand that wasn't holding Max in her own. 'I'm sorry about the other baby, Anne . . . I was wrong . . . at the time, I really thought we were doing the right thing . . .' Both women's eyes filled with tears, as Max lay in Anne's arms. 'I was wrong.'

Anne shook her head, the tears spilling onto her cheeks. 'I don't think you were . . . I don't think I really had a choice then. I was fourteen years old . . .'

'But you never got over it.' Faye knew that now.

'I've accepted it. It was right at the time. Sometimes that's the best you can do.' And with that, she took her mother in her arms, and held her there with Max. It was like saying 'I forgive you for what you did', but more importantly, she had forgiven herself. And now she could go on. As she walked her to her car later on, she held her hand again. 'I'm going to miss you, Mum.'

'I'm going to miss you too.' She was going to miss all of them, but she was hoping they would all come to France at one point. Once, after all, none of them had been a part of her life. And she had to let them go now. They had accepted her, in the end, and she had accepted them. All of them.

On the way to France, she and Ward stopped in New York and saw Jason and Van, happy in their loft, he writing his play, she working at a publisher's and writing her book at night. There was no talk of marriage there, but no hint of either of them going anywhere. And as Ward and Faye flew to France, she smiled over at him. 'They're all quite something, aren't they?'

'So are you.' As always, he looked proud of her. He had been for thirty years . . . since the day they'd met on Guadalcanal. . . if only he'd known then what he knew now . . . what a full life he had lived with her. He said as much as she reminded him that it wasn't over yet, and he kissed her over the champagne the stewardess had just handed them, as a woman stared at her and whispered to the man she was with . . . she looks just like a big film star I used to love thirty years ago . . . the man smiled at her. Everyone looked like someone to her. And Ward and Faye went on chatting quietly, planning their year in France. Eventually they spent ten years there.

They never quite understood how the time went so fast. The children came and went. Valerie married George, and they finally had a child, a little girl they named Faye, after her. Anne had four more, and everyone teased her that she should have been as lazy as their mother and had twins. Vanessa published three books, and Jason was still working on his plays; he had moved to Off Broadway now, from Off Off Broadway, and Faye was impressed at how good his productions were when they saw one once in New York. Valerie had won the Academy Award again, and finally so had George. Everyone was doing well, and after eleven years abroad, at the age of sixty-four, Faye quietly died in her sleep one night. They were in Cap Ferrat for the autumn, in a beautiful villa they had bought there, which they wanted to leave to their children one day. It would make a perfect place for them to come, all of them.

And now she came home to them, with Ward looking stunned. He was sixty-seven, and she had been his whole life from the age of twenty-five years . . . forty-two years . . . He brought her home to Hollywood, the place she had loved, which she had conquered so many times, as an actress, a director, a woman . . . as his wife . . . He remembered those desperate years when he had lost everything, when she had pulled them all together so valiantly, and started a new career, with all of them in tow, when she had helped him get back on his feet . . . and he remembered the years before . . . and the years long afterwards, as they made film after film for MGM . . . and the big break she had given Val . . . what he could not remember any more were the years without her. That wasn't possible. It couldn't be true . . . it hadn't been true . . . and yet it was true now. He was alone, she was gone. Anne and Bill met him at the plane, and mercifully, they had left the children at home. They watched the casket being lowered from the belly of the plane, as the wind whipped Anne's hair, and in the twilight she looked so much like Faye. She was thirty-one years old, and her mother was gone . . . Her eyes rose towards Ward's, and she quietly took his hand. She and Bill had talked about it the night before, and they could at least offer him that. They had built a guesthouse behind their house in Beverly Hills, and it would be nice if he came to live there. Ward and Faye had long since sold their old house in Beverly Hils. They hadn't lived there in years. And Anne looked up at him now, as Bill watched.

'Come on, Daddy, let's go home.'

For the first time, he suddenly looked old. He couldn't believe she was gone. Anne wanted him to rest. There was a lot they had to do, and the funeral would be in two days' at the church where they'd been married, and then Forest Lawn. And everyone would be there of course . . . everyone who had ever been anyone . . . everyone except Faye Thayer . . . but her family would be there. All of them. And Ward . . . it was difficult to imagine a world without her. He couldn't imagine it at all, as tears slid quietly down his cheeks, as they drove into the night, with Faye in the hearse behind . . . he could imagine her everywhere, if he just closed his eyes . . . she was still there with him, as she would be with all of them . . . always, for the rest of time. Her films would live on . . . the memories . . . the love and above all the family, each one of them, touched by her, a part of her, just as she had been a part of them.